Legacy of Dragons

An Espionage Novel
by
Michael Kendall

Legacy of Dragons is a powerful espionage story, set in the post 9/11 World of nuclear uncertainty.

Sea adventure, spiced with murder, blackmail and espionage, are all set against the fear of a terrorist nuclear capability that forms this fast moving drama of human relationships.

When his father dies after a diving expedition in the English Channel, the protagonist Dr. Peter Senden, begins a quest to discover the cause and becomes caught up in what he believes is a search for a sunken wreck and gold hoard. He is entangled in a web of obstacles created by his fathers past relationships, as he slowly unravels secrets about his family. He discovers that he shares part of a deadly WW2 nuclear secret with the daughter of one of his father's past associates. She is a young woman, who exhorts revenge on the man who raped her as a fifteen year old.

Major intelligence agencies thread together the story to prevent a disaster, as a mixed terrorist group of N.Korean and religious fundamentalists seek the major constituents for a dirty nuclear bomb. An equally ambitious covert plot by a section of the CIA counterpoints the action as the World's media move in.

The story weaves between the south coast of England, Washington, Hong Kong, London and post 9/11 New York.

To Elaine & Gordon
Best Wishes
Mike Kendall

© Copyright 2006 Michael Kendall.
All rights reserved. No part of this publication may be reproduced, stored in a retrieval system, or transmitted, in any form or by any means, electronic, mechanical, photocopying, recording, or otherwise, without the written prior permission of the author.

Note for Librarians: A cataloguing record for this book is available from Library and Archives Canada at www.collectionscanada.ca/amicus/index-e.html
ISBN 1-4251-0775-3

Printed in Victoria, BC, Canada. Printed on paper with minimum 30% recycled fibre.
Trafford's print shop runs on "green energy" from solar, wind and other environmentally-friendly power sources.

TRAFFORD
PUBLISHING
Offices in Canada, USA, Ireland and UK

Book sales for North America and international:
Trafford Publishing, 6E–2333 Government St.,
Victoria, BC V8T 4P4 CANADA
phone 250 383 6864 (toll-free 1 888 232 4444)
fax 250 383 6804; email to orders@trafford.com

Book sales in Europe:
Trafford Publishing (UK) Limited, 9 Park End Street, 2nd Floor
Oxford, UK OX1 1HH UNITED KINGDOM
phone +44 (0)1865 722 113 (local rate 0845 230 9601)
facsimile +44 (0)1865 722 868; info.uk@trafford.com

Order online at:
trafford.com/06-2533

10 9 8 7 6 5 4 3 2

CHART SHOWING PART OF
THE ENGLISH CHANNEL

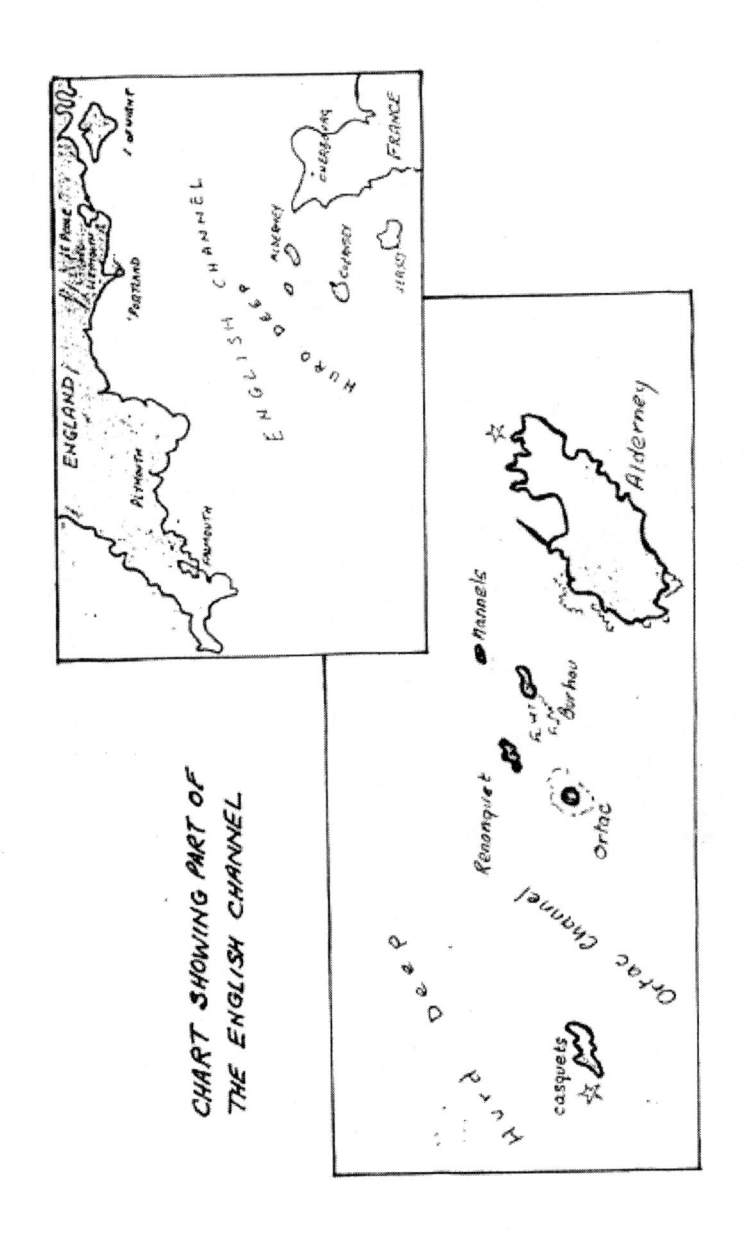

Michael Kendall

Legacy of Dragons

Prologue

*New hatched to the woeful time. The obscure bird
Clamour'd the live-long night. Some say the earth
Was feverous and did shake.*
                                    Macbeth.

Tinian US Airforce base, N.Pacific. August 7th. 1945

It could have been that obscure bird that Shakespeare heard and saw in his mind, the bird of darkness, the owl, lumbering slowly into the early morning sky as in Hiroshima people were fevered and the ground still shook with horror.

The sound on this early morning came from the droning, clamorous, Doppler noise of the four Wright Cyclone engines, lifting the B-29 Boeing Superfortress bomber slowly from the vast concrete runway and circling its darkened shape into the moist air of the North West sky.

The ten man crew including observers settled into their routines. Flight checks, meticulously practised and polished over the last two months, as the modified aircraft left the North Field US airforce base on the Tinian atoll behind them, nestling in the moonlight reflections of the Pacific Ocean. The same moonlight washing over the blacked out airfield, where the ground crew watched their silver charge until it dissolved into the liquid darkness.

Members of the flight crew were unusually subdued, carrying out their individual tasks as they had done since the end of June that year when they had been brought together for the first time as a team. But on this morning their thoughts were also on what had happened the day before. The classified meeting of the 509th. Composite Bomb Group they had attended and the debriefing of the Enola Gay crew following the successful mission number thirteen and return from Hiroshima where the *Little Boy* uranium atom bomb had been dropped.

As far as they knew, today's flight to Kyushu and the city of Kokura was not another practice bombing mission dropping "pumpkins". The briefing room had been tense. It was for real, as had been the flight commanded by Col.Paul Tibbets to Hiroshima the day before.

Each man worked his equipment, waiting tensely for the flight commander to announce whether this was to be another reconnaissance flight for some future mission, or to confirm that the single pod shaped device hanging in the forward bomb bay like a monster's egg, was the real thing. Ahead of them, the advance weather reconnaissance and instrument aircraft were keeping radio silence in accordance with the mission instructions of their Operations Order, small visible dots on the radar screen raster as the formation flew through thick cloud towards their destination.

Five hours after take off, the decoded radio messages from the weather planes announced their worst fears. The operation was to be aborted because of thick cloud cover, thicker than yesterday, with no chance of achieving their target.

Then the first disaster struck as they banked over about to turn for home. A fire in the communications wiring harness that was quickly extinguished but left a mass of charred rubber, noxious fumes and knocked out fuses.

Next, the primary and secondary power supplies to the navigation gyros suddenly gave up.......

Dawn was still an hour away and Tinian was in the middle of a torrential downpour as a tropical storm worked its way across the region. The room in the US Airforce base HQ radio ops building was thick with cigarette smoke as Capt. Roger Kirk entered brushing water from his wet rain cape and shaking off his hat. His eyes took in the worried expressions of the night staff operating the plotting tables and the array of radio communications, faces glinting sweat, and answering Kirk's question, even before the shift supervising lieutenant turned to him and saluted.

'We received their mayday call a few minutes ago Sir, just after the top brass retired for a couple of hours. Relayed from one of the weather aircraft. We understand that they're making for the nearest land in the Ryukyu Islands. They've made brief contact with Okinawa who are evacuating all but essential personnel; the landing could be highly dangerous to our own troops there. We also understand that all their navigation equipment is out. Sir'

Kirk referred to the large regional map on the wall. 'Anything heard since Lieutenant?'

'No Sir.'

'Nothing from Guam?'

'No Sir. Guam is still heavily engaged in their search operations for the Indianapolis survivors. Our last communication was the abort signal when we closed mission fourteen down. We're now operating on the emergency procedures.'

Kirk sucked air through pursed lips. 'Oh, Holy, Holy shit!......... Get General Farrell and the science personnel back up here immediately and stand by to relay signals via. the Pentagon to Gen. Groves and the President on USS Augusta.

Prepare standard code rescue signals to Air Command and Marianas Command, Anything else?'

'They suspect sabotage Sir. Incendiary devices reported that started fires in various parts of the aircraft. They're trying to defuse *Thinman* before they reach Okinawa, Sir.'

Yesterday's uranium bomb had been fused in flight; this one surely could be defused before landing.

Kirk's eyes went back to the map and the outline shape of Japan as the unwelcome news and its implications sank in.

Was this to be the first dissenting demonstration of the new atomic age? The nemesis for the preceding days work? Could someone have gotten through the cordon of security, enraged, fearful, horrified, at what the future might hold following the awesome terrible devastation at Hiroshima the day before? Sabotaged by their own personnel?

'Get the security cordon around the Bockscar compound and scientists' building doubled, immediately. My orders.'

'Affirmative. Sir.'

Coded messages clacked out their noise from teleprinters and Morse keys buzzed their endless dots and dashes, but all that could be heard from the receiver loudspeakers was the relentless crackle of side band background static. A female member of the plotter staff sobbed quietly as they stood in silence looking at the stationery icons on the table. *Thinman* was missing and would be neatly catalogued later as the World's first major nuclear accident.

Two days later the weather cleared and this time the Bockscar flight crew commanded by Charles W. Sweeney ran the mission to Kokura, but again the cloud was too dense to accurately locate the target.

So they flew on to Nagasaki and dropped *Fat Man*, the first plutonium atomic bomb with the power of 22,000 tons of TNT.

Part One
The Retirement Fund

Chapter 1. Capt. Gilbert Piltcher. 15th. August 1953.

The old court house that stood behind the Commercial Road had emptied.

Chauffeurs who'd waited in wet side streets or parked on bomb-site car parks adjacent to the court building in Southampton were now driving their legal charges back along the A33 trunk road and Winchester by-pass. Back to offices, homes and clubs in London. All of them financially better off for the few days' work that the out-of-town enquiry had thrown at them. None of them with any concept of the giant slash that forty years later would scar the Twyford Downs above them with the remorseless roaring torrent of the M3 motorway.

Those members of the media who relied on small court trivia for income had also left, most of them heading for hotel bars and a telephone over which to dictate their copy to distant editors. Then, heading instinctively towards the bar to wait for opening time and a drink.

In the courthouse basement, the prison cells were empty. No one had been found guilty or had been charged for any misdemeanour. In fact there hadn't been any attendant policemen as unlike a criminal court, this had been a court of enquiry.

The merchant navy accident investigators were gone as were the bowler hatted insurance company assessors and Board of Trade examiners. No one seemed to have gained and no one seemed to have lost (except that is for the Falcon Star Insurance Company). The suppliers of the mounds of paperwork, like the lawyers, had also made money out of the hearing, an official Board of Trade enquiry into the sinking of an elderly tramp steamer and the deaths of five Chinese seamen by drowning in the English Channel.

A story that none of those newspaper reporters, who were now drinking and flirting with colleagues, could have imagined the impact that the resurrected case would have some fifty years later in a new century when the world's media would go into a desperate frenzied search for the truth, the real story of the ship's truly deadly cargo. How the worlds first nuclear accident at the end of the Pacific war could resurrect itself as a terrorist activity a few miles off the South Coast of England.

On the other side of the city, four of the men who'd been at the heart of the inquiry had paid off their taxi and now stood in the saloon bar of a quiet dockside pub, chatting over the day's events.

Their body language indicated a nervous wariness of each other, polite but not communicating the conversational warmth of close friends.

Simon Carter fished some tablets from a pocket and took them in a gulp of his whisky before raising the glass again in a final salute. His eyes glanced around the small bar room to make sure the four of them were alone. There would be another hour before the steam whistles signalled the end of the second shift and stevedores poured back into the place from the nearby docks.

'Bottoms up gentlemen. That's all over and done with then.'

No one else spoke, all eyes on the man whose normally sallow facial flesh now showed tinges of colour excited by the day's proceedings.

'I suggest we meet up again in a couple of month's time when this lot has blown over. In the mean time,' he patted the side of his nose, 'keep your mouths buttoned up. You'll all get your share.' He grinned out the dismissive words, and as if prompted, the young physicist Dr. Tony Holmes looked at his pocket watch.

'Sorry chaps but I've got to get away, must be back at Aldermaston this evening for a new series of heavy water experiments we're doing. The steamer leaves for Basingstoke shortly. How about you Senden, didn't you say you'd got to get back to your ship at Portsmouth?'

The Royal Navy sub lieutenant downed the rest of his pint, placed the glass on the bar counter and reached for his raincoat and number one.

'Afraid so, we've a new ship in commission, leaving the dockside early in the morning, lots to do before then. I'll share a taxi with you doctor, to the station if I may. What's heavy water for God's sake, a new fangled kind of bottled drink?'

They all laughed at the innocent remark. Tony Holmes grinned knowingly. 'You know damned well that I can't discuss what I do.'

The four of them said their goodbyes, Tony Holmes and Philip Senden departed into the rain. Carter and Gilbert Piltcher watched them go and then sat at a small table, appearing like silhouettes in the dim daylight that filtered through the acid etched frosted pub windows.

The trumpet sounds of the Billy May Orchestra strained from a wireless loudspeaker somewhere in the distance behind the empty bar counter and the stale body smells of lunchtime, beer and cigarettes, clung with uncertainty to the air. The landlord who had served them could be heard at work somewhere in the back of the building, stacking empty beer bottles in crates, whistling something that vaguely resembled the air vibrations of the music.

Carter put his glass down and sat with his arms folded on the table in front of him. A well built man in his late twenties whose neatly trimmed beard under the pale blue eyes gave him the appearance of being older, Caucasian but with oriental features, wearing a light coloured trench coat that he had undone as he placed his trilby hat on the chair beside him.

He chuckled benevolently as if to himself and then in a low voice.

'Well then captain, that's all over and done with. I'm glad to see the back of that damned courtroom, the enquiry, the insurers and all the other bloody people involved. No one's lost face and no one's to blame.' His hand went to his beard, stroking it downwards as though feeling for any out of place hair.

'Our friends Senden and Holmes acted out their part of the story like little lambs. We wriggled out of that horse shit smelling like roses. We won.' He beamed the statement at the other man, probably five years his senior and continued.

'Now that we're over the hurdle of the enquiry we can start talking seriously about money.' He paused as if savouring the thought. 'The deal that you and I made still stands of course and your help in all of this mess will be rewarded as soon as the assessors have paid up and I can make the necessary salvage arrangements.' He lent forward patting his hand on the man's sleeve and with another furtive glance around the bar room said in a confidential tone, 'I promise you that your little secret is still safe with me.'

The other man withdrew his arm from the brief contact as if by instinct and removed the pipe from his mouth, prodding the dying embers without comment, wiping the powdery finger tip against his trouser leg, eyes lowered and studying the head on his beer apprehensively, as if waiting for the niceties to finish. He went to speak, but Carter raised a silencing hand to him and continued.

'Now, my friend, all I need from you are the correct co-ordinates for that wreck.' And then in a quickening voice, 'you have them with you I presume?'

He looked expectantly at the man he had referred to as a friend, as Captain Gilbert Piltcher, shifted the position of his backside on the uncomfortable bench seat running along the wall. In reality, the sub conscious act was nothing to do with the comfort of his buttocks, or indeed the coarse material of his seaman's trousers, but intended to ease his mind into what he was going to say. The man in front of him had defiled the court with his deceit and got away with it. Gilbert's own parallel deceit was a secret that only he knew about and still guarded. He struck a match to the pipe that became two flames reflected in his eyes, and when he answered it was in a slightly arrogant careful voice as he kept his eyes on those of the man sitting on the other side of the small marble topped table.

'I think that what you meant to say Mr. Carter was that it was you yourself who won. It was nothing to do with me or the others, we merely collaborated your story as agreed. And with respect to the information on the ship's position, I'm afraid you presume wrongly.' He drew heavily on the pipe and huffed out a plume of blue smoke into the thick air, flicking the spent match to an ashtray. 'Having fudged the true position of the ship with the authorities over the last few months since the sinking, and then this last week in that court room, there was no way that I would have brought that information along with me to the hearing now was there? No way at all.'

An expression of annoyance flashed over Carter's face, forcing the benevolent smile on his lips into a thin line as he realised the truth behind the statement. The captain was not going to bend easily to his request. He leant forward until his face was very close to the other man and hissed.

'Now, you listen to me you depraved little queer. I want the position of that ship and I'm going to have it. Don't think you can betray me now, not after all that we've been through.' He stopped, sitting back, slowly shaking his head from side to side as if to emphasise what he had been holding back.

'You and that nancy boy Senden.'

His contempt of the man sitting opposite him, dammed up for the convenience of the court and now out in one great outpouring as though the number one flood gate-valve had been opened. There could be no holding back now, no niceties, no polite haggling, the torrent would be unstoppable. And then, stabbing the table with his forefinger, his voice still lowered but menacing.

'I demand to know the correct position of that bloody ship, you hear? Otherwise I tell the authorities and newspapers about your little affair with that sub lieutenant and you both lose your jobs, commissions and reputations. Royal Navy and Merchant Navy, it doesn't matter to me. You understand me eh; it'll be fucking prison for both of you.'

The other man rose slowly from the seat, dark eyes now careful to avoid the disapproving stare with which Simon Carter regarded him. During the course of the official enquiry it had been all smiles. Now, with just the two of them, the perception of empathy that had been between them was gone. Reduced to an empty shell, like the court room they had just left. He placed his pipe on the table in front of him as he folded his arms in a defensive pose, feet spread apart and eyes watching Carter's clenched fists as he replied in a voice over which he tried to maintain a firm level of cadence.

'What you've just said is a very serious accusation Carter. You've never had any proof that the relationship between Philip and me during that voyage was anything but,' he paused for the word he was seeking, 'anything but platonic.' He dropped his pose as his voice rose. 'You know bloody well that we were just good chums. Anyway, you can say what you like as far as I'm concerned, you'll have to give me time, it wasn't safe to .....,' before he could finish the sentence, Carter had risen and lent across the table grabbing the captain by the lapel of his seaman's blazer, the previously restrained voice now raised in a hoarse shout as they faced each other and Piltcher's body took up a defensive shape as he half turned and ducked his head in anticipation of a punch.

'I've not sat through months of sodding argument with the insurers or the last week of wrangling court officials to be fucked about by you Captain. I return to Hong Kong two days from now. You hear, two days. And if I don't have the information by then, the press will get the full story, the real story, and you'll both be finished. Fucked up in prison where you can hold hands for as long as you like.'

Carter released his hold with a flourish, as though letting go of something unsavoury and sat back heavily on his chair, looking around again to assure himself that no one had seen his outburst. A man of various moods, very violent on occasions and now looking as dangerous as the captain had ever seen him. And he knew the homophobic ship owner, who had until recently been his employer, could be very dangerous indeed. He'd seen him in action in Aden, Alexandria, Gibraltar and he'd heard stories. But, right now the captain considered he was reasonably safe with so much at stake.

Captain Gilbert Piltcher's normally florid facial colour paled so that the pebble black eyes contrasted their annoyance with his self restraint. The music had changed to an old Glen Miller number with soft trombones as he smoothed down the blazer material with his fingers, replying in a quieter voice that was more defensive than defiant.

'I don't have to listen to this shit you know, believe me, when I say I haven't got the co-ordinates with me I mean what I say.' He shrugged his shoulders. 'That gold was sunk with the ship and she's lying too deep to do anything about it.

Anyway, Carter, bully boy tactics, lies and deception have always been your weapons, but you can keep your bloody hands off me in future because I'm finished with you. Your father was a good man. But you?' He sat again but with every muscle tensed as he surveyed his lost livelihood. 'I've lied for you, perjured myself in that court room, and for what?' He didn't wait for or an answer , his face now shaking with ambivalent anger, the pitch of his voice higher and louder, clenching his fists in readiness this time of the man who had touched a poisoned nerve..

'To keep your dirty mouth shut to protect others that's what, and I'll have to live with that stain on my conscience for the rest of my life. That arse hole ship of yours was a death trap, an accident waiting to happen. I just thank God that I don't work for you any more.' He lifted his glass and took a long pull of beer, wiping away with the back of his hand the froth that disguised the perspiration that had formed on his upper lip, his eyes watchful in case of another onslaught.

Carter appeared to freeze with rage, the psychosis turning his eyes to wicked slits that matched the meanness of his tight lips, and then quite suddenly, as though some great pressure had been released within him, he scowled again at the captain.

'You have my address captain; two days that's all.'

The greenies he'd swallowed earlier, the amphetamine tablets that he used as a stand by when he couldn't get his usual fix, were already doing their work.

Piltcher retorted with an upward shrug of his head. 'What about the others, what did they do for you? What about your poor old father? I suppose you've tried to pay them off with the same vague promises that you've given to me. And those poor devils who perished.' The eye contact had now become intense. 'Suppose I decide to tell my side of the story, the true story of what really occurred on that ship. You'd be finished as well you know. Fucked up and finished.'

The landlord's banal whistling and the chinking sound of beer bottles continued to float on the air as the whisky glass was emptied in one swig and Simon Carter, ignoring the questions, rose, picked up his hat and turned to go. As he stood, he twisted slowly round wagging with his forefinger at the captain and with a menacing grin growled out his warning.

'Do that my friend and you would be signing your own death warrant. There's a great deal at stake here, more than you could possibly know about. And in case you're thinking about doing something yourself, forget it. That ship and the gold are guarded by a terrible secret. Remember, two days that's all you've got.'

Then he departed into the rain, leaving his reluctant drinking partner and past employee to consider what had been said, and what hadn't been said.

Captain Piltcher remained, sitting there sipping his beer and chewing on the empty pipe, as a vision of the freighter and his last fearful moments on board her flooded back into his memory.

The voyage from Hong Kong and the way the Russian trawlers had shadowed them. Why? He didn't know. The ship's manifest only declared small machine tools and cotton jeans. They had also been carrying British Army military supplies of an unspecified nature, but certainly nothing explosive. No munitions. They would have had to be declared. Was it the gold he had discovered? Surely that would not have warranted a fleet of Russian trawlers crawling up their backsides.

The storm of a few months ago that had caused such havoc and death both ashore and at sea on that terrible January night. The night of the Irish ferry disaster and North Sea floods that had struck so silently and quickly. Of those enormous seas and the pitiful screams of the crew members who had been swept away. Then his escape from the ship as he struck out for the island that had once been a Nazi Todd stronghold. And before that, those glorious evenings in the Indian Ocean he had shared with Philip before the voyage had become fraught with suspicion and frayed tempers.

Why, he pondered, had Philip Senden and Tony Holmes only been called as secondary witnesses?

There would be plenty said and done over the years before the separate covert deceptions of all those involved were conjoined and the legacy of their actions touched others at a later time. His ship, now lying out there somewhere on the bottom of the English Channel, bore a secret story, a legacy greater and more deadly sinister than even the Captain could have possibly imagined.

Chapter 2. Philip Senden

Over five decades had passed since the Board of Trade enquiry of 1953

The site of the pub where Philip Senden, Tony Holmes, Simon Carter and his captain had argued after the enquiry would be hard to find by anyone now except the archivist in the City Architects Office. Who, after rummaging in old plan file drawers, would have to cross refer to newer CAD generated drawings and eventually, with a satisfied nod, move the mouse pointer at a spot somewhere in the middle of an eighties industrial estate.

The four young men who had deceived the court all those years ago were in a new century, elderly now, having lived their lives under the same shadow of lies for over fifty years.

Those events and indeed the significance they would have over the next few weeks were unknown and of no consequence to Dr. Peter Senden as he drove through a maze of Hampshire country lanes looking for an address on an e-mail print out.

He came across the place quite suddenly and stopped the car. A small nameplate, mounted on one of two ivy clad pillars, was the only indication that this was the address he'd been looking for. The pillars, standing like sentries each side of the entrance, breaking the uniformity of the sunlit red brick estate wall which swept alongside the country lane.

The e-mail on the seat beside him was checked again before he turned the hire car into the dark void of shadows that was the entrance to Downshall House Sanatorium.

He was in a reflective mood. His first trip back to England for months, the greenness of the place always gratifying to the eyes, after the washed out colours of some of the dismal places he had visited during his tour of duty.

This time he had returned out of necessity rather than by his own volition, servility to others, but now wishing he'd returned earlier. The e-mail only told him that his father had been taken ill, requesting his urgent attendance and he tried to leap his mind forward to what he would discover at this remote place. His requests for more information when the embassy official in Berlin had first rung him had been stone walled, professing to know everything and yet nothing over the telephone. His subsequent e-mail attempts to find someone with the authority to outline the seriousness of his father's illness had been unsuccessful. Phone calls to his father's flat in Weymouth went unanswered. Then this e-mail had arrived at the hotel in Cologne, giving him details of how to find the Downshall House Sanatorium where his father was, together with an appointment and time to meet someone he didn't know. His attempts to establish the source or even a phone number for the place had been unsuccessful. The place didn't exist, wasn't listed and the international directory couldn't help him. He held down a sense of anger that this might just be some complicated ploy to get him back to England earlier than he had planned.

A cattle grid drummed its noise on the car's tyres, jerking him out of his cerebrate visions as he drove slowly along the tarmac drive, bounded by large rhododendron bushes, the flowers still resplendent in the variety of their colour against the cloudless June sky.

A hundred yards and the driveway became more formal where white painted kerbstones had been laid and various official signs indicated that this was a British Government Ministry of Defence property. Ahead he could see a barrier across the drive and a small gate house where he stopped the car as a security guard emerged, wearing the summer issue uniform and flack jacket of the Atomic Energy Authority Constabulary and carrying a Heckler and Koch sub machine gun slung across his chest.

Peter opened the side window as the security man walked round the car and enquired.

'Good morning sir, do you have an appointment?' It was an obvious enough question, but one that had an overtone of addressing an uninvited or underdressed guest at a yacht club ball. His gravel voice, which although polite in its demand, had been moulded from an earlier unpolished stone.

Peter looked at the man, taking in the armament, the security cameras, wire mesh fencing and barrier that lay beyond them.

He'd been expecting something different, a rest home for the elderly perhaps, with blush cheeked young nurses pushing their charges around in wheelchairs against a background of peaceful urbanity, uniforms emphasising the sexuality of their female body curves, with starched caps and long legged black stockings. This formal place seemed to be out of keeping with those images and the sterile simplicity of the e-mail message.

'My name is Peter Senden and I'm here to see a Dr. Wilson concerning my father, Rear Admiral Philip Senden, who I understand is a patient here.' He waved the paper in front of the guard who grinned back at him now as he bent to read it.

Then he was escorted into the gate house where a phone call was made and his credentials checked before signing a visitors' form and obtaining a lapel pass badge. The guard, friendlier now that the formalities were in place, directed him with the voice of official politeness left over from his military days.

'Proceed along the drive to the main house sir; you'll see where to park.'

As the red and white security boom pivoted upwards, Senden got back into the car and drove a few hundred yards until he rounded the last bend where the front of the old Victorian red brick building came into view. Here the drive opened up onto a large expanse of gravel, bounded by lawns, flower beds and backed by more rhododendrons. They appeared to be a screen for the high security fence he noticed that stood behind them.

There were about a dozen cars and an ambulance to one side of the building and Peter Senden parked the car there, grabbed his jacket from the passenger seat and strolled casually over to the main entrance.

Stone mullion framed windows echoed back his footsteps on the gravel as they looked down onto the quiet frontage from four gables, dominated with decorated pinnacles. A seated stone lion sat at the side of the entrance holding a cartouche, an ornamental scroll of paper on which the engravings of the building's original owners had long since disappeared. A building that seemed to retain the ghosts of it former splendour and now stood there on this warm summer day dutifully serving its incumbents in the new century.

Two large men appeared at the front door and he was ushered into a reception hall where another constable, sitting behind the reception desk, raised his head from the closed circuit television screen and enquired.

'Dr.Senden?'

'That's me.' Peter Senden acknowledged his name and the lapel security badge was swiped by a hand held scanner.

'Would you read this Health and Safety notice and the F.C.O. Security Notice and sign both please sir.' A couple of signatures as the bored desk man stifled a yawn and one of the heavies escorted Senden along a passageway, opening a door and ushering him into a small waiting room.

It was hot, very hot and humid too. The small room that he had been shown into was stuffy and had that distinguishing smell that somehow abounds in institutional places. A smell of disinfectant mixed with the faint odours of urine and yesterday's cooking, verifying the extra load now put upon the ancient drainage system of the old building. There were a few chairs and a table on which the daily papers had been neatly laid out. A large radiator belted out heat even though it was the start of the English summer.

'What is this place, a hospital of some sort?'

His escort sat with his arms folded, nodding only and making no verbal reply, his breath humming the gentle spice song of a Lamb Jalfrezy from the previous evening.

In a nearby room, Cmdr.Hank Hoskins, of the U.S.Naval Security Group Intelligence and assigned to the Central Intelligence Agency, sat with his British Secret Service counterpart.

The American looked too old to be on active service. Dressed in a conventional civilian suit; balding with short crinkled hair, a pale lined face with jowls that showed the micro thin reddish threads of surface blood vessels. Heavy eyelids covered small twinkling eyes and dominated the features. He wore half moons on the bridge of a pugilistic nose over which the eyes peered out with intelligent concentration as they watched Senden on a small closed circuit colour screen. For the Commander this would probably be his last major assignment pending retirement. He looked at the dossier in front of him that Maj. Jack Fellows had given him earlier.

'You say this guy of yours is security cleared?' His voice was a cultured drawl and bore the hallmarks of the North West States, Washington or Oregon.

Jack Fellows's gaze remained on the screen.

'Yes sir, as it says in the dossier he's a chartered engineer contracted to the M.o.D. Intelligence Service on a freelance basis, checking advanced engineering systems data for them. Not our own equipment you understand.' The Major's loquaciousness hesitated as he sensed Hoskins's acceptance that the man on the screen in front of them was an industrial spy working for the British Government on defence systems counter espionage.

Hoskins flicked casually over the pages as Fellows continued.

'He was recruited about ten years ago from one of the U.K.'s largest defence electronic companies and has been vetted by our B1 section annually. Worked on the design and development team of the communications intelligence gathering systems used by G.C.H.Q. Had an input into locating and verifying comms equipment used by the terrorists in Afghanistan. Also it was through his vigilance that the al-Qaeda anthrax bio weapons programme was reduced when he helped our Excise people to seize German made fermenters that were being illegally exported to Middle Eastern Universities. An exemplary record and good education. Finished off at Imperial College.'

'Who pays his salary?' Hoskins drawled out the question as he continued to peer at the screen, watching Senden with the casual interest of someone adjudicating at an audition of mushroom pickers. The years had taught him that this was a question that seldom got a direct answer in this business. He asked it anyway.

In the adjoining room the escort sat stolidly with his arms folded, casually examining the finger nails on one hand, oblivious of his personal fragrance that was gently filling the room and mingling naturally with the background air.

Peter Senden had lost interest in the mute and thumbed open one of the newspapers half looking at the headlines as the paper rested on the table. He appeared a relaxed lanky framed man with a young face for his thirty eight years. Lightly tanned skin with a mop of fair hair, sort of parted down the middle that flopped over the left side of his forehead and which he habitually smoothed back from time to time with his hands, whether from habit or the uncertain nervousness of the occasion the Commander could not judge. The grey eyes, if the television monitor had portrayed them correctly, appeared to be trained eyes that, although they had been on the newspaper, were now taking in the surroundings. Assessing, noting everything they surveyed, eyes that in spite of their young years already showed crinkled weather lines at their corners. The straight nose over a generous mouth and firm jaw line indicated an intellectual character, a face with two days of dark stubble that even so, would command attention in a crowd. Those eyes had already detected the tiny watching device which Peter now looked at directly, so that Hoskins could see the impatient energy of that face, the straight mouth now wearing a slight smile on one side that raised and accentuated the cheek, causing a small indentation to appear below the cheek bone, waiting to see his father, oblivious of the more sinister reasons for his being in that unusual building.

Maj. Fellows clicked the monitor off, as though showing his slight irritation at the Commanders apparent natural distrust of anything British and turned to Hoskins.

'He supports our Special Operations T2 Technical Branch, as I said, working on industrial counter espionage. Not had much experience at the sharp end as far as I can see from the report, mainly support roles I believe. Even so he carries a high security category. You'll see from the file that in addition to his Masters degree he's also an active yachtsman; has his own boat.' He paused as the Commander nodded his understanding of the man's CV.

'Married, kids or anything?' The details were in the file but Hoskin's felt the need to ask. He noted that his earlier question, regarding who paid Senden, had not been answered. Fellows replied.

'His wife died about two years ago in a tragic ski accident. There was no issue from the marriage. No regular partner at present as far as we know.'

The file was flicked through again as Hoskins considered the man whose father could now be another cog in a number of problems he was considering. Intertwining back over nearly sixty years, problems that had been forgotten with time, dispersed like a fuzzy image and now suddenly brought back into sharp focus.

'Well he's close enough. Let's hope he's not too close, I guess we'll find out in a few minutes.'

He closed the file and stood looking out of the window whilst he considered the value, if any, of Peter Senden's input in assisting the *Thinman* team. The young man's father, the old Rear Admiral, was the only clue they had after weeks of unsuccessful ambulant investigation.

'O.K. let's go ahead and see how he reacts to what they're going to show him. I would prefer that he didn't know the details of the *Thinman* assignment at this stage, let's just see if he leads us anywhere. If he proves to be useful we can decide later how much he should know.'

Major Fellows smiled inwardly at the Commander's resigned sigh, lent forward and switched the monitor back on.

'My department has arranged for our pathologist Dr. Wilson to effectively partner him, even though neither of them will be aware of the official relationship as yet.'

The waiting room door opened and the two military men bent towards the monitor screen with anticipation as the man who had shown Peter to the room stood and a white coated young woman entered, accompanied by another man.

She pushed a wisp of fair hair up into her hair band before extending a hand to Peter who rose to her greeting.

'Good morning Dr. Senden. I'm Jessica Wilson in charge of looking after your father.' She checked her voice to one of careful sobriety whilst at the same time, with no conscious effort, projecting her female charisma of friendly concern towards him as she tilted her head slightly to one side, her eyes looking up at him.

'I'm afraid you're only just about in time. The Rear Admiral is very ill which is why we requested the British Consulate's office in Bonn to try and track you down.' She hesitated for a moment as if waiting for some response but he nodded his acknowledgement of the situation, being impatient to see his father.

'If you'll follow me please doctor.'

They left the room and as they walked along the passageway she spoke back to him over her shoulder.

'Before we get to his room, I must warn you to be prepared, he's very ill and you may have difficulty recognising him. He's been asking for you but is now having periods of mental confusion and is just about in delirium.'

Peter had not seen his father for about nine months. He'd been travelling back and forth across Eastern Europe and Asia most of that time on a series of engagements for his department, Foreign Office delegations to Kabul, Bosnia and visiting various engineering exhibitions, most of which had now come to an end. He had been enjoying a few days holiday in Cologne when the phone call had come through from the embassy official, informing him that his father was ill. How ill or serious the situation was they could not tell him except that reading between the lines the request had seemed more like a covert demand for him to return to England.

They stopped in a corridor outside a small medical ward on the ground floor of the building where there was a large observation window that looked into the room.

Peter could not disguise a shocked gasp at what he saw as the curtains were drawn back. A shrivelled body lying in the bed. Eyes closed, the lips approaching a purple blue colour, under a clear plastic oxygen mask, the face puffed up, blotched and puce in colour. Various intravenous pipes emerged from the mouth and nose and suspended sachets dripped their essential liquids into the body. The hands resting on the counterpane were swollen, red and shiny, covered in erythemal sores with ice packs around them. The full head of hair that his father had been lucky to retain into his seventies was now gone, a few tufts amongst the sores being all that remained. A fully gowned orderly or nurse, complete with mask and umbilical air line, stood next to the bed making adjustments to the array of monitors and suspended sachets of liquid that fed the body through the plastic tubes.

Peter looked in shocked disbelief at the scene that presented itself through the observation window. He heard his normally assertive voice as if at a distance as he asked in a croaked whisper.

'Christ Almighty, what's happened to him?'

Dr. Wilson turned him gently away.

'We would like to know that as well. The Rear Admiral is suffering from acute radioactive irradiation, so acute that I'm afraid there is nothing we can do for him except to keep him as comfortable as possible.' She broke off and looked through the window at the bed and the remnants of the man laying there, all but his soul fading into mortality. She preferred not to look directly at Peter as she said in a quiet voice.

'I'm afraid I have to warn you, he is going to die.'

Peter glanced back into the room, a thousand questions tumbling over each other, littering his brain, queuing up now to be answered. What the fuck was going on? When he asked the first of many questions, his voice was recovered, firm and assured.

'Surely you can do something for him, how on earth did he get in that condition anyway? He's an old man for Christ sake.'
Dr.Wilson replied.
'Your father was referred to his local hospital in Weymouth by his G.P. three weeks ago, suffering from acute sickness, diarrhoea and dizziness. It wasn't until the hospital staff there saw the result of blood tests that they realised how serious his condition was.' She paused and looked sympathetically at Peter. 'His blood count is down, and the white cells have stopped reproducing. His gastrointestinal system has broken down completely. I'm sorry Dr.Senden, but his body is breaking down, dissolving into protoplasmic debris. He's now in a coma which I regret he will not recover from.'

She took his arm and led him back to the waiting room, passing the windows of wards where he had the occasional glimpse through open curtains of other patients, lying in bed or sitting, reading, watching television, sleeping or just staring into space. They in turn glanced up at the unscheduled party as they passed by, breaking the monotony of the warm midday, a time that normally heralded the clanking and clatter of the lunch time trolley. His technical eye noted some of the monitoring equipment and he wondered, Christ what was this place?

He was given tea as he sat there his mind already clearing the debris of shock at what he had seen and now thinking of the vibrancy of the man as he remembered him from their last meeting. He had never been terribly close to his father and now wished he had been more attentive to the old man. He cursed himself for not returning sooner.

Sipping the tea brought his thoughts back into focus as his mind roamed around what he had just seen and recalled visions of the past, when they had been a family.

'Has my mother been informed about his condition?'

Dr.Wilson had taken a seat opposite him and lent forward with her reply.

'We understand your parents were divorced some years ago. Due to the circumstances of your father's illness, it was not considered to be appropriate for your mother to be involved or to see him like that. You're his official next of kin which is why we asked you to come here.' She put a hand to her mouth and cleared her throat. 'Because of the nature of his illness, it is of paramount importance that what you have seen here is not communicated to anyone else, especially the media.'

Peter put his teacup and saucer down on the table, the grey eyes under the frowning forehead searching the group, his manner now more assertive.

'Why not, for God's sake, what's all this about, I'd like to know how he came to be here and who you people are?' He waved his hands around the three of them in protest, his voice impatient as he asked. 'What's going on, how did my father come into contact with radioactivity in the first place?'

The doctor stood and folded her arms as she glanced at the other man, as if asking for the right to reply. He gave an affirmative nod and she turned back to Peter.

'Dr. Senden, this building is a secure hospital, not a normal hospital you understand but a place especially intended for incidents such as this. Its existence is not in any published directory and officially it doesn't exist. It is only used in extreme cases where, for the sake of public interest as well as the interests of our own organisation, it is felt better to keep such cases out of public view.'

Peter snapped his interruption.

'Gulf War Syndrome patients I presume; exposure to depleted uranium that no one wants to admit to.' He didn't dwell on the subject. His engineering background told him that there were many other substances, PCB's, asbestos and beryllium, for instance all used in the defence industry and just as dangerous if the dust was inhaled.

'What organisation?'

The doctor again faltered, exchanging a glance over to the other man and it was left for him to explain.

'This sanatorium, as my colleague Dr. Wilson has just said is a secure hospital dealing with specific cases where nuclear irradiation is considered to be the cause. It is also a pathological establishment run by the British Security Services for the purposes of examining nuclear radiation related incidents. You've been allowed to visit here because according to our records you've been security vetted and cleared up to a suitable grade with your T2 departmental involvement on sensitive defence projects.' He folded his arms in front of him as though trying to build a barrier between them.

'It's quite simple really. It means that within the provisions of the Official Secrets Act, you are bound to consider what you have seen here today in the same context as your routine work for the Government.' He gave a casual shrug of his shoulders, 'that is, not to say anything to anyone about this visit, or what you have seen here without being subject to the normal severe financial penalties and long term imprisonment.'

There was a pause as Peter considered what had been said and remembered his obligation to the State when he signed the documents relating to the Act and his annual vetting by the B1 department, in London. He shook his head in astonished disbelief.

'Yes, I suppose I'm bound to agree. I'm sorry but I just don't understand what's happened. My father has been retired for years how could he have possibly become contaminated by radioactivity? When did all this happen?'

It was the doctor who again replied.

'The Rear admiral was found in his home following a call out to his doctor saying that he felt ill. As I've said, he was admitted to the local hospital that, on evidence of his condition, rang a special number which alerted our organisation. As far as his doctor and the hospital are concerned, your father has been taken into private care, through the Royal Navy Association. A decontamination team then supervised the removal of everything he'd been in contact with. They also went to his flat and carried out checks there but everything was clear. We would have expected for instance that some of his clothing such as metal buckles on belts or his watch would have shown signs of radio active contamination. Unfortunately, there was nothing in the flat or on his body that showed any sign of him being in contact with radiation. When he developed ulcers in his mouth we discovered that he had a denture and the metal inserts were radioactive.'

Peter interrupted her impatiently.

'Yes, yes, but how and where did it happen. What was he doing?

'So far we haven't been able to establish how he could have come into contact with, what was apparently, an enormous dosage. An IRC or immediate risk check has shown that there is certainly nothing in the area of Weymouth or the old decommissioned Portland Naval Base that could have caused his injuries. Unlike the base at Davenport where the MoD store nuclear waste from decommissioned Trafalgar subs, nothing of that nature was ever stored at Portland. That's why the press have not as yet been informed. The Operations Directive Committee on this one has taken the decision that such an announcement could cause panic amongst the local population.'

Peter was still shocked at the whole scenario, his thoughts of those tranquil scenes of sexy long legged nurses pushing gentle old folk around in wheelchairs now kicked forcefully into oblivion as he considered the secrecy that now surrounded the situation he had unsuspectedly walked into.

'Surely he said something, I mean, didn't the doctor who attended him ask him where he'd been or what he had been doing?'

'Absolutely. Dr.Caplin was of course questioned. He told us that your father was in a state of collapsed shock when he found him and was already becoming delirious. There was a delay in visiting him, the doctor had several urgent emergencies that evening and from the symptoms had concluded that your father probably had a dose of flu.'

Jessica Wilson fished in a pocket of her white coat and pulled out a folded paper that she referred to.

'The only information we have is that in hospital he told them he had been diving, didn't say where or when. By the time he was questioned professionally he was delirious, his words nonsensical and gibberish, his mind had gone back in time to his Naval days, seemingly shouting at the demons and nightmares of his life. The only tangible words were about something he called the *Dragon's Morsel* and someone or something called Carter.' He kept repeating this thing about him finding the *Dragon's Morsel* and Carter almost hysterically.' She looked at Peter in expectation. 'We were hoping you could enlighten us as to what he might be referring too or who this Carter is.'

Peter frowned as his mind rushed over the words. Nothing made sense to him.

'I'm afraid it means nothing to me, I've no idea what he could have meant, or who Carter is, have you checked back through his Naval records or anything like that?' He felt his inside wince with acute embarrassment. The question was so damned obvious. If it was obvious, she gave no indication of her thoughts as she replied.

'Every angle on the name has been checked. Your father never had any contact with an operation or assignment of that name whilst he was in the Royal Navy. The other thing of course is that the reference could have a connotation towards narcotics language.'

The room was becoming unbearably hot and Peter loosened his tie.

'You'd be way off beam there, I can't believe it's drug related.'

He looked at the other three, his private thoughts turning over what had been said. Drugs? Christ anything was possible in this scenario; he didn't know that much about his father's private life of recent years.

'What happens now?'

The man, who was in fact a plain clothed Special Branch sergeant, replied.

'I'm sorry you had to walk in here and find your father in that terrible condition but because of the security surrounding our investigations it wasn't possible to forewarn you in any way. As you've heard, this is now a security matter and you'll need to be questioned further...... . I hope you'll understand the need for secrecy with respect to what you've seen here. Our orders are that complete confidentiality must be maintained until we can find out what happened. Because of constant terrorist threats that we're dealing with, we're able to blanket this event through the Prevention of Terrorism act.'

He nodded his head as if trying to recall anything else that had to be said.

'So, no leaks to the media.'

He stood, as if it was the sign that the meeting was over and then, apologetically.

'I'm sorry about all this; you may of course see your father again if you wish before you leave.'

Peter stood, as an orderly came into the room and drew Dr. Wilson to one side. He instinctively knew what was whispered before she turned to him.

'I'm so sorry.' She put a hand out to his sleeve, her fingers gripping him momentarily in an unspoken token of sympathy.

'Your father was seventy four, the temporary death certificate will specify a cardiac arrest as the cause of death and our own undertakers will take care of the funeral arrangements for you in due course.'

Peter turned away from her, upset at the sudden news. News that was only just beginning to sink in as he thought about the upright father he had known and the shrivelled body that lay in that ward. He spoke quietly.

'In the case of an unusual death isn't it normal to have a Coroners inquest?'

'We'll be holding our own post mortem. The Coroner has to be informed of course, but a Public or Naval Coroner's inquest would be out of the question at this time. I'm sorry about what's happened, but you can understand that due to the circumstances we wish to keep this matter out of the public domain, at least until we know what happened. Our own enquiries will continue for as long as it takes to establish the source of your father's contamination. There will be an enquiry in camera chaired by the local Coroner. Depending on the outcome, a decision will be made as to how any future enquiry is conducted and what the media should know.'

Peter Senden tried to recover his composure, the axiom of death taking time to sink into the minds intimate labyrinths. At first, the visions of his father came flooding back, then a burning disbelief like waking from a dream, a calmness, perhaps it wasn't true, a terrible nightmare maybe. Questions started to scream their messages, why? His body system grappled with the inconsolable enormity of what had happened before the real shock and finality of death set in and his mind shuddered with the thoughts of what has been irrevocably lost for ever. Then the cyclic feeling of helplessness heralded the bereavement he would feel.

The strange account that he had been given still baffled him as he turned the conversation over and over in his mind, dragons, drugs, terrorists? That Friday morning when he had boarded the plane at the Cologne/Bonn airport he had already been informed that his father was ill but he never imagined that it could have been this bad.

During his childhood his father had seemed to be frequently away from home and on his brief leaves from the Navy he had never been at ease with Peter. When his parents divorced they had grown apart and Peter had only seen him rarely.

He was still contemplating over what had transpired when Dr. Wilson's voice filtered through the haze of his thoughts.

'I'm sorry to bother you with this but there is one more thing I need to ask you. Your father owned a small boat I believe?' She had been looking at the paper she had referred to earlier and now looked up in anticipation.

Visions of his father on the boat, the fishing trips, sailing and learning to dive flashed through his mind, tangled with the branches of endearing memories from happier days, of sailing holidays, that now flooded through his consciousness.

That's correct although I'm not aware that he ever goes near it these days.' He was still thinking in the present tense.

We would like to check the boat over but we need the details of where it's moored and if possible, its movements before he became ill'

Peter shook his head the request didn't seem to have any relevance to the enormity of what had just happened and he replied sharply.

'I'm not sure, the last time I saw it was about three years ago in one of the old boat sheds near Ferrybridge, out on the shingle bank behind the northern corner of Portland Harbour.'

The sergeant moved immediately to the secure wall phone and rang a number with the information Peter had just supplied.

The two men in the adjoining room stood back from the monitor.

Major Fellows gathered his hat and briefcase and with a brief nod at the screen said.

'Well Sir, I think that's about it. We'll monitor progress and see if Dr. Wilson comes up with anything. In the meantime my department will keep in touch with yours.'

Hoskins nodded slowly, as if a little uncertain at the Major's loose organisational grasp of the situation.

'It's another path we can try, it'll probably lead nowhere, but we'll make sure they are kept under surveillance, we're dealing with something mighty dangerous here and the less the two of them know the real situation, the less likelihood of them getting into serious trouble.'

'We'll continue to keep this whole thing under wraps for the time being, as agreed between our respective governments, but we know the media are snooping about out there, with their usual hankering thirst, don't know how long we can hold them off.'

'You just make sure there are no leaks on your side. We must find *Thinman* before those fundamentalists; otherwise there will be a hue and cry that could cause public panic on a massive scale if this whole thing gets out.'

'You can rely on that old boy. Our intelligence agencies have already rounded up most of the known terror groups that could be connected with this operation, and there are plenty of them. Our Joint NBC Regiment is also standing by for action as soon as something is known. I understand that your C.I.A. chaps are also now liaising with them.'

The commander gave him a quick sideways glimpse. He'd been warned about some of the peculiar British colloquialisms.

'My chaps, as you call them, operate on the basis of an autonomous need to know. I guess they'll tie up when they think it's necessary. I'm more concerned that we find out what this *Dragon's Morsel* refers to, who Carter is and if there's a lead to the nuclear material that we're looking for.'

The Major, tallish with thinning grey hair and active eyes that twinkled behind the owl like glasses perched on the small hook of a nose, wore the old establishment neat moustache that bristled as he took the rebuttal without comment. He picked up his umbrella and doffed his brown Windsor hat.

'Till the next time then Commander, I'll bid you good morning sir.'

The Commander nodded his good bye as he picked up the copy of the dossier the major had given him and placed it into the briefcase, removed his glasses and stroked between his eyes with finger and thumb.

Together with a few others, he was the guardian of the longest standing nuclear secret of the U.S. Military, a secret that went back nearly sixty years, the loss of the World War Two nuclear mission now designated with the protocol title of Broken Arrow- *Thinman*.

But he bore a much heavier burden behind those hooded eyes that was beginning to show. A burden that gave him restless nights, had him waking bathed in perspiration as he thought about the plotters at Langley who were relying on him and his team to locate *Thinman*.

The *Crusader* Project they called it. A covert CIA plot that had got him involved unenthusiastically. A killing plot, unapproved by their government, to rid the World of leading al-Qaeda fundamentalist terrorists. A plot backed by hatred and fear following the fundamentalist attacks on Western ideals around the World.

The plotters at Langley had him over a barrel because of previous cover ups by his department over the suspected loss of the American W88 nuclear warhead secrets, through a Chinese espionage group at Los Alamos. He sighed as he stood at the window of the small room and watched the Major depart to his waiting car. What the hell did the guy want with an umbrella on a day like today? The Anglo American co-operation ordered by the respective governments on this one appeared to be working but he wondered what the Brits were holding back from him. The task force that had been quickly formed had found nothing to date. The old man in the adjoining ward had been the only lead that had come up on *Thinman*, but that mention of *Dragon's Morsel* was puzzling, it could not be coincidence that he had come across the mysterious metaphor in the past. Had the Chinese communists now come full circle after nearly sixty years?

He glanced again at the small monitor, showing the young man who had just learned about his father's demise. Sitting there, head cupped in his hands, his elbows resting on top of the long haunches. So, Senden's son was one of their own and he had no doubt that the British authorities would be bringing pressure to bear on him for the sake of their own national pride.

Chapter 3.   Simon Carter

Those tourists and business people travelling on the upper deck of the Star Ferry between Kowloon and Hong Kong Island that morning would not have given Mr.Simon Carter a second glance. An elderly man, he was not chatting into a mobile phone like most of them and was not a tourist engrossed in looking through the glass eye or the LC display of a video camcorder. He was smartly dressed in a light grey suit, of medium build with a good head of silver hair and could have passed for a European or Australian on a business trip, except that the high cheekbones and sallow complexion of his facial features, showing over the short beard, indicated that there was a slight trace of Chinese somewhere in his background.

He sat in a window seat, his pale blue eyes looking out over Victoria Harbour towards the Central and Wan Chai skyline of glass architecture, dominated by the seventy-eight story high Central Plaza building.

The Bank of China and the Hong Kong and Shanghai Bank Towers, loomed over the old Queens Pier and other ferry terminals, like giant ancient warriors guarding their kleptomanic plunder. Victoria Peak was slightly obscured by cloud that rolled across its upper reaches of green parks providing nature's emblematic mantle as a backdrop to the colourful foreshore development.

The waterway was busy as usual, with pleasure boats full of tourists, churning up the short sea, bow waves crossing and colliding into larger waves. Motorised junks plied their trade through the turbid brown water, laden with everything from market produce from the 'Territories' to decks piled high with waste cardboard. Fishing boats arrived from Lantau with their catches for the thousands of restaurants located on the Island and in Kowloon. He watched as large barges chugged their way down stream, fitted with special derricks for unloading the cargoes of hundreds of ships moored in the sheltered waters off Kennedy Town. In spite of the vast airport at Chek Lap Kok most of the supplies necessary to keep the vast six and a half million population going, still had to be shipped in by sea and ships still queued in the shipping roads where their essential supplies were unloaded.

In return for those supplies, the vast outpouring of exports from the Territory and Pearl River Delta were then embarked for destinations all over the world.

The water churned with so much activity going on, but the stable little green ferry ploughed on its course as its predecessors had done for the last one hundred years. The main difference over that period of time was that the crossing, which in Simon Carter's youth had taken twenty minutes, now only took ten minutes due to the reclaimed shorelines on both sides of the harbour.

Mr.Carter wanted to think and had chosen the ferry as the more relaxing way of crossing that afternoon.

The ferry pulled in to the pier head and the hundred or so passengers in their colourful look alike designer embossed clothes jostled to disembark, avoiding the spray pushed up between the craft and the pontoon, then climbing the noisy wooden stairs to the ferry hall, teeming with tourists all talking and shouting in their various tongues. Carter took his turn, climbing the stairs more slowly than the rest of them, avoided the illicit traders hawking their miscellany of wares to the tourists and found his way out of the terminal into the Connought Road. There he hailed one of the many red taxies waiting outside Jardine House and growled his instruction to the driver. The taxi took him to the Peak tram station, where he purchased a concessionary ticket for the funicular that would take him up to the Peak

Simon Carter's face was expressionless and no one could have guessed that his mind was reeling over so many problems as he left the Peak train and walked down to the view point. There he leaned on the edge of the parapet and gazed out, his head stooped disconsolately into his shoulders, as he looked down on the territory where he had spent most of his adult life.

Had he been asked for the time of day by one of the many tourists there, he could have answered in one of the local Cantonese dialects, Japanese, a smattering of Portuguese or perfect English, his mother tongue. That's if he had heard them, for he was deeply engrossed in his metaphysical self.

Simon Carter, like many others, had speculated for years on the vast property developments spread out below him and grown rich on the proceeds. Rich enough to own his own racehorses on the course at Happy Valley that, from that height, looked like a small green postage stamp set amidst the Lego like concrete structures. Many of the tower blocks had been built and successfully run through a maze of companies that he had owned, in many cases with exclusivity.

On the darker side of his conscience, much of the funding had come from his old masters in Beijing before they retired him off. He had no inclination towards the communist ideological dream, but had been drawn into their web through his own fickleness as a young man. He smiled grimly to himself, recalling those old days when he had acted as go between for the Peoples' Government and Asian subversive groups, supplying them with essential information about the business community in Hong Kong. Now they had suddenly given him one final assignment. A simple task, with a small payment up front, though nowhere near the money he really needed.

The losses on the Hang Seng since the decoupling of the Hong Kong Dollar from the U.S.Dollar at Beijing's insistence, followed by their currency devaluation had been crippling enough. His over stretched speculative borrowings from banks in Singapore and Djakarta had collapsed causing him to sell off properties to the new Chinese at ridiculous values, well below the exaggerated prices that he had thought would go on for ever. He had found out that, like Lloyd's investors a few years previously, high capital returns on investments are seldom long lived. His investments on Nasdeq technical futures had proved that. He had gambled as he had done throughout his long life and lost. His directorships on other conglomerate boards had gradually evaporated away as he became older and young Chinese entrepreneurs had moved in swiftly to take up the rich spoils.

The new Chinese had quickly taken over his other covert activities and associates had left him for more lucrative pickings and spat him out in the cold. Spat him out, the way the traders habitually disgorged their phlegm onto the ubiquitous easel of tarmac street coverings around the many market places in the conurbation that is Hong Kong. He cursed under his breath as he considered what they had taken from him and the irreverence they now showed towards him by the small emolument he had received for this final mission.

His only retained asset was the property that was his home in one of the most exclusive areas of the Peak. His liabilities on the speculative loans he had arranged were now out of control. Creditors were circling him like wolves waiting for the first one to pounce, bringing him down, tearing at the entrails, stripping him to the bone and baring his innermost secrets.

In order to retain some dignity that was so important to the Chinese side of his psyche, he knew that he had to retain the home he was so proud of and to find the extra cash required to cover the ever increasing costs of living there. He was not alone of course. Many of his associates who had climbed aboard the economic miracle that had been Hong Kong and South East Asia, had crashed, many harder than himself. He also wanted to be seen as the prosperous racehorse owner again, mixing with those who had cast him aside at the Hong Kong Club as a lost cause.

His mind wandered back and forth over his rise and fall in fortunes. His seventy odd years may, with God's willing, extend to a few more, another ten maybe. He stood there thinking about the conversation earlier that morning in Kowloon with the men purporting to be fringe Korean bankers and the exorbitant interest rates they had demanded on the mortgage he was trying to raise on the property. They had suggested another way out, a dangerous way out that he was unable to refuse and now, with promises of their help and the Beijing assignment, he would hopefully be able to raise some desperately needed cash. How the Koreans knew so much about his private affairs he didn't know, he was just thankful for the proposal they had put to him.

To negotiate and complete the transaction, they wanted him to go to their City of London offices. Their proposals to help him did not afford him the free hand he would have wished for, but he was desperate and any glimmer of hope was worth clutching at. He would work out how to cheat them for his own benefit later. It was fortuitous that his mission visit to England for his old masters could be easily combined with the requirement of the Koreans.

Simon Carter had arrived in Hong Kong with his English father and Chinese mother in the late thirties where they had sought refuge along with thousands of other middle class families who had fled from the Japanese invasion of China. His father was a marine salvage engineer at the time and had managed to transfer his family and business assets by sea from Shanghai.

Simon had spent his first few years with his English grandparents in England and later at boarding school, whilst his parents steadily built their colonial life style around the commercial opportunities that abounded at the time in China. Later, after a brief time at the engineering college, he followed his father into the business. After the Second World War, a small shipping line was developed which had somehow developed into property and big business. And now he was in this mess of business affairs.

The cloud had thickened again and the view had become largely obscured. He watched as he flicked a cigarette butt and it arched away on the slight breeze before he turned and walked back towards the upper funicular station where he stopped at a small bar for a local German style beer and another cigarette. As he sat there, his mind went back again to his beginnings in his father's small marine salvage firm.

Within a few months of him starting work, the Japanese Imperial army had three divisions massed on the border with the mainland. Low level air raids started over Kowloon and his mother had been killed by a ricocheting round as she had run for cover during a strafing attack by a squadron of Nakajimas.

The border with mainland China was crossed shortly after by the Japanese invaders in spite of heroic defences put up by a platoon of Royal Scots and Canadian reserves who were rushed up to the front to support them. A few days later the Japanese forces had advanced through the New Territories and were on the northern outskirts of Kowloon and the Empire troops had to be evacuated by an armada of small boats. Simon and his father had assisted with their own craft carrying troops, their equipment and wounded to Victoria City on the Island where the forces were redeployed.

The loss of Kowloon was serious and enabled the Japanese to deploy their heavy artillery across the narrow strait opposite Victoria City where the continuous heavy bombardment caused severe damage to the lightly armoured defenders. All the fixed heavy artillery had been installed for naval defence and pointed in the wrong direction.

As the next few days ground on, the superior Japanese forces gained their foothold on the eastern side of the Island. It was here that the main food and water depots were situated and their capture meant that without outside help, the Colony was bound to fall. The Middlesex Regiment, Canadians, and Royal Marines fought bravely on against mounting odds, but on Christmas Day 1941, Hong Kong Island was overrun. Sir Mark Young, the Governor of the colony had, with great reluctance, to accept the third and last demand of the Japanese C in C. to surrender and was taken across to Kowloon where the capitulation was signed at the Peninsular Hotel.

There had followed a time of great barbarity. Officers and men of the British Army bound and bayoneted to death, survivors of the garrison, including Indians, Chinese and Portuguese imprisoned in huts without light, food or sanitation and the wounded left to die where they had fallen. Permission to bury the dead was refused by the Japanese Command, the civilian population suffering terrible deprivation, starvation, indiscriminate imprisonment, rape and killing by beheading and drowning.

In London, House of Commons members listened horrified to Mr. Anthony Eden as the terrible story and barbaric abuse of power by the Japanese in the Colony was related. The British public received the news with dismay and some anger having been told that the island was strongly defended and could hold out indefinitely, even though the garrison only numbered a mere eight thousand compared with the forty thousand Japanese troops waged against them.

Simon's father was initially imprisoned, but the salvage firm had been considered useful to the invaders and was requisitioned by the Imperial Army to salvage some of its own local shipping losses, mainly from American aircraft. Simon and his father could not be considered as collaborators as refusal would have meant certain death.

Simon sat there, his hand around the cold beer glass, as he recalled the day that they had heard the drone of the American B-29 Superfortress bomber somewhere overhead. A sound recognised by all in that part of the world that was the theatre for the mass American bombings as they started to take the upper hand in the Pacific conflict.

The muffled explosion that followed lit up through the low cloud as the smoking wreckage fell into the sea about a mile away from where he and his father's crew were manoeuvring over the wreck of a Japanese freighter. They had been instructed to salvage part of the cargo from the freighter consisting of small machine tools and had just arrived at the location, near to a small island. He knew that they were at the southern end of the Ryukyu Islands, the Sakishima-Shoto group, which run from Southern Japan down to what is now Taiwan and included hundreds of small islets and islands including Okinawa.

The crew had all run to the side of the ship and later seen only one lone parachute flop into the water from what must have been an air crew of at least a dozen. Their Japanese army guards waved the men back to work under the threat of their bayonet mounted carbines, laughing at the airman's plight as he fired his Very signal pistol in an attempt to attract their attention.

The date was 7th.August 1945.

The short wave radio had been alive all day with jumbled reports from all over the area that the city of Hiroshima had been razed to the ground by American bombs the day before and the guards were intent on listening, not that any one of them had families there, but the incredulous news could not be ignored. A whole city eliminated from the Earth in one day.

One of the Chinese crew had shown his delight at the news of the bombing too obviously and had been bayoneted by their Japanese guards and thrown overboard. There was talk of the Pacific war ending and their four guards, whilst still watchful, were more relaxed than normal as they crammed around the door to the deck radio shack, smoking and listening intently to each report that came in.

Two days later they heard about the gigantic mushroom cloud and fireball flash as reports came flooding in over the radio, twenty-two thousand souls had perished to the north of them at Nagasaki and another seventeen thousand became statistics to pick over and draw on for all time.

Simon couldn't remember how it started, but he could still see the look on those soldiers' faces as his father and the crew caught them in their off guard state, garrotted them with lengths of chain and tipped them into the shark infested sea. The operation had been planned for days and young Simon had crouched and watched from behind one of the main deck derricks as the older men carried out their swift reprisal.

His father and crew debated whether to go back to Hong Kong, sail north to Okinawa, which had been taken by the Americans a few months previously or try and run south to the Philippines and risk the Japanese blockade that existed around many of the small islands. Instead, they had stayed a few days replenishing their starving bodies with the soldier's rations and listening to the radio reports pouring out of the short wave receiver in every regional tongue. Describing a new sort of bomb, called an atom bomb, with the destructive power of thousands of tons of T.N.T. A bomb that in the future would put fear in men's hearts whenever war was contemplated. A bomb that could be used as a deterrent in future wars, promising long term peace.

On the fifth day they heard Emperor Hirohito's surrender broadcast. The Pacific war was over.

Simon Carter's mind came out of the past as he finished his beer and looked at the groups of Japanese tourists having their photographs taken around him. They all seemed happy enough with their digital cameras and camcorders in spite of the political and banking problems they had left behind at home. Young students, who knew little of the past and could only see their immediate future, dogged with unemployment, which would have been unthinkable to their parents. Their parents who, flushed with the past success of their giant automobile and electronic industries, were now feeling uncertainty about the ability of the State to provide for them in their old age. He bore no grudge towards them, what was the point, these were different people to those who had murdered his mother and devastated his family all that time ago.

He had been daydreaming instead of trying to resolve his problems. He lit the last cigarette from the packet he had started a couple of hours earlier, stood up and wandered past the crowded tourist shops to another less crowded view point.

The view from the other side of the Peak concourse looked out towards Lantou Island and beyond that to the South China Sea. He stood there, and the casual observer would have considered that he was preoccupied looking out to the sea and distant islands. But his eyes and optic nerves were not communicating with the geniculate part of his brain. Instead, his visions were memories of the long distant past.

His meeting with the bankers had reminded him how his life had also involved others, in particular how the paths of four young men had crossed all those years ago. The English sea captain, the Royal Navy lieutenant and the scientist who could, even now, still hold the key to his future. This one final mission could solve his problems.

After the Pacific war, his father had borrowed heavily and invested in a couple of old freighters that joined the supply line to ship in the goods and machines which were so desperately needed by the Colony as it then was. Each outward trip carried low priced exports that were finding favour throughout the World and with each shipment a little more was added to the bank's coffers that enabled further investments to be made in land infill sites. His father had created one of the colonies smaller trading conglomerates or 'hongs' that he had steadily built up in the volatile market place.

At that time, Simon Carter was on the steep learning curve of business and trading. Wheeling and dealing, ducking and diving as each situation necessitated. Corruption was widespread and he was an excellent pupil. He travelled widely, setting up deals, arranging shipments and cross carrier agreements. He was also responsible for the salvage firm operation that he ran for his father who was by then concentrating wholly on property deals. The salvage operation had been reduced in scale and only retained one small vessel equipped with diving gear and limited lifting tackle. Simon treated it almost as a hobby, sailing occasionally with the crew when he needed a break from business or needed to get away from the girls and marijuana in the night clubs around Causeway Bay and across the water in the gambling casinos at Macao.

It was about seven years before he returned to the site of the wrecked plane, and located the position that he had plotted after the murder of the Japanese soldiers. It was during the Korean War and the salvage firm had been commissioned to salvage medical equipment from a British support vessel that had sunk a few miles away.

The American B-29 bomber fuselage was lying in about fifteen fathoms of clear water, wingless, mainly on its side and in three pieces that were partly buried in the sandy bottom. The centre section lay on its back with the bomb bay doors burst open revealing the content of its belly. Embedded in the sand some distance away he was delighted to see at least two of the engines that he knew would be worth salvaging.

When he clambered inside the fuselage, taking care not to catch the rubberised fabric of the heavy diving suit he was wearing, Simon could see racks of control panels and other electrical equipment in a great jumble of corroding wires. An untidy pile of gas cylinders lay on what had been the ceiling of the cabin, now littered with twisted chairs and other debris, covered with sea anemones and crustacia which had taken up residence in the sheltered undersea haven. A leopard shark, startled by his presence, glided past his visor as the small groupers and other fish continued their feeding on the kelp that rose from the sea bottom like a miniature forest.

When lightly rubbed with his gloved hands, it was still possible to read the engraved instruction labels on the various dials, meters and coded thumb wheel switches mounted on two identical racks of equipment, each one with its own central key panel.

Simon had gone to the wrecked plane mainly out of curiosity and he remembered very well his astonishment and horror at what he then saw through the window of his cumbersome diving helmet.

Before returning to the surface he recovered what turned out to be a waterproof attaché case. It was the contents of this case that gave Simon Carter his first clue to the enormity of his find; drawings, technical specifications, test results and setting up procedures for the strange equipment he had seen down there on the seabed.

On that occasion he had skippered the boat with a crew of Cantonese speaking seamen and his number two and co-diver Cheng the only one who understood some English. The rest of them had no idea what the Latin characters and figures on the various pieces of equipment meant. Simon Carter quickly established in his young mind that he had stumbled onto buried treasure that he decided could fund the high living style to which he was becoming accustomed. His gambling debts at the racecourse and in several Macau casinos were becoming troublesome and his father, who was now considering retirement, refused to help financially.

On the evening before they departed the wreck site, he had taken Cheng aside when the rest of them were playing cards on the fore deck. The little man limped badly and had arms, crippled from pressure strokes caused by nitrogen embolism from the bends and a lifetime of unsupervised diving.

'Cheng, I am not happy with the suit I was wearing the other day, could you help me to test it out?' The little man had looked up to his boss and given him a toothless smile.

'Course a will skipper, wha you wan me do.' Cheng dressed himself in the diving suit and started the air pump. Simon checked the helmet and non return pressure valve before placing it over Cheng's head and screwing it on. Cheng descended the steps still smiling through the observation window and fitted his ballast weight belt before entering into the sea and vanished below the waves, never to see the light of day again. With the air pump governor jammed and the non return valve securing screws loosened he never stood a chance. He couldn't read either but Carter never considered that.

When the crew helped him to raise the mess that had been his best diver, they considered it an unfortunate accident, one which Simon Carter had no hesitation in entering in the ship's log as such, making him the only witness to what had been seen in that underwater tomb.

Simon knew from the waterfront gossip of the time that the U.S. Navy survey ships that occasionally called in to the British Naval Base for supplies, were desperately searching for something in that area. Nobody knew what it was except that they were operating in a vast triangular area of the Pacific between Guam, Okinawa and the main Japanese Island of Honshu. He guessed that what he had found lying out there in the China Sea was the object of the spasmodic American activity he had seen over the last few years. It would require a great deal of thought on his part to decide what to do with his discovery.

The cigarette had burned down to the filter bringing him abruptly out of his daydreams and his fingers fished for another only to feel the crumpled empty packet in his pocket. It was time to stop thinking about the past and return home for more arguments with his young wife, his second and thirty years his junior. She hadn't yet come to terms with their demise, the cook and house girls having been dismissed along with the two gardeners a few weeks before and she was not happy. In any case, he had to get away from the crowds and decide how, if at all possible, he could contact the only persons who may now be able to help him. An ex Royal Navy lieutenant by the name of Philip Senden, a scientist, Dr. Anthony Holmes and Gilbert Piltcher an English merchant navy sea captain, the one time master of the Acacia Lady.

The Acacia Lady had been one of his father's ships. She was an oil fired old fashioned steam tramp, built in the mid thirties on Tyneside and had seen most of her useful life transporting copper ore from East Africa to places as far afield as the Port of London and Tokyo with her holds on return trips full of rolling stock and signal equipment for the rapidly developing African railway system. She had run aground on a reef in Malaya trying to avoid pirates who prevailed in the Malacca Straits during the post war period. After salvaging, she had been patched up and sold cheaply to the Hong Kong firm where she had joined the other two ships of the fleet. Now she lay in her grave on the other side of the World somewhere in the English Channel.

As Carter strolled out of the concourse to where he had left his car that morning, he was also preoccupied with the thought of two million dollars worth of Chinese gold bullion laying down there on the sea bed, probably worth between ten and twelve million dollars at today's prices.

Most predominant in his mind were the memories of that voyage in the Acacia Lady, the three young men, Philip Senden, Gilbert Piltcher and Tony Holmes, who had been his unwelcome companions and the lies that had been told in the Southampton court room on that wet English day some fifty odd years before.

Chapter 4. The Retirement Fund.

When he left the sanatorium, Peter Senden drove to his Dorset home, on the outskirts of Upwey, his mind full of what he had seen and the secrecy and mystery surrounding his father's death at Downshall House. What had his father meant by the references to some sort of dragon and something or someone called Carter?

His spirits rose as he drove into the familiar surroundings that he had not seen for months, the tranquillity of the place refreshing after his long overseas tour of duty. The cottages and old houses, down in this part of the village, dappled with shade in the afternoon sunshine, always gave him a welcome home feeling as he drove through the lanes and on to his home.

On his way back from the Downshall Sanatorium, Peter had phoned his part time housekeeper Mrs.Lyonns and was glad to see that she'd been there and prepared a meal for which she'd left written instructions.

There was a neat pile of mail on the kitchen dresser and a parcel she had taken in for him. Whilst he had been away, most of the mail had been forwarded to his known destinations so there was unlikely to be anything new. The junk mail was sorted to one side and binned in the garbage container as he read a couple of letters from his bank, confirming investments made on his behalf and examined the paperwork for the new car he had ordered on the Internet to be delivered from the Netherlands. There was a pile of subscription magazines all of which he piled on a kitchen chair for later reading.

He phoned his mother and warily outlined the news of her ex husband's death, giving her the official version of how Philip had died of a heart attack, possibly after a diving expedition. She took the news well but Peter could sense a few tears as they talked about his father's past life when they had been a family. She chatted for a while about a miscellany of things that had gone on whilst Peter had been away until she came back again to Philip and the funeral arrangements that would have to be made. Peter was deliberately vague and she didn't pick up on his explanation, that there could not be a funeral until a coroner's inquest had been held. They agreed to talk again over the next couple of days and make the arrangements for a Memorial Service the following week.

After phoning his mother, Peter followed Mrs.Lyonns' instructions, attended to the microwave and got on with his meal and unpacking before settling for the evening, catching up on correspondence but with the inexplicable mystery of his father turning continuously in his mind. What had he been doing to receive those awful rays that had broken his mind and body, what had he found during his last dive?

Mrs.Lyonns was round early the next morning and the aroma of bacon and a full English breakfast was in the air by the time Peter was up and showered.

'Good morning Dr. Senden, nice to see you back home again.' She was a jolly lady, always chatting about her grandchildren and the various indiscretions that went on around the village.

'Thanks Mrs.Lyonns, nice to see you too, any news?'

About half an hour later he downed his third cup of black coffee, the breakfast things had been cleared away and she had filled him in with every detail of local gossip and shown him numerous new photographs of her grandchildren.

Peter told her that he had been called back from Europe earlier than anticipated because of his father's death. To his surprise she burst into tears.

'Did you know my father?' He enquired.

She wiped away the tears and composed herself.

'Not very well Dr.Senden, but I presume you mean Rear Admiral Senden who lives down on the front at Weymouth.' After Peter had confirmed her question, she told him that she had done some temporary work there on occasions when his father's regular cleaner had been ill.

'By the way, where's the parcel I left here last night?'

She finished dabbing at her eyes.

'I've put it in the study for you Dr. Senden.'

The sanctuary of the study was a welcome relief from the chatter of the last half hour and he carefully opened the parcel to reveal its contents. It was from his father and Peter guessed it must have arrived some weeks previously. An old green cardboard file full of share certificates, insurance policy documents, papers, letters and a scrapbook of newspaper cuttings.

He glanced quickly at the cuttings, coverage of court cases involving nuclear test veterans who claimed that they had been used as human guinea pigs to measure radiation effects at Christmas Island in 1958. Yellowing musty newspaper reports of an inquest into the sinking of a merchant ship in 1953. Another clutch of cuttings covered the case of a scientist who had sold laser secrets to the Russians in 1985. There were others covering events over the years to do with naval exercises that Philip had probably been involved with in some way. They seemed to be a scrap book collection of events that would only mean something to the collector, all unrelated and he was about to turn his attention to the other items when the doorbell rang and Mrs.Lyonns called him.

It was Dr.Wilson, except that she now wore her hair down and was casually dressed in a navy self stripe fabric shirt style jacket and matching trousers over a berry coloured linen top. A plain medallion necklace and matching earrings completed her outfit. She looked stunning and Peter faltered for a moment before asking her inside.

'I'm off now sir if that's O.K. Coffee's on the perk in the kitchen.' Mrs. Lyonns smiled coyly at the doctor as she went out. She would have plenty to gossip about now for the rest of the day.

He led the doctor into the drawing room and they sat down.

'Can I get you a coffee?' She gave him an affirmative smile, which lit up her eyes and accentuated her wide mouth and the facial bone structure, making her quite beautiful to look at, something he had not even considered at their meeting the previous day. Then she had just been someone bearing bad news, today she was something else, very female and he felt a sudden pang of guilt as he let his eyes dwell over her for those extra few milliseconds. If there was a Mr. Wilson, he was a lucky guy but there was no ring on her left hand.

He opened the kitchen dresser and pushed the old coffee mugs he would have normally used aside, selecting the bone china cups and saucers his wife had bought when they were first married.

'So Dr. Wilson, what brings you rushing down here, any fresh news?' She accepted the cup of coffee and put it on the side table as she glanced at him, an unspoken apologetic glance, overcoming her intrusion into his recent bereavement.

'Dr. Senden, we found your father's boat, chocked up on the side of the Fleet, the lock up shed he used out on the beach was full of diving equipment and a lot of it was contaminated. Our Special Branch colleagues had to remove it all last night when it was quiet, wearing contamination overalls and using specialised equipment and vehicles. The local police sealed off the area as a health and safety exercise and were told that some old asbestos sheets were being removed and there was no need for alarm.

The contamination was caused by an unusual radio isotope.' She stopped and glanced at him with her pool like eyes and he could not help his attention wavering from their conversation as he returned her glance momentarily. Long enough to feel her searching as if probing for something deeper in him For that fleeting moment he could only think how he would like to feel the touch of that wide mouth, the perfume was gorgeous. She continued.

'There were no traces on the boat itself, so he must have been on another vessel, anyway, the main reason for my visit is to hand over the temporary death certificate that you will need, presumably when you or your lawyers settle his affairs, but you will no doubt be getting a visit from the Special Branch shortly.'

Peter took the document and placed it beside him.

'Surely you didn't come all this way on a Saturday morning just to deliver the death certificate.' He cursed himself inside, it sounded like an unfriendly comment, if he was to make any progress with the private thoughts he was having about her, he shouldn't have said it.

She looked embarrassed at the question.

'Dr. Senden, I live just outside Dorchester, I thought that as you lived so close, I might as well drop it in to you and have a further chat about your father to see if it was possible to piece together any more information you may be able to help us with.'

He apologised.

'Sorry, I didn't mean to appear rude.' He fumbled over his words. 'I think what I meant to say was that it was kind of you to spare your time in coming over here. By us, I presume you are talking about the Atomic Energy Authority.'

She gave that smile again and he knew instinctively that he was forgiven as she continued.

'Not exactly, the A.F.A. merely provide us with a security force now that we live under constant threat from terrorist activity.

As I said yesterday, Downshall caters for interactive cases between the Police Special Branch, MI5 and other forces including the Defence Ministry. The special facilities of the pathology laboratory there are used by all of those organisations in any incident that involves radio active substances. I'm connected to the Police Special Branch as an M.O. I also advise the U.K. Marine Agency Accident Branch.'

'Seems that we both work for the same employer then.' Although Peter worked for the T2 Technical Branch of the Defence Intelligence Service, and variously with GCHQ and MI5, he didn't know too much about the other sections even though his initiate training at Fort Monckton at Gosport was shared by the other special branches. His combat training with the SAS section at their Hereford HQ and camp outside Brecon and his long nights and days on the Welsh moors of Mynydd Eppynt and the Black Mountains had prepared his body and mind for the job, as had the crash course with the Marines in Poole Harbour. However, his job did not demand the physical efforts of most recruits. His time was mainly spent with foreign delegations at overseas conferences, looking behind the scenes when required, teasing out technical information on foreign defence systems that could not be interrogated by covert British Government listening stations, probing with their satellites.

He was an unusual recruit who had been plucked from the industrial sector rather than the normal route through the armed services or public schools. Like most engineers, he had a different approach to life than many others that his section found useful. An enquiring mind, demanding a precision and logical approach to problem solving that had brought him to the attention of the M.o.D. when he was working as a Project Manager in the communications industry.

There was that embarrassed silence again, as if they were each weighing up the other. He was subconsciously aware of the perfume she wore and enjoyed her fragrance as his mind came back to their discussion and he asked.

'Why is the Special Branch involved in this case?' Christ, why did he keep asking such bloody obvious questions! She seemed to be seeping past his primary ring guard fences that had been erected subconsciously after his wife's death. Fences that he was unaware of but that had become apparent to some of his closer friends, especially their wives or partners.

'Let's just say that it is unusual for anyone to receive such a high dosage of radioactive irradiation in the public sphere of things. Even industrial accidents with radio active substances rarely prove fatal or long term in their effect these days due to the stringent handling rules and procedures which are now incorporated into any processing of these materials. The authorities therefore treat an incident such as your father's very seriously. The most obvious cause is through unauthorised handling of these substances, for instance by terrorists or people trying to smuggle material for covert uses by non nuclear countries. I am sure that I don't have to spell out for you the worlds' fear of nuclear proliferation these days with so many wild- card countries and terrorist organisations trying to outdo their neighbours.

Most worrying these days are the efforts of fanatical terrorists getting hold of material. Splinter groups from the al-Qaeda network of terrorists, or North Korea for instance, Iran, Syria or the leftovers in Iraq.'

She didn't need to voice her concern. Part of his recent tour had involved him in Budapest and then the bleak city of Bratislava farther up the Danube in the Slovak Republic, quietly following up field agent reports of the Russian Federation Mafia attempts to deal in plutonium and other nuclear materials. Deals that were becoming uncontrollable; sending the deadly materials to the highest bidders without recourse to international convention on treaties or safety. And always with a rag tag of terrorist agencies in the background.

'Your telling me he was involved or somehow came into contact with weapons grade plutonium or enriched uranium?'

She looked around the neat drawing room, neat because of Mrs Lyonns's attention to detail. Two beautiful flower arrangements in the room, but no family photographs or other feminine touches. A large set of book shelves crammed one wall. All in all the room indicating that the occupant was a bachelor living alone.

This had been a difficult one, MI5, SO13 and other branches including the CIA all tumbling over each other for information. She had no idea why the CIA were involved in something that had occurred in England or why the Anti Terrorist Branch were showing interest, but guessed that at her level as an M.O. she was not being told the whole story. She had not been specifically told to conceal anything from Senden.

'All I can say is that we traced the contamination to the radioisotopes of uranium-235 and plutonium-239. The highly radioactive isotopes of iodine-131, strontium-90 and caesium-137 were also present together with certain nitrates indicating that a nuclear supercritical chain reaction may have been set up somewhere. It's an unusual combination and we do not consider that it's weapons grade plutonium, at least, not by today's standards.

So, you can see why the authorities are so concerned. It doesn't make any sense that an elderly man could be found suffering from such an acute radiation dose or indeed has come into contact with one.'

Peter pushed his hands through his hair and tried in vain to recall those few lectures he had attended on the subject. Nuclear physics had only been touched on and was not a subject he had been over interested in or assessed on until his more recent involvement through the T2 department. Even then he had always had others he could refer to.

'Bloody hell,' he said quietly. 'What happens now?'

'Well, as I was saying, the induced isotopic irradiation that the metal parts of your father's diving kit exhibited is of a rare combination and it will be imperative that we discover where your father had been and what he was doing.

As we told you yesterday, his normal clothes were clear. We can assume maybe that he was wearing his diving equipment when he came into contact with the substance and changed into the clothes he was found in later.' She glanced again at him as she took a sip of her coffee. 'Considering your father's age, do you know if he dived on a regular basis, or with whom he dived in company with?'

'I'm afraid not. He used to belong to a small diving club at Portland but that was years ago. Of course, he was an accomplished diver at one time when he retired from the Navy it was his main sport.'

'Well, no doubt our people will probe about until they find out something. From the little that I know about diving, I wouldn't have thought it to be a lone sport. If he was diving at the time he encountered this *Dragon's Morsel* thing, he must have had someone with him. Perhaps it was this Carter person.'

She smiled again, 'it's all right Dr. Senden, your recent travels are apparently well recorded through your Section, but we must find out who was with him and where he was.'

His thoughts, whilst still considering the possible exquisiteness of knowing her more intimately, went back to the Downshall Sanatorium and the other patients he had seen there.

'What about the other people in your secret sanatorium, were any of them involved do you think?'

She answered casually. 'Most of our patients are service people who are usually only brought in for surveillance. People who believe they are contaminated by depleted uranium for instance. A lot of it is used, as you're probably aware, in munitions. Supposed to be safe but after each area of combat, the Gulf, Bosnia, Kosova, Iraq, there is a statistical rise in unusual complaints that we have to look into.'

She replaced her coffee cup and rose from the settee, not wanting to be drawn into discussing or divulging the many other cases that were being studied at Downshall. Cases that she was bound not to talk about; the effects of war that governments on all sides would not discuss. The birth disfigurements, cancers, leukaemia, brain tumours, unusual illnesses called syndromes all apparently with a mysterious link to handling radio active substances either knowingly or, mostly, unknowingly.

As she reached down for her briefcase, she paused momentarily, aware of his eyes playing over her cleavage as she bent forward, the motion accentuating the plunge of her breasts as they vanished into the shadow of her soft cotton jersey top. His eyes dwelt there for those exquisite couple of seconds, long enough for him to feel the sudden imperceptible pump of his arousal, the first for a very long time.

'Please call me Peter.' The words sounded strange and he wondered if she'd noticed. She glanced up at him and that smile flashed across her face again. She had felt genuinely compassionate for him yesterday but she felt it had been an excuse to touch him. A fine looking man she had thought, tallish with intellectual features and that mop of fair hair that he constantly pushed back with his hands. She had seen his genuine grief the previous day, but something else had touched her, twitched her inside and now as their eyes met again for that fleeting allowable moment she saw his sensitivity, felt his appeal, knew she would think about him a lot.

'Well Peter, I must get back, thanks for the coffee, no doubt we'll touch base again soon. By the way my name is Jessica.' She walked towards the door and he searched for words that would ensure that they met again.

'Absolutely. Yesterday came as quite a shock as you can imagine and I'm baffled by what you've told me, just can't understand it, my father handling nuclear substances, it's incomprehensible.' He stood shaking his head slowly, indicating his disbelief as she waited for him to open the door.

'If anything comes to light I will of course get in touch.'

He didn't want her to go and as they shook hands politely at the door he stammered out a suggestion that they might meet for dinner some time. The thought had also gone through her own mind. She was delighted to accept his invitation and wrote down her private mobile number for him. She had already read about his previous tragic loss in the abbreviated registry file sitting in her briefcase.

Peter returned to the study, his thoughts still on her as he turned over his father's papers amongst which were a couple of Admiralty charts covering the Channel Islands and the Western Channel, his blue diving qualification record book and diving log, none of which had been filled in for some considerable time.

The charts were old and well used and didn't give any clues. They had been Sellotaped in places where they had come apart along the folds. In some areas the detail had been erased completely by constant rubbings out of pencilled- in positions. The only other item was an instruction handbook for a hand held electronic navigation unit or GPS (Global Positioning System), used by walkers, airmen and sailors to accurately pin point their position and altitude anywhere on the earth's surface from satellites. There was no covering letter or any indication why Philip Senden had parcelled them up and sent them to him. Peter could only think that the old man must have guessed his impending demise and prepared the parcel on the spur of the moment.

He put the GPS handbook in the bookcase, moved the charts and diving documents to one side and glanced quickly over the newspaper cuttings again, not reading them in detail as he turned instead to the bank correspondence, investments and insurance policies.

His mobile rang and Doug Lawson his T2 Section Leader opened the conversation with his condolences.

'Christ, how did you hear so quickly, I was asked to keep the whole thing buttoned up?'

Lawson gave a low laugh on the other end of the line.

'You forget Peter; we are the Technical Branch and can hack into most of the Services computers. You'd be surprised at some of the things I see up there. Anyway, the other reason for phoning is to pass on the good news that you've been granted a months leave on your contract to give you time to get the funeral and your father's affairs sorted. That's after you've submitted your latest reports of course. Oh, and John Cooper will be taking your place on the Balkan tour two weeks from now. Perhaps you could contact him with some of the details. Cheers.' The phone went dead and Peter sat there, slightly perturbed that the information he was supposed to keep confidential was already on the system computer net. If his leave was good news, what was the bad news, he hadn't thought to ask, but suspected that there was a lot more to his father's death than he was being told. What had his father been doing? Surly not attempting to smuggle nuclear material out of the country.

Later in the morning he drove down to the Fleet at Portland and had a look at Philips small diving boat, drawn up on the shingle beach behind the Chesil Bank and in need of maintenance, it hadn't been to sea for a long time, the paint work was blistered and the bottom was in need of scraping and anti fouling, with the rudder stocks stiff with corrosion. The shed on the beach still had police incident tapes around it and he was stopped from going inside by the duty constable, who told him that the health and safety officers were still in there, removing asbestos.

He made enquiries with a group of divers along the beach as they checked over their equipment, but none had seen Philip down there for some time, they directed him to the local club house where many of them congregated, a sort of drinking club for divers and those who shared the same underwater interests. Will Smith the club bar steward was busy but spared the time to come out to the bar and chat to him.

Peter described his father and asked if anyone there would know about his diving programme.

'Yes I know old Phil, haven't seen him in here for months, I wouldn't think he has been out in that boat of his for at least a year, but ask the lads over there, if he's been around they'll probably know.'

The small group, mainly young men and a couple of girls were all in high spirits and laughing loudly as they ranged over their stories, exchanging rhetoric with a couple who had forgotten to check the fuel level in the outboard before going out that morning and requiring to be towed back.

Peter asked if any of them knew Philip, but as soon as he was described as elderly, it gave them fresh fuel for their merriment. No, they didn't know him, had he enquired, amongst sniggers, at the wind surfing club.

He went back to Will and explained that his father had died from a heart attack, probably after a diving outing. The group's merriment stopped as they now realised the significance of Peters request for information.

'Is he the bloke over on the beach with the asbestos problem?' Peter looked over at the sunburnt young man with anticipation. 'He was around here about four week's ago. With some foreigners, Chinese I should say, been out wreck diving I think. On a boat from Falmouth.'

That's all they could tell him, they had seen Philip from time to time, usually alone but on some occasions he arrived in a small van with a couple of people they described as Chinese looking. Also on occasions he had been with Arab business types, drove out along the beach to the hut, loaded the diving cylinders and gear and driven off. They were all in agreement that he had not been out on any of the local dive boats.

Peter thanked them and returned to his car in thoughtful mood. Foreigners? What in Gods name would his father have been doing with a group of Chinese or Arab business people?

His visit to Philip's physician, Dr. Caplin, confirmed all that Peter had been told at Downshall except that, as far as the doctor was concerned, his father was now being looked after by the Royal Navy Benevolent Association. It transpired that it was the doctor who, at Philips request, had driven over to Peter's house and delivered the parcel.

His next call was to the Weymouth Marina where he called into the dock master's office for his boat keys and strolled along the pontoon, to where Seamaiden was moored. He climbed aboard the sloop, feeling that slight movement beneath his feet that always induced a sense of expectation and adventure in him. The hollow sound of his feet on the cockpit sole always welcoming as he padded to the companionway entrance, unlocked the washboards and went below.

He was pleased with the way the maintenance firm had looked after her during his absence. Everything in place, clean and ready and he knew he must take her out again soon.

The late afternoon was spent with Scotland Yard Special Branch officers who visited the house and spent a couple of hours interviewing him into the evening. The discussion was informal, but Peter was perfectly aware that he was being interviewed in a very precise and methodical way that left no stone unturned. Superintendent Malcolm Seiger left his card and requested him to keep in touch. A very serious matter he had said, an understatement as far as Peter was concerned, nuclear material that an elderly man had somehow come into contact with and died from was indeed a most serious matter.

The next couple of days came and went as he dealt with a pile of paperwork resulting from his F.O. tour for the T2 Section, finalising his reports, visiting his researcher in the London office and dealing with those affairs of Philip's that could be attended to quickly.

His assistant, Grace Pettyforce was loaded up with unusual research requests from him, to find all that she could on a long string of reports that covered nuclear accidents, hundreds of them going back over the years from all over the world.

He picked up his new compact sports saloon from the dot.com. distributor but the anticipation of driving his dream car, that had fostered over the last few weeks, had left him.

Peter kept thinking over what could have happened to his father, the contamination, the foreigners he was reportedly with a few weeks previously. A boat from Falmouth they had said down at the beach.

Philip had become a private reclusive type in retirement, rarely attending association or ship reunions. He had given up his golf membership and had died with few friends. The local vicar had only known him slightly and had relied on Peter to prepare a summary tribute to his life for the Memorial Service.

In its preparation, Peter Senden had suddenly realised how little he really knew about his father as he contacted old naval colleagues and went through Philips commendations and service medals. He also roughed out an obituary notice which he e-mailed to the *Daily Telegraph* and was surprised when they printed it the next day. It was in much more detail and with additions to the service career in the Royal Navy that Peter had not known about. The journalist given the task must have referred to the newspaper's own extensive files covering his action during the Suez crisis, his involvement with the Atomic Mosaic project in 1956, work on the first guided missile destroyer Devonshire and his first command on a corvette patrolling the new Polaris submarines at Holy Loch. His special commendations during his spell in the Middle East during the Rhodesian oil blockade were covered. Then his staff appointments and commands before his retirement after the Falklands War in 1982. His DSC and DSO and the photograph showing him holding his MBE award outside Buckingham Palace.

On the following Tuesday he phoned Jessica and they lunched together before visiting Philip's sparse apartment at the top of one of the buildings on the Weymouth sea front where two Special Branch officers were still searching through the remaining pile of files and papers looking for anything that would give them a clue to where he might have been. Older correspondence was discarded and more recent papers, bank statements, letters and notes were boxed up and taken away for detailed inspection, together with the sea charts and diving books that had been sent to Peter.

The ansaphone bore two untraceable messages from someone called Gilbert Piltcher saying that he was anxious about contacting Senden and would ring at a later date.

Neighbours were interviewed but Philip Senden had been a private person and no one in the apartment block knew him except to say the occasional, good morning. Peter reported what he had been told down at the Ferrybridge beach by the divers, but the officers thanked him politely. Their foot soldiers had already been making their own enquiries and had come up with the same information.

As they were going through the items list, checking off what was being taken away, Peter started to look through the desk drawers again.

'That's strange, has anyone seen a diary during the search?' They all confirmed that they hadn't. 'There's something else missing as well that I haven't come across, in fact there are several things missing. He had a small hand held GPS, you know, the sort that tells you where you are if you're out walking or out at sea. Also he had a rather nice brass binnacle compass that sat over there on the sideboard together with a sextant he kept on display in its open box.'

'How long is it since you were last here Peter?' Jessica asked him.

'Well, it's probably twelve months ago, maybe longer.'

'Perhaps he sold them. They wouldn't be of much use to him if he wasn't getting out and about.' Peter said nothing but he knew that his father would not have disposed of the sextant, his Royal Navy leaving present from the Officers Mess.

The rest of Philips papers, share certificates and insurance details, including his old scrap book were re-parcelled and sent off to Barrett and Godchild, the solicitors who would deal with Philip's Will and probate. John Barrett was a close friend of Peter's and was named as the Executor in the Will that John's father had drawn up for Philip a few years previously. The books, chattels and furniture were left for later disposal through agents.

Peter also contacted his mother on the telephone again during the week and between them they drew up a short list of acquaintances and friends whom they considered would like to attend the Memorial Service for Philip.

On Thursday, John Barrett rang to offer condolences to his friend and confirm receipt of the share certificates, insurance policies and other paperwork from the bank, credit card issuers and so on. They knew each other well, boarding school, flatmates at university, sharing the same old jokes, drinking partners on more occasions than they would like to admit. There was a certain sobriety in his voice on this occasion.

Peter, I've not had time to go through Philip's papers in any great detail but as sole executor I've been through his Will that was lodged with our offices here in Winchester. Nothing unusual to report, most of the estate will go to you as his immediate next of kin of course. There's one bequest that outlines some sort of retirement fund. Know anything about it?'

'A retirement fund you say. Sorry can't help you on that one. Perhaps it was a delayed annuity or something like that.'

'Well, there's a peculiar wording around it. Do you know any one by the name of Carter, Piltcher or Holmes?'

Peter stiffened, 'Did you say Carter?'

'Yes, do you know him or how I can get hold of him?'

Peter hesitated, how much should he tell his friend. 'What's it in connection with John?'

'Well the names I just gave you are people who apparently had some sort of agreement with your father over this retirement fund.' John sensed the pause in the reply as Peter recalled Philips last recorded words and his reference to Carter. He couldn't tell John the circumstances of his information and just said.

'I believe he may have been a diving friend but I don't know who he is or where he can be contacted. Piltcher must be a local friend. He left an ansaphone message at the flat.'

'That's O.K., thought I'd ask. I'll put out some enquiries and notices over the next week and see what comes up.'

Peter was thinking. 'Should he involve his friend?' He had decided to go to Falmouth for a few days sailing once the Memorial Service and its attendant obligations had been dealt with. Whilst in Falmouth, he intended to see if he could follow up the information given to him by the divers.

'Whilst you're on the 'phone John, do you fancy a sail down to Cornwall next week. Before all this happened I'd planned on taking Seamaiden for a short holiday sail, I've decided to go to Falmouth, well St.Mawes actually for a few days, wondered if you'd like to join me?'

'Hang on a minute.' John picked up his diary and thumbed through the pages covered with his secretary's jottings of appointments and engagements. He had sailed with his friend on numerous occasions around the Solent and on the duty free booze run to Cherbourg before the E.U. shot it into oblivion. The sunshine outside his office window kept reminding him that he needed a break. He grimaced as he looked at the full pages. 'Sorry old mate, no can do until the end of next week, say Saturday. I'm expecting George Fuller to be back in the swing of things by then.'

Peter sounded disappointed. 'How about we meet up in St.Mawes then, on Saturday week. I'ii be staying at the usual place, the Black Rocks Hotel down there on the front by the harbour. We can hopefully get a sail around to Helford. Perhaps you could book a few days, we might even make the Scillies. I'll leave the keys to my new car you wanted to try out at the marina, you can park yours there, drive down in mine so that you've got your car to get home in when we return to Weymouth.'

They confirmed the arrangements and John sat back as he contemplated his friend's kind offer of a sail and loan of the new car. He hit the intercom button to his secretary.

'Sally, can you book me into the Black Rocks Hotel at St.Mawes for next Friday night, no, see if you can make that a week, the change will do me good and I'll take some work down with me. Oh, and can you see if anyone on the staff would like my tickets for the Hampshire v.'s Gloucestershire match at the Rosebowl on Monday week?'

Chapter 5. Anthony Holmes.

When Simon Carter left the Peak concourse, those few days after the events at Downshall, he reached his parked car and drove the short distance to his home. The front security gates swung open as he pressed the button on the hand commander and drove past the ornamental gardens, now becoming overgrown and in need of attention. He parked at the front of the house, his memories flowing over him of how Philip Senden, Gilbert Piltcher, and Tony Holmes had crossed his life over fifty years ago, the ship, the court case and their subsequent relationships.

The curt note that Carter found from his wife when he arrived home confirmed his other fears. He had suspected for some time that his wife fulfilled her pleasures elsewhere. Now that the trappings of wealth were falling away, she had gone, and as he went through the small pile of mail that had arrived that morning, it seemed strangely quiet in that large property with no staff about.

Most of the mail concerned his desperate finances, letters that in some cases conveyed veiled threats on his life unless he paid up. He pushed them to one side and curiously turned over in his hand an envelope that bore a British stamp and postmark. It was a note from his errant son David in London. He sighed as he read through the brief. His son had got out of the mess several years previously and now spent most of his time in London and Central America. Carter suspected the merchandise his son was dealing in, but his requests for financial help in that direction had been ignored. He only received information from him on rare occasions or when he wanted a favour, such as a contact name. The letter   included a copy of the obituary to Philip Senden from the *Daily Telegraph* covering his naval career and special commendations. The cause of death was attributed to a heart attack.

Carter read through the letter again. He only had a vague recollection that he had ever mentioned to his son the long passed connections with Philip.

So, already his plans were going to be upset. With the Rear Admiral dead he wondered if he was going to be able to gather the information that was part of the deal with the Koreans. He resolved to book his airline ticket to the U.K. that day.

Simon Carter stood there in the emptiness of his study, contemplating, thinking, trying to scheme things out. He looked at his watch. It would be early morning in Europe. He picked up the phone and dialled a number in England but found it unobtainable. He dialled another and spoke briefly to the recipient. He then phoned his small office and issued instructions to his secretary to shut the office until further notice.

The recipient of his call to England was about Carter's own age. He had been sitting on the sun terrace at Oldbury Hall in Devon, enjoying his breakfast as he gazed out over the park land surrounding the house. On the patio table was the script for his latest television series that he had pushed to one side. Something on engineering achievements and their importance to contemporary society, Sir Anthony Holmes was writing some notes to his estate manager when the call had come through. Now, the aged scientist sat there, his head in his hands, in desolate melancholy at the thought of his life being shattered once more by the man who had crossed his path several times in the past. His mind, hovering over the memories of that voyage all those years ago.

Fifteen minutes later, a recorded transcript of the call appeared on Graham Nicholson's DICTIONARY computer screen at the COMINT Morwenstow secret listening station in North Cornwall. The number dialled had activated several system parameters used for examining voice communications on GSP mobile phones. One such system, the Calling Line Identification Data, detected the Carter synonym and number. Then, one word used in the brief conversation had caused the Echelon 2 system 'key word' voice pattern recognition scanners in the satellite receiving station to lock onto the call and pass the remaining part of the conversation to his briefing department. He saved the data for onward transmission to K Division at GCHQ, Cheltenham.

Holmes sat there for a while, thinking back to his encounters with Simon Carter during the Black Sea deal that had caused such painful press coverage. Unfounded as it was, the media at the time had hounded him and resulted in his forced resignation as a Senior Scientific Adviser to the Joint Intelligence Committee of the Cabinet Office. He glanced into the room behind the patio and his eyes fell on the framed photograph that sat permanently on the table. The memories of his wife's support at the time and how she had been driven to her death privately haunted him to this day.

After an hour he rose and walked through to his study where he searched through a drawer in his desk for a well-thumbed card index box that contained telephone numbers he had not referred to for a long time. The people he wanted to contact were unlikely to have e-mail. He ran his finger over the cards and extracted the ones for Rear Admiral Philip Senden and Merchant Navy Captain Gilbert Piltcher. There was no reply from the Weymouth number but when the Truro number rang it was immediately answered by Gilbert Piltcher.

The tap had been placed on Holmes' telephone line minutes before he lifted the receiver. No warrant had been requested officially under the Interception of Communications Act, as by a clerical error the original fifteen year old warrant had never been cancelled.

'Just thought you'd like to be forewarned that Carter's on his way over here from Hong Kong, say's he's been trying to get in touch with you and wanted your address and 'phone number.......Yes, that's right......after all these years. He expects to be here in the next day or two for some meetings with bankers........yes, just thought you should be forewarned my old friend. No, I didn't give him any information, said I didn't know. He has an old telephone number for you.'

At the other end of the line there was silence and the special services British Telecom engineers assigned to the telephone tap thought the conversation was over.

A gravel like voice responded. 'Thanks for letting me know Tony, that's about the last thing I would wish to hear, thought it was all over with him, never thought he'd be coming back after all this time. What do you think he wants?'

'Well he said he needs your help to assist him in finding the retirement fund. He's getting the backing from some bankers to make up a salvage expedition for the search. Reckons the gold is worth about ten million U.S. dollars at today's rates. Say's he's tried to contact you without success as he believes that you are the only one who knows the true position.'

There was a growl like laugh from the other end of the line. 'Well for my part I know what I shall be doing.'

'What's that Gil?'

'Get out of here and lie low for a while, that's what I shall do, go to you know where, until the coast is clear again.'

Sir Anthony sat heavily in the leather upholstered chair in front of his desk. 'Jesus Christ Gil, what am I supposed to do. I can't just vanish off the scene, my profile on television is too high and I've a new series starting soon.'

'You're just fortunate that you were never fully involved with him in the earlier years after that bloody ship's inquest! As it is, you suffered enough at his hands. Presumably he only 'phoned you to get my address, can't see any reason why his search should involve you.'

'What about that Senden fellow, did he ever find anything?' There was a pause on the other end of the line as Gilbert Piltcher chose his words.

'Haven't seen or heard from him in years. Last I heard was that he was taking out diving parties to that area. I'm sure Philip would have told us though, I'll ring him later and see what he knows.'

'Good. Look, I've got to attend a meeting in Truro next week with my production team, how about we meet up. I shall be staying at St.Mawes as usual. I could visit you if you like. At the same time I think I'll try and get hold of Senden, this thing goes back fifty years now, it's time we put it down to history.'

'O.K. brother in law, haven't seen too much of you recently. We'll meet up somewhere and have some lunch.' The line went dead and the special British Telecom operatives at the Devon exchange started their transcript from the tape.

Chapter 6. Paper Tiger.

Commander Hank Hoskins sat at his desk in Grosvenor Street, a temporary office in the heart of London's Mayfair and a block away from his Embassy. He read the decoded e-mails on the desk console screen that contained the telephone transcript of the call from Hong Kong starting with the *Dragon's Morsel* phrase that he had requested to be set into the COMINT (communications intelligence) scanning electronics at Menwith Hill. Other parameters such as name, area, communications type etc. had also been fed to the powerful Cray interrogation systems The rest of the telephone conversation was brief and there was no indication of the preamble leading up to the time that the computers had locked into the set key words and Hidden Markov Modelling (HMM) applied for the statistical analysis on all calls where the sender was named as Carter or *Dragon's Morsel*.

Hoskins had been intrigued by Philip Senden's last known words. He knew very well what the Rear Admiral had found, but where was it and why had he referred to it as the *Dragon's Morsel?* The phrase and name had also been inserted on the British Secret Service computers and hooked into the National Security Agency systems at both Morwenstow and Menwith Hill along with other key words, purely at his request. And here it was on his screen.

The telephone conversation monitored from the Hong Kong source referred only to a retirement fund estimated to be worth ten million US Dollars after the keyword alert and arrangements being made for the correspondent to visit the U.K. and set up a salvage operation for its recovery. There was no other information, nothing to which he could refer to or that would help him on the *Thinman* project.

The next message was the transcript of the land line telephone call made by Sir Anthony Holmes to someone called Gilbert in Cornwall. A conversation that sounded wary of the impending visit by Carter, but no further mention of the *Dragon's Morsel*. The transcript ended with the name of the recipient of the call, Gilbert Piltcher, traced quickly through directory from the number dialled by Holmes.

There followed the usual decoding and security narrative, the name of the recipient, telephone tapping authority reference number and primary telephone number. The copy had been channelled to him by Major Fellows's department and there followed a string of other intelligence reports.

Hoskins lifted the phone. 'Nancy, get the guys in here pronto. Darn me if something hasn't come up at last.'

There was a knock on the door and agents O'Brien and Hansdorf entered, unshaven and looking slightly dishevelled having been disturbed from their short sleep in the outer office. They had flown in from Washington that morning at Hank's request and after a short conference, were catching up on the time zone change and a sleepless night aboard the noisy Hercules C130.

Hoskins tore off the printer output and showed it to the two men.

'Our British partners are probably miles ahead of us already on this one although we have no interview reports as yet. I want our own intelligence reports, everything we can find on these three guys, Carter, Holmes and Piltcher. . .' He paused as he scanned through the sheet. 'George, get your team to follow up on this guy Carter. I'm particularly interested in him and see if our operators in the Hong Kong station have anything on him.'

He looked at O'Brien.

'Jesus, O'Brien you look like shit, for Christ sakes get washed up and get onto this Piltcher guy, find out where he breathes, what he eats, what he does. I'll make arrangements to see this titled guy but I'll do some background on him first.'

Horace O'Brien was the older of the two agents and made no comment at his apparent dressing down by the Commander. They had known each other a long time. Somalia, The Gulf, Bosnia, Afghanistan, it was like a reassuring compliment, one that covered old associations. They went back a long way.

Hoskins winked at him as the two agents turned to leave and he reached for the phone again.

'I also want our own tail put on Peter Senden, not sure how much reliance we can place on the British surveillance.......Hello Nancy, get Major Fellows on the line tout de suite and make an appointment for me to visit his records department, tell him I want to see everything they've got on Sir Anthony Holmes. Any news yet from Inspector Seiger? We were supposed to get copy from his department at Scotland Yard following Senden's interview and search of his father's apartment.'

He crashed the handset down at the negative reply.

'So much for the co-operation we're supposed to be getting from the Brits.'

Hoskins sat back and removed his glasses, rubbing his eyes as if to clear his thoughts. The Congressional Select Committee were screaming for information from him but what could he report to them? All he had so far was a story about a contaminated elderly diver and a phone conversation about a retirement fund valued at millions of dollars, somehow connected with the *Dragon's Morsel* thing.

The small task force of US and Royal Navy ships had been quickly assembled and were waiting at Portsmouth for further orders as were the French Navy and British Joint NBC Regimental group. His own team had been flown into London a few weeks before and spent most of their time sifting computer dross. The French DST and British Secret Service groups were also on full alert for the tiniest clue that would throw some light on the *Thinman* situation.

Fifteen minutes later, O'Brien was back, shaved this time.

'You were right about our partners, they have already been down to Cornwall and interviewed the guy Piltcher, this report just came in to the outer desk from the British Special Branch.'

'What does it say?'

O'Brien read through the contents.

'Says here he knows nothing about a ship called the *Dragon's Morsel*, the last time he had any contact with Carter was about fifteen years ago. Holmes is his brother in law but he hasn't seen him for about ten years, except on the television. Holmes is apparently a programme producer and presents his own T.V. show here in the U.K. They questioned him about Rear Admiral Senden. Seems he knew him years ago but no recent contact, they also did some background on him. Piltcher was a merchant navy sea captain until he was retired after an abortive court case over gold smuggling in the Black Sea about fifteen years ago. Apparently nothing was proved even though there were suspicious circumstances. He was a heavy gambler, lost heavily on the horses. A suspected homosexual who, according to the interview transcript, seemed to be afraid of Carter.'

'Did they find out why?'

Horace O'Brien read through the sheet again.

'Yes, he said he suspected it was Carter who informed the authorities about his suspected gold dealing. He was also beaten up many years ago and puts that at the door of Carter. It also says here that Piltcher is over eighty years old and is considered to be an unreliable witness.'

Hoskins looked disappointed, 'O.K., let's concentrate on the other two see what we come up with on Carter and Holmes. This gold smuggling, you say the Black Sea, any leads on that?'

'No. Piltcher was acquitted, apparently not enough evidence.'

Simon Carter had a window seat on the Air China Boeing 747 and sat with his head propped against the edge of the seat as he gazed down over the vast expanse of the Siberian forests below him. The patchwork quilt of the flat China plains was well behind him now as were the gold and brown shades of the Gobi Desert and Mongolian Plateau. Mile after mile of endless terrain which in some places looked like a forested lunar landscape, with great circular outlines of what he could only imagine were the edges of ancient meteor craters. The few roads from his high vantage point ran dead straight for miles connecting clearings with small communities of buildings and machinery. The occasional lake was all that broke up the endless wilderness of forest that stretched out for as far as he could see. His mind was still on the sudden desertion of his wife and he fished in an inside pocket of his jacket to read the note again. He rested his head back then and thought about the meeting that he was scheduled to attend with the Korean banking arm in London. He wasn't sure why they appeared so eager to help him with an expedition to recover the gold or what they really knew about his earlier background. He just contented himself with the thought that his share of anything recovered would enable him to pay off some of those debts on which interest was mounting daily.

Some of the loans had been arranged through fringe financiers to piggyback others that, besides interest, were now a threat on his life, for if he didn't settle within the new terms he had managed to negotiate with them his very being could be at stake, they would wipe him out. His mind trolled over what he knew. Was he on a hiding for nothing? He couldn't be sure that the bullion would still be there. That's if he could get that old bastard Piltcher to cough up his secret. His son was the key to that one. He could extract water from stone, or blood when required. It was a chance he had to take. There was nothing else except humiliating defeat at the hands of his creditors. More importantly, the few years he calculated he had left could be foreshortened after the painful revenge he knew would be due to him if he didn't succeed on this one.

His wife's desertion was a disappointment. He still loved her but the physical side had become difficult. His weekly trysts with his young secretary drained his energy in that direction. Sirin probably knew what was going on, or one of his enemies had told her. He wondered who, but there were so many. His life had been full of deals that had gained him friends in some quarters but many enemies. His mind drifted on, to those early, exciting days when he had so much energy, his dealings with the people from Peking.

In the early fifties the so called World Powers had all demonstrated their ability to explode nuclear devices many times more powerful than those that had ended the Pacific conflict in 1945. All, that was, except the new Communist Peoples Republic of China and Simon Carter had resolved that the significance and value of his scientific find out in the China Sea would best be rewarded in that direction rather than any salvage deal he could do with the Americans. In any case, the Americans were then tied up in the Korean War and the search vessels he had noted previously no longer came into the old naval dockyard at Hong Kong.

The Chinese Communist victory in 1949 had caused thousands of refugees to flood into the Colony, but there was a two way traffic going on and many refugees were not what they appeared to be. Simon Carter had been surprised how quickly his covert enquiries at the time had resulted in a contact from the Peking regimes secret service, run by the shadowy figure of Kang Sheu.

The Social Affairs Department was the Chinese Communist premier intelligence service, but the department that dealt with intelligence operations in Hong Kong was the Ministry of Public Security (M.P.S.) It was two agents from that organisation who eventually contacted him.

Simon Carter had negotiated cautiously with the communist M.P.S. agents. Firstly they had needed to be assured that what he was offering was in fact genuine. He'd dived a couple of times on the wreck by that time and was in possession of documents from the briefcase he'd found, which clearly identified the purpose of the bomber. His main concern was that he would be followed to the secret location or that one of his original crew would guess the deadly secret. For that reason, he had dived on the wreckage alone on a subsequent trip undertaking the dangerous diving tasks himself. Unlike the first dives, when he wore the cumbersome helmet suit with its lead weights and air lines to the surface ship, he'd used the new aqua lung and face mask, imported from France and which enabled him to glide down to the wreckage with ease in his frogman's outfit.

He had asked the Chinese agents for three million U.S. Dollars to be paid in advance on sight of the satisfactory evidence, with another two million on the retrieval of his find. His intention was to give them the position of the wreck where the equipment could be brought up to the surface by their own people. He also thought about the time after delivery when he knew his life would be in jeopardy and he knew he had to secure certain guarantees. He split up the secret documents and deposited them with sealed letters in safety deposit boxes in a number of banks in Victoria City, London and San Francisco.

The requests and proposals were circulated around the communist hierarchy in Peking and the scientific chiefs, ensconced in their new military research centre at Shuang Chengzi in the western Gobi Desert and the highly secret and restricted nuclear complexes at Qinghai and the Lop Nur region of Xinjiang.

There was controversy between the two overlapping security departments as to who should be responsible for the management and control of the young salvage engineer's proposals. Communist bureaucracy took up a great deal of time and no one seemed prepared or in the right position of power to make such a monumental decision. At various meetings, Carter edged his contacts on with threats that he would be offered far more if he went directly to the American or British authorities.

The Chinese mandarins on the grey edge of government subvention thought otherwise. They were very aware of what was going on and knew about Carter's gambling debts and narcotic habits at that time in detail. In fact, after the opening negotiations, they made it their business to be largely responsible for his mounting losses and increasing dependence on drugs.

Eventually, the communist contacts arrived with a deal that seemed to amount to what the Chinese research chiefs could scrape together out of their meagre budgets. They were not interested in the secret American technology. It was the manufacturing techniques that were the real key to what they wanted.

Their scientists knew the theory, which had been freely available in scientific papers and circles for many years, but an incredible development cost was involved in attaining the objective. A cost that could not be reconciled against the general obligation to rebuild the proletariat state. Their political leaders preferred to play a cat and mouse game with the West. Did they have a nuclear research programme or not? No one in the West really knew and the policy of deterrence seemed to be working as they were finding out during the Korean War.

The M.P.S. agent explained, 'Our revered Chairman and philosopher, Mao Tse-tung has said,

"*This technology is a paper tiger which the United States reactionaries use to scare people. It looks terrible, but in fact it isn't. All reactionaries are paper tigers.*"

Our politicians are not interested in acquiring the knowledge or equipment you say you have discovered, they are too busy feeding the mouths of our people. However, our scientists are curious to see the American equipment and have requested that we follow up the matter, which may be of some academic interest to them. We have therefore been instructed to offer you three million U.S.Dollars only, two million to cover the initial cost and one million on completion, all to be transferred in gold bullion due to our shortages of foreign currency. This final amount to be held for two years whilst our scientists analyse your find.

The guarantees you have sought with respect to your future will be maintained as long as you are prepared to cooperate in the future with our Social Affairs Department, as and when they may require your assistance.'

Carter calculated that the International Maritime laws on salvage would net him less than a tenth of that amount if he went through the correct channels and declared his find. His agreement to the deal had to be taken on trust and could not be verified in any way, but his gambling losses were growing and he had to take the chance. He was also now in so deep that he had to commit. He wanted currency, and eventually an agreement was struck whereby an advance of one hundred and fifty thousand U.S.Dollars was deposited in a Swiss bank account for his use. The Peking manipulators however still stipulated that the balance be paid in bullion as before.

He was still deep in thought as the stewardesses came around with the mid flight meal and he fumbled with the fold down table noticing his hands were trembling. If only he could somehow manage to get his hands on the balance of that bullion, lying lost in a rusting rotting hulk on the seabed of the English Channel. It would be the answer to his problems.

The twelve hour flight from Beijing to Heathrow London was tortuous as another benign announcement over the aircraft's PA suddenly woke him. Since leaving his home yesterday morning, he had already been on the go for hours. By taxi, hover craft and train to Guang-Hou on the Chinese mainland, then the internal Chinese flight before changing at Beijing. He had considered that the more obvious flight from Hong Kong to London might be detected by his creditors. His tired eyes watched the in flight movie, with no sound, as his mind went over the past.

He had hoped Philip Senden would be able to provide a lead to the position of the old wreck and its gold, but he was now dead.

At one time he had corresponded with Senden on another matter, but the most recent letters that Simon Carter had received from him had been left unanswered. The last letter a couple of months previously had inferred that he was getting close to discovering the whereabouts of the retirement fund and had obtained some financial backing, something that did not please the man from Hong Kong. He had not corresponded for many years with Piltcher and even now he wondered if his old captain would still bear previous grudges and be antagonistic to his plans. If Piltcher was already dead, then his secret would have died with him. Carter considered this possibility and frowned to himself. He was already bolstered by the recollection of the events surrounding the bullion and the glimmer of a chance that he might somehow be able to regain the loss. The loss, which had become insignificant all those years ago when his father had died. As his only son, Simon had inherited the salvage and shipping businesses plus many other business interests he had no idea existed. He had joined the Colony's multi millionaire club over night. The loss was significant in another way. He had committed himself to work for the Chinese Communist S.A.D. organisation and he had murdered for it.

The 747 droned on over the Gulf of Bothnia towards Kattegat, Denmark and the North Sea. The cloud had descended again, like a cold wraith around Carter's shoulders and he shuddered as he remembered that night so long ago which had tormented him ever since.

The killing night, which had been followed by the secret loading from the salvage ship onto the Acacia Lady, moored up in the roads opposite Victoria City at the dead of night. The night he had lined up eight crewmen for their wages and the soldiers had machine gunned them down with his assistance.

The night had produced the usual low fog over the bay that enabled the remaining crew of covert Chinese soldiers to toil for hours, operating the winches, overcoming exhaustion. The American equipment, in the new heavy lead containers inside their wooden boxes, placed in the deepest part of the No.2 hold with some of the boxed machine tools stacked over them, the bullion, still in the No.3 hold. The remaining machine parts stacked in the No.1 hold. The next day, an additional cargo of cotton jeans was quickly embarked to cover the illicit cargo.

The ships manifest for customs purposes simply stated the legitimate transport of second hand machine tools to Shanghai and clothing bound for Sydney together with supporting Waybills, Certificates of Origin and other clearance paperwork from his customer and from his salvage firm, which was an independent subsidiary of the shipping firm that owned the Acacia Lady.

He remembered his apprehension as the customs officer went through the paperwork and then, unusually, requested an inspection and descended into the cargo hold inspection hatch. The wooden crates were smaller than some of the others and as per. the paperwork, they were designated as spare milling machine arbours. The officer, satisfied, stamped the clearance documents and departed to one of the other dozen or so ships awaiting his authorisation that morning.

Captain Gilbert Piltcher was a young man who wore his green white and red mercantile marine ribbon alongside the Pacific Star and war medal decorations with pride. Simon's father had taken him on to command one of the other ships in the small fleet, but on this occasion, Simon commissioned him to captain the Acacia Lady. Her long voyage, first to Shanghai and then down to Australia. There would be several stops on the way to load and unload various cargoes which had been pre arranged..

As he sat back in the economy class seat of the 747, he paid no attention to the landing safety announcements. Instead he thought back to the words spoken by the young Royal Navy Sub. Lieutenant as he came aboard the Acacia Lady that afternoon in the autumn of 1952. Words that still rang like cold lead in Simon Carter's ears after all those years.

'Mr.Carter? Shipping agent for this ship?

'I'm Carter; the ship's owner, how can I help you?'

'Sub.Lieut. Philip Senden Sir, I have a note from the High Commissioner which requires and gives me the authority to requisition this ship for the use of His Majesty's Government,...... sorry I should say Her Majesty's Government.' The wartime king had died at the beginning of the year and Philip Senden was still getting used to the new nomenclature.

'As you've probably heard on the radio, there's trouble in Africa with the state of emergency that's been declared in Kenya this morning, caused by the Mou Mou activities there. We also need supplies for our troops in Egypt because of the coup d'etat there in July, following the abrogation of the Anglo Egyptian Treaty when King Farouk was ousted by a group of Egyptian army officers, led by that chap, Muhammed Nagib.

We have orders to send some comfort to our troops over there in the form of backup material, which we happen to have here in H.K. It's likely that the situation in both counties will worsen and we need to be prepared..........'

Carter's remonstrations had been of no avail as the young Naval Officer explained that there were only four British registered ships in the roads that day and two had already been requisitioned for the exercise He also pointed to the copy of the ship's manifest that he held, showing that there was only a limited cargo on board as notified by the Customs Officer. Philip Senden would be accompanying them and the convoy would be protected by a corvette until they reached the port of Mombasa and finally the naval dock at Alexandria. Simon Carter could only stand by and watch as the sappers loaded four stripped down light observation aircraft on board together with dozens of boxes of spare parts and other general supplies.

And then the scientist had arrived with his boxes of equipment that were to be shipped back eventually to England. Dr.Anthony Holmes had headed one of the many scientific teams measuring radio active fall out from the first British nuclear test on the Monte Bello Islands off the N.W coast of Australia that October. He was required to set up equipment and take measurements during the voyage.

And so, on that day at the end of October 1952, Carter's masters in Peking were informed that their prize of American nuclear technology and part gold payment were under the control of the British Royal Navy. They were compromised and could only stand by as the Acacia Lady set sail with the four young men, Simon Carter, Captain Gilbert Piltcher, the Sub. Lieutenant Philip Senden and the scientist Dr. Anthony Holmes. A carefree group by all accounts but a group whose relationships would become inextricably linked in the future as the Chinese made hasty arrangements for a fleet of Russian trawlers to shadow them.

Chapter 7.   Captain Paul Rogerson (R.N.Ret).

Following his telephone conversation with Gilbert Piltcher, Sir Anthony Holmes had sat there, still thinking about Carter. Why of all people had he phoned him that morning after all this time? Carter had ruined him once, years ago, but he had never divulged his other secret. Perhaps he had been keeping that one for this occasion. If Carter now intended to use that old ammunition it would mean disaster for him and all that he had managed to build up over the preceding fifteen years.

He showered and dressed and went back to the study where he started to read through the script again. He couldn't concentrate and instead decided to go outside for some air to clear his thoughts. Carter's reference to the ship as the Dragon also puzzled him. Why had he referred to the old ship and the retirement fund with that name, as though something about the wreck still haunted him?

It was Thursday morning and he decided it was time to visit his brother-in-law down in Cornwall and try to sort out once and for all what was currently known about the retirement fund. The fund that they had all agreed to share after the arguments on board the Acacia Lady all those years ago which, with time, had faded into obscurity.

He returned to his study and tried to contact Philip Senden again on the phone. The Weymouth number just rang until an ansaphone message came up which he ignored, and instead, sat at his P.C. and typed out a letter to Philip Senden suggesting a meeting between the three of them.

Had he been patient enough to listen to the answerphone message he would have learnt about the Rear Admiral's recent demise.

The Memorial Service at St. Michael's Church was a very quiet affair   The twenty odd people who attended the service, included Peter Senden's mother, his friend John Barrett and Dr.Jessica Wilson, together with a few friends and family. Some of Philips old Naval colleagues were there but many others he had tried to contact were too old and infirm or too disinterested to attend. There also seemed to be a few watchful faces there who were not accountable.

Peter stood under the church porch, as he waited for his mother, still in conversation with the vicar somewhere inside. The rain that was now drumming its presence on the porch roof brought a freshness to the air after the past several days of sultry heat and he was breathing in its sweetness.

A voice beside him said.

'So what happened to your father?' An elderly gentleman had sidled up to him on the church porch as he watched the others dashing off through the light rain to their cars.

Peter glanced down at the man. Grey wings of swept back hair and a large hawkish nose that dominated a deeply wrinkled and weather beaten face. Bent over, supporting himself on a walking stick and carrying a raincoat over the other arm of a well-pressed blazer that had seen better days as he then introduced himself as a one time friend of Philip's from the diving club.

'I'm sorry; my name is Rogerson, Captain Paul Rogerson R.N.retired. Knew your father years ago, we dived together on many occasions.' He spoke with a smile that indicated cheerfulness in an otherwise empty life of retirement, his head cocked over on its side so that he looked up at Peter like a bird looking for tit bits.

Peter looked out at the rain.

'The Rear Admiral suffered a heart attack I'm afraid, but under mysterious circumstances, we believe he had been diving and collapsed on his return.'

The captain donned the ancient raincoat in readiness for the rain.

'With those foreigners no doubt; seen him from the Quay. Lovely boat.'

Peter suddenly came out of his remoteness and regarded the old man thoughtfully.

'Fancy a drink before you leave Captain?'

They had said their goodbyes to the Reverent Martin and a taxi had been arranged for Peter's mother. Jessica had to rush off and Peter Senden sat in the local pub over a couple of pints as the Captain happily poured out his naval memories and experiences from his diving days. He found Peter a more than attentive listener and relished an audience that he had not experienced for many years.

'You say you've seen my father recently on a diving boat?'

The captain replied.

'Several times and on different boats though I wouldn't exactly call them diving boats, more like floating gin palaces,' he rasped a cackle of a laugh, ' but they all had diving gear on board, I saw it being loaded. Always foreigners. Looked like business people. Last time was about a month or six weeks ago.'

'What was the name of this boat?'

'Can't remember, haven't seen it now for several weeks but the harbourmaster's office down at Weymouth may be able to help you.'

'Any idea where they went on those trips?'

'Well I suspect that if he was taking these business people out and getting paid for it, they probably went to a spot west of Alderney in the Channel Islands, your father was always there, I dived there for years with him.'

'Why did he favour that particular area, it's pretty murky all around there, what did you dive on?' Captain Rogerson looked quizzically at Peter, the little circles of energy that were eyes looking up at him from the delicate petal like folds of skin that surrounded them and, after a downing the rest of his pint, looked towards the bar. Peter took the hint and ordered a fresh round.

'I must say I'm surprised you didn't know. He had this thing about a sunken treasure ship but like all those stories, we never found it.' The old Captain gave a gurgling laugh, 'wouldn't tell anyone the details, kept the information close to his chest you know, we used to go along with him because he had a boat and all the gear.'

Peter frowned, 'You mean he was looking for a Spanish galleon from the armada or something?'

'No, more recent than that, an old freighter I think it was went down in a storm during the fifties.'

Peter thought back to the sanatorium and what Jessica Wilson had said. 'This ship, it wasn't called the *Dragon's Morsel* by any chance?' The old man took another sip and wiped away the froth from his mouth. His day was looking up, unlike most days that were spent in his lonely flat overlooking the harbour, his usual company being the voices in his head.

'No, he never told us the name although he did refer to it as his retirement fund on occasions.' He gave another cackle of laughter, 'leaving it a bit late at his time of life to be worrying about a retirement fund.'

Peter lifted his glass and drank for a few moments as the importance of the chance conversation sank in. 'Where exactly did you say he used to dive?'

'Couldn't give you an exact position. In the earlier days it was somewhere off the South West Casquet Bank towards Hurd Deep. It's an inhospitable place about fifteen to twenty miles south west of Alderney. I remember it as a place where there were always over-falls and strong tidal eddies, a difficult place for diving.' He gave that gurgling laugh again, 'black as the ace of spades down there, had to use tri-mix due to the depth.'

'You say the earlier days, does that mean there was somewhere else he searched?'

The captain then recounted the story of his last dive with Philip that set Peter on the edge of his seat. It appeared that Philip Senden had on several occasions taken the diving boat and crew to a position west of Alderney on the edge of the Ortac Channel that lies between the Island and the Casquets, a predominant group of rocky outcrops and the most westerly point of the Cherbourg Peninsular. The old Trinity House lighthouse is situated there, now unmanned and automatic, guiding commercial shipping bound from Biscay to the Channel and the North Sea ports in France, England and further afield. Ships have to round those rocks to the West, where there is a shipping traffic separation zone. The Ortac Channel itself is seldom used by shipping due to the many off lying rocks, which in many cases are unmarked and dangerous in all except very calm weather. The uneven seabed causes heavy over falls and rip tides in the area, being one of the first obstacles for the Atlantic rollers as they smash through the rocks causing a swell that can rapidly uncover and cover rocks, and a spray which can shoot over one hundred feet in the air when adverse wind against tide conditions prevail. The most prominent feature is Ortac Rock that lies at the south east end of the channel, being some twenty metres high and a nesting place for Gannets. The Eastern side of the channel is marked by some low lying small islets of which the main one is Burhou Island, another nesting place for a variety of seabirds. The whole area can be wild place with tides running at up to seven knots and only a few local fishing boats and bird spotter parties ever go there.

They had been there many times but the captains last trip with Philip had ended in tragedy.

Against all the basic safety rules used by divers, none of the crew were ever allowed to know what they were diving on or the reason for diving. Philip had done several deep dives on the day in question, with the Captain assisting him on the surface and another diver going down with Philip. All the diving table information had been complied with as he had laid out a series of marker buoys along a bearing roughly south west from the diving boat.

Apart from the secrecy, all had been normal and the weather had been fair enough for Philip to take the tender to a nearby Islet for some bird spotting.

During the last dive, thick fog, which is a characteristic of the Channel Islands, had descended. The second diver had failed to resurface and they had put out a Mayday call. Lifeboats from Alderney and Guernsey were there within the hour but the fog hampered the search. A thorough search was started as the fog lifted after a few hours and lasted over twenty hours, but no trace of him was found. Local divers were called in later to search and found the remains of his body, caught up in thick fishing netting that was snagged on an underwater obstacle.

The coroner's conclusion was death by misadventure and an open verdict had resulted.

Peter looked at his watch. He was meeting Jessica for dinner that evening and time was getting short. He bought another drink for Captain Rogerson after checking that the old boy was not going to drive and exchanged addresses before ordering him a taxi and departing. Peter knew his father must have been in his late sixties at the time of the accident. He had taken up diving as a recreation when he was in the Royal Navy and after retiring from the service, had taken frequent holidays in the Bahamas to indulge the sport. His amateur diving licence had not been renewed, due to his fitness. He had, nevertheless, continued to enjoy the sport as a recreation. In fact, his enthusiasm had become too much for his wife Monica and they had divorced on amicable terms many years before.

So, without a licence and with his previous record, it was difficult to understand how he could have been involved with the foreign business parties that Peter had learned about from Captain Rogerson and the divers at Portland. Surely they would have looked for a recognised and qualified diving firm to indulge their sport.

The rain had stopped and it was a fine summer's evening just over a week since they had first met at Downshall and she looked stunning. They sat together in a small Italian restaurant on the high ground of green fields overlooking the shimmering sea, towards the Chesil Bank with Portland Bill standing out low on the horizon in the evening sunshine. Peter wanted to tell her how he felt about her but somehow the main subject of conversation centred on his father, the treasure ship and what Captain Robertson had told him earlier.

The meal came to an end all too quickly and they sat there idly chatting over their coffee. Jessica looked at her watch.

'I ought to be going, Friday tomorrow and I've got a heavy day, then I've got a few days off, shopping in New York. I will of course be debriefed about what we've discussed this evening.'

He looked at her with a sheepish grin.

'I suppose I should have guessed that you have been sent along to spy on me?'

She lent across the table and looked at him solemnly as she grasped his hand.

'Peter, we both know how important it is to find out what happened to your father. I was not ordered to extract information from you but you must agree that what you have been telling me could have an important bearing on this whole matter. As you said earlier, we both work for the same people. In any case, it was my decision to accept your invitation to have dinner with you, not theirs.'

He looked down at her hand, still clutching his own and squeezed his fingers slightly on hers.

'Sorry that was silly of me, of course we both have a job to do in tracking down what happened. Now, how about a night cap, we can stop on the way back at that pub we passed earlier or you're welcome to come back to the house for one.'

She lowered her head slightly as she felt the blush rise to her face and smiled.

'That last suggestion sounds nicer.'

Peter had been out most of the day but had received visitors without realising it. The tiny radio microphones were installed by the time they arrived back at the farmhouse.

A blacked out transit van was drawn up on a farm track off a lane couple of miles away on the high ground at the end of the valley. It looked like any other vehicle of its type, except that it had an unusual number of aerials mounted on the roof. Agents' Jack Brady and Stan Whitehouse sat there on the night shift sipping their coffees when the couple entered the house.

The listeners started their recording tapes as the couple quickly finished their drinks and Peter led her upstairs to the bedroom. Brady had only been half listening up to that time and turned to his colleague with a grin.

'Better put a spare tape on for this. I think it'll be one for the private library.' Stan turned away, pretending to read the newspaper in the dim light, embarrassed at his partner's obsession with other people's private games.

'Turn the sound off Jack, listen to it on the cans if you must. Thankfully the video channel isn't working.'

The next morning, Peter made two 'phone calls, the first to Supt. Malcolm Seiger, outlining his findings of the previous day. The second call found John Barrett sitting in his Winchester office, sorting out the post and various e-mails that had come in overnight. The same age as Peter, but with a slightly rounded body that, with his jacket removed as it was this morning, showed his past indulgences as his immaculately pressed shirt bulged over the trouser top. He frowned over the round bespectacled face as the desk telephone rang and reached for it. Early calls didn't usually please him, he liked a few minutes at least to catch up on his mail before the working day started and his secretary, Sally Denning, was under strict instructions not to disturb him until nine o'clock.

'Sorry to disturb you John, but Peter Senden is asking for you. Says that it's reasonably urgent.'

John's expression of slight annoyance turned into a smile of recognition. His old university friend had never had the same strict convention of time that he applied to himself.

'O.K. Sally put him on.' The hold Muzak started and he held the ear piece at a distance until he heard the familiar voice before replying.

'Morning old mate, how are things, sorry I had to vanish so quickly after the service yesterday..... what can I do for you at this unearthly time in the morning, thought you'd still be in bed?' Peter chuckled; he was sitting in the kitchen with a plate of croissants in front of him whilst Jessica, still donned in one of his bath robes, perked more coffee.

'Thought I'd just confirm the arrangements for Saturday.' There was a slight pause in his voice. 'Actually John it's about work that I'm phoning you, wondered if you'd had a chance yet to go through those share certificates and letters of Philip's that I sent you last week, any news on those names you wanted?'

John looked across to the various piles of documents on his work table and located the old green file that had belonged to Peter's father and which was now under a number of others.

'Sorry Peter, been so tied up on other things, had four court attendance's to deal with last week and one of our partners is off sick at the moment. I did make some enquiries with respect to the people mentioned in your father's Will though and my clerk has put out some legal notices. A few days ago I should think. Sally tracked down a Captain Piltcher living in Cornwall and I'm hoping to visit him whilst we're down there.'

'Well, I said there was another motive for 'phoning, sorry I didn't get round to it yesterday but with the rain, everyone seemed to want to make a quick get away. I thought whilst we were together we could have look through those letters to see if we can throw any light on what Philip was up to before he died. I'd also like to see if I can find out anything about a ship called the *Dragon's Morsel*, I think my father may have been searching for it before he became unwell.' He paused as Jessica poured his coffee and kissed him on the forehead before sitting beside him with her arm curled up around him inside the loose robe. I'd also like to find out more about the diving accident he was involved in; I believe your father was his solicitor in those days.'

'This ship, the *Dragon's Morsel*, was it British registered do you know?'

'Don't know John, all I know is that an old diving friend of his told me yesterday that Philip had dived for many years looking for a treasure ship, I've heard from other sources that the ship may have been called the *Dragon's Morsel*, sank around about 1953 somewhere west of the Channel Islands.'

'We'll have a look in Lloyd's Register, around 1953 you say, I'll have to get Sally to go down to the Reference Library, see if they hold any registers going back that far. See you on Saturday.'

John replaced the phone, reached over and took the green file out of the pile, placing it on the desk in front of him along with Philip Senden's general file that the clerk had put out for him a few days earlier and which contained the Will.

Peter sat there after the 'phone call, the softness of her body beside him as she twiddled the hairs on his chest with her finger tips. He turned and kissed her gently and she looked up at him, her hair falling across her face, which he brushed to one side before reaching into her gown, cupping her breast in his hand and feeling the taught nipple.

'Thought you said last night that you'd got a heavy day ahead, had to get up early.'

She smiled pulling him closer and murmured quietly.

'It can wait.'

Two miles away the listening post magnetic tapes were rolling for the day shift.

John Barrett was engrossed as he read through the file.

His father had represented Philip Senden, at the Bailiwick of Guernsey Coroners Court Inquest in St.Peter Port that had lasted for nearly a week.

At the inquest, the crew of the diving boat were all questioned and it was established that against all the basic safety rules, Philip had kept the destination secret indicating only that it would be near Alderney. When they approached the Casquetes, he then took over the navigation of the craft himself using transit sight triangulation lines between the Ortac rock, The Nannels and the high cliffs on the south side of Alderney.

The coroner's conclusion was death by misadventure and an open verdict had resulted. Philip had been severely reprimanded for his actions but surprisingly no legal action had ensued from the family of the drowned diver.

He tapped his teeth with his fountain pen as he continued to thumb through the paperwork on Philip the trip to Cornwall would also give him the opportunity to check the whereabouts of Jacksnest Cottage at Trevello Cove where he had established that Captain G.Piltcher lived. Apart from the Will, there were several references to this gentleman in the old correspondence of Philip's that Peter had sent to him and he had decided to try and locate him.

Philip had not left much in the way of personal paperwork. A few share certificates, old bills and receipts, pension details, photographs and the usual bits and pieces that one builds up over a lifetime. His Will contained the usual bequests. However, one bequest had proved difficult to arrange in spite of the usual notices in the public and legal press. It referred to a retirement fund, the word retirement being in parenthesis. The wording was also strange and referred to, 'my share of the 'retirement fund' as agreed with Capt. G.Piltcher, S.Carter and T.Holmes. My share of the proceeds, when found, to be divided equally between my ex wife Monica and her two sons, Peter Hillary Senden and David.'

John had not as yet been able to disclose the Will contents to the Senden family, but why that odd reference to 'her two sons' and only one complete name. John had known the family for a long time and had never questioned their family relationships. His enquiries through the Inland Revenue and Benefits Agency of the Social Security Department had both indicated that, apart from his service pension and state pension, there were no other retirement benefits due to Philip Senden. From all his gathered information Philip Senden only had one son and that was Peter.

To complete probate, John had to ascertain as far as possible that there were no other funds attributable to the Estate for tax purposes.

Another item was a wallet file that contained a bundle of correspondence going back to the early fifties with, 'Our Retirement Fund, DO NOT DESTROY', scrawled in faded ink across the cover. The file contained a scrapbook collection of yellowing newspaper cuttings and some letters, old by all accounts, faded and some in a type face used by a typewriter that had seen better days.

There were two correspondents, variously named Gilbert Piltcher and Simon Carter. Some of the letters were difficult to read, some were straightforward. None bore addresses. Several referred in various ways to the mysterious retirement fund.

He had found out through the Seamans' Union Register at Southampton that the sea captain had been employed through the late fifties and sixties by the Blue Star Company on its North Atlantic and W.Indies lines. The Liverpool firm had been acquired years before by a Greek shipping firm and records were scant. He had later left and become Captain of a cruise liner operated by the Volostok Shipping Company, sailing the Black sea resorts until his retirement some time in the mid eighties. Those tourist areas had been opened up to foreigners at about that time by the Russians, eager to earn western hard currencies.

A call to the London offices of Volostok (U.K.) Ltd. gained his last known recorded address in Cornwall. This after much questioning and the convincing story from John's secretary, Sally Denning, that she needed the address because her quarry's daughter was in hospital and she needed to trace him.

John had immediately drafted a letter to the captain requesting a meeting but the letter had been returned a few days later with unknown, return to sender scrawled across the unopened envelope. So the paper chase would have to continue.

There was no telephone number or postcode for the address. He had seen Peter's invitation to Cornwall as an opportunity to visit Jacksnest Cottage in the hope of meeting someone who could point him in the right direction.

John's enquiries about the other correspondents had so far drawn a blank.

Peter's enquiries at Weymouth had failed to establish the name of the yacht that Capt. Rogerson had described. Several vessels matched the description, but it seemed that different yachts had been used by the foreign businessmen and had only ever called in on occasions to embark equipment. There was only one vessel that was thought by the harbourmaster's staff to fit the description fully and it came from Falmouth. At least that was the port of registry they had noticed on the stern transom. The mooring fee records were scanned but there were hundreds of them and there had been numerous boats of similar description in during the summer.

At Downshall later that morning, Jessica Wilson reported to her immediate superior and head pathologist, Dr. Bill Wright giving him the details on Peter's chance conversation with Capt. Rogerson. It all seemed quite straightforward. The nuclear contamination probably came from a wreck that the Rear admiral had dived on. His reference to the *Dragon's Morsel* could only imply that he was referring to the ship's name.

When Jessica had left the office to clear her laboratory desk and attend to outstanding reports before flying to New York, Bill Wright phoned a London number. As he waited for the connection, he looked at Capt. Rogerson's card. There was something that Jessica had said that didn't quite tie up something he would have to check on. If the ship had sunk all that time ago, before the day's of the Worlds covert abundance of plutonium, it was unlikely to be the contamination source.

The voice suddenly came on the line, 'Fellows.'

'Hello Major Fellows. Dr. Bill Wright here, nuclear pathology lab at Downshall, you asked me to contact you if anything came up on the *Dragon's Morsel*. I'll be sending you a confirmation report of course but ....yes, the line is secure, the digital encryption is changed here several times daily.' The doctor then outlined Jessica's report to Dick Fellows, who listened intently to the story that was a repeat of what he had already heard from Supt. Seiger that morning at the briefing meeting. An old wreck of that date was unlikely to be the source of the contamination. No, the Rear admiral if he was in fact diving before his death had to be somewhere else, but where? The department had trolled the files and there were no reports over the last forty five years of any nuclear loss that would have caused the contamination in that area. Even so he called in his secretary and went through the motions, requesting a Lloyds List for ships in operation between 1945 and 1955.

Major Fellows sat thoughtfully in his Thames House office, its windows looking out over Millbank and the River Thames beyond. Even here, on the sixth floor of the building, above the great arched portico designed by Sir Frank Baines, the windows were protected with steel grills, guarding the nation's secrets in the British Secret Services Headquarters.

Nineteen forty five to fifty five. That should be a broad enough scan he thought casually as he returned to his crossword.

"Cheat gets a quick pint, 5,1,4,3."

He smiled to himself as he sorted out the encryption in his head, and pencilled in, "Pulls a Fast One."

About one and a half miles away in the Grosvenor Street office, the unauthorised tape transcripts of Peter Senden's conversation with his solicitor that morning were being scrutinised by members of Hank Hoskins' CIA team. They were not however treating the information with the same irrelevancy as Major Fellows, it was their first clue coupling to the *Dragon's Morsel* and within the hour they had operatives searching archival documents in the Public Records Office at Kew for the period, whilst over on the west side of Washington at Langley, they trolled the international directories of maritime nations looking for any ship registered in that name.

Chapter 8.   Terrorists.

When Simon Carter collected his small suitcase from the luggage carousel at London Heathrow, he walked through the green customs channel and out onto the terminal concourse.

At the arrivals' barrier, a small man with Korean looks stood patiently holding up a piece of cardboard with the name 'Mr.S.Carter' heavily inscribed on it with black marker pen.

Simon ignored the notice and looking straight ahead, went instead to the Bureau de Change and changed his fist full of Hong Kong dollars into Sterling. There were no travellers' cheques to sign or anything that could later identify him. Then he followed the signs and caught the Piccadilly Line tube train into London, changing once before arriving at Waterloo station.

He hailed a taxi outside the station and asked for an address in Soho's Chinatown.

It was Wednesday evening and Peter Senden planned to take Seamaiden round to Plymouth the next day, sleeping on the boat overnight so as to make an early start in the morning. From Plymouth he would then catch the west going tide for Falmouth and St.Mawes. He had gone to the local chandlers in Weymouth to purchase a few spares but found them closed and was on the way back to the marina.

It had started to drizzle and holiday makers had left the streets for the comfortable confines of the pubs and clubs in the area. Peter emerged onto the empty quay side running alongside the river and started to walk briskly towards the Marina entrance where Seamaiden was moored. He passed the boat yard on his left hand side, where small yachts and other craft sat in cradles or shored up on baulks of timber awaiting maintenance, their owners having given up work for the day as the rain had settled in. His eyes glanced over them, boats of all shapes and sizes, sailers, motorboats, small fishing boats, sitting there, waiting for their owners' dreams of the sea and adventure.

He heard the motorcycle engine start somewhere behind, turned and stopped as it drew up alongside him. The pillion passenger casually dismounted and asked him for directions to Dorchester. In the next instant Peter was fending off the blows from a baseball bat wielded by the helmeted passenger who shouted obscenities as he swung the bat in vicious circles at him.

Peter took the first glancing blow on the shoulder as he instinctively turned and ducked, the second blow caught him off balance and he fell to his knees, raising his arms in front of his face and took several blows as he knelt there, the thick waterproof sailing jacket and Guernsey sweater taking some of the force. The assailant was not an expert with a baseball bat. He had probably purchased it thinking it was an easy weapon, but he used it more like a truncheon, loosing the lethal power ineffectually.

Peter located the kerbside with one foot, then using the purchase as a spring board he shot forward under the man's guard hitting him with two fists with a force that made the man double up. As he swung round to deliver his next blow, the driver of the machine dismounted and threw himself onto Peter, knocking him backwards where his head made painful contact with the road surface. He heard the running footsteps behind him as his first assailant suddenly looked round within the limit of his black visor in time to see the short wooden scaffolding pole hurtling towards him. Agent George Hansdorf was holding it two handed like a medieval pike man as he rammed the end at the side of the helmet. The man dropped the bat and shrieked in agony as he struggled to remove the helmet and the bat rolled away under one of the shored boats.

'Get on, get on.' The driver screamed as he leapt back onto the machine revving the engine and his accomplice staggered to the pillion seat still struggling with his helmet, blood beginning to ooze from under its protection onto his neck. The back wheel skidded on the wet steel rail tracks that ran along the middle of the road, turning the machine around and they roared off into a small side road leading to the swing bridge that spans the River Wey. As Peter lay there semi conscious, he heard the engines high revving sound echoing and re echoing off the road and around the wet buildings as it crossed the bridge to the other side of the river. The noise seemed to be changing to music and coloured lights whirled around him. His mind told him that he was on a theme park ride that was hurtling towards a black tunnel and darkness.

Bob Jones was just accelerating his tanker out of the Harbour roundabout with eleven thousand litres of kerosene behind him, destined for the fuel depot on Portland. He'd just been chatting on the telephone to his wife back in Cardiff and told her that he had found a bed and breakfast for the night. The woman who looked forward to his weekly visits to Castletown was, at that moment, busy smoothing the warm bed sheets from her previous client.

Other traffic braked to a halt as the motor bike turned out from the swing bridge, swept across the road and shot off so fast that the passenger lost his balance and fell off into the road, still clutching his head as he somersaulted under the wheels of the fuel tanker. His crushed helmeted head rolled out from the other side, as the bike vanished at high speed and the tanker's tyres skidded on the wet road losing their grip.

The jack-knifing vehicle hit the kerb sending up pieces of rubber as the tyres burst with quick reports and the tanker rolled over, slewed along on its side, metal screeching in distress as it hit the first car blocking its path. Then knocking it into a second and third which burst into flames with an explosion that shattered windows in the buildings on the other side of the thoroughfare.

Peter was on his knees as he heard the explosion followed by a few microseconds of silence, and then there was just the smell of burning and distant sound of women screaming on the other side of the river.

Bob Jones disengaged the ignition, even though tiny accelerometers would have already operated automatically to close down all the electrical systems and baffle valves. As if driven by an unknown energy source, he reached up and hauled himself out of the cab without any thought of injuries and jumped down to the road below. He could hear liquid gushing from somewhere and had jumped into a pool of the pungent stuff as it spread towards the other cars.

The car on fire was sitting across the carriageway and must have been previously parked because there was no one in it. The next car contained a woman sitting transfixed in shock at what she had seen, but he could see a small child in the back, its face pressed against the side window, full of terror as it beat with tiny hands at the glass. The pool was spreading but the road camber had slowed its progress and directed it towards the gutter. Jones splashed through it, wrenched open the door and the child fell into his arms. 'Run, as quick as you can,' he yelled as he turned to the other door and pulled the woman free. 'Run, for god's sake run before this lot goes up in flames.' She ran after her child, sobbing and gasping as the slight wind wafted the heat and acrid smell of the black smoke from the blazing car over her. The storm drains were taking the liquid that was already pouring into the river. Spreading its thin film of rainbow colour hues across the water; beautiful colours from a filthy scum. Soot particles were falling like satanic snow and covering the polished topsides of cruisers and yachts moored down in the town marina.

Peter staggered to his feet as the sound of the explosion ricocheted around in his head. He was dazed by the fall and was suddenly aware that he was falling again as he felt a pair of strong hands grabs him from behind. He had a vague awareness of being pushed into a car and held on the floor as it accelerated off. He felt weak, too weak to struggle as he felt himself held there in an iron like grip.

On the other bank, crowds had started to gather. Cars had emptied and women stood screaming in shocked horror at what they had seen. Others, with various bleeding wounds caused by the flying glass, had poured out of the couple of nearby pubs and windowless local shops and cafes that were still open.

All three services were there within minutes, police, fire brigade and ambulance. Chief fire officer Don Neil soon had the area cordoned off whilst his officers manned the foam spray, which quickly turned the damp summer evening into a snow scene. Two police constables closed the road and directed other curious car drivers away from the area whilst another two ran around with notebooks spitting information into their communicators.

'Who saw what happened here?'

None of the onlookers had seen the actual baseball bat attack. That would have been seen on the other road by any passing vehicles that were now off the scene. In any case most witnesses were in shock from the nightmare scene there before them. The sight of a severed head and the pool of blood around the decapitated body was too much for most. A couple of hundred years before, their ancestors would have queued up in the square to see the tumbrel deliver such a sight. These days, even with the violence perpetrated each evening on their television screens, reality came as a terrible, sickening shock.

Witness's details were written down as a police hearse drew up and screens were hastily erected around the body ready for the police doctor's unsavoury task of examination.

Bob Jones sat on the kerb, a grey blanket around his shoulders, his head in hands, a medic sat with him as he told a police constable what he had seen.

Peter was still dazed when he came to and found himself sitting in the car outside the entrance to the Marina where his yacht Seamaiden was berthed. There were two men in the car, both wearing ski masks.

The man sitting beside him just said, 'nothing you can do here Senden, say nothing and you'll be O.K., just get out of here as you intended to and go.' The accent was American.

'Thanks but what's all this about who are you guys? Who the fuck hit me?' The American made no reply but the accent had already answered one question for Peter.

'OK tell me this. What's the CIA doing here in Weymouth of all places? I've noticed your surveillance over the last few days. It's my father isn't it?'

'Senden, it was just lucky that we were around when you were assaulted. We're sorting it out for you. No police or anything like that, this is a security matter that you walked into by mistake. Now, just get out of here and go.'

What was it all about? He didn't know and still felt groggy, but he decided to take the advice of the mystery men who had saved him and sail for Plymouth that evening.

As he slipped out of the harbour a little later, he was oblivious to his part in the disaster that had occurred on the opposite bank, as he motored Seamaiden past the flashing lights of ambulances, fire engines and police cars still assembled up there on the quay side. He had been too busy trying to fathom out who could have possibly wanted to attack him, or whether it was a case of mistaken identity. It was pretty obvious now that the Americans had been tailing him, but why? He guessed that it centred on the demise of his father. Only when he had passed the raised bridge and was motor sailing out towards the twilight and flashing buoy lights of the Shambles shoal bank, did it occur to him to question in detail what had happened.

After assuring himself of his anonymity at Waterloo, Simon Carter had arrived at the address in Lisle Street, a place he remembered from his early days in England as a street devoted to shops selling surplus Word War II equipment but now devoted to providing epicure Chinese food adapted to the European taste. Not all the premises in the small street behind Leicester Square were devoted to restaurants. This one had its windows painted out so that passers by could only see the signs that promised erotic sexual aids for sale inside. He climbed the scruffy wooden staircase to the first floor landing, piled high with cardboard cartons presumably full of stock for the premises below and found his son's flat.

The key was where his son David had told him it would be and he let himself in, surprised at the opulence of the place compared with the outside surroundings. He dropped his luggage in the small hallway and went straight to a cupboard in the kitchen where he found what he wanted, exactly where his son had said it would be. Then he fell into an armchair and smoked the joint he had been craving for and slept until the telephone woke him a few hours later.

It was David. Greetings were quickly dispensed with as Simon spoke to his son and outlined the reason for his visit to England, the desertion of David's step mother and the financial problems in the Far East. Carter embroidered the story, explaining how he was re organising his finances with the help of a Korean bank and hoping to raise about four million.

David apologised for having been called away on urgent business that would last several days, but he now found himself listening intently to the old man's news. Four million or even a small share of it was what he needed for his Costa Rica project. He didn't tell his father about his own plans. They could wait until later. Instead he readily agreed to assist where necessary. In the same way, Simon was wary of his son, not divulging too much detail about the gold search plans. In any case his head and body were weary from the drug and he was glad to end the call and return to his fitful sleep.

Over the next couple of days, Simon Carter made several trips from the flat being careful always to ensure he was not being followed. He travelled by train and taxi and on one of those trips he went to an isolated country house a few miles south of Basingstoke, deep in the wooded Hampshire countryside, and took delivery of a small parcel of compact discs from a nervous gentleman, going through a prearranged preamble given to him by his old masters and which he had learned by heart before leaving Hong Kong.

They were both surprised as they came face to face again, recognising each other after all those years but neither of them exchanging names, just the few innocent sounding phrases of conversation to establish the contact authenticity. Their eyes avoided contact as the transaction they had both been paid for was completed, both aware of their past and the dangers that each man posed to the other. The man watched as Carter's taxi drove away, remembering back to his period in Hong Kong when Carter had held his future in the palm of his hand, a future that since that time had involved him in petty espionage resulting from the depraved sexual weakness that Carter had discovered in him. His thoughts were interrupted by his wife, still in jodhpurs and riding gear as she strolled over from the tack room, her loud voice bellowing out in the parlance of her county set accent.

'Jackson, who was that man? What did he want?'

The man looked over to her, the overindulgent backside and bulging bosom, bristling with her self importance borne from the nemesis of her titled birthright. She was the youngest daughter of a peer and they had married twenty five years before when he was in the Guards, a marriage of convenience that her desperate parents had sanctioned for their ugly duckling after she had become pregnant by him. She had later miscarried, but the opportunity of wealth and position had spurned him on. How he hated her.

'Just some private business my dear, he was a courier from the London office.'

She brushed past him into the house, passing wind as she did so, as if oblivious of his presence. His fleeting thoughts at that moment were on how he would like to get rid of her, but his main thoughts were his memories of Hong Kong, how he had been trapped by Carter into serving the Chinese as well as his own Government.

On his way back to London, in the taxi, Carter casually looked in the parcel and found about twenty CD recordings of Chinese folk music. What on earth did Beijing want with these? He was still wondering what significance they could have as he deposited them in his luggage back at the flat in Soho.

His other visits concerned tracking down the whereabouts of Gilbert Piltcher. The man whom he hoped still held the clues to the gold. He dialled the numbers of a few past contacts without success and then phoned someone that he knew would have the information. His first wife.

On the third day, he rang the London telephone number he'd been given for the Korean Bank on his mobile and apologised for the delay in meeting, saying that the original flight had been delayed and he would now be arriving on a flight in the morning.

At Heathrow the next morning, he hung around the various shops near the exit barrier until he saw the short oriental man again holding up the same notice with Carter's name on it and went up to him.

The man swung round and enquired, 'Mr.Simon Carter?'
Simon confirmed the question.

'I am directed to take you directly to the bankers meeting if you would kindly follow me sir.'

Simon followed the man to a shuttle bus that dropped them off at one of the airport's vast parking lots. The man had not spoken much up to that point as he produced the keys to a Seven Series BMW loaded the small attaché case and drove them briskly out of the airport onto the M4 motorway heading west. Carter gazed casually out of the window as they turned south onto the M25 orbital motorway. There was little exchange between them and Carter assumed the man to be a private chauffeur doing his job.

A few miles and they joined the M3 motorway heading west towards Southampton. Carter's senses told him they were heading away from London and he leaned forward apprehensively from the back seat and tapped the driver's shoulder.

'Shouldn't we be heading in the other direction?'

The driver smiled apologetically at him through the rear view mirror, fished out an envelope from the glove compartment and handed it back to Carter.

The envelope was open and a letter inside bore the logo of the Peoples Bank of N.Korea with instructions for the driver to collect Simon Carter and take him to Weymouth, a seaside resort and small port on the south coast, about one hundred and twenty miles south west of London.

Simon read the letter.

It was not what he had been expecting. He had never queried the Korean bankers and had assumed wrongly that they were from South Korea. There it was plain to see. He was dealing with the North, a whole different ball park. Nevertheless, as he considered the change of circumstances he now faced what could he do? They had offered him hope and he settled back in the seat for the journey.

When Simon awoke, he felt refreshed even though his sleep had been restless. He glanced at his watch. He'd slept for most of the two and a half hour journey and they were now on the outskirts of Dorchester. A road sign at a roundabout indicated another six miles to go, that they made in twenty minutes, arriving on the Weymouth Custom House Quay beside a large trawler yacht, its Arab crew standing by and ready to cast off.

There were four men sitting in the comfortable surroundings of the saloon when Simon Carter boarded the yacht and they rose as one to greet him as he entered. The cabin was thick with cigarette smoke as though they had been waiting there for some time.

The short man who had met Carter at Heathrow looked around the cabin.

'Mr.Carter, can I introduce Mr.Chi Ling a director of our bank. These other gentlemen are our accountants, Chungai, Shinsa and Yoido.' The three men bowed their heads in greeting.

The man standing at the head of the table was dressed in a dark double breasted suit white shirt and an Amani style coloured tie. He inclined his head towards Carter with a slight court bow of acknowledgement, but, unusually did not present his card. Instead he sat and waved a hand limply, indicating a place for him at the table.

A cocktail cabinet made its silent rotation from the aft bulkhead of the saloon and a steward served drinks before being dismissed by the short man who then gave orders into a telephone, in a language that Carter did not understand. He felt the slight vibration of engines and activity on the side decks as the ship edged slowly out from the quayside berth.

The director looked at the papers in front of him, one elbow on the table, holding his cigarette aloft between a heavily nicotine stained finger and thumb whilst the others sat back in polite silence waiting for him to open the discussion.

He was a stocky man with heavy black eyebrows and a black head of hair that presented a straight line where it was combed back from the forehead. He wore thick black rimmed glasses that dominated his flabby Korean facial features. He raised his head and peered at Carter through the thick lenses, his pouchy eyes narrowing down against the cigarette smoke curling from his nostrils. He seemed to be summing up the man across the table, as though deciding there and then his future fate.

He spoke in English.

'Mr.Carter, I will come straight to the point. We have been examining the figures you supplied to our associates in Hong Kong showing your various balance sheets. They do not make good reading I'm afraid. The four million dollars you require would only be secured against the property at the Peak under the terms already outlined to you. Your other ventures are insolvent even if we acted for you and could arrange to put them on the market, they would not cover your debts.' He paused, craning his neck slightly to a side window, watching the quay sliding away before concentrating again on the papers in front of him. 'Notwithstanding that, we find we are also representing certain other parties who are your creditors. They are going to be most upset if we divulge our findings and searches to them on your unhappy financial affairs.'

Carter sensed a trap, a set up, but why bring him all that way just to tell him that?

They discussed aspects of his finances, circling like vultures after the kill, blocking all Carter's attempts to get onto the subject he thought he was here to discuss, the funding of a salvage operation to raise his gold. Gold that he had risked his life for all those years before when he had been indebted to the gambling casinos as a young man. Gold that he'd given up as lost and written off when his father died. More significantly, gold that had drawn him into the Chinese Communists' espionage web, changed his life as he followed their instructions and gnawed into the business community that had trusted him. Shit! Here it was again, a different organisation, probably more dangerous than any he had dealt with before. So what were they really after? His assignment for Beijing that he had combined with this visit to England had not been divulged to anyone. Then the awful thought struck him, was he being set up by his old masters, was this the final trap to conveniently get rid of him, wash their hands of him? Why? They had had ample opportunity to do that for years.

He sat there, trying to raise within himself the old confidence that had seen him through so many deals during his lifetime. There was a void. It wasn't there. Instead he felt inwardly sick at the thought of what the outcome of their discussion may involve, his final humiliating defeat with no money and no wife. To be compromised into possibly working for these people in exchange for his life and old age.

The young accountant, Yoido, sitting opposite Ling tapped his gold capped propelling pencil on the table.

'Mr.Carter, I believe our colleagues in Hong Kong told you there is the possibility of another way that we may be able to help you.' He looked to the director for permission to continue which was granted by a curt grunt and small nod of the head that made his glasses slip slightly down his nose until the bridge came to rest above the broad nostrils.

The accountant continued.

'Until ten years ago you were working in part for S.A.D. the Chinese secret service, or Social Affairs Department. Is that not so, ha.?' Simon Carter shuffled his feet uncomfortably and made no comment.

'We gather from information in our possession that you were disgraced over the Holmes affair in 1985 and ignobly retired with no pension. Is that not so, ha Mr.Carter? You were also considered to be undermining your responsibilities to that department by your son's fringe dealings in drugs and pornography ha. We also know that you were not exactly honest with the Peoples Liberation Army and worked also with the MI6 British Secret Service organisation in Hong Kong, ha?'

They were all looking at him for a response, as he considered the turn of conversation, and his silence prompted Ling.

'Come now Mr.Carter, you must consider yourself......... amongst friends here. We wish to help you in exchange for,' he paused and looked at the others, choosing his words, as he pushed his glasses higher, 'for certain information that we believe could be of use to us.'

'And what would that information be?' Carter replied cautiously, this was his last chance to raise the funds he so desperately needed but what was the line of questioning leading to? The Koreans like so many eastern nationals had this peculiar way of circling the main subject of discussion. His discussion with the Koreans in Hong Kong had implied that they knew all about the gold and were prepared to help in a salvage operation. These people were being evasive to the point of unreality.

'We have information that you found a certain object some considerable time ago which the Chinese Peoples Republic paid you for but, the goods were never delivered. In fact they were lost, is that not so, ha?'

Carter toyed with the documents in front of him, so that's what they're after he thought.

'I'm not sure what we are talking about here, or what this line of questioning has to do with the financial points we are supposed to be discussing or the reason for me being here in the first place. I thought you were interested in helping me to raise a considerable amount of gold from the seabed. I don't give a fuck for the past, only the future.' His inside felt knotted as he craved for the drug and he reached for a cigarette from the carved jade box in the middle of the table and lit it, watchful and acutely aware that a deal was in prospect, almost on the table, but he wondered at what cost.

Ling raised his hand to silence the accountant.

'Mr.Carter, don't play games with us. You know very well what we are referring to. In 1952 you employed a Chinese skipper on your salvage boat in Hong Kong. You may not have realised it at the time but he was an officer of the Chinese Peoples Liberation Army and a member of the Central United Front Work Department, a good communist.' He paused to light another cigarette and wafted the smoke away with his hand. 'He has recently told us about your exploits at that time in some detail. How you helped to murder his crew for instance.' He pushed the glasses to their normal position and for the first time made direct eye contact.

Carter hoped that the shock revelation of his past did not show on his face. His inside was churning in a way that he thought he had learned with time to overcome. He opened his arms and fanned them in front of him with a transitory flourish 'The man you are referring to must be at least eighty five years old by now, how do you know that there is any truth in this preposterous story?'

The accountant lent forward with an earnest hesitation that told Carter they needed him.

'Mr.Carter, in exchange for our possible financial help, we need something in exchange from you. Something that we believe we can come to an amicable financial arrangement over that would benefit both sides.'

Carter wondered what side he was supposed to be on as he carefully replaced his papers in the leather document case he had brought on board with him, hoping this action may indicate to the others his apparent unwillingness to discuss anything more. This was not going the way he had anticipated.

Ling whispered to the man sitting next to him. It was one of the other 'accountants', a man who so far had said nothing but whom Carter had observed from the others' body language, was probably the senior of the negotiators purporting to be accountants. He was a young man with Eastern features, Mongolian maybe, with cold unusual blue eyes that suggested a mixture in his background, smartly dressed in a blue serge suit as the others were but tie less with a shaved head and powerful shoulders. He smiled and addressed Carter in a thin high voice that seemed to be a couple of octaves higher than his looks would have supposed.

'My name is Johnny Chungai. Please, Mr.Carter, don't be too hasty in dismissing the proposal before you hear what we have to say. What we may be offering you could be your salvation, the help we require would bear rich fruits for yourself. Indeed, there would be enough to cover your paper debts and leave you with a considerable sum for yourself. Say five million dollars. Now please listen whilst we give you a brief outline of what it is we wish to propose.'

Carter stubbed out the cigarette and sat back, his arms folded in a gesture of defence, pleased that there was still the prospect of money on the table. The Korean continued.

'We have a complicated contractual situation that I will briefly explain. Our banking organisation is involved with certain friends in North Africa. In fact we are contracted to supply part of the know how on building an atomic power station for them. At least that is what they would like the Western powers and International Atomic Commission to believe. In fact much of the activity is being devoted to the development of a plutonium plant specialising in the manufacturing capability for a nuclear bomb.'

He looked at Carter for any response, but Carter sat there, poker faced, thoughts whirling through his head of the fundamentalist Islamic Holy war being raged throughout the World, waiting to see what card they were going to deal him from the deck.

'We are looking for sources of weapons grade plutonium to use before our main production plant at Keumjangri in our own country comes on stream.' Again he hesitated, expecting a response from Carter. Simon just sat there thinking to himself that what had already been said meant that if he did not commit to whatever it was they wanted, he was already dead meat and would not be allowed to walk off the yacht alive. He could feel the swell of the open sea now and he knew they could read his thoughts.

'And suppose I decide not to assist you.?'

Johnny Chungai rose from his seat and walked casually over to one of saloon windows, flexing his fists and glanced out, as though answering Carter's feeble question.

'We are well out at sea here my friend, I doubt anyone would recognise you when your dismembered parts were eventually washed up on some remote shore. However, I'm sure that won't be necessary.' He turned back to Carter, his mouth widening into a broad grin, as though the inevitability of the idea appealed to him.

'Your old skipper, Ho Sin I think his name was, co-operated with us in great detail before his unfortunate death that only occurred after we had wrung every last fragment of information from him. He sang with the confidence of a sweet song bird before it is slowly crushed in the hand.' He paused and placed his strong hands on Carter's shoulders as he stood behind him, as if to emphasis the point. 'Told us all about your ship, the Acacia Lady up to the time she sailed from Hong Kong.

Come on Mr.Carter, you need money and we are reasonably certain that the equipment you found all that time ago contained a small quantity of weapons grade plutonium that we could use to give our friends the confidence that we can supply them in the longer term. It would of course be a short term solution, the twenty kilograms of material that is involved would enable us to construct two nuclear devices these days, using modern machine tool technology from our friends in Iran, that would be used in a situation that would shatter the forthcoming Middle East Cease Fire Conference, disrupt the European Community's confidence and bring disgrace to the American imperialists once and for all, hopefully making their position in Europe, the Middle East and Asia so untenable in the future that their so called allies will disown them.

The fragile political compromise between the states of the European Union would become fragmented with accusations, a good time for our fundamentalist Islamic friends around the World to take their full revenge and regain the control they once enjoyed over those sanctimonious peoples. As for the Israeli cease fire, we do not.....'

The director put out a hand to silence the enthusiasm of Chungai and exclaimed.

'Mr.Carter, we need only one thing from you, the true position of the Acacia Lady. It is not where it should be according to the reports we have. We have had a team of specialists looking in that area under the guise of treasure seekers for the last six months and can find no remains of the ship.

Another old friend of yours, Rear Admiral Philip Senden, was employed by us in the belief that he knew the position of this ship but he wasted our time and has apparently since died. Now we are running out of time because we know that the British and French Navies have also started searching during the last few days under the command of a U.S. Navy task force lead by the special survey ship, the U.S.S. Phoenix. An unfortunate leak by one of our Middle Eastern partners alerted them, but the offenders have been suitably dealt with. Time is running out and it is absolutely essential that we find the material before the Americans or British.'

Carter felt the hairs on his beard tingling, possibly from the fright of the situation he now found himself in. Possibly from the horror he felt as he remembered the barbarity he had seen as a child in Victoria City, but mainly, he knew, from the desire of stimulant that the circumstances had triggered. When he spoke, he found his mouth dry even though perspiration trickled down his back and he could sense the droplets forming on his brow. An experience he had not felt since dealing face to face with Chechnian rebel leaders, an occasion even worse than in Afghanistan or Iran, and he was now fifteen years older.

'Surely there are enough nuclear devices around the World for you to arrange to steal one. What about the stockpiles of nuclear devices in the former Russian satellite countries?'

Ling replied. 'No, no, Mr.Carter, we have compiled a very detailed feasibility study into our requirements. In spite of the Worlds' belief that the Russians are unreliable, all the stockpiles of warheads you refer to were removed and are carefully accounted for in secure Russian Federation arsenals. The so-called Russian Mafia professes to ownership of such material, but in practice once money is paid up front they never seem to be able to substantiate their claims. In any case, our studies have shown that these modern devices are much too complex for our use. No, we require something very simple. The equipment you found in the China Sea was of prototype construction and hence the protective triggering devices are very simple by today's standards.' He lit another cigarette. 'We already have an expert on triggering devices with us, a scientist who I believe you know.'

Carter looked around the faces at the table.

'What you are considering is preposterous, I imagine that if the equipment you speak of was lost years ago in the English Channel it would have been detected and removed by now.'

'We think not. Since we detected a leak in our proposals, we know that the American task force have, like us, been conducting a desperate search pattern. As I said, there is enough plutonium to build two nuclear devices, one for our Middle East friends and one for ourselves. The information we require from you could be worth substantially more than we have indicated.' His face crinkled into a friendly smile, as if anticipating an argument won.

'Why should a bankrupt country like yours require a nuclear capability, surely you've already proved with your underground tests that you have the technology, surely there are enough trigger happy people in the world without you joining in?'

Ling laughed. 'Why should we let the western powers hold the rest of us to ransom Mr. Carter. We have a right to reinstate Korea as one nation and remove the absurd artificial demilitarised zone that has been in place now since 1953. The Americans deployed 45000 soldiers there until recently to keep our people apart.

Our nuclear programme was stopped by the U.S.A. at the Geneva Convention back in 1994 when they suspected that we could be producing weapons grade plutonium at Keumjangri. In exchange for our generosity they were to supply light water reactors for a new plant at Yongbyon with international supervision. They promised to supply us with oil to meet our energy requirements whilst the new plant was built. But the U.S. Congress withheld the necessary funds and the oil has never materialised. Now the World tries to hold us to ransom with U.N. sanctions.'

Carter tried a brave smile as he looked across at him.

'Why tell me all this? The only fast breeders I ever came across were rabbits.'

Ling glowered, as the others looked puzzled at his remark.

'Very funny Carter, but let me tell you more. We have had more recent encounters with the West when unfulfilled promises have been made to our Government including the big issue of reunification. The Japanese and Americans are riveted with fear over such a prospect and are doing everything that they can to delay such a long delayed reunion of our families. Now Mr.Carter who would you consider as being the aggressor in such a situation. No, the Americans have held their cosy world position of dominance for too long and the time has come to change history and hit them hard from two directions. We've demonstrated that we are a nuclear power. With our long range three stage ballistic missile, the Taepodong-4 we can now deliver our package into the American heartland. The al-Qaeda organisations for their part have already substantiated several severe blows to the Americans, but this time they will deliver their part of the bargain in Europe to put a stop to the false Middle East Cease Fire Conference to be held in London in a couple of months from now. The catastrophe will be blamed on the Americans and people of all races will rise against their respective Governments and demand a de-coupling from the U.S. who will then become isolated in world affairs. Their economic strength will be severely weakened and their people will demand that their politicians withdraw support for the various puppets who administer their unpopular policies especially in the south of our country and in Israel, Iraq and Afghanistan to name only a few.'

Carter sat there, bathed in sweat at the thought of the proliferation that could result if their plan succeeded. His inside was pounding, he was losing it.

Ling, or to give him his correct title, Colonel Chi Ling, one time head of the overseas section of the Peoples Secret Services of N.Korea, continued.

'We understand that our Chinese friends now have many of the latest secrets for the American W-88 warhead. It will not be long before there is a stand off between China and the Americans. The diplomatic breakdown during the early part of the Bulkan conflict indicates how insecure their relationship is. We intend to get there first, the sixty year old nuclear deterrent has been used for too long and it is our intention to break it.'

'I can't help you, your plan wont work.' Carter's words came out in a whisper. 'I was led to believe before I came here that you were bankers interested in providing the funds for a salvage operation of which I would benefit in part. I was only interested in finding the gold with your assistance, sharing the proceeds and paying off some of my outstanding debts. I don't even know the true whereabouts of the Acacia Lady.' His voice faltered as if trying not to pour out the next sentence, but he couldn't stop it. 'I thought I'd be dealing with bankers, you're just a bunch of terrorists.'

Ling rose rather quickly for his bulk. 'No Mr.Carter, we are not terrorists, we are the hero's of a new world order that is about to be put in place. You have seen part of that power recently when the American people were punished at New York and Washington.' He nodded to Chungai and turned to stare out of the cabin window.

Chungai looked over to the colonel and clenched his fists.

'So Mr.Carter, we are wasting our time with you.'

He clutched Carter by the shoulders and lifted him bodily out of the seat and threw the old man to the floor.

Chi Ling suddenly turned and wagged his finger at Chungai, indicating him to stand back from the cowering heap on the saloon floor.

'Mr.Carter I cannot believe that you were naive enough to believe that we were only interested in the humble pickings of your ill gotten hoard, even though the sum is significant. 'How were you hoping to make arrangements to salvage the gold if you don't know the position of the ship?'

Carter rose unsteadily and clutched the edge of the table with one hand whilst he fished out his handkerchief to wipe away the blood oozing from his nose. He looked around the table, with fear now positively showing in his eyes. He knew they had told him too much about their intended plan for him to be allowed to depart that boat on the same terms he had joined it.

'How will my life be guaranteed if I tell you anything?'

Chungai let out a high pitched laugh, almost hysterical in its sound.

'We've gone too far to offer guarantees my friend.'

He turned with a vicious energy and kicked Carter to the floor again, where he lay, curled up and groaning, his hands clutching his testicles where the blow had made its contact, the pain signals now rushing in confused panic around his body.

He looked up, in terror as Chungai moved in to deliver another blow.

'Wait, I'll tell you who has the information.'

Chungai smiled again reached down and lifted him to a seat. Carter stared out in front of him his eyes dazed by his craving.

'Anything going on here? Got any horse on board, you know, smack?'

They looked at him coldly and Chungai grinned.

'I'm sure we can find you something but, before you take your trip, we want the information, then I promise we will find something for you.' He thought, why hadn't anyone told him about the old mans weakness, It would have made his job easier, putting Carter completely in his power, making the man scream and cry for his craving, though he would not have had the pleasure of imagining for himself the exquisiteness of the pain he had just inflicted.

Carter looked furtively around the table.

'The old captain of the Acacia Lady has hung on to his secret for fifty years, he must know the position, he was smuggling gold into Turkey a few years ago, you'll find him at this address.' He pulled a small note book from his pocket. 'Capt. Piltcher is his name, at Crows Nest Cottage in Trevello in Cornwall.'

Chungai smiled at him.

'Thank you Mr.Carter, excellent, I knew we could do business, I hope for your sake that this is the truth, we've wasted too much time over here as it is and what started off as a simple search for the Acacia Lady has now become a very tight schedule to keep.' He moved to the wall telephone and gave instructions to the bridge and Carter felt the yacht heel as it changed course.

'How may I ask do you intend to lift the device and the gold if you find it, this boat doesn't have the capability?'

'Our crew are experienced Arab divers selected by our Middle East friends; it probably hasn't occurred to you that our race is, let's say, rather conspicuous in this country. The Arabs on the other hand are fully accepted here. They will do the lift using special air bags. We then have a small freighter standing off in the Western Approaches ready to come in and do the final collection.'

'What about your promise?'

Yoido went to a wall cupboard and extracted a box that he handed to Chungai who opened it and placed a ready made joint into Carter's begging hands.

'We only serve the best here, these are a batch of made up flame-thrower samples for smoking, or would you rather chase the dragon with your own paraphernalia, we have fresh artillery if a bang is your preference.' As Carter grabbed for the proffered joint Chungai gave his high pitched laugh again as he withdrew it in jest before offering it again holding it high in the air so that Carter had to beg for it like a dog. Carter was given matches and conducted to a small cabin and the door locked.

Back in the main saloon, another man had joined the group. Tallish with thinning fair hair over a pale face dominated by a large moustache.

'I said no violence Johnny; he is after all my father.'

Chungai shrugged and grinned at Carter's son as David sat down, and took the note book in his hand.

'So this is all he had? Was there no actual position given?'

Ling lent forward, glancing around the group.

'Another false lead Chungai?'

Johnny Chungai's eyes hardened like sapphire diamonds.

'We'll know that once we have visited this old captain. We'll get the information out of him even if I have to skin him.' He looked directly at David. 'Now my dear sir, if you want to continue dealing with us on the Middle East cocaine run, I hope for your sake and your fathers that we are not on another wild goose chase.'

David smiled confidently, speaking in his clipped whining accent that gave away his colonial beginnings.

'We're partners Johnny, remember? You would not be here if I had not made the introduction to my father in Hong Kong. You were only able to start this venture after I searched his office and found his private files about the gold. I promised you we would find the ship and the gold, one of these four old men must know the position because we know that gold bars with the old assay numbers turned up in Istanbul. As I've told you before, find the Acacia Lady and we have enough gold to capitalise on our main merchandise deals.'

Chugai stared at the minion in front of him. A means to an end, someone who through his own greed for gold had helped them fill in the finer details of the fifty years old story. Someone even he could despise for tricking his own father. Someone they could dispose of once their main aim was achieved.

Simon Carter was still in some pain as he dragged himself to the porthole and peered out. It was getting dark outside. He lay on a bunk, smoking until the pain fell away and he fell into a scag nod, dreaming a fitful golden sleep.

Breakfast was delivered to his cabin by the steward who carefully locked the door again as he left. It was now lighter outside as the door was again unlocked and a crew member conducted him back to the stateroom where the Koreans sat as the previous evening.

'Good morning Mr.Carter, I hope you're feeling better for your sleep. We called in to Plymouth during the night to replenish stores and we're now bound for Falmouth to visit this man Captain Piltcher. On the way we would like you to go over the history of the Acacia Lady once more for us..........' There was a sudden commotion on the deck above and shouts echoed dully in the saloon as crew members could be seen through the windows running along the side decks.

Colonel Ling motioned his head to the door and Chungai and the others ran to the door as it was flung open by the short man who poured out a torrent of foreign words as gunshots were heard and the yacht slowed and cut engines.

Chungai shouted an order to one of the others and Carter was propelled to the spiral staircase leading down to the lower deck where he was thrown down and bundled into a small cabin and the door locked.

As he lay on the floor retching from the drug and rough handling, he opened his eyes and realised he was not alone.

Painfully he raised himself up and stood there swaying in the dimness of the cabin as he looked down on the figure laying on one of the bunks, dressed in jogging top, trousers and trainers, his wrists and mouth bound with tape, as frightened eyes looked up appealingly at him. Carter fumbled with the mouth tape first and the man gasped for air as the remnants were removed. The tape binding the hands was not so easy. The man sat up awkwardly and Carter sat down on the edge of the bunk as he tried unsuccessfully to unravel the wretched stuff from the mans wrists.

'Carter.....Simon Carter?' The man gasped out the name as he tried to ease off the tape over his hands that only made it more tenacious.

Carter stopped and peered at him.

'Well I'll be damned, Tony Holmes if I'm not mistaken.' They looked at each other, both much older now but still recognisable after over fifteen years

'Damn you Carter, what's this all about? Trouble seems to follow you around, but thanks anyway.' Sir Anthony raised his taped wrists to his face and rubbed over the sweaty stubble as he looked around the cabin. 'Are you part of this bloody set up?'

'I don't know what set up you're talking about Holmes, I'm here on a business trip that appears to be getting out of hand.'

'Your so called retirement fund trip that you phoned me about? Are these terrorists your partners?'

Carter was bending over the floor retching again and Holmes continued.

'For Christ sake man, tell me what's going on. Are my brother in law and Senden involved?'

Carter wiped his mouth.

'Senden is dead, died about two weeks ago. I've not seen the captain for years. I've walked into something here that I didn't expect. It goes back to our days on the Acacia Lady.'

Holmes was still struggling with the wrist tapes.

'I doubt it Carter. These people are a serious threat to the forthcoming Cease Fire Conference between Israel and the Palestinians. A project and something I've worked hard on for the past six years.'

Carter's head rose slowly.

'So you're still involved with them?'

They both stopped as overhead they heard the sounds of running footsteps on the decks and sudden bursts of gunfire. The engines were restarted and they felt the vibration from behind the cabin bulkhead. Then the door was unlocked and Yoido was beckoning Carter to follow him as two crew members moved into the cabin to reinstate Holmes's bonds.

Chapter 9. Seamaiden

The westerly breeze had dropped to practically nothing. The sails started to slat in a lazy arc as the yacht wallowed in the shallow troughs, hardly making any way. They had been set for a close reach and the mainsheet now needed to be slackened to give Seamaiden better stability.

Peter Senden lent forward from where he was sitting at the tiller and loosened a few turns on the jib winch and then sheeted out the mainsail. The surface of the sea was like gunmetal now between the slight trough to peak of the waves and pockmarked by the rain that was falling steadily and stinging his face and hands. The visibility had reduced to a few hundred feet and the whole scene around Seamaiden was of a dismal Bessemer pig iron grey, blending into a pale ochre murkiness that was neither sea nor sky. It reminded him of an unfinished Turner seascape he had once seen in the London Tate Gallery collection and he could suddenly appreciate the subtle colours and brush strokes the artist had used so skilfully in the painting.

He glanced around his restricted horizon before lashing the tiller with a staying line and going below to check his position for the umpteenth time since leaving Plymouth early that morning. At times like this it was useful to have a chart up in the cockpit to refer to, but the rain was heavy and the chart table easily accessible at the foot of the companionway stairs in the protection of the saloon where he now stood, steadying himself against the wallowing swell.

He had sailed for about twenty five years, firstly with his friend's parents on their yacht, then later as Commodore in the University Dingy Club. His post graduate days at Imperial College in Kensington had allowed him to crew in a number of large yachts on the East Coast as well as from the club out of Lymington. He'd met Yvonne there, when they were both crewing for friends during the Admiral Cup series.

After they were married, one of their first priorities had been to purchase Seamaiden, a thirty eight foot auxiliary Bermudan sloop designed and built by Nicholsons at Gosport. The yacht was their pride and joy and they had spent every holiday cruising the Channel Isles, Cornwall and Brittany coast in her. That was until the day he lost her, nearly three years ago, killed by an avalanche when skiing off piste with a friend where they shouldn't have been. She had loved skiing and begged him to go with them to France, it was their one difference of opinion, she loved the sport and he didn't. He had cheerfully waved her and her friend Susan off at Gatwick: Three days later he saw the news on the television, with the first dreadful reports that had made him sick with worry. Then the notification that she was dead. The memory of that day repeated and repeated on him, hitting him at times with a fury he had somehow learned to control.

He marked up his dead reckoned course on the chart, adding an allowance for leeway, and then copied the Lat. and Long. position from the G.P.S. and transferred it to the chart noting that he was slightly off the track he had set earlier.

The G.P.S. was a godsend at times like this. Being single handed, he was pleased to see his worked up position verified by the satellites orbiting 12500 miles above the earths surface. Ensuring that their ephemeral data controlled by atomic clocks gave a position that was, on occasions, more accurate than the charted information used by sailors.

There had been a head wind to contend with earlier and his E.T.A. at St.Mawes would be later than previously advised to John Barrett.

Rivulets of water dripped off his waterproofs and the brim of his cap onto the chart, smudging his pencilled annotation. He cursed quietly and reached for a towel to dry off the droplets and as he did so he felt the boat movement change. It was almost indiscernible against the general movement caused by the swell, but even to a recreational sailor, the slightest change to the normal sea motion stiffens the back and cues up the reflexes for action. He was up the companionway steps and into the open cockpit in a few strides and quickly looked around. The rain had increased now, sending up tiny plumes of spume from the sea surface that was still relatively calm whilst the wind was only indicating a few knots on the wind instruments. Apart from the hiss of water on water, it was eerily quiet and the visibility had decreased. Peter guessed that as the rain increased there was a possibility that the squall would suddenly hit.

There it was again, the same movement, lifting and rocking the yacht as she rose and fell gently, except that this time Peter saw the small cross eddies, foaming white and bubbling as they rolled across on top of the normal wave shape. His immediate reaction was to scan the vicinity for another vessel, but he could see nothing in that damp clinging blur of fog. The moisture particles wafting in, opening out the space around them and then, just as quickly, closing in on the limited horizon. He listened for a couple of minutes in case he heard a fog horn or engine noises but there was nothing. He'd switched on his navigation lights earlier as the visibility had deteriorated and now reached down for the fog horn he carried and gave a long blast. He listened again. Any other boat in the vicinity should have heard it despite the rain and responded in a similar way but he heard nothing and after looking around again, he decided to go below again to brew up before the squall struck.

Possibly the wash from a large vessel that had passed some way off he thought, sometimes you just didn't hear them as sound could be deadened by the rain and air density. Sound could have a peculiar effect at sea. He had often sailed at night with good visibility and a full moon and heard engine noises that must have been miles away.

That morning he had left Plymouth on the west going tide, having sailed there from Weymouth the previous day, the day that the mysterious assailant had attacked him with the baseball bat. He rubbed his arms in recollection of the event and the people who had stepped in so quickly for the unnecessary rescue. He had only noticed a couple of other yachts leaving at that time, but from

Drakes Island they had taken a more southerly course, probably bound for Braye on Alderney or St.Peter Port he thought.

He glanced instinctively at the navigation instruments again, mentally noting depth, log and barometric pressure that had been falling slowly for the last couple of hours but now appeared steady. He heaped a generous spoonful of instant coffee into the mug he had been using and topped it up from the kettle. He didn't normally smoke below, but with the weather being wet and anticipating worse to come, he lit a cheroot before poking his head outside again for a look around from behind the protection of the spray hood that straddled the companionway.

A thin tongue of lightening struck the sea somewhere off the port bow followed by several other strikes nearby, which momentarily loomed through the fog with a ghostly brightness, then the inevitable rumble of thunder that rolled around the heavens.

The gloom was lifting slightly now and the wind had increased and backed a point to the west. The precipitation was down to a light drizzle again although the visibility had not improved. It was time to adjust the sails and take any benefit from what little wind there was. He finished his coffee and threw the butt of his cigar over the side as he bent down into the saloon.

As he placed the empty mug in the galley sink, he heard the VHF set burst into life with a flow of excited foreign language followed by a sharp report like a gun being fired. He jerked upright, banging his head on the cabin ceiling. Crack; another report. He hauled himself into the cockpit, his mind seething with visions of a broken shroud or a torn sail headboard. His immediate upward inspection assured him that neither was the case. He made a quick visual inspection of the boat, the teak decks glistening with the wetness as he reached for the tiller, but he could see nothing out of place and quickly adjusted the sheets to the improved wind speed. It was still murky ahead and for good measure he let off a blast with the foghorn as he shifted his seat to glance under the jib sail.

And there it was, looming out of the mist a few feet away, a small ship or perhaps a large luxury trawler yacht of about ninety feet used for diving, straddled across his bows and apparently not under power. Just sitting there with a slight wallowing motion and not showing any lights.

Peter heaved on the tiller and ducked as the boom smashed across the yacht and came up hard against the mainsheet as he gybed around the rear of the ship with only inches to spare. As he did so he glanced quickly at the other vessel and saw two figures, as if in slow motion, manoeuvre a body over the stern push pit rail. He looked over his shoulder in horror as the lifeless body, clad in a divers dry suit, hit Seamaiden's transom, resting there for a moment before sliding into the sea and vanishing.

There was a terrible wound in the forehead and that fleeting moment was enough time for Peter to see the staring eyes looking out from the blood covered head. .

Crack, crack, crack, Peter now recognised the sound as he realised that he was now a target and rounds from the Walther PPK were tearing into the sea's surface around him sending up small spits of spray. An automatic joined in and he ducked instinctively as he glanced back at the stern of the cruiser now being swallowed by the mist. There was no ensign and he could not make out the name on its transom. And then it was gone, enveloped in the mist somewhere off his starboard quarter. He could hear shouting and more rounds were discharged although he guessed that they couldn't see him as they hit the water harmlessly behind him. He was numbed by what he had seen and within seconds of the cruiser being lost from sight had heard powerful engines being started up.

In those few moments, the rain had started again and the wind increased to about fifteen knots that easily lifted the sails and gave the yacht the power to sail into the wafting fog.

On the Koreans' vessel, the crew were scanning the same early morning translucent English Channel fog for signs of the sailing yacht that had nearly collided with them. Chungai looked around and quickly assessed the situation.

'Do you think they saw anything?'

Shi Ahidrah the Libyan senior diver came bounding up the steps to the fly bridge and spoke in Arabic.

'They would have been blind not to see the body, it hit the transom of the other boat as we tossed it into the sea, but we got the name, Seamaiden, a sailing sloop of about twelve metres in length. We only saw one occupant but there may have been others on board.'

Chungai fitted a new clip to his Walther, replaced it in the hip belt under his jacket and looked at the damaged radar screen.

'O.K. Order a search pattern to be started. When you find the yacht, we'll board her, dispose of the crew and then sink her. Get a couple of the crew to start scrubbing down the deck over there with the power hose and remove those blood stains..........Captain, get this boat started again and make sure we find them before this fog lifts. Keep those Ak47's handy and shoot as soon as you have them in range.'

Having issued his orders, Chungai swung himself down the ladder to the side deck and strolled back to the state room where the others had re-gathered. He looked grimly around at the four Koreans.

'Appears one of the Arab divers may have been an infiltrator. He used the VHF radio, spoke in his own tongue, Hebrew I believe, but the captain understood some of it. He was broadcasting the information Carter gave us and must have been listening outside.'

Ling's dark eyes glittered with anger behind the thick lenses.

'Pity you shot him Chungai, it would have been useful to know who he was and the people he was communicating with. As it is, we must now assume that some other organisation, the CIA for instance, is privy to the information. Do you think he was talking to the sailing craft that was suspiciously close to us?'

'I doubt it Colonel, but we can't be too sure. The crew have orders to track her down and sink her. Unfortunately, the radar screen got a direct hit during the scuffle and the main radar is no longer functional.' He nodded to Yoido. 'Get the old man back up here. I haven't finished with him yet.'

'Chungai, I haven't finished with you yet.' Lings's hoarse voice lifted to a shout. 'The water around here is cold, no sharks to dispose of the body, it will be washed up somewhere and the British in their methodical way will want to identify it.'

Chungai gave him a recalcitrant stare.

'Yoido, get Carter up here.

Peter's mind was in a whirl. Were they after him, would they see his wake? He glanced nervously over the stern at the creaming broken water stretching out behind him until it became indistinct at the edge of the fog. They must surely see this as clearly as a pilot sees an illuminated landing strip.

In his haste to gybe, he had not hauled over the jib sheet and the yacht had slowed with the jib sail backed. So he gybed again to starboard and hauled in the sheets so that the boat was reaching and now quickly picking up speed. He scanned his limited circle of visibility for any sign of the motor yacht but there was nothing and he could just discern the throb of engines as the sound was reflected and re-reflected by millions of tiny airborne water particles that made it impossible to judge the sound direction. A sudden swell lifted the transom causing the yacht to rise and fall so that he lost some of the power in her sails. He heard the throb of an engine making low revs somewhere behind him. If it was the other vessel, it had gone of at right angles somewhere off his port side, probably following his initial wake. He considered that the speed of the other craft would also create a wake that would confuse the sea patterns much more than his own craft. In any case he decided to tack back roughly in parallel with his original course that he gauged would be a few hundred metres over on his starboard side. In this patchy fog and mist if the other craft did a box search they would soon become confused between their own wake and any others they came across.

After about a mile, during which time he had tried to tune his ears to the slightest sound of any engines, he went onto a starboard tack to regain his original direction. He would have to recalculate his actual course once he had time to pin point his position. The compass indicated west.

The hiss of the rain and the bow wave were all that could be heard now as Seamaiden slid easily through the water. The fog was still patchy and Peter scanned all around him continuously looking for a glimpse of that vessel that he had seen so fleetingly but which now haunted his mind. He glanced at his watch and guessed that the incident must have occurred about an hour before although he had not thought of looking at his watch at the time. Again he thought he heard an engine but it was further off this time. Had he now eluded them?

He was now back on a broad reach and Seamaiden was creaming along at about 6 knots. He daren't sound his foghorn in case of detection and had to hope that any other craft in the vicinity would be observing the collision regulations for fog.

Suppose the other vessel had him on radar.

'Shit!'

The expletive was the first word he had uttered in hours. The sudden thought hadn't occurred to him before as the vision of the fluorescent dot on the radar screen recording his every movement reeled through his head. Most craft of that type had a radar set installed. If so, why hadn't they seen him? Perhaps there were other craft in the area, the couple of boats that had accompanied him out of Plymouth early that morning may have turned back when the weather deteriorated. He listened again but could hear nothing against the sounds of Seamaiden's sails and shrouds humming as she sped through the leaden sea into a continuous blanket of wafting fog and rain.

Peter Senden's mind was still racing back over the incident. It would be just his luck to be in the wrong place at that time. Had he imagined it? Had the body he had seen been real? The gunfire and little spouts in the water that each report had thrown up convinced him that he had come across some sinister act that he could not begin to come to terms with. His mind went over the motorcycle incident a couple of nights previously when he had bowed out of Weymouth. The Evening papers when he arrived in Plymouth had reported the incident as a road accident, no mention of his own painful experience. Who had pulled him away, was it CIA operatives or his own organisation or someone else? What were they doing there? He knew the answer, he was under surveillance, being tailed but if so, what was the reason? He had told Special Branch everything he could and Jessica had presumably passed on the latest information he had gleaned from Captain Rogerson.

He had been sailing for about two hours since the incident and about six hours since leaving Plymouth early that morning. . He became aware that his hands where they gripped the tiller so tightly were getting sore, his bruised arms resulting from the baseball beating were painful and his forehead ached from where he had hit it on the cabin ceiling stringer. He had been transfixed in that position all that time, straining his ears and eyes for the slightest sound or sight of the cruiser that he had only seen for a matter of a few seconds. There was only a light drizzle now and water droplets hit him as they sprung free from the rigging and sails. He realised that he was also stiff and quite hungry, although the feeling of hunger could have been the nervous tension he now felt in his stomach.

Peter took another look around, re-fastened the tiller with the stay and went below so that he could set the kettle to boil for some instant soup whilst he quickly peeled of his wet waterproofs and hung them to drain off in the wet locker. He took a few sips from the mug of steaming soup and popped his head out for another look around. The rain had stopped and the fog seemed to have lifted here so that his horizon had enlarged to a circle of about a mile of empty sea that had now developed more of a swell, so that spray occasionally broke over the bows. He ducked below again to determine his course when the VHF suddenly came alive on the listening and emergency channel sixteen.

'Sailing yacht Seamaiden in approximate position six miles due south of Dodman Point, this is the motor yacht "Friendship" do you receive, over?'

Peter stared at the set. Apart from the four hourly weather reports from the coast guard, there had been very little traffic. He had deliberately avoided sending a call to the Falmouth Coast guard in the fear of having his position verified by GMDSS (Global Marine Safety System), or having to identify his yacht's name. The call came again and again. Peter ignored it and was now staring in disbelief at the GPS set which was flashing "Error Message" on its small flat screen. He pushed the Enter button on the keyboard and the screen indicated Position unreliable. His mind turned back to the lightning that had struck the sea so close to his boat earlier and suspected that it had upset the delicate electronics. Then he heard something that every sailor dreads, the sound of surf breaking on rocks.

Chapter 10.   John Barrett at St.Mawes.

John Barrett had motored down to Cornwall the previous evening in Peter's new car as arranged and now gazed out over the harbour and the Percuil River beyond from the vantage of his window at the Black Rocks Hotel. It was not his first visit to St.Mawes and he now looked out at the hundreds of boats of all shapes and sizes as they clung to their various moorings. The jingling musical sound of their halyards, mixed with the hum of tourists and cries of seagulls that came to him through the open window. The breeze was light and the wide mouth opening to the River Fal and the Carrick Roads that he knew so well was just about visible in the hazy mist that had insistently hung in the air since early morning.

Even the trees that came down to the water's edge on the other side of the river had their tops obscured in a light bridal veil of mist as he watched the little Place ferry making its course, past Amsterdam point, back to the harbour. The tide was flooding but the mild smell of seaweed was still on the breeze as the Adrian Gilbert ferry from Falmouth nosed into the harbour and disgorged its first issue of day trippers.

The St.Mawes Sailing Club burgee flew proudly on a high mast next to the Harbourmasters office alongside two red ensigns and tourist cars were already arriving in the small car park on the harbour groin.

The only compensation for the restricted view was that it was very warm. The weather forecaster on the early morning television programme had predicted that the sun would soon burn off any sea mist and a beautiful hot sunny day was to be expected now that the low pressure front had passed. Climate change or not, it was good news for the thousands of holidaying families in the area.

He didn't hear the knock at his door at first. He was totally absorbed by the view and the small cluster of people who had gathered on the quay below. They were obviously a boating family. Mother, in her jeans and sailing smock in charge of a large cold box the contents of which he surmised would contain salad, cooked chicken and all the trimmings for a family picnic. Father with his sailing cap, shorts and monogrammed tee shirt carrying an inordinate pile of wet gear and shouting out instructions to the various children who appeared to take no notice as they skipped along in happy anticipation of the day ahead.

He watched as they waded out their tender that was now being lifted by the incoming tide and piled it up with their various bits and pieces. Then heard the various arguments as to who was to be first in the boat, who would push off and who would control the outboard.

John smiled his thoughts as at last the family got under way, released the long painter that secured them to the quay and started the outboard that spluttered into life and took them off to one of the waiting boats. He remembered his own anticipation of a day's adventure as a child when his parents used to take him sailing.

He heard the knock, louder now, as the maid outside decided she had been too polite with the first quiet tap on the door. He left the window and crossed the room to the door where the young girl proffered him a tray of breakfast.

'Oh, thanks, put it down over there on the table please.' She placed the tray and removed the cover revealing a very full English breakfast.

'There's a Fax for you in the envelope Mr.Barrett.' She indicated the white envelope on the edge of the tray. 'It arrived a few minutes ago.'

He thanked her as she adjusted the coffee cup on its saucer and with a final glance to ensure everything was all right turned and left the room.

John sat at the table and his hand hovered over the envelope but instead, following the habits of many years, he reached for the table napkin that he placed on his lap, poured his coffee and started the meal. After his fourth piece of toast and delicious home made marmalade, he took a final sip of coffee dabbed his mouth with the napkin and reached for the envelope. He hadn't expected a Fax, as his secretary usually contacted him on his mobile phone. The topography in this part of Cornwall made reception patchy and the mobile was not always reliable. Then he remembered, it wasn't even switched on.

As he suspected, the fax was from his office in Winchester and relayed a message from Peter Senden indicating that his planned overnight sail from Plymouth had been delayed and that he now hoped to arrive in St.Mawes late morning. There followed the usual apologies.

John sighed as he scanned the message. Not unusual for Peter he mused, always late and full of excuses. It was part of his character that in twenty odd years as friends had never changed.

He recalled Peter's phone call the previous week. Apart from a firm friendship, John had acted as the family solicitor for many years and had spent some time over the last couple of weeks dealing with Philip Senden's affairs and probate.

The inquest involving Philip Senden's death had been a curious affair, opened and then closed indefinitely at the request of the Crown Solicitor. The body had not been sent to the local undertakers, but instead had been released from the Haslar military hospital to the Naval Coroners mortuary in Portsmouth which John considered most unusual. Peter knew more about the background to all this than he was saying.

He rose from the table and passed back to the window where he scanned the river through his binoculars for progress on the family he had been watching earlier whilst he considered how to fill the day ahead. He spotted their small boat, a twenty-five footer he thought, just making way with main sail up and flapping and the jib being hoisted. Judging by the father's gesticulations from the bow the family were still not listening seriously to his orders. John shifted the binoculars to a large trawler yacht coming up the river at quite a lick. The father, as John had assumed him to be, was now running back to the stern of his craft as the wash of the passing motor yacht sent the boat tossing and bobbing in the after wake causing him to go crashing into the cockpit on top of the other occupants. Angry voices floated across the otherwise calm view and could be heard above the sound of the motor yacht's engines that had now slowed as the crew picked up a river mooring. The strange thing was that the crew John could see on the yacht were all dressed in dark suits, a rather odd contrast to the attire of other yachtsmen he thought. Probably a charter of businessmen returned back because of the earlier poor visibility. Christ. One of them already drunk he assumed as he saw an elderly man being supported by the others into the tender.

John turned back into the room and picked up the local guide book but decided to fill in his time with a visit out to Trevello Cove to see if he could locate Captain Piltcher's cottage.

He took another look out of the window. The mist was clearing as the forecaster had predicted and he could now make out Pendennis Point across the estuary and the Black Rock beacon in front of it. On the other side of the estuary, the isolated clump of Scotch pine on the downs leading over to St Anthony's Point was now clearly visible and small twists of mist rose upwards from the trees opposite. He wrote a quick note to Peter on the hotel stationery explaining that he would visit Jacksnest Cottage during the morning and gathered up his jacket and keys.

The Black Rocks Hotel was one of those typical old buildings that had been added to over a period of its history as a coaching inn. Its whitewashed walls and private promenade made it stand out from other buildings along the front. The rooms were full of character, large and comfortable and scrupulously clean. In the reception lobby, the wood panelled walls were discretely hung with numerous oil paintings and prints depicting both country and sea scenes. The beamed ceiling and plaster work gave a warm feeling to the area where the reception counter was located. Beyond this area was a comfortable lounge with nicely proportioned windows overlooking the sea and framed with curtain drapes that had been carefully selected to blend with the other soft furnishings. On one side, a large open fireplace with an ornate carved dark oak surround was home to an arrangement of dried flowers that were placed in the grate at this time of year. Comfortable armchairs abounded and there were adequate small tables on which drinks could be placed from the bar that was in a smaller ante room. Another door led one into a tastefully decorated and well laid out dining area with cosy wood panelled alcoves and murals of sailing ships. The unrestricted views from the dining room looked straight out over the water at some of the most glorious soft landscape in Cornwall.

At that time of the morning, John found several people at the reception, paying their bills, adding their compliments to the visitor's book and generally looking at the various pamphlets and books on local walks that seem to abound in such areas. He was not in any great hurry now and was happy to wait for the people in front of him before handing over his note for Peter

A woman in her late twenties stood in front of him and had now reached the attention of the busy receptionist to whom she enquired.

'Have you seen my father this morning? I haven't seen him since yesterday morning, he doesn't appear to have been back to his room overnight and I'm a bit concerned for him. I'm supposed to be in Truro at 11.00 o'clock and he has the car keys.'

The receptionist ignored a telephone ringing behind her.

'Sorry, Miss. Holmes isn't it? I usually notice him when he goes out for his jog, but I don't recall seeing him this morning. I'll see if any of the other staff have seen him if you like, after I've dealt with this gentleman.'

Miss Holmes nodded her assent and stood back for John to hand in the note and ask the receptionist to hand it to Dr. Senden when he arrived. As he turned to go, he noticed the agitated look on the young woman's pale face.

'I hope you don't mind me butting in,' he said, 'but I couldn't avoid overhearing what you just said and I'm heading in the Truro direction if you'd like a lift.'

She looked up at him and smiled politely. He was slightly taller than her, dark receding hair with a fresh bespectacled face, slightly overweight she thought, someone who indulged his tummy, with a friendly though authoritative air of one used to handling others' situations, not a glamorous man but even so, attractive.

'That would be most kind of you, but I'm a bit stuck. I must find out where my father is and at the same time I'm due at a lecture in Truro in about an hour and a half.' She felt awkward and a little uncertain of the offer. She had noticed John at dinner the previous evening and wondered casually why such a man should be dining alone. What if anything went wrong?

She pushed the thought from her head. John looked at the receptionist who had picked up the telephone and now stood with her hand over the mouthpiece.

'If I leave my mobile number with you, could you kindly ring us when he comes back?'

The receptionist nodded and indicated a notepad on the counter for him to write down the number.

'That's very nice of you, I accept,' she said, smiling up at him so that he now saw her face in a relaxed expression crowned with dark auburn hair, green eyes and waft of perfume that he found inwardly pleasing. 'It's O.K., I have my own mobile.' She scribbled the number on the receptionists pad.

'My car is in the car park on the other side of the road,' he indicated the foyer door and she picked up her shoulder bag and moved off in front of him her hair picking up the sunlight as they emerged onto the street . They didn't notice the seated man sitting nearby who had apparently been engrossed in the morning paper that he now folded as he stood to leave.

The engine of Peter's new Jaguar purred into life and after a quick look at the local map, John drove off in the direction of Tregony where he could join the main road to Truro. He was not aware of the blue Mercedes that pulled out shortly after him and followed at a discreet distance.

'I'm John Barrett by the way,' he said giving her a quick glance.

She smiled and half turned to him. 'I know. I saw your name on the letter rack that your note was placed in. Then almost as an afterthought, 'I'm sorry, my name is Katherine Holmes. My father is Sir Anthony Holmes.' She looked at him to see if the name meant anything to him.

'You mean Anthony Holmes, the scientist on that T.V.programme?'

She nodded. 'The same guy.'

They drove on in silence for a while.

'So, where do you think he's gone, didn't he leave a note or anything?' It was an opening question and not really his business but he sensed she wanted to talk.

'I've no idea, we've been down here for a few days whilst he was preparing for a new programme. I help on occasions by researching background material for him and it was convenient for us to be here together. I am also attending a lecture this morning and speaking to some local environmentalists.'

'What are you lecturing in?'

She looked across as though assessing if he would understand what she was about to say.

'I'm actually attending the lecture on underwater holographic photography and its advantages in statistical analysis on alluvial contamination in the local rivers caused by tin mining.'

She grinned over at him. 'Sorry that's a bit of a mouthful, basically I'm a physicist, an investigative journalist looking at some of the effects of marine pollution, you know, all those plastic drink containers that float up on beaches, oil spills, sewage, radioactive waste and a whole lot of others. I consult for a section in the Department of the Environment.'

'Sounds awfully clever, what on earth does it all mean?'

They chatted about her project and he outlined the purpose of his visit to Cornwall as the anticipated sailing trip. It transpired that she was also a keen sailor and had crewed on a friend's yacht on the Round the Island race on a couple of occasions.

The time passed quickly and they were soon on the outskirts of Truro looking for signs that would direct them to the City Hall.

'I presume you were going to Truro, hope I haven't taken you out of your way.' Secretly she didn't care. She'd enjoyed his company.

'Not at all. I'll drop you off, then I'm off to meet someone.' The door clicked shut and he sat there for what seemed an age as she stood there waiting for him to drive off so that she could cross the road. He opened the electrically operated near side window.

'Would you care to join me for dinner at the hotel tonight?' His words came out in a firm voice but he was surprised to find himself shaking slightly.

'That would be very nice. See you at about 7.30?'

'Great, look forward to it, have a good day.' He slid the automatic gear lever through the J box and signalled to pull out, suddenly aware of the traffic that had piled up behind him in those few brief moments. The situation was not helped by the Mercedes that had drawn in to park several car lengths behind him causing congestion in the narrow street.

As he drove back across the town towards the coast and Tevello Cove, he thought back over their conversation and his inspired moment in asking her to dinner. He was in a happy mood and hoped that Peter Senden would understand him bringing her to dinner that evening.

Chapter 11. Crow's Nest Cottage.

Peter Senden picked up the chart he was using and climbed up into the cockpit. The rocks were clearly visible off his starboard bow, and he could see that they fanned out around a high predominance of rock outcrop separated from the headland by a couple of cables and surrounded by others that were awash. He established that they must be the Whelps group that lie off Nair Head and were now exposed on the falling tide. The tide had inset him into Gerrans bay and he adjusted Seamaiden's heading to give him a reasonable offing to Zone Point and Falmouth.

As the weather improved over the next hour and the mist burnt off, he continuously scanned the horizon for the trawler yacht. All he saw was the occasional sailing vessel heading eastwards, probably out of Falmouth and taking advantage of the tide that was now running up Channel.

John Barrett saw the signpost that pointed to Trevello on the right hand side of the road and turned the Jaguar into a narrow winding lane bound by stone walls and high hedges which separated the fields each side. The car's four wheel drive gave meticulous balance and all too soon the lane brought him out to a flat area of ground and a small car park that he turned into to examine his map again. A couple of other cars were parked there and a party of walkers chatted whilst donning their walking boots and preparing rucksacks for a trek along the coastal path that he saw from the map ran along the top of the cliffs. He locked the car and strolled over to the cliff edge and looked down on the bay before him.

The view was typical of the Cornish coastline, rugged undulating cliffs dropping down to small coves edged by rocks over which the sea broke in a constant deluge of spray as the fetch of the Atlantic waves that had travelled so far were flung on to them. There was still some mist here and he could see a small fishing boat quite close in tending to an orange buoy that probably marked a lobster pot. Further out a high rock jutted out of the sea and was surrounded by others on which the surf pounded with relentless regular energy as if in a vain attempt to reach the shore. A yacht suddenly appeared from behind the rock and turned offshore in a south westerly direction. John couldn't be sure at that distance, but thought it looked like Seamaiden. If so, he thought Peter was taking some uncharacteristic chances coming in that close. He watched the yacht for a while but failed to notice that he was also the subject of observation by two gentlemen sitting in the Mercedes just up the lane from the car park.

He opened up the map he was carrying and located Trevello as a small group of cottages about half a mile along the coast from where he was standing. It was a nice day now and the splendid breakfast repast he had finished earlier needed to be worked off, besides that he had the happy prospect of dinner that evening with a young lady whom he could not stop thinking about. So he set off to walk the rest of the way along the cliff top path.

'Shit Horace, where's he off too now?' George Hansdorf's accent was North American and Horace didn't respond straight away. 'These son of a bitch British just love to walk all over the place but he's gotta come back for that beautiful set of wheels sometime. He may have gone off for a pee of course.' He picked up the hand held and called the communications vehicle, 'you hang on here and I'll follow on foot. If I need assistance I'll call. The Senden guy won't be arriving at the hotel until later, may as well find out where his associate is headed.'

The going was harder than John had thought. He hadn't noticed that there was a deep ravine cut into the cliffs between his starting point and the cottages at Trevello. The path had taken him down almost to beach level and was now taxing him on the steep upward climb which lead him through a small wood of oaks, stunted and bent over away from the prevailing winds.

Further up the hill a pair of buzzards were making their strange kitten like meowing calls as they circled and zoomed on the zephyr up-draughts from the cliffs. John stood and watched them as he recovered his breath and admired their faultless acrobatic air displays. A twig suddenly cracked somewhere behind him and he turned instinctively. The gorse was high here. The path had weaved in and out so that it was impossible to see more than a few yards along it. A couple of walkers had passed him going in the opposite direction a few minutes earlier and exchanged the usual courteous, good day, observed amongst walkers. It was after all a fine Saturday morning and he thought nothing more of it.

He climbed a stile and found himself in a narrow lane, probably the one that he had been on before turning into the car park earlier. A signpost simply read Trevello Cove.

A few minutes walk brought him to a neat row of stone cottages, slate tiled and individually colour washed in shades of white and pink, facing out towards the sea. A grassy bank covered in wild flowers separated them from the road and baskets of trailing fuchsias covered the walls on one cottage. Even at this time of the year, smoke could be seen coming from a couple of the chimneys.

The tranquillity was broken only by a dog barking somewhere behind the properties.

John imagined there had once been a small community living here based around a coast guard station, as the other side of the road looked out over a windswept hedge of broom and hornebeam with a view of the whole bay. Nowadays the remoteness of the place probably housed home workers as they tapped away at their workstation keyboards in the idyllic solitude of their surroundings, surfing the indulgent excessiveness of the Internet.

He quickly located Crow's Nest Cottage at the end of the row, next to a farm track leading off to one side of the road that dipped inland here around an old barn and then down towards the beach. So, it wasn't Jacksnest Cottage at all.

Sally Denning had been given the wrong name, which accounted for his earlier letter being returned.

The front door was slightly ajar but John used the ornate unpolished brass door knocker shaped like a folded fisherman's anchor. There was no reply, but he sensed that someone was inside and gently pushed open the door to announce his presence.

His gaze immediately told him that something was wrong. The door had swung open into a small sitting room that appeared to be in chaos. Furniture was overturned, drawers were hanging open and papers were scattered around the floor. The sound of a door creaking came from somewhere, he thought in the back of the house. John ducked through the doorway and in a few strides had crossed the room and opened another door that led him into a short passage with stairs on one side and a kitchen beyond. A creaking floorboard, that had offered its warning to past generations sounded and John felt a bit self conscious as he cleared his throat and called.

'Hello. Captain Piltcher? Anyone at home?'

There was an ominous silence except for the loud tick of a grandfather clock in the corner and the dog barking in the distance. John placed a hand on the wooden banister and eased himself quietly up the stairs, his body sounds seeming to crash in his ears, relaying the thick aortic thumps of his heartbeat. He should have turned and got out of the place and didn't know why he crept forward instead.

The landing showed the same signs of a search as he pushed open another door into one of the bedrooms. There it was the same again. Mattress turned off the bed and clothing scattered around from upturned drawers.

The punch to the side of his neck came from behind him and was like a million stars exploding, sending him crashing to the floor in a tumbled heap. He was dazed as he laid there and sensed the warmth of the oozing wet patch on the back of his head where he had hit the king post of the banister rail. Footsteps sounded down the stairs as someone made a hurried escape, crashed against the clock that gave out an anguished jangling cry of sufferance. He tried to stand but his legs felt like India rubber.

The dog was barking louder and more urgently now as the roar of a motorcycle diminished down the lane outside followed by a screech of brakes somewhere as a car swerved to avoid it.

John staggered down the stairs to the front door as two bodies suddenly blotted out the sunlight. 'I think there's been a robbery here,' he blurted out the words that seemed to be disjointed and rubbery lipped as if he had been drinking and then his head was reeling, spiralling him into the black tunnel of unconsciousness.

When he came round, he was propped up in one of the armchairs and the two men were standing over him.

'That's a nasty cut you've got there, better get it seen to.' The man was American from his accent and enquired.

'What happened here? We were nearly driven off the road by a couple of guy's on a motorcycle who suddenly appeared out of a cart track going hell for leather.'

John looked up at the two of them but couldn't speak.

'Sorry Mr.Barrett.' It was the second man who spoke, 'you seem to be badly shaken sir, get on the phone George and call an ambulance.'

It never occurred to John that, as passing motorists, they called him by name.

Horace O'Brian winced at his mistake in using John Barrett's name, which, if discovered, would probably mean a reprimand and a quick return to the States.

The listening team at Weymouth had told them that Peter Senden was sailing to St.Mawes and they, like John had motored down the previous evening.

The unforgiving floorboard creaked again somewhere upstairs. O'Brien was across the room in a flash but was careful not to draw his Smith and Wesson 38 piece until halfway up the stairs. He did the usual thing that one sees agents do in films. The gun in a two-handed hold, barrel pointing upwards. Kick open the door, duck and point. Lying on the floor in the second bedroom was an elderly man, badly beaten by the look of him.

The agent checked behind the door and then checked the other rooms before returning to the body and securing his weapon in its shoulder holster.

'Gilbert Piltcher I presume,' O'Brien whispered the words to himself as he leaned cautiously over the man and checked that pulse and breathing were O.K.

'Another one up here George,' he shouted down the stairs. 'Unconscious and beaten up, get that ambulance on the way urgently.'

The call had to be made from the neighbour's house as Piltcher's telephone did not appear to be working and the agents could not use their handhelds for fear of detection by scanning and lock on. With the knowledge that had been imparted to them during the briefing with Cmdr.Hoskins the previous day, they knew that there could still be other operatives in the area. This was not a simple burglary and they had already broken the rule of non involvement with a subject under surveillance.

On the brow of a hill overlooking the cottages from the back, a tallish man with his long white hair flowing in the breeze had been out walking. He ducked down behind a cattle trough and observed the comings and goings at Crows Nest, which seemed to be suddenly drawing a lot of attention. When he saw the police arrive at his home he made a hasty retreat across the fields to where his car, packed with a few belongings, was parked in another lane that ran down to the cove.

An hour and a half later, on a small run down housing estate on the outskirts of Plymouth, two Suzuki motorcycles were parked outside one of the houses, the engines still warm from their sixty mile run, through the Cornish lanes to St.Austell, then up to Bodmin where they joined the A38 trunk road to Plymouth. Inside the house three men sat in silence as Major David Hessel, head of No.3 Special Overseas Squad of the Israeli Mossad stood, jacket less and with his tie unusually loosened off, glowering at three of the four man team.

'A right cock up you made of that, nearly caught out by our American cousins at Trevello by all accounts, what went wrong?'

'Sorry chief didn't expect visitors had to make it look authentic.' The tough looking Sergeant Micha Karishova, Sayeret Matkel Naval Commandos Parachute Corps, stood his ground as team leader of the abortive break-in that was supposed to look like a burglary.

'Well what happened?' The Section Head demanded.

Sergeant Karishova then outlined how they had lain behind a hedge row as they had firstly surveyed the cottage they had been told to search, seen the Koreans running out and decided to split the team, two following the suspect terrorists while the other two entered the cottage.

Once inside it was obvious that a thorough and untidy search had already taken place.

'Then this guy just turned up out of the blue, walked straight in on us. We were upstairs at the time and about to attend to the old boy lying on the floor, badly beaten up he was, presumably by the terrorists. Isaac was looking out of the window and spotted someone watching the place, we believe it was one of the C.I.A. people who had arrived in St.Mawes yesterday. Then this guy comes creeping upstairs and we had to do something to protect our cover. I hit him where I knew it would put him out for a few minutes without much harm done. It was the CIA all right, they get provided with nice cars, we nearly hit theirs as we escaped.'

Major Hessel glowered at them and Karishova's grin at his dig about transport vanished as Hessel turned to the other two.

'So, where did the terrorists go to?'

Zak Heinz replied. 'They scooted back to the dinghy park at St.Mawes. The tall one whom we identify as the N.Korean mercenary, Johnny Chungai and another guy seemed interested in one of the yachts moored up out in the river. They went into the workshop and came out with a large pair of wire cutters, then they took a tender and went out to this particular boat, a vessel of about eleven or twelve metres in length.' He referred to his note pad, 'Yes here it is, the name on the transom was Seamaiden. Chungai climbed aboard and bent down in the cockpit, had his back to us so we couldn't see what he was doing. Then he went below for about ten minutes, came back up, got into the tender and they pushed off up river to a very large motor yacht.'

'Did you get the name of this yacht?'

'Unfortunately not sir. Tide was on the turn and she was lying with her stern pointing away from us. They both went on board for about five minutes. When they reappeared there were five of them, three Koreans, including the first two, our target and a Caucasian.'

'You mean there was another Englishman?'

'That's right, a tallish man but quite old, seemed a bit doddery. He kept stumbling.'

'What happened next?'

Zac removed his leather jacket, as Matt came into the room from the toilet.

'Believe it or not, a small police van drove up as the others were getting into their car. The officer got out and told us we shouldn't be parked there, you know how fussy the Brits are about parking. Then he asked for my driver's licence and checked the tax disc. By the time he was finished, the car had vanished off the scene. We met up with Micha and Isaac at the usual rendezvous and came scooting home.' Matt nodded his compliance at what had been said.

'What about the police check, was that O.K.?'

'No problem, our documents were fine.'

'Well on this occasion you were probably too polite, it seems that the Koreans beat us to it, that's of course if they found anything. They were obviously on the same highway as us, suspecting that this man Captain Piltcher held the clue to the real shipwreck position.'

Sergeant Zac continued to remove his leathers, the British climate at this time of year was fine but the humidity at times did not lend itself to wearing this sort of gear indoors. He sat in his vest and underpants.

'What's the next move chief?'

Major Hessel sat and rolled up his sleeves.

'We're really only here as observers. Our Government is co-operating as much as it can officially with the Americans and British on this one. Unfortunately, they're making a hash of the whole thing. That gang of Koreans and their fundamentalist partners should have been picked up by now. Trouble with this country is that everyone is allowed to come and go without question, no I.D. requirements no checks. I suppose that's what they call democratic human rights.'

He looked into the scruffy back garden of the house, the grass knee high. The neighbours thought they were immigrant labourers working in the docks. They only knew that the men kept themselves to themselves, never venturing down to the pub or joining in anything local.

'I say observers but we do know from our own intelligence sources that the CIA has brought in about two hundred extra operatives on this one including the FBI. We don't know how many the British have allocated. Our Government raised the whole issue with the Americans when we discovered the terrorist plan a few months back, we're supposed to sit back and observe, no direct involvement because of the forthcoming Cease Fire treaty between us the Palestinians and Syrians. The radio call from our agent Abrim on the yacht, confirmed the address that you men visited this morning. It's now our duty to keep tabs on those involved and with our team in London and other undercover agents, to find out who else is involved and why this exercise is taking so damned long. We also have the security of the Cease Fire Treaty conference to worry about. The fundamentalists' plans have not been fully divulged to the other governments. Apart from this nuclear material they are looking for we know they also have plans to wreck the Conference. Could be on the same scale as nine eleven in New York if were not all careful.

As for Sergeant Abrim, we've heard no more since he broke his cover and made that radio call. We have to assume from the abrupt ending of his call that he is now out of the game.'

Isaac asked, 'who was Abrim?'

'An operative from one of our North African cells who infiltrated the group a few months ago. We have heard nothing from him since he made a desperate call this morning that was received by SAUL Group. According to his brief transmission, the scientist Holmes was on board the terrorist's boat as a prisoner together with our target and a man identified only as Carter. Your account of the terrorists' movements in Cornwall would imply however that he is no longer on board the motor yacht. Our orders now are to keep up observations on the terrorists and assist in any way we can to find Holmes. London has informed the appropriate British authorities that the terrorists have Holmes.'

'What's the Holmes guy got to do with this exercise?'

'Not sure about that except that I understand he was helpful to us in the past, something to do with laser technology the Brits traded for information we had on hostages way back. I understand that he has also been one of the key UK background figures in helping with the negotiations for the Cease Fire Conference.'

Zac looked outside.

'Raining again, what a goddamned awful climate this is.' He looked across to Micha. 'Those fundamentalists could turn up anywhere. They seem to operate out of various ports on the south coast. What about us chartering a motor yacht, we could probably keep tabs on them then.'

Major Hessel glanced over at Zac, it was a good idea and he should have considered it before.

'Firstly we need to track them down and find out from the other cells exactly where these terrorists are operating from. Then we'll do something about it. In the meantime, as I said before, we can only observe.

That same morning, Seamaiden had entered the white occulting sector light of St. Anthony's Lighthouse situated on the eastern peninsular guarding the Fal Estuary. Half an hour later she was at the pre arranged visitors mooring buoy and Peter Senden was chatting to the harbour master's assistant who had motored out in the harbour launch to collect his mooring fee.

Peter tidied up the lines and sheets on deck and then went below to change into shore clothes. He disconnected the G.P.S. from its mounting and slipped it into the holdall before locking the washboards and hailing a passing water taxi to take him to the landing stage on the harbour quay in front of the Black Rocks Hotel.

The receptionist looked up as he entered the lobby. 'Ah, Dr.Senden, it's nice to see you back again.' She checked the booking and handed him a room key as he signed in.

'Thanks Nicki. Any messages?'

'Mr. Barrett left you this note earlier, oh, and a Dr. Wilson rang. She will ring you again later.' She passed over the envelope that he read and folded into his hip pocket.

'Can you give me the number for the local police station?'

She referred to a chart of emergency numbers behind the counter, wrote out the number for him and asked.

'Anything wrong Dr. Senden?'

He hesitated but assured her that he just wanted to report an incident he had witnessed and made his way up to the room where he watched the lunch time news over a small beer, whilst he mulled over what he had seen that morning. Then he dialled for an outside line as his mobile was dead as usual.

A woman operator answered the call. 'Devon and Cornwall Constabulary, how can I help you?'

Peter hadn't thought out his reply in advance and faltered.

'I want to report a suspected murder.'

The operator replied casually as though he was reporting the latest fish prices.

'I'll put you through to the duty sergeant's desk. One moment please.'

He repeated his statement to the sergeant and outlined the events of the morning. He sensed the momentary pause at the other end of the phone whilst the officer considered what he had heard and made up his mind as to the reality of the situation. There were plenty of hoax calls at this time of year.

The policeman confirmed Peter's details and location and ran over the story again.

'Right sir, you are through to our divisional headquarters in Truro I'll arrange for one of our inspectors to come out to you, may take about half an hour but please remain where you are until he arrives.' Five minutes later a patrol car drew up in the narrow street outside the hotel and Detective Inspector Robert Evans entered the reception area with two constables.

Peter was at the door of his room as soon as the knock came and ushered the Detective Inspector and one of the accompanying constables to the two armchairs whilst he seated himself on the edge of the bed.

Robert Evans looked young for the responsibility he carried. Crew-cut hair showing signs of balding, but alert eyes with a fresh complexion and neatly trimmed moustache that moved in unison with the wad of gum he was chewing.

Peter went over the details of the sea encounter he had witnessed that morning and substantiated parts of the story when prompted by Robert Evans. The constable made notes as they spoke.

The telephone rang. 'It's a call for Inspector Evans,' Nick in reception was enjoying a chat with the young constable at the desk and tried to sound incurious.

The inspector used few words on the 'phone, only glancing at Peter from time to time and uttering affirmatives.

'Do you know a John Barrett?' he asked Peter who confirmed his friend.

'Was he driving your car sir?' A picture of his wrecked new car flashed across Peter's vision.

'Well, yes he drove it down here for me yesterday. Why do you ask, is he O.K.?

'Your car is O.K. sir, but I'm afraid your friend is in hospital.'

'Jesus, what's happened to him?'

The Inspector chewed in silence for a moment as he considered his reply.

'Don't worry Dr. Senden, your friend is in good hands, I understand he was caught up in a burglary. Unfortunately, he hit his head though when he fell against the banister king post. Also, he received a glancing wound on his shoulder.' He consulted the notes he had made and rose. 'I'd be most obliged sir if you could accompany us to Truro where we can prepare a statement on what you've told us.'

Peter hadn't expected this.

'Am I under arrest or suspicion?'

'No sir, but certain other facts have come to light and we need to discuss them in more formal surroundings, we can also drop you off at the hospital afterwards if you like.'

Nicki had now been joined by the manageress and they looked on in disbelief as the party left the hotel. The staff would certainly be agog with speculative gossip that evening.

'That radar screen is irreparable.' Jake Higgs of Higgs and Freeman Marine Electronics (Falmouth) was on the fly bridge. The boat was a large charter trawler yacht, used by divers and he had taken the dory out to her that afternoon at the request of the owners to effect repairs. He was now standing and looking at the damaged set.

'God knows what did that,' he said to his teenage son who was assisting him. He surveyed the remains of the smashed liquid crystal display and electronic integrated circuit module. The back of the casing had disintegrated and remnants were embedded in the perspex spray screen.

'Looks like a bolt of lightening or something went straight through it, we'll have to go back to shore and order a replacement.'

It was the repeater screen that relayed information from the main radar set located in the control cabin to the open fly bridge above. They went below and disconnected the repeater cable from the main unit and reset the electrical contactor to the radar circuit.

'That's all working now.' Higgs adjusted the controls and satisfied himself that the radar was functioning correctly. 'Better go up and get the repeater off now.'

He released what was left of the casing from its side mountings and disconnected the cables on the back that appeared to be undamaged.

'Bloody hell! Look here. There's a hole in the spray screen behind where the unit was.' The two men looked at the small 9mm hole, visible now that the unit had been removed.

'What d' yer make of that then,' said Higgs. He had been told by the syndicate owners that the charter party had reported some lightning damage during their trip that morning. It would not be an insurance job as the party had waived the considerable damage deposit paid with the hire charge in advance and in cash. Enough to replace half a dozen radar sets, the syndicate representative had said with a laugh over the phone.

Higgs had seen lightening damage to pleasure craft before. Fortunately, it didn't happen very often but when it did the result was usually catastrophic. The electric field in a lightening strike could produce hundreds of amps that usually blew out all the wiring and damaged the electronic equipment beyond repair. In severe cases, it melted plastic insulation and welded wires together and could even blow a hole in the boat around the zinc anode that provided the sacrificial earth or electrical contact with the sea water.

He went below again and examined the cable looms where he could and did a radio check on the GMDSS V.H.F set. (Global Marine Distress and Safety System). Everything worked. He was puzzled as the damage obviously hadn't been caused by lightening and if not by lightening then by what. Some sort of explosion? Or maybe a bullet?

'It's none of our business. Better report back to Derek that he will need a new spray screen, a polycarbonate one this time, as well as a repeater.' He lifted his hand held marine radio and called his office with details of what to order. 'Tell Derek I'll cost it out later. We're on our way back in the dory.'

The police interview room was bare except for table and chairs and recording equipment on a side table. A constable sat by the door and Peter sat at the table smoking the last cheroot he had found in the packet. The interview had been conducted in a most professional manner and he had dictated a statement of what he had seen that morning. D.I. Evans re-entered the room accompanied by an older man.

'Please feel at ease Dr. Senden. We're processing your statement and you can sign it shortly, but firstly I'd like to introduce you to Commander Hank Hoskins. Commander Hoskins is an American security officer from the CIA.' He glanced at Hoskins as though to confirm the accuracy of what he had said.

'He has some questions with respect to your story and your friend's involvement with the burglary at Trevello this afternoon and what you have told us in your statement, but I must emphasise that this is informal you are under no liability to answer anything you don't want to.' Peter sensed that there was a certain brittleness between the two of them as he rose to shake hands.

Hoskins carried a small sheaf of papers that he placed on the table and carefully straightened them top and bottom with his long well manicured fingers, before removing his spectacles and facing across the table.

'Dr. Senden, please excuse my intrusion to what must have been a most upsetting and disquieting day for you.' The commander spoke with a firm cultured American voice and Peter felt the authority in it as soon as he continued. 'I'm over here at the invitation of your government who are helping us with a certain problem that may or may not have involved your father.'

Peter looked at him incredulously. 'How do you mean,?' He looked at Evans who sat impassively looking into space.

'Your father met with a fatal accident a few weeks ago under mysterious circumstances I believe?' He looked directly at Peter as if expecting or searching for some reaction.

Peter merely acknowledged the fact with an affirmative but disconsolate shrug, remembering his obligation under the Official Secrets Act not to divulge the true nature of his father's death. 'Died from a heart attack I'm sad to say, about three weeks ago.'

'You have been trying to contact a Capt. Gilbert Piltcher and a certain Simon Carter amongst others since your father's demise, through your solicitors, Barrett and Godchild. I understand also that Mr. John Barrett is acting directly from your instructions.'

Peter hesitated, what on earth was it to do with this official of the U.S. government. The commander saw his unease but continued.

'Dr. Senden it is most important for us to know if you have managed to speak to any of these people yet, Captain Piltcher is in hospital under police guard but apparently is not well enough to throw any light on today's incident. We are also anxious about locating the whereabouts of the other man, Carter, who is also wanted for questioning.' He made no mention of Sir Anthony Holmes, his main reason for being in Cornwall that day. Holmes had not attended his pre arranged appointment that morning at the hotel and nobody seemed to know where he was. Then he had received the news from Supt. Seiger about a mysterious report that Holmes had been seen with the suspect group on a motor yacht. A group which had since dispersed.

Peter confirmed that as far as he knew, neither of them had come forward with respect to John Barrett's notices in the press.

'Can you tell us why you are seeking to make contact with these gentlemen?'

Peter looked over to Evans who was now showing more interest in the proceedings and said. 'If this is a security issue what has it got to do with my father? The people you have mentioned are completely unknown to me; they were merely friends who corresponded with him years ago. I understand that there is mention of them in my fathers Will and Mr. Barrett, as my solicitor, and as my father's executor has tried to trace them. That's all there is to it.'

The commander donned his half moons and examined one of his sheets of paper before again addressing Peter.

'May I suggest to you that you are interested in these correspondents because a great deal of money is involved, something to do with the *Dragon's Morsel* maybe.'

Peter was stunned. Evans was looking directly at him for any reaction. The constable shifted his position slightly to ensure that he didn't miss anything.

'I'm afraid I know nothing about any money. My father was reasonably provided for through his savings and state pension. He also had an ex service pension.'

He was interrupted by Hoskins who now smiled for the first time. 'Young man, we're talking in terms of millions of dollars here.' He stopped short as if not wanting to elaborate on the subject and removed his half moons as his eyes twinkled at Peter. 'We believe Mr.Barrett's encounter with the unknown assailant at Trevello could have been a case of mistaken identity. Any idea who might have wanted you out of the way Dr. Senden, after all it was your automobile he was driving and we now believe that the blow to Mr.Barrett was aimed to kill?'

'I.......just don't know..... I'm sorry but this has all been a great shock to me, this morning's shooting and now this.' Peter stammered out his reply. The profound shock at the thought of his friend being so nearly killed in mistake for himself, making his thoughts flash back to Thursday evening and the motorcycle attack. He decided to say nothing.

There was a knock on the door and the statement was handed in to the constable. Evans broke the silence after the commander's extraordinary assertion.

'I think that's enough for the time being.' He turned to Peter who was sitting in disbelief considering the unlikely hood of his father being involved with large sums of money. After probate it was unlikely that his estate would be worth more than £250,000 after any tax was paid. As for the blow that John had received, how did they think it was aimed to kill? He asked the question.

'We believe the punch he received was a professional body blow aimed at the nape of the neck, in the event your friend was lucky, it missed the cervical nerve by a few centimetres but if it had made the right contact, Mr.Barrett would almost certainly be dead by now.'

He turned to the Inspector, 'could you leave us alone for a few minutes please?'

Evans protested, but gave way when Hoskins reminded him that Peter Senden was not under arrest and waved the constable outside. Evans left the room in protest. This was his territory after all.

'Dr. Senden.' The Commander's words continued and came through the haze of Peter's thoughts. 'I understand that you are an engineer working under contract to the British defence industry, and that you have been vetted by your Government's security agency up to the equivalent category of *Top Secret*.'

Peter hesitated again; he could not see the reason for the Commander's line of questioning or what all this had to do with the chance sighting of the abhorrent act he had witnessed that morning or how it was connected to the incident two evenings ago. He remembered the similar phraseology being used during his visit to Downshall House.

The room was very quiet with just the two of them sitting there facing each other across the table. How did this American know so much about his private affairs and who his employers were? He gave a guarded reply.

'That may or may not be correct, but I don't see what any of this questioning has to do with the statement I've made to the police about the incident I witnessed this morning. If this is a security matter I'm sure you will know the correct procedural channels to use.'

Hank Hoskins looked directly at him, the young man whom he had guessed was now trying to find out what had been going on before the unfortunate demise of his father.

'There are some dangerous people out on the streets Dr.Senden, how are the bruises on your arms. No, don't say anything, let's just say that you owe the CIA one, the man on the motorcycle in Weymouth was a local man, apparently a cousin of your Mrs.Lyonns. Have you any idea as to why she or her family should wish you any harm?'

Peter s expression was one of unconcealed surprise

'Mrs. Lyonns is my contract housekeeper, looks after the place whilst I am away on business, a very efficient and nice lady.'

'How long has she worked for you?'

'About two years I should think, are you sure it was her cousin, in which case, what did they hope to gain by beating me up, they could have actually killed me with that bat if they'd wanted to.'

'So you've no idea why they would want to harm you?'

'None at all. I would doubt that Mrs. Lyonns would have had anything to do with it though. We get on well on the rare occasions that I see her.'

'Senden, I would suggest you do nothing at the moment to alert her to what I have just told you. Be watchful though.'

He asked other questions, mainly repeats of what Peter had already been asked by the Special Branch.

'Am I under surveillance because of my father? Or is it perhaps something to do with my recent trip in Eastern Europe?'

The commander stood and gathered up the file of paper in front of him, carefully tapping them on the table again to straighten the edges. He smiled, as if to himself.

'Dr. Senden, the reasons cannot be made known to you at this time, but we are trying to piece together all the facts relating to an event that happened many years ago. Something that has re-emerged and is so serious that my Government together with your own and others are highly concerned about the security surrounding our enquiries. I'm sorry that I cannot elaborate at this stage, but I must insist that you keep our conversation private. Any requests by the press for information on this subject will be dealt with only by the proper police channels and press releases.'

Peter nodded his assent. 'Yes, of course, Commander but surely I have the right to know what my father has or was supposed to have done.'

'As I said, we are conducting an investigation and your father may have been able to help us. It does not mean that he was necessarily involved. By the way please accept my condolences over your loss. Now, I have another appointment and must get going, good afternoon Dr. Senden.' He handed his card to Peter, turned and was gone, leaving a silence in the room that was only now broken by the faint whine of the recording machine as it relentlessly continued its obligatory eavesdropping.

Inspector Evans and the constable returned to the room.

'Dr. Senden, I'd like you to read through this and if you consider it to be a true statement of what you have told us, please sign it where indicated.'

The D.I. was burning up inside with curiosity, why weren't they telling him what was going on. The American CIA man had suddenly made his appearance and been introduced to him by his superintendent.

Here he was with a suspected murder at sea with the Marine Accident people breathing down his neck. A break-in, which looked like more than just a casual affair, with two people in hospital, one an old man, severely beaten. And now a bulletin on a missing scientist had been issued. When he listened to the recording disc replay he was even more mystified. Weymouth he had said and a motorcycle. The news wires had been buzzing with the horrendous road accident for the last couple of days.

He returned to his office and called in one of his detective constables.

'Mike, can you pull out all the reports we have on the incident in Weymouth the other night? You remember. The road accident.'

Chapter 12. The MI5 Registry.

On the fast track train back to London, Commander Hoskins turned over the pages of the Senden file and puzzled over the cross referencing of the various events and people concerned. Then he turned to agent Hansdorf's account he had obtained on the beating that Peter Senden had received at Weymouth. He looked again at the photographs of the man who had lain in the mortuary at the special isolation wing at Downshall Sanatorium and chewed thoughtfully on an arm of his half spectacles.

Philip Senden along with Carter and Piltcher had featured in another of many reports that had crossed his temporary desk in Grosvenor Street since arriving in England. Carter especially warranted a closer inspection but where was he. From documents supplied to him that morning from old files gathered up by the Section in Hong Kong, Carter was known to have been actively supplying information to the MI6 British Secret Service before they had officially left Hong Kong. They had also confirmed that he worked for the Chinese communists until the mid eighties when he had apparently been retired. However, the documents contained no references about the *Dragon's Morsel* or what it referred to.

He raised his eyes and looked out of the carriage window at the passing scenery. English countryside, with its small fields, numerous hedgerows, copses and villages. It was getting gloomy outside and rain was already falling. He wanted to get this thing over and done with and thought about his retirement shack on the lake, back in the mountainous expanses of his native Oregon.

The transcripts of the telephone call three days previously that Carter had made from Hong Kong started with the *Dragon's Morsel* phrase that had alerted the computerised scanners. But the rest of the conversation referring to a prospective search for a retirement fund worth ten million dollars bore no clue to it's meaning or in helping him to complete the *Thinman* project.

He knew the *Dragon's Morsel* was unlikely to be a ship; even so the registers of every maritime nation had been searched at Langley. The metaphor appeared to connect Philip Senden who was now dead, the scientist Anthony Holmes who he had learned was reported missing and the brother in law Gilbert Piltcher who was lying in a beaten up state in hospital. Then there was the radio message in a foreign language that Peter Senden had heard on the yacht that morning. No one seemed to have picked up on that one yet. He rang his office on his mobile, requesting a transcript of the tape from the coast guard.

Then there was the man Simon Carter from Hong Kong who, according to the intelligence reports he had received from Major Fellows, had been identified by MI5 computers at Heathrow and had somehow shaken off the British Special Branch tail on the London Underground.

He needed more information on Carter.

By mid evening, Commander Hoskins was sitting in an ante room connected to the computer complex at the R1 registry in Thames House, together with the Secret Services Registry Section Controller, Don Holliday. They drank coffee as they waited for information on Sir Anthony Holmes to be printed out from the vast data banks held there. Permission had been unusually granted for him to view the top secret files that were not even available to Special Branch without special dispensation.

As he sat there quietly observing Holliday, a man in his early thirties with thin wispy ginger hair over a long face that bore the pallor of his indoor labours, he thought to himself, old Maj. Fellows was certainly keeping to his side of the bargain even if other sections in the British system were not.

Special Branch had their own computer system, the Police National Computer that was linked into parts of R1 and other National systems including the vast data banks at the DHSS in Newcastle and the Immigration system at Heathrow. That computer system was also being trolled and cross referenced by their officers for information on Holmes and cross linking to any subversive organisation or group who might be connected to him or come under suspicion of a kidnapping exercise

The security door blipped its signal in recognition of the PIN number as it opened and the data processing manager Betty Jennings entered with a sheaf of printouts and without looking at Hoskins, handed them to her section boss.

'That's all I could find Don, but there's probably more there than Commander Hoskins really needs to see.' It was a typical remark and reflected the reluctance of anyone in the registry to disgorge their closely guarded information. Information that covered everyone from Cabinet Ministers and their lovers to subversive authors and playwrights. Lowly secretaries of any organisation that branch sections in the Service thought it necessary to monitor, right down to pimps, pop stars and street traders. Don Holliday scanned the sheets, carefully holding them away from Hoskins' direct line of sight even though it would have been impossible for him to read anything at the distance between their two seats.

As he read, he made margin notes. Occasionally he would tear out a page that he handed to Betty Jennings for disposal in the shredder, the only other piece of furniture in the room besides the three chairs and a low glass coffee table.

After what seemed an age to the Commander, Holliday looked up.

'Right sir, I think we have enough information here to give you the rundown on Sir Anthony Holmes's background.' The effete top drawer English accent grated on the American's ears.

Holliday read through the record. Born 1929 in Palestine of Jewish parents and moved to this country obtaining British citizenship in 1939. Educated Brunel University, obtaining a first class honours degree and PhD. Career details next, then where he had worked, what he had done, his wife's details and background, maiden name Piltcher, married with one daughter and when they were married. Parents murdered May 14. 1948 by rebels, during a trip to celebrate the formation of the new State of Israel. Knighted in 1980 in recognition of his work in electro optics and high power lasers. He stopped as though finished and smiled almost apologetically to Hoskins.

'I sincerely hope that what I have imparted to you will be of use sir.'

Hank Hoskins showed no sign of surprise when the name Piltcher was mentioned. So, Holmes had been married apparently to Piltcher's sister. He stood and removed his jacket, placing it on a spare chair and patting it into a neat smoothness. He bent to his wallet file on the table and extracted a letter on pale cream paper with the black logo heading of Downing Street.

'I got that much from leafing through a copy of Who's Who before I came here. Now, may I remind you what this letter says? It is personally signed by your Prime Minister and the Director General or chief executive of this organisation. It gives me the authority to seek information on specified people and organisations that we do not have at Langley in the States. Because of the urgency in my investigations, our respective governments have agreed at top level that our various national security organisations should co-operate within the area of interest. Now Mr.Holliday, stop farting around and try and enter into the spirit of things by providing the information I have requested.'

Holliday smiled. His anaemic smooth face showing tiny pinpricks of perspiration on his upper lip which he proceeded to wipe away with the silk handkerchief, plucked from the breast pocket of his immaculately hand cut Jamie Smith suit.

'I was of course going to do that.' He omitted any polite preposition as a silent protest at his admonishment.

'Sir Anthony was, until 1986, one of the senior scientific advisers to our Joint Intelligence Committee. At that time he was heading a consortium of Government research organisations looking into the feasibility of developing high power laser weapons. Your country and others were also busy at the time on a parallel course that it was envisaged would eventually be used in the Strategic Defence Initiative or Star Wars weapons scenario, the outlandish laser systems approach to near space war sanctioned by your President Reagan in 1983.'

Hoskins made no comment. The Star Wars strategic defence system was up and running again, replaced by the National Missile Defence System or Son of Star Wars. A space shield that his government thought necessary to implement since reports that the Chinese had managed to get hold of America's most sophisticated W-88 nuclear multi target warhead design. The crown jewels of America's nuclear secrets with on running implications for the security of the British Trident defensive weapons missile system. A breach of security at Los Alamos a few years previously that, if it were true, had allowed a Chinese espionage ring to provide the Peoples Liberation Army with the secrets that could leap frog the Beijing government forward a whole ten years in their nuclear weapons development programme at Quinghai.

The Chinese Government of course had denied any truth in the matter, saying that it was wholly concerned with internal American politics. Hoskins knew the details by heart. Since the watered down version of the Congressional Cox

Committee report had been issued in 1999, it had been the job of his team of CIA agents to continue tracking the penetration. The most comprehensive espionage disaster since Ethel and Julius Rosenberg sold the secrets of the US atom bomb to the Soviets in the forties. Holliday extracted several sheets outlining references to similar work by the U.S.A. that the service had obtained through its covert MI6 overseas operators and passed them over for shredding before continuing.

'Holmes was a reasonably high profile character. His picture had been published in technical journals, the mass media and on television during interviews about the SDI project. He took cruise holidays on the Black Sea where he went largely unrecognised.

However, our people over there were aware that the Russians knew exactly who he was and he was constantly under MI6 surveillance in case any contact was attempted.'

Hank Hoskins interrupted. 'And was any contact made?'

'Not with the Russians directly, but he was approached by a middle man operating out of Hong Kong for the Chinese. An agent now retired, that we knew as Simon Carter. They wanted information on the lasers used on the particle accelerator weapons triggers that were being jointly developed between the British and Americans. Holmes immediately reported the incident to the appropriate committee and it was agreed that we would feed misinformation back to them.'

'How was that done?'

'Well, without getting too technical, it seems that the optics involved on the lasers were very highly specified, platinum free quartz and so on. Any tiny defect in the lens mouldings, polishing or coatings could have lead to catastrophic laser damage within the systems themselves. The thin film coating technology was especially important as designs had to be incorporated that transferred the high energy laser pulse levels through the optical systems as though they were invisible. New methods of centrifugal spinning were developed for these coatings that employed some very exotic rare earth materials, made up to precise ratio mixtures and applied in hundreds of thin layers, thinner than light wavelengths. It was not too difficult to change some of the formulations, knowing that it would take their scientists months, if not years, to work out that the information Holmes passed over was useless. The computer aided design programs also had bugs deliberately inserted which moved the errors around so that results were hard to define.'

Hoskins was listening, assessing the information in his mind, not making notes as that privilege had been specifically denied to him.

'What did he receive from the Chinese in exchange for this information?'

'One hundred thousand pounds Sterling, deposited in an East German bank and later transferred indirectly to our Revenue Section.' Holliday folded down the sheets and looked over at Hoskins. 'Do you have any specific questions on this character? Most of this is ancient history you know.'

Hoskins was silent. Then. 'Why did your authorities agree to supply those secrets, even though they were adulterated?'

'Holmes was able in return to assess how advanced the Chinese were on their materials technology, information that was fed through to your own people at the Lawrence Livermore laboratory.'

Hank asked. 'His earlier work was involved in passive activation links on your nuclear weapons programme according to our files on him. Was he ever involved in the nuclear bomb factory near Aldermaston?'

Don Holliday wiped above his top lip again and brushed back his thinning hair with his fingers. What the fuck was all this about?

'No, his main expertise was in engineering physics and electro optics. He was never involved as a nuclear scientist.' Holliday read on about Holmes's work on electro optic counter measures and his involvement with the secret laser anti-dazzle sight designated LDS and developed during his brief time at the Royal Signals and Radar Establishment at Malvern. This information was too classified to pass on to the Commander and he kept quiet about it.

Hoskins thought for a moment.

'His resignation was very public at the time, the press crucified him. How did that come about?'

Holliday referred again to the print out.

'Deliberate leaks appeared on editors' teleprinters in the major media newspaper offices. They purported to originate from Government sources, but they were traced back to a small news agency in Hong Kong which was quickly shut down by the police over there. We believe that Simon Carter perpetrated them as some sort of revenge when it was discovered that the information he had obtained for his masters in Beijing was useless. Basically, the leak exposed Holmes as if he had actually sold secrets and in spite of Government intervention and denials his credibility was badly damaged. The anti Semitic organisations of the time worked quietly in the background and his reputation was also damaged by accusations that he was homosexual.'

'And was he?'

'We had our suspicions but nothing was ever proved. In any case, he would have had to admit any gender problems when he was periodically vetted by our security people in personnel. He was married with one daughter and appeared to be heterosexual. He had a mistress for a short time when he was at the Atomic Weapons Research Establishment.' He paused whilst he looked back over the now untidy pile of paper. 'Yes here it is, a female scientist.' He looked up at Betty Jennings and handed her the sheet. 'See if we have anything on this woman.'

Hoskins interceded. 'Can your machine print out a list of his other contacts at the same time, for instance can you see if he ever came into contact with anyone by the name of Senden?' Don Holliday nodded his approval to Betty who had been standing whilst the two men discussed Holmes and was glad to get back to her computer work station.

Holliday referred to the sheets, 'The data base summary says that there are over five thousand contact names, let's see, Senden you say.'

Hoskins eyes followed the long legs up to the short skirt as she left the room. 'Holmes is a widower I believe. When did his wife die?'

'During the scandal and considerable press coverage, it appeared that she stood by him during a nervous breakdown that led to a suicide attempt. After that of course, he was taken off any work of a sensitive nature. She later committed suicide, blaming the media for the break up of their marriage and the downfall of her husband whom she said she still believed in. That softened the public's attitude towards him and he started to make guest appearances on scientific television programmes. Now of course he has his own very popular series, feeding simple every day science to the masses.'

The door tone heralded Betty Jennings back into the room, looking pleased with the result she carried and gave to Don Holliday.

'Well that's a surprise; we have Holmes's gender as a passive male. It seems that his mistress, a Dr.Hilda Johns, later vanished. Turned up in Israel working in the secret nuclear weapons laboratories south of Beershiba, at Dimona, retired and later died in 1997.'

'Any contact between Holmes and Johns after she left?'

'Negative. We don't think so, although they were seen together at one time at a scientific conference in Geneva.'

'What about the other name, Senden.'

Holliday thumbed through the new armful of computer printout.

'There are two Senden's listed. Lt. Cmdr. Philip Senden, who was the Naval Officer in charge with Holmes during sea trials on laser weapons and a Dr. Peter Senden who worked indirectly for Holmes through a GEC Marconi subsidary, who were contractors on the passive activation links through one of their divisions. It appears from a recent update that the Lt.Cmdr. was later promoted, eventually to Rear Admiral and is now deceased.'

His eyes continued to scan the information until he suddenly stopped and frowned as though thinking to himself.

'I'm not sure that I can tell you any more about Peter Senden.'

'That's presumably because he works for your T2 Section.'

Don Holliday looked surprised. Here was this total stranger who had turned up out of the blue with the highest authority one could obtain to look at his files. How much he should tell him he wasn't sure, he just shrugged and said.

'I'm afraid Commander that your letter only gives me the authority to seek information on Sir Anthony Holmes and Rear Admiral Philip Senden, I believe it would be a breach of security to comment on Dr. Senden.'

'O.K. let me ask you about Holmes's daughter.'

This time Holliday looked directly at Hoskins without referring to the sheets.

'Her name is Katherine, a physicist working for the Environment Agency.'

'And?'

'I'm afraid that once again that is all I can tell you about her.'

'Is that because she also works for your organisation?'

Holliday shrugged his shoulders. 'I regret Commander, that I am not permitted to say anything about Katherine Holmes, my brief as you have already pointed out, was for information on Sir Anthony.' He handed the copy back to Betty for shredding and turned again to face Commander Hoskins.

'Well sir, I think that is about all I can tell you about Sir Anthony Holmes, it all seems a long time ago now, about twenty years I suppose. Have they found him yet?'

He hoped that the barest details he had conveyed would be enough to keep the American happy. There was a lot more in those surprisingly detailed files that he considered unsuitable for the Commander to be told, even though he appeared to have the highest authority.

It was now the turn of the Commander to give up secrets. He just shook his head, picked up his jacket from the chair, thanked Holliday for the information and rejoined his escort who was waiting outside the room. The lift took them down to the vast underground parking area where his car and driver were waiting.

They went through the security formalities and drove up the ramp as the giant armoured gates of Thames House rolled open and the car turned out into Thorney Street behind the British Secret Service building and headed north towards Parliament Square and St James's. It was black dark and the London rain showed up the street lights as blurred streaks as the wipers worked to clear the screen.

'Where to sir?'

Hoskins long fingers were resting on his overnight bag on the seat next to him and he ordered the sergeant to take him to the Wiltshire R.A.F. base from where he would fly overnight to Washington and the CIA headquarters at Langley.

Chapter 13.   The Newspaper Journalist.

'For Christ sakes, what happened to you?' Peter Senden was sitting beside the hospital bed where John Barrett lay, his plastic neck brace in place and rolls of bandage and wadding curled around his head like a turban.

John Barrett was more coherent now and expected to be discharged the next morning.

'I went along to Piltcher's place this morning and interrupted a burglary.'

Peter's reply was guarded and he turned so that his back was towards the door. 'But what are the police doing here for God's sake; they appear to be guarding you.'

'It's a funny thing old mate but I think they believe I had something to do with the burglary. They want to question me tomorrow as to what I was doing there at that time. Unfortunately, I gather that Captain Piltcher was beaten up badly and is still unconscious in intensive care and.....' He paused and looked past Peter at the constable sitting outside the private room and mouthed at Peter to close the door. Peter shook his head and lent close in a whisper.

'They only let me in here after a lot of argument and the door has to stay open. I've been questioned about Gilbert Piltcher by some American Naval officer this afternoon, what's he been up to?'

John shifted his position on the bed that was fast becoming uncomfortable.

'That's odd, it was two Americans who found me semi conscious but they vanished off the scene before the ambulance arrived. I obviously went in and out of consciousness because the last thing I can remember was a lady neighbour of Piltcher's sitting with me when the ambulance and police arrived with sirens hooting like the cavalry in one of those old Hopalong Cassidy films.'

Peter thought back to the incident on the quay side back street in Weymouth. His rescuers had been Americans, but why was the CIA so interested in the two of them that they were both under surveillance?

'Can you do something for me?' Peter nodded his assent. 'Can you ring the hotel and ask for Katherine Holmes. I had invited her to join us for dinner this evening.'

Peter smiled 'Rotten old sod, I thought we would be eating on the boat this evening so as to get an early start in the morning. Didn't know you had a romantic liaison on the go. Anyway of course I'll ring her for you.' He gave an exaggerated chuckle, 'perhaps she'll have dinner with me instead.'

The two men had been friends for a long time and any likelihood of competition was only meant as a joke. In any case, unlike John who had had an unhappy divorce two years previously, Peter now had a relationship with Jessica that was developing quite rapidly.

'I had the most extraordinary experience sailing over here today.' Peter had gauged that his friend was well enough to receive an account of the shooting and the fear he had experienced out in the fog that morning.

'The local papers should have plenty to report on tomorrow. A suspected murder at sea, a brutal burglary and a missing scientist.' Peter stopped short as he saw the expression on John's face suddenly change.

'Christ, I had forgotten about Katherine's father if that's whom you're referring to.'

Peter looked at him. 'You don't mean that Sir Anthony Holmes is your date's father? It was on the local lunch time T.V. News. I saw the report in the hotel room when I was having a beer and contemplating if the police would believe my murder story. He's missing and there's a police search going on at the moment for him'

John looked agitated. 'I've got to get out of here and see her. She must be worried sick.'

Peter glanced at his watch, it was already 6.00 o'clock. John was looking tired so he decided it was time to leave and get back to the search.

'Don't worry, I'll try and contact her when I get back to the hotel, I presume she's staying there as well?'

John confirmed the question, gave him his car keys and described where he had left the Jaguar.

'Oh, by the way, did your office find out anything about the ship, you know, the *Dragon's Morsel*. You were going to look in Lloyd's Register?'

'Nothing there mate, Sally did a thorough search. There was no ship of that name ever shown as being registered, so it wasn't worth doing a search on wrecks.' He never thought to ask how Peter would get back to the hotel, he was already dozing off.

Peter Senden hadn't told John that he was also helping the police with their enquiries. In fact he was due to return to Pendennis Castle in Falmouth. It was from there that the police had set up an incident room and were liaising with the coast guard and SAR helicopter from Chinnor together with the RNLI lifeboats from Fowey and Falmouth.

The search for the body Peter had reported, had commenced during the afternoon from the information and chart position that he had given them in his statement.

Everyone was being nice to him, but he had a certain feeling of scepticism from D.I. Robert Evans who was running the investigation. The whole story seemed so outrageously far fetched that during the interview he suggested that Peter may have suffered concussion or delusion when he hit his head on the bulkhead. There was also the question of whether the various events that had emerged during the day had any connection.

The radio reports between the various organisations continued through the evening until the search was called off as darkness fell. At about 10.00 o'clock, Peter was returned to the hotel and was requested to remain there by the police until the morning.

As he collected his room keys, he enquired about Katherine Holmes but she had not returned to the hotel. Nicki motioned to him and whispered.

'There's a man waiting to see you in the lounge, he's been here all evening and left this card for you, he's a reporter from the *London Daily Chronicle*. Oh, we've had the T.V. people here as well, quite exciting, Sir Anthony who is staying here has vanished and we've all been questioned by the police. They wanted to know what time you arrived here as well, all very mysterious I must say.' She looked at Peter hoping for some possible enlightenment.

Peter made some light comment, took the card and entered the empty lounge, empty that was except for a robust looking middle aged man who was sitting drinking from a large brandy glass, and from the colour of his complexion probably not his first. He rose as Peter entered and proffered a large hand which Peter shook.

'Dr. Senden, thank you for seeing me. My name's Ian Porter, I'm the local news gatherer for the *London Daily Chronicle*, can I get you anything.'

Peter sank into a chair beside the man. 'No thanks, too late for me. So, Mr.Porter, how can I help you?'

'There are reports that you are the person who witnessed someone being thrown overboard from a ship somewhere off Dodman Point earlier today.'

Peter didn't reply but turned to see Nicki hovering by the open doorway. 'Nicki, could you get me a pack of Hamlet cigars from the bar please?' He turned to Porter. 'The police have issued a statement to that effect I believe.'

'Oh, come on Dr. Senden, their report is as brief as a Sumo wrestler's jock strap; I need words to feed to my editors not the tit ends that the police have poked out.'

His florid face smiled as he breathed out his brandy fumes and Peter was inclined to turn away and leave him to his imbibing.

Porter fished in an inside pocket of the well-worn tweed jacket he was wearing and pulled out a photograph that he waved in front of Peter. 'Do you by any chance recognise the people in this picture?'

Peter took the photograph and looked at it. There were three men, one in a ship's captain uniform and a teenage girl standing together beside a swimming pool on what looked like a cruise ship. The picture was blurred and appeared to have been enlarged from part of larger group.

'That looks like Sir Anthony Holmes the missing scientist, his picture was on the television earlier today, but I haven't a clue who the others are. What's its significance anyway?'

The photograph was returned to the pocket and Porter with a peculiar nodding of his head suddenly seemed more sober. The nodding seemed to emphasise the main features of his face, the large thick eyebrows that ended in curly bushes that matched the equal abundance of hair protruding from the nostrils and ears.

'Could any of those gentlemen have been the person you saw out there earlier today?'

Peter was musing over those eyebrows, had he had a pair of scissors he would have been tempted to lean forward and offer him a quick trim. 'That'll be ten bob sir, anything for the weekend?'

He brought his thoughts back to what had been said and surmised. Poor sod. Here was the local reporter trying to join up the stories of the day and make some sort of sensational scoop for the papers he served.

'I'm afraid I didn't see the features of the person. It all happened so quickly.' He looked around and half rose indicating from his body language that the interview was closed.

'You're not very inquisitive are you Dr. Senden. Would you like to know who the other chaps in the photograph are?' The question was given in a slow coy way, the head tilted to one side, so that the hairy nostrils seemed to fill the man's face. The question could only demand an affirmative answer to Porter who had put out a restraining hand that now clutched at Peter's shoulder.

Nicki appeared with the cigars and both men paused whilst she removed the cellophane covering and opened the packet for him.

She hovered within earshot.

'Thanks Nicki, you can leave us now.' Peter sank back into the chair and lit his cheroot.

'Mr.Porter, I'm tired, I've had a hell of a long day and I'm ready for a shower and my bed. Why should I care who's in your photograph?'

Porter parried the rebuttal. Having a thick skin was part of the job.

'That photograph was taken on a Russian cruise ship about eighteen years ago. You were correct in recognising Anthony Holmes. The significance of the photograph may become apparent to you when I tell you that the other gentlemen are Gilbert Piltcher who was the captain and a Far Eastern businessman by the name of Simon Carter. The young girl is Holmes's daughter. Holmes lost his job as a result of that picture. Accused of spying but not proven. Passing secret laser information to the Russians.'

Peter Senden was an engineer, a thinking man, considered by his friends as clever, solid, reliable and fun loving when it suited him. By his own volition he wasn't an excitable or voluble person. He had a logical and precision approach to life and its problems. If an infra red camera had been trained on him at that moment, the effect of Ian Porter's casual comment would have shown instantaneous tiny changes in the screen colours as the adrenaline suddenly pumped through his system and heartbeat raised, increasing his skin temperature by minute amounts.

Peter's look of surprise was immediately apparent to Porter, who now sat back as if he had played a trump card and awaited the outcome with his arms folded and a knowing half smile now crowned his expression. He had cast his line, captured his quarry's curiosity and now intended to reel him in little by little.

Up until that time, Peter had not made any association between the various events of that day, treating them all as separate entities. Here was a set of situations that now established definite links between his father and the mysterious Gilbert Piltcher and Simon Carter. The names stated in his father's Will. So, Sir Anthony Holmes was probably the same person as the T. Holmes also mentioned in that same document.

Anthony or Tony, they were the same name. He thought back to the hospital conversation with John. Was it coincidence that he had met up with Holmes's daughter, or was there a more obtuse reason?

One man dead, one man missing, one man beaten up and lying in hospital and his friend in the same place, possibly there instead of himself.

Peter was suddenly cautious. This man was no ordinary local reporter; he wasn't interested in the body floating somewhere out there at sea.

He obviously knew who Peter was and was on some sort of assignment, but how much did he really know. This would be a cat and mouse conversation from now on.

Porter had been watching him closely. 'I see I've surprised you Dr. Senden. You see I'm not the old hack that I pretend to be. I have been following a story line now for several weeks and I can assure you that you have become involved in something very big. Something that the authorities are hiding from us, something that has involved the Government spending out millions of pounds worth of tax payers' money over the last month or so.

My newspaper, along with others, has been digging and prospecting ever since we received a minor leak from a rating on board the Portsmouth based Royal Navy survey ship H.M.S.Seeker. He was overheard in a pub sounding off about his restricted leave. It transpired that for the last month the Royal Navy together with the French Navy and a U.S.Navy task force, including a recovery ship, have been trolling up and down the Western end of the English Channel in search of something. Official sources of course deny that there is anything unusual in this.

We've checked through the NATO Navy List and all ships including our own nuclear submarines are accounted for, most of them being in repair yards at the current time. We can surmise therefore that they are not looking for a hitherto unreported sinking. Similarly if a nuclear warhead had been lost, a massive number of ships would have been concentrated in one area. An A.R.T.S. or Accident Response Team comprising anything up to five hundred specialists would have been involved. However, we do know that virtually every wreck in the area is being surveyed using both conventional means and the unmanned naval submarine known as the 'Remote Counter Mine Disposal System.' We know that the Ministry of Defence has recently placed urgent orders for two more units costing a quarter of a million pounds apiece without going through the normal Parliamentary procedures on the procurement of such equipment.

We got another clue that a massive survey was being conducted through the 'Admiralty Notices to Mariners' published weekly by the Navy Hydrographers Department. As you know, these notices are used by commercial and recreational sea goers and give up to date information on harbours, lights, buoyage, wrecks and so on. Well, the last few weeks have seen a large number of hitherto unknown wrecks and other underwater obstructions notified mainly in the shallower parts of the Channel.'

His glass was empty again, and this time Peter accepted his offer of a whiskey as Ian Porter waved towards the barman who was clearing glasses from another table.

He continued. 'Back in 1989 after the Tiananmen Square outrage, there was a rare defection of a Chinese clerk from the New Chinese News Agency. He was not a large fish by any means but he poured out his soul to the MI6 contingent based in Hong Kong. I was assigned to that story and the fragments I was allowed to see and later able to piece together included a seemingly unimportant account of a British merchant ship called the Acacia Lady that sank in the Channel back in about 1953.

I will not bore you with the details now as to why the Chinese were interested in that particular vessel, but when I did a search through the newspaper archives for the period, I found an account of the old Board of Trade Enquiry into the sinking.

Your father was the Royal Navy officer on board at the time along with Captain Piltcher, and a director of the shipping company named Simon Carter.' He could see straight away by Peter's guarded expression that he had hit a nerve somewhere.

'You mean my father and those two were on the same ship, the Acacia Lady you say?'

'That's correct.'

'So how does Sir Anthony fit into all of this?'

'How do you mean?'

'Well, it seems from what you have said that my father may have known these three people some time ago, but I don't know in what context.'

Porter looked away as if thinking.

'That photograph was taken years after the Acacia Lady affair, during a holiday on a Black Sea cruise ship. It was fished out of my newspapers archives when it came to light through lists put into the public domain by MI5 in 1995, that Holmes and others had been under surveillance. We believe that they suspected them of feeding the Russians with information on secret high power laser weapons that were being researched at the time when he was working at what was then called the Atomic Weapons Research Establishment. It was after Holmes got his knighthood of course. He got that for his research at Rutherford and later with the Helen laser system at A.W.E. at Aldermaston. Something to do with nuclear fusion I believe.'

Peter had been listening intently to Porters story and now interrupted again.

'I think you'll find that Sir Anthony's work was connected with P.A.L.'s or Permissive Action Links that are very complex electronic keys for nuclear weapons. The key effectively locks the weapon and renders it inoperable in case it falls into unauthorised hands such as terrorists. My old firm, as I am sure you will already know Mr. Porter, was Marconi Switching Networks that handled some of the contracts that are still highly secret in their content. But how do you get the connection between what the Navy are supposedly doing at this time and an event that happened fifty odd years ago?'

'Intuition dear boy. Born out of twenty five years of old fashioned foot slogging.' Porter paused as if deciding how much to say. 'On the one hand we have the Navy and for all I know, the rest of NATO, searching for something out in the English Channel. On the other hand we have a group of old men, suspected of covert dealings in the Black Sea but knowing that they were also involved years ago in a mysterious sinking. Then I find out that one of these men was in Weymouth hospital with severe burns, possibly radiation burns.'

He picked up the brandy glass and peered at the last few dregs.

"Sorry to hear about your recent bereavement by the way. What really happened?'

Peter thought. 'Is this the keystone question of the conversation? Is that what he is fishing for, does he really know something?' He shrugged off the question with his usual response about a heart attack whilst diving and followed it up quickly by asking. 'Was my father also on that cruise ship?'

'Yes, although he was not suspected of any complicity according to the released MI5 records. It is generally considered in media circles that he worked for MI6 after taking retirement from the Royal Navy.' He looked expectantly at Peter for a response.

So that was it! Peter had been away at University just after his father's retirement and saw little of him at the time. He knew that Philip had spent a lot of time abroad.

'What's this all about Mr.Porter?'

Porter looked disappointed at the side-stepping of his statement on Philip Senden's injuries and MI6 involvement, but then, it was just possible that the young man sitting beside him would not have known. He took on an air of careful conviviality as he stood.

'Dr.Senden, if I told you that, I wouldn't have a story for my editor. Be assured though that through other sources I hope to establish a tentative link that now needs to be substantiated.'

Peter had other questions about his father's involvement, but Porter had finished his drink and the bar had closed. So had his mouth for the time being. Without knowing it Porter had just furnished him with another small piece of information in the jigsaw of his father's death that he would tuck away for future use. The Acacia Lady must have been the treasure ship that Philip was trying to find. If what Porter had said was correct, why were the Navy looking for it?

Could it have been the wreck of the Acacia Lady that contaminated Philip? How could Porter have known about Philip's radiation burns?

As he lay in bed, sleep didn't come easily as he turned the events of the last few days over in his mind. He remembered the scrap book of newspaper cuttings he had received from his father and hoped John had brought it with him to Cornwall. The scrap book had suddenly taken on a greater significance than the share certificates and other items. He eventually dropped off thinking about the strange interview with the American C.I.A. man, why was he involved, what had his father been up to, was it this tentative statement by the newspaper reporter that his father was ex MI6? He consoled himself with the new knowledge he had gleaned from Porter that evening, The Acacia Lady had to be the treasure ship that his father had been searching for. He had to decide whether to pass the information on to Malcolm Seiger at Scotland Yard, or keep it to himself for the time being. What was the *Dragon's Morsel* if it wasn't the ship? Was it by chance that John had become associated with Katherine Holmes?

Why had he been beaten up at Weymouth?

He hoped the morning might throw up other clues when he was due to visit a couple of charter offices over in Falmouth. Capt. Rogerson had said, a gin palace; a yacht from Falmouth

Chapter 14. The ship's chandler.

Peter Senden woke suddenly to the sound of the telephone ringing. A check on his wristwatch indicated that it was only 7.00 a.m.

'Ah, Dr. Senden?' It was the stand -in night porter. 'Dr. Senden, I have a policeman here who would like to speak to you.' The voice was curious. The night porter had heard the gossip from the night before and was now more alert than he would normally have been at that time of day. He had already agreed with his cousin on the local press that any small piece of news on the various happenings would be immediately reported.

'O.K., give me a few minutes to dress and shower and I'll be down there.'

It was one of the constables from the previous afternoon.

'Sorry to trouble you sir, but you are required at Truro and I have a car waiting outside for you.'

Inspector Evans looked tired. The plastic coffee cups and piled ashtray in front of him indicated he had had a busy night. He waved Peter to a seat across from his desk.

'Thanks for coming over so quickly.' He proffered his cigarette packet but Peter declined. 'Have you ever met Captain Piltcher?'

'I hope you didn't haul me out of bed just to ask me that.' Peter had imagined that there was some news on the search for the body that had been scheduled to start at first light.

'In answer to your question, no.' Evans gave him a long glance as he stubbed out another cigarette. 'So you would not be able to identify him?'

'Of course not. All I know is that he was an old friend of my father's. Mr.Barrett has tried to locate him because he may be a beneficiary of my father's Will.' Peter was still annoyed at the way he had been questioned the previous day and now reached forward for the last of the cigarettes and lit it.

Evans remained passively quiet, he hoped he had another packet in the drawer though he had lost count of how many of the hateful things he had smoked. His mouth told him it was quite a few, and then, 'Do you know anything about the court case that Capt.Piltcher was involved in back in 1986 concerning a gold smuggling incident?'

Again Peter gave a negative reply.

'Did your father know a Mr. Luk?' Peter's mind went back to the file his father had stored so carefully over all those years. He had only had a cursory look at it before handing it over to John.

'Not as far as I can recall, I don't know who he is. Why do you ask?'

The Detective Inspector leaned forward now, his shirt sleeves had been rolled up and he flicked ash off the desk top before resting his bare arms on the table space in front of him.

'We made enquiries with the letting agents for Crows Nest Cottage, where your friend went yesterday. Captain Piltcher negotiated by post and nobody there could identify him.'

Similar enquiries with the neighbours confirmed that a gentleman had been seen there but had not made any attempt to talk to them. In fact none of them could give an accurate description of him or even knew his name. All they knew was that he came and went at odd times and drove an old Morris Traveller. In short, Dr. Senden, the car is not at the cottage and it was not Captain Piltcher who we found unconscious there after your friend said he was attacked.' He slumped back in the chair as he looked at Peter and shrugged his shoulders in a vague, tired gesture of incertitude.

Peter thought back over what had been said during his visit to the hospital. Were the police trying to make a case against John Barrett?

'The neighbour who called the ambulance was told by your friend that the unconscious man was Captain Piltcher and he was admitted to hospital under that name.'

'Surely you don't think that Mr.Barrett or I had anything to do with what happened yesterday. Anyway, who was it if it wasn't Piltcher?'

Evans paused again as if trying to get a detective's intuition as he now looked directly at Peter Senden.

'The neighbour only assumed the man was Piltcher. During our search of the premises we found a wallet that had apparently slipped under the bed. Its contents identified the patient as a Mr.He Luk who is visiting this country from Hong Kong. His identity was also confirmed by the hospital a short time ago. We also know that a car was seen at about the time the burglary was taking place, driving away from the beach car park just below the cottages at high speed. When we searched the area we found a Hong Kong passport in He Luk's name lying on the grass verge.'

Peter sat forward on his chair. 'Well, who is he?'

Evans's tone was harder as he replied. 'I had hoped that you would be able to answer that question Dr. Senden. You see, we found both your address and your father's in a notebook he was carrying. The address of the incident yesterday was also in there. It seems strange that this person came all the way over here to the U.K. with only a few contact addresses and yours was one of them, and yet you deny any knowledge of him.'

Peter opened out his arms in a gesture of disbelief.

'I just don't see how I can help you. You give the impression that you think we're mixed up in some smuggling or money laundering exercise. That American Commander yesterday, can't remember his name, but what was all that about millions of dollars and how does it relate to my father? What's happening about the search? Have you found a body yet?' The questions tumbled out in a jumble. What was all this questioning to do with him?

'The problem I have Dr.Senden is that a number of cases I have at the moment seem to be connected with you. You are an intelligent man, so it should not seem strange to you that I see you as a key component to my enquiries. In answer to your question, the coast guard search and rescue organisation have failed to find a body but they're starting their search again about now.

I have your report and statement about a gruesome murder you say you witnessed when you just happened to be at a position miles from anywhere. You are also connected with Mr.Barrett who just happens to be assaulted by an as yet unknown assailant. Your friend is found on the premises where an old man is nearly battered to death. You say you don't know him and yet he is carrying your address around with him. You are linked indirectly with Katherine Holmes through your friend whom we are interviewing separately about her missing father. We are now aware that your father was being sought by the U.S. Central Intelligence Agency over some financial thing that they refuse to give us details about. What the bloody hell do you expect me to be doing?' His voice had risen as he swung back and pivoted his chair so that he was looking out of the window where the dawn shadows were shortening as the morning sun rose.

Peter Senden put out the foul tasting cigarette.

'I'm sorry I cannot be of more help, honestly. I can confirm to you once again that neither John Barrett nor I know what is going on.' He then outlined his conversation with Ian Porter but left out certain items.

The inspector swivelled his chair round to face him, his hands now clasped behind his crew-cut head.

'Thank you, that's interesting. We know Ian Porter but not what he is essentially seeking. He's been down here for weeks, poking around the naval ships at Drake in Davenport. He's been warned by the M.O.D. police at Portsmouth to keep out of the Naval dockyard. It is not against the law for investigative journalists to go around questioning people. Whatever it is he is trying to find out, we know nothing about it.' He stopped, realising that he was saying too much to the man across the table whom he had not yet made up his mind about.

Peter guessed that the Inspector knew more about Ian Porter than he was prepared to admit.

'Have you heard how Mr.Barrett is this morning?'

Evans lifted the phone and made the enquiry.

'Well, you'll be pleased to hear that his X rays are O.K. He's had a quiet night but is still under medical observation. The inspector eyed him thoughtfully. Having listened to the recording disc and the conversation between Hoskins and the man across the table, there were other burning questions he would have liked to ask. He decided to save them until the reports of the Weymouth incident came through from the Dorset Police.

The interview had petered out and both men sat in silence.

'I'll arrange a car to get you back to your hotel but I would like to keep in touch in case there are any developments with respect to the search. We will also want to go on board your yacht. Perhaps we could do that this afternoon if that's convenient.'

Back at the hotel, Peter had breakfast. The Sunday papers were full of speculative stories over the disappearance of Sir Anthony Holmes. He enquired at the reception desk about Katherine Holmes again but they had not seen her since the previous day. Surely she was not still at the police headquarters.

Peter remembered the GPS set in his holdall.

He located the Higgs and Freeman Electronics workshop at the back of a boat yard, full of puddles, blocks of shoring up wood, paint tins, abandoned rope and an assortment of old and rusting marine gear. Electric cables snaked across the ground along with a leaking hose pipe that made the whole place look lethal. Racks of upright tenders stood against an open fronted shed where masts and rigging were laid out on wooden horses, waiting for the stresses of their next outing. Dingy trailers took up a large part of the open spaces between silent cradled yachts full of their owner's dreams, some of them merely hulks and so old that it was unlikely they would ever sail again. The spot was reasonably sheltered and the smells were a mixture of putty, mould, paint and epoxy resin clinging to the natural odours that rose from the nearby seashore.

The door rattled open to his touch and inside the building to one side was a small office, relatively tidy with a young woman busy at the keyboard of her computer. A large glass fronted display cabinet housed an extraordinary array of electronic gadgetry for sailors. Infra red binoculars, computerised charts on compact disc, flux gate compasses, radio equipment, satellite communicating distress beacons together with many types of navigation equipment. A dusty bench ran along one wall with various oscilloscopes, test meters and soldering irons with racks over containing reels of cable, and an array of dismantled bits and pieces, equipment cases and cardboard boxes were stacked in heaps on other shelves that also served to house the bits of chandlery that were displayed for sale and illuminated by a couple of dusty fluorescent lights.

Peter explained to the girl about the lightning strike and the demise of his G.P.S. set.

Whilst she was explaining that they were about to shut up for the day, Jake Higgs emerged from the inner gloom of the place, took the set and turned it over in his hands for a cursory examination.

'These things are unrepairable I'm afraid, all we can do these days is to fit a new module. The days of getting the old soldering iron out and replacing components are long gone. The innards are assembled by computer controlled robotics for a few pence. The price the consumer pays is all down to the cost of marketing and getting the product on the sales stand.' He sighed, remembering the days when he could replace a vacuum tube, capacitor, resistor or transistor and charge a commendable price for the privilege especially in the limited yachty market as it then was.

Peter said nothing. A lot of his work had been concerned with the design of the mechatronic equipment that Jake Higgs was complaining about.

'It's most unlikely that lightning upset it, more likely to be a connection to the aerial. I'll stick it on a power pack and aerial and give it a try.' It took less than a couple of minutes for Higgs to hook it up and for the unit to establish contact with its orbiting satellite system. The screen indicated its ground position to within a few metres.

Higgs looked satisfied that his diagnosis was correct. There would be no business for him here but he had a few minutes to chat.

'You've probably damaged the aerial or its cable on the boat. When was this lightning strike?' Peter explained it had been on his voyage the day before but did not enlighten on the other happenings.

'Funny,' Higgs frowned, 'We had another report of lightning damage yesterday or the day before on the large luxury yacht moored up in the river, the Starlight Princess. We're certain that it wasn't lightning though.' He gave a nervous laugh, 'looked like someone had used it for target practice.' He gestured to a pile stacked in a corner, the remains of the radar repeater and the damaged spray screen that he had since removed in readiness for fitting the replacements due in that day.

Peter said nothing but bent down and examined the 9mm bullet hole.

D.I.Evans was there within the hour, together with a forensic team who, with their clinical condom thin gloves, packed the parts away in plastic bags for later detailed examination. Their unenviable task of sorting out Higg's fingerprints from anything else useful would be a challenging job for someone later in the laboratory as they applied their scruitinous tests.

The find at last gave some credence to Peter Senden's statement and now gave the police a positive lead to the syndicate boat owners and their cash paying charter customers. Peter watched from the shore as the loaded police launch threaded its way through the moorings to the large trawler yacht moored further up the river.

Chapter 16. Conspiracy at Langley.

When Hank Hoskins arrived with his overnight bag at the Andrews Airforce Base to the south east of Washington on Sunday morning, there were no immigration formalities. He was met off the Lockheed Hercules C130-H by one of the Assistant Station Commanders, Michael Bull and whisked off by limousine to the heliport where a company Sikorsky waited, its four rotors already powered up from its powerful turbines.

He found the Virginia climate sticky after his few weeks in England where the summer was beginning to provide above average cloud cover and rain nearly every other day. As he transferred from the car he glanced upwards, as the Pratt and Whitney engines of two F-22 Raptor stealth fighters screamed their approach on the overhead flight path towards one of the vast concrete runways.

Hank heaved himself up into the jump seat and donned a headset as the helicopter lifted off and headed away from the US Air Force complex, turning west to pass over the Potomac River.

It was a route he knew well. This morning the Fight Lieut. at the controls informed him that heavy flight traffic out of the Washington National Airport, following the Independence Day holiday celebrations, meant they would be detouring to the west before turning north towards Arlington, rather than the normal direct flight along the Potomac. A few miles to the east, the dome of the Capitol building stood out in the hazy morning sunshine and then they were soon alongside the George Washington Memorial Parkway, running along the west bank of the river, heading north east now towards Fairfax County and the C.I.A. Headquarters buildings at Langley where another car was waiting for him.

Hoskins instructed the driver to take him straight to the records bureau library building and spent some time on the microfiche machines, where he scanned the images of old intelligence records for the Hong Kong section. He suddenly found what he was looking for and let out a quiet yelp. There it was in front of him, the Chinese metaphor that had puzzled him over the last few days, a Maoist reference to the *Dragon's Morsel*.

He had the information digitally scanned onto disc, signed for it and addressed a security envelope for the diplomatic bag to his office in Grosvenor Street London.

As he hurried back to the CIA HQ main entrance and through the security barriers, he was hailed by a tall man with a pale round face waiting at the elevator lobby.

'Hi Hank, how you doing, what brings you here on a Sunday morning?'

Frank Gibson put his briefcase down on the polished floor and hitched the belt to his pants before extending his hand. Hoskins gave a tired grin to the Section Assistant Deputy of Overseas Nuclear Affairs. A shock of prematurely grey hair crowned the features of the face, dominated by strangely black eyebrows. He could not be classed as coming from any original ethnic or immigrant background, not Italian, nor German. Not Irish or Jewish or Spanish. Just a tall pale faced American dressed in a pale grey suit, out of keeping with the normal dress for a Sunday morning.

'Hi Frank, nice to see you, just been doing some background work in the library, I'm on the way over to my office.'

Gibson looked around the empty lobby and put a confidential arm around Hank's shoulder and in a quiet voice said.

'Hank, this is a good opportunity to talk whilst the place is quiet, I've got a meeting arranged upstairs for the guys, sure like for you to join with us if you've got time.'

They entered conference room C2103 and Hank took a seat, extracting his glasses from a top pocket of his lounge suit and gave them a methodical polish.

Around the table were six faces that the Commander knew well and who had nodded or saluted their greetings to him. The faces did not bear the relaxed features of a normal Sunday morning in the office. A time usually spent in a casual mood, an excuse to get away from the grasps of the family for a while. These faces tried to hide and disguise the hidden tension of over tuned guitar strings.

Gibson addressed the meeting.

'Just bumped into old Hank here, thought it would be a good opportunity for a verbal update on what's happening in the U.K., then we can get down to the main agenda.' He passed the onus on Hank to reply.

'Nice to see you guys in here working on a Sunday morning, I was not briefed for this meeting, but I'll try and outline what we know to date.

The co-operation requested between our Government and the British since the Israeli Government first brought this whole damned matter to our attention is working reasonably well over there.' He stopped as if searching for a different logical starting point.

'When Mrs. Maya Dersch, the Israeli Prime Minister, first flew in for confidential talks with the President about the suspect fundamentalist plot, we were of course alerted.

A plot to disrupt the Middle East Cease Fire Conference in London next month, was probably to be expected and the security forces of the countries concerned were already considering such a possibility and taking the usual precautions. The Islamic nuclear bomb threat was treated with a certain amount of sceptical indifference, there had been plenty of similar threats over the last few years and our intelligence reported that no sources existed for procuring enough fissionable material to build such a wild card bomb. Things suddenly turned very serious when we picked up the story about the search for *Thinman*, a situation we found hard to digest given the history of that occurrence. The contaminated British diver, Philip Senden, was our first clue. The isotopic fingerprint we found was a direct match to *Thinman*. How it ended up in the

English Channel we shall probably never know, but we are certain that it is the source that the fundamentalists are looking for.'

He stopped again. 'But there are too many organisations over there. I would suspect each one trying to outmanoeuvre the others.

'How do you mean Hank?'

Hank looked around the table, all eyes on him. They knew the reasons; now they were all waiting for the detail.

'To be fair, the Brits are keeping us informed up to a point, but I have a feeling that because we are in their own back yard, they feel they should be sorting the whole thing out for themselves. Due to my request, we put up keywords on the communications network over there and our Echelon System scored pretty quickly, but by the time we heard about it, their own people had already conducted interviews, so anyone who was hiding anything would have been warned that something big was under investigation.'

'What about the Israeli suspicions and the group of terrorists?'

'The suspect terrorists are over there all right but they're keeping a pretty low profile. We understand that they could have been operating as a group of treasure seekers diving west of the Channel Islands.

I have already reported on the other people whom we believe may be involved.

To summarise progress to date. The late Rear Admiral Philip Senden's background is hazy. All we know for sure is that he was probably diving somewhere in the English Channel when he became contaminated and died. We are certain that he was employed unknowingly by the terrorists. From the research I've done in London I believe it was somewhere near the Channel Islands but that area has been searched by USS Phoenix and so far they have come up with nothing. We've got the British and French part of the task force searching some distance away, mainly in shallower waters. We now know that Philip Senden was associated in the past with Sir Anthony Holmes on sea trials with secret laser equipment, some details of which Holmes later sold to the Chinese through their agent Carter. I have to add that the sale was with the full knowledge of the British Ministry of Defence and substitute data was supplied. Even so, Holmes was later branded by the media as a traitor and resigned his job. He's now missing and the SO.13 British Special Branch Anti Terrorist squad have been tipped off that he could have been kidnapped. At the present time we can find no connection between Holmes and Senden which would suggest any joint complicity. Holmes also had a girlfriend who defected to Israel to work on their nuclear programme. Nothing is known that could substantiate any complicity on Holmes's part but we have people digging around to see what can be found. Unfortunately, it was all a long time ago and not of any great significance with respect to contemporary technology.'

He thought back over the other events of the last few days and continued whilst the others sat and listened in the air conditioned atmosphere, making occasional notes in the bare wood panelled room, the sun shades drawn down over the windows, the walls surmounted with framed photographs of more recent Presidents, now faded both by the sun and time.

'Then we have Piltcher. Special Branch has interviewed him but he's pretty old and they believe that what he says is unreliable. Apparently he's shit scared of the guy called Carter.

Carter is the other one who we are sure is involved, a small time double agent and businessman full name, Simon Carter, who was working for the SAD, the Chinese Communist Secret Service in Hong Kong. We also know that when it suited him he fed information to the British MI6 station in Hong Kong. He was sacked by SAD a few years back when they discovered that they had been fed misinformation by the British. We believe they also knew he was moonlighting.

You will have seen in my department's report the other day that the research led them to believe that *Thinman* could be on a wreck called the *Dragon's Morsel*. It's the only thing they have found that connects all of these names together. The time period is also about right. However, our records department could find no record of any ship of that name being registered in any maritime country at the time.' Hoskins thoughts were on what he had found earlier in the library, He knew very well that the *Dragon's Morsel* referred to something else that he could not communicate in this company.

'We have since discovered in old British newspaper reports that a freighter by the name of the Acacia Lady sank back in '53. There was a British Government enquiry directed by their Board of Trade at the time. We checked back through the official court transcripts and discovered that the ship was owned by a company run by Carter's father. Carter was on board at the time along with Senden. Piltcher was the captain of the ship and he quite clearly specified the Decca co-ordinates to the court at the time of the enquiry. These were passed on to the task force who then searched that spot and there is nothing there. We also know that Pitcher was the captain of the cruise ship in the Black Sea when Holmes was dealing with the British laser secrets. Piltcher was also suspected of smuggling gold into Turkey at about that time, but nothing was ever proved, due mainly to alibis given by his brother in law, Sir Anthony Holmes.

To bring you up to date, there was a bungled burglary at Capt. Piltcher's place on Saturday. Piltcher was beaten up, I suspect left for dead by someone looking for information .and the police there are still looking for the culprit or culprits. We believe that the culprits are a mob from N.Korea who are liaising with the Middle East fundamentalists. Our men arrived just after the burglary and found Holmes's daughter snooping around there. Said she was visiting her uncle and saw a number of Chinese looking guys running from the scene. Then this solicitor turned up, John Barrett, apparently acting for the Rear Admiral's son Peter Senden and whoever was in the house slugged him one. My view is that it was a professional hit that this guy Barrett just walked into, I say professional because he was punched just right to make it look like a serious attempt on his life. Three nights ago, Senden's son was attacked by two assailants. One was killed as they attempted their get away and we're awaiting formal identification from the Dorset police department to be fed through. In fact we know that the assailant was a relative of Peter Senden's housekeeper. Coincidence maybe, but pretty close to the boiling pot. The death is being treated as a traffic violation as it happened shortly after the attack. Senden is also involved with a reported killing out at sea that I shall come too shortly.

We haven't been able to put a trace on Carter yet. His home in Hong Kong has been shut up and his offices are locked. His wife was contacted, now living with a Chinese diplomat, but knew nothing about his movements at least that's what she says. His secretary was just told to lock up until further notice over the phone. We understand that he was identified last week when he entered the U.K at Heathrow but somehow shook off the surveillance that MI5 placed on him. There have been no reported sightings of him since then. We also gather that he is in very deep shit with his creditors.

One additional point. There may have been a load of bullion on the ship according to a telephone conversation that MI5 monitored. We believe they refer to it as the Retirement Fund. Philip Senden's son Peter has this solicitor seeking information on Piltcher and Carter apparently to do with the will that Senden senior left. Barrett is the executor of the will and the U.K. probate laws demand that the executor of the Will should investigate all funds or possible sources of income to the deceased estate for their Inland Revenue Service. The bullion theory is of course enforced by the Black Sea gold smuggling dealings of Piltcher.

Finally, Senden got mixed up with this incident at sea when he says he witnessed a murder. The British police haven't connected it yet, but when I read the statement that Senden gave to the police there was one little bit that puzzled me. Before he witnessed the man being thrown into the sea, he heard a message in a foreign language on the ships R/T. All messages are recorded in the same way that the US coast guard record messages, the only difference there is that unless there is an emergency, no one takes any notice, the messages are just archived. The English Channel is full of shipping and all sorts of messages are passed in a variety of languages. My office requested a copy of the recording and the embassy ran it across our language experts. It was quickly identified as Hebrew and translated. Gentlemen, the man would appear to have been an Israeli Mossad agent apparently working undercover with the group of Koreans. We believe they are the group that the Israelis identified and warned us about.'

The other men had sat in silence during Hanks report, nodding approval or acknowledging points as he spoke.

'Thanks for that update Hank, so, apart from the terrorist group, we've got a few outsiders nudging in on the project, presumably because of the gold. Get your guys there to keep them away can't have amateurs prodding around into our business. What is Mossad doing over there?'

Hank grinned, 'you know as well as I do that every European country seems to have its quota of Israeli agents. My guess is that having instigated this whole thing, the Israelis are keeping a watchful eye on our progress. There is of course the Cease Fire Treaty conference coming up shortly. The British have told us that in addition to our own security arrangements being made for that occasion, the Israeli, Syrian and Palestinian organisations have also poured in a few extra people.'

'Any news yet on how this terrorist group is getting on.'

'If *Thinman* is in the wreck of the Acacia Lady, we're still not sure how it came to be in the English Channel but we're pretty damned sure that the terrorists are being co-ordinated by a N.Korean mercenary by the name of Johnny Chungai. A vicious piece of work by all accounts. The MI6 contacts still operating covertly in Hong Kong believe he is behind the Moslems who are taking over the heroin trade on the Chinese mainland. He's also been associated with a number of bombings over there, which the Chinese keep quiet about. Seems they suffer from these fringe fanatics as much as we do, they just keep quiet about them. When they get near suspects, there are no show trials, they just make sure they're shot there and then.'

'How do you know it's Chungai, has he been seen?'

'Let's just say we got a pretty good description. The British police are aware of the group but have associated them with trying to get a foothold in the U.K. drugs market.

The authorities over there have been useful but no one has established yet what Senden saw on his last dive or where exactly he was diving. The nuclear isotopic fingerprint definitely points to *Thinman* but it's been like looking for a needle in a haystack. One final point. Senden's son works part time for the British Secret Service, some technical department called T2. However, we do not believe he is involved in subversive activities. I also believe that Holmes's daughter is somehow tied into the same service.'

'What about the Chinaman they found at Piltcher's place, do we know who he is yet?'

Hoskins faltered for a moment.

'I'm sorry, what Chinaman, there were only two people found there, Senden's solicitor John Barrett and Captain Piltcher'

Frank Gibson looked around at the others before closing his eyes and sitting back in his chair, the black eyebrows wrinkling into the forehead.

'Sorry Hank, got a bit mixed up, what I meant was how's the Piltcher guy, there are so many over there I'm getting confused. He laughed with nervous embarrassment and the others joined in. Hank reported on the man's condition as he knew it up to the time of leaving Cornwall on Saturday afternoon. He was suddenly cautious and kept what he had learned in the library that morning to himself.

    Frank Gibson thanked Hank and patted the document in front of him before pushing it across the table to where Hoskins sat.

'I have to presume you're still with us on this one Hank, spend an hour on that and then we'll talk later.' The others rose and left, leaving the Section Deputy alone in the room with Hoskins.

The departmental 'Eyes Alpha' report entitled Project *Crusader* consisted of a couple of dozen sheets which Hank scanned quickly before settling to read them slowly and in more detail. What he read was an amplified version in line with his previous discussions even though the concepts as now presented filled him with disbelief and a desire to absence himself from the company. A blueprint to turn the tables on the terrorist's plans that had been outlined by the Israeli Government. A plan to rid the Middle East of the leading fanatical trouble makers who had plagued them for so many years, blown up the heart of America's financial centre, tried to destroy their defence organisation at the Pentagon, embassies, killed hostages and committed a growing number of horrendous crimes against innocent Americans on their own front doorstep. All in the name of fanatical religious splinter groups.

A plan which if successfully executed would look like the most unfortunate accident with no trace of blame or identification attached to the proliferators.

As he read the detail, he was worried and addressed questions to Gibson.

The Section Deputy rolled a Havana cigar across to Hoskins who lit it with some relish. He'd spent the last couple of weeks smoking things he suspected were tobacco impregnated paper on the other side of the Atlantic.

He smiled. 'I'm not sure you should have shown this to me Frank. Hell, it looks like the Nicaraguan contras and Irangate all over again. How's it being funded?'

Frank Gibson sat back in his chair, his hands held together with the fingers interlaced, his index fingers touching at the tips as if in prayer. A younger man than Hank, probably in his mid forties and a company man through and through. He had started his C.I.A. career after leaving Wall Street as a financial adviser and dealer to the Hindes and Stern brokering house and had been recruited for his detailed knowledge of Middle East financial affairs.

The firm of Hindes and Stern was a broking house used by many of the minor Princes in the oil rich Emirates, who turned a blind eye to the fact that the firm's directors and partners were all Jewish. In the same way that they ignored their minority Shi'ite subjects who were so antagonistic towards the Americans. They just ran their Ferraris until they became too dusty from the desert sands and turned them in for new ones. Their money couldn't be in safer hands, or so they thought. It was ironical that millions of dollars had already been peeled of certain accounts to fund the secret project that had been designated project *Crusader'* Gibson was not going to tell Hoskins those finer details that appeared in a closely guarded safe of a Senator at his holiday apartment in New York.

His face was now flushed.

'Don't worry Hank. This sort of thing is being propounded all the time, it's a case of what the government doesn't see it doesn't want to know about it. The funding has come from private political sources who are sympathetic to our cause.'

'Has the President approved it yet?'

Gibson looked down at the table. 'The plan has changed from its original concept Hank. We consider it best that the President should not be informed in case of implication later in the unlikely event that anything goes wrong, he doesn't know, only a few outside of this room know the exact implications of what we have planned. Our overseas boys are not senior enough to know the finer implications, they just follow orders.'

'What about the Select Committee on this, don't they report to the President?'

'Hank, when this whole thing started and we discovered that *Thinman* could be in the English Channel, the select committee agreed that the British and French had to be told at the highest level. As far as the Europeans are concerned, they are assisting us to clear up our own shit, put there years ago by persons unknown. It's being treated as you know as an urgent environmental problem over there. All they know is that it's nuclear material that has to be found and contained before serious pollution starts. They're doing the work covertly as we requested and they agreed so as not to arouse public suspicion and cause mass panic. They are treating the terrorist threat as a side issue.'

Hoskins nodded his approval at the official understanding of the *Thinman* status in the U.K. as Gibson continued.

'That feasibility report, now designated Project *Crusader*, has grown out of the original discussion on the subject when the possibility of turning the tables on those fanatical bastards was first raised.'

The others filled back into the room and Graham Erricsmann wearing the uniform and pips of a US Army Colonel flopped his large frame onto one of the chairs and spoke.

'Well, what do you think then Hank?'

'I'm frankly worried at the scale and possible aftermath of what is being contemplated.'

Erricsmann grinned, his protruding lips griping around the cigar stub in the corner of his mouth.

'We're not contemplating Hank boy, this is a green go go go, a carefully thought out exercise to rid the world of these fanatical fuckers with one quick sharp blow.' He lent forward and lowered his voice. 'They think they're going to get their hands on our property, but we'll turn the fucking tables on them, they'll never know what hit them. When they find what they believe to be *Thinman* and cart it back to their rat infested conference, we'll blow the fuckers to the four corners of the globe. The aftermath will allow the stable Middle East governments to take control moving in after the event on the wave of uncertainty that will follow. We will then offer them our assistance as the good guys.'

Hank looked at him, trying not to show the concern he now felt.

'What's the downside of all this?'

'Leave that to us Hank. You'll not be implicated if things go wrong. You have our word on that, the same way you were kept you out of the limelight after your involvement with the W88 nuclear warhead secrets when they were lost to the Chinese. Your part in this is simply to find *Thinman* before the Brits or the Frenchies do. I cannot overemphasise that point'

'The report states that you still have to specify the satellite. Have you sorted out that side of it yet?'

Agent Tim Gregson spoke up for the first time.

'Yep, we'll be using the old European Space Agency Afriscan II Satellite. It sits in a convenient geosynchronous orbit and has all the digital telemetry we require. The NATO military decommissioned it last year and it's now operated commercially. The arrangements are in place and the hire of air time will be untraceable, our own departmental technicians will then do all that is necessary to trigger the explosion.'

Hank looked over to Gibson.

'I've not had the opportunity to meet up with Admiral Sam Mcready yet but I gather that this team is prepared for immediate deployment of the plan on board the USS Phoenix.'

The Section Deputy nodded.

'Everything will be ready. We have a small conventional Daisy warhead which has been dismantled and is on immediate standby to replace *Thinman* when it's found'.

Hoskins looked around the table at the faces of the conspirators, all looking at him.

'How's the fundamentalist conference being organised, do we know the time scale yet?'

Frank Gibson dropped his holy pose and lent forward his eyes roaming around the faces at the table.

'Christ Hank, you worry too much, leave all that to us and the mercenaries operating in Algeria on our behalf over there The less you know the better you can protect ass if there are any comebacks. Just locate *Thinman* Hank and our guys will then see that the plan goes into action.'

After Hoskins left the room, the other men sat in an awkward silence broken finally by Charles Muller who said.

'Are you all thinking what I'm thinking? Can we really trust that fucking old son of a bitch? He seemed a bit worried by it all.'

The colonel smirked at them through his cigar smoke.

'Don't forget Charlie boy, we've got him by the goolies, his balls would be off and paraded in public if he said anything. He's coming up to his retirement at the end of this project. I guess he wouldn't want to lose that by wising up on us. He's in too deep now and he knows it, if his part in the old Nic episode was ever let out he would whistle a big goodbye to any pension and be stripped of his tags.'

'Does he actually know who our partner in the U.K. is on this?'

Gibson looked around the table at the expectant faces.

'It's a FAQ I'm not prepared to comment on. No one except the senator knows who our contact is over there.'

'So you don't think he suspects anything?'

'No way Charlie boy, that report he's just seen was a special issue just for him. As far as he is concerned, it's going to be a conventional warhead that is swapped for *Thinman*.'

They were right to worry about the Commander. The plan that had been lightly discussed those few weeks earlier when *Thinman* had suddenly been moved to the front burner, had grown from a simple drunken comment over beers one evening, rolled into an idea that had been developed, moulded, barbecued, and was now cast into a fully fledged conspiracy.

Substitute the *Thinman* material, let the terror group find it, take it back to their conference and then remotely blow them all sky high. Hank abhorred the morals of those who were fanatically ranged against his country, killing innocent people in the disguised name of religious fervour. As Americans, they were all still reeling from the disaster of Dar es Salaam and the epochal horrors of New York and the World Trade Centre. Did the conspirators have to stoop to the same low depths of unethical depravity?

Hank had seen war at close hand in the early nineties and the after effects during the Desert Storm episode in the Gulf. His war had been mainly spent on board one of the US Naval command ships sorting out the hundreds of Iraqi intelligence reports as they were intercepted by AWACS aircraft flying overhead.

His whole vision of the war, had been concentrated in one area when he had visited the fire control operations deck, where the scene was one of detailed electronic screens and radars on which targets were depicted in different coloured symbolism, console operators moving their icons about, shouting, alarms sounding and fire buttons being pressed on the orders of computers.

The nightly briefs flashed to the ship from Riyadh in the Saudi desert showing images of laser controlled weapons devastating the enemy installations with such apparent deadly accuracy and cheered by the crew.

It was only later that he saw the real effects of those buttons. The photographs, showing the charred bodies of mothers' sons, women's lovers and children's fathers.

Then there was the intangible long term legacy that governments preferred not to discuss, the effects on their own side as well as the enemy. The long term after effect of child deaths from cancers and pollution caused by the depleted uranium weapons used with such devastation. Micron sized particles of uranium lodged in the bodies innermost life support cavities, causing strange illnesses, miscarriages, appalling deformities in newly born babies. A wind borne poison that would roam parts of the planet for thousands of years to come when present national boundaries would no longer exist.

And for what end, the World was still the same old place and history would go on recording the futility of modern warfare when ranged against the impossible odds of the heterodox hatred amongst its diverse population.

The festering Iraqi war and ethnic cleansing of populations together with attrition in other parts of the globe indicated to Hank that history would go on repeating itself as long as mankind existed. The atrocities by the Nazis, the pre-war annihilation of the Chinese by the Japanese, the Tibetans by the Chinese, the African genocide, Stalinism and twenty seven million souls lost. And now the Islamic jehad. There would probably never be an end to it. Like pimples the problems would keep on erupting. Why did they even bother about things so far from their own doorstep?

Before his war in the Gulf, he had purposefully sought out for his own mental picture, information on the people they were going to war with.

Moslems like any other people on earth seemed to want to get on with the job of living, working and enjoying their families. As usual it was the demigod leaders and religious clerics who combined politics and religion as one, but Islam was more complicated than the Protestant humanistic beliefs that he had grown up with.

His brief study of Islam and The Five Pillars of the Qur'an, the Moslem Holy Book, had informed him that at least one fifth of the population of the Worlds surface, or over one billion were Moslems and worshipped Islam believing as Christians and Jews do in monotheism or one god, and in fact the same god, with the same prophets and old stories, something that Hank found puzzling. An approach to life that combined religion with politics and a tax system, a whole variety of sects, brotherhoods and organisations that had taken many different routes through the course of history. Not unlike the schisms in most other religions including his own, which had caused so much human misery and suffering since the Middle Ages.

Hank had reached the elevator and stood there thinking about the men in the room he had just left with such hatred in their hearts. Hatred against something he considered they did not fully understand and that could not be stopped. It was true that the militant fanatical groups had killed and maimed. The solution his colleagues were proposing was like a mere fly on the anus of an elephant. Kill a few and more would quickly and gladly take their place.

Back in room C2103, Muller was thumbing over the dossier that Hoskins had been shown.

'Hell Frank, who word processed this for Christ sake.'

Gibson broke his conversation with Erricsmann. 'I did, wouldn't have let one of the clerks prepare anything as secret as that. Why. You got a problem with it?'

'I'm not sure Frank, but there's a double line error in here, Para.24.3 has a line repeated twice, the first line specifies the conventional explosive's warhead handbook and then the same line is repeated again beneath it with a handbook number that is the nuclear W85 warhead for the Pershing MGM31 battlefield support system.'

Gibson grabbed the document and referred to the offending line that should have been removed during his re hash for Hoskins.

'Shit, that should have been wiped out along with the other items.' He read the referring paragraphs again and scanned the rest of the *Crusader* document.

'Well, he read through it pretty damned quickly, he'd have been sure to mention it if he'd seen it, you know how worried he is about the whole fucking concept. No, my guess is he probably missed it.'

Hank departed the elevator and went straight back to the library where he looked up the reference handbook he had noted in the document prepared by the group. What he then saw confirmed his fears and told him that something was terribly wrong. This was a complete change of scenario, but what was the object? He thought back over the conversation on his way over to his office in the Naval HQN building. They had said something about a Chinaman at Piltcher's house, was it a genuine error on Frank Gibson's part or was information bypassing him. Back in his office he took D.I. Evans card out of a pocket and slung his jacket over a chair. He entered the 44 prefix number for the U.K. then immediately cancelled, any international call from there would be recorded on a disc somewhere in the bowels of the building, picked up by surveillance satellite systems and analysed by half a dozen security organisations. He sat there thinking over the conversation again and what he had discovered in the library. Then he called the duty officer and ordered a car.

He drove across Washington, keeping an eye on his rear view mirror until he was satisfied that he was not followed. Then he looked for a pay 'phone booth and put the call through to England where DI Evans picked up his personal office phone, looking at the clock on the wall.

'Hi there Inspector, Hank Hoskins here .... that's right, calling you from the States, guess it's getting late there right now but I need your help......yes.

Do you have any information about a Chinaman being found at Piltcher's place yesterday?'

On the other end of the link, Robert Evans confirmed the mix up of identities between Piltcher and the man they now knew as He Luk.

'Who would know about that over there Robert? Has it been released to the media yet?

Evans frowned, Robert was it, Hoskins wanted a favour, he thought.

'Well, there's the hospital for one, our men who did the search, a few in Special Branch, Oh and Peter Senden. This man Luk had Senden's address on him and so we interviewed Senden this morning. Says he's never heard of Luk. Some strange goings on though we found the evidence linking Senden's story about the man thrown off the luxury yacht. I have to say I still have my suspicions about Senden's story. In answer to your second question, the press have not as yet been informed.'

'Why the suspicion with Senden, Robert?'

'Well it was Senden who led us to the evidence, bullet damage on a spray screen said to come from the yacht; I can't really comment though until I have the forensic report that I expect tomorrow.'

'Thanks for the update Robert, have a nice.......I mean sleep well.'

He phoned the office in Grosvenor Street, but there was only the night duty man there. Then he phoned George Hansdorf.

'George, Hank Hoskins, here where are you? ....Have you heard anything about the police mix up over the man you found at Piltcher's address in Cornwall yesterday, or was it the day before, guess we're on different time zones.'

Hank put the 'phone down following George's negative reply. So there had been a hurried cover up in room 2103, how had Gibson known? Only from someone in England who had direct access to Gibson. So, who was feeding him information? There was nothing he could do here now except to return to England as soon as possible.

He caught a late flight out of Dulles to London and settled down to think. It looked like the *Crusader* plans had probably changed to something so horrendous that he found it difficult to contemplate the outcome. If they were planning to nuke the Islamic fundamentalists there would be all hell let loose. Accident or not the World would point the finger at the U.S.A. as the culprit. He couldn't understand the minds of the conspirators but they had him over a barrel, or so they thought. When the crazy scheme had first been suggested he had thought it a joke. Then Gibson had come to him with the original proposal, as the senior representative of the U.K. end of the operation he needed Hanks co-operation. When Hank had declined and told him where to go, the nastiness had started, his past had been gently raked over, threats made. The suggestion of exposure of his part in the Nicaragua affair in the early eighties would lose him his commission, job and pension due in four years time.

The Chinese spy ring at Los Alamos should have been detected before they were able to transmit the W-88 warhead design to Beijing. Other heads had rolled in Hanks department when Congress had discovered that an attempt had been made to cover up the security breach. He had escaped the witch hunt but Gibson had made oblique references to Hank's part in the abortive investigation and attempted cover up that had resulted.

Gibson was not aware of the special role Hoskins's team were involved in or the ongoing search for the truth over the Chinese espionage spy scandal.

Hank had decided to monitor the situation and take what action was required if and when it happened. But who could he trust, who was the mole on the British side? It couldn't be the hospital or the police. They had no direct contact with Washington, knew nothing about the structure of the American organisation or who to contact. That meant it had to be someone in the British Secret Service

Senden? No, he was too far down the chain, not really connected, too specialised in his own field of technology to be implemented.

Major Fellows? Too old; too established in the hierarchy of the organisation to be involved in such a dangerous liaison.

There were others he had met but, like Senden, they were small fry. No, this had to be someone higher up the tree, someone with connections into the Middle East.

Sir Anthony Holmes was Jewish; his parents had been murdered on that night that had meant so much to Zionists when the State of Israel had been born.

Unlikely he thought, in any case the scientist was missing, presumably kidnapped by the terrorist group for his knowledge that could help them. Or was he kidnapped? Could he be the one the terrorists needed help from to decipher the safety interlocks on *Thinman*? Was he their sleeper?

He had met many of the MI5 and MI6 senior people over the years both privately and professionally, his meeting with Sir George Longland, Maj. Fellow's chief, had been brief when the *Thinman* liaison between CIA and MI5 had been agreed at ministerial level. If he was involved, then the whole British Secret Service could be riddled with maggots.

The Select Committee through which his own direction emanated could also be corrupt.

He turned the problems over and over in his mind. There were the others who had broken into the Cornish cottage after the terrorists had been there. Major Fellows had denied that it was SO13 anti terrorist group operatives If he was being told the truth, who was it? How were Mossad involved? Perhaps there were just too many different organisations falling over themselves in the quest to gain over their colleagues in other departments.

Hank awoke as the aircraft started its descent to Heathrow and the other passengers started to stir in anticipation of grabbing their hand baggage and entering the usual airport queues before the stampede to the luggage carousels. He felt tired, not from his flight or the time difference, just tired, irritable and disillusioned with the whole set of affairs that now confronted him.

The leak of nuclear weapon secrets in recent years had been considered to be disastrous by the Department of Energy who bore the ultimate authority for the US nuclear weapons production. The espionage associated with the W88 nuclear range of weapons, ten times more powerful than the *Little Boy* atomic bomb dropped on Hiroshima, had been further compounded by other leaks on missile technology and the advanced submarine radar tracking system. A system developed at the Lawrence Livermore Laboratory, and theoretically capable of detecting the covert deep sea movements of nuclear submarines. Enough to undermine the West's deterrent including the British Trident fleet and possibly promote China to the status of a super power, dominating the Pacific basin and ultimately causing confrontation over Japan, Korea and Taiwan.

Hank's team was only assigned to track down the W88 computer leaks that had occurred from the Los Alamos National Laboratory in New Mexico. Nearly six years of foot slogging hard work had still not identified who had the secrets or even if the Chinese had the technical capability to develop systems based on the thousands of missing files. It had been widely reported that they were close to deploying a mobile intercontinental nuclear missile based on the American designs, the Dong Feng-35 but no hard evidence had yet emerged that this was the case. The committee he reported to were becoming increasingly impatient at the lack of hard information, unable to properly assess the future defence strategies needed to face the impending emergence of China as a super nuclear power or N.Korea and Iran as a nuclear wildcards. All they could do was to promoting their missile space shield.

Now he had been thrown like a ball at a coconut shy into the *Thinman* assignment, just because he happened at the time to be in England, a seemingly simple search that again was producing nothing. Hank Hoskins grabbed his overnight bag and stood in the gangway queue waiting to disembark. With the *Crusader* plot now hanging over him he felt disillusioned, helpless as flotsam borne along a strong tide as he struggled with his lonely conscience, considering the after effects of what would be the worst nuclear disaster on record.

Chapter 16 . Gas on board Seamaiden.

That Sunday afternoon at about the time when Hoskins was on his way to Langley, Peter Senden was having a late lunch and considering the purpose of his visit to St.Mawes that was fading fast. He had hoped to have a few days sailing on Seamaiden in the company of his friend and to discuss his father's affairs before finalising the details of his next overseas appointment. He'd also hoped to trace the diving boat that Capt. Rogerson had told him about but his visit to the Charter office had resulted in nothing. The mystery surrounding Philip's death was still no nearer to being solved. Now there were new considerations to think about, the treasure ship story that Captain Rogerson had related, was it the Acacia Lady that Porter had told him about? Perhaps the *Dragon's Morsel* was a name for the treasure his father had been searching for. Who were the attackers on Friday evening in Weymouth? He rubbed his arms that were still bruised from the baseball bat his assailant had used.

John Barrett was still in hospital and Peter 'phoned when he returned to the hotel from Higgs boatyard, to check his progress. The ward sister who answered sounded hopeful that he would be allowed out the following day assuming the doctors approved on the evening round, he had already had a visit from the police that morning and made a statement.

Peter decided to go out and check Seamaiden, run up the auxiliary engine and charge the batteries. At the same time he would re -fit the G.P.S. navigator and check the cables and aerial installation mounted on the pushpit.

As he climbed on board from the yacht club water taxi, he noticed straight away that the padlock clasp that secured the washboards was broken. His pulse increased as he went below and saw the mess. Nothing appeared to have been taken. His valuable binoculars, wet gear and various navigation aids had not been touched. The expensive new 406 MHz. EPIRB, (emergency position indicating radio beacon), purchased in Weymouth was there, surely an obvious target for boat thieves.

He picked the pilot books and charts up from the floor where they had been strewn in what appeared to have been a frenzied search and sank down on the saloon settee berth. The base cushions had been removed and slashed open, the contents of the compartments under them turned out, crockery smashed and cabin sole covers to the bilge removed. Looking forward to the foc'sle cabin he could see that sails had been pulled out of their lockers and left in a mangled heap. In places, the head linings had been ripped down and now displayed the bare inner carcass of the fibreglass moulding. Even the small drinks cupboard and galley cupboards had been left open so that the doors swung and clattered in slow unison with the water movement around Seamaiden, like the sound of falling dominoes, as she rolled gently to her mooring chain.

Peter sat for a while, head in hands as he surveyed the damage. His love affair with Seamaiden had grown from the moment he first saw the curvature of her lines and felt the security of her embrace as he went below. He knew her moods, indulged her demands for cash, and knew her fickleness. They shared the exhilaration of sailing through the tiller and the balance of her rudder. Her rigging sang to him when she was happy and she never complained when he couldn't visit her, lying there in her lonely waterbed. Whenever he was aboard, she was there, uncomplaining, always ready to do his will.

It was as though she had been raped and was now unable to tell him what had happened and or who had invaded the privacy of her sanctity. The anger suddenly welled up in him, as he sat there, wondering what the hell they had been looking for.

He pulled a cheroot out of the packet he had purchased the night before and fished in a pocket for his lighter. Something he sensed stopped him, was she telling him something, her movement was suddenly different, a wash from a passing boat caused the saloon door to bang as it swung to and fro. Bending down to the floor he caught the faint smell of propane gas that, being heavier than air, can collect in the bilges with disastrous results.

It was part of his ritual on leaving her to turn off the gas supply at the cylinder in the cockpit locker and he was sure that he had done that the day before. He stood and went gingerly over to the galley and saw that the oven tap on the cooker had been turned on and heard the quiet hiss of escaping gas. Christ, he was sweating now as he considered the explosion that would have racked them both with flames had he lit up.

With the tap and gas bottle switched off, he sat in the cockpit and operated the hand bilge pump that he hoped would disperse the gas safely overboard, after which he opened all the deck hatches in order to allow air to circulate.

His attention had been fully on these tasks, when he was hailed by the passing police boat that had slowed down for Inspector Robert Evans to come aboard. The sensitive nose of the onboard gas detector that he'd reconnected after finding the wires cut, had at last indicated that the gas had been dispersed and Peter waved him over.

The helmsman brought the police boat skilfully alongside the yacht that enabled the Detective to step quickly over the gunwale. He was smiling now and advancing in a friendly manner towards Peter who said nothing but pointed him below.

Within minutes the D.I. was on his mobile phone and arranging for another forensic team to come out to the yacht. He looked quizzically at Peter whilst they waited, chewing gum rather than chancing a smoke. He hesitated before breaking his professional etiquette, but he thought first name terms might soften the conversation considering the shock that the forlorn man sitting with him had just had.

'Trouble seems to be following you around Peter,' he said as he again surveyed the yacht interior. 'Do you know what they were looking for?'

Peter knew his reply was doubted as he shrugged and answered with negation. Evans looked out across the river.

'I hope you really have told me everything, seems that from an unassociated incident yesterday you have now become a victim. If your boat had been blown out of the water with you on it, we would probably have been reporting it as an unfortunate yachting accident.'

Peter chilled at the thought as the detective continued.

'As it is, we'll now have to treat this incident as another possible attempted murder connected with what you witnessed yesterday.' Evans turned and looked at him now with concerned eyes. 'It may not yet have occurred to you Peter, that whoever did this is obviously seeking something in common with yourself and Captain Piltcher. We're reasonably sure now that nothing of value was taken during the break in at Trevello, God knows where Piltcher is. We have an A.P.B. out on him at the moment and the Chinaman is not responding to questions.'

The mobile rang and Evans bent his head away to answer. The conversation was brief but Peter gathered from the snatches he heard that the correspondent was talking about Sir Anthony Holmes.

He cupped his hand over the instrument.

'I would like to arrange for a contingent from the Dorset police to visit your home if that's OK with you. We need to check and make sure there has been no forced entry there.'

Peter nodded his agreement and the tired Evans went back to his contact and made the arrangements with Peter reminding him of his address at Upwey. The phone call over, he told Peter that Katherine Holmes had returned to her father's home to await any further news of his disappearance.

He continued by telling him that when they questioned the owner of the cruiser, the Starlight Princess, he was only able to give the police a description of the charter party representative. It seemed he paid cash and didn't even go back to claim the damage deposit. Apparently the boats that were chartered were always skippered by their own people. On the occasions that the party had chartered, they had their own D.T.I. registered skipper who had all the correct qualifications. The cruiser and other craft had been chartered several times by the group over the last six months, always foreign businessmen keen on diving. All transactions were in cash and no records kept.

They had been seen in various locations west of Alderney, always paid cash and the latest charter had been for a week. Police enquiries along the South Coast marinas had indicated various sightings from Weymouth to Alderney. Even so, they had failed to register any of their destinations with the coast guard and on the latest trip, only the departure and arrival times from Weymouth to St.Mawes were known.

Peter sat there, feigning only a remote interest in what the Detective Inspector was saying. The Starlight Princess had to be the boat that Capt. Rogerson had seen in Weymouth. It all fitted, a diving party of foreigners, Weymouth, Alderney, a boat that fitted Rogerson's description.

Evans chuckled suddenly which broke the sobriety of the two of them sitting in the cockpit as they waited for the others to arrive.

'I'll bet that the owner's agents couldn't get back to their office quickly enough to amend the books and show the correct VAT on those cash transactions. I shouldn't think they get too many cash deals in that sort of business.'

His comment was meant to be jocular but Peter Senden wasn't in the mood.

Then he suddenly asked. 'Why didn't you report the attack on you in Weymouth?'

Peter was uncomfortable with his reply. 'How do you know I was involved?'

'I don't officially. The Dorset police are handling it as a motoring incident. However, I do know you were there and your statement as a witness could be very useful in their enquiries. I'm reluctant to push it because of the CIA involvement, but I need to know what it was all about.'

'I wish I knew. All I can tell you is that the motorcycle pulled up, this chap jumped off and laid into me with the baseball bat. Someone, whom I now believe was attached to the CIA, ran up and intervened. The next moment, I was bundled into a car and later told to piss off which I did. I knew nothing about the full impact of the accident that occurred afterwards until I read the newspaper reports the following day in Plymouth.'

'Surely you must know if someone has a grudge against you, or perhaps you've upset someone.' Peter considered the detective's understatement as they watched the police launch returning up the river. On board were two forensic personnel, their box of equipment and supply of sterile plastic bags held ready to transfer onto the yacht.

'Inspector, I've been abroad for nine months, returned a couple of weeks ago and ever since I seem to have been surrounded by misfortune. In answer to your question, I can't think of anyone over here who would wish to harm me.'

The detective eyed him for a moment. 'Your statement yesterday said that you were a self employed engineer. What exactly do you do? What sort of overseas clients do you have?'

Peter stepped forward to assist the first of the forensics aboard.

'Sorry Inspector, all my clients are dealt with on a confidential basis. You have my statement from yesterday to that effect.'

The inspector thought back to the recording and what Hoskins had said about Senden's top secret vetting by the MOD, he suspected this man was either working in association with the CIA or possibly MI6. If so, what were they all up to? He hadn't told Peter that when he went aboard the Starlight Princess, the Special Branch were already there, an overlap of enquiries that would have to be sorted out higher up.

'I'm afraid we will have to impound your boat for a while whilst we do our forensic checks. We'll be as quick as possible and I hope you will not be too inconvenienced.' Evans obtained Peters agreement.

'Doesn't look as if I shall be going any where now anyway.'

Senden and the inspector returned to the harbour quay to see Ian Porter heading the crowd of inquisitive holiday makers who had gathered there. He fell into step with them as they walked to the waiting police car, his questions brushed aside until they were free of the crowd.

At the car, Inspector Evans turned to him.

'Essentially we have found the motor yacht that we suspect a drug gang has been using. However, we cannot make any official statement until the Customs and Excise department have carried out their own examination. Dr.Senden's yacht appears to have been sabotaged. We believe by the same people, however, at this stage of our investigation I can say nothing more.'

Peter 'phoned the hospital on his return to the hotel to be told that John Barrett would be discharged in the morning. He hadn't done anything about collecting his car and ordered a taxi to take him out to the spot along the coastal path where it had been left. He hoped John's diving gear would still be in the boot.

Chapter 17. Surveillance.

When Peter Senden arrived at the hospital, his friend was waiting in reception wearing a large yacht cap to hide the bald area on his scalp where the skin had been stapled together to repair the gash that he'd received.

They walked back to the Jaguar and drove in silence for a while and Peter decided to take the quiet route back to St.Mawes via. the King Harry chain ferry. This part of Cornwall has many creeks and rivers that infuse their waters into the River Fal and Carrick Roads and the chain ferry was a crossing point on the Fal River that would take them over to the St. Just peninsular where St.Mawes is situated.

As usual there was a small queue of cars waiting on the steep narrow approach road and they left the car to lean over the parapet and look out over the river. On the downstream side, dense woodland came down to the shoreline on each side of the waterway where the green foliage ended in symmetrical straight horizontal lines on both sides of the river. As though the forest's hem had been coutured by some giant dressmaker's scissors. Up river from the ferry, the deep water provided a mooring for numerous redundant large ships, which looked totally out of place in the woodland setting. It was interesting to see the old dredgers and freighters here, their paint work blistering and rusting and pulling on their anchor chains, as accountants and maritime insurers in far away city centres decided each ships future. Estimating the scrap value to the companies that had been so faithfully served by these ships, many now redundant and facing a tow to an ignoble death at the breaker's yard.

'They wouldn't allow me to go into the intensive care ward to see Piltcher.'

John Barrett had been half listening to Peters small talk about the river and apologised as he realised he had cut across his discourse. Peter was quiet again. He hadn't yet told John about the police interviews, the mix up over Gilbert Piltcher or the damage aboard his yacht.

'It wasn't Captain Piltcher that they found in the house. It was some Chinaman from Hong Kong by the name of He Luk.'

John's head jerked back with surprise. 'You mean he was one of the burglars? I thought they found him beaten up and unconscious, no, wait a minute, I heard only one person run down the stairs and out of the house. Whoever it was had a motorcycle waiting outside in a side turning. The two Americans, who stopped their car and helped, must have confirmed that point.'

Peter thought about the incident a couple of nights previously and the Americans who had bundled him away from the accident in Weymouth. He decided to say nothing of the affair to John even though he still had some questions about that incident.

'The two Americans haven't been interviewed as far as I know. I thought they drove off before the ambulance arrived.'

'Do you know Peter, it's coming back to me now, those two fellows did seem in an awful hurry, but thinking back on it, it was they who said it was Captain Piltcher. How on earth could they have known his name? They had just come in off the street as bystanders. Another funny thing, I believe they used my name as I was coming round. The lady neighbour certainly seemed to know who we were. She said she was a first aider and kept calling him by name, you know, something like, can you hear me Captain Piltcher, I'm a first aider. I assumed that as a close neighbour she must have known who he was. Anyway the Chinese guy, must have been a visitor of Piltcher's don't you think.'

The ferry was returning across the river and they went back to the car and sat there waiting to drive on.

'A lot seems to have happened over the last couple of days John. Some of it you haven't heard yet. Let's get back to the hotel and have some dinner.'

Peter Senden wanted to think. His mind was turning over all the events of the last few days, like a corkscrew roller coaster at one of those theme parks. Stopping occasionally and then off again with a great rush of jumbled information. He still had to ring the insurers about the damage to Seamaiden and wondered how long she would have to be out of commission, the paperwork involved and what he would tell Jessica when she phoned. The search, the missing men, a shooting, the newspaper man, the police interviews. It all seemed like a strange nightmare and as they drove onto the ferry he glanced in the side rear view mirror to see an Audi A4 about three cars behind them driven by one of the young police constables who had been at the hotel the previous day. Christ, what was all this about? Once off the ferry, he drove the rest of the way in silence, keeping an eye open for the Audi somewhere behind but when they reached the first and only stretch of straight road there were several cars behind them and the Audi was not there.

Cars driving on to the ferry formed four rows and did not necessarily get directed off the other side in the same order that they had driven on. The Audi had obviously been delayed. Peter took the next left hand turn and drove along until they were out of sight of the main road and stopped.

John had been relaxing with his eyes closed, wondering how the girl he had only met yesterday was getting on with her terrible worry over her missing father. His first enquiry of Peter at the hospital had been for news on her. He opened his eyes as they came to a stop and looked up.

'What's the problem?'

'I think we were being followed by an unmarked police car, not that there are many places to go to around here. God knows what they think we're up to.'

The constable's voice came over the radio room operator's headset as he reported in.

'Lost them I'm afraid sir. They came over on the King Harry ferry and by the time I was waived off by the ferry people, they were well ahead and must have turned off the road somewhere.'

The message was immediately telephoned to Robert Evans who at that time was in the Falmouth dock yard to where Seamaiden had been towed. He was watching as the Customs and Excise dog handler encouraged her retriever to sniff out every locker, sail bag and item of clothing on the yacht. The cabin sole floor boards had been carefully removed to expose the bilge areas and the various pipes leading to the heads and engine had been checked for any obstruction. Optical fibre endoscopes were being used to probe fuel and water tanks and the numerous inaccessible places that every yacht has, had been searched in the same way using miniature CCTV cameras.

'Nothing sir.' She called up to the Inspector as he finished his call and replaced the mobile phone in his pocket. 'If there was anything here Judy would have found it.' The dog nuzzled her for commendation, its tail beating back and forth and she bent down and jostled the intelligent head.

Evans continued to look at the yacht from his vantage point on the dock side. Surely there had to be something there. He had worked a long day and with only a couple of hours rest in the office. Evening was now approaching and the forensics had taken their various samples and left. He was disappointed that the search for drugs had proved negative.

'Do you think anything could have been thrown overboard?' He knew it was a damned stupid question, but she answered, with her candid opinion, her rank in H.M.Customs being lower than the police detective inspector.

'Had there been any trace of an illegal substance on board Judy here would have nosed it out sir.'

The dog jumped ashore followed by the handler and Evans was left standing there, hands in pockets, weary, disconsolate and uncertain now as to his line of enquiry. Up until that time his mind had been working over the various facts and he had convinced himself that the drug running theory was the one to pursue

He had assessed that Peter Senden was probably on the level but couldn't be sure that he was not part of some covert operation. If that really was the case, why bring in the police service, surely the undercover services would have cleared up their own mess if that was the case. The check on Senden's home near Weymouth had not indicated any break in there and he hoped his sergeant had relayed the information. The man overboard story had not yet been substantiated. The lifeboat search had continued throughout the day with negative results. Was there really a body in the sea or was it just some sort of subterfuge to direct the authorities away from another drug related event?

The damage to both the vessels was real enough. It was indisputable that the spray screen from the cruiser had been shot at. The broken aerial mount on Seamaiden certainly appeared to have been hit in a similar way. The two break-ins with no obvious motive of theft, missing persons, a Chinaman. Was it just an argument between drug gangs? Was that what the C.I.A. involvement was all about?

The report from Weymouth appeared to be unconnected. Just a tragic road accident caused by a motorcycle, but the CIA seemed to know more about it than he did. He had conveyed the information gleaned from the interview room disc recording to his counterparts in the Dorset Police who would now widen their enquiries. Other enquiries by his staff had established that Captain Piltcher, although cleared at the time, had certainly been on the fringe of a smuggling organisation some years previously. Where was he now? Why couldn't they find him? The enormous amount of money outlined by Commander Hoskins had also pointed to something of high value like drug trafficking, smuggling or maybe money laundering. Then there was the hospital's report on the Chinaman's blood samples that he had received during the afternoon with traces of illegal substances.

His Detective Sergeant came up to him.

'No luck I hear. I gather from forensics that most of the fingerprint and hair fragments will probably turn out to belong to Senden. The motor yacht, Starlight Princess, had been cleaned up but they found traces of blood and a palm print that they have matched with some finger prints found here. They're being scanned through central records at the moment for a match. I gather no other naughties found here.'

'Matching prints on both vessels? That may be significant. It will be interesting to see if Senden's prints are also found on the Starlight Princess.

Arrange to have this lot tidied up please Jim and make sure the boat is left secure. Customs and Excise will be having another look at it all in the morning. As for me, I'm whacked and am going home, but please call me if anything comes up on the sea search or on Sir.Anthony' As he walked away, he called back over his shoulder, 'Did you call Peter Senden and confirm that the Dorset police found his home intact?'

The sergeant affirmed that Peter had been telephoned earlier.

'You can call off the tail we put on Senden. I don't think he will be going anywhere tonight.'

The other tail was still there. The blue Mercedes had overtaken Peter and pulled up a little further around the next bend. Horace O'Brien called the communications vehicle. 'Jack, this surveillance is leading nowhere, were going to call off for the evening.'

Chapter 18. The scrap book.

The two men were finishing their evening meal in the Black Rocks dining room, which was now gradually emptying of other guests as they wandered off to the small bars that abounded along the sea front and in the little town of St.Mawes.

Peter had told John in confidence about the yacht incident and the mix up of identities over Captain Piltcher. He also outlined his conversation with Porter, the reference to Sir Anthony Holmes, Philips old associates mentioned in the Will and what had been said about the Acacia Lady.

They had dined on roast duck, served slightly pink on a bed of chestnuts, parsnips and bacon in a rich sauce, having started with locally caught spider crab accompanied by an avocado salad and Dijon mayonnaise. They waived away the puddings and concentrated on cheese and the remains of a very good bottle of Burgundy.

'Feeling better for that?' Peter put the question as he finished the wine. 'I presume you brought Philip's papers down here with you.?'

John nodded. The last couple of hours were more akin to what his body and in particular, his stomach enjoyed. Now he had to go back to work and he drained the last drop of the grape from his glass.

'They're in the hotel safe, I'll collect them and we can go through them in my room. I suppose you realise that strictly speaking they form part of Philips estate that is still subject to probate.' John had already looked through the file briefly but considered that Peter probably already knew their content. In any case, there was something puzzling him that he knew only Peter would be able, he hoped, to supply the answer.

'Peter, you don't have any brothers or sisters do you?'

Peter smiled, the question seemed out of context with what they had been discussing.

'No, you'd have met them by now, anyway why do you ask?'

'Oh, nothing really, it's just that there is a reference in Philip's will to someone called David, a cousin perhaps?'

Peter looked puzzled. 'Not as far as I am aware. Is he also connected to the retirement fund and the other people we've mentioned?'

John decided not to press the point at that stage and just said,

'The retirement fund, whatever it is, is a mystery. I'll have to talk to Piltcher if we ever catch up with him. See if he can throw any light on the matter.

Back in John's room, they spread out the various contents of the old folder, consisting of the newspaper cuttings and letters, over the bed and attempted to put them into some sort of chronological order. It was difficult as some of the letters bore no dates.

The old newspaper cuttings covered reports of the Board of Trade enquiry in 1953 which Ian Porter had already mentioned to Peter and which he now read in detail.

In the spring of that year, the London registered Acacia Lady owned by a shipping firm in Hong Kong had been on voyage from Alexandria in Egypt to the New Surrey Docks in London. She sailed in convoy with two other small freighters and a corvette and carried a small crew of Chinese seamen together with her captain, Gilbert Piltcher, Simon Carter a director of the shipping company and Philip Senden who was the Naval Officer responsible for part of the cargo that comprised undetailed British Army military equipment. She was lightly laden and the rest of her manifest consisted of a cargo of salvaged machine tools and cotton merchandise. The only passengers on board were a group of scientists doing some sort of environmental measurements during the voyage, although in the paper they were called climatic measurements.

Whilst crossing the Bay of Biscay, the vessel had taken on water and started to list badly. The sea pumps were employed but failed to hold and it was suspected that her plates had been damaged or that the cargo had shifted. They made for St.Nazaire where they expected to effect repairs, but the French authorities at the port refused entry when they were told that military equipment of an unspecified nature was on board. Inspection had shown that the main bulkhead between the number one and two holds, where she had been damaged years before, had weakened and temporary repairs were made with bulks of timber and auxiliary pumps taken out to the ship by a French tug.

They limped on as far as Ushant where the Army equipment was transferred to one of the other ships, along with Philip Senden and the scientists. The Acacia Lady took on ballast to adjust her trim and continued on her way.

As she sailed on towards the Casquets, she ran into a typical Atlantic low pressure system. The storm produced enormous seas to such an extent that the bulkhead again started to buckle and she started to take in water. She was soon down by the bows, and this time, even with the extra pumps, she was wallowing as her thrashing propeller constantly rose from the sea. Captain Piltcher ordered the crew to the lifeboats and radioed a Mayday call to Portishead who arranged for them to be picked off by a nearby trawler and transferred to one of the other freighters.

According to the translated testimony of the surviving crew members at the inquest, the Captain and Carter refused to be taken off when the trawler arrived and stayed on board with a skeleton crew as the ship drifted northwards on the tide.

They had been arguing and shouting at each other, but the mainly Chinese crew could only glean parts of the conversation that had inferred that in addition to the main cargo, there was something else on board that the two men were eager to save. The voyage had started in Hong Kong and had been uneventful until they reached Gibraltar. The crew stated that from Gibraltar there had been many arguments between the three senior men, Piltcher, Senden and Carter.

The next day the ship was still afloat. A Dutch salvage ship arrived out from Cherbourg and was standing off to take a line. Simon Carter had transferred to the salvage vessel to negotiate terms within the provisions of a Lloyd's Salvage Contract and discuss the matter with the insurers.

As evening approached, a new low pressure system hit them and the salvage vessel kept a radar watch on the stricken Acacia Lady as she drifted over the Hurd Deep west of Guernsey until she disappeared off the screen. The salvage ship had then returned to Cherbourg for the night. The next day there was no sign of the Acacia Lady, she had vanished with the crew and her captain.

Three days later, an exhausted Captain Piltcher was rescued from the small island of Burhou to the north west of Alderney by a fishing boat that spotted a flare he had sent up. Five Chinese crewmen had been washed overboard in the storm and the ship had sunk.

At the inquest into the deaths of the men and the loss of the old ship, Carter's testimony gave an account of how the ship had been requisitioned by the British Government to carry military supplies from Hong Kong to Egypt.

Philip Senden had been called to give his account of the voyage.

There was much cross examining about the arguments between Piltcher and Carter but they were put down to the heat of the moment and the attempts to save the ship.

Piltcher had abandoned the ship before she went down near the Hurd Deep and had sailed the lifeboat tender for many hours before sighting the small island of Burhou where he beached the tender and sheltered in a small hut until his rescue. The tender had been snatched away by the strong tidal currents.

The Falcon Star Insurance Co. was unhappy. The liability for the ship and its cargo had been with the Government up to the time of disembarking the military supplies to another ship and had been transferred back to them by agreement over the radio. The next day, the ship had sunk, leaving them with a loss that they could not recover.

Most of the correspondence from Piltcher was written in a scrawl that was difficult to read in places and addressed to Dear Philip, whereas the Carter letters were mainly typed on flimsy airmail paper, indicating that they were probably received from abroad and addressed Dear Senden. All the letters were short and in places cryptic. As Peter read out the letters and interpreted the writing, John used his computer note pad to make readable transcripts.

After about an hour, John looked up.

'These are not normal letters you would expect to see from a group of friends. It would seem as though we have several separate subjects here. I would guess from the earlier letters that your father was receiving covert threats from Carter about some concealment. Then from about the early seventies, regular amounts of money from him, which are described in various ways as advance donations coming from the retirement fund.

Look here. He says, 'I cannot emphasise enough that the Dragon should not be touched. Leave it where it is for all our sakes." In another reference he says, 'You are all milking me over and above the value of our agreement. You know the Dragon has not yet been found. I suspect Piltcher has tucked it away somewhere for his own benefit.' So, you were right, the *Dragon's Morsel* is not the name of a ship as you originally suspected but something else, the treasure Philip was seeking perhaps.

The Acacia Lady must be the wreck he was looking for or maybe *Dragon's Morsel* is some sort of code word for the ship.'

There are also references to phone calls. Here Piltcher says;

'Carter has rung me again about our retirement fund. He wants to end it. He wants you to find it and bring it up."

In this later letter he says, "Only I know where the retirement fund is hidden."

The last letter from Carter in 1985 seems to finalise payments, he says, he has stopped the funding, says he's too old and no longer cares about the Dragon. Sounds to me as if some sort of blackmailing was going on between them all. It must have been something pretty big to have gone on for over thirty years.'

Peter's ears pricked up on the Dragon references, he couldn't tell John about the reported last words his father had uttered with respect to the mysterious metaphor, but was Dragon merely a shortening of *Dragon's Morsel*?

'This is a strange one,' Peter had turned over what they had considered to be the last letter in the series from Piltcher that just ended with the words, phone me when you know something.

'On the back there's a telephone number scribbled in pencil followed by a list of elements. He must have taken them down from a 'phone conversation. Indium, lithium, nitrogen, etc., there are eight in all.' He handed it to John who gave the list a cursory scan before dropping it back on the pile.

Their conversation was interrupted by the telephone ringing. John picked up the handset and mouthed to Peter that it was Katherine Holmes enquiring how John was feeling. There was still no news about her father and the police frogmen had started searching along the river bank where he had his morning jog. She sounded depressed and thanked John for his concern, agreeing with him to meet up some time in the future for lunch.

John, still on the 'phone, picked up the letter Peter had given him. 'Katherine, you're a scientist, before you go, would you know what the following elements have in common?'

He read out the list to Katherine who sounded surprised at the request as she listened and then told him that there were numerous cross links but nothing she knew of that could combine them all. Beryllium was poisonous; Nitrogen was an inert gas, another one was an isotope and so on. She then asked the reason for his interest and John explained that they were written down on the back of a letter and he was just trying to see if they had any significance. She laughed for the first time at the inconsequent reason for his enquiry.

'When I was at school we used to write letters in a simple code based on the chemical periodic table, you know, the atomic numbers. Hydrogen was H or the number one, Oxygen I believe was eight, and so on. If you'd like to hang on, I'll get one of my chemical books and look them up for you.' She was soon back and John read her the list.

'O.K. the first element is Indium followed by, Technetium, Lithium, Nitrogen, Helium, Argon, Beryllium and Tungsten.' He beckoned to Peter for his pencil as she checked her book on the other end of the line.

'The symbols do not seem to spell out anything intelligible,' she paused as she looked through her list and then tried to sound out the result. ' What you have given me produces the letter combinations, In, te, li, n, he, ar, b, and w or, by numbers, 49, 43, 03, 07, 02, 18, 05 and 74. Does that mean anything to you?' John looked at the incomprehensible list and had to agree with her that they made no sense at all. He passed the scribbled information to Peter who looked at them and shook his head.

'If you dial Germany from here, I believe the suffix is 049, I'll give it a try.'

John stayed on the phone chatting for some time and Peter decided to give him some privacy and adjourned downstairs to the public call box and then to the bar.

The call went through before he had used up all the numbers and a female voice answered.

'Gut Abend. Kan ich Ihnen behilflich sein?'

'Ya, Guten Abend. Ich Heisen Peter Senden, Ich telefon von U.K. Kennen Sie Die namen, Piltcher, Senden oder Carter bitte.'

The startled German lady on the other end of the line turned out to be the proprietoress of a massage parlour and answered Peter in English saying that she gave complete confidentiality to all her clients and couldn't help him.

He replaced the receiver with a half smirk on his face, a massage parlour for elderly gentlemen he wondered as he strolled through to the bar, ordered a pint and sat there thinking over what had been said upstairs.

In his younger years, his father had been away from home for long periods and it was only in adult life that they had got to know each other. Peter had previously never heard about the Acacia Lady and his father's involvement with her, in fact he knew very little about Philips early years in the Navy, they had never been discussed at home and he had never thought to ask. How he now wished that he had given the old man more of his time. Now he was gone and the chance would never occur again.

He sat at the bar with his beer and a cheroot as he looked at the peculiar list of letters and numbers that John had written down and suddenly had an idea.

John had finished his phone call and started to tidy up the papers on the bed when Peter knocked and entered the room.

'I think I've got it.' Peter was grinning from ear to ear as he thrust the Admiralty chart down on the bed and pointed to a position he had marked with a large cross.

'Luckily I usually carry a large detail chart of the Western Approaches in my holdall in case of emergencies and look what I've found.'

John just looked at the cross on the Admiralty chart and wondered how much his friend had drunk in that short time. He was a non smoker and could certainly smell the odour of cigars and beer.

'If we assume that Nitrogen indicates north and that the symbol for Tungsten, which is W, indicates west, then we have a position of 0494303 north and 021805 west. That could be the spot that Philip was diving on before his heart attack. Look, west of Alderney.'

He stood back as John examined the chart.

'If you're certain, then it looks as though you've cracked it, but having done so, I don't see how it helps us at all. I'm sure Piltcher isn't sitting out there.' The slight sarcasm was ignored by Peter as John again realised that Peter knew more about the details of Philips death than he was saying.

'I would say it's very significant, here look at the chart. From Piltcher's account at the enquiry, the Acacia Lady went down over here in Hurd Deep with something on board that Piltcher and Carter wanted. So why was my father diving nearly ten miles away in the Ortac Channel?

Dragon's Morsel must be the code name for the Acacia Lady, also, one of those letters from Piltcher states that only he knows the wreck's true position. Don't you see? The Acacia lady was sunk in the Ortac Channel and not in Hurd Deep as stated at the enquiry. Hurd Deep is up to one hundred metres in depth and would have been very difficult to dive on in those days. The depth around Ortac is only twenty to forty metres. I believe that Philip was trying to retrieve whatever it was that the arguments were about.'

Peter gave a flourishing bow, convinced of his explanation.

'I rest my case M'Lud.'

John remained impassive as he considered the tentative links to the past together with the various options and translation into reality of their evening's work. His head now felt better and the trained legal mind went logically through what they were now considering as a solution to what the letters implied, but why? The question kept rebounding back. What reason would Captain Piltcher have had to lie to the Board of enquiry about the vessels resting place? Peter was probably correct in his assumption that the Acacia Lady would at that time have been difficult to locate by the insurers had they wished to examine the wreck. So, what were the three old men trying to hide?

From the various comments in the letters from Carter, it could be construed that he was being blackmailed, but what was Philip Senden's connection, after all, he had departed the ship before the Mayday had been sent. What were the payments to Philip for? Was Philip also involved in some blackmail plot? His mind roamed around and played with all the facts as Peter Senden waited for his answer.

'I believe that our three gentlemen were involved in something that happened before the sinking. If I remember correctly from the testimonies of the crew, a change in the attitude of the three became apparent after they left Gibraltar, when the arguments started. Whatever it was, they struck a deal of secrecy or came to some agreement. It would also seem to me, if your analysis is right, that your father risked his life to dive on the wreck for something that they called the retirement fund. Perhaps it was smuggled diamonds or something. I don't know. I suppose that if they were smuggling, they would not have been too happy when the ship was sunk and may have wished to conceal its exact whereabouts. I suspect that the childish code used to conceal the position could have been written down during a 'phone conversation, possibly with Piltcher.

Anyway, all of this is very speculative and doesn't explain why someone took pot shots at you yesterday or why you are apparently being followed by the police.'

Peter yawned, 'Sorry mate, long day I think I shall turn in shortly, lets put this lot away. See you at breakfast?'

Chapter 19. Monica Senden.

It was very dark when Peter Senden's head surfaced above the water of the Percuil River. The only sounds he could hear, other than the water lapping gently at the hull, were the voices of a crew returning to their boat somewhere down river and the faint base beat of someone's car radio over in the town.

He had entered the river using John's wet suit gear at 12.30 a.m. and now checked his watch again as he looked at the hull of the Starlight Princess looming above him. As far as he could see, the ship was in darkness as he swam silently to the boarding ladder, which he had observed from the shore earlier had not been taken up. A small wooden tender rubbed its fenders on the side of the yacht at the foot of the steps, its slight creaking hiding any sound he made as he gripped its edge and pushed up the face mask. He waited for any sign that the sound had been heard before removing the flippers and pulling himself out of the water. He tried to remember. The tender had not been there a few hours earlier when he had stood on the shore with a compulsion to visit the yacht. He was now sure this was the boat his father had probably spent his last hours on as he cautiously ascended the steps.

The teak decking had retained the heat of the day's sun and felt warm to his bare feet as he crept along the side deck where he tried the wheel house door. He was surprised when it opened and he let himself into the dark interior. He stood there whilst his eyes accustomed to the darkness, what was he looking for? It was unlikely that the charter party had left anything that would be useful to him, but he had to check. He moved aft and made a search of the stateroom cabins and saloon, peering in cupboards and drawers with the aid of the pencil beam torch he had purchased earlier. All as empty as a parson's purse. A fast cursory search of the other cabins indicated the same.

He froze as a creak somewhere below sounded. His own boat creaked at night and he relaxed, working his way forward to the pilot house. There the drawers and shelves contained only pilotage reference books, operator manuals, signal flags and other items that would be essential for the running of the ship. The chart table drawer contained charts in their unopened cellophane packets and looked unused. The whole place was clinically clean. He turned his attention to the array of instruments at the helm station, radar, weather fax, navigation instruments, chart plotter, radio, and sonar.

The chart plotter! That was what he was looking for. He switched it on and the screen threw an eerie glow along the polished wood surround as he sought the menu and went into the stored waypoints mode. Waypoints are navigational aids that define a location or position, such as a buoy, that can be stored for future reference. There seemed to be hundreds of waypoints as he scrolled the screen and was thankful that they had not been erased. Then he saw it, ACACIA LADY 0494303N 021805W. He unzipped his latex suit and pulled out the paper in its waterproof wrapper he had written on earlier in the hotel. The positions matched, he was right, there was now a definite connection between this vessel and his father. He listened as somewhere behind him the yacht creaked again as he placed the paper on the console and went to re-zip his suit. The pull tag had corroded and came away in his fingers and he was concentrating on pulling up the zip slider.

The voice came suddenly as he felt the sharp jab of the gun barrel on the back of his neck and an arm reached round him to pick up the paper.

'That was clever of you who ever you are; I'll look after that if you don't mi.......' Before the sentence could be completed, the man was reeling away unbalanced from the back kick that Peter had managed to contact onto his assailants knee. He turned, rolled and dived at the attacker as they fell in a tumble on the cabin sole, blows raining at each other as they fought on the floor. It was something that the other man was not used to, Peter brought his fist into contact with the mans jaw who lay there, moaning his hands showing the blood oozing from his mouth and nose. Peter bent briefly over his assailant and stabbed the torch on his face, a face that somehow looked familiar. Who was he? Peter didn't stop to find out; if the man was a police guard he didn't want them to know he had been on board. Anyway, he had found out what he wanted to know.

The man was sitting on the floor still moaning as Peter retrieved the paper, threw the gun over the side and departed into the night.

Breakfast was over. Seamaiden was still being checked by the Customs and Excise officers and John had arranged to return to his office by train. Peter placed his napkin on the table, stifling a yawn from his late night and suggested that he could drop his friend off on the way at Weymouth so that he could collect his car. He hadn't seen his mother since their brief meeting at the Memorial Service and had telephoned her earlier on the off chance that she may be available for lunch. Since the separation from Philip, some fifteen years previously, she had been living at Lulworth, a small village not far from Weymouth. It would also give Peter the opportunity to call into his home on the way there and collect some extra clothes.

The two men chatted about the various theories of the previous evening during the journey to Weymouth, but all the ideas they had considered seemed very speculative in the light of day. Peter kept his midnight adventure to himself as he dropped John off at the marina and then drove to the village, arriving at his mother's old cottage at midday. Monica was out there to greet him as soon as the tyres crunched on the gravel drive.

They embraced quickly and he put his arm around her as they walked to the door. She was beginning to look frail even though she was only sixty nine years old. Her hair, once flowing and blond was now grey and drawn straight back from her face and fastened with an elastic band in a small bunch. She folded her arms into her cardigan even though it was very warm.

Peter felt the guilt of a son who found private and business commitments encroaching more and more on his life, with less and less time for visiting his mother.

They entered the cottage and straight away Peter could smell cooking. He turned to her in mock surprise.

'I said we'd go out for lunch.'

She just smiled and waived him to a seat in the kitchen whilst she turned on the coffee percolator.

They chatted about the memorial service, traffic through the village during the summer holiday season and the garden, where they now sat with their coffee.

The cottage was a couple of hundred years old, and typical of many properties in the area. Built with a mixture of mellow brick and napped flint and with thatch on the roof that came down to the first floor level and then gracefully curved up and over the two small upstairs dormers like well manicured eyebrows that reminded Peter of his encounter with Ian Porter a couple of evenings before. The garden had been developed and nurtured with much care since she had moved there and was looking its most colourful at this time of year.

They sat on heavy old cast iron chairs, that screeched their presence as they were scraped across the small patio of York stone and herring boned bricks. Her terracotta flower pots abounded with fuchsias, colourful geraniums and other perennials, with blue lobelia cascading and tumbling over their edges to the ground. A large umbrella over the table provided welcome shade from the meridian sun high above the trees in the southern part of the garden.

The small talk continued over their coffee until Monica rose to go indoors and check her preparations for lunch. Peter sat there smoking in the comfortable surroundings, the peace of this place far removed from the day to day problems of work and the last few hectic days in St.Mawes. It was very different from his father's stark apartment on the sea front at Weymouth, where everything there was to serve a purpose. No photographs, flowers or mementoes, just essential furniture and books.

'I've prepared a hot pot for us, hope that's all right.' Peter thanked her as they entered the neat dining room and he considered her inappropriate choice for such a hot day.

Lunch over, they retired again to the patio to finish the bottle of wine that she had rushed out to purchase that morning after his phone call. During lunch they had talked a lot about Philip and the great loss they now both felt. She couldn't understand why there could be no funeral yet and Peter consoled her to the fact that the authorities could not release the body until the exact cause of death had been established.

'John and I have been going through some old letters of father's.' He tried to slip into the subject as though it were of trivial importance and not his main reason for the visit, but he felt his face flush slightly and hoped that his mother would not notice.

She didn't seem too interested as she bent down to dead head a nearby rose stem, well past its prime and threw the withering hips towards the back of the bed.

'Did you know any of father's friends before you were married?'

His mother looked up and somewhere in the infinite depths of her brain, an imperceptible pulse of warning bells sounded.

'Well, we knew each other for a long time before we were married dear, he had lots of friends in the Navy and in business together with his golf club cronies and others.'

Peter felt awkward at questioning his mother about things that were long in the past and would probably turn out to have no significance in the future.

'Did you know anyone by the name of Simon Carter or Gilbert Piltcher in those days? Another one is a T.Holmes.'

As her son looked at her for an answer, she felt as if she had been suddenly rocketed back nearly forty years as she considered the implications of her answer. The warning bells were ringing so loudly now that she wanted to cut their campanile strings for ever. In all those years of raising him as a son, nursing him through his childhood illnesses, seeing him progress through his education, his professional career and marriage, the question of her past had never been a topic of interest. Certainly, they had discussed where she was born, went to school, worked and so on, but never who her associates were or her detailed lifestyle before she married Philip. It's often surprising how little is known by an offspring about a parents life, previous to their arrival on the scene. Grandparents are often the catalyst when they tell their grandchildren stories such as, 'when your mother was a little girl, etc.' Often there is an unknown gulf between those early years of growing up and the re-emergence in adult life as a parent.

Monica knew the two names very well. She had been married to one of them before her affair with Philip had ended in her first divorce.

Her marriage to Philip had been a wonderful experience in the early months. They had bought a house in Portsmouth overlooking the old waterfront which she had furnished during his duty tours, so that during his shore leave they could relax and enjoy each others company. Peter had been born a couple of years later and from that time the marriage had turned cold. She knew the reason but she and Philip had slogged on, trying to keep up appearances with his naval colleagues and their wives. They lived their own compartmentalised separate lives and although she still had some love for him, they eventually agreed to live separately. Then they had divorced.

It seemed an age ago as the thoughts slipped through her memory in a few seconds. She had no idea what the letter contents may have revealed about the various relationships of those long past days.

Peter, seeing her hesitation, prompted.

'Are you OK mum, you seem to have been surprised at the question. I only asked because John needs to contact them about father's will and we don't know where to start.'

'Darling, it's getting chilly out here that's all, let's go inside and talk.' Peter hadn't noticed any change in the temperature and assumed his mother had disregarded his question, whether through discretion or uncertainty he didn't know.

They sat beside the inglenook fireplace, in which she had stood a bucket of freshly cut flowers whose perfume filled the cool room. The tea tray she had prepared bore a plate of biscuits which, years ago had been his favourites and for a moment he felt like the small boy again, being spoilt by his mother.

Monica lifted the teapot and concentrated on keeping her hand steady as she poured.

'We've never talked much about the time before we were a family.' She paused as she offered the biscuit plate as if trying to find words which would not shock or hurt him. Even though he was thirty eight years old, she still thought of him as the teenage son before he went off to university and she thought she had lost him.

'Your father knew Gilbert, Tony and Simon long before I came on the scene. As you know, I was previously married before I met Philip but I'm not sure that you would know it was Simon Carter I was married to.' She paused as though her thoughts were far away.

'After the divorce I reverted to my maiden name which appears on our marriage certificate.' She paused again, looking at the grown man sitting there, wishing she had said something to him years ago.

'You have a half brother living, I believe, still in Hong Kong but it is a few years since I've heard from him.'

Peter sat back in astonishment, feeling a nervous quiver running around in his stomach. A half brother he knew nothing about, someone else out there sharing his own mother. He was suddenly uncertain, unsure of his own independent birthright. A feeling that momentarily pressed hard on him, causing him to control his inner feelings in front of his own mother. The revelation of this piece of news was new to him and immediately the letters he had been reading the night before and John's odd question took on a new significance as she continued.

'When Simon and I broke up, your brother was only two years old. His father absconded back to the Far East with him and eventually won custody through the courts. You will gather from that, that the courts considered the matrimonial breakdown was my fault.'

She quite suddenly started to sob and Peter went over to her and put his arms around her so that she cried even more, her small body shaking as the pent up remorse of all those years flowed out from the deepest part of her soul. He assumed she was crying over the reminiscences she had just described. But Monica's private grief was from a far deeper chasm that she had tried unsuccessfully to conceal and forget over the years as her memory again recalled, as it did most days, that awful afternoon when Simon Carter had raped her.

She and Philip had been married for about six years when Simon had called on her unannounced in Portsmouth. He was on one of his rare visits to the country and wanted to see Philip who had departed to his ship the previous evening. Carter had pushed his way into the house demanding to know what Philip knew about the position of the Acacia Lady.

It was the first time they had met since their divorce and she despised him for the loss of her son. She had laughed at him, flaunting her genuine ignorance of what he was demanding. He had hit her with the back of his hand, drawing blood to her lips, as she fell on the floor where she lay and continued shouting her contempt of him. He stood over her, furious, hands clenched and perspiring. Her contemptuous voicing turned to frightened protest and then pleas as he loosened his belt and unbuttoned his trousers, lunging on to her, ripping her light summer dress and slip as he pulled them up above her waist, tearing at her lingerie in a frenzy of flaying arms and legs, gripping her to him, forcing himself into her, slapping her about the face until she bled further and, taking his ruthless fulfilment with a thrusting strength she could not escape. He had left her there semi conscious, lying on the floor bewildered, not knowing what to do.

She couldn't contact Philip, he was away at sea and in any case she could not at that moment have shared the disgust and self effacement she felt for herself, the violation of her body right, Carter had ruined her virtuous dream of serving her new husband faithfully. She had bathed, scrubbing herself almost raw as if to remove his smell and during the next few days she had ticked the calendar days off with increasing alarm. Her period date came and went and another month went by with no showing until her doctor told her the news she had been dreading.

There were no rape councillors as such in those days, no sympathetic ear to help the burden. She had no close family to turn to. Only her husband when he returned on leave, who took her story sympathetically, but either through embarrassment or his own weakness would not discuss it further. As she grew Peter's seed, abortion was out of the question. She knew other Navy wives who had vaguely hinted at similar experiences but her pride overshadowed such ideas.

Rape, unless witnessed, was a private affair which was not spoken about. The scars had to be somehow healed in a woman's own mind, not admitted to others, not spoken about for fear of reputation. She had borne those scars all her life, scars that she would never ever admit and couldn't admit to her son, who now held her so fondly, in the inviolable belief of his parental background.

When Peter had been born she had proudly presented the boy to her husband as his own. Unbeknown to her at the time, his last Naval medical had discovered his impotent low sperm count. Philip never found the right time to question her and never spoke of it again, so that they steadily grew more remote from one and other. He could never know if the baby was from their own union or from Carter but he accepted Peter without question.

Mother and son sat like that for some time in silence, both thinking about what had been said about her past, Monica, now fearful that her second born son would despise her for her impropriety all those years ago over her affair with Philip. And Peter feeling sympathy for his wretched mother whom he loved so much.

She sat up and looked at him, her eyes red from crying, and the little makeup she had applied earlier, now smudged around her cheeks.

'What do you think of your mother now then?'

Peter released her and sat on the arm of the sofa they had shared.

'Mother, nothing's changed between us. Whatever happened before I was even born can't possibly change the love we have for each other, or what we have stood for and shared through our lives. In hindsight and maybe a little selfishly on my part, I wouldn't have had the gift of life if it hadn't been for you and Philip.' His consoling words were meant as a sort of forgiveness. What would a priest have said to such an emotional outpouring from the confession booth? He didn't know. His industrial psychology training didn't go this far.

He poured another cup of tea for her, questions beginning to form in his head like giant cumulus clouds before a cold front. He took her hand tenderly and said in a quiet voice.

'Do you feel like telling me more now, I mean, who is my half brother, how old is he; where is he?'

Monica had recovered now. She knew there was no going back or keeping her secrets from him now that she had revealed so much.

'Your brother was born in 1956, that makes him about forty seven years old now. I was only twenty one when I met Simon. We were married and your brother, his name is David by the way, was born about a year later. Simon was and still is, as far as I know, a businessman in Hong Kong and was frequently over here on business where he had a flat in West London. After we were married I thought we would be moving to Hong Kong, but he insisted on me staying here in the belief that the new National Health Service could provide better pre natal services than over there. His absences grew longer and longer and on his infrequent visits he was moody and often violent. He suffered from terrible nightmares and often woke screaming at night, as though he had been to hell and back.' She stopped as though the thoughts, now flooding back through the mists of time, were focusing more sharply.

'He suffered you know at the hands of the Japanese during the war.

Eventually, little David and I saw less and less of him. Philip used to come up to town when he was on leave and stay over at the flat in West Kensington and that's how it started. We just fell in love and there was nothing I could do about it.

Simon came back to the flat unexpectedly one evening after being away for months and, well, he found us……. asleep in bed.' She stopped her narrative there, embarrassed and uncertain at confessing her former adultery to her son.

Peter had listened intently to her emotional outpouring. Outwardly he appeared strangely calm at the news that somewhere he had a half brother he never knew existed. Inwardly, what she had said had shocked him. He felt like a trapeze artist caught in slow motion, his hands grasping for the missed bar, plunging downwards, his inside trembling with the insecurity he now felt, imagining the pulp as the final consequence of the fall.

He managed to keep his voice steady as he asked.

'Do you still communicate with them, by letter for instance?'

'Not for years,' she hesitated. 'Peter, I have to tell you, Simon phoned me here last week. It was a call out of the blue, took me by surprise I can tell you. We chatted about old times and I told him about your dad's death, the family and so on. But he seemed preoccupied with how he could locate Gilbert Piltcher. You wouldn't remember him. He used to visit us at the house in Portsmouth, a Captain in the Merchant Navy who had known your father for a long time.'

Peter broke into her effusion. 'Were you able to provide him with Gilbert's address?'

'Yes dear, I hadn't seen or heard from Gilbert in the last twenty years, although I knew he lived in Lyme Regis and then Lymington for a while. I wrote to him informing him about the memorial service but the letter was returned from his landlady in Lymington and she gave me an address in Cornwall. By the time I received the new address, Philip's service had come and gone and I must confess that I never wrote to Gilbert. I knew you were dealing with your father's papers and so I gave Simon your address and the address of the flat in Weymouth where your father had been living. He had already heard about your father's death through the newspapers.'

Something jogged in Peter's mind, something he had heard over the last couple of days. Inspector Evans, that's right it was Evans who told him that his address and his fathers were in a notebook found on the Chinaman from Hong Kong who was now residing in the intensive care unit of the Mid Cornwall hospital.

'Mother, was Simon Carter an oriental, you know, a Chinaman?'

She smiled for the first time at his apparently innocent remark.

'No darling, of course not, he was as English as you and me. He had a British passport and had residential status both in this country and in Hong Kong. I only met his father once, a charming man, and that was at the wedding. Sadly his mother was killed during a Japanese air raid during the last war.'

Peter sat there thinking of the associations his mother was now recalling. She seemed to have recovered and it was nearly time for him to leave.

'Do you know if Gilbert Piltcher or Simon Carter ever sent sums of money to my father? I guess it was during a period fifteen to twenty years ago.'

She had risen, holding the tea tray and half turned towards him.

'Your father always lived beyond his means, especially when he was in the Navy. We lived very well considering his service pay was not a lot, but it must have been enough, after all, he paid for your private education and saw you through university. I know he borrowed money but I wouldn't have thought that he borrowed from those two. You see, I always left the family finances to him. Didn't really understand mortgages and things like that, it wasn't a woman's place to be involved in those days.'

'I'm sorry to press you but did father ever mention a retirement fund or something called *Dragon's Morsel*?'

Monica looked at him in the disapproving fashion he remembered from times in his childhood when she was about to scold him for some misdemeanour.

'I thought you'd come over here this afternoon to see me, I had no idea you were going to bring up all that stuff from the past, haven't you already heard enough today.' Then, after a thoughtful pause. 'Yes, your father did mention the retirement fund. It was a name he used in connection with an old ship that was sunk in the Channel, loaded with a golden cargo he used to say. That's where they all met, Gilbert was the ship's captain and Simon was one of the owners. Your father had some connection with it through the Navy when he was in the Far East. The retirement fund was something to do with your school fees, I remember him talking about the Dragon with Simon at one time but I've no idea what it was. Why all these questions Peter?'

He had not given her any indication over the last few hours about the events during his voyage to St.Mawes, or about John's encounter, at the home of Gilbert Piltcher. The police enquiries and the fact that he had been beaten up and then nearly blown to kingdom come on the yacht had also been carefully withheld from their conversation. He hadn't wanted to alarm her, and now wasn't the time, considering her upset state. He decided to stop his probing.

He kissed her gently on the cheek.

'No more questions then. Let's go back to the garden and you can show me your latest plants and what else you have been doing out there before I have to leave.'

Chapter 20. The Chinaman.

When Peter arrived back at the hotel, there was an envelope waiting for him with the Devon and Cornwall Constabulary logo printed across its top. The contents merely informed him that the yacht had been returned to the mooring but that he was required to sign the enclosed indemnity receipt and return it as soon as possible. It reminded him that he had done nothing about the insurance claim for the damage that had been caused. It was getting late and he went to his room in the hope that the insuring agents in Liverpool would still be manning their 'phones. He carried the insurance documents in his holdall and now proceeded to read the fine print of his 'plain language policy' before lifting the handset.

The exclusions, warranties and claims procedure appeared to be in conflict in places and he threw the document to one side for John to look at later. He'd heard nothing from John and could only assume that he was either on his way back to the hotel, or would be staying overnight at Katherine's place.

He lay back on the bed, hands clasped behind his head as he considered the day with his mother, her distress and revelation about his half brother whom he now thought about as he also considered what the golden cargo of the Acacia Lady might have consisted of and why his father had risked his life in his old age to dive on her.

He looked at his watch. Half past seven. He hoped Jessica might phone even though it was probably late evening in New York. He had a lot to tell her and wondered what she would say when he told her about David.

The ideas that he and John had come up with the previous evening were fitting together now and an idea was starting to form, which, the more he thought about it the more enthused he became. He swung off the bed and undressed for a shower before picking up the 'phone and asking for the Mid Cornwall hospital.

'Hello, yes, I would like to enquire how Mr.He Luk is this evening..... Yes, I'm his son from Hong Kong. Landed at Heathrow a couple of hours ago, I'm on my way down there now.....I see, so he's out of intensive care. That's good news. Can you tell me his room number......thanks. No, don't tell him I'm coming, I'd like to surprise him if that's OK........ great, thanks a lot, cheers.'

Peter put the phone down and considered what he had just done. Totally out of character, but what the hell, he had to find out if his suspicions were right. He knew John would never approve and hurriedly showered and went down to his car.

As directed, he arrived outside the small ante room at the end of a corridor that led to the main ward, He felt conspicuous with the bunch of flowers he had purchased in the hospital reception area. It was beginning to get dark outside and the Raybans he was wearing made him feel rather silly as he approached the woman police constable sitting outside the room.

'I'm Mr. Luk's son, David, have the hospital informed you about my visit?'

The constable looked at her note pad. 'That's OK Mr.Luk, your father is sleeping, don't be too long.' He quietly turned the door handle and entered.

There was only the one bed in the room and a man lay there, the television was on but with no sound and the man was dozing. A half open door led to a bathroom. The main room was dim, with the blind pulled down. Peter stood there, quietly observing, wondering what he would say if his idea was wrong. The man suddenly turned and looked at him. He had a fleshy face, still badly bruised, with a great shock of silver hair. He had probably been quite handsome as a young man, but now the face bore the sallow colour that comes after years of living in the East, his eyes puffy from sleep, narrow and suspicious over his high bearded cheekbones.

'Hello Mr.Carter, I've brought you some flowers to cheer you up.'

The man was suddenly wide awake and heaved himself up in the bed.

'And who the hell are you, bursting in here like this, what do you want, my name's Luk.'

Peter played it out. Watching, to make sure the man didn't press the call button lying on the counterpane.

'Oh, come on Simon, I know who you are, and what you are doing here in England.' The man's hand reached out but not to the call button. Instead he turned up the volume of the television set on the remote control.

'Do you now.' The man answered in almost a whisper. He had still not reached for the call button and eyed Peter with a mixture of apprehensive interest in his eyes.

'I've come to save you, you old bastard.' Peter was now beside the bed and moved the call button out of the man's reach as he sat down on the edge of the bed. 'Simon Carter, pleased to make your acquaintance.' He offered his hand to the man who was now nervously looking towards the door, but then slowly raised his hand and shook Peter's.

'Who the fucking hell are you young man, coming in here, scaring me to death and calling me names Have a look at the room chart will you, you'll see that my name is Luk. I'm on holiday here from Hong Kong, although you wouldn't think it. Been beaten up which is why I'm banged up in this bloody place.'

'Oh, come off it Carter, I'm your son's half brother. You did know he had a half brother didn't you?' Peter had still not given his name in case he was barking up the wrong tree.

The man peered at him more closely and adjusted the volume control to a higher level.

'You're Senden's kid, Peter isn't it?'

At last, Peter felt jubilant that his hunch had been correct. No stranger to the old trio could have been in Piltcher's house that day when John had visited and interrupted the search. The coincidence of someone else from Hong Kong being there on that day was too great after what his mother had told him that afternoon.

Carter looked nervous and perspiration had started to stand out on his forehead. Just then there was a tap on the door and a nurse came in with a small phial of medicine, which he took as he continued to stare at Peter.

'My word Mr.Luk, we'll have to check that temperature again, seems your son's visit has excited you.'

Carter gave no reply to the young nurse, who now busied herself, smoothing the bed and adjusting his pillows whilst the thermometer was stuck in his mouth. He never took his eyes off Peter, watching him now as Peter put the flowers in a spare vase.

The nurse retrieved the thermometer and read its digital message that she transferred to the chart at the end of the bed.

'I was on holiday in Hong Kong earlier this year, had a wonderful time.' She started describing where she had been to Peter. The Space Museum, Ocean Park, Jardine's Bazaar, the Jade market. She rambled on in a friendly way.

'But I expect you know all of those places. Where do you live in Hong Kong Mr.Luk?' Peter suddenly realised she was addressing him. He had never been to Hong Kong and had no idea what to say. His deception was about to be betrayed when Carter suddenly spoke up.

'Forgive my son, nurse. He's had a long journey before coming here tonight and is very tired. We live in the Peak area, one of the finest neighbourhoods of the old territory.' He smiled at her in appreciation but she wanted to continue about her holiday experiences.

'The Po Lin Monastery was wonderful. I expect you've been there Mr.Luk.' Again she looked at him in expectation of a reply but he could only nod in agreement. 'That new airport, can't remember its name.'

This time Peter butted in. 'You mean Chek Lap Kok, yes, a wonderful modern airport and so large.' He had seen a programme about it a few nights previously on the television. 'Better than the old Kai Tak one in Kowloon.' He hoped he had remembered the name correctly and looked to Carter who gave a slight nod.

'Well Mr.Luk, you should be out of here tomorrow with any luck.' As she realised the pun she put her hand to her face and giggled, 'Sorry sir, it just slipped out.' She turned towards the door and was gone.

When she reached the ward sister's office, she knocked and entered.

'As far as I could tell he seems genuine enough, Mr. Luk certainly acknowledged him as his son.' The immigration officer who'd been called in nodded his thanks as he turned over the pages of the passport belonging to Mr.HeLuk.

'Thanks for that.' Peter looked at the man he accepted as his half brother's father, slightly at a loss for words or what he should now be doing. The television sound was very loud but as he attempted to zap it, Carter put a finger to his lip and shook his head.

Luk, as he was known according to his hospital notes and name at the top of his bed, hadn't taken his eyes of Peter.

'For fuck sake take those ridiculous dark glasses off and let me look at you. So you're the little brat of Monica's that I supported for all those years. Yes, I can certainly see the likeness now. Your brother is just an older version of you, slightly less hair, but yes, you could almost be twins.' He laughed as he withdrew his other hand from under the covers to reveal a large oxygen cylinder spanner that he put down on the bedside unit. 'Sorry, heard the door knob turning, wasn't sure whom it was going to be.'

'Bloody hell, Simon, you could have killed me with that thing. Who the hell were you expecting?'

'Aye lad, it wouldn't have been the first time I'd killed to protect m'self. Some very nasty people put me in here. Well now.' Carter felt in command of the situation now and beckoned Peter to sit closer so that they could talk against the indecorous sound from the television. 'I suppose you're wondering why I'm Mr.Luk and not Mr.Carter,' he laughed again over Peter's obvious discomfort at the presence of the potential weapon.

'You know Simon, the last few days I've been slugged with a baseball bat, used as target practice, nearly blown up, tailed and now nearly beaten over the head. I guess that's some sort of record. By the way, the police are still here, there's a lady constable sitting outside the door.' He scanned the old man's face, still swollen and red from his beating. 'Who did this to you Simon?'

Carter ignored the question and looked at him, serious now.

'Peter; I hope you don't mind me using your first name, we are virtually family after all. I've got to get out of here. I've been pretending I'm much worse than I really am. The immigration people got hold of my Hong Kong passport that I dropped in the car park at Trevello and tried to question me about illegal entry to this country. Each time, I've pretended to doze off but they will be closing in tonight or tomorrow, I'm sure.

In fact, I still have British Citizenship and my British passport in the name of Simon Carter is still with my luggage at Waterloo Station. I used that one to travel here from Beijing, the Hong Kong one is useless, takes days of paperwork before the Chinese even get down to allowing you to fill out the exit visa. Trouble is, I didn't want to travel around here as Carter in case certain people got to hear about me. It's all very complicated, in fact from what you just said about being blown up, it could be that you are also in great danger.' He looked over to the door again, 'turn the volume up a bit more on the telly can you, that's better, at least if we speak quietly we may not be heard on the bug that they've probably planted somewhere in here. I've searched all over this damned room but couldn't find it. They must think I'm quite ill, my clothes are still in that locker.'

Peter glanced over to the open fronted locker where there were certainly clothes hanging there.

'I'm sure that little nurse's conversation was a ploy to find out who you were. How did you manage to get in here anyway?'

Peter told him about his earlier telephone conversation with the hospital. This time Luk laughed with a roar of approval.

'They'll be checking your name on every immigration computer up there at Heathrow, when they don't find it they'll be down here so fast you'll not have time to shit yerself.'

Peter Senden had not imagined there would be complications like this, he hadn't really even thought about what he was going to do when he confronted Carter. He had made a spur of the moment decision and now cursed himself for not having more sense. He remembered his conception of the idea in the hotel, 'totally out of character' to his normal reasoning.

'What danger, what do you mean, something to do with Acacia Lady?'

Carter's reply was guarded. 'There are other people out there, looking for the wreck, you know, the Acacia Lady.'

'You mean there are treasure hunters out there?'

'Not exactly lad, let's just say that there are some unsavoury characters floating about out there who are interested in the wreck.'

Peter considered what had been said but decided to delay the questions burning inside him.

'Where are you staying at the moment, it may be possible for me to get your British passport and then we can sort it all out. By the way, do I call you, Carter or Luk?'

'You call me what you like lad, Luk was my mother's maiden name and in China I'm allowed to use it. Since the hand over to China a few years ago, I found that a Chinese name on my business literature was essential if I was to continue doing business there. I have other assumed names as well. It's common practice in the Far East.'

The television programme droned on as the two men from different generations sized each other up. 'Anyway, what do you want with me?'

Peter looked down at the bruised old man. 'I want to know what's going on Simon, why I was beaten up the other night for instance, do you know anything about that, was it connected to whoever beat you up at Trevello and put you in hospital?'

The reply was met by a negative silence and Peter continued.

'What are you doing here anyway, looking for the Acacia Lady treasure, or is it something to do with a *Dragon's Morsel* or retirement fund?'

Carter gave him a long look. What did this young man sitting on the bed really know of the past and the dangers of what he was saying?

'I can't tell you anything here.' He put a finger to his lips and swept his arm around the room as if suspecting that listening devices were secreted in every recess.

'What you want to know will depend on other people as well as me. You'll have to wait.'

'Was it those other people who did this to you?'

Carter looked at him coldly. Peter could upset the remnants of his plans. The Koreans had turned very nasty when they got to Crows Nest Cottage and found nothing to help them. The psychopathic Chungai had nearly killed him in his rage and had been pulled away from Carter by the other two. There was no way that he wished to share the spoils with anyone else, but the Koreans were now his only link to the gold. He heaved himself up on the pillows, his eyes narrow with suspicion.

'What do you know about the gold? Have you found out the true position of the Acacia Lady?'

So it was gold and not diamonds as John had suggested the night before.

Peter eyed the old man. 'So the stories about treasure are true then, who else is searching out there for it, did they kill my father? Were you involved?'

Carter lay back on the pillow, 'No lad, I haven't seen your father for thirty odd years. We had occasional correspondence on the subject; he was trying to locate the gold by all accounts. Sorry to hear that he died, heart attack wasn't it?'

'My father died searching for the Acacia Lady, of that I'm sure.' Peter paused. 'Was there anything else on board that ship, you know, any military equipment or anything dangerous? What is the reference to the *Dragon's Morsel* for instance?'

Carter sensed the urgency in Peter's questions.

'I can't say anything, but I am sure that turd Piltcher is the only one who knows the true position. He was caught dealing in gold you know, a few years back in Turkey. Anyway, the gold, if it is still there, belongs to me.' His voice had risen and he looked about the room as though someone was listening. 'You keep away from it, you hear.'

'What's the retirement fund then Carter? According to papers and the will that my father left, he had some sort of agreed share in the fund. My conclusion now is that this fund refers to gold that was somehow smuggled onto the Acacia lady before she sank. I say smuggled because the ship's manifest, outlined at the time of the court case at the Board of Trade, makes no mention of any bullion being on board.'

'Fuck off and leave me in peace, I've no more to say to you. The gold is mine and I've made arrangements to salvage it.' Carter's face had turned to a scowl as he tried to end the conversation.

Peter was thinking, 'there's no reason why I shouldn't just walk out of here, after all they don't know it was me who made the phone call. If the immigration people are here there's no way that they can suspect any complicity on my part.'

He eyed Carter. 'I shall tell them who you are of course.'

Carter grabbed Peter's arm, 'If you do that lad, I'm a dead man. Just be patient and I'll see you get a share.'

Peter looked down on the sweating old man in the bed. They were going around in circles, getting nowhere.

'If you tell me where you're staying, I'll try and get your passport.'

Simon Carter lent forward so that his voice was a quiet whisper.

'I'm staying at a location that I'd rather you didn't know at the moment, write down where I can contact you and we'll see what transpires tomorrow.'

'I'm not sure where I shall be tomorrow. I'll give you my mobile number and the number of my solicitor, John Barrett, who would also like to speak to you.' Peter tore of a piece of the wrapping paper from the flowers and wrote down the numbers for him.

'Now, turn that infernal noise down and get out of here, If anyone stops you on the way out, play along with it for as long as you can, I promise we'll be in touch. Good night.' Peter turned the set off and left him there. Both men had plenty to think about that night.

When he strolled down the corridor, a door suddenly opened.

'Mr.Luk, can I see you for a moment,' Peter kept walking and heard footsteps behind him that drew level as he reached the lift. 'Mr.Luk, I must request that you come back to the office with me sir, I have some questions to put to you.'

Peter swung round. 'Are you referring to me, if so my name is not Luk, its Senden, I think you have the wrong person.' The man was shorter than Peter and was wearing steel rimmed glasses with thick lenses that made his eyes look larger than they really were as they looked up at him.

The lift arrived and went, the official still repeated his request but in a much firmer manner and Peter noticed a police constable emerging from another room and hovering in the distance. Peter protested his annoyance at being detained as they returned to the sister's room.

'Sit down Mr.Luk. I am Alan Woods and I work for a department called SO1, the Special Branch Immigration and Passport Control Squad. I am detaining you in accordance with the Immigration section of the 2001 Terrorism Act. and must request you to empty out your pockets please.' The constable had joined them and watched as Peter emptied the contents of the slacks he was wearing, whilst he argued about his human rights at this humiliation. The official sat tight lipped, as car keys, money, loose change, pen, sunglasses and lighter were placed on the table and he examined each item, including every coin, presumably to see if any of them were of foreign origin.

It was a warm evening and Peter was only wearing slacks and a shirt.

'Would you remove your shoes please Mr.Luk.' Peter did as he was bid and the official examined them closely before returning them to the table.

'You have a good taste in shoes sir, Churche's are a British make, although I imagine they can also be purchased in Hong Kong.'

'Your passport, please sir, you must have it with you if you've just arrived here, or perhaps it's with your luggage in the car. Do you know the car number?'

He was interrupted by the telephone ringing which he answered with a brief acknowledgement and then sat there listening before replacing the handset without comment. The impassive voice of the civil servant droned on.....

'Sorry sir, but we were expecting you to visit your father and I have to inform you that we are waiting for his health to improve so that we can caution him as an illegal entrant. There is no record of him having passed through any British airport and his passport doesn't bear a visa for this country.

In your case, I have just been informed that we have a record of your legal entry earlier this month at Heathrow, unfortunately, there is no recent record of your father's entry.'

Peter took in the incredulous news that now seemed to pin point him as the person who they thought had arrived earlier. Was it his half brother?

'Christ, can't I get it through to you that I'm not the person you want. Can we go to my car where my wallet and driving licence are, that should prove to you once and for all who I am.'

Peter explained to the constable where he had parked his car but insisted that because his wallet and credit cards were there, at least two persons should be involved. It took ages for the plain clothed colleague to arrive and the keys were taken. They were soon back again with the wallet carefully placed in a clear plastic bag. The civil servant emptied the contents onto the table and dutifully examined his drivers licence and credit cards. Still he seemed unsatisfied.

'You say you are not Mr.Luk's son, in which case I must ask what your connection is with him.'

'He's my uncle, well not quite; he's my mother's ex husband.'

The officer looked at him as though it was at last beginning to dawn on him that he may be interviewing the wrong man.

'The car you are using is not on hire is it, I presume you can you tell me in what name your car is licensed.' Peter gave the details and another 'phone call was made. The receiver was replaced and this time the civil servant smiled at last.

'You will appreciate Dr. Senden that our Government puts a high priority on immigrant security and in this case we have obviously made a gross error as to your status. May I, on behalf of my department, offer you our sincere apologies for delaying you and wish you a pleasant evening. You are now at liberty to leave.' He waited as Peter replaced his shoes and reclaimed his possessions, then stood and opened the door.

Peter got up slowly, 'Before I go, perhaps you would be kind enough to tell me how I can claim compensation for wrongful detention and the time I have wasted.' It was cheeky but so what.

The civil servant bent and fumbled in his briefcase.

'This leaflet explains the legality of our processes and the procedure should you wish to go ahead with a complaint. My card and details are attached. However Dr. Senden, impersonation can be a serious crime and I would be very careful in future not to try it again. Good evening sir.'

Senden stepped into the lift which transferred him from the ground floor to the floor above where the main entrance was situated. As he emerged onto the reception concourse, and headed for the side exit, he could see security guards running to the main entrance

He drove slowly back in the direction of the hotel as his mind poured over all that he had learned that day. Nicky, who was on reception duty for the evening, handed Peter a note. It was a telephone message informing him that John Barrett was staying overnight at Katherine Holmes father's house and hoped to be back in the morning. He strolled into the lounge bar for a night cap and his heart sank as he saw the hairy eyebrows of Ian Porter wending their way across to him.

'Good Evening Dr. Senden, great news if you can call it that.' Peter lit a cigar and ordered a whisky.

'Same for you Mr.Porter?'

The newspaperman surprised him as he declined, 'Got a large one over there old boy, bring your drink over and join me.' They sat in one of the alcoves and Ian Porter pointed to the headlines in the Western Evening Gazette. 'Have you seen this yet?'

Peter picked up the newspaper. The headline on the front page was set in large print and read;

'SIR ANTHONY IS KIDNAPPED'

'Late this afternoon the Devon and Cornwall police issued a statement that Sir Anthony Holmes, the eminent scientist and broadcaster who has been missing since taking an early morning jog on Friday, is suspected of being kidnapped.

A witness walking her dog near St. Just saw a man in running kit answering Sir Anthony's description as he ran past her early on Friday morning. She saw a small car draw up behind him and three men get out and manhandle him into the vehicle that was then driven off at speed. As yet, no responsibility has been admitted by any organisation and the police are appealing for any other witnesses to come forward.'

The report went on to describe how Holmes was discovered missing early on Saturday from the Black Rocks Hotel in St.Mawes, where he had been staying for a few days whilst preparing material for his new television series. The alarm had been raised by his daughter later in the day when she realised that he had not returned to the hotel on the Friday evening from a filming session. Further enquiries established that he had not in fact returned from his morning jog. Later paragraphs covered the presenter's work and his past, including the suspicions at the time that he had sold laser secrets to the Soviet Union in 1986. His wife's subsequent suicide was also unnecessarily dwelt on at length.

Senden handed the newspaper back to Porter.

'What on earth would anyone want to kidnap an elderly scientist for?'

Porter nodded his head knowingly.

'As I told you the other night Dr. Senden, the mystery surrounding the Acacia Lady and its officers may be coming home to roost after nearly fifty years. Seems strange that within a matter of a few weeks, since the Channel search I told you about was started, firstly your father dies I gather in mysterious circumstances, then Captain Piltcher is beaten up and my researchers in Hong Kong tell me that the infamous Simon Carter has gone to ground. Then to top all of that, Holmes who has been associated with Piltcher and Carter is kidnapped' He gave Peter a smile. 'You could hardly call it coincidence. What I want to find out is how the association between them, struck up all that time ago, could now be causing these, er, problems.'

His expression turned to one of expectation but Peter looked at him angrily.

'I'm sorry Porter but I don't see any sinister mystery over the Acacia Lady. The accident and sinking were well documented in the press at the time, I've read them and I see no connection between that event and the current search in the English Channel. I don't know what it is that you are trying to rake up but I'm afraid I can't help you.'

The reporter flopped back in the chair and reached for his glass. He looked up thoughtfully as Peter rose to go.

'So you've been to the Records office at Richmond since we last spoke, or were you already aware of what I told you?'

Peter glowered at him and said nothing.

'Don't be so sure Dr. Senden, forgive me for saying so but three of those men all have histories of shady dealings........'

'What the hell are you implying, Porter? That newspaper report on Sir Anthony Holmes just builds on past speculation, it was never proved or substantiated.' Peter stood over the seated man, his anger now apparent to other drinkers in the lounge. He glanced around at the faces that had turned in his direction and sat again Then in a quieter voice, 'What is it you're trying to winkle out of me Porter? Why can't you put your cards on the table?

Porter accepted the more conciliatory tone and lent forward in a whisper.

'I want to know what was on that ship when it sank. You see Dr. Senden, I am convinced that it is the Acacia Lady that the authorities are searching for, but for what reason I do not know. It was carrying undefined military supplies that would not be of much interest these days but I am intrigued as to the mystery that now seems to surround the people involved. That search, if it is for the ship, is costing the taxpayer plenty and they have a right to know through my newspaper what is going on, it's as simple as that.'

'What do you know about the other people involved, Piltcher and Carter for instance, you say they have shady pasts, enlighten me?'

Porter waved the waiter over and ordered another large brandy, 'same for you?'

'No thanks, all I want is some answers.' Peter stubbed out his cigar and sat there as Porter's empty glass was exchanged.

'Piltcher was involved with gold smuggling some years ago, that's all I know. We, that is our research department, believe that Carter was involved in subversive activities for the Chinese. He was, of course implicated with Holmes when the Black Sea spy scandal blew up. Then we have your father whom we suspect was acting for MI6 at that time. I have to admit that those events do not seem to be related but something tells me there is more to those gentlemen than we know about.' He downed the remaining dregs of liquor from the glass and stood to go.

'By the way, you probably will not yet have heard that a body was found floating in the sea early this evening, no doubt it will be in the local papers tomorrow.'

Before Peter could answer, he turned abruptly and was gone, threading his way through the tables to the exit.

Peter ordered a club sandwich in his room as he sat with pen and paper and tried to write down some of the facts he had assimilated and put them into some form of order. The 'phone rang and it was Jessica in New York.

Next morning, Peter had showered and was dressing before going down for breakfast when the 'phone rang. It was John.

'Why don't you keep your mobile turned on, I've been trying to get you for the last half hour. Had to stop and find the hotel number.' He didn't sound in a good mood. The last few days had gone by, the short leave he'd taken was about to run out and he would have to get back to his office again the next day. He had a court appearance to attend on behalf of a client and was now driving back to St.Mawes to retrieve his luggage from the hotel and book out before returning to Winchester.

Peter put the phone down. He'd a lot he wanted to convey to John. His hunch about Simon Carter and the illegal entry Carter had made into the country as He Luk. The news about his half brother and what his mother had said about the Retirement Fund. The suspicion he had that the payments, referred to in the letters from, Carter were to pay for his education. Also, the apparent animosity that Carter had for his parents.

The dining room was not so busy this morning. He picked up the *Daily Telegraph* and scanned the headlines, which, as on the previous day were full of speculation about Sir Anthony Holmes. At the bottom of page three a short article caught his eye.

A body had been found floating in the sea somewhere off Dodman Point by fishermen and taken into Falmouth harbour last evening. The police had not identified it and could not say if it was the body that a yachtsman had reported seeing thrown from a cruiser three days earlier.

Peter quickly finished his breakfast and went back to the room. The mobile was now charged and he phoned the police H.Q., asking for D.I.Evans after announcing who he was.

'One moment please Dr. Senden.'

'Mortuary here .... Yes, I'll get him for you.' Evans came on the phone.

'Hello Dr. Senden, you certainly pulled one last night, I was hoping to talk to you this morning about the escape of the China man.

'I can explain last night but firstly, I presume you have seen the newspaper reports on the body found floating off Dodman and that you now believe the statement I made to the police about the shooting I witnessed?'

'Never doubted you sir. Right now I'm looking at the body of someone who has a 9mm bullet hole through his head. However, I would like to know how you suddenly became acquainted with Mr.Luk, having told us previously that you had never heard of him. I'm not aware that you've broken the law in any way, but I would appreciate speaking to you again on the subject.'

'I'll explain what transpired when I see you, too complicated over the phone.'

They arranged to meet early evening at the hotel.

When Peter returned to the hotel reception, Nick informed him that there was someone waiting to see him and gestured to Hank Hoskins who was sitting in the lounge with another man and rose to meet him. The other man remained seated but Peter's trained eye noted the unusual bulge in the suit jacket.

'Hi there Senden, can we talk somewhere private.'

The breakfast period in the restaurant was over and the place was empty as Peter ordered coffees and guided him to one of the alcoves. Hoskins looked around. He didn't like being directed to a specific place and instead went to another alcove. Peter guessed his reasons and they sat down.

'Well Commander, this is a surprise what can I do for you?'

The coffee arrived and Hoskins poured his cream with slow deliberation as though thinking about what was to be said.

'Senden, I'm going to come straight with you. You've already been informed at the police interview the other day as to who I am and whom I represent. To put you at your ease, I know from my associates in your British Secret Service that you are employed by them as an engineer in the T2 Section. I also know about your father's death and the cause through radio active irradiation and may I say how very sorry I am.'

Peter started to interject but the Commander held up his hand to silence him.

'You are aware that we, that is the U.S.Government through the C.I.A., have been anxious about finding out all the facts leading up to your father's death. We were especially interested to know what he meant by his reference to the *Dragon's Morsel*. It now seems that he found something in the ocean that belongs to us and which we are anxious about locating; however the position you kindly passed on to Major Fellows via. Jessica Wilson is not correct.' He stopped as he tore open the sugar sachet and poured its contents into the coffee.

'Who's Major Fellows?' Peter had lit a cheroot and drew heavily on it as the question was asked.

Hoskins looked surprised. Was Senden genuinely unaware of who Fellows was or was he just putting on a front?

'Major Fellows is my counterpart in your Security Services organisation. He knows everything that is going on. The story is beginning to take on a form now how your father, Carter and Piltcher came together back in '52 on board the freighter Acacia Lady. She was carrying military equipment, the property of the US Government; how it got on that ship we do not know. Our subsequent enquiries also point to there being a substantial amount of gold on board, hence my comment at your police interview. Its authenticity cannot be proved although if it is there its probably Chinese gold. The ship sank somewhere in the English Channel, we believe near the Channel Isles, which is where it gets difficult. The military equipment for sake of description, contained radio active material and it is this that we are sure your father came into contact with. We have been searching for the wreck unsuccessfully for the last month together with the help of the British and French Navies as obviously it constitutes an environmental hazard and has to be removed.'

Peter considered what he had also heard a couple of evenings before from Porter and the newspaper clippings in his father's scrapbook. Things were beginning to stack up.

'There couldn't have been much nuclear material around in 1952.'

The commander ignored Peter's remark

'I have to tell you that we are not the only ones looking for the Acacia Lady. I understand that Carter has arranged some sort of consortium to help him raise the gold.' He stopped and opened his briefcase and pulled out a small notepad.

Peter sat tight, what was the commander fishing for?

'Senden, you're an engineer; what do you know about satellites.' The question was blunt and he looked directly at Peter who was caught left footed at the sudden change in the conversation.

'What sort of satellites? Do you have anything specific in mind?'

'Let's say a geosynchronous one used for telemetry or maybe telecommunications.

'They're complex bits of kit and rely on their ground stations or other satellites for the information they receive and transmit. They're like repeaters in many ways. A signal from the ground goes in one end, is amplified and retransmitted from the other end. Depending on the bandwidth over 100,000 separate signals can be amplified, switched, processed and then retransmitted, sometimes down different cones to areas hundreds of miles apart. A lot of other things can happen as well, there are innumerable combinations. A geosynchronous unit is exactly that, in synchronisation with the earth or what could be called a stationary position in the sky.' Peter stopped he felt like a walking technical dictionary. 'What exactly do you need to know?'

The Commander looked around the room as if deciding how to put the question he vitally wanted to know.

'I need to know how you would go about stopping one from transmitting if that is possible?'

'Can't your own people tell you that?'

'Afraid not, it's just a hypothetical question I need to know for my own information, just thought that as a technologist you may be able to help me that's all.'

Peter felt apprehensive and looked away from Hoskins gaze. His eye caught a pale blue document in the open briefcase which from the logo and code number on the right hand corner, Peter knew was so confidential that few existed. Even then they did not exist for the use of individuals.

It was the access code book for an old 5/50 kiloton selectable yield W85 nuclear warhead. He recognised it from the work he had done for his Section in Germany when he had secretly assessed the capability of the American two stage solid propellant MGM-31 Pershing 1. A short range battlefield support missile most of which had now been decommissioned under the Salt Treaty.

'I'm not sure I can help you on that one. There are thousands of satellites up there working in the gigohertz band of frequencies. Also it would depend what switching system it uses, could be on the IMMERSAT system or the latest Advanced Communications Technology Satellite system, called ACTS for short.' He looked quizzically at the Commander. 'To stop transmission the best thing would be to locate the ground station and switch off there. Even then there would be no guarantee that you'd stop transmissions because many communications sats are inter-linked and channels can be independently switched from other sources.'

'So your saying it is not possible for instance to jam the transmitting frequencies.'

Peter smiled and opened out his hands.

'I wouldn't think so, unless you could somehow break into the transmission cone or shoot the thing down. Anyway Commander, I'm intrigued, what's on your mind?'

Hoskins replaced the notebook in his case and twirled the combination locks.

'Wish I could tell you Senden but as I said it's a hypothetical question from a non technical guy whose mind sometimes wanders over these things.' He laughed and the subject was closed as abruptly as it was opened. 'Now as I was saying, we know Carter is after raising the gold but has vanished into oblivion since he landed last week at Heathrow. Also this guy Piltcher has gone to ground and we have Holmes missing, who was also connected in various ways with the others. You're the son of the fourth man in this mystery and I must emphasise the importance of letting us know if any of them tries to contact you.'

The situation and conversation were somehow unconvincing. It was obvious to Peter that the Commander's real concern had something to do with communication satellites. He considered the rest of the conversation to be small talk, nothing he didn't already know. The main question reeling in his head was what was the U.S.Army handbook, that he had glimpsed, doing in the Commanders briefcase?

Was he being taken as a sucker or was Hoskins concern real? He rose from the table and shook hands.

'I'll let you know Commander, I still have your card.'

Back in his room, Peter thought over what had been said and what he had seen. He picked up the mobile and dialled a number that was immediately answered by his Section Chief Doug Lawson.

'Doug, its Peter Senden here. Sorry for ringing you on this number but it's urgent and I'd like to meet ASAP........... that's right, Peter Senden. I can't tell you what it's about on the open line but it's important we meet.'

Doug Lawson was at that moment touring the facilities at HMS Sultan the marine and aircraft engineering training school near Gosport.

'Where are you Peter, thought you were taking some leave.' Peter told him he was at the bottom end of Cornwall.

'Look, I shall be over at Drake Naval base in Davenport tomorrow, how about we meet up there.'

Peter replied. 'HMS Drake sounds fine.' They made their arrangements and Peter rang off satisfied that he'd made the right decision in phoning his superior.

Hank Hoskins went back to his hotel after meeting Peter and replaced the copy documents in his room safe. He had concluded that the leak of information back to the Langley conspirators about the Chinaman, He Luck, could have only come from someone in the British Security Service, probably someone close to Senden.

He already knew that Senden should have recognised the handbook.

It was only a minor consideration to the growing complexity of the *Crusader* Project that he knew had to somehow be stopped. If his suspicions proved to be correct, Senden would inform his superiors and the mole would get back to Frank Gibson with the information of his conversation. Things would then start to happen. His main concern was how the conspirators and their wider circle of contacts could be safely flushed out.

John arrived an hour later and met up with Peter who had been hanging around in the lounge near the reception area, so as not to miss him. He was looking anxiously at his watch but conceded to Peters request to stay for a coffee whilst they discussed the new information that had been gained during the previous day and the encounter with Carter. He said nothing about his conversation with Hoskins.

John had listened patiently and looked at him, an incredulous grin forming over his previously serious features.

'Frankly old mate, I'm astonished at what you did at the hospital. I think you may be deeper in the brown sticky stuff than the client I'm supposed to be representing in the morning. Shouldn't you be telling the police all this?'

The coffee had become cold and Peter downed the last dregs before replying.

'There's a lot more to this retirement fund business and the Acacia Lady than we know. I want to leave it for a while and see if Carter bothers to contact me with any more information.'

John said nothing, he suspected that there was more to the story than Peter was prepared to admit. He thought for a moment before 'phoning his office and spoke briefly to his secretary. He put the mobile on the table and looked at Peter.

'Who would believe it, as if I haven't got enough on my plate listening to your problems, the little shit I'm supposed to be representing has got caught up in another burglary. He's in jail pending an appearance at the magistrate's court tomorrow morning.

One of my junior partners will have to deal with his application for bail and contact the court on the other case.' He looked round and called over to the receptionist to keep his room. 'Come on Peter, I'll make the necessary arrangements with my office and then, were going sailing, we could both do with the break, clear our thoughts a bit.'

'How is Katherine Holmes by the way, you've not said anything about your trip to her father's place?'

'She's bearing up under the circumstances, she's a wonderful girl. The news on her father is not encouraging, but at least she believes he is still alive. She's been called off to some conference in London, got a call from her department at about eleven thirty last night and I gather she was virtually ordered to go there. It must have been important though because she's being picked up by a chauffeur driven car at about three o'clock Thursday afternoon.'

'You're keen on her then?'

John smiled and declined his head as if unusually bashful at his reply. 'I'm not sure Peter, it's early days yet. You haven't met her but I believe she has some sort of problem over and above her missing father.'

'How do you mean?'

'Well, you've not met her yet. She's very attractive, intelligent and all those things, but I felt there was some sort of inhibition there, you know, a sort of frigid barrier that was drawn up whenever I got too close to her, may have just been me of course, but , well I'm not sure that I shall be pursuing the relationship.'

'What about the retirement fund? Was she able to throw any light on that?'

'Well it would seem that there is a copy of Sir Anthony's will at the house. Apparently the police requested it, but the family lawyer wouldn't let it go. Said there was nothing there that would have any bearing on the disappearance. Katherine had seen it and when I asked her about the retirement fund she implied that there was a clause in the document similar to your father's Will. Afraid that's all I can tell you.'

Chapter 21. Senden in custody.

The two men climbed aboard Seamaiden. The police and customs people who'd been on board had left things tidily stacked in the saloon. Peter went about the business of stowing equipment back to its rightful place and making a temporary repair to the head linings whilst John bent on the sails, checked over the deck items and then ran up the diesel engine.

They released the mooring buoy and Seamaiden swung away on the tide under the power of her engine. With John on the helm, Peter went forward and started to winch the mainsail halyard, pulling up the sail, with its Terylene crackling its sound as the folds fell out, until the right luff tension was reached for the light wind that afternoon. Next, he adjusted the out haul controlling the foot of the sail, pulled up the kicking strut and loosened off the topping lift before making his way back to the cockpit. John sheeted in the mainsheet from his position at the helm as the sail filled. Peter was already busy letting out the control line to the roller reefing on the jib sail, setting it most of the way out, adjusting the track positions and starting to winch in the jib sheet.

It was a glorious sunny afternoon, with a light north westerly breeze, the conditions that cruising sailors dream of. Seamaiden picked up on the starboard tack, her keel biting in to the slight sea to produce the reaction to her sails as her speed picked up. It was as if she acknowledged the freedom from her mooring chain and lifted her skirts to dance across the stage that was the sea's surface.

Peter took the tiller from John and cut the engine, his face beaming with the pleasure that is the solitude and quietness of sailing. They were not going fast, a few knots now, equivalent to about ten miles an hour. Not fast compared to the few cabin cruisers, that spouted their white wakes out across the roads, but a magnificent feeling of harnessing the freedom of nature's power. It was an exhilarating feeling as the craft heeled and he felt the slight weather helm through the tiller and the warm air drafting across the deck. He brushed his hand through his hair as he looked around them. John was making a final slight adjustment on the sheet winch and then sat back on the cockpit seat, taking in the sounds around them, of the hull smacking water, the creaks as the sails strained their aerodynamic shapes, enjoying every second like Peter.

Seamaiden stayed on the same tack across Falmouth Bay to the entrance of the Helford River, where they anchored for a while and had a brew up before returning homeward.

They both concentrated on enjoying the exhilaration of the perfect sailing conditions, as though they had a secret pact not to discuss the last few days or what waited for them ahead. Peter was constantly aware of the small motor cruiser that kept a reasonable distance off with what looked like a fishing party on board. Nevertheless, he knew now that he was under constant surveillance, even out here at sea.

As they luffed up to the mooring buoy and secured the line, they saw the police car arrive along the shore road and park outside the hotel. Evans was slightly early.

'Dr. Senden. Mr Barrett.' The detective had been waiting with another man who rose to greet them as they entered the hotel lounge 'I trust you enjoyed your sail this afternoon.

Now, Dr. Senden, I'd like you to meet my superintendent Gordon Shepherd.' They shook hands and moved over to a group of seats by the window. Gordon Shepherd drew his chair a little closer to Senden.

'I see from my reports that we've had quite a bit of contact with you recently Dr.Senden. I hope you'll be able to assist us a little further. We've now seen the post mortem results of the body that was discovered yesterday and would like you to come along to the mortuary and see if you can identify it as the one you saw the other day. Unfortunately, it will not be a pleasant task, it never is, but the cadaver had been in the water for some time and, well, it's a bit disfigured.' He looked at Peter who agreed to the request and continued. 'The Coroner has been in as well as the Marine Safety Agency people, also, forensics have informed us that it is male of Middle Eastern extract, identified by the teeth and hair apparently. We have no record of a missing person of that description on our files at the moment and he carried no identifying marks except that his sports clothing was all purchased here according to the labels. We now have the task of trying to find out who he was and what he was doing if he was on the Starlight Princess you very nearly rammed.' He didn't go into other finds they had made, such as the minute particles of sand under his fingernails. These were now being compared with soil samples from areas around the country. They had already been compared with fragments taken from Seamaiden the previous day that had shown negative results.

John agreed to meet Peter later and went off to sort out his programme for the next few days. Peter went with the other two to the mortuary.

The visit to the mortuary proved inconclusive. When Peter gazed on the dead mans face, he could not be sure. His previous encounter had been so brief. The face was now blotchy and swollen and the eyes were closed. The blood around the wound had been cleaned up and a small plug of lint filled the hole in the forehead, probably to save Peter from seeing the gory mess inside. The sheet covering the body was replaced as Peter shook his head and told Evans that he could not be positive in the identification.

As they left the clinical sparseness of the mortuary, Evans asked Peter about the man he had visited in hospital the previous evening, Mr.He Luk. Why had he visited him and the subterfuge used? If Luk was his uncle or a relative, as he had claimed, why the pretence at being his son? Why had he denied all knowledge of him at the earlier interview? Did he know who David Luk was? A person who had apparently entered the country, quite legally, but had not shown up at the hospital.

Peter went over his previous suspicions that He Luk was in fact the man his solicitor had been looking for.

And then there came the awful declaratory statement.

'Dr.Peter Senden, I am arresting you on suspicion of complicity on three counts. Firstly with respect to our investigations into Mr.He Luk, an illegal immigrant. Secondly, on suspicion of being involved with the traffic of illegal immigrants into this country. Thirdly, as a party to the murder of Abrim Sharghan, an illegal immigrant and an Israeli subject, who was suspected of importing drugs to this country.'

The policeman recited the statutory rights to Peter Senden who stood there, mouth suddenly dry and lips sealed in a thin line, stunned and speechless at the new twist he had not even imagined could happen.

The police station cell door was opened and John Barrett entered and looked around.

'Cheer up mate, I've seen worse places than this.' Johns opening remark was meant to sound jovial but it was lost in the overpowering smell of disinfectant that emanated from the latrine in the corner. He sat on the opposite bench and concentrated the concern on his face that he felt. He had been shocked at the news and clutched a copy of the charge in front of him.

Peter looked up from one of the low bunks where he was sitting.

'Christ John, what on earth have I done to deserve all this, I've told them everything I know, and I just don't know how to get through to Evans and his superintendent Shepherd. What happens now?'

'They will interview you again in my presence as your solicitor, they have the necessary powers to hold you for, I believe, thirty six hours if necessary. After that the charge must go before the local magistrate when we can arrange bail. Now, tell me as calmly as possible, what happened at the mortuary? What questions were asked and what you said in reply?'

They continued to converse for a while until the door was opened and a constable requested them to attend in an interview room where Robert Evans and his Detective Constable were waiting.

They went through the formalities of the compact disc recording machine, noting the time and occupants of the room. The detective then outlined the charges again before starting his cross examination.

From the questions it quickly became apparent that he thought that Trevello Cove could have been a convenient landing place for a small yacht to disembark, unnoticed at night.

'We have checked the Lloyd's and Small Ships registries and see that Seamaiden is still registered in the joint names of yourself and your deceased wife. Is that still correct?' Peter confirmed the details.

'During our examination of the craft we noted that you carry an inflatable tender on board, an Avon according to my inventory. Although it was stowed in its bag, we found that it was wet on the inside. Can you explain why that should be?'

Peter thought. Obviously not a sailor or he would have known that it takes ages for an inflatable to dry out properly once it is rolled up. Invariably, the small craft can be rubbed over with a cloth when brought on board, but the restrictions due to deck space on modern yachts make it difficult. Peter answered that he had used the inflatable a few days previously in Plymouth and it had been stowed hurriedly so that he could get under way to St.Mawes.

'So you deny using it to go ashore at Trevello Cove?'

'Certainly. I've never been there from the seaward side and I would think that the approach could be quite dangerous to attempt a landing there.'

'We have a reliable sighting from a fishing vessel that saw your yacht very close inshore on Saturday morning, about half a mile from Trevello Cove. How do you account for that? There is no entry in your log to confirm that you were in that area.'

'Well of course not. I don't make entries directly to the log book anyway. I use a note pad to log weather conditions, times and courses and then write them up in the log later or at some convenient time. If you refer to those notes you will see that I recorded a change of course off the Whelps, by Gull Rock.'

The Inspector opened a large envelope and slid the log and Peter's notes out on the table and thumbed through the note pad. Peter hadn't noticed that they had been taken. He'd been too busy preparing for the afternoon sail to notice their absence.

'O.K., I acknowledge that you have noted here your position and change of course at ten o'clock, but there are no entries in the notes or the log before that time. How do you explain that?' Peter went over the events again, how he criss crossed his original course after nearly hitting the motor yacht and in his panic to get away from the area and just sailed wherever the yacht would pick up the most speed. He had already given the police the position he had plotted immediately before the event and written on the chart.

'Dr. Senden, we now know that He Luk, an illegal immigrant, hired a car in London. Had he flown into Heathrow, he would presumably have hired a car there where his passport would have been required as identification. As it is, the small hire company he used didn't even check his drivers licence. We believe that he was transported ashore by you some time ago and was at a holding post at Trevello waiting for you to pick him up.

We have evidence that the people on the yacht Starlight Princess were also on your own yacht, Seamaiden. We found the fingerprints of someone known as an international drugs dealer, Johnny Chungai. Traces of cannabis have also been found together with soil samples on your vessel that matched the area around Crows Nest Cottage.' The inspector referred to a long list on the sheet in front of him and after a long pause, 'how do you explain the fact that your fingerprints were also found on board the Starlight Princess?'

Peter sat there, as John and the policemen waited for his reply.

There was a knock at the door and a police woman beckoned to Evans. He terminated the recording equipment and followed her out, leaving the two men to sit in uncomfortable silence with the constable, John wondering just how much his client really knew and what he had not been told.

Assistant Chief Constable, Malcolm Archer was waiting in his office with Cmdr.Hoskins and Chief Supt. Gordon Shepherd as Robert Evans knocked and entered. Maj. Jack Fellows stood quietly by the window and was not introduced.

'I believe you met Comdr. Hoskins the other day. On his initiative, I have just finished speaking to the Home Secretary who has informed me in very strict confidence that the man Abrim Sharghan, whom you have identified as the dead man from Israel, is in fact an American citizen and was working for the Commander on a matter of US national security. It seems that this man was involved in undercover work for the C.I.A. and infiltrated an offshore drugs gang that has been active between France and this country. His murder is almost certainly a gang killing and most unlikely to have involved Dr. Senden whom I see on the charge sheet that you are currently holding in connection with the case.

Now, Supt Shepherd has just had some information from Hong Kong with respect to your Mr.Luk.' Archer sat back, still privately glowing inside and indulging in his self importance of speaking personally to the Home Secretary.

Gordon Shepherd took over the conversation.

'As you know, we have been in touch with the police in Hong Kong about this gentleman. Difficult now because the old channels and contacts have changed. Apparently he is known there under various names, one of which is Carter. According to the emigration and airline ticket information they have supplied, Mr.Simon Carter travelled to China from Hong Kong several days ago using his British passport. It would now seem that if our Mr.Luk is the same person, he arrived in this country quite legally from Beijing on that British passport. Major Fellows here has requested his immediate release from the immigration department and that request has been dealt with.

Also, I have been informed that the CIA investigations into Senden's father may be connected and we have been requested by the Commander and Superintendent Seiger in Special Branch to give Peter Senden a free rein at the moment so that those enquiries can be continued.

Whilst I appreciate your reasoning behind arresting Senden, we have no alternative at this stage except to drop all charges and release him. Your earlier deductions on drug smuggling now appear to be correct.'

Evans looked crestfallen as he took in his superior's orders and was politely dismissed from the gathering. As he reached the door, Hoskins enquired.

Any news yet on the A.P.B. you have out on Capt. Piltcher?'

Evans replied. 'Afraid not sir. In fact we don't know that he is actually officially missing. It was only as a result of the break in to the cottage in Trevello that, you sir, asked us to trace him. He must be in his early eighties and we conducted a line search yesterday in the nearby fields with thirty five men in case he had collapsed or been taken ill somewhere near the house. I regret that nothing was found.

If you have read my report of yesterday, you will have seen that we have gained a little more information on his background. It seems he used to stay at a friend's house in Lymington. Before that, he owned a substantial property just outside Lyme Regis. Apparently he was also a keen racegoer and placed large bets at meetings around the country. The cottage at Tregello was rented. The two mysterious American tourists who found him have not as yet been traced.'

He hadn't liked the way that Commander Hoskins had been thrust on him earlier in the week by his Super during his interview with Peter Senden. He hoped his last remark hadn't missed its point on him. He knew nothing about this American Intelligence Officer who seemed to know plenty about Senden's affairs. He hadn't had time to really consider the Commanders role, except that when large amounts of money had been mentioned his mind had automatically sensed that drug trafficking or illegal immigration could be the basis of his involvement. It now seemed, from what had just been said, that he was probably correct in that assumption. However, he still could not understand why an American should be involved. There were no communications from Customs and Excise on any joint operation, either with the police or, with the French or other continental authorities, as was the usual case relating to drugs events.

'From the report, you will have also seen that Piltcher was suspected of smuggling gold bullion between the Russians and Turks whilst he was commanding a Russian cruise ship on the Black Sea in the mid eighties. The court records of 1986 show that he was acquitted after the Crown failed to substantiate the claim. We gathered the basis for our enquiry into the court case from the lady who he stayed with at Lymington. She also provided our colleagues in the Hampshire force with a photograph, but its years old and he's probably aged since.'

Hoskins thanked him. The remark hadn't missed its point. He secretly wished he could take the well meaning detective into his confidence, as he had done with the mans superiors, to the real involvement of the man who had died out there at sea.

'I have an urgent meeting to attend in London this evening I have your report Inspector and will be reading it on the way.'

Major Fellows spoke for the first time. 'And now we will bid you good evening gentlemen.' He hadn't uttered a word during the meeting and had not been introduced. He left with the Commander.

The two men sat silently in the car as it sped along the A30 towards the M5 motorway and London. Hoskins read through the relevant parts of the Police Inspector's report before replacing it in his briefcase.

'Nothing new there, I'm afraid, the people we want to talk to seem to have gone to ground. I'm most disappointed that you did not confer with me before ordering Carter to be released from hospital.'

Fellows looked up from the newspaper crossword.'Can only apologise old boy, no idea you wanted to question him or that he was the Carter referred to in the sanatorium the other week.'

There was a stony silence between them as the car manoeuvred its way onto the M5 motorway. Then Fellows asked.

'Gather you spoke to young Senden yesterday what was that all about?'

Hoskins thought, so the bait had been taken.

'Major, since I've been over here I haven't had the opportunity to assess Senden myself. I wanted to make it clear to him that finding these people is of paramount importance to our search. Just had a quiet chat to make sure he knew, that's all.'

The Major looked ahead. 'How's your search for the W88 warhead secrets progressing?'

'So you know we are still looking into the espionage matter at Los Alamos.'

'Of course we do, what we would like to know is why your team are poking around in the U.K. Do you believe there is a British link connected to the affair?'

The Commander grinned. 'You don't really expect an answer on that one Major but let me tell you that our investigating team are looking at many aspects of the security breaches of recent years, which are now public knowledge. Some of course affect your own security here in Britain, Trident for instance. Our brief is to keep searching world wide to find out where those secrets ended up. Over here of course, this *Thinman* business has taken precedence for the time being.'

He couldn't tell the Major that many of his specialists were now confined to the *Thinman* task force. Some had returned to the States and Germany where they were trolling through records and bank accounts looking for any indication of a missing W85 warhead. He shuddered at the thought of the CIA conspirators back in Langley and had started his own covert investigation into how they would acquire the nuclear device to sustain their ill thought out goal for the *Crusader* project.

The Major persisted. 'So do I take it that you are not investigating anyone over here with respect to the loss of the W88 nuclear multi warhead designs?'

'Let's put it this way Major, all our main efforts at present are confined to *Thinman*. When we hopefully find what we are looking for it's my intention to retire from active service and the Los Alamos espionage affair will be taken over by someone else.'

He glanced at his British counterpart and changed the subject.

'Any plans for retirement yourself?'

The major chuckled. 'Couple of more years yet. Then I hope to be able to concentrate my entire time to my collection.'

'What sort of collection do you have?'

'Motor cars dear boy, motor cars and lots of them, over forty, mainly pre war you know. I keep the collection in a series of barns at the moment. My aim when I retire is to build one large covered area in which to bring the whole collection together.' The Major then went into detail on his favourite subject extolling the virtues of the many cars in his care, the private maintenance team he employed and his latest acquisitions.

'It sounds like an expensive hobby.'

'Married money dear boy, money. What about you, are you married? Any children?'

Hank always dreaded the question whenever it came up as it invariably did from time to time. The question was constantly with him. Why had his life been so severely penalised? It made his inside shudder just to say those words again and try to sound casual about their awful content as he tried to remember their faces.

'Wife and two kids, killed in a ballooning accident many years ago. My son and daughter would have been in their mid thirties by now.'

'I'm sorry.' The Major spoke sideways at the window, avoiding any eye contact. His own life could have been different had his wife allowed them to try for a family. Instead all he had was a car collection. There was little said between them as they continued their journey, each man thinking and trying to get behind what the other had said.

'I'm going back to my office tomorrow morning.' The two men were driving back to the hotel and John broke the silence that had lasted for the last couple of miles.

Peter looked straight ahead; he was still in the after shock of his arrest and release with an apology but no explanation given by the police as to why they had so suddenly decided to drop all charges. He felt that he was still on the hook and suspicions about his involvement with illegal immigration would not be going away. He turned the rear view mirror to look for the car that must surely be tailing them but the road was empty. The Mercedes at that time was driving carefully a few cars ahead of them.

'A lot has happened in the last few days Peter, I came down here for a couple of days sailing with you and all we have managed is to get constantly involved with the police. You seem to be sitting under an unfortunate star sign or something for so much to have happened.'

Peter turned on the car radio. 'I don't blame you for wanting to distance yourself from the events I seem to have invited on myself, but I still need your help. Christ knows, we haven't even started to get to the bottom of what is implied by my father's letters. If they were smuggling gold or something all those years ago, I'd like to know where it was. Surely, you as the administrator of his will must establish without doubt that everything is tidied up.'

'That's true, but I said this morning I have other clients waiting on my time which is not exactly cheap. What about you, have you completed your overseas contracts or do you have to return to Europe after this?'

John had suspected for some time that Peter's work was not as free lance as he would have him believe. He remembered six years previously when he had acted as a reference for Peter when he had taken a position in one of the Home Office departments. The detail on the form John had filled and the subsequent interview had told him that this was no ordinary job.

Peter laughed, 'I'm supposed to be on leave, should be thinking about future work but I want to get this lot cleared up first. I must try and establish what really happened to my father.'

'I thought you'd satisfied yourself that he had a heart attack after a diving expedition.'

The silence that greeted the comment told John once again that Peter was holding something back.

'Well, if you can't tell me the whole story I can not help you on that one.'

'John, you have a good idea whom it is I really work for and due to reasons of national security I'm not allowed to say how Philip died.'

'But you do know?'

'Yes.'

Again there was silence between the two friends. The same impenetrable silence of people indulging in their own private thoughts, as in the other vehicle carrying the two military men, speeding them towards London.

The local news was on the car radio with a brief report that a man had been arrested in connection with the case on illegal immigration. He was reputed to be a member of a gang responsible for the death of the unidentified body found in the sea earlier in the week.

John reached over and turned the voice down.

'That station is either a bit behind the times, or the police don't want to release too much information. I get the feeling that there is a lot more behind what has been happening than I have been told.' Again he fell into silence as his friend said nothing. 'Look, it's only Tuesday, why don't we meet up later in the week again, perhaps by then the police will have tracked down Piltcher or Carter and we can ask them directly what they know about this retirement fund business.' Then, as if it was an afterthought. 'Oh, by the way, in the confusion over your arrest I forgot to tell you that a David Luk phoned my office this afternoon and has made an appointment for Thursday with respect to the notices we put out about Philips death.'

So it was true, his half brother was here. The immigration officer had mentioned that Luk's son had flown in to Heathrow the previous week, but he hadn't expected the name to be Luk.

'What on earth has he contacted you for, how did he know your office address for God's sake. What's going on John?' Peter was suddenly annoyed and roused himself out of the self pity of his arrest.

'You know him then? He has apparently responded to one of the legal notices our firm put in the press with respect to your fathers will. You know we advertised for information on the whereabouts of Carter and Piltcher some time ago. From what you told me about your encounter with Carter in the hospital I gather that David Luk is his son.' He gave a quick sideways glance at Peter, remembering the strange wording of Philip Senden's Will that he had still not confided to Peter. Why had Philip stated 'her sons' as benefactors, could David Luk be the son referred too as just David, or was he here to represent his father in some way. The answer would not be known until he met the man on Thursday.

The next morning Peter was in Plymouth and going through the formalities of admission to HMS Drake. He was escorted to a conference room where Doug Lawson and Major Jack Fellows were waiting for him. Lawson reiterated his telephoned condolences as Peter looked across to the Major who Doug then introduced.

'I hope you don't mind me bringing in Major Jack Fellows. He heads up the Special Services Branch in MI5 that deals with military liaison in MI6 and foreign services such as CIA. .....Well Peter what's on your mind'.

Peter Senden would have preferred to have spoken to his section head alone but decided that that Fellows was a safe bet. Hoskins had also mentioned his name during their strange conversation. He started at the beginning, outlining his visit to Downshall and everything that had happened since, including his encounter with Carter and his suspicion that he himself was under surveillance by the CIA.

He then outlined his suspicions concerning Hank Hoskins.

Fellows had been making notes.

'I agree with you Senden. It would be most unusual for anyone, even Commander Hoskins, to have an individual copy of the W85 nuclear code manual. Did he say which satellite he was interested in?'

'Unfortunately not. All I know is that he seemed worried about asking the question, I gathered that for some reason he didn't want his own people involved. Just seemed highly suspicious to me, knowing that the W85 handbooks come in pairs under lock and key and require a satellite confirmation code from the White House before the final action links can be deployed.'

'The man Carter. Did he say who beat him up or where he had been since landing at Heathrow?'

'He wouldn't tell me anything. I believe he may have thought I was somehow thrust on him by the immigration people.'

The three men fell silent while Jack Fellows consulted his notebook.

'Mr.Lawson, would you leave us for a few minutes. I'd like to speak to Senden alone.' Doug Lawson looked at the Major, slightly bewildered but seniority prevailed and he left as requested.

'Senden, There is a lot going on that I can't explain to you at this time. I want you to attend a meeting with me at Thames House on Thursday evening. I have to rely on you not to mention what has been said today. In the meantime I will speak to the Deputy Director General on the matter of Hoskins even though I cannot think what he could be up to. Till Thursday then, you may be in for some surprises, we'll get Lawson back and I'll bid you good morning.'

Chapter 22. Carter and Son .

John Barrett's office was situated in a small Georgian house that faced out on to the cathedral close at Winchester. A tranquil area of mown lawns surrounded by plane trees, which allowed dappled sunlight to pattern the grass in various shades of green. It was a quiet corner of the city and cordoned off to the tourists by wrought iron fencing. The Wessex cathedral with its spireless tower and priceless ancient library rose majestically from its medieval foundations and was the picture frame scene visible from the various partners' rooms.

At ten o'clock that Thursday morning, two men arrived at the front door and rang the bell.

Sally Denning phoned through to John who was again looking through Philip Senden's file and checking the various actions he had already ticked off in preparation for his ten o'clock appointment with David Luk.

'Your ten o'clock appointment Mr.Barrett; Mr.Luk and his father are here.'

His father! Was this at last going to be his introduction to the elusive Simon Carter?

'Bring them up straight away Sally.'

The large oak door to the office opened and John's secretary showed the two men in. John leant across his desk and shook them both by the hand and indicated seats while Sally took their requests for coffee.

The three men sat there and John opened out his arms in a gesture of indication to start the meeting.

'Well Mr.Luk, you requested this appointment but I need to know, am I speaking to two Mr. Luks or two Mr.Carters or what?'

David Luk glanced at his father who remained silent. The son was in his mid forties, with receding hair that he occasionally swept back with his hands even though there was not much hair to arrange. John could see without doubt that the man in front of him could be Peter's half brother, the similarities were quite startling. He wore a charcoal grey suit and carried the air of a man who had made his way in the world. He lent forward, fingering a plaster on his chin.

'Thank you for seeing us Mr.Barrett. I know some explanation is necessary before proceeding with the purpose of our visit. My name is David Luk. My birth certificate gives my name as Carter but some years ago I had my name changed by Deed Poll to Luk which was an old family name. In fact some of our businesses registered by my grandfather bore the name somewhere in their title. Although I considered myself to be British, I was registered as a resident of Hong Kong before the colony was handed over to the Chinese. To enable my children and indeed myself to blend into the new community and administration more easily, I decided to change our name. I was divorced some time ago and now live between apartments in London and San Jose in Costa Rica.

My father has developed several names over the years depending on his circumstances. Most of his business is carried out in the name of Luk, but his real name is still Carter.'

John addressed himself to Simon Carter.

'Well Mr.Carter, according to the police service you are classed as an illegal immigrant within the meaning of the latest amendments to the Immigration Act. One who has absconded from custody and I'm not sure that I should be speaking to you, unless of course you have come here to give yourself up. Perhaps you could tell me what's going on.'

Simon Carter felt in an inside pocket of his suit jacket and slapped his British passport down on the desk in front of John.

'Who says I'm illegal, there's a fucking passport to prove who I am. Go on, look at it; it's quite legal until it runs out in three years time.' He was a different character to his son who looked on uncomfortably at his father's aggressiveness as John darted a surprised glance at him.

'It's the sodding British authorities who got it wrong. I entered the U.K. quite legally as Carter, as I'm entitled to. I'm sure you can check that out with the people at Heathrow and, incidentally, as far as I am concerned I was never in custody or charged with any offence. I just got up and discharged myself from that bloody hospital. Also, for your information I have already been questioned by the police down in Cornwall about my perfectly legal entitlement to be here. Kept me bloody well locked up they did.'

John had examined the pages of the passport during Carter's vehement outburst.

'Well sir, your passport looks fine to me, why didn't you show this to the officer who came to see you in hospital. It could have saved a lot of time and your own inconvenience at being questioned by the police.'

'I have my reasons,' the old man growled the words and his son took up the dialogue.

'I had no idea that my father had been in hospital or that a problem had arisen over his citizenship. I've persuaded him to come here in the first instance because he wanted to get hold of Peter Senden but couldn't raise him on the 'phone and your number was the only other point of contact we had.' John thought, typical Peter, phone not charged up as usual.

'My father is having some business problems at home and he asked me to join him here in the U.K. to help him find someone whom I gather he thinks has the financial backing to his current problems. Unfortunately, my stepmother has chosen this particular time to shove off with someone else and it has affected him quite badly. I've no idea why he should have tried to hide his true identity.'

'Oh shut up you little turd you know I'm broke. It will affect you soon as well; you're still a shareholder and director of a lot of those enterprises.' Carter had turned on his son his voice raised as Sally brought in the coffees and raised her eyebrows to John. David Luk gave her an apologetic look.

'Please gentlemen. We are not here to argue. I would like to know why you are here and what I can do for you. I have presumed that this visit concerns the death of Philip Senden who, I believe Mr.Carter, you knew quite well and with whom you had spasmodic correspondence until quite recently.'

Carter looked at John and still with a raised voice. 'That bloody thief and his accomplice Piltcher owe me and I'm here to get what's due to me.' He stumped the desk with is fist which John thought probably hurt him.

'Please Mr.Carter, if you can't conduct yourself more modestly I shall have to ask you to leave.' It was the last thing that John wanted but if he was going to learn anything the conversation would have to be rational. 'Now, please let me hear your side of the story. As you must be aware by now, I am the sole executor of Philip Senden's Will and therefore the administrator representing his interests. His papers suggested that you and he were connected along with a Capt. Piltcher and a T.Holmes in what he called a retirement fund. This suggests that there may be some asset value which, by law, I have to investigate in connection with his estate and in assessing his tax situation.'

Carter thought for a minute and then in a slow voice as though his mind was somewhere far away he started to talk.

'Senden has blackmailed me for most of my life, I'm getting on now and don't give a sod who knows, or the reason why.'

His son bent close and whispered in his ear, a reminder perhaps to moderate his language a little.

'Yes, there was something we called the retirement fund but it was lost with the Acacia Lady. In spite of that, that shit pulled my tits and milked me over the years because of what he knew. I could afford it then, but now I'm broke as I said before and I'm here to find out what your client knew about my gold.'

John had started to write some notes and butted in.

'Let's start at the beginning. What exactly was this retirement fund and how was it lost?'

The old man lent forward and looked at them, a tiny thread of saliva clinging to his chin.

'About ten million dollars worth of gold I should think, guarded by something so terribly abhorrent and horrendous that I have constant nightmares over it. O.K., we made a pact on that ship that the gold would be shared but they never knew the truth about the dragon that now guards it night and day and will do for the next ten thousand years. They found the gold all right, after we left Gibraltar. Wanted to know where it came from, silly sods as if I was going to tell them. Argued and threatened to expose me. Me, the owner. Mutiny I'd call it. Then it was lost due to the incompetence of Piltcher.'

His face went ashen and he was talking almost incoherently in short bursts as though in a dream. David Luk put his hand on his father's arm.

'Father, you're not making any sense. Are you feeling all right?'

Carter brushed the hand aside and rose shakily to his feet, his mouth dribbling.

'I've kept the secret for all these years. Those bastards knew I would be done for if the truth had been told at the hearing. If I'd told the whole story I was a dead man.....the Chinese you see......' He clutched at his chest as his legs crumpled and he crashed onto the floor before either of the other two could catch him.

John punched the telephone. 'Sally, get an ambulance here urgently, I think Mr. Carter has had a stroke.'

The two men were immediately on their knees beside the still form of Simon Carter, the ammonia smell of urine from his involuntary loss of bladder control strong in their nostrils. David loosened the tie and felt for the cartoid pulse at his father's neck.

'His pulse is there, pounding away and he's breathing.'

Sally burst into the room as David made the announcement. She went down on her knees beside him.

'Help me to role him over to the recovery position.'

They rolled him over and Sally adjusted his legs and arms to what she considered to be the correct recovery position. Another member of the staff came in with a blanket that was carefully laid over him and people crowded around the door all offering advice before the ambulance siren announced its arrival and Simon Carter stirred and tried to sit up.

Peter Senden was sitting in a small waiting room in another part of the building. He had asked to be present at the meeting with David Luk whom he wanted to meet. John had told him that it would be improper for him to attend. Instead, he had advised him to wait in case a suitable opportunity arose for them to meet after the appointment. When he heard the commotion and the ambulance, he put down the newspaper he was reading, wandered along the corridor and out of curiosity peered into the room from behind the others who were standing there.

The eyes of the two brothers met in instant recognition as Peter pushed through the crowd and entered the room. They had fought on the Starlight Princess the other night. The eyes were the only exchange and the reason for his half brother being on the yacht would have to wait until later.

The paramedic team arrived behind him and ordered the room to be cleared except for David Luk and John Barrett, sitting on the floor beside the patient, who had forced himself up on one elbow with the colour flowing back in his face. He was coherent now as he looked around, slightly dazed and fished in his pocket, pulling out a small pump spray.

'Angina attack,' he gasped as he sprayed the glyceryl trinitrate under his tongue and fell back into the protective arms of one of the paramedics.

The sound of the ambulance siren grew weaker as Simon Carter in company with his son was driven away to hospital.

Sally brought fresh coffees into the office where John Barrett and Peter Senden sat discussing the circumstances that had led up to Carter's collapse.

John was looking through the window where a sudden summer shower was beating its rhythm against the panes of glass. The area in front of the cathedral was emptying as visitors scurried with their umbrellas to shelter in the small antique and book shops that abounded around the Close. He asked Sally to drive over to the Royal Hampshire Hospital and find out from David Luk where he was staying or how he could be contacted. In the resulting confusion he had completely omitted to ask for details.

He looked over to Peter as he retrieved an ashtray from the bottom side drawer of the desk and pushed it towards him.

'Please feel free to smoke if you wish I'm certainly having one in spite of my resolution not to.' He lit up a panatela and exhaled the smoke before continuing. 'Well Peter, I am not sure where to start. Carter seemed to be very agitated about your father, quite vehement about him actually and also Piltcher. His son David said very little, very business like though.' He picked up the brief notes he had made and scanned through them. 'They are over here to see someone about finance for their business interests in Hong Kong but we didn't get very far on that one. Unfortunately, as soon as I mentioned Philip, Carter just took off, accusing both him and Piltcher of blackmail, and mutiny. I'm not sure if he was really aware of all that he was saying.'

'It looks as though your interpretation of those letters the other evening may have been correct then, but I don't understand what my father could have been doing. Blackmail you say. That's a very serious accusation and I would want to know a lot more about the details before I could believe my father was involved.'

'I understand that they discovered a hoard of gold and had some sort of agreement to share it. The problem seems to be that it was lost somewhere along the way and is guarded by what he calls the Dragon whatever that is. Did your father never mention any of this to you? Carter said that over ten million dollars worth of gold was involved.'

Peter stiffened at the mention of the Dragon again. It hurt him that due to the secrecy surrounding his father's death he could not say anything to John about the last words his father had uttered. What was the object referred to by the strange metaphor? Instead he feigned surprise as he remembered Capt. Robertson's conversation and what the US Navy Commander had said to him at his first interview with the police in Truro.

'Christ John, that's a lot dosh to be arguing about. What exactly did Carter say, I mean about my fathers share, was that what they meant by the retirement fund do you think.'

'Well, the old boy was getting a bit upset by then, just started to blurt out all sorts of things, but when I asked him what the retirement fund was he just said ten million dollars worth of gold.'

'Didn't he say what this dragon was? Did he say Dragon, or was it *Dragon's Morsel?*'

'Just that a dragon was guarding the gold that Piltcher lost and would do so for the next ten thousand years, I presumed it was just an expression meaning something like, the sea is guarding it until some time in the future. I doubt that there are any dragons out in the English Channel, he made no mention of the *Dragon's Morsel* only a dragon,'

He stopped as he recalled Peter's earlier instructions to him. 'Didn't you say earlier that you thought the *Dragon's Morsel* was the name of a ship?'

Peter blew out a large cloud of smoke, as though not listening. His previous seriousness was suddenly broken as he grinned and said thoughtfully.

'Bloody hell mate, this talk about treasure must be serious, the old man was searching for it when he........ suffered his heart attack.'

John nodded his agreement. He didn't comment on Peter's earlier slip of the tongue or his apparent selectivity in answering questions that he didn't like.

'Certainly seems that way but I'm not sure that you can lay claim to any of it if that's what your thinking.' John had been taught to be cautious and seeing Peters rising enthusiasm was wary of his friends new thought processes.

'How do you know he was looking for the gold before he died?' John's eyes narrowed. He had started to realise as before that he was not being told the whole story.

'Pure conjecture, he must have been looking for the gold, everything points to the fact that the gold and the retirement fund are the same thing, remember what Captain Robertson told me after the Memorial Service, father had been searching for a treasure ship for years.

They sat there for a while, contemplating what had transpired over the last half an hour and looking through the letter transcripts again together with the Admiralty chart that Peter had left with the papers.

At last, Peter stood up and did a slow pace around the room, his arms folded across his chest as if thinking deeply. He stopped suddenly facing John across the desk.

'Have you kept up your British Sub- Aqua Club Certification John? I believe last time we spoke about it you were up to 'Sports Diver'.'

John feigned surprise at the question; he'd been half expecting Peter to come up with something like this. 'If your thinking what I think your thinking the answer is definitely no.'

'But you are a qualified diver. It's the only way John, we've got to go out there and find out for ourselves what this is all about.'

John raised his head slowly, thinking about the horrors of diving in the gloomy waters of that part of the English Channel, with its low visibility and strong tidal currents. Most of his qualifying dives had been made in the Med. Only a few had been in the Channel, mainly on wrecks off Anvil Point in Dorset. He was looking forward to another visit to the Aegean later in the season.

'Actually, I'm now qualified up to Dive Leader level. I'm supposed to be taking the Advanced qualification with my club in a couple of week's time.' He grinned at Peter as he leant back in his chair and took another cheroot. 'Anyway, what you are thinking is highly speculative. We don't know for certain that there is any gold out there or where it is. To be quite frank, I think we should be relying on more than the ravings of an old man before rushing to conclusions. If there was gold down there, it could have been salvaged long ago. In any case, if Philip knew about it, why didn't he bring it up years ago when he had the diving boat and ample opportunity to spend time searching?'

Peter had sat down, the ideas and thoughts of the treasure running around his head like excited competitors in a sports arena, running a race where the finishing line had been taken away. Surely there was some way of verifying the story. The Captain had spoken of a treasure ship, Hank Hoskins, the American commander, had mentioned gold on both occasions he had met him. His mother had described the Acacia Lady as a golden ship; if blackmail had taken place for all those years, surely there must have been some foundation for the story and the so called retirement fund. The last time he had met Carter in the Truro Hospital, he'd seemed perfectly sound of mind, hardly a person likely to be off his rocker. Why had his father made all those trips to Alderney surrounded by secrecy if there was nothing there? He thought back to the fight on board the Starlight Princess, Carter's son David, seeking the same information.

John knew his friend well and could sense his frustration.

'Let's talk to Simon Carter again, he may have calmed down a bit now. We'll try and find out what he can add to the story and also what David Luk's interest is in all this.' He was thinking about the wording in the Will again and looked directly at Peter as he carefully couched his words. 'I haven't mentioned this to you before, but your father's Will.' He hesitated again feeling slightly uneasy as he looked at Peter, 'Your father's Will has a specific clause which mentions something about your mother having another son named David who is supposed to share in this retirement fund.'

To John's surprise, Peter laughed. He then went on to explain the conversation with his mother and the account of her previous marriage to Simon Carter.

There was a sudden tap on the door and Sally Denning came in soaked by the rain in spite of the small umbrella she was now folding down.

'Afraid he got away and didn't leave his details with the medics. That bloody car park, by the time I'd found a parking space and got my ticket, they were long gone.'

'Are you saying he discharged himself from the hospital in that condition and his son allowed him to?'

'I'm afraid so Mr.Barrett, they just bundled out of the ambulance straight into a taxi and left. I did get the taxi operator's number if that's any good.'

'Thanks Sally, seems to me they don't want anyone to know their whereabouts, I wonder what they know that we don't, perhaps there's a more sinister reason for them being here.'

Sally left the room and Peter picked up the file and tapped it with his finger.

'The answers still in here somewhere, I'll bet you they know exactly where the gold is and right now are on their way to finding it. Then they'll do the vanishing act again and we'll never know the answer.'

'There's still one person we haven't heard from yet, the mysterious Capt. Piltcher. I wonder where he's vanished to.' John tapped his pen on the desk top as he thought.

'Look Peter, how long do you think it would take to get down to Alderney, we could possibly fly there from Southampton. Take our diving kit and hire a boat. Go over to the position you found in the notes the other night, have a quick dive on the spot.'

'Now you're talking, but why make our attempt so public. All that gear and other people involved as crew. Why not get down to Seamaiden again this weekend and sail there. At least then we are unlikely to be under scrutiny from the locals and our time will be our own.'

The two men continued discussing their plans until Sally 'phoned through to remind John about his train to London and the appointment he was to attend with another client.

Chapter 23. Rescue at sea.

There was a neap moon with low scud cloud cover, very dark with the usual clamminess in the air caused by the night fog. Tiny moisture particles, lit up by the red and green navigation lights, cast ghostly shadow halo's around the bows of Seamaiden, with little sparkles of light falling on the black sea ahead and reflecting off the wet fore deck like a candle lit cathedral window.

Jessica had joined them and they had left at 4.00 o'clock in the afternoon. Peter Senden had calculated that they would arrive at Braye Harbour on Alderney as the tide turned at about 5.00 o'clock on Saturday evening, a voyage of some 120 miles. The wind was light as they left the mooring and Seamaiden slipped out under engine, past the Black Rock beacon on the starboard side and St. Anthony's Head lighthouse on the eastern protective arm of the Fal estuary.

The yacht was on a port tack making a good 7 knots over the ground with the force 4 north westerly wind on her port quarter. The weather forecast for Portsmouth, Plymouth and Fastnet was for the wind to back slowly south westerly and then veer north west later with wind force increasing to strength 5 or 6 possibly 7 later The coastal reports announced the barometer dropping in the Western Approaches as another low pressure system approached, typical of that summer even though it was now mid July.

It was John's turn on watch and he sat huddled over the tiller, watching the pale glow of the compass card as it swayed in its sealed gimballed world, the apparent wind indicator digits rising and falling slightly with each wave. When they had set off in the afternoon it had been very warm, he was glad he'd taken Peters advice and packed his thermals. His waterproofs were dripping wet from the night mist that could just be seen as a dim white circle around the yacht where sea and mist combined. It was their own small world, a circle that occasionally became larger as the visibility increased and then smaller as the patchy fog became denser. A shower of cold sea water added to his discomfort as the bows plunged into a rogue wave, sending up a spray that, by the time the wind and gravity took its inevitable course, landed on top of him, the salt stinging the eyes.

As the previous evening had waned away to darkness they had seen the great loom of the Eddystone lighthouse, flashing its position, two every ten seconds, but now the low sea mist had closed in with just an occasional glimpse of the stars overhead. They had seen little else, a few fishing boats and another small craft running parallel with them, about a mile to the north, its green starboard light dipping and rising.

The cabin lights had been dimmed and Peters shape appeared silhouetted against them in the companionway as he climbed into the cockpit and stood balancing himself with his knees against the portside seating. He was grinning in the enjoyment of the night air, his hands holding two steaming mugs of soup.

John accepted the soup gratefully. Apart from dry water biscuits, it was about all his stomach would accept. He was not inclined to sea sickness, just slight queasiness from the constant motion of the yacht as she ploughed her furrow through the water.

'Anything around,' he enquired as he checked the Wichard snap hook on his safety line that connected him with the yacht. He knew that Peter had been playing with the new toy, a radar set, that Higgs had installed for him the previous day.

'There's a whole cluster of big ships right out on the limit of the range scale, could just be clutter or the Casquetes starting to show up.' He looked puzzled. 'May be finger problems on my part, I'm still getting used to the tuning control. Probably tankers entering the shipping separation zone. I saw another ship passing some way behind us a while ago which I would think was the Plymouth to St.Malo ferry. I've seen other small targets but they come and go, probably reflections off waves or other small craft. I'm also getting an occasional blip from the racon on the Channel Light Float.'

'What about the lights we saw previously.'

'Oh, I think it's something quite small, been travelling on a parallel course as far as I can see, I'm only getting an occasional blip from the radar.'

The two men sat there drinking, John getting wet and Peter sheltering under the protection of the spray hood. Peter had planned watches of three hours apiece and John had about another hour and a half to go before handing over the tiller and going below to the comfort of the quarter berth for a couple of hours of shuteye.

The tide had now turned in their favour again and the velvet black sea surface carved past them, each wave with its breaking foam top illuminated firstly by the coloured navigation lights the as the wave went sliding under them and then the small white stern light as the transom lifted to its power.

Peter looked at his watch. 'Two thirty five. The coast guard weather forecast is due in a few minutes, I'd better get down there and have a listen before I come on watch, I'll check the dead reckoning position against the G.P.S. as well.'

He went below leaving his helmsman watch keeper sitting there as sailors have done since time immemorial, alone, staring at the compass, adjusting the tiller to the feel of the yacht, glancing at the sail trim and getting cold and wet.

When Peter relieved John's watch it was getting light and he shared the solitude with the fishing boat about a mile off their port side that would vanish for a while and then appear again according to the sea state. The view behind him was not so good, with high cumulonimbus clouds shining white over the lower grey ominous cumulus clouds bellowing up against a darker western sky. The wind was now a point abaft the port quarter and after dropping for a short while had increased as daylight presented itself. The apparent wind indicator showed fifteen knots, which implied that the true wind strength was already reaching force five. Seamaiden was now downwind sailing at eight to nine knots with her jib and main sails straining at the taught sheets that had been gradually let out as the wind backed.

'I've been watching her for some time.' John indicated the other boat to Peter as he took the watch and raised his binoculars to it.

'She's a small fishing boat the sort used for day sea angling, about thirty feet having a rough ride I should think, taking a bit of a risk being out here with the worsening weather forecast. It's strange that she's been on that course all night, she must be capable of a few more knots than Seamaiden. I'll alter course a few degrees to port to get a little closer just in case. See if you can raise her on the radio when you go down below.'

John descended the steps into the saloon that felt warm after his long sojourn at the tiller. He looked over at the mop of fair hair that was Jessica, in the starboard bunk her sleeping bag pulled up around her head and in a deep sleep, oblivious to the morning outside. He discarded his wet gear as he reached for the thermos left strapped down in the galley and poured out some hot chocolate that Peter had prepared before taking over the watch. He felt the warmth of the liquid taking its effect as he sat at the navigation desk and checked the GPS position against Peter's plot on the chart before reaching for the radio hand mic. and pressing the talk button on low power.

'Fishing vessel in approximate position 14 miles due west of the Channel Light Float, this is the yacht Seamaiden calling you on channel sixteen, over.' The hiss of the VHF squelch came through the loudspeaker but no reply. John tried several times but the radio hiss was not broken by a reply.

Suddenly the VHF came to life but not with what John was expecting.

'Seamaiden, Seamaiden, Seamaiden, this is patrol frigate HMS Pembroke calling you, over.' John acknowledged the call and changed to the channel that was then requested by the frigate's radio officer.

'Seamaiden; this is Pembroke, your position and course please sir.'

John found himself perspiring suddenly, he wasn't used to radio procedures and thought of calling Peter down. He qlanced quickly at the G.P.S. screen.

'HMS Pembroke, this is Seamaiden. My current position is 49 degrees 55 minutes North, 03 degrees 15 minutes West. Our course is 95 degrees magnetic. Over.' There were a few seconds pause, then, 'Seamaiden, Pembroke. I have to advise you sir that you are sailing towards a twenty mile diameter exclusion zone. As of 0400 hours this morning all ships and seagoing vessels are prohibited for safety reasons from entering the zone that consists of an area bounded by a radius of ten miles from the position that I shall now give you and will then repeat.'

John took down the position and affirmed the details before ending the transmission and returning to the hiss on sixteen the calling and safety channel. Almost immediately he then heard an emergency navigation warning broadcast from Portland coastguard. It was procedural practice for such warnings to be given on an alternative channel to the calling and safety channel. This time the Portland operator called for 'radio seelonce' as he gave out the same details that John had just received from the frigate. The urgency was emphasised to the extent that merchant ships in the area were advised to ignore the shipping lane traffic separation zone where the prohibited area overlapped. The coastguard broadcast was closely followed by broadcasts from the French Crossma safety organisation and then Cherbourg Radio, adding information about severe penal fines introduced for any ship ignoring the emergency regulation jointly declared by both the British and French governments that morning.

John looked at the chart with the circle he had drawn and then bounded up the companionway steps to Peter, sitting at the helm, looking and pointing into the air as a Fishery Protection surveillance aircraft circled them.

Peter started to say something but the urgency in John's voice stopped him.

'We've got to change to a northerly course. I've just been speaking to HMS Pembroke, there's some sort of exclusion zone ahead which we've got to circumnavigate, you'd better come down and check the new course I've laid on the chart.' He described the various broadcasts he'd heard and that 'radio seelonce' was in operation.

'I'm already sailing a more northerly course to try and get nearer to that other boat, strange thing is that as soon as I started to converge, she also altered course more northerly to keep roughly the same distance between us.' Peter swept his eyes around the horizon before going below with John to examine the chart.

'Phew, that's a massive area to close off, must be some sort of naval exercise. They're usually announced in advance although I've never heard of them closing an area like this. Accounts for all those ships I could see on the radar.' He stabbed on the Navtex, which immediately confirmed on its print out that the information had been available for the last three quarters of an hour. The radar had been switched off for the last hour to conserve battery power and when Peter switched it on again, the screen on its long range scale showed over a dozen ships off their starboard bow side with some large echoes that could only be tankers moving up from the south. The most prominent feature was a large echo about three miles ahead of them.

Peter went on deck and scanned the sea forward of them. It looked like a large building at first, a block of flats where it was impossible for a building to be. Then the tanker gradually appeared out of the horizon mist with its bow wave now clearly visible, as it lunged towards them at about twenty knots.

Only a few minutes separated them and Peter pulled in the mainsail sheet hard before gybing Seamaiden onto a port tack and bending down to start the auxiliary engine.

The tanker continued her course, passing them within a few hundred yards off their port side. Peter scanned the area where the fishing boat had been, but there was no sign of her.

He called down to John.

'How far are we from that exclusion zone?'

Johns reply informed him that they were still a few miles off but that they needed to start going north east if they were to avoid it.

Peter scanned for the fishing boat again.

'I've lost sight of that small boat. I presume he didn't reply to our radio call?' John came up on deck and joined him with the binoculars.

'Better head over in that direction and see if he's O.K. that tanker put up a series of quite large waves as she passed. Hang on a minute I can see something. Yes, there she is, almost abeam, looks low in the water though, she keeps vanishing in the swell.'

They adjusted the sails and Seamaiden swung onto a close reach on her new northerly course crashing through the swell and eddies that the tanker had left in her wake. They could occasionally see the cabin top of the fishing boat that was no longer under way.

Peter steered Seamaiden on a course that, allowing for the tide, he estimated would bring them up just down wind from the other vessel.

Jessica was up now and poked her tousled head out of the companion way to say good morning and see what had suddenly changed the motion below. As she took in the scene, she dutifully went below to put the kettle on.

'Look, there's someone waving.' John was kneeling on the port cockpit seat trying to balance as he attempted to keep the boat in the binoculars' field of view. 'There are two of them and I don't need to give you two guesses who they are. It's Carter and son and by the look of them they're in big trouble.'

As they approached the other vessel, they could see that it was lying low in the water, not under power and rising and falling sluggishly to each wave. David Luk was waving frantically and someone was in the tiny cuddy at the controls.

'The engines been swamped and we're sinking.' David Luk called across to them. Their boat had settled lower in the water now with every wave and water was spilling over the gunwales.

Peter luffed Seamaiden into the wind so that her sails were flapping and flogging wildly. The engine was still on and he motored as close as he could to them before John threw them a heaving line.

'Mind telling me what's going on and why you were following us?' Jessica poured them hot drinks and filled a hot water bottle giving Peter a scolding look. 'Here take this first Mr.Carter. It'll warm you up a bit.' She crawled behind Peter and dragged a sleeping bag out from one of the lockers. 'Put this around your shoulders you really mustn't get cold.'

The two rescued men sat there in the saloon. Blankets draped round them with the cups of hot chocolate cuddled in their hands and their discarded wet clothing lying on the cabin sole. Simon Carter looked grey and slumped back into the seating. Jessica had put a dressing on the gash in the old mans forehead from where he had slipped as they abandoned their craft. It was full of water and had sunk soon after getting the two men aboard Seamaiden, leaving a mess of floating debris and cushions and fenders on the surface that had quickly dispersed behind the waves.

'I suppose I owe you one Peter.' The old man growled the words as if with reluctance. 'We would have drowned out here without your presence of mind and seamanship. We were on a bloody daft mission, thought up on the spur of the moment.' He seemed uncharacteristically reticent looking for words that he could not find. His son interceded.

'I told him it was too dangerous in that tiny boat, we're lucky to be alive. The fuel lines were foul and I had to blow them out. We were constantly bailing and when that tanker approached we were unable to get out of the way. We were swamped and I don't suppose their watch even saw us.'

Peter looked at his half brother. 'We've not had time to introduce ourselves or talk yet, but what were you trying to, do why were you following us, what were you doing on board the Starlight Princess?'

He glanced up through the companionway. John was busy at the helm again and oblivious to their conversation.

David seemed at a loss for words and it was Carter who stirred and sat forward pulling the blanket closer around himself.

'Same as you were lad. Trying to establish the correct position for the gold. We guessed after our little conversation the day before yesterday that you would be after the gold like a jack rabbit. We hired that boat and kept watch on Seamaiden in anticipation of you setting off to find it and, judging by the diving gear we saw you loading, it wasn't too difficult to guess where you were off to.'

Peter looked at them both with a wry smile.

'So what did you expect to do when we arrived at our destination, come aboard like pirates I suppose? Honestly, you two defy belief. You're lucky we got you out in time, I don't know what the temperature of the South China Sea is at the moment, but here in the English Channel, you'd be lucky to survive for a few hours, even in the summer. As it is, I'm surprised that you are not suffering from hypothermia, no proper sea clothing, lifejackets or anything you must both be insane.'

'Be fair Peter, we did purchase a couple of ghastly looking anoraks and there was some food on board. Unfortunately, the radio didn't seem to work and there was no gas for cooking. Fortunately the radar worked and we were able to keep you in our sights.'

'Well David, you are remarkably lucky that's all I can say. Now, what happened to you two when you left John's office the other day, you just vanished into thin air.'

Carter pulled the sleeping bag tighter and said nothing. David replied.

'My father needed to rest after that incident, I took him back to the pub I'm staying at outside St.Mawes. The stupid man got talking to a fisherman about hiring boats and this fellow offered him one down near where your yacht had been moored. He insisted on going there to keep a watch.'

In reality, Carter had hoped it was a good hiding place from the Koreans.

Peter sat on the opposite berth and looked at the two dishevelled men.

'What do you both really know about the retirement fund and this *Dragon's Morsel* thing? Is there really gold there as everyone seems to think there is. '

Carter looked at him, a slight smile on his face.

'Wouldn't you like to know my lad and wouldn't I like to know. I can tell you,...........nothing.' Peter looked at David Luk who just shrugged his shoulders.

He stood and looked out through the companionway to where John was helming. He had to shout to make himself heard above the noise of the sea.

'Is everything all right up there?'

'Aye aye Skipper; still on course.'

'Then turn her around, were going back to St.Mawes, head as close to 270 degrees until I can work out a new course.' Seamaiden turned easily and John now felt the full strength of the wind as she heeled over to the close reach and he hauled in on the sheet winches.

Simon Carter jumped to his feet, his blanket falling away to where he clutched it around his waist, his eyes narrow and treacherous.

'What the fucking hell are you doing, I thought you were going to Alderney.' Peter looked over his shoulder as he studied the chart table.

'So did I originally my friends, so did I. However, we don't know what we're looking for when we get there do we, so what's the point. We're actually on the way back, the holiday is over.'

'Get this boat of yours around, were going where I say.' Carter screamed his demand together with a long stream of obscenities as he reached across to grab Peter. David Luk was on him in an instant and Peter could only stand and watch as Carter was forced to the cabin sole by his son. Father and son then remonstrated with one another. David fending off the punches aimed at him until Carter tired and fell back on the settee, still shouting abuse.

David looked to Peter for help and Peter lent forward and added to the pressure of holding him down, surprised at the strength he found in the old man that, quite suddenly, ebbed away.

The two brothers looked at each other, not knowing what to say. David broke the short silence.

'Sorry about all that, he'll be O.K. now. He's getting worse as he gets older.'

He turned so that his face was out of sight to Carter and mouthed to Peter.

'Early stages of dementia.' Peter looked at the old man, now quiet and sitting there as though nothing had happened. Christ, if it was true, nothing he had heard in the last week could be relied upon. Carter opened his eyes and this time pleaded in a small voice for Peter to turn Seamaiden back towards Alderney.

Peter looked at David Luk.

'Can you confirm if anything he has said in the last week is true, or is it just a figment of his imagination, I mean, is there gold out there or not. If there is, do you know its accurate chart position?'

'Oh, there's gold all right, he's spoken of nothing else for days. I've also seen his old letters from your father and a Capt. Piltcher that seem to confirm the story, but we believe that Piltcher has never given a true indication as to where the Acacia Lady really sank. We had to assume that you were in possession of that information.' Occasionally, David seemed to become a different person, more assertive than his mild manner would suggest. Peter looked at him as he took in what had just been said about the letters, the other half of the puzzle.

'That's why we were following you, although God knows what he expected me to do when you arrived at your destination. Try and join forces I suppose.'

Peter flopped down on the settee on the opposite side of the cabin pushed his hair back and looked at David, really for the first time. It was like looking at himself in the mirror, the same facial features, slim nose and fair hair of his mothers, slightly almond shaped grey eyes. His half brother sported a moustache that he didn't have, but imagined he might try one some time in the future. It suited David and it would probably suit him. They both sat there for some moments sizing each other up, as combatants might do before deciding their opponents weak spots, but they were not opponents in that sense. They had both been nurtured in the same womb and suddenly felt their fraternal cord. Peter got up and they shook hands, marking their solemn new-found fraternal bond in silence

'We can't go to Alderney for one simple reason. The Navy have just issued an instruction to all shipping to stand clear of an area west of the Channel Islands. Our position is just outside the edge of that exclusion zone and I don't want to run into any further trouble with the authorities.'

David looked at the chart and the position Peter had marked with the rather juvenile annotation, 'here lies treasure.'

'From memory, that's nowhere near the position that the Acacia Lady was supposed to have been sunk. How did you arrive at that?'

Carter had been listening and now stirred.

'Told you they knew more than they would admit, I want that position, after all the gold still belongs to me.' He closed his eyes again and said with a gurgling chuckle.

'The dragon guards it though, you'll never see it.' He lay with his eyes closed as if asleep, then suddenly sat up and discharged the contents of his stomach into the bowl that Jessica had left on the seat. David went over to him and covered him with the blanket. The old man's complexion had turned to that grey shade of green that every skipper knows will only be cured by sitting under a shady tree on the shore.

'I would appreciate it if you could get us back as soon as possible, he's not too well.'

Peter had been thinking as Jessica boiled the kettle and filled another hot water bottle for the old man before going topside. He climbed out into the cockpit after her where the full force of the wind suddenly struck him. John was bent over the tiller and Jessica was sitting in the shelter of the spray hood and pointed to the weather ahead. Great black clouds that were now much closer. He ducked below again to put on his wet weather gear before climbing back to the cockpit.

'I'm reefing down a bit John, head further into the wind for a while then we'll put her on a heading of about thirty degrees. We're heading back for Weymouth.'

'O.K. skip, any reason for the change of plans?' Peter had turned his back to them and didn't hear as he worked the winch to furl the jib on its roller down to about two thirds, hauling up on the sheets as he went. Then he clipped his safety harness onto the jack line and climbed forward to adjust the mainsail reefing lines at the mast base, reducing them to balance the jib. The wind was howling through the shrouds with a large sea beginning to kick up waves over the fore deck as lines and sails rattled, spun and shook with every new wave whilst he made the adjustments and dogged down the folds of sail into the reef ties. Then, he signalled John to turn to starboard as he started to move slowly back along the port side, making sure of every handhold before regaining the shelter of the cockpit.

His adjustments completed he told John that Carter was suffering from sea sickness and possible hypothermia. David Luk wanted to get him back to terra firma as soon as possible. Dartmouth or Brixham were the nearest harbours and would be well sheltered from the westerly weather but Weymouth, being his home port, would be the most suitable.

Peter looked to the weather on Seamaiden's port side. She was whistling along at a steady nine knots with a few degrees of heel but too much weather helm. He made the final adjustment to the jib until Seamaiden rejoiced in her balance as she rose to each wave with John working the tiller bringing her firstly closer to wind and then loosing off as the wave passed.

John was pretty wet again from his windward spell on the helm.

'I'll take over in a minute, must work out the new course first.' Peter went below to the charts again, there would be time later to tell John about the reciprocal letters that David Luk had, that might form the other part of the jigsaw.

Carter was looking worse. Peter put a call through to the Portland coast guard outlining the sinking of the other craft, its position and details about the rescue of the two men. They were offered a helicopter lift off but agreed to have an ambulance standing by at Weymouth so that Carter, due to his age, could be checked over after his ordeal.

They were lucky with the weather, the worst of which passed south of them, the steady wind on the edge of the front allowing them to catch the tide inside the Portland Race and make good time on the passage. Carter had slept most of the day between his trips to the heads, were he retched until there was nothing further to come up.

Peter had put David on the helm for a while and on one occasion had chanced to ask him about Carter.

'I'm surprised your father is so seasick, I thought he used to be a ship owner.' David had grinned and half tilted his face, that uncanny look that Peter knew so well from his own features.

'The English Channel has a reputation for some reason. Something to do with the swell frequency I believe.'

It was nearly five o'clock in the afternoon when they tied up at the visitor's pontoon on Custom House Quay on Weymouth harbour wall, whilst they waited for the Town Bridge to open and allow them access to their marina berth. The ambulance was there but what they hadn't expected were the press and local T.V. cameras. Simon Carter refused the medic's plea for him to attend the hospital. David Luk and Peter had to go over the details of the rescue several times for the journalists, all anxious about meeting their deadline schedules.

They missed the bridge opening and had to wait for the next one. When they eventually drifted up to their pontoon in the marina, Peter was dismayed to see Ian Porter standing there ready to take their warps and, Peter thought grimly, ready to Hoover up any other tit bits.

'Hello sailors, I've just seen your bit on the local T.V.'

One of the millions of viewers sitting in the south of England and watching the regional television news that evening had also pricked up her ears when the rescue interview had mentioned visitors from Hong Kong. When she saw Simon Carter, she made a phone call to an office in London's Soho district, a tourist office by all accounts, but the phone rang in an inner office. The man who picked it up listened to what she had to say with great satisfaction. He replaced the receiver and then rang a mobile number in South Devon.

'Ling I have excellent news for you, we've found your Hong Kong friend.'

'Look here Porter, we're very tired and we've said all there is to be said down on the quay. Now, be a good boy and bugger off for goodness sake.'

'What's all this I hear about an exclusion zone? Do you know what they're up to out there?' Porter was insistent for a reply and wasn't going to budge that easily.

'What's it to you then, any money in it for a real story?' It was Simon Carter, as he let himself down onto the pontoon, seemingly now fully recovered. 'I know exactly what they're out there for but it'll cost you plenty if you want to know.' They all looked at him in amazement, standing there in Peter's spare clothes that were too tight for him. That was except Porter who now put on one of his benevolent smiles.

'There could be a couple of hundred quid in it for you.'

Carter's face blackened. 'Not for what I could tell you, I'd want ten times that and more for my story. I'm off for a drink.' He knocked past Porter with his shoulder as he strolled casually off the pontoon onto the walkway and continued walking without looking back.

The pontoon was narrow and Porter was caught off balance so that he crashed into the side of the yacht. He made a desperate grab and caught hold of the guard rail which pushed Seamaiden gently away from the pontoon until she came up hard against her spring warps. He stayed suspended over the water between the yacht and the pontoon, but couldn't keep his footing and slipped so that he dangled there, his legs flaying to keep them above the water but without success. As he clung there, his hat fell into the water, the place that Carter had intended Porter to be.

David darted off after Carter whilst the other two helped the furious journalist to regain his footing on the pontoon. His hat was floating away in the weak current but was quickly retrieved with the boathook.

'Who the hell does he think he is? I'll bloody well sue for that.' Ian Porter's voice was raised and croaky as he stood there, in squelching shoes, wringing out his hat that Jessica, saying nothing, had handed to him. Then, as if a curtain had come down on the incident, he suddenly regained his composure as Carter's words came back to him. 'What do you think he knows that could be worth so much?'

The event had been quite dangerous, but to the onlooker, Porter swinging there attempting to walk on water, had looked very funny, especially as his hat slid over his face almost in slow motion before dropping on the water. Peter concealed his smile.

'All part of a day's work in your profession I should think Ian.'

The irritated journalist had bent down to remove his wet shoes and socks and looked up at him.

'I've known worse days than this. You need to keep that old bugger under control you know, he's a bloody liability. Anyway, how about an answer to my question? What does he actually know about the naval exercise and the prohibited zone they've stuck around that area?'

John had clambered back on board Seamaiden and was standing on the side deck as he looked down at Porter. It was the first time he had met him.

'Surly the Royal Navy has put out a press release on their exercise, or do you mean to tell me that you've not had anything.'

Porter glowered at him.

'There's been nothing. The media have been pressing for an explanation since it came into force this morning. The Navy PR department, what used to be called the Flag Officer's HQ for the Plymouth sea area, has put up a stone wall. All we've had is a communiqué from them, stating that it's a normal joint services exercise with other NATO units, to test emergency procedures in the event of a terrorist attack from that area. I ask you, who do they expect to attack them from that direction, the Vikings? The answer is no one. They're up to something out there, have been for months and we mean to find out what it is they're doing. They owe it to the British tax payer.'

'We know no more than you do, I saw about a dozen ships on the radar, but some of those may have been commercial shipping. It's a busy area out there, rather like a motorway, with west bound ships on the north carriageway and eastbound ships on the southern carriageway.' Peter spread his hands, 'I'm afraid that's all we know.'

Porter looked at them both. 'Well that old man seems to think he knows something, what's his name, I'd like to speak to him.'

Peter suddenly laughed as he coiled the surplus warp and thought. 'You should know my old mate. It was you who showed me his photograph the other night'

John was concerned about what Simon Carter had said. Was he about to gab about the gold, or was there something else out there he knew about, the *Dragon's Morsel* for instance. What was this mysterious thing that he had spoken about, that guarded the Acacia Lady?

He said. 'I'm afraid the gentleman is ill which probably accounts for his outburst and bad manners, I'll speak to him when we get him home and see what he was talking about, see you around tomorrow.'

Peter indicated the boat. 'We'll be down here to clear up then. Now, please excuse us, we've had a long day, we've still some clearing up to do and then we're off for a swift pint.'

'Look, I want answers not bloody fobbing off, by the likes of you. Who is that old bugger?'

Porter was prodding at Peter, who gently pushed him to one side as he bent to continue the final tidying up of the warps and fenders.

'My friend, if you continue prodding me like that, you'll end up in the place that the old boy intended for you. Now piss off before I change my mind.'

Porter backed off hastily, his eyes darting from Peter to John.

'O.K. gentlemen, I've asked you nicely, you may not realise it but if that old chap really has something to tell which my editor approves, it could be worth plenty, you tell him that from me.' He turned and squelched off up the broad walk, rubbing his aching arms, hat, shoes and socks in hand.

John looked down at Peter.

'What was all that about then, wonder what he's really after. Do you think he knows about the gold?'

Peter stood there thoughtfully. The Navy would hardly have thrown a cordon around such a massive area for a few bars of gold. John ignored Peter's silence.

'If I were you, I'd find the pub they've gone to and get Carter back here as quickly as possible. That's probably what your newspaper friend is about to do. Leave the rest of this until later, let's find the Carter's and wring out of them why they're here and what they want.' They secured the companion way wash boards and headed for the marina entrance.

Tim Porter stood under the cover of the entrance porch way, shoeless as he talked earnestly into his mobile. He turned his back to them as they approached and lowered his voice.

Chapter 24. Schizophrenic Carter.

John Barrett and Peter soon located Carter and Luk in the nearest tavern to the marina and invited them back to Seamaiden. Jessica gave her apologies and left having prepared some instant coffee for them as they sat around the saloon table.

'You're very quiet Simon, lost your tongue suddenly or are you not used to this sort of thing.' Peter had related to them how he had been attacked along the road outside the marina by the motorcyclist wielding his baseball bat, the shooting incident at sea and John's encounter at Crows Nest.

Simon Carter glowered at Peter. 'That little episode was nothing to some of the things I've seen during my lifetime lad. However, for a couple of posies like yourselves to have been duffed up so frequently is, I admit, unusual.' He looked at them, as his eyes narrowed down to slits. 'Does anyone else know what you were looking for when you set sail for the Channel Islands?'

John replied. 'I think more to the point Carter, we should hear what you know about all this. What was it you said earlier, if I recall it was something about you knowing exactly what that Naval exercise was all about. Come on now, tell us all about it.'

David Luk sipped the hot coffee whilst Carter scowled at them all.

'As for the Navy, it's true what I said, that story is worth money but it's also my life forfeited if I tell it.'

Peter looked at the old man. 'For God's sake Simon don't be so melodramatic, who on earth would want to bump you off at your age, you old fool.'

The old man cackled a laugh. 'You youngsters, so bloody cock sure all of you, living your nice safe little lives. Tell me lad, do you have a mortgage on that house of yours?'

Peter looked embarrassed how did Carter know anything about his house.

'Since were all trying our hardest to be honest with each other, I'll give you a blunt answer that is, no. My parents lived there for a while and after the divorce they let it out and eventually agreed that we should have it as a wedding present.

Carter looked at him in thoughtful silence before turning to David.

'And who provided for you son before you decided to sod off to England, saw you through university, bought off your embarrassments with young tarts and saw to it that you always drove a new sports car.' It was David's turn to squirm as the others looked at him with fresh interest.

'Look father, where is all this leading to you're embarrassing our host and his friend.'

'I'll tell you where it's leading. To me. To me. Do you understand, to me. I've been the fucking paymaster for you both.' They were getting used to Carter's lack of adjectives but Peter now protested.

'I'm sorry Simon but you'll have to moderate your language a bit, especially as you've no basis on which to make such sweeping statements or inferences. Don't forget that my father is dead and can't defend himself against your slurring remarks.'

John cut in across Peter.

'No, let him go on. I'm interested to hear a bit more about our friend here; he keeps avoiding the direct questions. Why did you say you knew exactly what the Navy were up to? Now Mr.Carter or whatever your name is, give us a straight answer for once.' John's tone was harder now. He was in court, questioning, twisting, teasing out the truth if he could, as though the man across the saloon table was the accused, sitting there in the dock, with no brief.

Carter lent forward, one elbow on the table his head cupped in his hand whilst the other coddled a large whisky glass. He glanced at them one by one and started to unfold his story, a story of four young men who had met under strained circumstances on the Acacia Lady nearly fifty years before. The three of them were listening to Carter's story. Even his son David hadn't heard it in such detail before, although he had guessed many years previously that the old man kept a lot of his past from his family.

He had just completed the story up to the dive on the wreck of the American bomber on the seabed in the China Sea. Peter had opened another bottle of 'Famous Grouse' and the kettle was reboiling in the galley for more instant coffee. John had hoped to get away before this but was engrossed in listening to the intriguing life that Carter had been through, his childhood, the Japanese invasion, the growth of his father's businesses.

They had come to a point again where the old man seemed reluctant to continue and John edged him on.

'Simon, all this is fascinating, it would make a great story in its own right but you still haven't given us any clue as to the original question. What do you think the Navy is doing out there in the Channel?'

Carter waved his glass and more Scotch was poured.

'Where was I. Oh yes, I didn't tell you what I found did I, you wouldn't believe me any way. Well needless to say, it was some American military equipment. I sold it to the Chinese Liberation Army and in return they bought what I had found and, my soul.' The last two words were spoken very slowly and deliberately, as though to emphasise that he did actually have a soul.

'So what did you sell them that demanded such a great sacrifice on your part?' Peter tried not to sound sarcastic, but he was tiring of the story which did not seem to be leading anywhere. Fifty year old military equipment couldn't have much significance these days.

Carter looked directly at Peter.

'As I said just now lad, you wouldn't believe me if I told you. What they bought from me they didn't get, but it paid for all this.' He waved his hand around the boat saloon. 'And your mother's place, and that house of yours. It also paid for your education and David's. I wonder looking at you both if it was worth it. All that communist money could have fed a few thousand Chinkies.'

'For Christ sakes Carter what is it that you are trying to say.' Peter was angry at the continuing innuendoes with respect to Philip.

'What I'm saying is that I sold my soul to the devil and have had to live with its advantages and disadvantages ever since.'

The three of them looked perplexed at his divisive and abstruse meandering account that continued to give no answer and yet demanded their attention. John was getting anxious about the time, the last train had left and his car was still in St.Mawes. This looked like an all night session.

'For God's sake man, tell us what we want to know so that we can get this over and done with. I'd like to try and get home tonight.'

'Ah, young people, so impatient. My story covers time, and yet, the true meaning of time is unimportant to you unless you have some immediate deadline to meet. Time has many dimensions you know, the present, the past, the future. When I was a small boy, my grandparents took me to see a performance of Julius Caesar in London at the Old Vic. There I saw a group of old men, plotting, ruling, arguing, determining the destinations of their people. I saw the same play when I was fifty. There were the same characters, saying and doing the same things except that this time they appeared to me as earnest young men. The same story in time, but not the same perception if you see what I mean.'

'Christ he's a flipping philosopher as well. Come on Simon, get onto the gold, you know damn well that's what we want to hear about, your just stringing us along.' Peter's outburst caused his half brother to put a hand on his arm.

'I think he will be coming to the point in a minute, a bit more patience and we may find out what we want to know and if what he has said makes any sense.'

Carter ignored them as he drowned another Scotch and continued.

'They're looking for something that could be on the Acacia Lady that's all I can tell you.'

Peter feigned disinterest and looked at David who shrugged his shoulders in disbelief. They all looked at him.

'Is that it then?' Peter thought it safe to be sarcastic now. They were not going to get anything sensible out of Carter that night. The old man was obviously hallucinating with the whisky he had drunk.

John looked at Carter.

'So, this Dragon you have spoken about, presumably the American equipment, is that what you were paid for.'

'You guessed it lad. Those Chinese scientists couldn't wait to get their hands on it for their own research. As for me, they paid in gold all right but in return I was recruited by SAD, you know, the Social Affairs Department, equivalent to the CIA in the US or your MI5, that is until I was retired about ten years ago. It was one of my jobs to assist in negotiating armament supplies to some of the less desirable inhabitants of this small planet. I also had responsibilities for recruitment to their cause in the Hong Kong business community.'

The saloon fell silent as they looked at each other in a mixture of incongruous disbelief.

'Come on John, you're a glutton for punishment if you don't mind me saying so.' Peter had also had a few scotches by now and it was showing. 'The silly old sod's fantasising,' he said sideways to John.

John was still sober and took another sip of his cold coffee carefully measured what he said.

'I believe him. Chilling and unlikely, horrendous and incomprehensible as it sounds, I think I believe him.'

Peter fidgeted with his glass as Carter continued.

'Believe me, I never believed in all that communist stuff. I was young and desperate for money, saw a chance to make a lot of it and swore my allegiance to their cause without realising the full consequences of what I'd done. It was like going to a tattoo artist's studio and having your girlfriends name blazoned across your chest and waking the next fucking day to the reality of never getting rid of it or her. Anyway, they looked after me, which allowed me to look after you two boys.'

Again there was silence as they took in what he had said. Peter, his voice impatient enquired.

'But, and I say but because the whole thing sounds implausible, if you sold this secret equipment to the Chinese forty odd years ago, how did the gold end up here in the English Channel. I presume that it is the same gold that we're talking about and that it was on the Acacia Lady.'

'That's a very long story my lad. It involved your father and Capt. Piltcher.' His words were becoming slurred. He suddenly stopped and peered at his empty glass realising that the drink had loosened his tongue and that he'd confided more to them than he wanted. 'I'm tired, can't think any more, must get some shut eye.' He yawned and his eyes closed there at the table.

'That's great, we at last get him up to the point of this outrageous story, the bit that may or may not be never never land and he nods off to bloody sleep.' Peter stood and lit another cheroot. 'And if you two think I'm going to believe all this rubbish about the secret service activities, well, if it did happen it happened so long ago I'm beginning to doubt if there is gold out there or if he's just fantasising over some book he's read somewhere.'

John replied. 'It's not a book Peter, we've already seen some indication of what was going on between those four men from your father's letters. What Mr.Carter here has said fills in the other side of the story, which, I presume amounts to blackmail over the gold. Is that correct Carter? I'd be interested to see the other side of the coin, the letters you received from Philip for instance.'

Carter was dozing and David looked at Peter with that slight upward turn of the head that he was beginning to get used to as his older half brother pushed his hands through the scant hair.

'You may not like what you find out Peter. I've seen them.'

'How do you mean? Surely they can't be any more confusing than those we have already seen, full of threats, the retirement fund and this thing they called the Dragon.'

'I've obviously not seen your letters from my father to Philip Senden. I'm still afraid there are events suggested by your father's letters that you will not like at all.'

Peter gave him a quizzical look.

'I think I shall have to be the judge of that, the important thing is to marry each letter to its reply if we can so that we can get the wider picture.'

'The letters are in his Hong Kong office, I read them one evening when he was passed out on grass, I presume you know he is drug dependant?'

So that was it, John thought about the old mans behaviour, normal one minute, irrational the next, showing all the qualities of a schizophrenic personality, a psychosis mental state in which mood and thought are marked by introversion of thoughts and delusions. Could there be any truth in anything Carter had told them?

It was getting late, none of them had eaten properly since leaving St.Mawes the previous afternoon and Peter suggested he and David should go off and buy some Indian take away down in the harbour.

John sat alone with Simon Carter, who was still wearing the old boat clothes that Peter had dished out to him earlier in the day.

'How long have you known young Peter then?' Carter, suddenly awake again, asked the question.

'I suppose about twenty five years, we became friends at boarding school, went on to university together.'

'You married,' the old man looked at him quizzically for his reply. 'Divorced two years ago I'm afraid. Wife ran off with a millionaire client.'

'So you're normal, you know what I mean, with women.' John smiled at him, what was this old rogue trying to find out about him?

'Yes of course I'm normal, in fact if it wasn't for you and trying to help Peter out, I'd be with a delightful lady right now.'

'Those other two weren't, Senden and Piltcher I mean, queer as farts in a bath they both were. Anyway, I'm sure you've guessed that already I should think, being a solicitor you must have worked that one out for yourself from the letters.'

John looked at him and reached into a locker where he knew Peter kept his supply of small cigars. He offered one to Carter who declined.

'Smoked too many of the other kind, you know, what they used to call marihuana. Why do you think I'm like this now? I used to be quite respectable you know. The long term effect of the drug causes attacks, trouble is they become worse and worse, but, so what, that's life.'

'Tell me about your son David, can you confirm that he actually is Peter's half brother.' He waved an arm to clear his tobacco smoke as it coiled around the cabin.

'No he isn't his half brother at all, they are blood brothers, Monica was their mother, and I'm their father.'

John was stunned at the news.

'Good grief Simon, is that what all this is about? Is that what Peter will discover when he finds the *Dragon's Morsel?*'

Simon was dozing again, his head back against the settee cushions, the silence of the cabin broken by the heavy nasal breathing of the old man as John thought about what had been said. He felt the slight movement of Seamaiden as the others climbed back on board and rose with his fingers to his lips as they descended the companionway steps.

'He's asleep,' he said in a whisper.

Peter looked round in the subdued lighting of the cabin.

'Good, I'll have his Onion Bhajis.' The meal was eaten and the Scotch bottle was quickly emptied before they tumbled into their bunks.

The next morning it was eight o'clock before Peter awoke. He lay there for a few minutes, listening to someone's snores at the other end of the boat, his mouth tasting the whisky from the previous night. He raised himself on one elbow and looked around at the remnants of the Indian meal, still lying in a messy clutter on the cabin table. The companionway wash boards had not been closed the night before, his half brother and Carter were gone and so was the chart. The snoring had stopped and John emerged from the fo'c'sle and looked around.

'They've gone then?'

'Looks like it and they've taken the chart as well.'

John reached back inside his sleeping bag and extracted the crumpled chart.

'Not quite as befuddled as the rest of you were last night.' He grinned at his friend as he dropped it back on the chart table. 'You'd better get moving mate. If I remember rightly, you told me you had an important conference to attend in London this afternoon. It would be funny if it turned out to be the same one that Katherine is attending.'

Early that morning, David Luk had shaken his father out of his sleep and they had crept off the boat. They didn't get very far. A large people carrier with blackened windows was drawn up outside the marina entrance. As Luk and Carter went through the marina exit gate, they were surrounded by four men, who nudged up to them close enough for the two of them to feel the concealed armaments.

'Keep quiet gentlemen and you will come to no harm, we just need to speak to you. Oh, by the way, we gather your performance on television last night was excellent.' Carter shivered as he recognised the pitch of the voice that came from behind him.

The back doors opened and they were hustled inside the vehicle, which moved off as the doors closed. Johnny Chungai sat inside and greeted them with an ominous silence, watching as the driver headed east out of the town. At last he spoke to them.

'So David, you thought you would play games with us.'

As Carter swung round to his son for some explanation, Chungai lurched across the vehicle and hit him so that the old man went down between the seats in a crumpled heap. David Luk protested but raised his hands at the gun that was then produced.

'Johnny, for Christ Almighty's sake, put that thing down and listen for a minute. We're supposed to be partners in this remember. Find the gold so that I can use my share to set up the supplies from my facility in Costa Rica. Your associates in Haifa will make fortunes if we cut out the Colombian barons.'

'I'm listening to you, you arrogant useless Britisher. You ran out on us.'

David pleaded his story of getting his father out of the hospital and then following Peter Senden's yacht after the apparent disappearance of Gilbert Piltcher.

'What happened to him at the hospital police interview, did he say anything?' David laughed nervously at Chungai's question.

'No, it was all a misunderstanding over his passport, honestly, Johnny you must believe that I have our joint interests at heart. I just couldn't get hold of you.'

Chungai lowered the gun.

'We managed to extract the whereabouts of this man Piltcher from the scientist Holmes. You will visit him on our behalf with your father who is apparently an old friend. We have much at stake as you have said David, but this time if anything goes wrong, you can consider our deal as closed as a virgin's thighs.'

Chapter 25. The Nuclear Conference.

The *Thinman* assignment document that sat on the table in front of Commander Hank Hoskins was a very thick file, and that was only the summary. Offices in the Pentagon, Newport and at the Langley CIA Headquarters in Virginia, housed thousands of documents referring to the project and scanning back over sixty years. In the file were photocopies of fading documents dating from the 1940's, with many paragraphs deleted by censors long retired from service. Virtually every document was stamped with security codes ranging from Nuclear Top Secret to the various inter service nominations.

He sat with others on the dais of the Thames House small conference hall as the fifty or so delegates settled.

Peter sat near Major Fellows and had been told to say nothing. Hoskins had greeted him with some surprise.

Major Fellows rose in front of the lectern and a hush fell over the audience as he introduced Commander Hank Hoskins.

'Ladies and Gentlemen.' Hoskins stopped and looked down at the file. 'I know you have all been security cleared and your credentials checked several times on the way in here. I thank you for attending this conference at such short notice and our partners in British Security for providing these facilities. To save further time I will introduce my senior officers to you

On my left is Anne Davies, she is in charge of all investigations with respect to any subversive terrorist action arising in Europe against the United States of America or which could affect our interests in Europe. Amongst other activities she acts for the National Security Agency in my country. Our Embassy is represented today by Mr.Reginald Kennedy and our technical adviser is Dr.Margaret Crawford from the U.S.Defense Nuclear Agency.

They are all supported by large teams of specialists who, for reasons of economy and space, cannot be here today, as indeed your own support teams cannot be here. Our Government has a team of Special Agents assigned to this project from the C.I.A. and flown over here a few days ago. Our FBI agency and other organisations are also involved. In case you have any doubts about their suitability to work alongside the British, let me tell you, in the confidence that this conference demands, that many of these agents have served previous undercover operations during the Gulf Wars with your Special Services personnel and in Northern Ireland during the troubles there as well as the Balkans, Afghanistan and Iraq.

As Major Fellows has told you, I am assigned by the US Naval Intelligence Department as the Naval Attaché to the CIA Committee of Foreign Nuclear Affairs. In addition to reporting through my normal channels at Langley, I also report directly to the Chief of Naval Operations who keeps the President of the United States personally informed on this project.

Major Jack Fellows here on my right represents the interests of the British Secret Service on this project. His teams have been assisting us with background information on various subversive organisations both here and in Europe and have liaised with the Royal Navy and Marine Nationale in France.'

The representatives in attendance that evening were from many organisations from both Britain and France. Service Chiefs and high ranking officers from all three Services, Chief Constables from the South Coast areas, Ministry of Defence, M.I.5., the French Direction de la Surveillance du Territoire (DST) and Direction General de la Securite Exteriere, the French equivalent to MI6. Others, because of their high security tags would only state that they were there by invitation but included various special operations groups including SAS and Anti Terrorist Branch officers. Interpreters with the necessary security clearances were also present.

Many of them had arrived over a period of several hours to avoid media suspicion that an important conference was in process and had then gone through the lengthy process of holographic retinal identification and other credential checks.

'O.K. Ladies and Gentlemen, some of you are already aware of the details in the *Thinman* project. Our respective Governments have already had preliminary discussions at top Ministerial level and are all agreed that the highest security level and co-operation must be maintained in order to retain both public order and confidence. We now have to inform a wider audience of selected people and those of you who have not been involved up to now, are about to be presented with an outline of what was Uncle Sam's greatest and longest standing military secret. I say was, because a couple of months ago we discovered that a group of Islamic fundamentalists had all the details.

Before going into detail, let me firstly outline some history that goes back to a period before some of you were born.' He paused to let the significance sink in as some of the younger delegates in their thirties and forties straightened up in their seats in anticipation of what was to follow. Peter lent forward with interest.

'You must be aware that on August 6th.1945, as a result of the Potsdam Declaration, the *Little Boy* atomic bomb was dropped by Enola Gay on the Japanese City of Hiroshima followed three days later with another bomb which was dropped on Nagasaki. The devastation was terrible and the Japanese Government capitulated, concluding what we in the States call the Pacific War, the official ending of hostilities to the Second World War. The event led politicians of all persuasions around the world to condemn the use of such a weapon in any future conflict and nuclear weapons have been used ever since as a deterrent against such an occasion.

It was four years before another nation detonated a similar device. That was the Russians. The British caught up in 1952 when they tested their bomb in the Monte Bello Islands off N.W.Australia. The U.S.A. at that time was already testing Hydrogen Bombs and the major powers such as Russia and China were getting mighty nervous. The next year the Russians had the Hydrogen bomb.' He looked at them with his penetrating eyes whilst they waited for the meat of the talk. Most of them knew their history.

He continued. 'Our area of concern goes back to the events in 1945 when our airforce was carrying out mass bombing raids on Tokyo. Then President Truman sanctioned the atom bomb to be dropped on Hiroshima on August six and Nagasaki, on August nine of that year after agreement with our allies at Potsdam, the so called Potsdam Declaration'

He paused, his eyes sweeping the hushed expectant audience.

'What the historians know is that three atomic bombs were originally sanctioned by President Truman to be dropped. What they do not know is that between those two dates another bomb code named *Thinman*, one of the three, was sanctioned to be dropped in Kyushu on the city of Kokura, known now as part of Kitakyushu. The B29 bomber carrying the second bomb never made it to the destination, it crashed and we lost an armed plutonium atomic bomb somewhere in the Pacific Ocean, what could be called the worlds first nuclear accident, what the US Military now calls *Broken Arrow Thinman*.'

The sound level went up as he referred to the small control panel by his side and lights dimmed as the huge audio visual screen across the far wall lit up with the computer icon display. He moved the mouse and clicked up a photograph of the old atomic bomb

'This is what we are looking for.' He pointed the laser baton at the screen. 'The bomb was constructed in two halves with a circumferential joint holding them together by several large toggle screws and weighing in all about 2000 pounds. At one end there are six aileron fins surrounded by a square box section made of several pieces of metal, riveted together.' The projected photograph was old and not of the best quality, showing the bomb, looking like any other, the rough riveting on the aileron fins giving it a DIY appearance. In fact the whole structure looked like some sort of hastily made prototype.

There was a general murmur around the hall as the delegates looked at the old photograph on the screen, took in what had been said and then fell into stunned silence.

'Unbelievable!' It was one of the Chief Constables who broke the silence and used the same words that many people over the years before him had come out with when they had received the confidential point of the *Thinman* assignment for the first time.

'Surely you had the means over the last fifty odd years to locate it. What about the Hydrogen bombs that the U.S. Air Force lost in Greenland and again in the Mediterranean, of the coast of Spain, 1966 I believe? You yanks managed to find that one.'

'I'm afraid not.' The Commander sat down at the table as though in thought. He knew from his experiences over the last few years since becoming involved with the *Thinman* Project that there would now be questions and some disbelief that, with all the technical recourses and military might of their great country, the deadly nuclear bomb originally destined for Japan had just vanished.

The official photographs of Major- General Delmar Wilson, head of the US 16th.Air Force and Admiral Guest, Commander of the US Task Force at Palomares were clicked by the mouse and shown on the screen as the commander took up the commentary again.

'The loss in Spain kicked off the biggest underwater search in history. Lasting over two months, it involved 33 naval vessels and over 3000 Service personnel at a cost of eleven million U.S.Dollars. The bomb was eventually discovered using a robot submarine in 600 meters of water, five miles off shore and recovered. Those are the official photographs.'

Hoskins continued, 'After the first bomb was dropped on Hiroshima, it was agreed by President Truman that if the Japs' didn't surrender unconditionally, the second bomb would be dropped in Kyushu on the city of Kokura on August 11th. Unfortunately, the weather was deteriorating and the drop was brought forward by four days to the 7th. We now know that the modified B-29 bomber assigned to the task developed some sort of navigational problems after it took off from Tinian Island and strayed way off course. Local electric storms interfered with radio communications that were primitive compared with those of today and the last transmission from the bomber commander was broken. They'd sent out a mayday call and implied that they were making to land at Okinawa to the south, in the Ryukyu Islands, that we had regained from the Japanese about a month earlier. The three weather planes that went out ahead of the bomber reported very bad weather and zero visibility. They, together with the observer aircraft, turned back and landed safely at Okinawa and no one at that time heard any more from *Thinman*.

The old B-29 Superfortress was about the most reliable bomber used during the Second World War and we now believe that this particular craft was sabotaged when people heard about the devastation caused by the first bomb dropped by *Enola Gay*. Extra security was then imposed at the North Field air base before *Bock's Car* flew the following day to Nagasaki.

The Tinian Island Command Office of the 509th. Composite Group 20th.U.S.Air Force, who were charged with the responsibility of the Japanese bombings, put out a communiqué to the personnel involved stating that the loss was unfortunate and that the exercise had been a dummy run for the *'Fat Man'* bomb dropped on Nagasaki the next day. Just one report out of hundreds of similar communiqués issued during the final days of the war.

At that stage, the engineers working for Robert Oppenheimer on the Manhattan project at Los Alamos had only been able to extract enough nuclear fissionable material to make four bombs. One of them based on uranium 235 and three based on the uranium isotope, plutonium 239.

The well documented Trinity Ground Zero or Alamagordo test in New Mexico used one plutonium bomb. The Hiroshima bomb was uranium and fired by a simple explosive charge. One plutonium bomb was used at Nagasaki and the remaining one; well you now know what happened to it.'

'Don't you know where it is?' It was one of the unidentified people who interrupted.

The Commander now smiled. 'Well it certainly isn't sitting at the bottom of the Pacific. We had the Navy search that area in the guise of exercises on and off for nearly eight years after the Pacific war. The *Thinman* project team which at that stage had given up searching the Pacific Ocean just kept a small team on standby to monitor reports in case any trace of the lost device was detected.

We found the B-29 eventually in 1953 on the Japanese continental shelf, or to be more precise, near a tiny island south of the Ryukyu Islands in the East China Sea. It was in a few fathoms of water, miles from where it should have been but the bomb and most of its control equipment was missing. It was towards the end of the Korean War and we were pretty certain that the Chinese had somehow found it before us. It was a revelation that was kept from our allies during the final negotiations at the armistice eventually signed at Panmunjom. In fact, it took China another ten years before she also exploded her first nuclear device.'

The Private Secretary to the Admiralty leaned back in his chair.

'You mean that you told your allies nothing about this at the time?'

The Commander looked uncomfortable with his reply.

'I am merely a servant of our Government. What the politicians do, or did at that time, was up to them but, one or two foreign Governments besides your own are now aware of the situation.'

Several low whistles were let out as the delegates noted the break of confidence in the Anglo American detente. Hoskins was embarrassed and looked around the walls of the hall, hung with paintings on loan from the National Gallery and depicting historic scenes of great British victories together with the generals and men who had fought so valiantly through history for the honour of their country. To some of the Frenchmen there, the scenes could have been considered offensive as they also depicted, what to the French in many cases, were humiliating defeats.

'Where do we go from here, what are you looking for exactly and why call us in, after all the Pacific Ocean is a long way from here?' It was the French minister with responsibility for civil defence in the La Manche region covering Brest in the west to Dunkerque in the north. He had been summoned at short notice to attend the meeting that had no title, no agenda and no briefing notes

The Commander looked directly at him. 'Our so called spy satellites have been taking measurements of radioactivity for a number of years now all over the globe. We've dotted the oceans with sensing devices that we pass off as weather monitors looking at the El Ni`no effect on global warming. We constantly fly missions over the Middle East and some of the remoter parts of the world on the same pretence, well, not really a pretence as we are actually measuring climatic changes. We also have side viewing systems in aircraft that are able to look deep into the Asian hinterland to detect radioactive sources. Over the last few years we have started to detect the characteristic plutonium isotope of uranium 235 from several areas.

The first and most noticeable is the Barents Sea around Murmansk, the Kola Peninsular, Severodvinsk and the island of Novaya Zemlya. That area contains over three hundred rotting nuclear reactors, nearly twenty per cent of the world's total, together with tens of thousands of spent nuclear fuel elements. It is a grave yard of the former Soviet Union's military naval might, nuclear battle cruisers and submarines laid up and rotting away..........'

Peter Senden remembered the place well. He'd been amongst the party who had visited the area a few years before with the Foreign Secretary of the day, pledging Britain's help to clear up the enormous quantities of nuclear waste. A northern wasteland, frozen for most of the year but where radioactive waste was seeping slowly into the fjords, poisoning and contaminating them for hundreds, possibly thousands of years.

Since that visit, the storage of enriched uranium waste from Russian ice breakers had been addressed and proper storage facilities built with some help from Britain. But it was only a small part of the overall problem.

The risk of uncontrolled nuclear chain reaction from the spent fuel and toxic waste far outweighing the meagre sums that could be applied for the clean up required, which most experts reckoned could take forty years to complete in that area alone.

He had seen the old November, Hotel and Echo-II classes of Soviet submarines, rusting hulks, moored up and still containing nuclear fuel. There was a total lack of clear planning or finance for dealing with the problem like the hundreds of other nuclear disasters around the globe that had taken place in the world's short nuclear history.

Then there had been the Kursk nuclear submarine disaster.

The mess was a thought provoking legacy for the future generations who would have to come to terms with the contamination in the seas as the nuclear poison was slowly leeched out of the casings dotted around the oceans. Eating anything from the sea might eventually become hazardous as the poison entered the food chain and spread. The sea itself could go on absorbing waste for many years but there would come a time in the future when the levels of contamination if not controlled more vigorously on a world wide basis could make swimming in the sea just a remote memory.

Toxic nuclear waste stored on land was equally dangerous. Plutonium burns readily and a fire at any one of the nuclear munitions dumps could send up plumes of particles into the atmosphere, spreading the deadly poison over thousands of square kilometres, knowing no man made boundaries, to be unknowingly inhaled by populations and resulting in long term cancer fatalities. Even under the highly controlled conditions that preceded the accident in 1999 at Tokaimura in Japan, accidents could happen, a blue flash of neutron radiation, an out of control chain reaction......

.........'Secondly, we have detected small traces around the Indian and Pakistani Atomic Research test areas where they have tested what we now know are similar crude enriched uranium devices mainly for political ends. However, the isotopic fingerprint doesn't match our own early nuclear devices'.........Peter thought, so what, it was still poison whoever's fingerprint it was. He thought back to the investigations he and his team had made on behalf of his department about four years before in India.

The stupid innocence of politicians in believing in such programmes as 'Atoms for Peace', that had allowed Delhi to acquire back door nuclear weapons. The programme had allowed Canadian designed reactors to be legitimately constructed from which Indian scientists had been able to extract enough nuclear material to manufacture its own nuclear bomb. And with all the implications of unstable religious groups gaining access...................... The Commander had, perhaps by design, not mentioned his own country's piles of lethal military nuclear debris or the ground water contaminated by depleted uranium munitions in places like Kosova, Iraq and Iran.

'The only area where we have started to measure radioactive isotopes with the correct signature in all respects is in the English Channel, in the strong tidal area somewhere north west of the Cherbourg Peninsular.

Recently a British amateur diver died of radioactive poisoning somewhere in the English Channel and as some of you know, a joint naval task force has been set up on a detailed search pattern of the area.'

Again there were murmurs of disbelief and several people trying to ask questions at the same time. The most prominent questions being, 'how do you know it's there?' 'Why has this not been made public before now?'

Peter remained grimly silent as he realised the significance of his being there and the reason for the secrecy over his father's death.

The Commander looked across to the old political campaigner Reginald Kennedy, survivor of many political wars and pulled out of retirement to act as the political arm on this occasion. Kennedy replied cautiously.

'Our respective Governments have requested that the *Thinman* search project be kept secret until such time as a positive position can be verified. This is to avoid the public panic and disorder that could result by the release of premature information.' The opening sentences had not been rehearsed and he was pleased that they came out naturally as his mind went over the question looking for avoidance material and parallel blame.

'There's a reprocessing plant at Cap de La Hague near Cherbourg that, like Selafield in England, processes used uranium rods but the plant uses plutonium as a fuel which has a different radiation characteristic to the 1940's bomb.

Greenpeace alerted the worlds press some years ago that there was leakage from that plant, like most of the others dotted around the world, but it is within the International limits for emissions which are being reduced as specified by the Sintra Agreement set up in 1998 at Lisbon. The reprocessing plants are fitted with things called, Actinide removal systems.'

He was now out of his depth and referred with an unspoken sideways glance to Dr. Margaret Crawford who continued.

'These systems remove the more dangerous radio nuclides, americium and plutonium but still allow the discharge of technetium 99 which is a soluble radio nuclide. The OSPAR treaty on sea pollution in the North East Atlantic aims to reduce those discharges over the next few years by the gradual closure of elderly Magnox nuclear power stations. ' Her brow furrowed as she referred to one of the papers from a huge pile in front of her and read on further, 'Technetium-99 has been detected in lobsters, shellfish and seaweed as far apart as the Arctic, the Irish and Norwegian Seas.

Further intense measurements in that area more recently indicated that although there were those leakage's, the main radio isotope nuclides detected were an exact fingerprint of the Kokura plutonium bomb, very weak but nevertheless it was there.'

Again Peter's mind went over the ongoing arguments between the Irish and British Governments over the nuclear pollution in the Irish Sea and the dozens of nuclear incidents that considered separately were treated lightly but in total, bore enormous consequences for the future.

Hoskins thanked the Doctor and glanced around the audience, his eyes appearing tired under their large hoods.

'What we did not know until quite recently, is how our bomb and about twenty Kg. of plutonium nitrate ended up in the English Channel or, where exactly the signature radiation came from.

I mentioned that there was a leak of information.

About six weeks ago, Israeli Mossad agents were given documents from a Palestinian group in Lebanon which caused their Prime Minister to get on the next plane to Washington for urgent talks with the President. The Palestinian government were horrified at the implications of the documents and in view of the forthcoming Middle East Cease Fire Treaty Conference, decided that their only course of action was to cooperate fully with the Israelis and U.S. They in turn are now liaising with the European governments.

We are no longer the only ones looking for the bomb, we know that there has been a terrorist group out there determined to find it so that the plutonium can be recycled into a new device. Our information also suggests that the threat of a wildcat dirty bomb could be used to disrupt the Conference. We know the media are already suspicious over the searches we are making in the Channel and if the news breaks before we find it, the Worlds press will be howling for our hides.

I report directly to The Chief of Naval Operations who is a member of our Joint Chiefs of Staff and advises the President on Naval matters. The President has recently taken personal command of the search and is advised daily on what is now known as the *'Broken Arrow Thinman'* project.

For those of you who are not aware of the euphemisms used by the US Government to describe significant nuclear incidents, let me just explain that *Broken Arrow* events signify occurrences that involve nuclear weapons or components that may result in situations where the risk of nuclear war does not exist. These may consist of, nuclear detonation, non nuclear detonation or burning of a nuclear device or component, radioactive contamination, seizure, theft or loss of a nuclear weapon, and finally, hazard to the public.

Broken Arrow Thinman, falls into several of these categories. There are other titles we use for nuclear accidents that need not bother us here today."

The British Under Secretary of State for the Ministry of Defence, Bob Darkins leaned forward and took a sip of his drink.

'How can you be certain that the trace you have recorded is the same bomb?'

Commander Hoskins removed his half moon glasses, gave them a quick clean on his sleeve and continued. 'I'm sure I don't have to remind you sir of the basic physics associated with radioactive radiation and the ageing process on the radioisotopes produced. We know without doubt, after checking all other sources, that the nuclear bomb originally destined for Kokura is lying somewhere out there in the English Channel probably in a wreck. After nearly sixty years we estimate that the steel shell containing the nuclear material has probably started to corrode through we also believe that the beryllium neutron shields and spacers may have shifted, causing the mass of the two halves of the device to become critical.'

'But the Channel is quite shallow, surely the detailed search by this task force should have found it by now?' It was the Chief Constable of Kent.

'You're quite right.' The Commander replaced his spectacles and flicked over some sheets of his file. 'It ranges from being quite shallow to depths around two hundred metres. The area covers thousands of square miles. Unfortunately searching takes time. We've only been out there for two weeks.'

The Secretary to the Chief of Defence Staff, Sir Martin Atkinson raised his hand.

'Mr.Chairman, I feel I am probably best qualified to answer Commander Norton's question. With the help of The British Admiralty Hydrography Department and the Hydrographique et Oceanographique de la Marine in France, the Royal Navy has been sweeping all the old wrecks in the vicinity, and there are hundreds of them. There are areas where very strong currents and some of the highest tidal ranges in the World have previously precluded reliable surveys. The US Naval Oceanography Command and the French Navy have also done sweeps but none of them have come up with anything positive.'

Hoskins reached under his file and pulled out two transparencies which he placed on the projector table.

'There are several anomalies that have shown up on our computers over the last two weeks by these latest moves which may have no bearing on the case at all but, nevertheless, need to be followed up.' He looked up at the screen and adjusted the image.

'The surveys have been so thorough that they found several wrecks that shouldn't have been there as you will see from those notes. That is, they had not been indicated in previous surveys which go back over one hundred and fifty years. Other wrecks have become buried in the sand and can only be located magnetically. Out of interest, the remains of several hitherto unidentified World War II planes that were shot down in that area have been found.' He paused again for a further sip of his drink whilst the others waited.

'Any unidentified wreck has been dived on by the British Navy using their latest lightweight submersible detection equipment and radiation checks carried out. None of them have been proved to be the source we are looking for. Other wrecks are just not there or have broken up so completely that they are not detectable. However, there is one wreck that the computers have thrown up which we calculate from the size of its engines and cargo of machine tools, should be showing some trace that just isn't there.

The Acacia Lady was an old pre war freighter bound from Alexandria to the London docks when she sank somewhere off the Channel Islands early in 1953.'

The shock announcement of the ship's name sent Peter's mind spinning back over the last few days. The treasure ship of Capt. Rogerson, the dragon ship his mother had talked of, the ship containing Carter's gold, the newspaper cuttings his father had stored for so many years and the oblique references by Ian Porter. Was this the American equipment that Carter had tried to sell to the Chinese. Was the dragon that Carter had waffled on about the other evening another name for the bomb?

Hoskins was still speaking as a copy of the Western English Channel Admiralty Chart was clicked up on the screen.

'Yes here it is. You will see on the Admiralty chart the area is called Hurd Deep that lies south west of the Island of Alderney and the Casquets in the Channel Islands.' He zoomed in closer.

'The Casquets are a predominant group of rocks and have a lighthouse situated just here.' He moved the mouse arrow to emphasise the position on the screen. 'Most commercial shipping bound from Biscay to the Channel ports in France and England and beyond has to round these rocks to the west where there is now a shipping separation zone. The water was considered deep enough there for a wreck not to be a hazard to shipping so it was only ever shown on the charts for the area as a deep wreck. In fact the area was used as an ammunition dumping ground after the First World War due to its depth. It's like a junk yard down there.

From about 1965 to the early part of the eighties, the place was also used to secretly dump nuclear waste. Some of you will have seen newspaper reports a couple of years ago about the MV Topaz incident when a glass flask of waste broke open, contaminating the deck and her crew.

Fishermen have known of a wreck in that position for years and regularly fish it for Conger eel. The French Navy who recently investigated it both magnetically and with radar sonar found that it was not a ship at all but the remains of an old wartime prefabricated caisson. There are other wrecks there that are well documented including the wreck of the submarine Affray, which went down with all hands on 17th.April 1951 and was eventually located three months later.'

He lifted one of the papers and adjusted his half moons higher on his nose as he read. 'Located by the Royal Navy 6th. Frigate Squadron on. June 14th. of that year following an intensive search somewhat similar to the one some of you have been engaged on over the last couple of weeks.'

Peter's mouth was suddenly parched, wanting to shout out about what he knew. He raised his arm to speak and as he did so a hand clutched his wrist and a finger on the Major's lips and slight shake of the head indicated him to keep silent.

Before Peter could protest, the Major rose and said. 'Ladies and gentlemen, we'll take a short comfort break now and reconvene in, say twenty minutes.'

Most of the delegates remained in their seats whilst others got up to stretch their legs.

Major Fellows drew Peter to one side and said quietly. 'I know you've made what you consider to be a discovery about your father and the ship, but this is not the right time or place to discuss it, O.k? There will be an opportunity later for us to discuss the various connections.'

Bob Darkins had sidled up to Hoskins. 'How did they manage to locate the *Affray* all that time ago?'

Hoskins smiled. 'I guess with a lot of hard work. I gather from the records that they searched an area of 6000 square miles, and thirty-one wrecks using Asdic. Eventually they found it by pure intuition like a lot of things that go on at sea.'

'This caisson you described, what sort of structure was that?'

'You've never heard of the Mulberry prefabricated harbour? Before those around him could assent, he continued. 'Now, that was one of the best kept military secrets of the last war.' He savoured the fact as though modern secrets could not be expected to last for long. There were so many counter organisations and so called leaks that every few days the World's media had a heyday on something to make politicians squirm.

'In 1945 the Germans controlled all the ports in Northern France. To back up the D-Day landings, Churchill had two floating harbours called Mulberry A and Mulberry B built. They were constructed during 1944 as gigantic steel and concrete caissons on separate sites all over the U.K. so that even your civvy Brits. didn't know what they were building. Some of the caissons were towed by tugs from as far afield as London, Glasgow and Birkenhead with the intention of sinking them at the two main landing sites in Normandy.

After the Bridgehead was established at Arromanches, the first Mulberry B caissons were towed in to the beach and sunk. They were then connected together by piers and floated into place so that they provided the basis for a harbour where supply vessels could unload and shelter. Unfortunately, on June 19th. the worst north easterly gale for nearly forty years struck the Channel. The partially completed harbours suffered immense damage and the A section that was for the use of our U.S. troops was largely washed away and ended up scattered along the Normandy beaches. Other parts of the harbours that were being towed across the Channel at the time were caught in the gale and had to be cut free. There were well over a hundred caissons, some weighing over 6000 tons, and most of them made it to their destinations. Those caught up in the gale had to be left to drift in the tremendous seas, unattended and a hazard to other ships. Eventually they were either beached, capsized or deliberately scuttled and sunk.'

Up to a few days previously the Commander had only vaguely heard of Mulberry but the French report had prompted some urgent research which was why he could now roll off the facts so fluently. He then proceeded to go into further detail about the block ships and many other tributes that had made the wartime project such a success.

Most of the delegates now sat waiting for the rest of the presentation. Many of them had other important meetings to attend after this one.

'So why choose this site as unusual from all the rest?' It was Bob Darkins again who seemed to have fired up his imagination to the night of the storm and its consequences. 'Surely there are numerous wrecks that are missing or misplaced, anyway, the bomb could have been in an aircraft that crashed.'

'Following every known sinking or plane crash in your territorial waters, there is always a board of enquiry set up by the appropriate Government department, regardless of nationality. Usually, by International convention, the enquiry is then referred to the governing body of the place of registration.

One of our jobs has been to sift back through all the official enquiries to establish each vessel's details, and any anomalies in those details.

The Board of Trade enquiry in 1953 that covered this London registered vessel was very thorough because a number of crew were lost and insurance fraud was suspected. The fraud was never proved, except that we now find that there is no ship, or should I say, remains of a ship in the position reported at the time. The authorities who control diving and salvage in this area have also allowed us to cross reference their files and no application has ever been made for salvage on that site.

We also know that this particular ship, the Acacia Lady, plied the East China seas and the Japanese Pacific both before and after the War. Before reaching Alexandria she had come from Hong Kong.'

He glanced momentarily over to Peter before continuing.

'We have recently established that the contaminated diver was connected in the past with the vessel and may have been unknowingly employed by a terrorist supported diving expedition in the guise of a treasure hunt.'

Hoskins closed his file. 'And that Ladies and Gentlemen is the situation at the present time, except that we know we are not the only ones looking for the bomb. We will now break into the groups as previously agreed unless there are any questions.'

'What about your Freedom of Information act in the States, Why hasn't the loss of this bomb become public information.'

Ambassador Kennedy cleared his throat and looked to the Chairman for recognition to reply.

'There are many instances of nuclear accidents in our country by which the act you have referred to has brought information to the public's attention quickly and efficiently. However, the occurrence we are referring to here happened many years ago before that act came into being in 1967 and no organisation has asked for an official enquiry. Also, the bomb was lost outside our territorial claims and the act would not have applied. The political consequences of the loss being, as we thought until recently, close to China and Japan, also had to be considered as did the integrity of our military forces in that area.'

A hand was raised from the front row.

'Mr.Chairman, Sir Terence Fletcher of the U.K.Marine Safety Agency. I see from this report and the brief visuals you have shown us, that the main concern is environmental catastrophe from increasing emissions as the nuclear device's outer shell corrodes away. What are the possibilities of this nuclear device exploding?'

Hoskins looked to Dr.Crawford for a reply. 'Unlikely to happen Sir. Even sixty years ago the safety mechanisms used in the high explosive charge used to set of the main nuclear reaction was quite sophisticated and, as now, required external control equipment to set off the sequence. Unlike the first bomb, which relied on a critical mass of uranium 235 detonated by a single explosive force, the Kokura and Nagasaki bombs were of the fission type where a complex array of explosive lenses was arranged around the central core of plutonium. The core was about the size of a grapefruit and consisted of two half spheres that were held apart by spacers The fire sequence had to be controlled to within less than a microsecond for it to succeed and drive the two hemispheres together for the critical mass to be achieved for detonation.

However, we are working on computer models to establish the effects that a spurious nuclear explosion could have even though we believe that such an event would be extremely unlikely. At the moment we're using informed guesswork as it would depend on factors such as the sea depth, tides and prevailing winds. If the bomb was in shallow water for instance, the sea would evaporate at the location causing a massive tidal wave to radiate out from the epicentre

Such a tidal wave, a tsunami, with no warning could, depending on the location, flood many Channel towns and cities and if combined with a high spring tide, could cause a great amount of destruction, causing maybe thousands of deaths along such a highly populated seaboard.

The other thing we have to consider, especially if the bomb is in shallow water, is the danger of detonation from an exterior source such as a mine or deliberate attempt to blow it up. In this case a nuclear chain reaction would not occur, but the result of the explosive force could scatter plutonium particles into the atmosphere over a wide area. Even microscopic particles of plutonium can cause severe health problems and if inhaled could cause death.

The main winds in that region are between the North West and South West and radio active fallout could extend anywhere from the Normandy peninsular and southern England right through to, the Low countries, North Germany, Denmark and beyond.'

She paused for the deluge of questions that were then directed at her. The recent events were still circumstantial and she could only give her own views based on data previously researched over the long search period.

Someone else raised a hand, 'The brief states that the control mechanism equipment is also missing, surely that must also pose the possibility that the device could be re armed.'

The Doctor looked around the table. 'The control equipment comprised many component parts such as thermionic radio valves, crystals, transformers and large paper capacitors as well as wiring, which in those days would have had rubber and cotton insulation. If that lot was also in the sea, most of it would have corroded to nothing by now. The main danger here is that if someone got through the security net to the old blueprints and circuit diagrams, the control equipment could be re- built using modern components. We have to also face up to the fact that we know a lot of the technical information has leaked over the years and is already in the public domain and on the Internet.' She continued. 'No, as the report in your briefing notes outline, the main concern here is to the environment from the very concentrated radio active emissions from the plutonium if the device starts to break up. There are also other highly toxic substances involved in the bomb's construction. These together with plutonium could cause a terrible long term disaster.

Firstly, the English Channel, which the European Union already considers is over fished, would become untenable as a fishing ground. Fish in the area could become mutated and pass genetic distortions down the food chain to other sea species and birds. There would be a total ban on fishing which could extend all over the continental shelf of Europe. That would cause thousands of jobs dependant on the fishing and associated industries in Spain, France, Portugal and Britain to be lost.

As another instance, wildlife reserves set up by members of OSPAR, known previously as the Oslo and Paris Commissions, would be put in jeopardy.

These coastlines are sensitive ecological areas for mammals such as seals that rely on fish as their diet and the migrant whales that pass through this area on their way to the Arctic. The computations of polluting the total food chain are enormous. The other mammals are, of course, human. The whole Channel coastline, north and south, is heavily populated and contamination on this scale could cause enormous economic consequences as well as a severe health hazard.'

She operated the lectern keyboard and flashed statistics on the AV screen with respect to Leukaemia, thyroid and other cancers that she then proceeded to expand on with statistical data taken from many sources.

Hoskins broke in again. 'Many of you will be aware that this is not the only nuclear accident to occur around the world, there are about sixty nuclear weapons that have been lost over the years mainly in very deep water, additionally, there are six missing nuclear submarines with ten nuclear reactors rotting away down there which at some time in the future will start to identify their presence and haunt future generations.

The Russian nuclear submarine Norsk was also a risk until its salvage a few years ago and Chernobyl, well, we all know the fallout effect that disaster caused.

There is also the international trade in uranium waste that is regularly shipped around the world and has been the subject of a great deal of public concern. Let me cite just as one example the case of the *Mont Lois* that sank in the English Channel in the eighties. She was carrying a cargo of Uranium hexaflouride, a basic material from which nuclear fuel is made, for the French company Comega and the Belgian power company Synatom. The material itself is not very radioactive, but a highly toxic gas and could have proved catastrophic had all the containers not been retrieved.

Thinman is only a small portion of the Worlds nuclear waste. We are however treating it with the utmost urgency because it is probably in shallow water and could be the cause of environmental catastrophe in the near future.

A member of the Environmental Agency directed her question to Dr.Crawford. 'Could you tell us please Dr.Crawford, how much radiation we are talking about, say, with respect to the discharges at the nuclear reprocessing plants at Sellafield, Cap de la Hague in Normandy, or the old Karlsruhe plant before the Germans reduced its output under their policy of withdrawal from nuclear power generation? All these plants have poured out enormous quantities of radioactive effluent into the sea for years.'

She looked over to the young woman and spoke carefully, for some reason she had not prepared for such a question.

'I regret that I cannot give you a straightforward answer to that one. Radioactive radiation takes various forms, what we denote as alpha, beta and gamma emission. These are measured in a variety of ways often relying on statistical data and result in units of measurement that can appear confusing. Most people have heard of the *Rem* or *Seievert* because these units define dose rates on living tissue and are used in medical establishments.

As I'm sure you are aware, the units used for the discharges you have quoted are more obscure. The most common one used to be called the *Curie* which has now been replaced by the *Bequerel*. Depending on the state of the bomb's shielding, the plutonium device could have an activity of about two thousand megabecquerels per second. The release of radioactive emitters from Sellafield has been reduced in recent years and is now about ten *Tetrabequerels* per year. If we assume that plutonium makes up about zero point zero one percent of the total discharge,' she stopped and did a quick calculation, 'well, I calculate that the bomb could deposit about fifteen times more plutonium radio nuclides per year onto the sea bed than the processing plant.'

Whilst she was speaking there had been some hasty finger prodding of quickly produced pocket calculators and Blackberries from some of the technical representatives around the table, who then proceeded to disagree amongst themselves as to the correct figure. Some delegates, having done their own calculations from presented data made it considerably more, some less than one thousandth of the figure she had produced.

The chairman intervened pointing out that such was the obscurity of reliable data, which was after all only statistical, those interested should gather separately after the meeting to discuss the reliability of the figures used.

Katherine Holmes had been stunned at the news of the bomb. Like most of those who were in attendance, she had not been forewarned of the real subject matter up for discussion. Somehow those responsible for preparing the delegate list had not connected her to her missing father.

Peter Senden sat in the silence he had been instructed to observe. He had noticed the young lady sitting at the end of the second row, attractive, green eyes and auburn hair. He thought he recognised her from somewhere in the past, but was soon engrossed in listening to the debate and the matter dropped from his mind. Earlier she had also given Peter Senden a longer than casual glance of recognition as he stood chatting to the meeting chairman.

'Commander Sir John Davey Mr.Chairman.' The Chief Constable of the Devon and Cornwall police had raised his hand to speak. 'May I ask a question about the control equipment? You say that the circuits have been released onto the Internet could Dr.Crawford expand on that for us.'

She looked through her papers again and extracted the relevant part of a report she had prepared for the *Broken Arrow Thinman* assignment.

'Yes Sir John, we have found many versions of the safety and control circuits posted on the Internet. The sources are not always known, but the worrying aspect of them is that the detonation radio frequencies , band pass filter information and sequences of transmission pulses are accurately defined on one of them. There is also information on pressure transducers that would have determined the detonation height above sea level. The designs are quite crude with respect to modern devices. There are only five interlocking safety devices and in anticipation of your next question I should state that, with the right knowledge, they could be easily re- instated using the current state of the art electronics. I should add however that the circuits only apply to the external control equipment and not to the bomb itself. As far as we can tell, no information exists in the public domain on the bomb circuitry or the method used as an internal power source.'

There followed a frenzied question and answer session by several delegates, on the technical aspects and feasibility of rearming the bomb.

Sir John was again waving his arm for recognition from the Chair which was granted as he read from his notes.

'Sir, as you are aware, Sir Anthony Holmes's team at what used to be called the Atomic Weapons Research Establishment in conjunction with engineers at the Royal Artillery Research Establishment at Fort Halstead, now known as DERA, was responsible for developing PALs, or Permissive Action Links which as I understand are the modern versions of the control equipment's you were describing just now and vastly complicated electro optic devices.

Some of you will have received my ALERT memo overnight informing you that we received information in Cornwall last night, that Sir Anthony has been kidnapped, possibly by the terrorist group you referred to earlier. I know some of your departments are already investigating that occurrence and the co-ordinating committee has been established and will meet later tonight after this meeting. It could be assumed, that with his special knowledge, Holmes kidnapping by this group could be directly connected with our discussions here today. Also, Commander Hoskins, you have not yet enlightened us as to the contents of the leak or the Mossad information that Prime Minister Maya Dersch of Israel took to your President.'

Mrs Davies replied. 'Thank you Sir John. Your senior Ministers are aware of the circumstances which are a complicated set of affairs. The Palestinians were horrified at their discovery and were actually instrumental in bringing the facts to the notice of the Israeli Government whom they felt would have more credence on the matter with our Government. Because they had stumbled on information pertaining to the device, they were anxious that they were not translated as a threat from their own organisation following the Middle East cease fire agreement negotiations that are now nearing a fruitful stage. The Palestinians have given us their full co-operation.

Weapons grade plutonium has been sought for many years by countries such as Algeria, Libya, Iran, Iraq and North Korea. The idea of manufacturing a fundamentalist dirty bomb is not new. Ever since the cold war ended, the major powers have been fearful that a black market would emerge, but so far, only small quantities of Uranium have turned up. It was also feared that nuclear technicians from the former Russian weapons programme would be coaxed by high salaries to some of the Middle Eastern wild card states. It turns out that most of the technicians on the Russian programme were pigeon holed into specific small areas of research and not many of them had an overall grasp of the total technology required. The handfuls of scientists who run the Russian Federation nuclear programme are all accounted for and are conscientiously engaged, like our own scientists, in keeping their knowledge from subversives. The basic contents of the fundamentalist documentation outlined several options ranging from the theft from nuclear stockpiles in the Russian Federation and the Ukraine to finding other sources of plutonium. The former ideas were concluded to be unrealistic due to the protective devices we have already discussed.

The terrorist group is not known although similar groups have committed the atrocities in New York and Washington, Madrid and London.

In the unlikely event of them finding the nuclear bomb, they would certainly need someone of Sir Anthony Holmes' knowledge if they were to reinstate it as a working device. Even then, it must be remembered that Sir Holmes only led the technical teams that developed the systems. He would need a vast team of experts in virtually every physical science to help him.

We cannot therefore deduce from your ALERT that this television presenter, who has made the application of science and engineering in everyday life so fascinating to millions of viewers, could be held for that purpose.'

Katherine had not been associated as being related and said nothing as she sat in stunned silence, thinking about her father.

'Apart from the surveys you are carrying out on wrecks, what else are you doing? For example the Acacia Lady, what do you know about her?'

Hoskins answered. 'Three central characters were involved when the ship was sunk. We have established that one of them is still alive and a resident of this country, although we are not aware of his whereabouts, one, the previously mentioned diver is dead, the third is a resident of Hong Kong and has also suddenly vanished. Since we discovered the disparity of information with our computers last week, we have been trying to trace them. They would probably be in their seventies or eighties by now. As you know Sir John we traced one of these men to a location in your own jurisdiction of Cornwall. Unfortunately, in spite of an active surveillance operation on a number of his contacts, we have not yet found him.

The conference droned on into the late evening as committees and sub committees were formed and the networking agreements established with civil defence representatives. Katherine was soon embroiled with the finger prodding calculator group as Major Fellows finished a conversation and turned to Peter.

'Senden while your here I'd like you to meet someone.' He beckoned towards the door. 'If you'd like to follow me please.' They left the buzzing conference room and walked to the lift where Fellows pressed the button for the eighth floor. Peter had never been on the top floor before and sensed the quietness of the quality carpet as they walked past the solid mahogany doors that lined the corridor until Fellows stopped outside the door of the Deputy Operations Director and knocked. The door was opened by a secretary who Fellows spoke to and they were shown into the Director's office.

Sir George Longland was Peter's ultimate boss although he had never met him and he indicated comfortable buttoned leather armchairs for them to sit. A large wall monitor screen was still recording the events in the downstairs conference room that was now emptying and he leant forward and turned it off.

Major Fellows and Sir George exchanged the usual pleasantries before Peter was introduced.

'Senden, my dear chap, so sorry to hear about your father, must have been a great shock after your other, er..... sad loss.' He closed the dossier he had been referring to a short time earlier.

'Conference went well I see. Now, Jack Fellows has told me about your observations with respect to our American friend Comdr. Hoskins. Probably nothing in it of course but the Major has requested that we release you to his department for a short period. I've spoken to Sir Paul Bane, my counterpart in your own department, who is happy with the temporary arrangement. I know you have been granted leave of absence but Major Fellows would like you to start sooner if that's all right with you.'

Peter took in the unexpected news as Sir George continued.

'This *Thinman* thing is nasty, very nasty, an atom bomb of all things, off the South Coast, you've just come from the conference so you know that of course Our department have received disquieting news that adds to a growing suspicion we have had that the Americans may be not be telling us the whole story. We picked up some information yesterday at the Akrotiri listening post in Cyprus. We've decoded traffic between an organised group of mercenaries who seem to be linked to a covert section of the CIA working between Lebanon and Somalia. Our friends in MI6 have been monitoring them for a few weeks now and these people would appear to be in the background of organising an Arab convention somewhere in the Algerian desert, close to a new nuclear power station that is being built there with the help of N.Korea. The names of the one hundred and forty odd delegates are some of the most dangerous terrorists in the World including, we believe, many disciples of the notorious al-Qaeda organisation.'

He smiled. 'Don't worry Senden, we're not thinking of sending you out there. We have others over at Vauxhall Cross covering that aspect. No, what we need is more information here. If your suspicions are correct, Hoskins is obviously trying to tell us something and he seems to have chosen you as a conduit, someone he can trust.'

Jack Fellows gave a polite cough.

'If I may say so Sir George, I have arranged to fly out to the task force sometime in the next couple of days, Hoskins will be there at the same time and it would be an ideal opportunity if Senden could be included on that trip and have a technical look around.'

'Capital idea Jack, this is a highly technical area which Senden is used to according to the excellent reports in his file, let's go ahead and see what transpires. Any questions Senden?' Peter asked a few pertinent questions and the meeting was over.

They were turning to leave when Peter enquired.

'Major, is *Thinman* also known as *Dragon's Morsel*?'

Major Fellows glanced over to Sir George, already engrossed in a pile of papers on his desk and drew Peter away. Outside the room, the Major said.

'The *Dragon's Morsel* your father spoke about has nothing to do with *Thinman* and I'd be happy if you didn't mention it again.' Fellows then took Peter to his own office two floors below, where the carpets were still good but not quite the quality he had seen upstairs.

Even at that late hour, a secretary brought them coffee and they discussed the *Thinman* conference.

'By the way, I understand our Dr. Wilson is getting on quite well with you.' Fellows's eyes gave that twinkle that came out every so often as he looked through the owl like glasses. 'Nice lady, wish I was younger, but then Mrs.F wouldn't allow it,' he chuckled to himself.

'So Peter, welcome to the team, you now know what *Thinman* is and that we desperately need to find it before we have a nuclear catastrophe or public disorder or both on our hands.'

The major seemed nervous as he lifted the coffee mug to his mouth and Peter's grey eyes noticed the slight shaking of the mans hands.

'I guess it was *Thinman* that my father found, presumably whilst he was seeking the treasure on the Acacia Lady. I would still like to know what this mysterious reference is to the *Dragon's Morsel* though.'

Major Fellows finished his coffee and gave the new member of his team a long hard look.

'Well I think it's time to leave. We'll tie up on the visit to the task force tomorrow. Until then I'll bid you a very good evening Peter.'

Part II.
The Acacia Lady.

The snot green sea. The scrotum tightening sea.
                                    James Joyce,   Ulysses.

Chapter 26. Ortac.

On the evening of the sea rescue and TV interviews at the quay in Weymouth, a man stood in the small bar at the Spring Head pub in the small village of Street, several miles away. In spite of a slight stoop he appeared reasonably tall, his receding white hair long and swept back where it curled almost to his shoulders. He had one of those fascinating faces, etched with deep wrinkles and weather beaten about a large sandblasted nose, the skin grey, showing through light stubble and eyes that were active and appeared like black shiny pebbles. The mouth was tight and drew on a small pipe that occasionally crackled as salivary juices mixed with the rough tobacco mix compressed into the bowl. He wore a short sleeved blue pilot style shirt, the pigmentation on the tissue- paper thin skin of his sinewy arms indicating that he was older than one might expect. He stood there, quietly as he had done at this time of the day for the last week, supporting himself with his hands on the edge of the bar. Between his hands stood a large whiskey glass from which he took the occasional sip as he watched the early evening news on the television set behind the bar.

To Captain Gilbert Piltcher the news wasn't of great importance, he watched it mainly out of habit, as the tinny voices came through his hearing aid. If business was quiet, he would usually ask the landlord to put up the Ceefax pages with the days racing results.

At this time of the evening, the bar was usually quiet and the clientele consisted of a few early drinkers who came in from the local farms to discuss the day's prices, argue over the latest E.U. missives and discuss the weather. They were usually huddled together in the small snug at the end of the bar, the smoke curling up to the old oak ceiling beams, where the ochre colour reflected the years of similar discussion from previous generations.

Sam Stephens the landlord of the Springs Head stood behind the bar looking into the small room, elbows resting as he politely listened to the various stories that he had heard, repeated over and over again night after night, joining in the laughter where necessary, making a comment when asked for on a football match result and drawing the pints of real ale as the next round came up.

To the outsider, it appeared that he had an indolent lifestyle. His wife could have corrected that misconception as she hustled her staff in the tiny kitchen behind the bars in preparation for the townsfolk who would drive out to the country pub later in the evening for dinner.

Stephens's ears were attuned to the latch on the old door leading into the premises, footsteps on the flagstone floor, the rustle of paper money or a tap on a glass. All signs that signalled a relief from the monotonous discourse.

'Another Scotch is it Gilbert?' He placed the glass under the optic in anticipation of the gravel voice reply. 'Yes please, but could you turn the volume up a bit on the telly for me first, there's something I want to watch.'

The Captain placed a twenty pound note on the bar counter for his drink as he watched and listened to the report from the Weymouth quay side. There wasn't much local news that night and the report had been padded out with interviews from the coast guards and the local representative of the Royal Yachting Association. One correspondent defending the rights of small boat owners, though specifying the stupidity of going to sea without proper preparation and safety equipment, whilst the other demanded proper licensed control which was being introduced by other maritime members of the E.U.

Piltcher had mildly recognised the name of Peter Senden and watched the interview account of the rescue at sea. When the name of Simon Carter a visitor from Hong Kong came up, he froze like the haw frost on a December morning.

The landlord heard the door latch and looked over in anticipation, only to see the empty bar. His regular for the past week had gone, leaving only the waft of pipe tobacco smoke, an empty whisky glass and his change from twenty pounds sitting on the bar top.

So Carter really was back and already in the thick of things. It couldn't have been a coincidence that Peter Senden just happened to be sailing back from the same area to effect that rescue. He walked down the road towards the Church, turned off across the fields and climbed the footpath that led up the hill behind the cliffs. Pausing occasionally to rest he entered the woods that, after a further short climb, brought him out onto a muddy flint lined lane that ran parallel to the cliff edge. It soon opened out with fields on one side and grassy tumuli along the cliff edge on the other side. As he strode down the narrow lane and turned off at the grass track, he mused over what he had just seen and heard.

'So the old devil really is back here, looking for his part of the retirement fund no doubt.' The words were spoken softly to himself as a pair of alarmed pheasants dashed out of the nearby hedge and took their flight low over the wheat field that ended at the cliff's edge.

He arrived at the steep winding path that led down to the remote caravan, hidden away on the sloping under-cliff between Branscome and Sidmouth, surrounded by wild gorse, brambles and hawthorn that bent their uppermost branches to the evening onshore breeze. A solitary blackbird sang its evensong as Piltcher fumbled with his key at the door.

Once inside, he went to a cupboard and pulled out a file consisting of letters, newspaper clippings and photographs. He sat there for a while as he turned them over, remembering his previous encounters with Simon Carter, in Hong Kong, Alexandria, the Black Sea and other places. His discovery of the gold aboard the Acacia Lady, the Court Room in Southampton forty odd years ago where he had lied under oath, his encounter with Carter and Holmes on the Black Sea cruise. He pondered over the thugs he had seen breaking into Crows Nest Cottage a few mornings ago as he had been strolling back across the fields. From his vantage point, he had crouched behind the cattle trough and seen the police car and ambulance that had arrived soon after. He had decided that too much interest was being shown in him. He decided to vanish for a while and was now holed up in this awful caravan deprived of the luxuries he had become accustomed to, no electricity and primitive sanitation facilities.

He had sat there for some time recalling the events that had landed him in this secret place of discomfort. It was getting dark and he turned up the Tilley lamp, reached for pen and paper and after a few thoughtful moments chewing on his pipe, began to write.

'My Dear Philip,
I've tried to 'phone you but can get no answer.
I know my time on this immortal earth will end soon. The cancer that is devouring me from within will see to that just as my wretched conscience has gnawed at my life these last fifty years, since I was unfortunate enough to meet up with Carter.
I have just seen your son Peter on the T.V., a fine looking boy if I may say so, but if he is associating with or assisting Carter he must be stopped.
I've no doubt that Carter is over here to search for the retirement fund. It's unlikely he will find anything as most of it has gone. I know from previous experience that he can turn very violent when things go wrong. He has contacts in the criminal fraternity who can break a man, but I will not dwell on that aspect of him at the moment.
What I am now about to confess has troubled my conscience for years.'

He stopped and read the first few lines and resolved to continue.

'When we left Gibraltar and the old Acacia Lady developed problems, you will remember that it was me who discovered the hoard of gold bullion that Carter had somehow smuggled on board.
We confronted him at the time and you will remember his rage. We were both, as far as I am aware, honest men until that time when he threatened the two of us over our innocent friendship. God knows how he knew. You could have lost your Commission in the Navy at the time and I would have been unemployable in the Merchant service, those days are fortunately gone now and the stigma associated with our love affair would not have arisen.
But it meant that he had a hold on us and we had a hold on him over the smuggling. Hence our fragile agreement not to report him as we otherwise should have done.
Let me go back to the night of the storm when the Acacia Lady was being swept towards the Casquettes. You had left the Acacia Lady by that time and Carter was negotiating a salvage contract on board the salvage ship as the bad weather descended and separated us'.

As he looked at the paper sheets in front of him, his mind was in another time, remembering that awful night.

'Tyne, Dogger, Humber, Thames, north easterly force 9, Dover, Wight, Portland........' The weather forecaster on the BBC's long wave *Light Programme* had continued his articulate drone as Gilbert Piltcher stood in the small radio room behind the bridge deck and waited for the Western English Channel forecast which he already knew. The coastal radio stations had been broadcasting gale warnings all that day on MF and the earlier news had been mainly concerned with the extensive flooding along the North Sea coasts of eastern England, the Netherlands and Belgium. It was the last day of January 1953 a day to be remembered both on land and at sea for the storms and high tides that came during the night with such terrible force and loss of life.

He triggered the microphone button again on the MF set, but the needles on the modulation meters didn't move. The radio transmitter set was dead.

Then he had walked crab like, bracing each step to the ship's motion, over to the starboard bridge door, and stepped out onto the wing deck, closing the door behind him, standing there in the howling cacophony of wind and water hitting steel, his legs astride as he tried to steady himself against the ships skewering movements, looking up at the dark grey cumbrance of sky and umbrella of cloud, the colour of Welsh slates, passing rapidly overhead. Another flurry of snow swept the ship as he had shivered and pulled the duffel coat tighter around himself sheltering in the lee of the bridge as another huge wave broke over them, with the deafening sound of steam hammers. He scanned the horizon for any sign of the Dutch salvage tug that had come out of Cherbourg but was then standing off, it's top lights occasionally visible above the white caps as she rose and fell about a mile away. The pipe clenched between his teeth had gone out again and he cursed as he removed it to his pocket. The seas were mountainous, worse than anything he had seen during the whole voyage from Hong Kong and he clung to a side rail as another wave buried the bow of the ship in its foamy grasp. She rose, slowly at first, and then faster as the wave passed beneath her old plates. And then she was going down again like an express lift, not allowing time for the fore decks to clear the tons of water pouring over her. Sea water rattling every wedge around the cargo hatch coamings, pouring along the gunwales, probing, tearing and seeking every weakness in her steel raiment as her head became more and more sluggish wave after relentless wave.

He returned to the relative calmness of the bridge where the Chinese helmsman, his face full of fear and shiny with perspiration, swung the small wheel from side to side. He called over to the Captain in Cantonese. 'She's not responding Captain, the bows are so low in the water.'

Piltcher knew it was useless, with the bows wallowing, the screw and short rudder were probably clear of the sea most of the time. 'Try and keep her bows on......'

The salvage tug's Dutch captain's voice crackled out from the radio set static saying that, due to the worsening weather, he would return to Cherbourg for the night.

The grinding wrenching movements and screaming sound of distressed metal that followed would remain in Gilbert's memory for ever as he came suddenly out of his dream and again addressed the letter he was writing.

' I was alone on that hulk with five Chinese crew, terrified, not sure what Carter would eventually say about us and the affair when the gold was lost and we had no proof as to his smuggling efforts.

What I said at the enquiry was true, the seas were tremendous, worse than anything we'd seen on the whole voyage from Hong Kong. There was a tremendous rending and grating and I guessed that the bulkhead between the number one and number two holds had at last been torn apart. She had been badly patched up in that area before Carter's father bought her. The fo'csle section and number one hold of the Acacia Lady just broke off and sank roughly in the position that I reported to the enquiry.

I had previously shut the watertight doors in the number two cargo bay and to my amazement and relief, the aft half of the vessel remained afloat, drifting with the tide and wind towards the Ortac Channel.

It was then I resolved that to keep our secret I had to somehow save the bullion.

I got the crew to rig the electric winch on the aft deck and removed some of the hatch coverings on number three hold. The sea was pouring in and the ship was settling lower as they worked through the evening to lift those machine tool boxes onto the deck and cast them overboard. It was at that time that an enormous wave suddenly welled up and washed them into the sea.

I was helpless as I looked down into that frothing dark abyss , all I could hear was their screams for help, becoming fainter and fainter until all I could hear was the winds screeching howling voice and the continuous crashing of the waves on that old hull. The men had gone. Perished in the darkness.

The small wooden boxes containing the bars of bullion were light compared to the equipment boxes and I toiled for hours on that winch, lifting them onto the deck.

Some were washed overboard. The rest I managed to put into one of the remaining lifeboats, each box containing two 400 ounce ingot bars of gold and weighing about 50 pounds.'

He paused with his pen raised and looked at the window that, with the outside darkness, now reflected back his image. A true image, of an old man, sitting there alone, as the events and effort of that dreadful night came flooding back to him. He remembered the sheer exhaustion on his then young body, the sores on his hands that had stung with the cold and salt wetness. The ship had suddenly shuddered to a halt under his feet and he had thought she was aground, but the waves lifted and pounded her. His eyes had become accustomed to the darkness and in the dim light he had seen a high rock off to his starboard side and heard the sound of thousands of gannets as they screamed their objections to the disturbance from their restless sleep. It had given him an immediate position, for he knew that this was Ortac.

The bottom plates cried out their agony, a sound that echoed and amplified around him as though the old lady was begging and struggling in her last desperate gasps for life, the seas occasionally breaking over her in great plumes of spray carried away by the wind like giant rocket trails.

He had operated the davits on the lea side of the hulk before shinning down a rope, bouncing himself off the sheer sides as she rolled to the waves pounding her from the windward side and dropped into the lifeboat. Thank god he had done his job properly in maintaining the old ship during her voyage, doing regular checks to ensure that everything was in working order. The petrol engine, under its waterproof canopy in the lifeboat, started with a single crank and he nosed out into the lighting gloom of the dawn, as the Acacia Lady heaved slowly above him, her bell tolling her death knell as she shuddered to shake herself of the shoal and rocks that surrounded her.

The Tilley was hissing and spluttering, he looked at his watch and saw that it was getting late but he knew he must finish his letter now, or it would never be finished. He rose to stretch his cold legs and fetch another gas canister, refill his pipe and then he picked up the pen and continued.

'I needn't expand here on how I departed that wretched ship, needless to say I steered the lifeboat with its cargo through those enormous seas to the small islet of Renonquet, a barren rock about one hundred metres long and half that in width, roughly three quarters of a mile from Ortac and on the North Western side of the Little Swinge, Alderney and Burhou. An old seaman I had once known, a Jewish Pole I believe, had been in the Alderney slave labour camp run by the Nazi Todt organisation during the war. One of his many stories was that he had helped to build an artillery gun emplacement on that island, the Germans considering it to be the closest piece of British soil to the southern mainland of England.

The reason for the story was, that unbeknown to the Germans, the labourers had constructed a small compartment within the cement foundation. Big enough to hide in should they ever manage to escape from the scourges of that dreadful main island prison camp.

The gun was never installed but as I steered for the Island through the fog, I prayed that I would find the right location and that hiding place. It was there sure enough, with the sea breaking great fountains of water over it.

I ran the lifeboat ashore on the lea side, where we bumped across the rock sills and the bottom planks of the boat were sprung. It was dawn by the time I scrambled ashore and secured the painter to rocks.

The heavy boxes helped to hold the craft in that position as I unloaded it and it gradually filled with the sea. And there, exactly as my old friend had described it was the concrete construction, its edges eroded with time and exposing the rusty steel reinforcement rods. The cavity was much bigger than I had imagined, hidden by hard marram grass and sea campions and sunk in the ground full of water.

The storm abated as the tide turned and after a short rest I used the starting handle as a jemmy, opened each box and just tipped the contents into the hole, each ingot bar vanishing below the surface of the water.

When I was half way through my work, I heard a strange gushing noise and thought I was discovered. From the top of an outcrop I was amazed to see the Acacia Lady lying low in the water at the edge of the mist that was now forming, I estimated about three and a half miles away. As the tide had turned North Eastwards, she must have loosened herself from the shoal around Ortac and drifted.

She was sending up great bubbles of air as she went down, slowly at first and then quite suddenly, the old lady vanished. I still had my hand bearing compass on its lanyard and took a quick fix on her position before virtually collapsing with exhaustion. When I came too, it was still light, although I'm not sure what day it was. The fog had thickened again and I found some Gannet eggs and swallowed them before completing the task of disposing the rest of the gold to the hiding place and then throwing in some loose rocks for good measure.

By the time I had finished the wind had dropped to practically nothing, the ebb tide had dropped to its lowest point, must have been a spring tide because every rock around was exposed . I remembered that Burhou Island lay three quarters of a mile along a bearing just south of east and proceeded to clamber, slither and drag myself over the rocks and seaweed in that direction, swimming across narrow gullies until I could just distinguish the slightly higher ground of the island and it's reef through the murky fog. I swam and scrambled across the southern edge of the Little Swinge and let the returning flood tide float me on to the foreshore reef of the main island, much to the disapproval of the many puffins nesting there. Here I found a bird watcher's stone built hut to shelter in for the night after dining again on raw eggs that I was able to find in abundance.

The next day, the fog had cleared, the Clonque Fort on the west side of Alderney looked so close, but I knew from the pilot books I had read in the Biscay that the dividing stretch of water, The Swinge, was reputed to be one of the most treacherous and dangerous races in the English Channel.

There were some flares in the hut, probably left there by bird watchers or a yacht at some time. I waited until I suddenly saw a small local fisher boat off the Nannels and sent one up.

Well, the rest of the story you know.'

The wind outside had increased and the rain had started, tattooing its noise on the roof of the caravan. The old sea Captain looked up and watched the diagonal patterns of water on the outside of the black window, highlighted by the light from his lamp, as each prismatic droplet of rain was blown across the glass by the wind. A sudden prickling felt on the back of his neck made him reach up and draw the curtain as though someone out there in the blackness of the night was watching him in his confession. He had filled and refilled his pipe as he sat writing and now looked at the many sheets of paper lying on the table in front of him. He had so much to say. If this was his life's confession he still had some way to go, it would have to wait though, he was tired and his watch told him it was three o'clock in the morning.

Chapter 27. USS Phoenix.

It was past midnight when Peter arrived home after the conference. Jessica's car was there and she greeted him at the door and hugged him. Fresh milk and provisions were sitting on the kitchen table and they sat over a pot of tea and chatted about the day's events. He drew her to him and they embraced briefly before he took her by the hand and led her upstairs.

Since Yvonne's death two years previously, Peter had avoided sexual encounters, much to the surprise of the women he had met over that time. With Jessica he thought at first that it was different, the chemistry had been there on that first day she had visited him. And now he tried to let himself go to her, the smooth curve of her succulent body above him, plunging down for that final ecstatic moment that he knew she had also reached as she lunged over him, writhing her thighs about him, her breasts caressing him , her long fair hair sweeping across his face those wide lips searching his.

He knew that he was only serving the physical needs of his body, the lust for something he had not experienced for a long while. His mind constantly went back to Yvonne, he still missed her after all that time and the deep wound was still there. He would somehow have to tell Jessica his true feelings in due course. He couldn't be certain that his organisation had not planted the two of them together for their own ends.

After they showered, she was rubbing his back with the towel and he had his back to her when she suddenly said. 'It's not working is it Peter.' He felt that strange tingle in his veins that told him he was going to lie. He wiped the condensation from the mirror and spoke to her reflection.   'How do you mean?'

She pulled back from him and picked up her dressing gown from the bath stool, knowing that he was fully aware of what she meant.

'I'm giving up my present job at the end of this month and moving up to London, I hope we'll still be able to meet, we've been good together and I've enjoyed it.' She turned at the door. 'I'm sorry Peter but I've had the impression the last few times that we were acting out a scene together, very nice at the time and I can't say I didn't enjoy it, but it's about as far as it went, I'm sure you'll agree.'

As she left the room, rubbing her hair in a towel she suddenly remembered and called back. 'Peter, I forgot to tell you, there's an e-mail from your department on the computer.'

Peter stood there in the bathroom. So that was that, so matter of fact and it had been much easier to extradite than he could have possibly imagined. He wasn't going to argue over it and that half smile of relief flitted across his face.

He followed her out onto the landing and they stood there saying nothing. 'I'll collect my things tomorrow Peter if that's O.K.' She reached up and pecked her lips on his cheek and was gone. So that was that, now he was a member of the Major's 'team' she'd gone, back to her controller for new instructions.

He heard her car departing. He didn't remember giving her his internet access keyword but put the thought to one side as he looked at the computer screen

The e-mail was from Maj. Jack Fellows with the arrangements that had been made for him to visit the task force, in particular the USS Phoenix and the Hecla Class Sonar survey vessel HMS Seeker early the next day.

Peter gazed down on the English Channel from his seat in the Royal Navy Westland Sea King HAS 5 helicopter, powered by its Rolls-Royce Gnome turboshaft engines. It was Monday morning and he was thinking back over the events since his recall from Cologne a month previously.

He was getting a running commentary through his headset from the flight deck observer who was pointing out the various ships now appearing beneath them.

'Those vessels with the black hulls and light brown superstructures are the Royal Navy support ships operated by the Royal Maritime Auxiliary Service, you can see the Roysterer Class Ocean tug over there. Just off its starboard side is a Rover Class fleet tanker and beyond her is a Clovelly diving tender. On the other side, I believe we can see the Sal Class Salvage vessel. She has a lifting capacity of 400 tons.

Now, below us is the Hecla Class Survey ship HMS Seeker, we'll be landing there on our second stop. Ahead of us just to the port side is one of the small offshore patrol vessels, probably the 'Alderney.' There's also a couple of Sandown offshore mine hunters around somewhere. Oh, look over to your left, that's a type 23 frigate, one of the Second Frigate Squadron. And now gentlemen ahead of us is the sovereign land of Uncle Sam, the USS Phoenix and her entourage.... Helicopter Golf Sierra One to command....'. The commentary ended as the official jargon for landing the chopper on the USS *Phoenix's* helideck started, and they began their descent to the ship as it moved slowly through the water .

The first thing that Peter noticed as he stepped out of the aircraft door was that the ship was much smaller than he had expected. An Officer welcomed them aboard and guided them forward from the quarter deck, past the deck hangar where mechanics worked on a Sikorsky Seahawk helicopter and along a side deck where equipment pipes and hoses seemed to snake in all directions. Whatever it was he was supposed to look for, Peter knew it would be very difficult.

They entered a side door and ascended a flight of steps towards the bridge deck but turned off and were shown into a ward room where Commander Hoskins rose to greet them. He saluted Fellows , even though the Major was dressed in a civvy rain jacket, more suitable for a wet afternoon of golf, and extended his hand of long fingers to Peter. 'Hi there Doctor, Major, welcome aboard the *Phoenix*. Hope you had a good trip over. I've arranged for you to have a look around and hopefully to meet our Task Force Commander, Admiral Sam Mcready.'

The ward room steward served coffee and flapjacks while Hoskins phoned through to the control bridge. 'Well, it seems that the Admiral is busy, has other problems on his mind right now. I'll have to give you a quick tour myself.'

He took them down to the crowded Sonar control deck room, and explained the complexities of the screens and equipment. Then off through corridors to another area, unmanned this time and showed them some of the latest experimental equipment being developed for anti submarine warfare. Then they watched in the task force room as operators mapped out the positions of surrounding vessels and logged the various flight paths of airborne traffic, using large electronic screens. From there they passed through the storage area, piled high with bags of special water repellent cement, crates and spares. It was here that Peter's eyes fell on something he didn't expect to see on a survey ship. A small crate with yellow radiation warning labels affixed to the outside.

He stood to one side, as Hoskins explained how the framework they would be seeing on the deck was to be lowered over the bomb once it was found and removed from the wreck. Divers in special suits would then suspend the device in the framework that, when the side plates were attached, would resemble a box into which concrete would be pumped from the surface. It would then be lifted with the aid of the salvage tug and air bags and shipped back to the States for decommissioning. Dredgers would then be brought in to vacuum the sea bed for a large area around the site and remove the spoils back to the U.S. where it would be buried in deep mine shafts. An enormous and expensive operation.

Back on the main deck, they were shown a large box like steel structure sat between heavy duty derricks, as welders worked with their oxyacetylene torches. It was surrounded by pumps the size of freight containers, together with divers gear, small submersibles and other equipment. The rest of the deck was surprisingly inactive with a few ratings propping up the guard rails and taking in the sun.

Commander Hoskins finished his dialogue. 'Well that just about concludes the tour, hope you found it of interest. Now I must get back to the control room. They're just about finished in this section search area.'

'No sign of the Acacia Lady yet then?' Peter asked.

Hoskins took off his half moons and replaced them in the top pocket of his uniform jacket. 'Unfortunately not. We are beginning to think that the Acacia Lady was a bum steer. It was only one of a number of suspect wrecks we had to consider. The circumstances surrounding it certainly led us to believe that it could be the source, but the evidence was not circumstantial. That is apart from the one reference to the *Dragon's Morsel* by your father and a similar reference to it on a telephone link we intercepted from Hong Kong.

When we finish here today we're moving to another area in Lyme Bay, about twenty five miles west of Portland Bill there are some wrecks there that need investigation. And now I must leave you with Quartermaster Mallesmann who will show you back to your helicopter.'

Peter thought about what the Major had said the previous day about the *Dragon's Morsel* being totally irrelevant to the search. If so, why had the Commander commented on its significance. He said nothing but decided to keep an open mind on the subject.

They said their goodbyes and Mallesmann guided them back to the heli deck where the Sea King had just returned for them.

As Mallesmann saluted and turned to leave, Peter said. 'By the way, I forgot to ask Commander Hoskins to convey our thanks to Admiral Mcready for a most interesting tour, perhaps you would do that on our behalf.' The lieutenant turned back to him. 'That won't be necessary sir, Admiral Mcready isn't on board at the moment, he was called Stateside a couple of days ago, he will not be back until this afternoon.'

The two men said nothing until they were back on board HMS Seeker and had been served tea in the empty ward room. 'So, you saw something.' Fellows dunked his biscuit and waited.

'I'm not sure how significant it was, but I should think it's unusual for a non combat ship such as the *Phoenix* to be carrying supplies of tritium gas.'

'Tritium gas, what's that?'

'Tritium, as I understand it, is used to boost the explosive power in a nuclear device such as a warhead. It works by adding extra free neutrons during detonation.'

'So, what's the connection.'

'Nuclear warheads are filled with the hydrogen isotopes , deuterium and tritium. Titrium decays quite rapidly over a period of time so that it's effectiveness to the boosting process degrades according to the age of the warhead. That means that it has to be replaced periodically, especially in older stockpiled nuclear weapons.'

The Major sat there thinking, idly dunking the rest of the biscuit until it suddenly disintegrated . 'I wonder what Hoskins is up to, why would he lie about Admiral Mcready do you think.' Fellows knew the answer but liked confirmation.

'I get the impression that the Commander is not a happy man. With his training and expertise in the U.S. Navy Intelligence core, he would not have taken the time to take me to one side and ask questions about satellite telemetry. The W85 nuclear warhead handbook in his open briefcase was deliberately displayed for me to see. He must have been aware that I would recognise it. Similarly, why stop in front of that pile of cement sacks to describe their operation. That could have been done up on the deck with the enclosure structure. I think it was a deliberate stop to ensure that we saw the gas bottles. We'd have had to be blind not to see them, covered with their yellow radiation labels. It was also rather strange that he, and not one of the ship's officers, showed us around.'

Fellows nodded and smiled. 'Well done my boy, exactly my own thoughts, I knew you would be well suited to working in my section. The Commander is trying to tell us something or point us somewhere, but I wonder where.'

'How about Lyme Bay Major.'

Fellows rose and called the steward. 'Can you ask Captain Williams if it would be possible to have a few words?'

Captain Williams, arrived after a few minutes , they had already been introduced as they came aboard on the Sea King and he had shown them the sonar control room. They had also watched Lynx helicopters with their dipping sonar anti submarine equipment suspended beneath by cable and trailed in the sea.

'Ah, Captain, can you tell me, have you carried out a box search yet in Lyme Bay?'

The Captain didn't need to refer to his ship's log, 'Yes Major, about two weeks ago. There are several wrecks up there and we did a thorough search . Nothing there that we didn't already know about. Our submarines use that area for exercises and there is also a gunnery range along the shore. There used to be a torpedo test range over there, as well as a small mining exercise area. So, as you can imagine, that area has been regularly surveyed over the years. Even so, we were most concerned to sweep that area again at an early stage of the current exercise.'

Dick Fellows glanced knowingly to Peter before asking the next question. 'Would the USS Phoenix know if that area had been searched.'

Williams smiled at them, took of his cap, with its single row of gold leaves on the black peak, and smoothed his thinning hair. 'A man can't have a shit around here without it being reported to the Phoenix. They know every inch that we search. The only secret we keep to ourselves these days is how we manage to remain the best Navy in the world.'

They all laughed as Captain Williams asked if there was anything else he could help them with before leaving. 'Yes there is as a matter of fact. Could you arrange clearance for our return flight helicopter to detour to an area twenty five miles due west of Portland Bill?'

With a 100 knots cruising speed and a slight north westerly head wind, they were over the area defined by Hoskins within thirty minutes and descended in a slow sweep looking down at the grey blue sea's surface.

When they first saw it from that height they thought it was a small orange life raft but as they approached they could see that the object below them was a large inflatable buoy, the sort used for ocean yacht races.

It bobbed up and down under the helicopters downdraught and was obviously anchored there for some reason. There were some small fishing boats about a mile away, but this object was too big to be a pot marker.

The observer's voice came over the headset 'Is that what we are looking for sir'

'I think it probably is, can you ask the systems operator to mark it on his GPS computer and then take us back to the ship. Can you also patch me through to Capt. Williams on board HMS Seeker. No, hang on. On second thoughts I'd like to keep radio silence, just get us back as quickly as possible.'

Pat Lloyd was attending his pots on the small open aft deck of his fishing boat, of about thirty five feet, with an array of pink marker buoys slung high on the rails as he heard the Sea King go over and circle the area about a mile south of him.

The seagulls following his wake didn't seem to notice the noise as he watched to make sure that the helicopter's point of interest was the orange buoy he had been shown earlier in the day, as it hovered for a while over the spot and then turned and headed south.

He finished with the pots before clambering over the boxes and coiled ropes on the deck and went to the cuddy cabin and lifted the hand mike on his VHF, making sure he was on the high power setting and selected a ship to ship channel.

'Control from Fishing Vessel Scorpion, the fish have taken the bait' An immediate reply barked through the loudspeaker. 'Scorpion, understood, thank you, out.'

He went back to his work musing over the quick one thousand pounds in cash he had made for sitting out there. It was a better return on his labours than catching fish. The stranger who had got into conversation with him in the pub the night before, a young crewcutted American had started to talk to him about diving and he had related the story of his father's drowning near the Casquettes during a diving expedition. His father had not been insured and the lousy solicitor at the coroner's inquest in Guernsey had argued successfully against costs. His family had received nothing.

Later he saw the machine return and drop two divers.

He referred to the small hand held GPS his aunt had given him as an unusually generous birthday gift and entered the position inshore where he would now go to pick up his crabbing pots. Then he would make his way inshore for the funeral of his cousin that afternoon.

On board the USS Phoenix, Sam Mandeville the duty radio officer took the message and passed it through to Admiral Mcready who had just returned to the ship. He dealt with many communications he didn't understand during the course of the day. Mcready's response and instructions were of no real interest to him, he just took orders.

His fingers moved quickly over the keys as he put in the non naval destination on his keyboard, entered the appropriate encryption code data and sent the message. 'The fish are nibbling the bait. Admiral Mcready.'

In Langley, Tim Gregson relayed the message through to Gibson. So the bait had been set and taken, easier than casting a fly for an elusive trout. Hoskins had given the false position to the British as they had predicted. He lifted the phone and called Graham Erricsmann who acknowledged the news with his usual acrimonious grunt of understanding.

Chapter 28. Capt. Piltcher's Confession.

Gilbert Piltcher read through the toils of the previous evening and nodded to himself. Now was the time to either tear up the paper sheets or continue.

He sat there over his light breakfast thinking about the consequences of the information he was now imparting to Philip.

His night had been sleepless even though he had increased the Diamorphine dose that seemed to be having less effect on him now and the pain was becoming almost continuous. The doctors at the hospital had given him three months. That now left him with a months to go before he would enter the hospice. He had nothing to lose by divulging his fifty year old secret as he took up his pen and after a few minutes started on a new sheet.

At the enquiry I did a terrible thing. I lied and inferred that the whole ship had gone down in Hurd Deep.

It was Carter who got me to lie. In exchange he offered me a share of the gold when it was salvaged. It was Carter who first called it the retirement fund.

I knew at the time that the insurers were unlikely to press for salvage at that depth and that Carter would think that his secret was safe. I never told him or you that the gold had been saved . I thought he would be happy with the insurance money. As you know, he picked up about one hundred and seventy thousand pounds from the insurers that covered his cargo and the ship, a fortune in those days, considering that the Acacia Lady was an elderly hulk even then.

But there was something else on that ship. He told me after the enquiry that the number two hold contained something that belonged to the Chinese Government , something so dreadful that he said he could not tell me what it was for fear of his own life. It probably explains why we were shadowed by those Russian trawlers all the way through the Med.

I never told him about the Acacia Lady breaking into two or gave him the bearing I had taken from Renonquet. Instead I gave him yet another false position. This information in exchange for him keeping quiet about the affair the two of us had enjoyed. I have to say Philip, that after all these years I still look back on our nights on the Red Sea with great affection.

Shortly after that, both my legs were smashed by a so called 'queer bashing gang.' As far as I was aware, no one else knew about us. It had all the hallmarks of Carter. I'd seen him in action in Hong Kong, Aden, and on other occasions. Vicious when he wanted to be.

As you will remember, he has a son who is just as bad as Carter. I came across news on him during a holiday on the Caribbean coast of Costa Rica. He was apparently in hiding from a Miami gang of criminals and was involved in several murders according to the newspapers there.

I only heard from Carter occasionally until quite recently. Don't know how he tracked me down but he did.

He sent me a letter requesting confirmation of the bearing that I had given him all that time ago, Apparently he wanted you to dive on the position I had given him, presumably to find the Chinese thing he spoke about.

You asked me many times for information that would enable you to find the retirement fund. I always desisted and claimed I didn't know until our telephone conversation last year when I gave you a chart position based on the information I had. I never heard from you after that and presume that you, like me, felt too old and tired to bother about it any more.

As for the gold, well there must still be a pile of it on that island, but the last time I went there the sea had gouged out the area around the concrete bunker and washed it into the sand and shingle on the foreshore. The broken remains of it were just about visible at low tide full of sand and overgrown with seaweed such that it looked like any other piece of the rocky shoreline.

I made several trips to Alderney in the fifties and sixties in a private charter boat, on the pretence of bird watching expeditions. On each trip I brought back a couple of the bars. My commission in the Black Sea gave me easy access to Turkey, where they were exchanged for cash. It supported my weakness for the horses, although I never learned and lost most of it. I also gave much of it away to charities supporting everything from gay rights in recent years to Ormond Street Hospital for Sick Children. You were lucky finding Monica. I found that unlike yourself, I could only find companionship in women, but never love. I had a lovely home at Lyme Regis, but what was the point, I had no one to share it with me. My sister who married Holmes died years ago and I have no direct heirs.

As I said earlier, I am dying. I could not go without at last telling you the truth.

The position I gave to Carter was not the correct one. I considered that the wreck would by now have disintegrated to the extent that it would be unrecognisable . So I gave him a false position in the hope that he would search and then give up the quest.

The old Captain coughed on his pipe and wiped his lips as he now paused in his writing. This was his last chance to make amends and he bent once more to his task. It was a long letter but he now felt as if the load he had carried all those years had suddenly been lifted. He felt better as he referred to a slip of paper and wrote the final sentence.

'The back half of the wreck lies about three miles and a couple of cables along a magnetic bearing of 355 degrees from the small predominance on Renonquet Island, the forward part taken from the Decca co-ordinates at the time lies SE of Hurd in the position previously given. Most of the gold is on the island, though it would be difficult to locate now. Some is here.

Well now you know the full truth . I hope you or your son Peter may find it of use. No flowers please when it happens.

Your most sincere friend.

He read through what he had said, he knew it rambled and was too long, it was an essay rather than a letter, an outpouring of the guilt he had lived with for all those years. He signed it and attended to the envelope before reaching for his reefer jacket and trudged up over the cliffs to the post box.

As he reached the top of the cliff path, Gilbert Piltcher cursed to himself. The sealed letter in his hand gave no address or point of contact. He hesitated but decided to continue to the post box. When he returned to the caravan he wrote out a second letter outlining the omission of an address in the first letter that he sealed and addressed to Philip Senden in Weymouth. He looked at his watch and realised that he'd have to hurry if he was to catch the last postal collection of the day.

Chapter 29. The New York Bankers

The man who gazed out at the panoramic view of lower Manhattan, where the World Trade Centre buildings had once stood, was of portly stature, immaculately dressed in a dark blue suit cut and fitted in Saville Row like his others, white shirt and, unusually for these days, a small bow tie. Harry Stern stood with his back to the glitzy penthouse office interior, looking worried, older than his sixty two years as he stood there intertwining his fingers with nervous fervour wringing his hands white behind his back.

He turned his heavy eyes to the office door as the knock announced his partner and Sam Hindes entered, dressed in a casual *GAP* patterned open necked shirt and slacks.

'Got your message about the need to talk. So, what's troubling you Harry?' Stern shrugged his shoulders and spread out his hands gesticulating towards the polished desk top on which one piece of paper lay. Sam walked across the thick pile carpet picked it up and scanned the page.

'Lord, that's bad news if it's true. Have you checked already.'

'Should I , checked and double checked since I called you back here last night Sammy. Sorry to disturb your vacation by the way, but I just do not understand what has happened.'

Hindes looked at the e-mail text from the Emirate Prince of Udiar, fifteen million dollars missing from the account that the broking firm of Hindes and Stern managed for him. A small amount when considered against the Prince's total funds but nevertheless fifteen mil. missing.

Sam turned to his partner, a man twenty years his senior whose Jewish immigrant father from the east end of London had started the firm in the late forties and ten years before he retired had head hunted Sam.

Sam had graduated from the University of Pennsylvania's prestigious School of Finance and Commerce before joining the Brookings Institute in Washington as an analyst, joined Hindes and Stern, worked hard in the firm and become rich enough through his Middle East dealing commissions to be offered a half partnership with Harry, when the firm's name had been changed to Hindes and Stern. A partnership that had proved highly successful as they now pursued their main area of business in the Middle East as NASDAQ listed brokers.

A printer started its clatter as fresh information on the Prince's accounts started to pour out. 'Well it's not enough to make them suspend our dealings on the Street, but our other investors may become jumpy if this gets out. When is the prince expected here.' Sam had picked up the first sheets of computer paper and was scanning the ledger entries as he spoke. 'Are any of our other accounts affected?'

'The senior account managers had their staff spend all last night looking through their dealings, but that one seems to be the only one where we suspect unauthorised withdrawals have taken place.'

'Did the Prince say in the earlier e-mail what entries he is not happy with?'

Harry went over to the desk and flopped in the chair behind it fiddling nervously with the bow tie. 'Let's go through things step by step. The prince is not coming over. He's asked us in his usual polite way to sort out what's happened and report back. He doesn't seem to be too worried. After all he can lose or gain up to that amount in a day's trading. There are thousands of withdrawals, but how are we to know if a drawing is legit or not. We manipulate the stocks and bonds on a daily basis depending on market forces at the time. Balances are paid into and taken out of nearly two hundred separate accounts, all carefully security coded through a maze of companies and trust funds in various countries on behalf of the prince.

He says he relies on his accountants for information, but like many of our customers he keeps his own rough tally on his fortunes. He just acted on a hunch that he was short of fifteen million even though it would seem like petty cash to him.'

The younger man asked, 'do you think anyone could have hacked into our systems?'

'I don't know Sam, if you remember, Frank Gibson set the system up before he took up his government appointment in Washington, should all be as safe as a Giddeon bible in a hotel room.' He spread his hands again and smiled at his partner. 'Who is to know these days, when we are dealing with so many accounts and networks, a virus or hacker could possibly get in. Frankly, I'm getting too old to worry about such things, leave it to the D.P. managers to worry about.'

Sam's forehead furrowed . 'Frank Gibson?'

'You remember him, worked on the early oil accounts, about six or seven years ago.' The desk telephone rang and Harry answered it. 'O.K. Ruth, would you send him in straight away.' There was a polite knock and David Milowsky the senior D.P.manager entered, jacket less and with shirt sleeves rolled up. 'Sorry to bother you Mr.Stern, but I thought you should see this.'

'What have you got for us David.' Harry waved him to one of the armchairs.

'Well, we've found that certain file entries on the Udiar computer software that hold these accounts have unusual root configurations that could......'.

Sam interrupted him with a benevolent smile, 'cut the technical jargon David give it to us in simple language.'

David faltered, searching for a non technical way of describing to his bosses what he had found. 'O.K. let's put it this way. a few years ago we went through our systems with a sieve, knocking out and checking that we would be compatible with the millennium date turnover, the Y2K thing.'

The others acknowledged the fact as he continued. 'On the 9th. September 1999, we had a hiccup when one of our Saudi accounts crashed. All nines you see, the system took the date as a four nine's error command. Part of the Udiar account was networked into it and we had to reconstruct a few megabytes of software at the time. Fortunately, it wasn't too difficult and with minimal alteration we were up and running again within hours.'

The partners sat there patiently listening, their minds could visualise dollars but found it more difficult when it came to computer bytes even though they relied so heavily on their digital investment. 'We've checked right back to the central computer in Trumbull and the backup Nasdaq system in Rockville and discovered that our own software was, shall we say, manoeuvred slightly. These accounts are protected by DES, you know, the Data Encryption Standard that we all use, plus our own security system. Well, it would seem that these protective devices in the software were removed from certain accounts of the Udiar prince and dummy accounts set up. The strange thing is though that they have lain dormant for a long time, and only started to be used about a month ago.'

Sam rose from the chair he had occupied whilst David Milowsky was delivering his findings. 'So it is a hack. Can we stop it?'

'Already done sir, got a programmer on to it straight away and closed the links.' Harry stared across the room to the panoramic windows as he offered up a prayer in a quiet whisper.'

'Well-done David, by the way how are Sarah and the kids keeping these days?'

Before Milowsky could answer the paternal company question of the older man, Sam cut across. 'Do we know the source or where the funds have been fed to?'

'I guess we'll never know the answer to that one, it's been widely distributed.' A thoughtful look crossed his face. 'We could reinstate one or two of the accounts as dummies, set up a telecoms piece of hardware that would trace the source if any further attempts are made . No withdrawal would be allowed of course.'

'Get to it David, find the putz who did this to us. By the way, do we know who programmed the system?' David had guessed he'd be asked, 'it was when I was working for Frank Gibson.'

Sam Hindes leaned forward to the 'phone. 'Ruth can you get human resources to pull out the old file on Frank Gibson for me. He worked here about seven years ago before he took up a government appointment in Washington. Also find out how I can get hold of the FBI fraud section.' Milowsky left the room and the two partners sat in silence for a while.

'I'll have to break the vacation and fly over to Udiar once our auditors have satisfied themselves as to the amount missing. Fortunately, we appear to have got on to it before it became a major disaster. Even so, fifteen million will take a lot of making up. We'll need to talk to the revenue about it and cut back on commissions, won't be very popular with the traders of course.'

There was another knock on the door and Ruth entered with the information they had requested and Sam rang one of his contacts in the FBI.

At Langley W.Virginia, Frank Gibson was looking concerned. The e-mail on his screen was not encrypted and had been there for a full half hour, long enough for any other casual user on the network to have picked it up even though he used his own turnkey password when accessing. It simply read.

Caution. Dragon's Morsel has a problem. Senden getting too near to the truth but now have him under control. British have suspicions concerning your senior naval man over here. Will do my best to avert the situation.

There was no name but the originators U.K. e-mail address was sitting clear and bold in the left hand corner. Had their contact in London gone suddenly raving mad? Transmitting on an open line, or was it a deliberate ploy to expose him and his colleagues?

Gibson shot his index finger to the mouse button and clicked the 'do not save' icon and the message disappeared as he cursed loudly. That message would still be in the system cookies somewhere. He sat there, his usually calm features creased in thought at the stupid break in security. He would have been there to intercept it if it hadn't been for the pile up on Dolly Madison that had caused traffic jams over a wide area as he made his way to the office that morning. He made some phone calls and booked the 2103 conference room down on the second floor, a room he knew was swept constantly for listening devices by his own authorisation.

An hour and a half later the conspirators were gathered as Frank Gibson told them the latest news.

'It's a bad situation Frank and it only endorses what I said about Hoskins the other week' Col. Graham Erricsmann, sat in his usual seat having driven up from the Pentagon building in East Arlington. 'If there is a leak we'll all go down the tube and all that hard planning with it. What do you think Hoskins has been up to?'

Charles Muller joined in. 'More to the point, who sent the damn message in the first place, we should know who the UK partner is Frank.'

Frank Gibson held up the palms of his hand. 'Whoa gentlemen, let's deal with one point at a time. I've already had some misinformation fed to Hoskins, to see if it filters back. I'll tell you the form that took in a minute. As for the reference to Senden, darned if I know. Can only presume our contact means Senden's son. He looked at his meeting notes prepared earlier. 'If you remember, Hoskins did tell us that Senden's son worked for the Brits., some technical department in their secret service. Guess it could be a covert cover but I don't understand why or how he could have gotten hold of anything to do with what we are planning.'

'We can't take chances Frank, we'll have to erase the Senden guy if he's causing waves.' The six men around the table took in what the Colonel had just said. None of them wanted a British assassination on their consciences at any future Congressional hearing.

'I'll talk to our U.K. contact before we take any action in that direction.'

The Colonel looked around the table. 'We'll have to act quickly. Our information is that the old *Thinman* device is probably in a lethal condition. As you know, the British diver Philip Senden, whom we suspect of finding it, died from a massive overdose of radiation. Because of its dangerous state, it will have to be properly contained when it is found and that'll bring a hell of lot of extra people on to the LAN team. Since this operation started the services have ordered another two hundred specialists onto the task force.

To ensure our plan works, I have arranged on our behalf and with Frank's knowledge for Sam Mcready's inner team to position the replica bomb somewhere else in the English Channel. The mercenaries in Somalia will leak a suitably convincing story to the fundamentalists that the bomb was never on the Acacia Lady. The information will then lead their Korean friends to find the replica and zip it off to North Africa.'

'It will have to be a convincing story Colonel .'

Frank Gibson cut across them. 'We know the fundamentalists have done a thorough exercise on this, much of it based on the same material sources as our own observations. We are going to leak through the mercenaries that *Thinman* was never on the Acacia Lady , put it over that it was transferred to another ship in Alexandria that also sank. Give them a new position on a wreck that has been surveyed, well away from the current mode of operations. In a position where they will be bound to find the replica.'

Charles Muller looked worried. 'How do we know they'll be taken in by the replica or that they'll even believe the new story?'

The Colonel grinned. 'You worry too much Muller, the casing of the replica has been artificially aged so that when it *is* found, they won't know the difference. The W85 nuclear warhead will have been armed by our operators and will be tucked up nicely inside the casing. All we want now, is for the fuckers to find it before the shit hits the fan and the task force find *Thinman*. There are so many of our people on the search team now that it would have been difficult to transpose the devices at that one site, wherever that is.'

Muller's black face was looking unusually pale and shining from the perspiration beginning to bead on his forehead as he suddenly leapt to his feet and thumped the table, shouting in a high pitched hoarse screech of a voice.

'Shit, Colonel, this has gone too far, I want out of here. Man, this *Crusader* project has been misconceived from the very beginning. The original concept we had of seemingly letting those turds find the modified *Thinman* bomb before we did , has changed. According to the project plan all this was going to be seen afterwards as an unfortunate accident. They were supposed to find *Thinman* with guidance from our own people and transport it back to the fundamentalist's conference. Then we were going to detonate it via. the satellite link. After analysis of the radio active fall- out, by the Russians, it would be proved beyond doubt that this was a missing World War II bomb stolen somehow by terrorists. Shit man, when the Russians, or anyone else for that matter, take their fall- out readings, it'll be obvious that it's not the old *Thinman* device at all but one from the US Military Arsenal, now designated as a warhead that's been Salt Treaty decommissioned.'

The other five looked to the Colonel.

'For fuck sake Charlie boy, get your black butt back on the chair and keep your nigger voice down. You're in deep like the rest of us, everything's on schedule except Hoskins and finding *Thinman*. I agree that the fall- out won't match. So what, it can always be argued that the terrorists could have found or stolen another bomb, there's still no connection to us.'

Tim Gregson their communications co-ordinator sitting further down the table had listened silently as he doodled on a pad in front of him. Before the enraged Charles Muller could reply, he interceded.

'We knew there were risks, and I agree with Charles here that now may be the time to pull the stops. Before we consider that though, let's look at what we've got. How for instance, do we know for sure that the terrorists will take the device directly back to the conference when they find it.'

Frank Gibson mopped his brow with a handkerchief and held up a hand for silence as he tried to reassert himself as the leader of the group and defuse the racial acrimony that had suddenly boiled up between Muller and the Army Colonel, an indictable offence in the department under normal circumstances. He cut across a stream of obscenities being hurled between them. 'Gentlemen please. Let's go back to the original concept of the *Crusade* project , which was a simple one.' The room quietened as they listened.

'When Mossad intelligence sources first identified that the terrorist group had somehow gotten information that *Thinman* was lying in the English Channel, we guessed that what they really wanted was the plutonium to complete the nuclear bomb with which they were going to threaten the Cease Fire Conference. The consequences of that occurrence need not be further emphasised here.

When we discovered through our Middle East contacts that a conference was being organised to assemble the heads of most of the World's terrorist groups in one place, we put our scheme to the Chief to turn the tables on them.

Find *Thinman* first, remove the guts, pack it with a conventional explosive device, put it back and let them find it. Then track it by satellite to the conference location where it could be remotely detonated. Hey presto and the thorn in our side would be removed.

Unfortunately, the scheme was turned down unconditionally by our politically motivated masters on the select committee running this thing.

That's when our own *Crusade* project was born but with the following difference. Instead of conventional explosives we have arranged for the modified and primed W85 nuclear warhead to be placed inside a replica casing. So with one push of the button, we alleviate the World of the leading terror group leaders, at the same time saving the Mid East Cease Fire Conference and stopping their future hopes of an independent plutonium production capability.'

Muller still sat there glowering at his clenched hands on the table, Erricsmann now more subdued, listened intently with the others as Frank Gibson continued.

'Now, let's look at the current situation. You have all seen the satellite surveillance photographs at our earlier meetings. The Libyan freighter is still standing off in the Atlantic, just outside the E.U. coastal radar range.

From our earlier intelligence, the terrorist group working in the U.K. has one prime objective, that is to find the device and get it shipped back to the Middle East. From there it will be transported to the restricted desert area where we know the Koreans are building a nuclear power plant that will at sometime be capable of producing weapons grade plutonium. It is only there that they have the scientific expertise, the scientists and engineers, to open up what they think is the old *Thinman* bomb and extract the plutonium for their own bomb or bombs. The conference centre at the power plant is where the heads of the various fractious terrorist groups are meeting . At that conference they will decide their future combined strategy from the strength of having a so-called Islamic nuclear bomb.

Now gentlemen, our own *Crusade* project group, if you remember, considered that something had to be done about it to protect the future interests of the U.S.A. which seems to have escaped the minds of the politicians.

With our nuclear bomb in position and one press of the satellite button, we will not only eliminate those bastards who have killed and maimed our own people over the years, we will also destroy any possibility of the nuclear plant being used against us in the future. The other benefits, if I might remind you, are political stability in the region that controls a major part of the Worlds oil supplies. When it's all over, the U.S. will be able to move in to exploit the situation.

Now, things have changed. The original concept that we could lead the terrorists to *Thinman* was ill conceived, we were not advised that it could be in a dangerous state, also the task force in the Channel is too big for our colleagues over there to do the switch without suspicion. The reconstructed W85 bomb will therefore be placed in another location that has already been swept and where it can be easily found and raised by the terrorist group. A place that is not under the gaze of the task force . Our problem now is to guide the terrorist group there as quickly as possible so that it can be found by them and raised'

'How you going to do that?'

'We'll make sure that our man in Yemen is given the position from the contingency plan. Sam Mcready will be given the code word to put the new package at that position. The information will be filtered through to the Koreans in the U.K. who will then find it well away from the task force.'

'What about Hoskins?' It was Muller asking the question, his face now taught as he still glowered at the colonel.

Frank Gibson spoke in a quiet voice, the situation around the table seemed to have calmed. 'Simple Charles, something I do not think you are aware of yet. Following our earlier uncertainty over Hoskins I decided to try and see how committed he was to the project. I fed the son of a bitch with a bogus position, let's say because of the delay in finding *Thinman*, to see if the information would be passed on. It was and Mcready signalled us yesterday that Hoskins had taken the bait and passed it on to the British.'

Mallismann sneered a grin at the black man. 'Hank is finished, I've seen to that.'

Muller crashed the table with his fist, his voice raised to a bellow.

'You're all mad I'm out of here right now, you hear, right now.' He was on his feet waving his finger at them all. 'I'm out you hear, I want no more to do with your fucking crazy scheme.' He picked up his paperwork and slung it at the table where it cascaded over the wooden top and fluttered to the floor before he marched to the conference room door and departed leaving the others staring after him. Whatever it was they had on him obviously didn't count any more.

The colonel sighed and popped a wad of gum in his mouth. 'Leave him to me, he's no problem.'

It wasn't as simple as Frank Gibson thought. The keyword that had puzzled Hank Hoskins until his recent visit to Langley had not been removed from the Echelon computer systems at Menwith Hill in Yorkshire, manned by the National Security Agency. The e-mail Gibson had turned up was passed, according to agreed protocol, to GCHQ who were at that moment passing the contents for forward transmission to an eighth floor office at Thames House in London.

Fifteen minutes later a door on the third floor was opened and two Scotland Yard special branch policemen stepped quietly inside the T2 Section Leader's office.

'Mr. Douglas Lawson ?' The first constable asked the question.

'We have a warrant for your arrest with respect to breaches you are considered to have made within the meaning of Section One of the Official Secrets Act..'

Upstairs Sir George Longland and Maj. Fellows were looking at the contents of the intercepted e-mail message and deciding the best way to proceed.

Over in the Grosvenor Street office, Hank Hoskins had gone onto the Internet that afternoon to check the Washington Post headlines of the American morning. There was plenty there as usual but one small news item sat him up in his chair. It was a late report on a suspected suicide by a Negro by the name of Charles Muller who had been seen falling from a multi story car park near his home in Bethesda. Mystery surrounded him and the CIA had admitted him as one of their senior operatives, although his exact function was not stated and there would be an in depth inquiry carried out by the FBI and by the local State Police force.

Hank sat there for a few minutes and reread the article. So, the conspirators were beginning to argue and now his own life could also be in danger. He had known Muller quite well, he left a wife and small child . Hoskins poured over his troubled conscience and decided that now was the time to come clean. He lifted the phone and asked to be put through to Jonathan Erkenham the Chief Advisor to the President of the United States of America.

In one of the Stern and Hines I.T. rooms, David Milowsky sat at his console tapping in data and checking over the new security system introduced that afternoon and decided to do some hacking himself. What he turned up surprised him and he went back up to the penthouse office where Sam Hindes and Harry Stern still sat, sharing a tray of tea and English digestive biscuits .

'Whoever hacked our system must have had a lot of confidence that they would not be detected,' he told the two partners. 'I've managed to get into one or two of their transfer accounts that have no guard shields. The surprising thing is that the accounts are set up within the General Treasury System in an area that normally restricts access.'

Sam sat up with renewed interest. 'You mean you've hacked into the Central Government accounting system? Lord God David, you'll get us slung out of the association.'

David half raised his hand's. 'Don't worry Mr. Hindes, it's untraceable, I only looked, couldn't change anything anyway.'

'So, what did you find there.'

'Well these accounts appear to be run like a bank as holding accounts, receiving funds from the Udiar accounts, holding them and then transferring them out to other accounts.'

'So we could get some of it back perhaps?' Harry Stern 's face was looking more cheerful than it had a few hours earlier.

'Not exactly Mr.Stern, that will have to be proved, presumably through prolonged litigation in the courts. No, these payments go through further breakdown accounts before they vanish into a maze of banks and other legitimate institutions.' Harry looked disappointed. David paused before delivering his coupe de grace 'There are one or two bank account numbers that we've cross checked with our own client accounts where we've found a match.'

'Go on, who are they?'

'Well sir, one belongs to Senator Humphrey McDonall and the other is an English bank account in the name of *Dragon's Morsel,* a strange name for an account. Most of the others are in the U.S. but we have found one in Lebanon, one in the Yemen and about four in Germany.'

Sam looked over to Harry. 'Dummy Government accounts paying out money and Frank Gibson sitting down at the CIA offices in Washington. Seems to me we could be inadvertently involved in something of a covert nature here. Who should we be trusting do you think?'

The three men sat there and Harry said. 'Leave it to the FBI Sammy, they should be up here any time now.'

'One further point sir, one of the accounts is connected into a Chinese bank, one that has been variously reported in the press as being a conduit for the Peoples Liberation Army, feeding funds into US political parties. You may remember that there was a similar exposure some years ago when a Congressional inquiry found out that cash was being channelled into the US banking system.' David fished in a pocket and pulled out the reference he had written down. 'Here it is, the committee heard that cash had been used to buy influence in the White House, the trail led back to the head of Chinas military intelligence at that time.'

Harry looked suddenly very old again. 'More bad news? I don't want to hear.'

Sammy stood and walked over to the tea tray only to find the teapot empty. 'O.K. David, it appears that we have been used to channel funds around through an unprotected keyhole. Make sure that the draft through that hole is stopped immediately.' He stopped and thought, his head supported in both hands. 'The last thing we want is to get involved in any adverse publicity, especially over this Chinese connection. We can take the losses if the amount you have detected is all that is involved, but I want an immediate in house audit on all accounts handling, say, fifty million or more. I should think that only involves about thirty clients I also want you to set up whatever is necessary to find out what those accounts you have identified as being client accounts are up to, who they are, where their funds are being directed and to what end.' David Milowsky turned to go but the partner called him back. 'How much did the Chinese connection cost us David?'

David looked through the sheets of printout, 'I would say we got off lightly, a mere two million one hundred and eighty thousand. It would have been slightly more but some of their own money has also been transferred to the *Dragon's Morsel* account in London.

Sammy frowned, he had hoped it might be more, if it had been used as before for political motives, it would be a useful piece of information to keep in his hip pocket. Depending on which party the funds had been channelled, his friends on Capitol Hill could use it and any favour given would demanded some form of return.

Chapter 30. Intruders

On his return from HMS Seeker, Peter Senden asked the Ministry driver to drop him off at the Weymouth Marina and Seamaiden, leaving the Major to return to London with his report on their suspicions.

Early the next morning, he decided to check on his fathers flat and walked down through the town to one of the Georgian houses that had been converted into flats with views out over the sea and along the Dorset coast, where the foreign trawlers and factory ships now stood off. He had already cleared most of Philips personal possessions and had arranged for a letting agent to view the property.

He tried to turn the key in the front door on the third floor, but it was unlocked and pushed open easily against the day's mail . As he entered , it was immediately obvious that someone had been there. He cursed under his breath, 'damned estate agents.'

Peter picked up the few letters from behind the door and looked around the main living room. On the table was a pile of old mail, all of which had been ripped open with the exception of obvious circulars that had been discarded on the floor in a pile. He looked through the half dozen envelopes that contained various bits of correspondence with respect to his father's bank account closure and a couple that still had cheques in them and one with cash. Peter was puzzled, if they were thieves what were they after, if they had not taken the cash? He took a cursory look around the other rooms, all neat and tidy as he had previously left them but with small clues of disturbance.

He discarded the new junk mail and opened the two new letters. One was a reminder from the Diver's Book Club about unpaid subscriptions that he would have to reply to. When he opened the other one he felt his pulse rate increase as he saw the signature. It was from Gilbert Piltcher and read;

Dear Philip,
I've suddenly realised that the long letter I wrote to you today with details of the retirement fund may have not include my temporary address. I've moved out of Crowsnest for the time being whilst Carter is around and if you need to contact me etc.

There followed a Post Office box number with a Dorset post code together with the location of the caravan.

Peter went back to the table and looked back through the opened envelopes for the first letter but it wasn't there, only one empty envelope with the same handwriting and postmark. So that was it he surmised, Carter was the probable culprit who had broken in and now had the letter with the retirement fund details from Gilbert Piltcher.

He looked around the room again, even though it was improbable that anything else had been taken. His eye caught the sextant in the open box on the side board and he went over and examined it. Surely it hadn't been there all the time. No, it definitely wasn't there on his previous visit, in which case, who had put it there.

He called the estate agent who was arranging the let and received confirmation that none of their staff had visited the property since the previous time that Peter had been there. Then he rang John Barrett. 'I've got an address for the elusive Gilbert Piltcher, seems he hasn't heard that Philip is no longer with us and he's written to him about the retirement fund. Unfortunately, the letter has been stolen and I bet you can guess by whom.'

He explained the circumstances of his visit and the findings to John. 'Not much point in informing the police, I reckon Carter came here yesterday after leaving Seamaiden or this morning.' As he was talking into the phone, his eye fell on a small embroidered handkerchief lying under the table and he reached down and picked it up. The perfume was vaguely familiar but he put it down on the table with the letter, must have been dropped by the estate agents assistant as she was measuring the room he thought.

He finished speaking to John saying he was going to drive over to the caravan later in the morning and had another look around the flat. He glanced out of the window towards the sea, watching a flotilla of Flying Eighteen skiffs skimming across the water in a competition, when his eyes fell on a man seated on a bench on the promenade opposite the flat. Peter stood back from the window and watched the man from behind one of the curtains as the passing crowds of visitors and holiday makers jostled around the seat. There was something odd about him. He appeared to be reading a news paper but would occasionally glance over to the entrance of the flats, as if waiting for someone.

Peter had only caught a fleeting glimpse of the man with the scaffold pole before the ski mask had been donned but the more he watched, the more he was convinced that it was the same man who had grabbed him after the motorcycle incident near Weymouth Marina.

He picked up the handkerchief and letter from Gilbert Piltcher and slipped them in a pocket, had a final visual check of the flat and let himself out of the front door, ensuring that it was firmly locked this time. On the landing, he slid open the window facing out to the back of the building and looked down into untidy yards of rubbish and old motorcars that lay behind a row of lock up garages facing out onto the street behind. He eased himself down over the windowsill until his feet felt the ridge tiles on the gable roof below and slid down the roof into a gully where he could see a drain pipe that dropped a few feet to a fire escape. He gripped the down pipe and slid over the gully and descended hand over hand and dropped quietly onto the fire escape and then into an alleyway that led him behind some of the lock up garages. He climbed a pile of rubbish and clambered over a wall dropping himself into the back street, and after brushing himself down, walked swiftly along to where it joined a side road. There were several cars parked there and he took no notice of the blue Mercedes as he approached the corner with caution and peered round the side of the building. Through the crowds he could see the seat across the road, now filled with a party of jolly lady pensioners eating ice creams. But of the previous occupant there was no sign. Peter stood there for a few minutes looking round the vicinity, scattered with holiday makers but there was no sign of the man. Perhaps he was dreaming something into the situation that just wasn't there and after another look round he headed thoughtfully back to the marina and his car.

George Hansdorf climbed back into the passenger seat of the Mercedes. 'That was a fucking close one 'ol buddy, you're going to get us both sent back Stateside if you're not careful.' Horace O'Brien muttered his reprimand, as a window cleaner sidled up to the car and tapped on the window. 'Our lads have still got the girl under observation, what do we do about him.'

'I'd love to follow the girl, lovely little back side, but, our orders are to keep surveillance on Senden. Your guys had better keep after her.'

Gilbert Piltcher had finished an early pub lunch of fresh prawns and bread washed down with a pint of the Spring Head's award winning real ale.
Now as he walked back to the caravan following his usual route over the cliffs, he had an uneasy feeling, a sixth sense prickle that he was not alone. He strode on, looking over his shoulder occasionally, his eyes scanning the undergrowth on each side of the path, drying out and steaming from an earlier shower.
It was one o'clock on a hot summer's day, the insects making their usual background noise. Something wasn't right the birds were too quiet. He arrived outside his temporary abode still suspicious, his eyes roaming the dense bushes and trees that grew there, as he fished in his pocket for the key that was not there.
The key was still in the caravan door that opened at the turn of the handle. Gilbert stopped, surely he had locked the door before rushing off to the pub. Careless he thought.

'Come on in Captain the door's open, it's good to see you after all these years.'
The old sea captain's physical awareness froze down to its tiniest nerve ends as his pulse increased to a base drum beat in his ears. He had half opened the door to the derelict caravan that was his temporary abode, hidden in a wild area amongst the thickets of bramble, hawthorn and gorse in the land slips between the Devon cliff top and beach.
It was Carter's voice all right, no doubt about that even after so many years, he still recognised its chilling tone. He turned to go as another man emerged from the dense shrubbery, a man in his mid forties, smartly dressed, brushing himself down from the debris of the bushes. He was tallish and ran his left hand through his balding hair, but more significantly he held a gun in his right hand and it was pointing at Captain Gilbert Piltcher beckoning him to go inside.

'What do you want of me? I'm an old man, there's nothing of value here.' It was a plaintive appeal that tumbled out in a trembling voice and Gilbert said it without thinking.

The man was beside him now and opened the caravan door wider, pushing Gilbert inside with the gun barrel pressed in the small of his back as gannets soared on the slight updraft from the cliffs and scolded them for disturbing the solitude of the place.

Carter was sitting on the settee in the diner area, his arms leaning on the table where he had pushed aside the remnants of Gilbert's breakfast.

'I think you probably have something of very great value here Piltcher that still belongs to me and I intend to have it.' He looked up as he spoke, his pale blue eyes over the bearded Chinese features observing his quarry with the hungry anticipation of a pole cat. He waved a hand towards the door.

'May I introduce my son.'

Gilbert was pushed to a seat, the pile of old yellowing newspaper cuttings on the table, that he had left from the previous evening, filling his vision. Carter's son put the gun in a jacket pocket as he made a quick visual inspection of the caravan's scruffy interior. Then he leant back against a wall, his arms folded, watching over the two elderly men as they faced each other, the afternoon sun etching its shadows across the small table between them.

It was Simon Carter who spoke again as his hands played over the newspaper cuttings.

'Well Piltcher you old sod, long time eh, I see you haven't forgotten our escapade at that court hearing, must be nearly fifty years ago I should think.'

'It was nineteen fifty three. What the hell do you want?' The captain replied shortly and felt in his pocket for the bottle of diamorphine from which he took a small gulp.

'You know very well what we're here for Gilbert. That weak brother-in-law of yours told us where you were hiding. Down here on the remote under cliff with only the sea birds for company.' His eyes met the captain's with a look of cynical mockery. 'Now, tell us where it is, the shipwreck and the gold. I know you've got the information because you were there, in the old days.'

'For God sake, what makes you think that?' Gilbert looked around at the two of them, fanning out his hands, trying to disguise the nervous tone of his voice.

'Come Gilbert, don't take us for fools. Who do you think shopped you for gold dealing in Istanbul back in 1985. You were alone on that ship before she sank, enough time I should think to grab a few ingot bars and note the real position for later visits eh.'

Gilbert Piltcher smiled thinly at them both .

'You know the gold was lost when the ship went down, that's what the court records showed or had you forgotten.'

Carter gurgled a laugh and looked over to the other man who was now holding back the rag of curtain from the window and peering anxiously back up the cliff path.

'No my friend, that story was acceptable fifty years ago. A lot of things were said in that courtroom that we both know were not the truth. But, the position you gave to Philip Senden a few years back was not correct. He dived there many times and never came across anything.' He hesitated as if waiting for another response from the captain and then continued, 'I now have certain, uh, ... newly acquired associates who are very anxious to find that ship.' He looked around as if making absolutely sure that they were alone, a characteristic that the captain recognised from the past.

'That ship contains something more than just gold, something that my associates might be prepared to pay for.'

The younger man cut impatiently across the conversation, his mind on the psychopathic Korean they had left in the car at the top of the cliffs.

'They could be here soon, get a fucking move on father, and get it out of him.' He lit a cigarette and looked at its glowing end before bending across and holding it close to Gilbert's ear.

'Look you old sack of fart gas, we don't have time for polite chit chat, just tell us the true position of that ship.' He blew at the glowing tobacco embers and jabbed the cigarette on Gilbert's right ear lobe.

The old man let out a cry as he stood and his hand went instinctively to the stinging ear.

Carter's son pushed him back into the seat and took a drag at the crumpled smoke.

'There's a health warning printed on the packet,' he said casually, 'now, let's see if it's true. Loosen off your belt and drop your trousers. I don't suppose you find much use for whatever it is you've got down there these days, but believe me, it will be very painful if I have to work on it.'

The octogenarian's eyes filled with horror at the thought of what his tormentor was about to do. He was in pain anyway, but the thought of his genitals covered in cigarette burns did not appeal.

Carter smiled. His nefarious son was more persuasive than he could have possibly hoped as he pushed a ball-point and sheet of paper over to Gilbert.

'Write the correct position down for us Piltcher, there's a good old lad, then we'll fuck off and leave you in peace.'

The pen was picked up and the reluctant Gilbert Piltcher reached over and pulled out a slip of paper from behind a piece of melamine panelling. 'There, that's what you want, that's all I have.'

David Luk grabbed the paper and looked at it. 'There are two positions here, what the fucking hell are you playing at Piltcher?' Gilbert Piltcher then recounted the story of the ship breaking in two but omitted to tell them how he had removed most of the bullion.

David Luk was again looking out of the window. 'Let's get out of here before the others arrive.' He grabbed Gilbert by the throat. 'Now you old cart load of shit, does anyone else have this information, Peter Senden for instance?'

Gilbert shook his head and Luk's long experience of looking into the eyes of terrified men told him that it was probably the truth.

They made for the door, locking it from the outside whilst Pitcher stood shakily holding his throbbing ear. Then he smelt it . Smoke and almost instantaneously, he saw the flames through a window, licking up outside the old plywood construction that was his temporary home. Within seconds the inside was filling with thick choking smoke as Gilbert stumbled to the door and fumbled with the handle but found it locked. As he turned in desperation there was an explosion at the other end of the dwelling as one of the gas cylinders went up and blew the end out of the vehicle.

About half an hour earlier it had stopped raining and the sun had come out producing a sultry heat as the moisture on the vegetation in the surrounding fields evaporated. A car, parked at the end of the farm track that lead down towards the cliffs and beach beyond, contained three occupants, Johnny Chungai, Yoido and the short man. Chungai had lowered the driver's window, wishing now that they had stolen a car with air conditioning. He caught the smoke at the back of his throat before he suddenly saw the black column reaching into the air from somewhere on the other side of the hedge and below them. He hesitated, Carter and Luk should have been back by now, he had seen the old man wandering back across the field some quarter of an hour before, from behind the hedge that separated the track from the field.

Then he heard the explosion and he and the short man were out of the car, over a gate to the field and running towards a small rise that looked down onto the wilderness of the under cliff. Half way down he could see the column of black smoke and flames bellowing up between the stunted trees and bushes. He shouted to the short man trailing some way behind and they bounded down the steep pathway as another explosion sent a gas canister hurtling through the undergrowth, hitting the short man and throwing him to the ground, never to rise again. Chungai looked on furiously at what had been the caravan, a blazing skeleton carcass with the flames licking their last taste from the girder framework and consuming the crashed in roof and walls. Any one in there would have perished very quickly.

The heat and smell tasted like the mouth of hell as it started to rain again. The licking flames of the carcass took no notice as they continued to devour every remnant of their prey, the blackened grass in the small clearing smouldering and spitting as water fought fire and a mixture of smoke and steam hung in the air.

Johnny Chungai stood there clenching his fists with rage, his hard blue eyes searching the vicinity. Where were Carter and his ignominious son who had promised to return to the car with the information they were all seeking. In the rough brushwood of the under cliff, narrow paths meandered in all directions, it would be useless to search. And then he heard the sound of an engine starting up somewhere down towards the beach and knew he wouldn't find them. How had they managed to conceal transport in that lonely place? They must have used accomplices, but whom?

He flipped his mobile open and spoke briefly in his own tongue, before he strode back to where the short man lay and dragged him back to the heat and flaming bed of embers. His eyes fell on a clothes line prop lying on the ground nearby that he used to push and roll the body into the fire. Then Chugai raked the embers over the body as firstly the clothing caught on fire and then the flesh started to roast and crackle as the flames picked over the new fuel. He turned away from the intense heat and awful smell of the pyre and ran back up the path and over to his car.

As he sat there with Yoido, shielded by the hedge, two farm workers went running across in the direction of the smoke column. He waited for them to disappear down the cliff path before starting the engine and driving quietly back along the track to the junction with the lane. The sirens came from somewhere on his right. He turned left and drove away.

The police car, followed by a fire tender and cliff rescue Landrover all arrived on the scene at the same time. Tom Parkins, one of the farm hands, was comforting his pal who was vomiting onto the charred grass as the constable came bounding down the path.

'Old Gilbert is in there, burned to a cinder,' he cried as he pointed to the burning heap and the protruding skeletal hand, charred and twisted by the heat. 'I was drinking with him only an hour ago.'

A party of onlookers was gathering from some of the other remote caravans and huts dotted along this part of the under cliff as the young constable took in the scene on his last few strides and was on his communicator within seconds calling for backup and reporting the scene in front of him. The firemen ran down their hoses from the tender in the field and doused the small bush fires that had started around the site before turning to the remains of the van.

Half an hour later, Detective Inspector Evans's mobile rang in Truro. It was his Super. 'Robert, you can cancel your A.P.B. on the man Gilbert Piltcher. Just heard from the Dorset Police, Piltcher is dead, his body was found half an hour ago in the burned out remains of the caravan he had been staying in somewhere near Seaton.'

Chapter 31. Gilbert's cavern and Katherine Holmes.

When he located the caravan that morning Peter Senden had found it unlocked with the key still in place. There was no one about and when the rain shower swept in he had taken shelter for a while in the van. When the sun came out he went back up to the cliff top and took a short walk. Taking in the magnificent view over the bay as the shower swept its way southwards out across the sea, the sun and blue sky contrasting majestically against the razor sharp outline of the black storm clouds with their murky grey underskirts.

The view along the coast stretched from the grey outline of Portland Bill in the east across the bay to beyond Dartmouth in the west and the sloping headland of Start Point. Now the storm had passed, the sea was calm with cats paws stroking its surface which shimmered with silver patches below him. The cliffs of red marle and yellow greensand were patched with outcrops of white chalk and red clay, topped by the icing greenness of the grass fields as they swept inland broken by small copses of beech and ash.

He had located Piltcher's caravan, partly hidden in the thickets of bramble, hawthorn and gorse, east of Strangemans Cove in an area called Littlecombe Shoot, a wild area in the land slips between cliff top and beach. An area where the paths were steep and rough, muddy underfoot where roots and loose flints made the footing difficult in places. Gannets soared on the slight updraft their noises disturbing the solitude of the place.

It was on his return that he had fallen prone on the grass as he spotted Carter and Luk making their way down to the caravan. He saw the old man return a few minutes later but was too far away to warn him, instead he had slithered down through the wet undergrowth and found another path over which the vegetation curled like a tunnel and allowed him to hide a few yards from the caravan whilst he considered his next move. It seemed only minutes before the two came out and locked the door behind them and he could see the old man's profile inside. To his horror what happened next rooted him to his hiding place as David Luk bent down and fiddled with the regulator on one of the propane gas bottles at the back of the vehicle. The next moment, there were flames licking at the old paint work on the plywood structure and the caravan was on fire. Luk and Carter turned and climbed briskly away along the path that Peter had found on the way down.

Without thinking for his own safety, Peter leapt forward from his hiding place.

They had left the key and he struggled with it for what seemed tens of seconds as the flames and heat spread towards him before he was able to wrench open the door. Dense black smoke, from the now smouldering plastic interior fittings, poured out through the door and he could just distinguish Gilbert Piltcher laying there on the floor of the passageway in a huddled heap. He took a deep breath, choking on the pungent smoke fumes and entered the door as the first cylinder suddenly exploded , sending blazing debris through the air. The table lifted in front of the blast and jammed across the end of the passageway, providing a temporary barrier to the heat and inferno that a second before had been the sitting room.

Peter pulled the heap that was Piltcher clear, dragging him away to the edge of the clearing, where he laid the man on his back, his clothes still full of smoke as he checked the air passage. It was clear and he was breathing. Thank God he thought as he dragged Piltcher further away from the burning wreckage that had been his home for the last couple of weeks. He was coming round and Peter held him up in his arms as he took those first deep gulps of air and cleared his lungs. The old man looked up at him with no recognition and gasped out his thanks as he struggled to his feet. 'Piltcher?', Peter enquired. Gilbert nodded as he looked wildly back at the blaze.

Suddenly Peter heard a shout from the top of the cliff . He beckoned to Piltcher with his fingers on his lips to be silent and indicated him to follow. But Gilbert knew these cliffs like the back of his hands and led them downwards along tiny meandering paths made by the cattle that wandered the area until they suddenly came out on a narrow beach. He crept out and looked up and down cautiously before stooping down into a gully and uncovering an inflatable craft, well hidden under throngs of gorse.

They covered the few yards of beach in seconds carrying and dragging the craft between them and waded it out through the light surf before rolling into its safety and firing up the outboard engine. Peter got Gilbert to lie in the bottom of the craft as he headed out to sea steering eastwards into Lyme Bay.

Gilbert Piltcher was lying, exhausted his head resting on his arms across the thwart. He glanced up at Peter and now recognised him as the young man who had been interviewed on the television two evenings ago. 'It's Peter Senden isn't it?' He croaked out the words from his rasping throat, 'thanks for that, thought I was a goner.'

'Keep your head down Gilbert, hopefully if anyone sees us from up there they'll think I'm a lone fisherman.' Peter kept his own profile as low as possible, with his back to the shoreline. 'Now we have to decide where to go.' Piltcher lay on the floor as the spray, sent up by the larger waves off the headland, flew over the bow.

Once they had rounded the predominant cliffs south of the little coastal town of Beer, Gilbert sat up and looked around. 'Let me take the tiller Peter, I know where to go. It's about three miles across Seaton Bay and in these light sea conditions we should be O.K. By the way, tell me now what you were doing over there, are you connected with Carter and his abominable son.'

Peter told his story briefly between ducking the spray as it shot over the bows of the small craft. About how everybody had been looking for Piltcher and the letter he had found at Philips flat.

Gilbert had not heard about Philips death and expressed his sorrow at hearing the news. Little else was said as they ploughed their way to the approaching coast line.

From their vantage point in a small copse where the cliffs suddenly lifted in height, the two US agents assigned to keep surveillance on Senden had kept their binoculars and telephoto lenses trained on the various events.

They had followed Senden after he parked the Jaguar in a farm yard off the top lane and had noted the other car as it had driven slowly along the muddy track and parked where it was partly hidden by hedges, a series 5 BMW about four years old from its number plate. Photographs of two of the occupants as they left the car and vanished out of sight below the cliff edge would later confirm their identification of Carter and Luk. Their notebooks recorded the time that an elderly man identified as Gilbert Piltcher had come wandering back from his midday tipple and vanished down the same path as the previous two. They had seen Peter Senden duck out of sight and were about to break cover when they heard the first explosion and saw the column of smoke rising from the trees. Two men ran from the parked BMW, a very tall athletic man and a short man. The tall man wore a Hawaiian style multicoloured silk short sleeved shirt and white jeans. The telephotos worked furiously before they broke their cover and ran to the top of the cliff in time to see the rib being launched off the beach below by Senden with the elderly man they had seen earlier lying on its floor. There was no sign of the others and agents Hansdorf and O'Brien decided it was time to leave and report back what they had just seen.

Then the tall man in the coloured shirt came back alone and sat in the car with the other occupant before driving slowly back to the lane. O'Brien pulled his eye away from the camera.

'That looks remarkably like the guy that the Holmes woman described.' He swung the camera to the tiny dot on the sea and pulled up the telephoto into focus. 'Senden appears to be safely away, but to where we can only guess. I suggest we follow the Korean pair and see what happens, although I would guess that somewhere around here there are other eyes watching.'

There certainly were. Special Branch DC Mike Parson's Audi was parked back at the main road and he and his colleague had to sprint along the side of a field, crouching low behind the hedge for cover as they ran.

Two other men lying prone on the cliff over on Hangman's Bay had also had their binoculars trained on the various happenings and now mounted their motorcycle and drove slowly along the cliff path to a point further along where they could join the main road.

Beer, Seaton and Lyme Regis are delightful coastal towns that lie on the South Dorset coast. The harbour or Cobb at Lyme Regis has been the basis for countless stories about the Duke of Monmouth's landing there on 11th.June. 1685. before the battle of Sedgmoor. A few years later in 1688, William of Orange landed his troops there before proceeding to Brixham and then on to defeat James II. An event that changed the history of the British Isles. Many authors have used the location as a basis for romantic novels.

Between Lyme and Seaton is a coastal area known as the 'Great Land Slip' that is a series of valleys and gullies extending along the coast for about eight miles. It's a wild, unpopulated area up to a mile wide with its own micro climate that has encouraged dense jungle-like undergrowth to cover the deep ravines, slime covered pools and muddy quick sands. In places towering sandstone cliffs stand, eroded and subject to land slips that constantly change the profile of the area. It is only accessible from each end and has a single footpath, precipitous in places, which meanders through its upper valleys and on a good day will take the experienced walker about four hours to negotiate. The seaward side offers only a few landing places along its rock strewn coast. It is probably the most natural and wildest place in Southern Britain.

The caves were so well hidden that few people even knew of their existence and there was no indication of them on Ordnance Survey maps.

They were not natural caves but had been quarried out since Roman times for their soft Jurassic sandstone and had been used during the First World War as an ammunition store, but the narrow military road that led down to them had long since vanished under the land slips and dense vegetation. Anyone attempting to get down there from the land ward side would have found themselves waist deep in the muddy fissures or impaled on ancient rusted barbed wire. The only record of their existence was buried in a dusty folder somewhere in the archives of the Crown Estates Office where the records were considered so old and unreliable that their existence had not even been computerised.

Inside, the cave system had been divided into a series of brick store rooms with heavy explosion proof steel doors that, although rusting, still served their purpose. An adequate supply of fresh water filtered through the limestone into a small reservoir that fed sanitation and other services. The original electricity supply had been D.C. laid in a conduit from an inland substation. Fortuitously, over many years of modifications to the sub station the electricity supply company had always reconnected, never questioning where the supply ended up.

It was to here that the thoroughly shaken Gilbert Piltcher his clothes still reeking of smoke had guided Peter Senden in the rib craft.

After crossing Seaton Bay, Gilbert Piltcher kept an eye on the steering compass and small outcrops of rock that he used as leading lines until he nosed the RIB craft carefully into a narrow tidal creek running between a break in the cliffs. All around were rock strewn muddy banks over which the ebb was dribbling its meandering trickles. He turned the craft to port around a low limestone stack and headed for what at first appeared to be a sheer rock face. The rib touched the soft bottom but the engine pushed them through. Gilbert indicated the muddy banks to Peter.

'All soft mud, like quicksand, if you got stuck there you'd be sunk up to your neck.' He rasped a laugh as they rounded another tight twist to starboard and the seaward cave entrance was right in front of them.

He stopped the outboard engine and tilted it forward as they both ducked down allowing the craft to drift into the low mouth of a cavern where it came to rest against a steep shingle bank.

After the brilliance of the sun, it was dark in there and it took a few moments for their eyes to adjust to the gloomy surroundings. The cave was small with the shingle bank running along one side. Peter looked around the claustrophobic interior and back at Gilbert.

'Christ Gilbert, what happens to us when the tide comes in, we'll be drowned in here.'

Gilbert pointed to the high ceiling that was just visible from the dim light that filtered through the entrance, throwing discotheque like ripple patterns around the rough walls and ceiling.

'There's another cave higher up and there's plenty of height here for the boat to float when the tide comes in and covers the entrance.'

Peter said nothing as he jumped out of the craft on to the shingle and took a line that he held whilst Gilbert climbed out.

'There's a ring up there on the cave wall, hitch the rope onto it.' Peter found the rusting iron ring pinned into the wall about six feet above the water line and stood, looking at the prison like surroundings, then turned to help the old man. But before he could say anything, Gilbert was clambering up the shingle pile, where he felt behind a crevice and pulled out a bunch of keys, then ducked out of sight into another small cave.

He heard the rasp of metal bolts and chain as Gilbert unlocked a padlock and opened the steel door into the main interior and turned a light switch, waiting as Peter, an incredulous grin on his face took in the faded warnings on the door and looked past him into the room, illuminated with bare light bulbs that reflected off the whitewashed brick walls and the arched ceiling. The floor was level and had been screeded at some time with cement, which was now crumbling in places.

Peter stepped into the room and circled round with his arms and hands extended . 'Good God Gilbert, those signs on the door are a warning that there are high explosives here, and those Ministry of Defence signs, what the hell is this place.'

Gilbert cackled a laugh and shook his head, the pain was creeping up again and he took the still intact bottle of Diamorphine from his pocket and swallowed a couple of drops. 'There have not been any explosives here for over eighty years. This place as you call it was once used as an ammunition store during the First World War but it has been shut up for eighty odd years and forgotten about. . It was probably used by smugglers before that. I discovered it nearly forty years ago and as far as I know , no one else ever bothers to come here. I call it my den. Those signs are mine to keep out trespassers there was no

Defence Ministry as such in those days.' He paused as Peter took in the security that the place offered

Peter was standing in the middle of the chamber, 'it'll be fine so long as you don't starve here, but this is quite a complex, where do these passages lead to Gilbert?

The chamber they were standing in was circular in shape. About twenty feet in diameter with a domed roof about ten feet at its highest point, all lined in brick and whitewashed. Four diagonal passages led off from the room and Gilbert beckoned him to follow. They walked past the first passage which was blocked a few yards in by a fall of rock but the second passage ended after about fifty feet and led into a room equipped as a kitchen, with a large old fashioned butler sink , trestle table and chairs together with a small propane gas stove. Gilbert went to a cupboard and opened it. There, shelves rose full of saucepans, cutlery and tinned food, some with peeling labels. Peter reached forward and took a tin in his hand.

'Peaches!,' he exclaimed, 'and here we have stewed steak, tinned potatoes, rice pudding, jam, peas; it's like a supermarket shelf, I take back what I said about you starving.'

He walked over to the sink and turned on the tap that rasped and gurgled until suddenly a brown trickle of water bubbled out. . 'Takes a few minutes to clear, it's fed from a small reservoir inside the old cave system.' Gilbert was beaming; very few people had ever seen his secret lair. 'Come and see the rest of the place.' Gilbert hobbled along in front of him as he led the way back to the main central room again.

Peter looked around in mused silence. It was the stuff of every schoolboys' dream, a secret pirate lair, or a smugglers haunt. A scene from one of those extravagant James Bond movies of the eighties, which always seemed to end up with the perfidious villain ensconced in such a place. They had just been imaginative film sets, but this place was for real.

The third passageway was longer and led them past a number of smaller rooms some with the remains of rusting steel doors, like a police station cell block. At the end of the passage, Gilbert stopped at a wooden door that he opened and turned the light switch on before standing to one side for Peter to enter. He took in the small sitting room in front of him as Gilbert went forward and carefully removed the dust sheets from the furniture, comprising easy chairs and a bed, and sat down in one of the armchairs. The room looked like something from the fifties, but had an air of comfort that that seemed completely out of keeping with the underground surroundings.

Gilbert smiled at Peter's obvious surprise. 'Not what you were expecting is it,' he said, 'afraid the television isn't any good now, it's a 405 line system from about forty years ago. The radio should be O.K. though, it was one of the first F.M. sets produced, before the time of commercial radio or DAB or anything like that of course.'

Peter looked around the room. It hadn't been used for some time by the look of it, the furnishings where dust covers had not been used were thick with dust and the paint work was cracked and peeling. 'Does this all belong to you Gilbert?'

Gilbert still sat there enjoying the disbelief on Peter's face. 'I put in all these facilities a long time ago when I had a house above the cliffs further inland. It was during the *real* cold war period when many of us at the time thought that the atom bomb could be used against us. I prepared this place for that eventuality. You see, my old house that used to be up on the cliffs inland from here had been used as some sort of army headquarters before I bought it and a clause in the deeds included this ammunition store. At that time it was inaccessible and I had to clear a way down here through dense undergrowth. The whole place when I found it was overgrown on the outside but much as you now see it on the inside. I cleaned it up over a period of a couple of years, painted the main chamber and rooms that I converted into living accommodation, sorted out some of the plumbing, mostly lead you know and fixed the electric.'

'So there's a main entrance somewhere'

Gilbert stood and indicated the door with his hand, 'Follow me and I'll show you around.'

Peter then explored the other parts of the complex with Gilbert leading the way, enjoying the satisfaction of showing the young man around his underground warren, like a stately home owner, welcoming paying guests.

Not a natural cave but one carved out since Roman times for its special soft sandstone, similar to the Beerstone quarries further along the coast. Then it had been abandoned for years until the First World War when it had again been used, this time as an ammunition store.

The third passage was longer than the others with empty rooms as before some with their rusting steel doors still intact. There were toilets and an old shower room, its iron pipes and contents now rusted and falling apart with water dripping into the dirty china trays.

'What's in here then?' Peter had arrived at the end of the passage in front of Gilbert where he was confronted on the left hand side by a steel door that was obviously newer than the others, with heavy duty bolts and padlocks. Gilbert turned him hastily away, 'just a place that I keep a few things' he said. 'Come back this way. I'll show you something else.' He indicated another opening on the right hand side, the old door fallen away from it's hinges so that they had to climb over it to a short flight of steep steps, cut out of the rock. Here the walls were not brick lined but appeared to have been hewn out of the natural rock. As they reached the top of the flight, and opened another door, Peter could see daylight ahead and they came out into another semicircular room, brick lined this time with narrow slits in the opposite wall through which the daylight cast shafts of brightness.

Gilbert went over to one of the horizontally shaped slits and looked out. 'This was once a pill box, probably housed a couple of Browning machine guns, giving almost one hundred and eighty degrees of cover to the seaward cave entrance.'

Peter cleared a pile of debris from the shelf of the other window slit, the dust hanging in the shaft of light, as he peered through. From here he could see a view looking back down along the chasm towards the rock face towering from the sea, which now completely covered the cave entrance. The view from the other window slit looked out over the stack they had rounded earlier, with the sea breaking gently around its base. 'This place is like a small fortress Gilbert, with the right equipment it would have been possible for you to hide away here for months. The only thing is that if there had been an atomic explosion out there, you've no way of filtering the air.'

Gilbert Piltcher suddenly moved away from the window slit as if to go. 'I suppose filtered air would have been ideal, but as I understand it, the radioactive dust could be blown for hundreds of miles anyway. Look at what happened at Chernobyl, Welsh sheep and land contaminated hundreds of miles away from the source. Fortunately, I never had to use it for such an occurrence. There's another passageway over there that leads down to the beach, but it's inaccessible due to the quicksand out there. Come, I'll show you what used to be the main entrance.'

They returned to the main chamber and walked along the last passage that led to another flight of steps which they climbed and stopped at a heavy steel door, its bolts rusted solid. A small Judas door had a double set of deadlocks which Gilbert unlocked and beckoned Peter to pull open. The sudden sunlight blinded them for a few seconds as they looked out through the twisted branches of a dead tree that camouflaged the flat rocky area around the front of the entrance. In front of them the rising ground was covered in dense undergrowth and trees, backed with wind mellowed sheer yellow limestone cliffs a few hundred yards away that rose inland of them. It was eerily quiet, no birds just the sound of the wind as it rustled through the trees.

Immediately above the door the ground sloped up to what looked like a level plateau of rock . Peter fished a cheroot out of his shirt pocket and lit it, blowing the smoke upwards in a spiralling cloud against the sunny sky as he surveyed the scene before him.

'There used to be a military road that zigzagged down here but it's gone now, I'm afraid it was devoured by nature and land slips. I cut a path through at one time but even that is lost now in the undergrowth and bogs caused by the winter rains each year.'

Peter was only half listening as he pushed the old branches aside and stepped outside to look at the impenetrable landscape when he heard a slight sound from higher up. He looked back to Gilbert who was already re-entering the door. 'Do you hear that ; sounds as if someone's up there.' The old man turned pale and he clutched his middle as another burst of pain welled up inside him like an inflating balloon. He clutched the edge of the door and turned his hearing aid up a little and listened intently. There it was again, a breaking twig and rustling as something moved slowly down the hill. Then a crash in the bushes as though whatever or whoever it was had fallen followed by another series of crashes and the rustle of foliage followed by a thump and a short lived silence, before the cracking sound of a breaking tree branch floated down to them.

Gilbert made to enter the door waving Peter to follow. But Peter stood his ground a few feet from the door, still listening his trained eyes scanning the terrain slowly for the sign of any movement as he had done during his training on those Welsh moors. He crouched and half turned to Gilbert and in a low voice said, 'I can see someone up there looking around, sitting in the branches of that tree. If I'm not mistaken, I think it's a girl.'

Gilbert was eager to secure the door but looked up in the direction that Peter was pointing. She was about fifty yards away and looking around at the ground as if deciding her next move. With that she suddenly saw them staring up the hill and dropped down out of sight. Gilbert pulled at Peter and nodded towards the door. 'Let's get inside, quickly now.'

'Suppose it's a ...., a walker perhaps.'

'There aren't any walkers that would want to come down to this place.' He was anxious to get inside and pleaded with Peter to follow. But Peter's curiosity had been aroused and he stood there watching and listening to the rustling sounds in the undergrowth. 'There she is,' he exclaimed with a glow of satisfaction as he darted forward towards a mop of dishevelled hair that had emerged through the edge of the undergrowth at ground level.

A plaintive female voice came up. 'Please help me, I'm hooked up on some barbed wire and can't move any further. I must talk to you.'

Gilbert leant back against the door and looked around nervously as Peter bent down under the low branches and helped the young woman to disentangle herself from the rusting remnants of barbed wire that he saw formed loops through the bushes. As he worked at freeing her, she slowly elbowed her way forward along the ground, her safari style jacket and jeans torn and ripped, one hand pulling a small rucksack.

As the last vestige of the vicious prongs was removed she staggered to her feet, her face filthy and bleeding from abrasions, her clothes trailing ground ivy and vetch and her hair matted with mud, bits of twig and pieces of beech- mast and Burdock heads.

'Thanks for your help, that last bit was tough going, I was crawling under the branches when I suddenly got caught up in that stuff.' She was brushing herself off with her free hand whilst the other clutched the rucksack.

Peter Senden led her to the door. 'Here, let me carry that for you.'

She shook her head and clutched the bag to herself as she entered the door and looked around at him curiously. 'Don't I know you from somewhere?' She hesitated the words, her mind trolling the recent past for the face and occasion. But her mind swiftly made a memory connection that went back fifteen years. She suddenly turned away from him, stepping over the door sill into the passage entrance so that he could only see her from the back.

Of course. The attractive young female environmental delegate at the *Thinman* conference. She had looked very different then, but even so there was something about her that seemed remarkably familiar to him. One of those feelings that told him he knew her from a different time domain and situation.

He turned and locked the door behind him and as he did so, he heard the oscillating beat of a helicopter, heading along the coast.

Gilbert and the girl were climbing down the steps in front of him as he found himself saying.

'I believe we attended the same meeting at Thames House a couple of days ago.'

She half turned and smiled back at him. 'Of course, I remember you now.'

He thought, there was something so familiar about her or was it the slight fragrance that despite her bedraggled looks still lingered. Peter dismissed the thought and showed the girl into the sitting room where Gilbert Piltcher slouched into an armchair. The old man looked tired, his face a grey ashen colour as he clutched his still painful ear in remembrance of the ingratuitous David Luk.

'Well, young lady what can we do for you . What do you want with this place.'

She gave Gilbert a long hard stare and he looked away from her as if feeling uncomfortable in her gaze. 'You don't recognise me do you uncle.'

Peter looked over at her with fresh interest. He'd remembered.

'Bunnybrains?' Gilbert asked, his eyes suddenly lighting up as he stood and came towards her. The dirt on her face disguised her blushes as he called her by her childhood name. 'Katherine,..... Tony's daughter?'

'That's right uncle the very same.'

'Good God.' Gilbert looked from her to Peter and back as though to confirm the reality of the situation and in a voice now firmer, 'so you know each other then?'

Katherine and Peter both smiled as their eyes met and she was immediately aware that he had remembered a time that went back years before their casual recent meeting in London. 'You could say that uncle but it was a damned long time ago.'

The introductions were re- made and the significant relationships suddenly became apparent to them all.

To Peter. Of course. Why hadn't he realised it before. Katherine Holmes had visited his parents' house years ago, they'd been out together. Different hair colour and glasses then. Her father had been a doctor of physics like himself and he hadn't connected John Barrett's description of the Knight's daughter.

So, here was the new lady friend of John Barrett and daughter of the missing Sir Anthony Holmes. He wondered what connection she had with the *Thinman* conference and how she had suddenly turned up here, the niece of the man everyone was looking for.

Following the disappearance of her father, Katherine Holmes had also been doing some background work. At the *Thinman* conference she had attended on behalf of her client department in the Environmental Agency, she had immediately recognised the name of the Acacia Lady. Her father had recounted tales on more than one occasion about his enforced voyage round the world on the ship as a young man. A few years later he had married Captain Gilbert Piltcher's sister, her mother.

Unlike Peter and his father Philip Senden, she had always been close to her own father and, after her mother had died so tragically, their relationship had been tied even closer.

She remembered only too well the visits to the Black Sea with her parents when she was fifteen years old and the awful events that had followed and caused her mother's death. Her own terrible personal experience that she had kept to herself for over fifteen years.

On her return to her father's home at Oldbury Hall, she had been desperate to find some clue to his disappearance. In his study she found the two cards her father had pulled out of the card index a week or so before. A letter, left ready for posting was on his desk addressed to Philip Senden, a strange letter requesting a meeting about gold and a retirement fund. His Will was also lying there on the desk, open at a page that had a paragraph circled in pencil and which referred to Philip Senden, Simon Carter and her uncle.

Her investigations had led her out of curiosity to Philip's flat in Weymouth where, getting no reply to her knocks, she had found the front door easy to open as she slid a credit card over the lock tongue.

As she searched through the correspondence, she knew it was wrong, but she was desperate to find any clue that might be of use in finding her father. The letter she opened first had hand writing on the envelope identical to those treasured letters of her mother's that she kept stored away.

She had been intrigued and opened it, and was surprised to find that it was from her mother's brother, her uncle, Gilbert Piltcher. She had not seen or heard of him for nearly fifteen years although she remembered that her father saw him on rare occasions.

As she sat and read the story that Gilbert had set out in the letter the previous day, the significance of its contents started to tie in with the things she had seen on her father's desk at Oldbury Hall. She had been saddened also to read that her uncle was so ill. There was no address on the letter and her only point of contact was the cave complex that she had visited with her father and uncle in her early teens. And here she was, back again and in a most embarrassing situation with Peter Senden. Someone who was a ghost from her past.

'I presume my father isn't here then?' She showed the disappointment on her face at Gilbert's reply.

'What's wrong with your ear uncle,' she had noticed the blistering. Gilbert looked at her.' Firstly young lady I'd like you to explain why you're here and how you knew where to find me. She looked across at Peter her embarrassment showing on her face as she searched for the right words and flopped into one of the armchairs.

'Quite honestly uncle I didn't know you'd be here. I tried to get hold of you at Crows Nest but your 'phone wasn't working so I went over there. I had no transport and by sheer chance I met Peter's friend John Barrett at the Black Rocks and he gave me a lift to Truro on the pretence that I was attending a lecture there.

From there I got a taxi to take me out to Trevello where I got the driver to drop me at the beach car park. As I walked up the hill everything started to happen. I was knocked flying by three Chinese looking guys, as they were running as fast as they could down to the car park. My skirt was ruined and I chased after them to remonstrate with the one who seemed to be the ringleader, a tall bald guy. Well, I didn't get a chance, they dived into a car and shot off like a fox running for its hole.

So I started up the hill again, in time to see a motorcycle draw up on the cart track. Two guys got off and one of them went into your house. Then to my great surprise, John turned up there and walked in. I hid just around the corner of that old barn place just down the road because the other motorcyclist seemed to be keeping watch. What happened next I'm not sure, a hand was clapped around my mouth from behind and a gun pointed at me. I was absolutely terrified. This American guy whispered to me to keep quiet but kept the gun pointed as he called someone up on his radio. The next thing that happened was the guy from the motorbike came rushing out of the house wearing one of those balaclava things with eye holes, joined the other one and they made off up the lane towards Tregony, just as another car came roaring around the corner and braked to avoid them. My captor flashed some sort of police identity card and told me to stay put as the car driver piled out and they went into the house together. Then a lady from one of the other houses rushed in there. The next moment they were out again, bundled me into the car and shot off.'

Peter was looking at her and suddenly felt that he was gawping, as she poured out the details that all seemed to fit like a jigsaw into Johns story and the police version. Gilbert had been listening intently, 'I'm sorry I didn't see you, couldn't have done much to help you though I was too far away, over the back there, on the hill behind the house. I only saw the group go in, pushing someone in front of them. I didn't like what I saw. I had already made up my mind to go to the caravan and decided to push off there and then. My car was already packed up and in the back lane.'

Peter butted in, 'that must have been Carter you saw. You may or may not know that it was Simon Carter as well as John who the police found there. Did you give the Police the descriptions of the Chinese people.'

The other two looked at him and almost in unison asked him how he knew about what had happened. Then they were all talking at once. The Crows Nest incident, Katherine's missing father, Peters encounters with Carter and Luk, Gilbert's rescue from the caravan and the likelihood that Carter was probably mixed up with a terrorist group.

The stories tumbled out for the next hour until Gilbert came back to the starting point of the discussion, asking Katherine again how she came to be at the caves. 'Let me continue where I left off.' Again she was searching for the right moment to explain her motives for breaking into the Weymouth flat.

'The two Americans told me that they were CIA agents working with the Police Special Branch, trying to trace my dad. Out of interest Peter, they were at the conference we attended the other evening with Commander Hoskins, strange that. Now, where was I. Oh yes, these guys dropped me in Truro by the hospital so that I could visit you, uncle. Except that when I got there, I discovered it was Carter. I recognised him straight away from our holiday in the Black Sea many years ago.'

Peter interrupted, 'why didn't you tell the police it was Carter?'

She looked at the floor 'I had my reasons.' She stopped as if her thoughts were far away. 'Before they dropped me off there they asked me not to say anything about what I'd seen or heard for fear of jeopardising the search. I was only able to give them a description of the tall Chinaman, bald with startling blue eyes, the rest all looked similar. The detective inspector in Truro, Evans was his name, was also given the description when he interviewed me later.

I then went along to see John but he was asleep. Poor John, he had asked me out to dinner that evening and I was disappointed.'

Gilbert suddenly excused himself, 'sorry got to go to the toilet.'

She continued, 'I went home and searched through Dad's study for any clue I could find. It was then that I came across all the newspaper cuttings about his time on the Acacia Lady . I knew the story of course, but then I found his Will and was amazed to find references in it to your father Peter, together with Simon Carter and Gilbert . A retirement fund was mentioned, apparently a hoard of gold that went down with the Acacia Lady.' Peter butted in at that stage with his own story of his fathers Will bearing similar clauses but not defining the retirement fund as gold, and how John Barrett had sought information on those named.

'I wondered if the gold was something to do with my father's disappearance.' She stopped again, her eyes filling with tears as her mind went back to the father she loved so much.

'Then that damned conference came along and I was nominated by my department in the Environmental Agency to attend. I was absolutely shocked to hear about that nuclear bomb that had been on the Acacia Lady when she sank.'

Gilbert Piltcher had returned to the room and reacted sharply for his age , his voice a semitone higher than normal as he cut in. 'What's this about a nuclear bomb, there were no bombs on board the Acacia Lady, her cargo consisted of machine tools when she went down. That is before the military equipment was unloaded in Biscay. What are you saying?'

Katherine looked at Peter, realising she had let out a secret confidence that even her closest relatives shouldn't know. Peter put out his hand and gripped her arm. 'It's all right Katherine, I'm sure we can rely on Gilbert to keep quiet about it.' He turned back to Gilbert, sitting there, his mouth drawn into a tight line behind the stubble as he realised that these two seemed to know more about his old ship than he did.

'I guess you didn't know Gilbert, I don't think any of you knew except that bastard Carter. The Acacia Lady was probably carrying an atomic bomb from the Second World War. The authorities are searching for it at this very moment. They also believe she was carrying gold bullion. My father had apparently searched for it for years.' He stopped there. He didn't want them to know the cause of Philip's death. That was still an Official Secret .

Gilbert took another sip of his medicine as the news sank in. So, was that the mysterious *Dragon* that Carter had referred to from time to time over the years? The ship had come back to haunt him again, with Philip gone, who had read his letter? Was it Carter? No, Carter had said he'd tracked him down through Holmes. So Carter must have seen Holmes since his disappearance.

Katherine was sobbing quietly and suddenly rose . 'Excuse me while I have a quick wash, I feel filthy.' She left them, and the two men started to discuss Anthony Holmes' disappearance and the Acacia Lady's long voyage from Hong Kong to Alexandria, calling in at various ports on the way to refuel. Carter had often referred to the cargo as the *Dragon* a euphemism they had taken to mean the military supplies they were carrying.

Katherine returned a few minutes later, her face now pink, and her eyes still showing signs of her crying. Peter suddenly noticed the sweet aroma of the perfume she had applied and his mind suddenly flashed back to his fathers flat . He fished in his pocket and pulled out the embroidered handkerchief he had found that morning and sniffed it. 'Yours I believe,' he said as he handed it to Katherine.

So, he knew. Her tears welled up again as she tried to stammer out her apologies. 'Please believe me, I was desperate, prepared to do anything to find my dad.' She bent down to her rucksack and extracted Gilbert's letter that she handed to Peter. 'I thought he may have been hiding here in the caves. Somewhere the authorities would not have known about.'

Peter read the letter and glanced over at Gilbert, the old Captains grey face showing the pallor of pain as he sat there , his lips colourless with saliva dribbling from the edge of his mouth. The opening paragraphs now explained the medicine bottle that the old man took his sips from.

He read on, the homosexual affair between his father and Gilbert, the story of the gold . It was all there and in the final paragraph, at last, the true position or positions of the Acacia Lady and her last fateful hours. He finished reading and there was a silence as his fingers went to the bridge of his nose and he wiped away the dampness that had drained from his tear ducts. He handed the letter back to Katherine. 'Here, keep it in your bag for the time being.'

He spoke quietly then, even though there was an urgency in his voice. 'That letter is very significant, those wreck positions must be reported to the task force as soon as possible. If Carter and his friends get there first, there could be a catastrophe out there. You said just now Gilbert that Carter got the address of the caravan from Katherine's father. Did he say when or how they had met?'

'No, he just said Tony had told him where I was holed up. I'm sure he would not have given Carter the information freely, so it must have been obtained under duress.' The old man started to cough into a handkerchief and Peter could see the droplets of blood that soaked into it as Piltcher wiped his mouth. 'Is there a phone here? We need to get you to a hospital as soon as possible.'

'No, it was disconnected, I have no way of making calls from here.' Katherine, stroked her uncle's brow, he was dying before their eyes. She pulled out her mobile phone, and Peter climbed the steps to the entrance, to make the call. He fished in his hip pocket for Hoskins' card. It wasn't there and he couldn't remember Major Fellows' number. Instead he rang his Departmental Section Leader in London.

'I'm afraid Mr.Lawson isn't here Peter, he's been arrested. Something to do with the Official Secrets Act.' Grace Pettyforce's voice sounded terse. 'Major Fellows has been trying to get hold of you though, I'll patch you through to his car.' Before Peter could reply, the voice suddenly changed to Major Fellows. 'Peter dear boy, where the hell are you, we've had some developments since yesterday, I've been trying to get hold of you.' Peter explained briefly where they were, including the circumstances of Piltcher, and within minutes, the Police helicopter he had heard earlier was overhead. The surveillance team, that had followed Katherine from the Weymouth flat, had called for its assistance when she had entered the wilderness of the land slips.

They clambered up to the small plateau of flat limestone above the caves and were soon crammed into the helicopter where they asked the pilot to head for the nearest hospital. The extraordinary news about Don Holliday that Grace Pettyforce had conveyed to him would have to be followed up later.

As they lifted above the ground and flew low over the sun drenched countryside, dappled here and there with fleeting cloud shadows, Gilbert looked down on the fields as they flashed by beneath them. Everything looked normal, sheep grazing, cattle standing in groups, the odd dog that rushed out as they passed overhead, barking its warning. This was Thomas Hardy country, the area that had nurtured him as a child, playing in the fields after busy school days as his parents laboured to reap the crop. Walking the cliffs that had given him a love of the sea as he had watched its changing moods and colour. In the homophobic circumstances of his adult isolation, not understood by others, he had grown to love the solitude of the sea and had taken her as his mistress. Above all he adored his native land, more than any other place he had visited in the World. His mouth was drawn tight and his eyes closed in his final rages of pain as he recited in his mind the words of a Thomas Hardy poem learned in the village school during his childhood.

> *Past the hills that peep*
> *Where the leaze is smiling,*
> *On and on beguiling*
> *Crisply-cropping sheep;*
> *Under boughs of brushwood*
> *Linking tree to tree*
> *In a shade of lushwood*

There caressed we!

He would never feel the caress of the wind or the soft brushwood of those Dorset woods again. It was too late. Captain Gilbert Piltcher, the old sea Captain, had entered through that veil where human reason ends and the long remembrance begins.

Chapter 32. Confrontation.

After the caravan incident on the under cliff, Carter and David Luk had fled from the scene of the inferno. They had been taken there by Chungai and two of his associates on the understanding that they would return with the information they knew Captain Piltcher would divulge with persuasion. Chungai had told them that the hostage they were holding would die if they didn't return with the wreck position information, vital to the Koreans plans. David Luk knew that the deal to cut him in as their main supplier in Haifa couldn't work. With what they knew, the terrorists would soon dispose of them once they had the information.

David Luk had looked back at the blazing caravan, satisfied that he now held the secret of the Acacia Lady's pot of gold, the treasure that would help to fund his planned syndicate between Florida and Cost Rica. It would make him one of the most powerful amongst the scattered drug dealers there, enabling him to set up direct links with the Colombian and Eastern organisations, regardless of his abortive talks with the Korean. He dragged his father, stumbling, half walking, half running, as they made their way along the narrow under cliff footpaths shielded by the ample vegetation. They paused in the undergrowth near the cart gap that lead down from the upper lane to the beach to ensure they were not being pursued. There was no one about here. It was an empty beach, and off the beaten track for holidaying sun seekers. He saw the small inflatable heading out to sea, the occupants back to him. Most likely a day fisherman on his way home. The fisherman ran his hand though his hair and Luk immediately recognised that the helmsman with his back to him was Peter Senden. Too far off now to put a bullet into the hull and he said nothing to his father as he grimly watched the small craft head off eastwards along the coast.

So Peter had probably seen them kill Piltcher in the caravan, his plans to involve him with finding the gold would have to be done cautiously.

After half an hour, Luk was satisfied they had not been followed by the Koreans and they crossed the open gap and ascended the cliffs on the other side and entered the woods. An hour later they were descending the steep coastal path down to the Branscombe Beach car park. They carried their jackets over their arms so as not to look too conspicuous as they joined the holiday makers thronging the area. Carter was moaning and complaining that he was tired and they sat on a bench outside the beach cafe overlooking the car park for him to rest. Luk sat beside him, watchful, and was suddenly up on his feet, dragging the reluctant Carter behind him. The object of sitting there and observing had paid off. A family had just parked a Shogun four wheel drive and walked off down to the beach, laden with the paraphernalia that children nowadays demand in such places. It was what Luk was looking for, they hadn't locked it and by the look of them they would be gone for some time.

They left the car park heading north along the narrow lanes and joined trunk road at Axminster. Here Luk turned the car eastwards. 'Where are we going now?' The tired Carter asked the question.

'Senden's place outside Weymouth, I got hold of his address while we were on the boat, he has the diving gear and a boat,' he grinned at his father, 'I'm sure we can persuade him to do the hard work for us, after all, he also has an interest in what we're after. We may be able to do a trade. He helps us in exchange for information on Holmes's whereabouts.'

'But we don't know what they've done with Holmes, he could have been moved again.'

'Oh shut up father, close your eyes and get some sleep, we've got an hours drive ahead of us.' He looked sideways at the tired old man sitting there beside him. What would he want with all that gold? He would only give it away to his creditors to save his neck. No, the gold would be his. He now had the location from the Captain but he had the problem of salvaging it from the sea and getting rid of the other interested parties.

George Hansdorf and his partner had followed the BMW for several miles now as it headed east along the same A35 road that Luk and Carter were to take later. The British pursuers had spotted the Mercedes and radioed to their American colleagues to take over for a while so as not to arouse the driver's suspicions.

The suspect's car drove mile after mile, not fast, keeping to speed limits, with the pursuit cars taking it in turn to keep the vehicle in sight. The Special Branch occupants of the second car radioed the Dorset Police Traffic Control centre with instructions to keep the car under surveillance without alarming or approaching the occupants who, from the CIA agents' description, could be the terrorists that the Special Branch was anxious to trace. The information had been cross checked with Malcolm Seiger and the descriptions matched.

They skirted the northern edge of Holes Bay, a backwater of Poole Harbour before they saw the BMW indicating to turn off towards Poole Town and head for the Quay.

The 5 Series slowed along the one way traffic system the driver looking for a parking slot. George Hansdorf was driving the Mercedes behind a couple of other cars which were also looking for parking slots.

The Town was teeming with cars and the BMW stopped a couple of times in anticipation of cars leaving, much to the annoyance of the following motorists.

George stood on the brakes as the car immediately in front spotted someone backing out and stopped, opening up a gap as the BMW drove further on. The car in front was a large one and the driver seemed to have problems manoeuvring it into the small space, turning, stopping, backing up again, waving at George to back up and give him more room. A motorcycle behind them overtook through the narrow space.

'If this son of a bitch doesn't move we'll lose them.' The large car at last moved forward into the space, but intended backing out again to straighten up.

George put his foot down to squeeze past and took the cars rear light cluster with him. The road in front was clear, but where was the BMW? In the rear view mirror George caught a glimpse of the enraged motorist; his car stopped half way across the road, as he looked at the damage to his precious car.

He drove slowly now, as Horace O'Brien scrutinised every car parked along there, every third car looked like the BMW to their eyes, unaccustomed to the European compact car. Then they saw him, the tall head shaven Korean in his gaudy shirt, accompanied by the other Korean, both of them smattered with soot particles. They had apparently parked further along the road and he was strolling back with the other car passenger towards the area of moored boats and yachts, rafted up alongside the Quay. There was nowhere to park without a parking penalty but they stopped the car where it was anyway and got out.

'You can't leave it there sir.' It was a traffic warden running after them. From the other direction, the motorist with the smashed rear light was approaching in the company of a beat constable. He shouted.

'There they are officer, arrest them, bloody road hooligans that's what they are.'

Any argument or raised voices in such a crowded area immediately draws the attention of the crowd and heads were turning including the Koreans. As Chungai saw the conspicuous American cut suits looking anxiously in his direction, he knew instinctively what they were and started to walk faster, breaking into a trot and then a sprint along the Quay, knocking into people in his haste, the other man running after him. Hansdorf and O'Brien started after them, but the motorist grabbed O'Brien by the sleeve and hung on. O'Brien grounded him with an apology and ran after George, hotly pursued by the traffic warden and copper. All heads were now turned to the commotion as people leapt out of the way of the running troupe. Fifty yards ahead of them, the Korean had stopped to look back for his companion before stepping over onto the quay side ladder.

There were two shots, it could have been a car backfiring, a rare occurrence these days, but the second man had caught a bullet in the throat and swayed in dizzy confusion before plunging off the quay edge into the water below as onlookers' first looked around and then flung themselves to the ground screaming and crying. The motorcycle with two riders was already away, weaving in and out of the oncoming traffic against the one way road system. No one saw the number plates. It wouldn't have been of any consequence anyway as they were changed almost daily.

The RIB waiting at the bottom of the iron rung steps, with one crew and the engine running took Chungai as he leapt aboard. Seconds later they were roaring out past the Oyster Bank beacon, the tall lean Korean half standing as he balanced in the centre of the craft looking back and grinning at them as they looked down at the body in the wash from the rib, bouncing in the waves between the moored pleasure craft and the wooden baulkworks of the quay.

Confusion followed, people screaming and running, and yacht occupants standing on their craft craning necks to see what had happened. George flashed his badge at the constable and asked him to call his station. The constable glanced at the badge and was already on his communicator with the traffic warden looking over his shoulder.

'Been to Disneyland have we sir? My son's got one of those. Now, quieten down please, until the squad car gets here, I'm arresting you and taking you both into custody.....' He gasped as O'Brien's hand clapped the back of his neck and the constable fell to his knees. The startled traffic warden backed away and the motorist did a quick disappearing act into the crowd. George snatched a pair of binoculars from a retired gentleman who had been standing there, spending his time harmlessly as he thought. A peeping Tom. Scanning the dozen or so yachts moored there, some with girls lying on the coach top coamings, sunbathing in very brief bikinis, others thinking they were out of sight behind the cockpit screens and wearing even less. All George was interested in was the RIB as it sped off down the Little Channel, sliding to port in a spray as it rounded the Stakes cardinal buoy and headed out along the Middle Channel. He heard the police siren behind him and the small patrol van as it pulled up. But he kept his binoculars firmly trained on the RIB until he saw the rising bow wave as it slowed beside a large motor yacht on one of the moorings. Then all hell broke loose, as a young male police constable together with his female counterpart tried to restrain them. Hansdorf told them who he was but they just looked at him blankly, preoccupied with their instructions to arrest them.

The Special Branch Audi drew up beside them and this time the identification warrants that were flashed received instant recognition by the police officers. Horace poured out his apologies to the first constable, now rubbing his shoulder and looking slightly dazed.

The motor cycle would later be found dumped on the foreshore behind the railway station when the tide went out. Similarly, checks on the BMW later showed it had been stolen.

D.C. Mike Parson looked around the dispersing crowd. 'Where did he go?'

George handed him the binoculars and pointed out the motor yacht to the D.C who focused on to it.

'Looks like they're preparing for sea, just seen a puff of smoke out the back, hey Charlie,' he called over his shoulder to his partner who had placated the beat officer and was arranging through his local net to get communications set up . 'Get on the blower to Portsmouth Fleet- Commander- in- Chiefs office, no wait, on second thoughts we've got the Marines here in Poole, get control to track down their number. And stress the urgency, no fucking about, tell them we need the top brass.'

A minute later he was talking to Colonel Teddy Beavis, at the Royal Marines base over on the other side of Hamworthy, losing precious moments as he explained the situation.

As soon as Chungai boarded the motor yacht he shouted his commands up to the Captain who had passed the afternoon listening to his iPod and improving his English. He liked it here in England and if the opportunity arose, he'd apply for political asylum. 'Get those engines run up and then cast off.' Chungai was looking back but no one seemed to be heading in their direction.

Chungai swung himself below and entered the main cabin where the other Koreans were playing poker, Ling bare to the waist his great belly flopped over the elasticated band of his old fashioned Hawaiian shorts.

Chungai shouted at them in their native language of Han-gu^l. 'We're out of here, get ready for sea, the CIA are on to us, I've just seen them back there crawling all over the quay.'

Colonel Ling looked up, 'So, after all our trust placed on Carter and his son you allowed them to get away. Our masters will not be pleased with today's work Chungai.'

'We're finished here, don't you understand.' Chungai's voice was even higher than usual. 'We must get to the harbour entrance before they start after us or we'll be boxed in here.'

He leaned out of the cabin side door and shouted directions to the Captain who already had his crew running around. This was the fourth boat they had chartered in the last fortnight, each one slightly different, and each one powerful.

Poole harbour is reputed to be the second largest natural harbour in the world but it has one narrow entrance to the sea and Chungai knew they had to reach it before it was closed off to them. He went outside and mounted the ladder to the flying bridge two steps at a time and looked around. Perhaps he had been mistaken. Then he saw the grey police launch edging out from the Quay, its polished blue topsides sparkling in the sun. He shouted in that high pitched voice of his, 'Let go that mooring line now, head for the harbour entrance Captain, and keep ahead of that police launch.' He pointed out the launch as the yacht turned slowly into the main channel and gathered way as the revs were increased. Chungai looked back at the police launch which was coming up behind them quite quickly. 'More revs Captain, we must lose them.' The Captain looked round. 'I'm only allowed to do six knots in this part of the harbour.' Chungai knocked him to one side as he pushed the throttle levers forward and the yacht went up on the plane, its wash tearing at the boats moored along the edge of the channel, sending them into chaotic rolling and pitching motions against their mooring chains.

Ahead of them a dingy race was in progress. It was the final race of the regatta that had started in a friendly way but was now deadly serious as the tiny Wayfarers set off for the last tack that would take them across the main channel.

The club commodore sitting on the committee boat saw it first, the speeding hull and white wash about half a mile away. He quickly calculated that at about twenty five knots, the craft would bear down on the tiny fleet in about one minute's time.. He yelled into his hand held radio to the rescue boat and recall horns started to blare. Then he looked on hopelessly a minute later as the motor yacht ploughed at speed through the fleet, capsizing and sinking several on the way.

Chungai looked back at the police launch as it slowed to assist in the rescue. When he looked forwards again they were almost at the harbour entrance and the Bramble Bush Bay, the chain ferry that runs between Sand banks and Shell Beach , loaded with summer traffic and holidaymakers , was pulling across the entrance, its black warning buoy still being raised on the stub mast. He pulled the wheel to starboard and the yacht broad sided sending a great sheet of water over those on the ferry deck, sending up screams of alarm as he then dodged between moored boats off the beach.

The ferry chains screeched and smoked as the donkey engine on the Bramble Bush Bay was slung into reverse, taking the chains and gear wheels up close to the safety margin allowed for by the designers. The police launch was still assisting the young regatta sailors as jet skiers headed out from the beach to play in the wash put up by the speeding motor yacht.

The Swash Channel spread out before him now with the Poole Bar beacon in the distance and the open sea around him. Chungai throttled back slightly and turned the boat eastwards but the Captain suddenly lunged forward and grabbed the wheel turning the speeding craft south east by south. Chungai screamed at him as he fought for control. 'Sand banks, all around here.' The Captain gasped out as Chungai started the turn again and sailing boats tried to tack and gybe out of the way. Small motorboats, their top sides gleaming with the polish lavished on them by their proud owners headed rapidly for the edge of the buoyed channel running alongside the Training Bank. No allowance had ever been made at their night school desks for this sort of flagrant disregard of the collision regulations.

Chungai released his grip as he looked over to the Hook Sands, with the seas breaking gently onto the shallows. 'Take command Captain, head for Southampton and put the false name plates onto the stern. We'll go into one of the creeks there and find another boat.' He swung himself down to the side deck and looked aft of the boat , over the white wake of water behind them. There was no sign of the police launch . He looked again before he entered the cabin where Ling was, now wearing a shirt and with the other Korean who had come in through the forward door from the wheel room where they had been watching the course of events.

Ling sat and scowled at Chungai. 'Well, you certainly got us noticed this time, what do you intend to do now?'

'I'm heading for the Southampton region, we can then either continue up Channel to Holland, go ashore or steal another boat depending on what happens over the next hour or so.'

Back at the Hamworthy Marines base at the back of Poole Harbour, Col.Teddy Beavis was in the communications room as operators set up the audio visual links with the Commandant General Royal Marines Headquarters of Commando Forces at Mount Wise , Whale Island and the Naval Southern Command in Portsmouth.

The men now charged with apprehending the terrorist craft decided a policy of containment of the vessel due to the dangers of injury to the hundreds of pleasure craft plying the seas off the south coast. Three Lynx AH7 helicopters of the Commando Brigade 847 Squadron were scrambled at the Yeovilton base in Wiltshire and the nearest fishery patrol craft, HMS Harlech Castle patrolling off the southern side of the Isle of Wight was ordered to steam into position. Two commando Merlin EH101 helicopters were hastily summoned at Plymouth and three marine craft on a training run at Studland Bay were ordered to pursue but not to apprehend the yacht.

Chungai stood in the cabin as Ling remonstrated with him over the abortive visit to Piltcher's caravan and the loss of two men. 'Look, we've been over here now for nearly three months and our search has covered hundreds of square miles. We've been ill equipped for such an exercise. Our masters thought it would be easy, posing as treasure seekers. That stupid old diver Senden they put us in contact with was useless. Then we were told to find the scientist who would unravel the secrets of the bomb when it was found, another useless old man . Then they sent us Carter who swore he knew where the device was located through his greed to find gold. His son who was only interested in setting up another heroin empire in Central America. He must have had the sense to know we would have to dispose of them later.'

Chungai hit the table with his fist. 'Shut up all of you, can't you see it's finished here, we've got to get out.' He went to the wall 'phone. 'Captain, how much fuel are we carrying.' The Captain was quick to confirm that they had taken on fuel that morning, two full tanks and five barrels, enough to drive the powerful petrol engines to Holland if they wished.

Ling stood and balanced himself against the sloping table, as the yacht continued to plane across Poole Bay. 'Chungai, we are not finished, our masters and indeed our customers are relying on this mission. Whilst you were away this morning we received new information, reliable information this time that the device we are seeking is not in this wreck of the Acacia Lady.' He rummaged in a drawer and pulled out a decoded fax sheet. 'This came in this morning from our Lebanese friends.' Chungai snatched the paper. 'What is it ?'

'It's a copy of a British Admiralty Board report, forgotten over the period of time, look read it.'

Chungai went to the cabin door again and glanced back towards Poole, shouting back over his shoulder. 'Tell me. I haven't got the time to read all this stuff.'

'That report states that the equipment was never on the Acacia Lady, she was used as a decoy. The Bomb was on one of the other ships which sank in the same storm and being still under Naval control the position of the wreck is clearly identified. Our new instructions are to go there and investigate.'

Chungai turned back and snatched up the paper, looking back at Ling. 'You must be mad, the whole Channel is now crawling with Naval ships, we wouldn't stand a chance, were being set up.' The Captain appeared at the door.

'Mr.Chungai we are being followed by three high speed small RIB craft, we think they are Royal Marines.'

Chungai checked his hand gun, 'Break out the Kalashnikovs and get the crew armed and ready.' He went out on deck and looked wildly around . The sea was dotted with hundreds of small craft, sailing boats and motor cruisers all out for the day, their crews made up of families and friends. The three small dots were becoming larger and he started to form a plan in his mind.

Peter consoled Katherine in the tiny space behind the helicopter pilot's seat as she held her uncle in her arms, remorse flowing through her body at her selfishness. She kept asking herself, why hadn't she seen fit to visit her ageing uncle before it was too late, the contents of his letter had shocked her, why hadn't he told anyone in the family about his illness ?

The helicopter flew them to Dorchester where the body was removed to the County Coroners mortuary. It took half an hour to clear the paperwork before they were in the police station .

Peter was patched through to the Major again. 'I can't discuss my findings over the net, but please be assured that I have the urgent information that's required by Commander Hoskins.' They agreed to meet in one hour at Peter's home.

The police car dropped Katherine and Peter in the road outside the old farmhouse where they thanked the driver and strolled up the drive. Peter frowned, 'funny,' he said, 'that's my girl friend Jessica's car, but she must have a friend with her, don't know who the Shogun belongs to.'

He was still looking back over the Shogun as he found the front door on the latch and ushered Katherine into the small hallway as he called out to Jessica.

There was an ominous silence and he suddenly felt his heart pumping faster as he sensed that something was wrong. A few strides took him to the drawing room door, the latch making its scraping sound as he lifted it and they were confronted by Carter and Luk. Well, not actually confronted, Carter was sitting in an armchair, smirking from ear to ear like the famous Cheshire cat. Luk sat on the settee, his handgun pointing to Jessica's head as she sat very still, the fear showing in her eyes and her face drained of colour.

'Welcome home Peter and who might she be.' Luk waved the gun at Katherine. 'I admire your taste brother, another lady expecting to share the delights of your warm bed no doubt.'

Peter's fists clenched with fury. 'Let her go you bastard, she hasn't done anything, as for this lady, she's Sir Anthony Holmes' daughter and you have effectively just killed her uncle.' He took a step forward towards David Luk but immediately checked himself as the gun was again pressed against Jessica's temple.

Jessica winced as the barrel cut into the side of her head. 'Sorry Peter, I came over to pick up my things.'

'Bastard am I, and what does that make you then dear brother.' Luk was enjoying himself, playing with them, taunting them to take up the impossible challenge of rushing forward to her defence.

'Come on David, remember were half brothers.'

Luk looked at Carter and laughed at Peter's misconception.

'Oh no, Peter we're blood brothers, isn't that so father.'

Carter looked solemn and nodded.

'It's true. That queer you called a father couldn't fuck a chick for his life. Impotent you see, liked playing with sailors.' The last acrimonious remark addressed to Katherine as Peter pushed her behind him, Luk emphasising the gun at Jessica's head in anticipation of Peter plunging forward, his obvious rage now showing.

'What do you think I made all those payments to him for? They were for your education my lad, blackmail, after that he tried to suck my tits dry, blackmailed me for years over the court findings of the Acacia Lady. He knew all about the gold and certain other matters you see.'

'That's not true. My father may have had certain weaknesses but he was *my* father. What the hell do you want from us for God's sake?' Peter's face had turned pale as he tried to contain the cauldron of anger boiling up inside him at Carter's new revelations.

Luk gave him a sardonic smile.

'Let's look at it this way brother, the World survives on trade and its trade we want to discuss with you, even though we are both so closely related. Now, you have something we want and in exchange we can give you something that you want. No, stand still please, I have killed many times, even lovely ladies like this one, any attempt to move forward and darling here dies, please understand that I mean what I say.

My proposal is this. A little family business. In exchange for using your diving know how and equipment, with you doing the diving of course, we will trade the hiding place of that young lady's father with you. You may like to know that we are now in possession of the true position of the gold and in exchange for your help will ensure you receive a small percentage of the proceeds, later of course when we have gone.'

'Why the gun David, if all you want to discuss is a family deal?'

'Let's just say that it ensures the odds are in our favour. I guess you saw what happened at the caravan this afternoon, the old man Piltcher is now out of the way and we have a clear pitch on which to operate.' Peter didn't comment on

Luk's assumption that the fire had killed Gilbert Piltcher or the rescue that had taken place, albeit too late to save the old Captain.

'And what's the alternative if I decide not to help you.'

'Like Piltcher, Holmes dies, it's as simple as that, this young lady beside me would take the place of Holmes quite nicely as a hostage, and I assume of course that you told the police what happened at the caravan?'

Katherine suddenly cried out. 'Where is my father?'

'You get him back when we have the gold, simple as that.'

Peter could sense the urgency of her cry as he put out an arm to push her behind him again as his mind rushed over the situation before them.

'What about the *Dragon's Morsel* Carter, didn't you say it guarded the gold for all time?' Luk darted a sideways glance at his father. 'What is this *Dragon's Morsel* you've been on about, what's it got to do with the gold?'

Carter replied slight apprehension now in his face.

'There's no dragon down there, unlike gold, anything else would have rotted away by now, if there had really been a cause for concern, the authorities would have dealt with it and removed it years ago.'

Peter sensed that the conversation could be prolonged and that David Luk had not been told the full story. Maybe he could be talked round by knowing the full implications and impossibility of a gold search, anyway it would prolong time and he hoped that Dick Fellows might arrive soon.

'Tell him the truth about the gold Simon.'

Carter could not resist the opportunity to gloat .'I told you the story about the B29 bomber crash and how I went there for salvage'.

Luk nodded. 'Get on with it then we can't sit here all day, I might get tempted.' He caressed Jessica's thigh with his free hand, pushing it up tight against the crotch in her jeans, watching Peter and moving his tongue provocatively around his lips as he did so. Carter didn't seem to notice the demeaning offence as he continued.

'When I did my last dive, I went over to have a look at the bomber engines, half hidden in the kelp. Except that one of them wasn't an engine at all, it looked like a bloody great big bomb. It was an unusual shape and I still remember that it reminded me of a giant chocolate Easter egg. Under the coral frost and barnacles that had begun to grow all over it, I saw the inscription '*Thin Man Mk one*' which I thought was a bloody good description of the device. I knew straight away that I had stumbled upon an American atomic bomb something that the whole world was desirous of having and yet no one really wanted. And, from my recollection of the time that I'd seen the plane go down, I reckoned this one had been destined for some poor sods in a Japanese city.'

'What are you trying to tell us father, that there's an atomic bomb on board the wreck?' Luk's eyes darted between his father and Peter now as the uncertainty began to register. Carter gurgled a laugh relishing in the story. 'There was once lad, but that was a long time ago.'

Peter broke in, 'I thought you said that the gold was guarded by the *Dragon's Morsel*.'

'A ploy lad, to stop your bloody father from going there. There is no Dragon out there, never was.'

'But I thought the *Dragon's Morsel* was the nuclear device you found. Surely that has been what all this is about?'

David Luk sneered across at him. 'An interesting story from the past and with no relevance now. Come on were running out of time, I've no doubt that the police will be here soon, we have to come to a decision Peter, your help or this lady of yours dies along with her father, I shall count to ten.'

Peter stiffened as he felt the movement behind him as Katherine fished in her rucksack. What the hell was she doing, he had to concede to Luk's terms, and sail with them to Alderney, there was no alternative and the Royal Navy would stop them anyway.

Luk drew away from Jessica as his attention was drawn by the movement and he pointed the gun in Peter's direction and started the count.

Everything happened then in less than two seconds. Peter felt the blast at his side as the handgun was fired and David screamed out as he rose clutching at the right hand shoulder of his torn suit as blood oozed over his hand. He tried to raise the gun and another shot shattered his right hand and sent his gun spinning across the carpet. Katherine came out from behind Peter, with her gun held in both hands, pointing alternatively between Luk and Carter, and beckoning with her head towards Jessica to move away.

'You bloody scumwads,' she screamed at them, 'you think you can trade my father for a pile of shitty gold.' She was fuming with anger as she waved the gun between the two men, one sitting bolt upright now in the armchair, wary eyes following Katherine's spiralling gun movements, the other moaning on the blood soaked settee.

'Killing is too good for you two, but I'm damned well going to do it. It will be difficult to choose which one of you goes first. Which one I give the pleasure of seeing the other die first, father watching son or son watching father. It doesn't matter anyway, neither of you have got an ounce of compassion or love in your bodies, just greed.' Peter bent forward and took her arm but she shook him off in her anger, raising her voice to a shouting fishwife's scream. The scream of the female gender protecting its young, or in this case, the life of her father.

'Let me tell you about these two.' She paused, the gun still hovering in her hands. 'David Luk nee Carter, drug trafficker, and procurer of small Latin American boys for the vice trade in places like Miami. David Luk, pimp, living off child prostitutes and pornography. Oh yes Peter, your brother there may have come from the same womb, but unlike you , he is a degenerate cancerous monster who deserves to die. The FBI know all about him and the Israeli authorities have pinpointed him as a main drugs supplier to their country. He is also a murderer, like his father and wanted in the Middle East. But what can they do? Nothing but tuck him up in a nice cosy cell for a few years. The World isn't going to miss him at all.

And this pile of shit , Simon Carter, a festering bloody coward who raped an innocent child. A fifteen year old girl, in her cabin whilst she was trying to enjoy a holiday on the Black Sea. Visited her cabin whilst her parents were ashore, beguiling her into thinking he was a friend of her father's. Then tormenting her with stories of her father's treachery and how he would expose him if she told. Yes, that young girl was me and the scar of that awful dirty experience has lasted to this day, to the extent that I have never had the privilege of enjoying a relationship with any of the men that have befriended me.

Simon Carter, whose wicked accusations poured disgrace on my family to the extent that my wonderful mother eventually killed herself.

Simon Carter, who ruined my father's career by those accusations, caused him to have a mental breakdown, …….. and threaten to take his own life.

Simon Carter, murderer of his ship's crew, oh yes Carter we know all about you.'

Her voice came down by a few decibels and she wiped away tears with her free hand. 'Simon Carter who through shock, shortened my uncle's life. A life worth a hundred of Carters.

And lastly, Simon Carter, who now thinks.' Her voice trailed of in a tremble before she breathed in for her last blast. 'Simon Carter who now bloody well thinks he's going to trade my dad for a pile of useless contaminated shit.'

She drew in breath, 'It's a sweet revenge I've dreamt about for years.'

Carter was still watchful, as she started to sob, still waving the gun at them.

'Now Carter, before you die, where……is……my…….father.'

Luk's left hand hovered between his right shoulder and hand as he lay back on the settee. 'If you kill us you'll never know my sweet lady.' Her gun hovered over them. 'O.K. who want's to be first.'

She fired another shot, the round pumping into the chair beside Carter's head, sending the upholstery up in a pile of feathery dust to float down to the carpet like snow flakes.

It was Carter who broke and in a gurgling voice pleaded with her. 'Spare our lives and I'll tell you.'

Peter put his hand out to the gun. When he spoke his voice was shaking. 'Put it down Katherine, let them tell us and get this over with. The authorities will catch up with them at some time.' She lowered the gun to her side, 'Well?' She demanded of them.

Carter sat forward a belligerent look on his face and glanced momentarily at Luk before speaking. 'Your father is being held captive by a terrorist group who are currently operating from a yacht in Poole Harbour. As far as I know he is being held at an old tin mine in Cornwall near St.Just….' before he could finish, Luk slumped sideways on the settee and rolled onto the carpet where his gun lay. He was up on his feet with surprising agility as he turned and fired left handed and Peter felt the bullet's draft as it grazed past his cheek and smashed a widow pane behind him. Another shot sent Jessica reeling against the wall, clutching her right side with a bloody hand as a vase of flowers went crashing to the floor from a table. Peter leapt forward to wrestle the gun from David Luk that discharged again as they fought. As Peter knew from their previous combat on board the Starlight Princess, his half brother was a gun man, not a fist fighter and he hit him where it hurt so that David Luk slumped back against the wall, but he still had hold of the gun and half raised it.

There were two sharp reports and Luk crashed to the floor as if thrown there like a sack of potatoes .

Carter was still sitting in the chair, his eyes glazed and staring into nothing, a small hole in his forehead and a tiny trickle of blood seeping onto his beard from one side of his mouth , his restless spirit now only in the minds of others. Others, most of whom would only remember him occasionally for his greed and double crossing, as those thoughts of him sank down into the dark labyrinths of their minds, where the spirits of the dead live on in the living.

Katherine just stood there the gun dangling at her side, as Jessica holding her bloody side staggered forward to the two men. She looked up in horror at Katherine and back at Peter, 'Both dead, you've killed them.' Katherine with tears streaming down her face looked on dazed at the two bodies in front of them, lying there like discarded crumpled gift wrappings. Peter went over and relieved the gun from her trembling hand, checking its chamber contents .

'Interesting,' he said as he turned it over in his hand, 'a .44 calibre Magnum, Desert Eagle, used to be issued to the Israeli secret police, where on God's earth did you get that from.'

She didn't answer, but took the gun back from him and put it in her haversack. A strange quietness had descended on the three of them since the shots only moments before and they could suddenly hear the sound of the rooks, disturbed by the echoing reports around the valley and wheeling in the sky making their noise above the trees along the top of the valley ridges. Peter stared at the two bodies. He'd been so near to finding the answer he desperately wanted to know, the meaning of the *Dragon's Morsel*. Now he would probably never find out.

Then they heard running footsteps outside as Peter glanced though the window and noticed the small starred holes in the upper glass panes of the window that had been behind him. He turned back into the room as Jessica collapsed beside the two bodies, her hand gripping her side her face drained of colour as he rushed over to her and knelt at her side.

In the beech woods that overlooked the house from the rear, a shadowy figure packed his gun in its sleeve, picked up a chewing gum paper and grinned up at the noisy rooks as he made his way silently back along one of the three escape routes he had planned. When he was a suitable distance away, he spoke quietly into his headset mic. 'Away here, did you get that about Holmes and the location of the terrorists?' A voice crackled in his headset. 'Team have connected at Poole, now going to boat.'

The old farmhouse drawing room was quickly full of people as Major Jack Fellows and Malcolm Seiger arrived followed by an entourage of armed police. The para medics followed close behind and started their routine examinations, attending to Jessica where she now lay on the blood soaked carpet, Peter kneeling there, holding a small cushion to her wound to stem the flow until the medics demanded more space.

He rose and introduced Fellows to Katherine, now shaking badly as she poured out to the Major what Carter had said about her father's kidnappers.

Fellows looked over to Seiger who had been examining Luk's handgun as it lay on the settee and now busily instructing his men. 'Get the local police in Cornwall to attend to the matter together with the Army, they can assess the situation and update directly to you on the search for this lady's father.' Instructions were barked into Seiger's mobile as Peter drew Dick Fellows to one side, 'how on earth did you know what was going on here?'

The Major looked around the room for the telephone and went over to it, flicking off the back. 'Our CIA friends seem to leave no stone unturned.' He waved the small radio transmitter for Peter to see, 'CIA standard issue.' His eyes suddenly narrowed as he spotted another device, smaller than the American one designed to look like a small electronic component of the telephone. He said nothing and replaced the back of the 'phone. He recognised it as another listening device, one issued to the Israeli Mossad secret service, but what was it doing there?

'As soon as the CIA control listening post heard Carter and Luk enter the room they realised what was going on and called us. They heard Dr. Wilson's scream as she pleaded with them not to shoot her. Wicked couple of bastards I would say, tormented her with that gun, discussing their plans and what had happened during the day before you arrived. A brave lady, she kept them talking for about half an hour which gave us time to get our chaps in position. Unfortunately, your mobile was switched off and it was too late to stop you going in.' He walked over to the two bodies and looked down at Luk. 'Shot at close range with a Magnum by the look of those wounds, where's the gun?'

Peter pointed to the holes in the window. 'Your marksmen took a chance firing at that range Major.'

Fellows surveyed the bodies and glanced up at the starred holes in the glass. 'They were not our marksmen dear boy they were too far away and by the look of those wounds they were not CIA. It was someone else who shot those two.'

Katherine suddenly felt the emotions of the last few hours well up inside, a terrible feeling of nausea that sent her rushing outside to be ill.

Fellows looked up at the holes in the glass and tried to judge the probable trajectories. 'Up there in the woods somewhere, we'll get someone up there in a minute, no rush, whoever fired those shots was a professional, they could be miles away by now.' He turned back, glancing around the room. 'Now, where's this information on Acacia Lady or *Thinman* or whatever we're calling it?'

In the confusion of the last few minutes, Peter had forgotten the original purpose for the Majors visit. 'Holmes's daughter has it in her knapsack.' He looked around for Katherine as the medics picked up the stretcher where Jessica lay and carefully took it outside to the waiting ambulance. They stood aside as a photographer crouched to take the official Special Branch photographs and Peter followed Jessica on the stretcher.

'Is she going to be all right?'

The medic replied. 'She's caught a bullet to the right of the liver, we think it's a flesh wound but we must get her off to hospital for a check up. She'll survive thank God.'

Peter found Katherine outside in the garden.

'Have you got Gilbert's letter?'

She produced it from her bag and gave it to him. 'Peter, you seem to know what's going on here, who are you, who are you working for?'

'More to the point Katherine, who are you really with, how did you learn to shoot like that?' She looked away avoiding the direct gaze of his eyes. 'Let's talk later, not here.'

He sensed her concern at the number of people around them, 'O.K., before further explanations, let's find out what we can do about finding your father.' He bent his head close to hers, picking up again her perfume and the slight waft of sickness on her breath and whispered, 'where's your gun by the way, they'll want to question you later?'

She hesitated for a moment, looking at him now, her eyes pleading. 'It's hidden in the blankets on Jessica's stretcher; I'm going along in the ambulance with her.' She turned and was gone, climbing into the back of the vehicle, the doors closing and siren starting as it drove down the drive and vanished along the road.

He returned to the crowded kitchen that now resembled a command post with everyone talking at the same time into their hand held radios and mobiles. The body bag with Carter zipped up inside it was removed to the coroner's department hearse that had arrived quietly on the scene and the dark suited officials were returning for Luk's body when they heard a shout from one of the medics in the drawing room. 'This one's still alive.' It was one of the Branch paramedics standing over David Luk and everyone jammed into the room. 'He's got a very weak pulse; we may be able to save him.'

Maj. Fellows hadn't stopped, the radio communications were going mad, messages being referred to him, talking earnestly into three different telephones as they were thrust at him, he turned as Peter re entered the kitchen and spoke rapidly. 'A lot's happening here dear boy, we believe the terrorist boat has been found, can't tell you everything now, the most urgent consideration is to get your information to the task force as quickly as possible, I've arranged for your information to be flown directly out there.'

A constable shoved another phone into the Majors hand. 'Hello......yes Sir George,.....I see, O.K. that's fine, my men will look after the arrangements.' He went to move back to the drawing room where there was another call waiting.

Peter asked, 'to the USS Phoenix?'

The Major hesitated. 'No to Captain Williams on HMS Seeker, We have received some information that I can't go into now, only to say that in spite of the excellent co-operation here I am concerned about the Phoenix motives. I've arranged for you to be picked up by helicopter from the field opposite, you'll be flown directly to HMS Seeker where they are awaiting your information.

Chapter 33. Poole Bay.

On the yacht speeding across Poole Bay, Chungai balanced himself on the fly bridge, estimating the closing speed of the approaching RIBs, his Kalashnikov AKM assault rifle resting against the bulwark. He bent back to the Captain at the controls. 'When I give the order Captain I want you to stop her dead in the water.' He shouted to the men crouching on each side of the craft with their weapons to get ready. Then he stood there watching, calculating the distance between them and the range when he would stop and allow the RIBs to overshot.

The AKM was lifted slowly and sighted up on the middle RIB as Chungai shouted the command. The Yacht sank on her haunches and then fell forward as the bow wave collapsed and she came to rest. The two outer RIBs immediately peeled off each side as the yacht stopped and the crew started to fire.

The coxswain of the middle RIB caught a round in the chest before he could react to the yacht that was suddenly within range. The men on board the Arctic 22 RIB had no chance as they attempted to fire back and their craft slowed as they were strafed like sitting ducks on the water.

The two other craft circled out of range and Chungai shouted the order to pursue the nearest one which had turned to escape but with one engine on fire. They drew level at speed and passed within a few yards firing as they went. The return fire was short lived as the marines slumped back from the onslaught. And then Chungai gave one of his high pitched screams of laughter and shouted.

'They're firing blanks.'

The young marine trainees had been on a training exercise in Studland Bay when the order had come through to pursue the yacht but keep out of range.

'Where to Mr.Chungai', the Captain was calling for orders and Chungai turned and pointed above the noise towards the open sea and shouting. 'Let's get back to the wheel house I want to look at the charts.'

Back at Hamworthy they were listening to the reports in shocked dismay, assessing what had happened. Ten young marines wounded or dead.

Colonel Beavis had received the Special Branch request and ordered the nearest available squad to pursue the yacht at a safe distance without engagement, they were new recruits armed only with SA80 light support rifles loaded with blanks and had been on training manoeuvres at Studland bay.

The command centre at Plymouth announced that the 847 squadron from Yeovilton had now scrambled the three Lynx AH7 helicopters, armed with TOW anti tank missiles but they had about thirty minutes flying time to the target area.

As the rogue yacht turned on its new course the Captain grabbed Chungai's arm and nodded to the patrol vessel's dark outline as it rounded the Needles on the southern part of the Isle of Wight.

'We can outrun her but she's probably armed, we'll be blown out of the water.'

Chungai was busy at the chart table and looked over at the vessel about two miles away. 'Turn back Captain I can see a way out where they will be unable to use their weapons. Head for the Solent waterway between the mainland and the Island, according to the pilot book, that area will be full of small recreational craft they won't be able to target us there.'

Ling pulled his heavy bulk into the wheel house. 'What the hell are you doing Chungai, we'll be trapped if we go back, and I'm ordering you to turn and head out to sea immediately.' Chungai turned to him, and nodded to the HMS Harlech Castle bearing in their direction. 'We'll be blasted to pieces out there, my option is the safest one, now get the men on deck ready to fire at anything that approaches.'

Chungai turned slowly and faced his colonel. 'Colonel, I'm taking charge and if you don't like it that's too bad. The Solent will be safe whilst we decide our next move.'

The four man high powered speedboat hired by the Israelis was manoeuvring out of the River Hamble on Southampton Water when the Solent Coast guard ordered radio Seelonce and started to broadcast a warning to all small craft that a speeding motor yacht was heading into the Solent area, its destination and erratic course unknown but a wide berth to be observed. On the mainland at Lee on Solent, the local gliding club received a message to ground all their craft until further notice, the message merely stating that commando helicopters were heading through the airspace and expected soon.

On the powerboat, Major David Hessel listened to the official reports over his head set as Max steered the powerful craft slowly through the water awaiting his boss's instructions. 'We're in luck they've left Poole by the sound of it and heading this way.'

Chapter 34. Question time.

Around the committee rooms and chambers in the Palace of Westminster that July afternoon, there was a holiday air as Members prepared for the Summer Recess.

Even Members of Parliament go on holiday and the Parliamentary Recess was due to start later in the week when the House of Commons chamber received its annual maintenance ready for the opening in two months. The Prime Minister was about to take his holiday in Portugal after attending the last P.M's question time that afternoon in the Commons and the Foreign Secretary was on her way back to the UK having spent the previous day of her Iraq tour trying to be diplomatic over the fresh atrocities in war torn Baghdad.

Ernest Doright, Member of Parliament for East Dorset had been watching events on the television in his chambers as normal programmes were cancelled and long range cameras on the shore picked up the course of the marauding motor yacht. The mid afternoon news reports from Poole Quay speculated that the dead man was a member of a drugs gang but then the awful news of the young marine recruits being killed hit the headlines.

He looked again at the anonymous fax he had received earlier in the day and ran through its contents again. He rang the Ministry of Defence Permanent Secretary Sir Nigel Hawks for a statement as to what was going on off the Dorset coast, outlining his concern for the public safety of his constituents.

There was no time to raise a standing order question. Instead, the permanent secretary arranged with the Chief Whip to allow the question and Doright went straight to the House.

The Speaker was handed a note and looked hesitatingly towards the Prime Minister who he knew would not be properly briefed about the situation.

The PM answered his last scheduled question at the despatch box and sat smiling amidst rhetoric laughter as he bent his head to listen to the urgently whispered briefing from Sir Nigel who had slid onto the green leather seat beside him. The Speaker called. 'The Honourable Member for East Dorset'.

Doright stood as the crowded chamber buzzed and Members craned their necks to see where the unexpected question would come from. 'Prime Minister, whilst you have been speaking this afternoon, there have been tragic events on the South Coast, a highly dangerous shooting and, I understand from news reports, that ten Royal Marines have been shot whilst pursuing a seagoing craft now marauding off the Dorset and Hampshire coast.' He paused as the murmur of voices became suddenly silent and Members listened with attentive interest.

'I have also received information that the Royal Navy task force currently operating off our shores is seeking to find an American nuclear device or to be more precise, a nuclear bomb. I am also advised that a terrorist group is........'

'Order, order.' The Speaker's voice cut shrilly across the assembly. 'The Member is perfectly aware that his question is limited to the tragic events of this afternoon.'

Doright stood his ground, 'Mr. Speaker, I apologise to the House for my oversight but surely my question demands a reply regardless of the formal procedures used here in the House.'

The Speaker stood. 'The Honourable Member for East Dorset will retract his statement which will be struck off the record.' Pandemonium broke out with Members waving their order papers at the front bench for a reply as the Prime Minister consulted with his colleagues before rising nervously.

He stood there as the uproar died to a whisper, head bowed, his shoulders square to his hands resting on the despatch box, the Questions Book portfolio in its red binding closed in front of him his nervousness apparent by the south Yorkshire that broke through his mid England accent. 'Madam Speaker, the Honourable Member for East Dorset has asked us about the tragic deaths of young Royal Marines this afternoon. Madam Speaker, this House is horrified that such an event should have taken place and our condolences and sympathy go out to their families.' He paused, the silence of the house pressing in on him as the secretary passed him a note. 'I understand that the events in question are still in process. Marine commando helicopters are now in pursuit of the offending motor yacht whose crew perpetuated the tragic deaths a short time ago and Royal Navy ships are converging on the area. The Defence Secretary's office will be issuing a statement when the situation has been assessed and dealt with. In the meantime, until I have more information, it would be imprudent of me to speculate as to who these people are or why they should have carried out this perfidious act of violence.' He sat as the Opposition Leader reiterated the shock and horror felt by all Members of this House, but was quickly on his feet again and together with the Permanent Secretary left the Chamber.

Ernest Doright had not had a chance to detract his statement and uproar prevailed again until the Speaker was forced to clear the Chamber.

Outside, in the Lobby hall, Doright was besieged by other Members, all baying for an explanation of his remarks, when a Sergeant at Arms approached and quietly conducted the MP to the Prime Ministers small private room. The PM was standing with Lord Younger the Chairman of the Intelligence and Security Committee and Sir George Longland who had been hastily called over from his office on Millbank by Sir Nigel Hawks who stood with the group. They were quickly introduced as Doright entered.

The PM extended his hand, 'Ernest, sorry about your treatment out there but we have a difficult situation on our hands at the present moment............'

The Prime minister explained the situation to Ernest Doright about the Israeli discovery and the subsequent arrangements between the Government and the Americans and the details on the task force set up to find the nuclear device. The shocked Doright handed over the anonymous Fax he had received earlier that afternoon to Lord Younger. 'If this came in to your Westminster office, it is most likely that the source can be traced. In the mean time, for the sake of national security nothing is to be said on this matter. I'll go back to my department now and put a trace on it.' He left with Sir George and the Prime Minister indicated a chair to the Honourable Member.

'Ernest, we have been having some thoughts on promoting you to the Junior Minister post in the Transport Department that I know you have been after for some time, and with your agreement, when we return from the recess, I will be writing to you to confirm the appointment.'

In the Press Office, mobile phones were running red hot as parliamentary correspondents contacted their media offices with the news of what had almost been said. Something about terrorists and a lost nuclear bomb. Journalists buzzed around their contacts like a locust's swarm, gobbling up any information no matter how slight or speculative it might be.

Chapter 35. Spithead.

It was young Adam Digby's eleventh birthday. His grandparents had decided to make it a treat day and together with his younger sister, were touring the Spinnaker Tower on Portsmouth's seafront to watch the boats and cross Channel ferries as they plied their way around Portsmouth harbour.

At the eastern end of the Solent, the terrorist yacht had reached the Needles channel on the western Solent approach and slowed within a group of pleasure craft making their way against the last of the ebb tide. The patrol vessel HMS Harlech Castle was closing but too distant to deploy her lighters and unable to use any form of firepower due to the close proximity of the other boats in the vicinity. All she could do was slow down and shadow the yacht as instructed with no engagement. Chughai was steering, keeping the yacht close to the other craft as they approached the NE Shingles east cardinal buoy and the narrow race opposite Hurst Castle Point on the mainland and Fort Albert on the Isle of Wight. The view into the western Solent was opening up and he could see hundreds of small yachts spreading out to the horizon. He grinned back at the Captain, these would afford adequate cover and the warship would not risk its fire power in the confined space. He handed the controls to the Captain again while he consulted the chart and ordered a course to the mainland shore south of Lymington where it would be too shallow for the warship to get close to them.

Up at Marchwood Military Port, at the head of Southampton Water, the Sandown class mine hunter HMS.Yarmouth had arrived the night before with a mainly civilian crew ready to go round to the Vosper Thornycroft yard in Portsmouth the next day to start her re-fit.

The few officers on board were getting ready to disembark when the order came through to proceed to the mouth of Southampton Water and set up a patrol routine but not to engage. They couldn't have engaged anyway because the lightly armoured vessel had no ammunition on board.

Chungai slowed the yacht again off Lymington, well protected amongst the convoy of small boats returning to their river moorings, and the Lymington to Yarmouth ferry crossing. A ferry passed close by and passengers waved to them little knowing that this was the yacht that had caused such mayhem an hour earlier out in Poole Bay. The patrol vessel had stopped out in the deep water area and was now guarding the narrow west Solent straits they had entered earlier.

Ling sat at the rear of the wheel house, his anger at the thought of failing his assignment predominant in his mind whilst he was further humiliated as Chungai now gave the orders. Seagoing orders that he couldn't aspire to, orders requiring special knowledge that was the same to seafarers the world over. He knew from the position of the warship behind them that they would not be able to retrace their course.

Chungai was consulting the chart again, this time with the Captain. 'O.K., we'll keep close to this northern shore until we reach this point on the chart.' His finger prodded the point off the sand banks at Calshot as the yacht edged forward again and lifted on the plane. The grey bulk of the patrol craft turned her 1427 tons towards them as the two 5600 hp Ruston diesel engines drove the propeller shafts churning through the water with her single DES 30mm cannon manned and ready for action.

The motor yacht took an irregular zigzag course keeping other boats between them and the line of fire from the patrol vessel, planing along the north shore and the shallower water with the other vessel running a parallel course further out. They saw the mine sweeper ahead of them as they approached Calshot. Chungai was enjoying himself, it reminded him of a few years earlier when he had been on a N.Korean patrol vessel guarding the fishing fleet that had strayed into S.Korean waters and the chase that had resulted. He looked back at Ling and the grin was suddenly wiped from his face as he saw the three Lynx helicopters approaching in close formation behind them. He turned again to the Captain and ordered full power.

Looking down on the zigzagging craft from the 847 squadron lead helicopter it would have been easy to trigger one of the wire guided missiles with a 99% chance of a hit. But the orders at this stage were to pursue and contain the vessel. In any case, there were too many small craft in the area and as they looked ahead they could see a large passenger liner turning out of Southampton Water.

The Digby family were now on the Spinnaker Tower observation platform 110 metres above Portsmouth harbour where they had been rewarded with the sight of a new type 43 frigate and two other grey naval vessels steaming out of the harbour and had a view over Spithead and the large cross channel car ferries plying between Portsmouth and Cherbourg.

The Digby's grandfather pointed out the off lying forts and was trying to explain their significance to the children.

Through the ages, Portsmouth has held a strategic position on the south coast, the British Navy using it at one time as their main base. Henry VIII had forts constructed along the coast and during Charles II reign, forts were constructed around the perimeter of the harbour to defend it from both land and sea. During the Napoleon wars, more forts were built out in the seaward approaches to Spithead and connected to the land by underwater barriers such that the eastern sea approach to Spithead and the Solent can only be made between No Mans Land Fort and Horse Sand Fort, an entrance about a mile wide.

From their viewpoint, the family could now see that the grey naval ships had taken up station there and were patrolling up and down between the forts. The car ferries further out were not being allowed through for some reason and three large vessels were now stationary outside the forts. As they watched, the sound of helicopters reached them from the west.

The minesweeper stationed on the entrance to Southampton Water was no match in speed for the terrorist yacht. It did however deter Chungai from any attempt to go ashore there and vanish with his men.
From Calshot the yacht passed on and took the shallow channel north of the Bramble Bank towards Portsmouth with the three helicopters following them.
There were not so many boats here and Chungai guessed that the helicopters had orders not to engage their weapons.

Suddenly they were not alone as a high speed powerboat joined them, running a course close behind. Chungai looked nervously over to the other craft as it drew level with them and saw flashes of automatic fire. The crew were firing back now as the speedboat suddenly dropped behind them again. 'SAS I should think,' he shouted to Ling who was already making a hasty retreat down to the cabin as the yacht slowed and the Captain rolled out of his seat into a lifeless crumpled heap of sea boots and wet gear. Chungai leapt the flybridge steps to the side deck stepped over another body and ducked inside the wheel house where he took up the controls and put the boat back on the plane. Down here with water breaking over the bows it was not so easy to see.
'Head them off to the north away from the forts entrance if you can.' Major Hessel shouted into the mic. to his speedboat driver in front.

The Digbys saw the yacht racing across Spithead heading almost due east with the three Lynx helicopters in pursuit now joined by the commando Merlins. As it sped towards the gap between the forts and the frigate picked up speed, another vessel, a racing powerboat appeared to come in close to the yacht and they saw tiny spouts of light coming from it causing the yacht to veer further north. Grandfather was now watching through the magnifying lens of his camcorder as he videoed the scene. 'Christ, they must be playing Russian roulette; they're heading straight for the underwater barrier.'

The ball of flame rose instantaneously in a great bellowing plume as the yacht hull came to a shuddering halt and the flaming topsides and barrels of exploding fuel flew forward in slow motion to crash in thousands of smoking pieces into the sea beyond. There were brilliant flashes of light as ammunition magazines started to explode and the sound of the blast and cracking after-explosions suddenly hit them as they watched speechlessly from the shore. All they could see now was a scene of vivid flames and dense black smoke as it spread across the water where the motor yacht had once been.
From his vantage point in the lead helicopter, the pilot looked down as the speedboat circled and took off at high speed out between the forts before he lost visual contact as the dense smoke rose and he pulled away. The black hulled speedster would be found later at the back end of the shallow neighbouring

Langston Harbour with three muddy sets of footprints leading to the shore and already being wiped out by the incoming tide.

It was 11.00 am Eastern Standard time at Langley, Frank Gibson and Tim Gregson had been called over to the 'comms centre where they were watching the messages being flashed up on monitor screens and reading the print outs that had been coming in for the last hour. The ground operators on the *Thinman* team in England reporting punch by punch the rapid events of the afternoon as it unfolded in England in innocent ignorance of the *Crusader* plot.

They watched the Internet pictures of the TV broadcast and saw the explosion followed by numerous interviews, as news programme producers scrambled through their lists of experts.

Gibson glanced nervously to Gregson and nodded his head towards the door. 'My office.'

The two men left the communications operatives, busily passing the information to other centres that had an appropriate interest in what was happening, including amongst others Jonathan Erkenham, the President's chief adviser. Nothing missed his attention. He even collected the Presidents nail clippings for examination. It was rumoured that if the President had a cold, his used paper tissues were put through the shredder. Someone had reported that he was in fact visiting the building that very day.

Back in Gibson's office Gregson 'phoned the other conspirators who were privy to the *Crusader* project with a covert warning message while Gibson frantically fed the shredder with documents and papers relating to *Crusader*.

At the Pentagon, Colonel Graham Erricsmann cancelled his appointments for the day and rang the motor pool for his car. Before leaving he went to his safe, removed the *Crusader* document and put it straight into the shredder. Fifty minutes later they were gathered in the conference room on the second floor at Langley.

The five men sat there and watched as Gibson strode up and down and suddenly stopped, smacking both hands on the table. 'It's finished, the plan has fallen apart and all we can do now is to sit back and wait for *Thinman* to be found, and then join in the jubilant celebrations with the rest of them.'

Erricsmann looked around the table. 'All my paperwork has gone and I hope you've all done the same, I'm worried about the weak links in the chain, the London guy and Hoskins. I've made arrangements for Hoskins to be eliminated but what about the other people involved over there. If they get grilled over this we could be implicated and in deep deep shit, what then?'

The others looked dismayed at the Colonel's matter of fact dismissal of Hank Hoskins. Tim Gregson looked over to Gibson, standing there pale faced, his fingers in their praying pose. 'Do we have to do that to Hank? Surely you said we had enough on him to keep him quiet.'

Gibson surveyed them through his haze of uncertainty. 'Don't you see, the man had a conscience, the same as Muller.' He stopped as though he had finished, then he said thoughtfully,

'labour to keep alive in your breast that little spark of celestial fire called conscience.'

He looked around the puzzled faces at the table.

'Attributed to George Washington gentlemen.' He stood and said quietly, 'George Washington who founded this great nation that we very nearly betrayed.'

Erricsmann gave him a half glance, the man was going off his rocker.

'Frank, we must know who the British contact is for Christ sake. With luck we can deal with it.'

'Luck? We'll be lucky to get out of this fucking mess alive. I've discovered that the bank accounts were cut off yesterday, probably by Stern and Hindes. They're on to us and the sooner we get out the better.'

Erricsmann insisted, 'for fuck sake Frank give me the name, we may still have time to extricate ourselves from this.'

He didn't get his answer as the conference room door was unceremoniously dashed open and six marines and a number of FBI personnel entered followed by two Fairfax County Marshals, all armed and pointing their weapons as the conspirators raised their hands and the Presidents Chief Adviser strolled in after them.

On board the USS Phoenix, embarrassed US Naval MP's arrested their Admiral and others under the direct orders of the President.

The Congressional committees and trial would cost the American taxpayer plenty in the months to come.

Chapter 36. The Acacia Lady.

Peter saw the commando Merlin helicopters flying back to their base in Devon from his seat in the Gazelle as the machine, taking him out to HMS Seeker, crossed the coast over Portland Bill, flying south to the British arm of the Channel task force. The Merlins hadn't managed to get to the operational area in time and had now turned back. A voluminous amount traffic had been coming in over the headset as they took off and only the clearance instructions with ground control units could now be heard and within half an hour they were hovering over HMS Seeker waiting for their landing instructions.

This time she somehow looked smaller than on his previous visit. She was small. 2510 tonnes displacement, 79 metres overall with a beam of 15 metres. As he looked down at the single stack, her topsides festooned with sensor aerials and turning radar scanners. he hoped this would be an end to his involvement that had lasted over the last few weeks.

Once on deck, he was shown to the bridge where Captain Williams and the other officers were waiting. The navigation officer, Lieut. John Barnes took the paper that Peter had prepared from the letter and went to the plotting computer where he called up his charts and data logging search records.

'Well the first position is out near the Casquet S.W.Bank, it was surveyed about two weeks ago when we were searching over near the Hurd Deep. There were echoes there that indicated something small. All we could find was a pile of old Japanese machine tools, sunk into fine sand and shells, there had been a wreck there, echoes all over the place but not solid enough for the size of ship we were led to believe would be down there. We dropped a probe down but no sign of radiation. The second position is on the edge of another deep channel, an old ammunition dumping ground about sixty to seventy metres deep, north of the Ortac Channel. That's miles away from the original position we were given, are you sure your data is correct?' Peter cross checked the readings with the letter. 'According to the ex Captain of the Acacia Lady, she sank in two parts. The front end sank over near the Casquet Bank, and contained a cargo hold full of machine tools.' He looked up pleased to confirm their findings. The main hull, engine compartment and No.3. hold sank in the second position after drifting in a storm overnight.'

Captain Williams was pacing up and down his hands clenched behind his back. 'It's a long way from the search centre. It'll be obvious to the USS Phoenix that we are moving to a substantially new area. Our orders over the last few days have been to steam up and down on a box search between Subfacts areas Delta 036 Papa 4 and Delta 038 Quebec 4, that means between the northern side of Hurd Deep and the Channel Light Buoy.' The professional surveyors were not taking kindly to the outside information being thrust on them. This Peter Senden wasn't even in the Service.

The Captain clasped his hands at his back again and looked out over the deck crane and grey coloured decks the colour almost matching the sea beyond. White foam crested waves were beginning to form in soldier lines with dark clouds ahead. 'Weather report please?' A rating saluted and handed him a satellite derived fax with the meteorological synopsis. 'Just ran it off sir, the weather is deteriorating from the west, visibility is falling, pressure dropping rapidly and we could be in for a rough night, sir.'

Williams turned to them as they all stood and waited for his decision. 'O.K. Senden we'll try it, ...signals, get a radio comm over to the Phoenix, say we're making for Braye Harbour to make a minor repair whilst the weather is bad, we'll re -join the task force', He looked at his watch , 'it's Zulu 1715 UTS now, let's say tomorrow afternoon, that should give us ample time. Were twenty miles away, say 1900 on site. We'll have an hour or so daylight and then continue through the night. Take over Mr.Briggs.' The Midshipman turned the tiny control wheel onto the new course set by the auto pilot computer and the quiet diesel electric drive drove the ship as she turned so that the wake appeared as a great white crescent behind her, breaking the seas as she set out on the new course and orders were given to deactivate the various sensors. From the radio room behind the bridge Peter could hear the operator whistling through his teeth. 'Quick come and see this would you.' They crowded around the door and watched the T.V.Screen with pictures of the explosion taken from an amateur video an hour earlier outside Portsmouth. 'Wonder who they were?' Peter realised that these men had been told nothing about the terrorist force in the area.

He went down to the ward room with John Barnes. 'You've been on board before I believe Dr. Senden, did you see the works downstairs.' Peter confirmed that he had been round very briefly, but wouldn't mind another look. 'Unfortunately the Chief has ordered the gear to be shut down. It's not worth running it at this speed. Any way I can explain things as we go round if you like.' Peter accepted the offer.

As they descended the deep stair well to the sensor room John Barnes was talking over his shoulder to Peter as he followed. 'Watch your head on the bulkheads! Seeker will be decommissioned after this little outing is over. She was built back in the late seventies you know, had several refits and acted as a hospital ship during the Falklands war crisis. The old man will be retiring at the same time I should think. Right here we are.'

They entered the control room with its screens, consoles and equipment racks. Rows of switches, coloured push buttons and custom keyboards seemed to be crammed into every available bit of space. 'That looks a bit more complicated than the depth sounder on my small boat.' Peter joked as he looked at the astonishing array of equipment and the large plotting tables.

Barnes grinned, 'we have everything here, she's a combined hydrographic and oceanographic vessel class, first used when the Polaris submarines came into service, if there's anything down there , we'll find it.'

Peter stopped beside a large console with keyboards and two screens. 'What does this do?'

'That's an operator's sonar console. The left hand display shows the predicted pulse transmission paths in ambient conditions, taking into account the seas measured salinity and temperature profile. The right hand screen is then used to input corrections made for propagation distortions on target contacts. It all relies on sophisticated digital acoustics, taking into account the variations in the speed of sound that vary according to the sheers in salinity and temperature that vary with the depth.' Peter knew the principles in some detail but his background training in industrial espionage always dictated that he should let the speaker assume he knew little about the subject. Not that there was anything to hide here, it just came naturally and occasionally a little gem would drop out.

Bill Barnes continued to chatter about his electronic charges over the next couple of hours as the ship grooved its way towards the target area. The position they were heading for had a rocky topography covered by course sand and signals were expected to be good although Barnes informed Peter that there was a lot of rotting rubbish on the bottom, mainly discarded World War I shells, all degassing slowly and allowances would have to be made.

Then they were getting ready as the six operators filed into the room ready to take up their stations and adjust their sets and data loggers for the search to come. Bill Barnes became engrossed with the technical running of the operation and Peter retired to the bridge.

The weather had deteriorated as predicted. Visibility had dropped to about a mile and outside the rain fell against the windows, and churned the sea's surface to a white greyish soup. Captain Williams strolled over to Peter. 'We would prefer it to be a bit smoother, our systems measurements rely on a reasonably stable base and we'll have to keep an eye on the main storm coming up from the south west.'

Peter looked on as instructions and orders flowed between the bridge, engine room and sensor room as the Seeker trolled along the course set by the information from Captain Piltcher's letter.

After half an hour, Lieut. Barnes appeared with an armful of printout. 'Nothing down there so far sir,' he said grimly as he spoke to Williams and darted a reproachful glance over to Peter, 'we've been over that position several times and there's not a trace of a target, the bottom's reasonably smooth and if there was anything we would have picked it up by now.' They both, without intending to, looked accusingly at Peter. Perhaps they had been right about amateurs. 'We are picking up stronger traces of radiation than in the other search areas, but it seems to be uniformly spread.'

The Captain stood beside the midshipman at the control wheel and gazed out to the middle distance and the deteriorating conditions before he turned. 'O.K. men we'll call it a day, switch off and we'll go back to normal stations.'

Peter was disappointed, surely after all this, Captain Piltcher's information couldn't be wrong. He followed Barnes back to the sensor room.

'Lieutenant, I see you use compact disc vector charts for everything you do on board here, plotting, navigating, etc. Do you have any paper charts I could look at?'

Barnes pointed to the large drawers under the plotting table. 'We have to have them on board as backup, why do you ask.'

Peter stopped, his mind had been turning over Gilbert Piltcher's story of how he had taken bearings from the Renonquet islet. 'Ask the Captain for a few more minutes, I've an idea that we may be in the wrong place.'

The Lieutenant lent to the phone with the request and asked. 'What do you have in mind sir, I thought from what you were saying earlier that the position you gave us was the one the original Captain of the Acacia Lady had admitted to on his death bed.'

'That's correct and I'm surprised you didn't find anything. By the way, how are your compasses set up on the ship?' Barnes explained the gyrocompass, other compasses were pre set to allow for deviation caused by outside magnetic objects such as the superstructure and other on board equipment, set by the global satellite systems for offset and magnetic variation.'

Somewhere in his mind something was yelling at Peter, then he had it and he pounced towards the plotting table. 'Pull out the largest scale chart you have of the area between Alderney and the Casquets, something that shows the Ortac Channel, small islands and rock outcrops around there, I have an idea.'

Barnes was taken up by Peter's sudden enthusiasm and leafed through the charts in one of the drawers, 'How's this, Admiralty Chart No. 60, covers Alderney and the Casquets including this area.'

They spread it out on the table and with pencil and parallel sliding rule Peter transferred the position Gilbert had given onto the chart and looked at it.

Barnes looked on expectantly.

'This position was translated into Latitude and Longitude from a bearing and distance taken from the top of Renonquet. He referred to the earlier part of Gilbert's letter, yes here it is, 3.2 miles along a bearing of 355 degrees, presumably magnetic.' He traced the position onto the chart using Gilbert's figures and stood back. Barnes looked at the chart with disappointment. 'It results in the same spot.' Bloody amateurs he thought as he went to turn away and order the equipment to be shut down. Peter grabbed him, 'Don't be too hasty Lieutenant, I haven't finished yet, do you have a pilot book or anything that would give us the history over the last fifty years showing the variation of the magnetic North Pole?'

Barnes was suddenly interested again as he started to grasp Peter's train of thought. He went to a side cupboard and pulled out several pilots for the area and plonked them onto the plotting table beside Peter.

Peter picked up the first one and ran through the index. Nothing. With modern global positioning systems, magnetic variation was an automatic input.

He looked at the chart bottom right hand corner Engraved in 1982 updated to the current time. The printed compass rose annotation read Variation 7 degrees 25 minutes west (1974) decreasing about 4 minutes annually. He stamped his finger on it and looked at Barnes. There's the culprit, what we need to know is what the variation was in 1953 when the ship sank, that's about 50 years of unaccounted variation.

Barnes could now see the logic in Peter's argument and reported to the Captain again before he started thumbing through the rest of the pilots and reference books.

They found the figure at last that would have applied at the time Captain Piltcher took his original compass bearing and transferred it onto the chart, resulting in a new position nearly half a mile away.

Captain Williams had just come down and joined the grinning faces. 'Weathers getting bad up there, do we have a new position or not?'

Thirty minutes later they got their first target indication, lying in a deep crevice between two underwater reefs that were not indicated on the charts and forming an underwater sonar radar shadow. The underwater TV cameras were lowered together with the submersible and were soon shooting pictures to the surface of an old ship, sitting upright in the gully, her superstructure outlined by the powerful lamps as a lacy silhouette of crustatia. As the cameras were manoeuvred around the remains of the ship, the stern name plate suddenly came into focused clarity, the riveted letters spelling out the name they had been seeking for so long, ACACIA LADY.

Peter was standing on the bridge, it was nearly dark outside, when the jubilant Lieutenant rang up confirming that this was the wreck and trailing probes down near the sea's bottom were picking up weak indications of radio active radiation, although it was no more than they had detected in the surrounding area searches.

Capt. Williams relayed the news to HMS Sutherland, the patrolling type 23 frigate guard ship that would stand by them during the night. The Acacia lady had been found at last and by the Royal Navy and the difficult task of containing her secret deadly cargo and guardian, would be dealt with the next morning by the Americans and their scientists.

PART III
Dragon's Morsel

*And thorns shall come up in her palaces,
nettles and brambles in the fortresses thereof:
and it shall be an habitation of dragons,
and a court for owls.*

Isaiah 34:13

Chapter 37. The Mossad Connection.

When the Gazelle landed early the next morning at Nelson Base in Portsmouth, Peter's one thought was for Jessica as he phoned and arranged for a departmental car to collect him and take him to the Dorchester County Hospital where he assumed she had been taken.

Whilst he was waiting his mobile rang, it was Jack Fellows. 'Congratulations dear boy I've just heard that the Acacia Lady was found last night by our own chaps and not the Americans or French. Your input into the proceedings was, by all accounts of major importance, well done, the Royal Navy is delighted.' He confirmed that Jessica was in the Dorset County hospital at Dorchester and that the car was on its way for him.

She lay there, her face a sickly chalk pallor, with Katherine Holmes sitting beside the bed in the small private room as a nurse tended to the various life support machines crammed around the bead head. He went over and gently kissed Jessica's forehead, felt for her limp hand and stroked it. 'That bastard Luk, I hope he gets life for this if he recovers.' He looked over to Katherine. 'Any news on your father yet, sorry, I should have asked before.' Katherine shook her head as the doctors entered the room and she rose to leave.

Outside the room Katherine came up to him and kissed him lightly on the cheek , 'I'm sorry, I feel pretty helpless just sitting in there, she's very ill Peter, they think it's her liver.' She stood there in front of him, her upturned face looking so concerned and then slowly she turned to go.

There was not the same sensual beauty in her face that he had first seen in Jessica. It was something else, her body warmth maybe, the hip movement, the lonely inner personality, the slight woody smell of her hair from the trees on the land slips. He thought about the teenage girl he had once known, the laughter they had shared and how they had parted. She had been different then, close cropped hair he seemed to remember. He felt an inner passion for her again, as he had felt when he held her to him after the shooting. This time it was greater than he had ever felt before, a welling up of feelings he couldn't control or understand, an emotional tenderness for her with a primeval desire to know her intimately.

He reached for her arm and pulled her back to him his eyes searching her face, his other hand holding the back of her head, fondling her auburn hair. Her eyes met his with the same understanding and desire as he pulled her towards him and felt the vital throb of her heart, pounding so loudly in her breast. She came gently into his embrace, pressing against him, their lips brushing, feather light at first and then firmer as they expressed the feelings they had both suppressed after he had comforted her after the shooting. Then she remembered back to their teenage days. She giggled as her head buried in his shoulder. 'Peter it was so wonderful meeting the way we did in my uncle's cave.' She looked up at his face as they both laughed and hugged each other again.

She suddenly broke away. 'Peter we can't, I feel so guilty.' She looked up at him her face shining in the new experience she had found. He gazed into her green eyes and realised how beautiful they now appeared, the wide generous mouth, and the lips that beckoned him.

'Don't be. Jessica and I, well it's difficult to put into words but we were using each other, we both knew in our hearts that there was no lasting depth in it. I believe we were thrust together by the people above us in the Service, hoping that somehow they would gain information leading to the *Thinman* assignment. We had agreed to part amicably, poor girl, she shouldn't have been there she was only collecting her things.'

They went back to the small ward, and looked down on the woman who had been so brave. 'Look lets meet later. I've got to get home and changed, I've had a long night. By the way, what happened to the gun, where did you get it?' She just smiled. 'It was my father's, found it in his study, it's now somewhere it will never be found. I retrieved it before we got here and managed to dump it.'

'What for? You didn't kill them, in fact Luk is still alive. Carter is dead, shot by a sniper but not one of ours.'

'That gun shouldn't have been in my father's study. I know very well where it came from and I don't want him implicated in any further complications. I just want them to find him.'

'There will be an enquiry you know, although I understand that everything that went on in that room was secretly taped by the Americans. Presumably they will be ordered to hand a transcript over to the enquiry committee in due course. By the way, where did you learn to shoot like that?' Her anxious countenance relaxed as she smiled, she knew she was good. 'I had lessons when I was a child and we lived in Israel for a while.' She broke off as if considering her next line of conversation.

'Peter you're obviously connected to the Secret Service with access to the files there. You must know that my father acted between the Israeli government and our own government at one time. It was a trade during the hostage crisis. He wrote a book on it afterwards but the MI5 through the Government got a court injunction and forbid its publication, it was before the time of the Internet and other ways of getting around it the way they do now. They raided the house and took everything.'

'Is he still connected?' It was an open question

'No of course not, but his old colleagues keep in touch from time to time. Now, let's stop the questions and leave this poor girl to rest.' She held his hand and somehow he felt a current pass between them, a tingling sensation that he had not felt since Yvonne. He took her in his arms again and kissed her. 'Until later' he whispered and she clung to him feeling her inner passion as their bodies pressed together, wanting him, craving for the chance of their union. 'Until later,' she repeated and let him go. They made their arrangements to meet that evening then she watched him walk down the corridor and waved as he turned the corner. She felt different today; suddenly relieved of the past and the stigma of that awful time she had spent in the cruise liner cabin when Carter had raped her. Exhilaration at meeting Peter and the elation she had felt in his arms. But underneath her new found ebullience was a great emptiness that she felt, at no news of her father.

As he went down to the car and it's waiting driver, his thoughts were of her but he would have to ask the burning question he now had in his mind. He had asked about her father's involvement with the Israelis but he needed to know the real truth about her own involvement. How did she know so much about his half brother David? He had also seen the small transmitter in the telephone casing that Major Fellows had opened in the drawing room back at the house and recognised it as a device used by the Israeli Mossad secret service. If that was the case what was their involvement, had they been the ones who had shot Carter and his half brother. If so, why? He asked the driver to take him back to the house that was now quiet, with one constable on duty.

Once inside, Peter went over to the telephone and carefully prised off the casing to ensure that the tiny listening device was still there. Then he removed the American device, put on walking boots and with his binoculars trudged off up to the ridge of the valley looking back at the house and the drawing room window to judge where the marksman had hidden. Sure enough he found the position. Not at the top of the ridge where he had started, the line of sight was wrong, too steep. Lower down there was a small copse from which he trained the binoculars on the house. This had to be the spot and he started a search of the area until his eyes fell on a chewing gum wad stuck to a fence post.

On his way back to the house he made a long call to Grace Pettyforce in the London office from a public call box in the village and then hung around there until the telephone rang with the answers he had requested from her.

He returned to the house and sat waiting for a while. The door bell rang and the constable stood there with an army despatch rider. 'Are you expecting a parcel Dr. Senden?' Peter affirmed that he was and that it had been despatched urgently from Bovington army camp a few miles away. It was the debugging detection equipment he had requested his office to arrange for him earlier.

He worked around the rooms, finding five American bugs, satisfied from the equipment earpieces that he had found them all.

As he worked on the removal task, he worked out in his mind what he was going to say and then, with all the American devices disabled he went over and stood beside the telephone containing the one remaining listening device he had checked on earlier and spoke slowly.

'This is Peter Senden speaking. I'm about to remove your listening device but before I do so I have a request to make. Whoever you are, I must speak to you urgently. Don't disconnect, please ask your controller to ring me in the next half an hour so that we can arrange to meet somewhere.' He felt self conscious standing there apparently talking to himself and went to the kitchen refrigerator for eggs and started to scramble them for his lunch.

Suddenly the telephone was ringing.

'Dr. Senden? I understand you wish to speak to me.' Peter detected the slight accent and occasional buzz of electrical feedback on the line indicating that the call was being made over at least two separate radio links to avoid detection. Peter said, 'can we meet somewhere?'

'Unfortunately that will not be possible, what do you want to know?'

'The truth, who you are and why you have illegally placed listening devices in my home. I also need to know what your connection is with Miss Holmes.'

There was the sound of laughter in the respondent's voice. 'You don't really expect me to give answers do you?'

'O.K. my friend, I don't know where you are located but I am sure you will want to protect your marksman from identification. The piece of chewing gum he left up on the hill has his DNA all over it.' It was a long shot, Peter had sighted up the rough trajectory that the bullets had made before walking up on the hill earlier where he had found cartridge cases and the piece of chewing gum stuck on a nearby fence post.

There was a pause at the other end of the link, and then the voice enquired, 'how does that help you?'

'Anyone who can hit a target at that range must be good, Olympic standard I would say.'

The line was quiet as the listener waited.

'At the Millennium World Games in Australia three years ago, Israel had one outstanding gold medallist in that field, Zac Heinz, an army paratrooper. All I have to do is to compare this DNA sample with the Games samples taken for drug tests and bingo.' Peter had taken a chance when he had phoned his office that morning and researched his idea. His hunch had led Grace to other useful information as well which, by the stunned pause on the line, he would now chance.

'So Major, I presume it is Major David Hessel I am speaking to, Head of No.3 Special Overseas Squad of Mossad. You are listed at MI6 as Heinz's commanding officer.' The line was ominously quiet as he continued, 'now, can you please tell me what's going on?'

'Dr. Senden, I must say that I have to admire your deductions. However, I am not in a position to help you.'

'Major, the range of this listening device is about half a mile. Your relay post has already been located and at this moment is surrounded by hidden police marksmen. Now, do we speak or do I bring your operation to a halt?'

Hessel made an immediate decision. 'O.K. Senden, I guess you deserve an explanation, we talk in exchange for continuing anonymity. Can you arrange that?'

'You have my guaranteed word on that my friend.'

His ploy had paid off and the Israeli major, who had warmed to the cleverness of the young mans deductions now gave him the basic rudiments of his assignment, the security of his country's delegation at the forthcoming Conference. 'So why eavesdrop on me?'

The phone suddenly went dead and Peter cursed himself that there was not an armed police ambush in the offing. He only had half an answer as he returned to his cooking in the kitchen.

As he was eating there was a tap on the kitchen garden door and he opened it to the constable who informed him that he had been recalled to the station. He sat and continued his meal cursing that his contact with Major Hessel had been terminated before answers were given to the burning questions he had.

An hour had gone by and he was sitting in the study when he heard the sound of a motorbike outside and the front door bell rang. A man of about his own age stood there, casually dressed, dark haired, bearing a grin that showed white teeth against the tanned face and brown eyes. He extended his hand.

'Major David Hessel sir, at your service. Sorry I had to break off but I had to be sure that our conversation was secure. Can we speak over there.' He pointed across to the other side of the lawn in front of the house where there was a garden bench.

'You came to our attention in our search for David Luk, a particularly nasty gangster and drug runner, wanted in our country and others for a variety of crimes. He was also associated with the group of terrorists who were killed yesterday. We were not sure what your connection was with him until recently. That's why we were monitoring you. You know of course that they were looking for the nuclear device out in the channel.'

Peter shrugged. 'Luk was looking for something else, but the important thing is that the device you mentioned has now been located. What about Miss Holmes, is she connected to your organisation?'

The Major grinned at him. 'There are important issues at stake here and you want to know about Miss Holmes. I guess it's more than a professional interest you have.'

Peter nodded slowly, 'I have to know.'

Hessel gave a guarded reply. 'She is one of our contacts with respect to security at the forthcoming Middle East Cease Fire Conference. That's all I know. She's certainly not part of our organisation if that's what is worrying you. You have my word on that.'

Peter looked puzzled, 'thanks for that. What was your man doing up there on the hill yesterday?'

'I was away on some other business. Heinz heard what was going on and decided to intervene, rather rashly you may think, but he took what he thought to be the right action.' He paused, 'gather Luk is now recovering in hospital.'

'How many people are on your team?'

Hessel shrugged. 'Enough to ensure the safety of our delegation when they attend the Conference. As I presume you know, our organisation discovered the terrorist plans some time ago. We were brought over in advance to ensure that your guys and the Americans found the nuclear device the terrorists were searching for.'

'Do you mean the *Dragon's Morsel?*'

Hessel laughed, 'is that your identification code, your shibboleth for the bomb? I've never heard it called that.'

Peter was surprised, he had still not been able to establish the real meaning of the *Dragon's Morsel*, whether it was the bomb or something else his father had seen.

'Do you know who attacked me in Weymouth or who tried to blow up my yacht?'

'Well as far as the first question goes, no, I can't help you. We know that the terrorists boarded your yacht though after the Trevello break in at Captain Piltcher's place.'

The major stood as his motorbike companion waved to him from the gate.

'Well, I must go now Dr. Senden. I do hope our chat has straightened things out a little.' He was halfway across the lawn before he turned. 'Oh, by the way, I forgot to congratulate you, the DNA ploy was very good, but our listening device is a remotely controlled transponder box, lying in a field somewhere up there.' He turned and was gone, climbing onto the bike pillion seat and roaring off along the road.

Peter remained sitting there, thinking over what had been said. It now seemed that nobody knew who had been responsible for the beating he had received that night in Weymouth. Hoskins had talked mysteriously about his housekeeper Mrs.Lyonns and he had not been able to contact her. He was still puzzled about Katherine. What role could a physicist working for the Environmental Agency have with the forthcoming conference?

He lit a cheroot and sat there, relaxing in the warmth of the garden, thinking over how his fathers demise had lead him to believe that there was a hoard of gold slashed away somewhere. His efforts had instead been directed onto the *Thinman* project. Could it be that having now found the wreck of the Acacia Lady, they may also unravel the mystery of the retirement fund at some time in the future. He thought not, the whole area would probably be sealed off for years if there was something else called the *Dragon's Morsel*, he would never know. At least he now knew who was responsible for the gas episode on board Seamaiden, but was that a police matter or a matter for Jack Fellows. In any case, officially he wasn't supposed to know. He would have to confirm his source if questioned and he had given Major Hessel his word.

Later in the afternoon Peter rang for a taxi and was again sitting in the small hospital ward with Jessica, now propped up on pillows with a large bouquet of flowers he had brought, sitting in a vase beside the bed. They chatted over the happenings of the last few days and her lucky escape from death. The bullet had missed her liver by less than a centimetre and the surgeons had now patched her up so that she expected to be out within the next couple of days.

They had parted on amicable terms that morning after the *Thinman* conference, but he felt more had to be said. He felt an awkwardness in his voice as he said, 'Jessica, I'm sorry our relationship didn't continue the way we had hoped, I feel sort of responsible for your current condition and.......' She didn't let him continue as she put a finger to his lips. 'Peter, don't blame yourself, we both felt the same way and needed to relieve the tension. You never asked me about my past, but last year I also lost someone very dear. We were not married but had been together for over five years when he was killed in a car accident.'

'I'm so sorry to hear that, you never told me.'

She looked over and smiled as she took his hand in hers and said softly. 'It doesn't matter Peter, you helped me over it, that's more than anyone could ask.' She paused, 'by the way, I didn't tell you that John Barrett came in to see me earlier. He's asked me to partner him next week at a Masonic Ladies Night, I hope you don't mind.'

'Of course not, John is great company when he gets going.'

'What about Katherine Holmes? I saw the protective way you looked at her yesterday. Is she interested?'

Peter looked embarrassed at the directness of the question and she smiled again. 'She is a sweet person Peter, sat with me for hours when I thought I was going to die, rely on a good lady friend's intuition, she should be good for you. Phew, I feel so tired, must be the anaesthetic.'

Her eyes closed and he sat there for a while looking at the beauty of her face and wondering what it was that attracted the sexes. Not necessarily physical beauty. Some sort of chemistry? Intellect? Or, was it just good old fashioned lust? He didn't have an answer to that indeterminable question and like psychologists all over the world, he never would have.

There was a knock and his inside gave a kick as Katherine's face appeared round the door. He rose and they went outside together.

She hesitated for a moment as she looked at him and then relaxed in his arms as he kissed her. She opened her eyes, 'how is Jessica now.'

'She's making a good recovery and should be out of here in a couple of days.'

They walked hand in hand back to her car, a small MG and Peter said, 'nice car, I've got to get over to Street sometime and collect the Jaguar. It's still parked there from the time I went down to your uncle's caravan.'

'It's a hire car. I left mine down at Axmouth before going into the landslips and climbing down to Gilbert's cave. I can drive you over to collect your car this evening if you like.' She looked away from him and bit the inside of her lower lip, was she being too forward, had she overestimated his feelings for her?

She quickly added, 'I can then drive on down to Cornwall and see how the search for my father is progressing.'

Peter's face broke into beam as he realised her uncertainty and bent a kiss to her cheek. He whispered quietly in her ear. 'Come over to my place and stay the night. We can pick the cars up in the morning and then go straight down to the search in Cornwall for Sir Anthony.'

She mused, so their thoughts were mutual. 'Peter, I've a friend who has a mobile home on the site where your car is, it's quiet there and, well.....' She faltered.

Peter smiled down at her, he hadn't stayed in a caravan since he was a child.

'O.K. pick me up at the house later.'

Chapter 38. Conscience of Hank Hoskins

It was dusk by the time Peter paid off the taxi and walked up the drive to the house. The duty constable was gone but as he unlocked the front door latch he heard a sound and turned.

Hank Hoskins emerged from around the corner and stood there, his finger to his lips indicating silence. Peter had noticed a car parked out in the road but had assumed it probably belonged to someone visiting another house nearby. He let him in and Hoskins went straight to the telephone in the drawing room and removed the back casing.

'If you're looking for listening devices I've removed them all, including the one in my bedside telephone.' He looked at Hoskins reproachfully, and guided him to the kitchen where a small Pyrex bowl of water sat on a work top with the devices sitting in the bottom. 'I've swept the whole house this afternoon, not only your devices I might add.' He looked accusingly at Hank who smiled and held open his arms, the body language for, sorry.

'What can I say Senden except that they probably saved your lives yesterday. Anyway, I'm glad they've been removed as I wanted to speak to you in private.'

They walked back to the drawing room and Peter said, 'I still don't understand why I was under surveillance in the first place.'

Hank Hoskins stood by the window and peered at the starred holes in the upper panes of glass before turning to face him.

'Let me try and explain.

When your father was found in such a distressed state, the co-operation between our respective Governments in the search for *Thinman* and the terrorist threat was well under way and I was called in as soon as it was discovered that the isotopic patterns matched. When he died, I thought your own search for the truth could possibly help to lead us forward. It was a chance I had to take, we had no other clues at the time. Then we picked up an international telephone conversation using the keyword computers at the Menwith Hill listening station and learned that something called the retirement fund, a gold hoard by all accounts, could be associated with our search, saw the newspaper advertisements with respect to your father's will that gave us a possible lead to three other people. Once you were on the gold hunt we thought that you may turn something up of significance.

Seiger at Scotland Yard has told us that according to some of your father's paperwork and bank statements, he was paid over the last few months to assist in finding *Thinman*, we believe he was contacted by the terrorist group using the ploy of promises of assisting him to find the gold that he had been searching for many years'

'Do you know how he was located by these terrorists?'

'We don't know how they tracked him down but suspect that it was through David Luk. Carter's secretary was interviewed in Hong Kong and told our people there that Luk had, unbeknown to his father, visited the office there one night and turned through the filing system. We also believe that David Luk was instrumental in luring his father over here. From our interrogation of the tapes we have made, it would appear however that his object was to locate the Acacia Lady and the gold.'

Peter butted in, 'Luk didn't seem to know anything about the deadly cargo she contained.'

'That observation was also apparent from the tapes.

We do not believe that he or your father knew about the bomb or who the real paymasters were; your father was too intent on his search for treasure. He found *Thinman* all right but didn't leave any clues. It was a long shot, but we hoped your own quest for the truth might assist in leading us to the contamination source. That's why you were placed under surveillance. As a result of all that, the Acacia Lady has been found thanks I gather to your own deductions. However, I have some bad news.'

'Bad news? Sounds ominous have you found Katherine Holmes's father?'

'I'm afraid not. That is not within my terms of reference, your own police and army are still looking at that aspect. No, the bad news is that *Thinman* was not on the wreck of the Acacia Lady as we had all supposed.'

Peter stopped halfway through removing his jacket and looked at the ageing Commander in disbelief. 'But everything pointed to it being there, Carter's confession, the letter from Piltcher and my father's death, it must be there.'

The commander just shrugged his shoulders, 'We've had your British divers and our own down and there's nothing there. The radiation background is about the same as that measured over the whole area, were back to square one again.'

Peter threw the jacket over a chair. 'Let's go into the study, this room is still in a bloody mess from yesterday.' He led the way through to the small study and they sat. 'Are you telling me that the terrorists found the bomb after all?'

'We don't think so. We intercepted a Libyan freighter that we had been watching on the satellites out in the Western Approaches to the Channel and the French Navy has been on board to interrogate the crew. There was no sign that the bomb had been taken aboard. Also, had the device been brought to the surface in the condition we believe it is now in, the radiation would have been detected by one of our satellites?'

'So perhaps there isn't a bomb out there after all, maybe my father was irradiated somewhere else.'

'Oh, it's out there somewhere, the measurements in the western English Channel that have been made over a wide area confirm the fact.'

'Does Maj. Dick Fellows know that your people haven't found the device?'

The Commander settled back into the comfortable easy chair and removed his glasses for their habitual clean before he looked up and replied. 'I'd rather we said nothing to Fellows at this time.' He looked at Peter wondering what the response would be but Peter sat there and lit a cheroot, delaying his reply as he thought over what the Commander had just said and why he had sought him out, after all there were a lot of people working on the *Thinman* project on both the British, French and American sides.

'I'm rather surprised to hear that Commander, what brings you here then?'

'O.K. let me tell you quite openly what all this is about. I'll start at the beginning when I was over here at the time your father was found and the isotropic radiation pointed to one of our early nuclear devices. It was a shot out of the blue, we had given up looking for it years ago but my department still controlled the old records as you are aware from the recent conference on the subject. I was here investigating something else which I shall come to shortly.

I did a lot of background work on *Thinman* when the story first broke from Israel and our Government Select Committee decided to ignore the terrorist threat and go straight to the job of locating *Thinman* with the assistance of the British and French Navies. They all considered it to be an environmental problem that needed to be cleaned up as soon as possible, even though the measurements were weak. The terrorists were considered to be amateurs and the plan was to lead them on to a location where they could be suitably dealt with.

As I believe you know, the Acacia Lady sailed from Hong Kong late October 1952 along with two other British registered ships. Her manifest stated that she was carrying salvaged machine tools and military supplies to Alexandria and because of those military supplies, the three ships were in convoy with a small Royal Navy corvette with a naval man on each ship. Your father was assigned to the Acacia Lady.

We know from our own old archives of the time that she was shadowed by the Russians on behalf of the Chinese Communists, who did not have the resources for surveillance that the Russians had. Our boys were shadowing the Russians, listening to their traffic. They knew that the Russians were keeping an eye on the Acacia Lady and assumed it was because there were some British scientists on board conducting radiation fallout measurements from their first atom bomb exploded at Monte Bello in October of that year.

The ships refuelled along the way at Singapore, Aden and Mombasa but when she arrived at Alexandria, the military supplies were not unloaded for some reason and the convoy set off again for Gibraltar with another fleet of Russian trawlers up their backsides.

From Gibraltar they set off on the final leg to London. The Board of Trade enquiry here in England clearly shows that when the Acacia Lady started running into trouble in Biscay, the British Navy removed the scientists and their equipment together with whatever the military supplies were and, from our own archive intelligence sources, we know that the Russian trawlers suddenly lost interest and returned to the Med.

The Acacia Lady continued her voyage and as I now understand it, split in two, sinking in different locations whilst the other two ships sailed on under escort to London.

We've looked at the official Board of Trade court records of 1953 in your Public Records Office at Richmond. The enquiry skipped over the voyage's history that only got a couple of paragraphs. Your father had left the ship before the tragedy and was only called to give brief confirmatory evidence. Holmes wasn't even requested to attend although he was in fact there. The main concern of the enquiry was the loss of life and the cargo value for insurance purposes.'

Peter interrupted. 'We know all this Commander, what's the point you're trying to make. We've found the Acacia Lady and according to what you have just said there is no bomb in the wreck. Perhaps it went overboard in the storm. You have not seen Piltcher's letter but he stated that the skeleton crew, before they were washed overboard, disposed of a lot of the remaining cargo into the sea.'

'Bear with me Peter whilst I deviate for a few moments and touch on recent information that I unearthed in our Langley archives. I'm sure you will find it has an interesting link. The papers that were handed over to our station in Hong Kong from the Chinese defector in 1989 mentioned the Acacia Lady in another vein, considered unimportant at the time and not terribly interesting from our point of view which is why most of them were made public. However, when *Thinman* came into the limelight and the Acacia Lady was suspected of being the source, I went back over the microfiche records again during my recent visit to Langley, in fact that was my main purpose for going back there.

Amongst the translations was a Chinese report of 1965 about missing gold bullion that appeared on their ledger sheets and had been written off secretly by their treasury. When the more liberal regime was installed there was an official internal enquiry into the matter. It transpired from that report that the bullion was an advance payment made in 1952 for something that they code named *Dragon's Morsel*.

'So *Dragon's Morsel* was the code name for the atom bomb.'

'Well, yes and no, I'll come to an explanation of that in a minute.

It appears that an advance shipment of gold was loaded onto the Acacia Lady before she sailed to the southern tip of the Ryukya Islands together with a salvage ship. The Ryukya Islands belong to Japan, Okinawa being the largest island in the group which most of us especially in the States remember well from the Pacific war battle that took place there. In recent times, conferences on World poverty have taken place there.

Being Japanese territory the Chinese presumably chose the British registered ships so that they could not be compromised for flaunting territorial waters. This is where the machine tools were salvaged as a cover for the old atomic bomb, our *Thinman*, in virtually the same place that the U.S.Navy found our B29 bomber wreck in 1953.

The report further stated that the Acacia Lady was expected to transfer her salvage near Shanghai where Chinese soldiers would board, remove the crew and sink her. But a typhoon blew up, the salvage vessel and the Acacia Lady somehow made her way back to Hong Kong. The report went on to say how the ship had then been requisitioned by the Royal Navy and how the Chinese had agreed the Russian surveillance, for a share of the American know how.

The report concluded that, either the Royal Navy had taken possession of the bullion or, it was lost in the English Channel.'

'That's all very interesting Commander, but your *Thinman* or *Dragon's Morsel* has not been found and from the information in Captain Piltcher's letter it would appear that the gold in fact is all gone.'

The evenings were beginning to draw in and Peter lent over and switched on a table lamp. 'Your talking in riddles Hank what point are you trying to make.'

'Let me finish my story Peter and you can then judge for yourself. You may be shocked at what you are about to hear.' He sat back with his legs crossed. '*Thinman* was one of my projects for years, not a burning issue of course, it lay dormant for forty odd years before I came on the scene. When it came to the boil again earlier this year I found myself on the edge of a conspiracy, one that I paid little heed to at first, as I thought it unlikely to succeed. I knew they thought they had me by the balls over something that happened a long time ago which I needn't go into here.'

Hoskins then outlined the details of the *Crusader* plot and how he had been hoaxed.

Peter thought, so that was the reason for the satellite questions. 'So you deliberately tried to lay out clues for Jack Fellows, the tritium gas, the W85 handbook and so on.'

'Not for the Major, he wouldn't have recognised his own mother out there. No, I aimed specifically at you because of your technical background.'

'So are you telling me there's another bomb out there?'

'Not any more, the W85 warhead had been shipped onto the USS Phoenix from our stores in Germany. It was disguised in the casing of the old '*Thinman*' bomb, presumably to fool the Koreans into thinking it was the original device.' He gave a sigh. 'The conspirators in the States have been arrested including I'm sad to say one of our most eminent senators who sat on the Select Committee when *Thinman* came up again. There have been other arrests on the ship. Admiral Mcready was one of them together with a number of arrests on our military bases in Germany. Their communication channels are still open and no one here knows that there have been arrests, the channels are now being monitored by other reliable members of the Firm.'

'But the orange buoy, what was that for, I understand that the RN divers found nothing there.'

'That was a decoy by the conspirators to flush me out, they suspected I wouldn't go along with anything so preposterous and gave me a false position.' He stopped and shifted his position in the chair. 'One of the conspirators in the States has been murdered and I suspect that I am also on their assassination list.'

'Sounds serious, but if they've all been arrested why tell me all this.'

'I've not come to the meat of what I have to tell you yet. Apart from myself and now you, I believe there is only one other person on this side of the Atlantic who knows the full story as I've now related it.'

'So what's your point?'

'The point is this Peter.' He stopped and looked hard at Peter over those half moons before continuing. 'The point I shall be coming to is that somewhere very high up in your British Secret Service, you have a double agent or what could be called a mole.' He removed the spectacles and sat fidgeting with them. There was silence between the two as their eyes met and Peter said thoughtfully.

'So why are you telling me this Hank, you know of course that someone in my department has already been arrested on suspicion of some sort of complicity with hacking into information that was secret. Surely you should be speaking to Sir George Longland or Major Fellows.'

'Young man, you haven't been in this awful cloak and dagger game long enough to have built up the contacts and recourses, or for that matter the political motive for double dealing which is the reason I have come to you. Your colleague, Lawson I believe, is not guilty of treachery, it's someone higher up the ladder who has used Lawson's computer hacking play games to his or her advantage.'

'So what happens now Hank, why don't you go to Fellows or your own department and tell them what you know. This is a serious situation that must be dealt with as quickly as possible and you still have to find *Thinman* before it becomes an environmental catastrophe in the Channel.'

'That's the whole point of the last twenty minutes Peter. I don't know who I can trust.'

Peter went over to the drinks cabinet, 'Scotch or Bourbon?' Hank indicated just water and Peter poured a good measure of Scotch for himself. 'I'm not sure I know how to help you or who to go to. How do I know that what you are telling me has any plausible truth, the threat on your life for instance, how do you know that you are not sitting there looking at your would be assassin.' He had direct eye contact now with the commander as he sat there sipping his Scotch.

Hank smiled, 'I gather that they were also concerned that you might find out something, as indeed you did when you spotted the tritium gas on board the Phoenix.'

'You mean I'm also on the hit list, was that what the baseball bat incident was all about, or perhaps they tried to blow me up on Seamaiden, or was it the mistaken identity at Crows Nest Cottage that nearly caused my friend's death?'

'No, those incidents were not connected. Look Peter, I've told my side of the story to the only person I feel I can trust over here. Yesterday I sent a full transcript direct to the White House, for the Presidents Chief Adviser, the *Crusader* plot had reached a stage where I knew enough about the people involved to have it shut down. My department were also informed by the FBI that irregularities had appeared in certain banking circles, enough evidence to nail the ringleaders who thought they had me over a barrel.' His face broke into a smile. 'They thought my earlier misdemeanours in Nicaragua had gone unnoticed, but I did a deal with our authorities years ago. Now, I will come to the main point of all this.'

'You mean there's more.'

'As I said earlier I was over here on other business. No doubt you will be familiar with the story that our latest W88 multi head nuclear device secrets were stolen a few years ago.'

'Yes, the Chinese got hold of them through a spy network at Los Alamos, some sort of cover up was attempted by your CIA people I believe.'

'That is what everyone believed at the time. In fact the cover up with respect to the loss to the Chinese over the W88 warhead was because I was charged with trying to establish the route that the information took. You see, we know that the route used was through London and that there were contacts used there. Unfortunately, the Senate committee hauled us in too quickly and I am not so sure that those secrets ever reached Beijing.

'Sorry I still don't see the connection between *Thinman* and what you are now saying about your W88 warhead secrets.'

'The connection is that the same metaphor, *Dragon's Morsel* was applied to both devices. When the *Thinman* project bounced back into life, I was surprised to suddenly find the same metaphor being used and it implied that the same people could be involved. I have my suspicions now as to whom the mole is but we need to lay a trap in order to flush him or her out.'

'Whom do you suspect for God's sake?'

'Let me tell you about one person in your organisation, someone who was stationed in the old MI6 operations in Hong Kong. The CIA had him under surveillance for some time and we know that he had contact with Simon Carter. When your father mentioned Carter's name in connection with what he had seen, we were immediately alerted to the possible connection.

We now believe that Carter may have been recalled from retirement by the Chinese secret service to complete negotiations here in London. The secrets of the W88 are probably contained on computer discs, a small enough package to be smuggled over to China. Every agency has been trawling the Internet over the last few years looking for the information. Any encrypted e-mail that is suspiciously long has by law now to be open to investigation if requested So we believe that the remaining information on LINKS is still around somewhere sitting on discs that can be easily transported.

My colleagues and I can't go crashing around making accusations about your top brass until we are absolutely certain that the discs are still here.'

'So how do I fit in?'

'We understand that you do not have a direct contract with the British secret service, we are therefore asking you to join our team. Assist us in finding and weeding out the spy in the British organisation.'

Peter sat and looked at the crystal glass of Scotch in his hand before taking another savouring sip of the golden liquid and rolling it around his tongue as he considered what had been said. It was malt and tasted good but what was being suggested was not so good.

'You're asking me to betray my own country?'

'Where's the betrayal? We are all looking to the same end.'

'I can't help you Hank. I'm too far down the line all I do is report on technical matters, I wouldn't do it anyway, Queen and country, you know, not cricket, still means something over here even in the twenty first century.'

The commander gave him a long stare and reassembled his half moons on the end of his short nose.

'Peter, this may come as a surprise to you, but we know exactly what you do and how your department have, like my own team, been trying to extricate information about what we have just discussed. In your case it is the security of the British nuclear deterrent, what you call Trident. Your Government, like ours has to know where those W88 secrets have gone, China, Libya, Algeria, Iraq, who knows who has them. Defence policy decisions have to be made by your politicians as well as ours. Your recent European trip was not restricted to that area, we know for instance that you were in the Middle East, North and South Africa and other places following up your own investigations along with others.'

'So Hank, if you know so much about what we are doing about your inept lack of security in the States on these matters, how come you can't tell me whom you suspect in our organisation.'

'If I told you, you would not believe me.'

Peter stood up and downed the rest of his Scotch at a gulp. 'Hell commander, you come in here with stories about conspirators, threats on your own life and possibly mine, asking me to act for your Government and an organisation that lets its crown jewels slip from its grasp and you can't answer a simple question. No, I can't help you. Let's restrict this conversation to the most urgent matter in hand, to find your shit that's lying out there on the seabed of the Channel.'

He looked at his watch, he was expecting Katherine at any time now and hadn't had time to shower or get changed.

The two of them sat in an embarrassed silence until Hoskins rose and drained his glass of water.

'O.K. Peter, I respect your feelings on the matter and I admire your integrity and loyalty, no harm in asking was there. I would have preferred an official liaison with you on this matter, as it is I shall have to trust the good judgement you have shown.' He gave a broad grin as though Peter had passed some sort of test. The young man in front of him was about the same age that his own son would have been by now had he survived.

'The person I suspect in your organisation is Major Jack Fellows or to give him his full name, Jackson Hoover Fellows. Needless to say, that with a name like that, his mother was an American.'

Peter's response was immediate.

'You can't mean that, surely you're joking, old Major Fellows is the heart of the establishment, ex Grenadier Guards, Jockey Club, horse owner, highly respected amongst his peers. Tell me you're joking for God's sake.'

'I wish I were Peter, the truth of the matter is that he has been moonlighting in a small way for years. The Langley plotters pulled out what they had on him when he was in Hong Kong and used him in a similar way to me, threats of exposure if he didn't conform. That's why he had you transferred to his own section where he could keep an eye on you He suspected you were getting near to the truth and might blow the *Crusader* Project.'

'But I don't understand it Hank, what did they have on him that would cause him to want to blow up half the Middle East.'

'He was probably under the impression as I was at first that only conventional explosives would be used. As to why, well, the usual old thing, more important than any other espionage dealings he had taken part in, I mean sex with a big S. He was and probably still is a pedophile. Married into money you see, his wife held the purse strings and would have cut him off if she ever found out. He would have lost that big house down in Hampshire and the automobile collection he dotes on. Carter discovered his weakness when he was stationed in Hong Kong and used him for his own benefit to infiltrate the police and other communities there.'

'Hang on Hank, how do you know all this, surely our own vetting at B1 would have found this out? Why haven't your own people informed my organisation if they know so much about him?'

A flash of guilt crossed the commander's face. 'Can't you guess Peter?'

'You mean your bloody organisation was using him before *Crusader*?' Hoskins shifted his feet again , 'you got it in one son.'

'So that's why Carter was released from hospital by the police.'

'That's right Peter, You may not have been aware of the meeting that took place when you were both being held at Truro. I was at that meeting and it was at Fellows official request to your immigration people that he was released, I suspect because he feared that Carter might blow on him.'

'So how are you hoping to flush him out?'

The banking heist I mentioned earlier. The FBI discovered money had been paid into a private account in London, now traced through your own banking system to Major Fellows, about one hundred thousand in your money. Are you any good on computers?' Peter shrugged, 'what do you need.'

The doorbell rang and Peter guessed it would be Katherine. He rose and said. 'Look Hank, I've got to go out, let me know what you need and I'll see if I can help.'

'Thanks Peter, let me give you a new card. They're moving my department into the main embassy building over the next few days.' He scribbled his name on the back of the card and handed it over.

It was the police constable , back again for a spell of night duty. He exchanged a good evening with Hank Hoskins as he left and Peter ushered the constable into the kitchen for a coffee. As he did so he remembered something and said, 'damn, he was going to tell me about *Dragon's Morsel*.'

Chapter 39. The newspaper.

The news on Wednesday morning was startling . The channel blockade, set up a few days before, had not missed the attention of every editor in Fleet Street and there had been pages of journalistic speculation devoted to the subject of the shooting at Poole and of the yacht blowing up off Portsmouth. . Now the parliamentary question of the day from the Honourable Member of East Dorset had been leaked and had alerted them to the fact that this was not localised drug dealing. International terrorism, its course and effect, were never far from the headline pages. The Parliamentary question had roused everyone. Foreign journalists and television crews were flying in like droves of starlings clouding the skies on a summer's evening.

Was there a stranded Russian nuclear submarine lying somewhere off the south coast or west of the Channel Islands? If so, then why the secrecy? Who were the terrorist group? Was it al-Qaeda? Who did they represent? What were they after? Was it connected to the forthcoming Middle East Conference?

The Russians of course denied the speculation and their diplomats were rushing between the Foreign Office, Ministry of Defence and other departments threatening a complete diplomatic breakdown between Moscow and the West, a return to cold war politics.

The Honourable Member for East Dorset had apparently decided to take a sudden holiday with his family, destination unknown. His country residence at Christchurch had been besieged with reporters only to find the resident housekeeper guarding the empty property, with no useful information to impart. Similarly, his London flat in Islington was also locked up and the curtains and security blinds tightly drawn.

Ian Porters piece in the *London Daily Chronicle* the day before, speculating on the loss of a Russian nuclear submarine, (even though he didn't believe it), had broken the seal. Now they were all on to it. Phoning well established contacts in various ministry departments, reliable moles, press officers, spin doctors and government PR departments. No stone was left unturned in their quest for some further glimmer of information no matter how small or speculative. There was a total clamp down and no Government department would comment. The Parliamentary Recess was about to start and was used as an excuse, most Ministers being on holiday or away on business, with Permanent Secretaries and Junior Ministers unable or unwilling to take the chance of commenting on such speculation.

Porter could see his months of hard work fading away as editors rammed their high flying youngsters onto the story, like cartridges into a hand pump shotgun, all anxious about carving their name in the annuals of journalism.

Porter had already done most of his background research over the last couple of months and knew that he was sitting on a story that could clinch his future promotion to one of the giant newspaper empires. If only he could find the connecting links in time and complete his piece, he knew he would be grasping the journalistic prize of his long career.

Philip Senden's terrible condition, when he had been taken to the Weymouth hospital, had been noted by a nurse who had told her boyfriend her suspicions after Philip had been transferred in a military ambulance to an unknown destination. The boy friend worked in the local newspaper office but remembered his earlier conversations with Ian Porter and received his handsome finder's fee in cash for the relatively unimportant piece of news at the time.

Ian Porter speculated that these were either laser burns or nuclear radiation burns. The latter seemed to be more realistic. But how did he get them? The background information gleaned on the retired Rear Admiral indicated that he had not been involved with nuclear devices, back during the fifties tests. However , he had attended the first hydrogen bomb tests conducted by the British government at Easter Island in 1958 and had shown a great deal of interest in the court cases of recent years. These had involved claims by ex service personnel that they had been used as human guinea-pigs and the Rear Admiral had supported their cause.

Radiation burns, if that was what they were, meant something had gone seriously wrong. What had Senden been doing and where had he been to get those terrible injuries. He read over his computer notes again checking every detail, cross referencing the stories and dates. Searching on names, places and times as the empty plastic coffee cups accumulated in his trash bin. The only places in the country where plutonium was being handled, apart from power stations, was at the highly secret and guarded Atomic Weapons Establishment at Aldermaston and nearby Burghfield, where the complex work involved in dismantling the old RAF free fall WE 177 nuclear warheads and the Royal Navy's Polaris missiles, now replaced by the Trident missile system, was in progress. No nuclear testing had taken place since the UK's twenty fourth and last underground test carried out in 1991, and there would be no future live testing since the Government ratified the Nuclear Test Ban Treaty in 1996.

All studies on weapons were now conducted using quantum physics experiments and complex mathematical modelling on computers plus implosion tests on heavy metals, using high power lasers. Latest reports from the consortium running the plant, indicated that the targets on environmental safety and health were all being met and any possible sources of contamination had been dealt with, even though this was contested by the local population. Porter read the latest company report in its entirety, no leads here. Certainly not to Philip Senden.

The office was an air conditioned non smoking area where an ash tray was as rare as a packet of bacon flavoured crisps in a synagogue. He was suffering withdrawal symptoms and went down to the ground floor for a smoke where again, he turned the facts he had over and over in his mind, like an overheated spit roast at a barbecue.

He returned to the office and rang the Haslar Naval hospital at Gosport trying to find out if that was the place that Senden had been treated. They would not have imparted such information and in any case they were deeply engrossed in trying to save the hospital from final closure due to continuing M.O.D. cutbacks.

There was the shooting at the Senden residence at Upwey near Weymouth. Neighbours had reported hearing shots and the next moment the place had been surrounded by police marksmen and all news blanked off. His assistant had been down there and heard about the body bag that had been transferred in the coroner's hearse. Who was it, was it connected with the suspected terrorists? He phoned the district coroner's office to hear that the body had been transferred to the local undertakers and once more, one of his assistants did some legging. All they would tell her was that the dead mans name was Simon Carter, a visitor from Hong Kong. So the old owner of the Acacia Lady *was* involved.

The woman injured in the shooting was fighting for her life, a Dr. Jessica Wilson. According to the neighbours, she had been a frequent visitor to Peter Senden's home over the last few weeks. Porter sent his junior hotfoot to the Dorchester hospital , to find out more, knowing that she would be one of many touting for a story line. He referred to the BMA register and discovered that she was an expert on radiation burns, where she worked was still a mystery.

It was at the hospital that his observant junior reporter picked up the news that Anthony Holmes daughter was somehow involved. She had been recognised as she left the hospital. She also picked up on the name Gilbert Piltcher, who had been burnt to death in his remote caravan.

A small piece in the local Dorset Evening Echo reporting Captain Piltcher's death from cancer had already filtered through on the media lines and been picked up by his staff. Porter noted the fact, but how could a man die from two causes in separate places? He put that piece of information to one side for later consideration.

Senden, Carter and Piltcher were all connected through the wreck of the Acacia Lady, the archival newspaper reports were clear enough on that. Now the three men were all dead.

The only other contact had been Holmes. Where was Holmes why was he still missing or was he also dead, inflicted with the same terrible symptoms as Philip Senden?

At the bottom of the deep discarded tin mine shaft, somewhere off the old A30 road in Cornwall, Sir Anthony lay on a dirty mattress, his mouth covered with tape and his hands bound behind him. The wounds from where they had tortured him over the whereabouts of Gilbert Piltcher, now beginning to fester in the dismal dampness and darkness of the place, the sound of dripping water all around him. The more he had struggled with his hands, the tighter his bounds had become and he lay there weakened and exhausted from lack of nourishment. His body shook with cold as he tried to keep his mind working, fearful that he had been left there to die in the smell of his own urine. He wasn't sure if it was day or night and forced his mind to remember, worked it on his old television scripts that he usually learned by heart, recited in his mind the line by line proofs of mathematical formulae he had learned in his younger days, surprised that they were still there. Most of all he pictured his daughter and the anguish she would be suffering, not knowing if he was already dead or still alive.

His captors had made two fundamental mistakes. They thought he could provide them with the information they were seeking about the Acacia Lady, in the same way that they had contacted Carter in Hong Kong and enticed him over with the aid of his greedy son, with promises of helping to find the bullion. Through his previously published works, they had also considered that he would have the technical knowledge to help them with the bomb. Neither was true and no matter what they did to him he couldn't help them. Not that he would have done anyway.

The terrorist interrogation had brought back vivid memories of the Acacia Lady. Memories he thought were lost with age. And his previous connection with the State of Israel his parents had worked so hard to achieve and the thought of the nuclear proliferation that would wipe out populations if the terrorists succeeded.

Before his acceptance as a Government scientist, he had taken time out to work on a small Kibbutz in Northern Israel. It was there that he had been drawn into a secret militia, a lingering offshoot of the Palmach , trying to run down the groups responsible for the murders in 1948 including his own parents. He had quickly realised the futility of such a venture, ten years had gone by since those awful events and he had returned to England. Hilda Jones had been his boss at the time her defection had come as a shock to him, they had worked jointly on the safety links for the British nuclear deterrent and following her vanishing act, many changes had been made which had projected him to the top of the heap. Now he lay there in the darkness, his mind wandering over his seventy odd years. His wife who he had loved so much and the villain Carter whom it seemed had followed him through life, after their encounter on that damned ship. His long standing affair with Hilda went back to the time when they were both young doctors, how had Carter found out, he didn't know but he had paid dearly because of that blackmailing, half Chinaman.

The sudden scraping noise above him and the sound of voices brought him out of his dreams, alert and fearful as he waited for their rough hands again. This time the voices sounded different as he sensed a glimmer of light and the movements became closer. He heard someone sloshing through the water that lay in the tunnel.

'We've got him.' The jubilant shout echoed along the mine shaft as he saw the beam of a helmet light approaching and the next moment the commando was there standing a short distance away. 'Bear with us Sir Anthony, we need a few minutes to do a wire check to ensure there are no booby traps in here.'

Then he was sitting up, his bounds released and sipping liquid from a flask proffered by one of the smiling mud smeared faces. It was six o'clock in the evening and he had been down there for about three days.

It would be a few hours before he was debriefed and a press release issued.

Ian Porter returned to his desk and went over the archive reports of the Holmes affair in the Black Sea scandal, trying to tie in Senden's connection with Carter and Gilbert Piltcher.

Philip Senden wasn't mentioned in any of the reports, there was no connection here, but he was there, old photographs had picked him up in the background. The missing reference to him only enforced the theory that he was working under cover for MI6.

He went over all the newspaper reports of the previous day, looking to see what other journalists had to say about the yacht exploding outside Portsmouth and the Royal Marine commando involvement. The shooting on the quay at Poole and the obvious special branch involvement. If these were drug smugglers as reported by the police, they had called up some very unusual armament.

Then he went down to the basement archives, old files that had not been microfiched but had been carefully removed from the old Fleet Street offices when they had moved into the glass edifice that was now the home of the Daily London Cronicle on the Isle of Dogs in East London.

He flipped through the scientific journals of the period, running his fingers down article indexes. Then Porter's heart bounded as he finally located a reference. The article was from an interview Holmes had given to one of the journals in 1980. Dr. Anthony Holmes had been a young scientist in charge of wind borne pollution measurements from the British atomic bomb tests at Monte Bello in the summer of 1952 and had returned to Hong Kong to await passage home to the U.K. He had voyaged on the Acacia Lady with some of his equipment, taking global measurements of radio active fall out during the voyage. When the Acacia Lady had started to list in the Bay of Biscay, he had transferred with his equipment and the other military equipment to another ship.

So that was the connection. The four of them had been on the same voyage from Hong Kong via Alexandria, Gibraltar and the Bay of Biscay. There had been no mention of Holmes in the main enquiry reports. In those he had just been referred to as a scientist.

Porter's copy writer had already written up his piece on the Royal Navy search that speculated as to why the American and French Navies were also searching in the western Channel. The article from yesterday evening speculating that the yacht blown up at Portsmouth was full of drug smugglers had now been rewritten as terrorists and combined and he was shouting from his keyboard workstation for more copy.

Then an extraordinary piece of information flashed up on Porters secondary screen from the newspaper's local reporter in Weymouth. A fisherman in a Weymouth pub had been spending money, sounding off about how he had assisted the American Navy in guarding a large marker buoy in Lyme Bay. A handsome payment had been made and he had seen Royal Navy divers in special suits, dropped from a helicopter and diving on the spot. Then he had seen a flotilla of Navy vessels descend to the location.

As he returned to his desk after this third trip for a smoke, Porters mobile rang. It was Sydney Parker from the Guernsey Evening Star. 'Hi Ian, just returning your call of this morning. The yacht you asked about, the Azzurra II, she's been into St. Peter Port several times over the summer months, also called into Braye on Alderney quite frequently. A foreign group by all accounts, wreck diving of the west coast somewhere. The same boat that blew up yesterday, there are people crawling all over the place here asking similar questions, got anything for me in exchange?'

'Thanks Syd, I owe you one for that , we'll see that you get full rights if anything comes of it. Oh, by the way, what about the other matter, the fax I sent you, any I.D. on that one.'

'Sorry Ian almost forgot. Yes, the harbour master here remembers him. The same party used other charter yachts as well, the Starlight Princess was a recent one, you know, the one they showed the Customs and Excise people searching on television a few days ago. Thought he was a bit elderly to be diving but told me that because of language problems, this guy, Philip Senden, was their spokesman when it came to mooring, refuelling and harbour dues. Oh, another thing, the Harbour Master at Braye told my man over there that he remembered Philip Senden well. He'd been doing a search off the Island for a treasure ship of some sort, searching for years apparently. He was always in and out over there, they nicknamed him Ben Gunn, you know, the funny old boy in Treasure Island .'

Ian Porter thanked his friend and rang off. So, Senden was definitely involved, but how did he tie in . The reports released to the press after the Tiannamen Square defection, only mentioned the Acacia Lady briefly, but there had been a suggestion that the ship contained gold bullion. Surely this story couldn't be about gold.

He mulled over the brief police press releases covering the strange break-in at Piltcher's cottage at Trevello and the drugs related report the police had issued about the man found floating off the Cornish coast. He couldn't connect these incidents and so far, he hadn't been able to tie Peter Senden into any of his speculation, but he didn't need to , he had enough to write his story line.

Ian Porter had put two and two together and started his final proof article. It surmised that after the British nuclear tests in 1952, equipment including a prototype nuclear device had been shipped back to the U.K. in a small convoy from the Far East, the convoy being protected by the Royal Navy. The Acacia Lady had been the carrier of the device before being lost in the English Channel during a storm. It went on to suggest that, due to a consignment of contraband gold being on board, the ship's owner Carter, had colluded with the Captain and a false position stated at the Board of Trade enquiry.

The ship had not been found at the time and over the years the bomb had lain in the wreck in Lyme Bay until recently, when a terrorist group had searched for it in the hope of using it to stop the Middle East Cease Fire Conference. They had employed Philip Senden as their guide, knowing that he had been seeking the gold reputed to be on board.

He sat at his console and tapped out the rudiments of the story, knowing he had a deadline to keep and called his sub editor Ray Barker who, when he had read the copy, put every reporter at his disposal and called an immediate meeting with the paper's editor and lawyers.
The story was speculative and after checking the many sources that Porter had used, the lawyers were against publication.
John Bradman the editor looked around the table. 'We can't miss this chance of a major story, if we've managed to get this far our competitors are not far behind. If we hold and they publish, we'll look stupid in the eyes of our readers.'
The older of the two lawyers, Paul Montgomery who had seen the paper through many previous similar news crisis replied. 'John, if you publish that article , even as a speculative story, you will cause mass panic amongst the local population down on the south coast. I do not think that this newspaper or its shareholders will thank you for that. I admit it is a story begging to be told and I appreciate the work that Ian has put into the research. Nevertheless, it is dangerous and I think we should obtain further opinion on it before we go for roll. I say that in view of the fact that the story has been as good as unofficially censored by the Government.'
John Bradman looked around the table at the sub editors and news feature committee members sitting there, strained faces, waiting for his reply. ' We do not have time to pussy foot around with this one Paul.
We need circulation and that item when polished up will produce an increase in our circulation with follow up material that we're now preparing for the next few days. Believe me Paul I know what I'm doing.'
Montgomery went into a huddle with his partner as they discussed the consequences between them in whispers before again facing Bradman.
Lord Dranscombe the chairman had unusually entered the room and indicated with his hands for the staff around the table to remain seated as he perched himself on the edge of the table and Paul started to speak.
'We believe that you and the newspaper will be heavily censured if you go to print with the story in its present form, we do however have a suggestion to make.'
'It will have to be quick. We want the machines down in Southampton to be rolling within the next half an hour.'

Paul looked around at the anxious faces, time was getting short and their deadline was looming up as deadly as a charging rhino. 'Right, chairman, ladies and gentlemen. We suggest that you address the article to the government. Don't pander over the story, just ask the question, we would see that as a reasonable approach and one that would be appreciated by our readers. If it causes concern amongst the population, all we can be accused of is opening the debate. It will then be the responsibility of those officially in the know to either reject the story out of hand or come out with the truth. Whichever way it goes, there can be no blame on this newspaper for irresponsible reporting. We are however, on behalf of our readers, expected to put the question against some of these facts that are already in the public domain. Once that is on the table, either of two things can happen. Firstly, the whole thing will be denied in which case we can keep nagging with follow ups and keep our readership happy in the thought that we have plugged away at an important issue. Secondly, we could be correct and if it flushes statements to that effect from the government we've won the day and it will be up to the government to state the case. Then of course we can go for the jugular screaming ministerial incompetence and demanding resignations, even a new government that I'm sure would delight many of our readers, in fact, I would say the vast majority of them. '

Lord Dranscombe cut in. 'I would be happy to see you proceed along those lines John, I've seen Mr.Porter's copy and I agree with Paul, just ask the question, our readers have the right to know what is going on and it will certainly help our circulation figures. Now, what have we got so far on this MI5 story and the arrest of Mr.Douglas Lawson.' The chairman had the final word and the copy setters got down to rehashing the headline and content of the leader article at their computers for that night's print run.

The lead editorial was rewritten with contributions from the newspaper's other senior journalists, based on the story that Porter had so painstakingly researched over the period.

The lead story asked the question. Was the task force searching for a nuclear bomb in the English Channel? It went on to speculate that the Acacia Lady had been carrying such a device when she had sunk in 1953 outlining that it was spare parts for the atom bomb tests in 1952 that were shipped and sunk with the knowledge of the Government and had been hushed up at the time . Probably because they knew little about the effects on the marine environment at that time. In any case, it was now established that the ship had sunk in deep water in the middle of Lyme Bay, a few miles from the coast and would have been difficult to salvage.

Most of the article was a repeat of the historical events and information that Porter had gathered during his investigations . In addition, the researchers pulled out all the old stops covering the many nuclear accidents sixty years into the nuclear age .

The support articles covered the Aldermaston marches, the lost hydrogen bomb at Palomares, the military nuclear waste of the world's armed services, the loss of four hydrogen bombs in Greenland in 1968 and Chernobyl in 1986. Three Mile Island and dozens of other case histories of outrageous loss of life, fires, neglect, Japanese fishermen and accidental discharges. There were other incidents going back to Windscale in the fifties and Tokaimura N.E. of Tokyo where plutonium had gone critical in 1999 and caused a neutron flash discharge. More recent revelations on the safety of Britain's top secret nuclear warhead factory in the Midlands and flagrant disregard of quality control at the Sellafield nuclear processing plant added fuel to the fire as did reminders of the tragic consequences of nuclear submarine accidents and reactors leeching out radiation on the World's sea bed's. Streams that meandered their way through the countryside around the UK Atom plant at Aldermaston were acknowledged to be contaminated with tritium and other radioactive chemicals and had concerned local residents for decades,.

The concern of investigative journalists over the increasing number of reported nuclear incidents was also evident from the number of television programmes which had been produced on the subject over recent times, in the USA, UK, and EU. The forest fires that so nearly caused disaster at the nuclear bomb factory at Los Alamos and the plutonium dump at Hanford in California. The Murmansk time bomb that would devour lives in time.

What else was being covered up in this industry that for some reason put itself above and before all others. Were Governments really in charge or were they being hoodwinked into supporting the never ending stream of denials and promises? Were Ministers with the ultimate responsibility of procuring nuclear services being given the right guidance? Were they even qualified to understand the finer points of the technology they controlled?

All this against the threat of the pre Saddam atomic bomb developments at Al-Jadria in Baghdad and the unknown consequences of such development. The activities of the al-Qaeda terrorist groups now scattered around the world since their routing in Afghanistan. What nuclear weapons did they now control?

The questions begged urgent answers for a World population who were becoming increasingly alarmed by the escalation of nuclear weaponry in unreliable hands.

Reported in isolation, all these events even though significant at the time were soon absorbed and forgotten by the public, more interested in the elitism of their sporting heroes and indolent pop idols. But, listed in their entirety, those incidents made a catalogue of disasters, demanding an urgent answer on the latest crisis from both Governments and the International Atomic Energy Agency and Commissions on Radiological Protection, set up to protect the world's population and future generations.

From the newspaper's terminal in London, the editorial and Porter's story were sent over digital lines to the printing contractor's works near Southampton over eighty miles away. (It could have been a thousand miles away, or one hundred thousand miles away by satellite link, it didn't matter). There the newspaper's contents were restructured onto the printing plates within minutes. The great rolls of paper that would be transformed into reading matter were transported along robotic tracks and loaded automatically onto hydraulically operated spindles which lifted each roll into the machine as the presses started to roll and the digital age compositors rushed about, checking their copy, making fine adjustments to print texture and colour balance of each printed page on their electronic checking tables.

The gigantic newspaper press started up, slowly at first, the paper ribbon moving miraculously through the six storey machine, changing its direction over hundreds of guiding spindles, passing over photo lithographic plates deep in its belly, the noise building up to a rattling crescendo as the speed gradually increased. Printing, cutting, compiling and sending the finished folded product along overhead roller tracks to the final binding machine stations. Then delivering bound bundles of the London Daily Chronicle to the handlers who stacked them into vans for distribution throughout the country the next morning.

Most readers as they picked up their daily from the doormat or the newsagents in the morning would not have considered the engineers who designed the miraculous system, central to providing them with the daily news. The material science that went into the structure of its components, the plastics technology, digital circuitry, power systems, chemistry, structures, hydraulics and many other branches of engineering that engineers provide with little recognition as to the central role they play in society.

Are they really nerds, anoraks, mechanics? Of course they aren't. The miracle of space exploration, satellite telemetry, the motor car, bar codes, entertainment systems, computers and cigarette production, (to name only a minute few), would not be possible without the brilliant creative minds of engineers, combining art form with science, economics with physics and public services with quality of life.

By the same miraculous token they are also responsible for taking the scientists nuclear theories and putting them into workable models that become Satan's toys.

Chapter 40. Panic in the South

Hank Hoskins had left the house at Upwey by the time Katherine arrived with her car. Peter called down the stairs to her as she waited patiently in the kitchen whilst he showered, changed and prepared an overnight bag . As he entered the kitchen, he immediately noticed the difference in her face, the pale worried look had gone and she had some colour in her face with minimal make up. The dark green trouser suit she wore emphasising her eyes and hair that he had suddenly found so attractive.

'Peter, they've found my dad alive and well and I've spoken to him over the phone.' She tugged him towards the car, confirming the few details she had in a torrent of happy conversation. They were moving off before she confirmed that the friend's holiday mobile home was all arranged and she would go straight down to Cornwall after he collected his own car in the morning.

Ian Porter stayed in the office overnight and grabbed a few hours sleep dozing at his desk. At six o'clock the following morning he read through the lead article and the supporting three page supplement of reports and articles for the fourth time as the other daily newspapers were delivered to him. The article was already the main news item on the major T.V. Stations and the telephones had not stopped ringing as interviews were hastily arranged.

Most of the other papers had lead to a lesser degree on the same storyline but had tried to tie it in with the arrest of the MI5 employee. Later editions were now flowing out and reporting a mass exodus of the population from south coast towns bordering the bay area as the alarming news spread. Roads were blocked with traffic at a grid locked standstill as fights broke out at service stations for petrol which was becoming scarce and supermarkets were looted for supplies.

Then the story of Sir Anthony Holmes had broken, causing a frenzied change of headlines in the later tabloid editions.

Katherine and Peter arrived at the holiday park late in the evening and located the friend's mobile home, having picked up her own car at Axmouth and returned the hire car. They sat there chatting about their lives since their brief meeting over fifteen years before. Their subsequent university experiences and careers came rolling out, his qualification as an engineer and her own qualifications in physics and journalism. She lived and spent much of her time on her father's estate south of Yeovil but had a small flat in Dorchester, a few miles from where he lived. Their discourse went on into the early hours covering news on their families and reminiscing over the times that she had visited Peter's parent's house in Portsmouth with her mother. She asked after Monica and then they talked about Peter's parents divorce, Philip, and her own great loss when her mother had committed suicide as a result of what Carter had done to her family. Peter did not raise the subject of the day before, or what Carter had personally done to her as a child. That could wait. Having disclosed her seventeen year secret in her rage the day before, he guessed that at as part of the healing process she would tell him some time in the future.

As Peter started to ask her about her work with the environmental department Katherine lent over and kissed him, 'it's getting late, we'll have plenty of time to talk more tomorrow. Now, we'd better turn in I suppose, I'll take the main room in the back if that's O.K.'

Peter was disappointed but said nothing as she sorted their things into the two separate rooms and they said their goodnights. It was a warm night and he wandered outside for a cigar, watching the smoke curl away to the sky, where the bright stars of Ursa Minor looked down on him as they pointed to the distant pole star. After a wonderful evening, she had thrown up an invisible barrier at the last moment, a light peck on the cheek, almost apologetic. Maybe John had been correct in his opinion of her.

He went to his room, undressed and lay there in the darkness, his hands cupped behind his head on the pillow, his eyes open to the ceiling as he thought about her. He thought back to the girl he had once known and how she had now developed into the desirable woman that he had fallen in love with and could imagine, lying in her bed and separated from him by a few centimetres of plastic panelled walling. He also thought about the scars in her mind put there by Carter and wondered how long they would take to heal.

He woke early, with the sunshine streaming through the lightweight curtains, donned a bath robe and after his ablutions went into the kitchen area. He started to prepare for breakfast with the unfamiliar cooking utensils he found there, when he heard her door open and she was behind him, putting her arms around his waist and hugging him. As he went to turn to her she said quietly, 'No Peter, please don't turn round. Not yet.'

She slipped his bath robe belt undone and eased the gown down over his shoulders, brushing her lips on his back and passing her hands up over his chest hair, caressing his nipples with her finger tips as he let the gown slip down his arms to the ground between them. He tilted his head back towards her closing his eyes in a mist as he felt his stomach muscles tighten in anticipation of her. The warm softness of her breasts pressed onto his back as he reached behind, running his hands over the smooth curves of her bare buttocks, pulling her closer as she rubbed her pubic triangle across the crease of his backside, passing her hands slowly down each side of his body, her fingers extended, stroking lightly over his thighs and then bringing them up until her thumbs combed through the hairs of his underbelly.

She let him go as he turned to face her, gently caressing her breasts as she pressed onto him, her head on his chest with her hair tumbling between them. Then she drew back, shaking her hair back so that he could now see her face, her eyes searching his, relaxed and shining, as if the clouds of the past had evaporated away. He bent and kissed her, his hand dropping to stroke the soft down on the mound between her legs. Then supporting her by her buttocks, he lifted her gently, drawing her tightly up to him as her legs opened and twined around his body, mounting him, her labia lips consuming his phallic sublimity, as they consummated their love.

She felt the ember's warmth of her inner glow and his sudden spasm and cry as his taught body relaxed and she clung to him while his thrusting vigour turned to prostration. Then they just stood there, for what seemed like ages, each in their own silence, their arms around each other, their thoughts on the union that had now transpired, perhaps by destiny, something they had now completed since she had glanced at him briefly so many years ago.

They breakfasted on the provisions that she had hastily got together the previous afternoon, crisp buttered rolls, bacon, eggs and coffee happily relaxed in the empathy they had found in each other in the early morning. Then they went back to the bedroom where she had lain that last evening, thinking about him, the previous revengeful memories of Carter raping her, now washed away in her love and desire for Peter.

They undressed each other and lay there in the coolness of the morning, a light sheet covering their bare bodies as they tenderly explored each other, thrilling with their lips, tongues and hands until she induced the flame of his readiness. This time their copulation was more enduring, beautifully long enough for her to feel that same warmth as he worked his magic in her. A euphoric warmth washing over her in waves as their bodies thrust in unison, rolling over so that she could look down at the elation in his face as he fondled and stroked her, then subjacent, looking up at him, feeling the strength of each vigorous thrust, moaning her pleasure as his eyes closed, panting in anticipation of those final moments of ecstasy. Then she suddenly felt a furnace door opening inside herself with a great surge of searing laser heat that sent its energy to the nerve ends of her body, causing her to convulse and shriek out in ecstatic pain and fulfilment of the orgasm she now felt as he also reached gratification. His love for her flowing out from his body, weakening him in the intoxicating tidal wave of loves passion.

She had never felt that euphoria in any previous liaison, the very few male acquaintances she had yielded to at university and over the intervening years having only had intercourse with her for their own pleasure, rolling away afterwards, sensing her involuntary frigid barrier. Now she felt free of the dirtiness of Carter and his pawing hands on her, as he had violated her young virginity, hurting her both physically and mentally. A mental hurt that had lasted until this magic moment with Peter. It had been wonderfully different from anything in the past. She had given herself to him as fully as her female instinct knew how. Now she lay there feeling a deep sense of serene calmness as her nostrils picked up the sweet odour of sweat, infusing between their bodies. He held her again in his arms, wiping away the strands of her hair sticking to her face, his lips brushing her closed eyelids, his hands stroking her skin that became alive with his touch.

It was nearly ten o'clock by the time they finally rose, showered together in the tiny cubicle, dressed and walked with their arms around each other, down through the deserted site to the farmyard where the Jaguar had been left before the caravan incident with Gilbert Piltcher below the cliff edge. There were about twenty other mobile homes on the site, but it was very quiet there, strangely no one about at that late hour of the morning.

The car wouldn't start and he cursed at the damage they quickly discovered, the siphon tube still hanging limply from the forced petrol filler cap. . 'That's just about how I feel at the moment,' he said.

She laughed, 'Never mind my love, I'm sure you will have recovered by tonight. Come on, let's drive down to the village in my car and buy some petrol.'

When they arrived at the village garage , they found the place locked up, everything was quiet, no vehicles or pedestrians. Katherine drove them down the deserted street past the Old Forge tea rooms that again like the garage and other small shops they found shut. Three coaches passed them full of people, as they groaned up the steep hill and they could see that they were packed to capacity, passengers standing and crammed together. A couple of open farm trucks passed them, full of campers from one of the local campsites. The passengers just stared at them in silence as the truck drivers went through the gears of the overloaded vehicles. It looked like a convoy of refugees from a television documentary.

Peter looked back at them, 'something strange is going here, this place is usually bustling with people, visitors and walkers.'

They drove down to the Branscombe sea front. It was the same, no one there, even the beach that was usually busy by mid morning was empty as was the car park where Luk and Carter had stolen the Shogun a couple of days before.

They drove back to the top part of the village, looking around them puzzled at the quietness of the place, parked the car and strolled back to the Square and Compass pub. Shut, but this time Peter heard a car engine start up from the back car park. The car pulled out into the road, over steering with its load of seven passengers. He waved the driver down, but the response was negative. The car groaned up the road a little way and came to a stop. The driver shouted back to him. 'Sorry no room, try the craft shop, they haven't gone yet.' The overloaded car started off with another groan of pain and was gone in a cloud of exhaust smoke.

The sound of breaking glass and exited voices suddenly came across the field from the Post Office along the upper lane and Peter turned to see four youths running off, one carrying the till as they bundled into Katherine's car and drove off at speed.

Peter ran after them shouting but stopped as he realised the futility of what he was doing.

They stood there in the middle of the road, confused at the various activities and apparent emptiness of the place.

'Do you two want a lift?' It was Sam Stephens the landlord of the Spring Head pub who had pulled up beside them.

'What's going on for goodness sake what's all the hurry.'

Sam looked at his watch, eager to be on his way. 'Haven't you seen the news this morning. Everyone's evacuating further north.' Katherine grabbed Peter's arm and looked at the driver in speechless amazement.

'You coming or not,' Sam Stephens cried out in impatience.' We're probably too late anyway, the radio is reporting solid traffic jams from here to Birmingham. There are fights going on up the M5 motorway as half the population on the south west coast try to get out of the area. Petrol is running out and the service stations are being looted.' His wife urged him to get going and Peter made the decision, pushed Katherine into the car and climbed in after her, not knowing why but instinctively feeling that it was the right thing to do.

Sam put the Volvo into drive and headed the car up the steep hill out of the village. 'I'm going to try and cut across country on the lanes rather than follow the main road. Christ, look at that will you.' They had just come up abreast of his pub, the front door had been broken down and people were coming out of the pub with crates of Scotch and rolling beer barrels back down the road. Others were sitting on the roadside drinking his stock as fast they could. He slowed and a young man jumped onto the back of the station wagon hanging on with one hand whilst waving a bottle of Vodka in the other like some fought for trophy. Sam took a right turn off the main road and the youth fell off swearing and gesticulating with two fingers in the middle of the road over the smashed bottle.

They drove on for a few hundred yards and Peter was about to start asking questions, when Sam suddenly braked hard and stopped there banging his fists on the steering wheel. 'Nothing I can do about it I suppose, there are too many of them, all our stock plundered by those mindless morons.'

'Let's keep going we've got a long way to go.' It was Sam's wife who broke into his heartfelt outpouring. The lane was narrow with high hedges each side and as Sam released the brake, an old van came down the lane from the opposite direction, blocking their way.

Two men got out and eyed the Volvo before simultaneously reaching back into the van and bringing out shotguns.

'Now what we got here Smithy, you reckon they got petrol in that nice motor?' The taller gypsy released the safety catch on his shotgun and walked casually up to the car and banged the side window with the barrels. Sam dropped the electric window a fraction and looked into the unshaven grubby face of the man as he smirked at them.

'You got any fukin' petrol fer us mister?'

Sam slammed the automatic into reverse and stood on the throttle as the station wagon weaved crazily back along the lane knocking the man to one side . The two gypsies ran after them firing off cartridges that crazed the windscreen as the car slammed its way out of range and continued in reverse back to the junction where he slewed the vehicle around and made off along the main road again.

No one had said anything. Peter and Katherine in the back seat had rolled around as the car had made its unconventional way back to the main road . 'Would anyone like to tell us what's happening?'

Sam's wife turned her head from the front passenger seat and shouted. 'Don't you listen to the radio or anything? The newspapers are supposed to be full of it but we haven't had a delivery. The post hasn't arrived today either, everyone's heading away from the coast because of the bomb, even the local radio has stopped broadcasting.'

Peter gripped Katherine's hand,

'Bomb? What bomb it must be a big one for all this fuss.'

They had driven down the previous evening listening to works of Vaughan Williams on Katherine's CD player and had not listened to the car radio.

Sam looked at him in the rear view mirror. 'A nuclear bomb, out there in the bay somewhere, the Navy is defusing it or something like that. They said on the radio this morning that there was no need for panic. Fat chance of that, everyone has upped stakes and run for it.'

The road ahead was suddenly blocked by cars and other vehicles. Sam stopped and leaped out.

'Wait there a minute, lock the doors, I'm walking down to see how long the queue is.' He was back in a couple of minutes with a grim look on his face. 'The police have set up a road block ahead and won't let anyone on to the Exeter road as its grid locked with stationary cars. We'll just have to wait here for a while.'

Peter got out of the car and they stood back as a car that had turned around further up the road shot past them. Ahead there was the sound of horns blasting as drivers lost their patience.

The Gypsy van drew up behind them and the tall man got out

'Thought you'd given the 'ol diddies the slip did you,' he said as he walked up to Peter and threw a punch. Peter ducked but as he came up, so did his head which caught the man under the chin. The gypsy's head shot back. He was used to this sort of thing and laughed as blood trickled from his mouth. 'Want to make a fucking fight of it do you, I'll sh…..' Before he had a chance to finish his inelegant sentence, Peter brought his knee up sharply into the mans scrotum, tipping him forward and brought down his fists on the back of the neck, sending the man sprawling on the ground.

Peter's training on the Welsh moors a few years previously hadn't left him, he acted instinctively as the other man came at him fumbling with the shotgun. He dived and rolled the few yards to crash into the mans legs, setting him off balance as Peter recoiled upwards jamming his fingers in the mans nose and then bringing his other hand cutting down across the forehead. The gun fell to the ground and discharged both barrels across the road in the direction of the tall man who now lay there motionless in the gutter.

The second man staggered over to the tall man who was now moaning where he lay. Blood streamed from his nose as his frightened eyes darted from Peter to his companion. 'O.K. Mister, you fukin' wait, we'll find you, don't you worry about that, we'll pile shit so high on you they'll smell it over in 'oniton.' He cowered back as Peter moved in with the shotgun and swung the stock at the mans head with a sickening thud that put him on the ground.

'Let's get out of here before I get really mean.' Peter swung back into the car as Sam moved the gear lever to reverse , pushing the gypsy's van backwards until it tipped over into a ditch on the side of the road. He then turned the car around and drove back in the direction of the village, past the drunks staggering about outside the pub and reached the tee junction where he stopped.

The previous events had taken a couple of minutes and Katherine was still coming to terms with the events of the last fifteen minutes.

'So, what are you going to do now.'

Sam looked up and down the road in desperation. 'I'm not sure, whichever way we go we'll run into a road block, but we must get away from here for the safety of us all.'

Peter caught Sam's eye in the mirror as he leaned forward in his seat and clutched the back of Mrs.Stephens's seat. He knew that to argue about the unlikelihood of the old bomb going off would be a fruitless waste of time and in any case without Katherine's car they had no transport of their own. 'Head out towards Seaton, we know a place there that will be perfectly safe.'

'You must be mad if you think we're heading back to the sea front,' it was June Stephens as she twisted round to face him, her eyes full of horror at the thought.

'I can assure you both that we know a place where we can shelter during this crisis and, if there is a detonation, we would have plenty of protection. Now get us down to the boat hard at Seaton, just before the river bridge over the Axe.'

They both turned and looked at him. 'What sort of place is it.' Sam was obviously of the opinion that to go inland was fruitless but he knew it was his responsibility to protect his wife and recent acquaintances who were now offering some sort of solution to their quandary.

'There's a deep cave on the other side of the river,' Peter offered.

'I've never heard of any caves over there, anyway, the local caves are full of people, we tried earlier to get down there. We heard that the quarry caves at Beer further inland were also full, people were fighting to get in there early this morning.'

'Look, just trust me will you, there is a cave over there that no one knows about; we can reach it by boat.' Peter looked at his watch. 'If we're quick we can make it, we need to be there at low tide.'

Sam considered the option, put the car into gear and turned south ignoring his wife's remonstrations of opposition. The road was empty in this direction and they soon turned up a single track lane towards Beer and Seaton.

The hill leading down into the seaside town of Seaton was empty. The view of the sea over the cliffs was tranquillity itself, silver blue and beckoning with its cats paws in the light breeze, giving no hint of its deadly secrets. On the far horizon they could see a cluster outline of grey warships as the Volvo headed for the sea front ignoring and driving against the one way traffic system and lights. An occasional car roared by in the opposite direction, with passengers gesticulating to them that they were going in the wrong direction.

'Stop here for a minute.' Peter climbed out and walked across the pavement that was littered with shattered glass from the small supermarket that had been smashed by looters. He was back in a few minutes, his arms full with milk, loaves and cans of drink. He also carried a newspaper. 'Drive on down to the boatyard. We should be able to find an inflatable RIB down there that we can use.'

On the deserted quay side they found a RIB, but when they checked the fuel tanks they had been siphoned and were empty. 'Spare can in the back,' Sam yelled and darted to the back of the car for the fuel. Katherine piled up the supplies on the gravel whilst Sam filled the outboard tank. Peter ran over to the locked harbour office and smashed a glass pane in the door with his elbow and let himself inside. He quickly located the key cupboard and extracted the engine keys for the craft. As he turned for the door, Katherine was beside him.

'They've gone,' she said. 'His wife insisted that they drove north.'

Peter hesitated. 'What do you think we should do?'

'Well I understood from the conference that the likelihood of that thing exploding was extremely remote. I was going to drive on down to Cornwall this morning to see dad in hospital.'

Peter looked at her sympathetically and drew her into his arms. 'Darling, there is absolutely no chance of you doing that, with this current crisis the traffic will be at a standstill, we're stuck here with no transport, can't even get back to the caravan now. I suggest we take the rib over to Gilbert's old cave and wait there until this thing blows over. Did he get any fuel into the outboard tank?'

'I think so, he was filling it when his wife went into panic mode and dragged him off.'

He fished in a drawer and found a note pad and pencil and scribbled a note of apology to the owner of the boat, hanging it on the key hook.

Once outside they dragged the RIB across the shingle to the muddy water's edge and loaded the supplies, wading it out into the ebb tide. The engines started straight away and they were soon threading their way out through the small mooring buoys and motoring down the middle of the narrow estuary, past the sand dunes and out into the seas gentle swell.

As they nosed into the darkness of the cave mouth, they grounded on the shingle bank next to Gilbert Piltcher's boat, still there from when Peter had taken him to the caves after the caravan fire. A glimmer of light filtered through from the lights in the cave chamber above which had not been switched off since their hurried departure two days before.

They clambered up the steps into the main whitewashed room and were about to enter the passageway to the living quarters when they heard voices echoing eerily around the tunnels. Peter stopped and beckoned to Katherine for silence as they pressed back against the wall and listened. As they did so a voice called out to them.

'Come on in Dr. Senden, we saw you rounding the stacks just now.' It was D.I. Evans from the Devon and Cornwall police and Superintendent Malcolm Seiger.

As the couple entered the living room, it seemed to be full of policemen. D.I.Evans came forward and greeted them. 'Fascinating place,' he commented, 'thought we would check it over following Captain Piltcher's death. Did he own all of this do you know.'

Katherine spoke up. 'My uncle told us he owned it and had converted it into a nuclear shelter, why what's the problem, what are you doing here, its private property you know.'

'Well Miss it would seem to be an ideal hiding place for the drugs gang we have been pursuing but I must say there is no sign that the caves have been used for that purpose. There's a locked steel door at the end of one of the passageways, do you know if there are any keys here that might fit the lock.'

The cave main entrance door had not been locked in the previous hurried departure. Peter climbed the steps to the main entrance and felt in the crevice he had seen Gilbert use and extracted the bundle of keys. 'One of these may fit but I think it should be Miss Holmes who opens it, after all, this place probably belongs to her now that her uncle is dead.' He offered her the bundle but she insisted on Peter taking the keys.

As they walked along the passageway Peter turned to the Inspector. 'How did you get here.'

'Our helicopter is waiting on the rock plateau above the cave, more to the point, what are you two doing here.' Peter explained what had happened and the panic they had seen as people tried to get away from the coast. The Inspector grinned.

'I gather from Supt.Seiger here that there is absolutely no chance on this earth of that thing going off. That's if it even exists. That stupid newspaper article has caused unnecessary panic from Brighton to Lands End.'

They all stood in front of the door as Peter tried the various keys in the locks that yielded one by one until with a final click, the heavy door was pulled open.

A musty smell came from the darkness of the room and Peter ducked inside and felt around for a light switch but there was none. From the echo effects, it sounded as though the room was empty. One of the constables switched on his torch and swung the beam around the glistening walls, caked over with calcium deposits. The floor was of roughly hewn flagstones and in one corner there was something covered under a tarpaulin sheet. Evans stepped into the room and went over to the pile and lifted the sheet.

The forty 400oz Bullion bars were dusty but still glinted their magic golden colour in the torches beam, sitting there, neatly stacked in a criss cross fashion in two piles

The group looked at the secret hoard in silence until Evans said quietly, 'so that was what the Commander was talking about. At a rough guess I'd say there is about, let's see, four hundred times forty that's sixteen thousand ounces. I believe gold is currently worth about $300 per ounce. That's something around four and a half million dollars or nearly three million pounds Stirling sitting there.' Peter grasped Katherine's hand as they looked at the small glinting piles.

'That must be what's left of their retirement fund. It was here all the time and now they are all dead.'

'What retirement fund?' Evans was looking at the pile as Peter tried to explain its origin. 'That story will of course have to be checked out Dr. Senden, but in the meantime we will have to check the legality of it being here and whom it belongs to. You say the people concerned are all dead?'

'Except for my father.' Katherine added, and then turned to the Inspector. 'We were on our way down to Cornwall to see my father, Sir Anthony Holmes, before this scare blew up, is there any way you can help us?'

Evans scratched his crew cut head and winked at Seiger, 'I should think we may find some room for you in the 'copter. We'll make security arrangements for this lot first and the Dorset machine can pick up these chaps when they're finished.' He fished out a notebook and began to write. 'Look, Miss Holmes, before we leave, would you check the contents of the cave and accept this note as confirmation of what has been found here?'

They all laughed at his fastidious attention to detail until he also saw the funny side of it and joined in their mirth. Supt. Seiger had been standing to one side and let the merriment die down as he then said. 'By the way, we have been trying to get hold of you on the phone earlier, you've obviously been away and not heard the news.' He looked steadily at them both as Peter said.

'What other news is there? We've been told about Miss Holmes's father being found, thank God he is alive and recovering.'

Seiger put on a good humoured smile.

'I am referring to the other day and the coroners post mortem on the man Carter. You may be interested to know that the shot that killed him was from David Luk's gun. We've now listened to the tapes our American friends made of the incident, in particular to the sequence of shots fired. It would appear that during the struggle for Luk's gun, it discharged, killing his father instantly.'

Peter groped for Katherine's hand in anticipation of what was to come.

'Luk is in hospital and is making a recovery following emergency surgery. His main wounds were from a high powered sniper's weapon that we still have to trace. He had other flesh wounds from a handgun fired by you Miss Holmes. It is unlikely that charges will be pressed due to the circumstances that prevailed that afternoon but your local police have been asked to inspect your firearms licence.' He paused. 'You do have one I assume.'

She looked around at the faces awaiting her reply as she faltered her response.

'Supt. Seiger, I am sure that you are very well aware that I do, but you will have to speak to my firearms issuing department in SO19 the Special Branch Firearms unit.'

Peter stood rooted to the ground and Robert Evans looked at her with astonished interest as Seiger asked her.

'Do you have your SO16 Warrant card with you ma'am, I believe that is the branch are you assigned to.'

She fished in the small shoulder bag she carried and produced her Diplomatic Protection Branch warrant card that he scrutinised and returned saying. 'Thank you, Superintendent Holmes ma'am.' She glanced at Peter with embarrassment. 'No time for answers now, we can talk later.'

An hour and a half later, they were sitting beside his bed, as Sir Anthony smiled tiredly at them. They poured out the stories of the last few days but he wasn't listening to half of what they said, her happiness and the new radiance he saw in her eyes told him all a father wanted to know. He started to feel very tired and they left him dozing peacefully to return back by helicopter to Peter's place at Upwey.

She knew Peter would be bursting with questions as soon as they were indoors.

'So, Ma'am, what's your involvement in all this? I thought you worked for the Environmental Department.' He seemed edgy, slightly annoyed, and she went straight to the kitchen to see if there was anything in the fridge to cook. He followed her in and stood in front of the refrigerator door. 'Well?'

'Darling I *am* connected to that department, it's my protective front and I do consulting work for them. You saw my Warrant card, I'm a Superintendent in the Special Branch concerned with Israeli diplomatic affairs.' She looked around the kitchen, 'You know my family is Jewish, I happen to speak half reasonable Arabic as well as Hebrew.' She tried to reach round him to the door handle but he stood his ground.

'You had bacon for breakfast this morning for God's sake.' She burst out laughing. 'Gentiles have funny ideas about modern Jews. We're a race of ancient people you know as well as a religion. It's true that orthodoxy demands certain rules and most orthodox Jews abide by them, but a lot of those rules are broken in the light of modern hygiene.' She gave him a mischievous grin. 'I didn't ask if you had been circumcised this morning did I?' And then, almost as an afterthought, 'anyway, I like bacon, as well! Life's a bonk darling and bacon is a bonus.'

He thought, was it only that morning that they had made love. He relaxed at her pun and drew her to him so that he could feel the contours of her body again.

'I'm sorry darling, didn't mean it that way, it just came as a bit of a shock finding out that you were a police woman.'

She pulled away in mock anger. 'I'm nothing of the sort, I'm a linguistic physicist attached to an organisation that finds my qualifications useful. I have that title because it is the only way that the organisational structure recognises itself. Like you, I'm freelance since the Government made its cuts a couple of years ago in the security services. In fact I'm not really Jewish in the true sense at all, the lineage comes down from the female side of the family. Now, question time is over, am I going to cook for us or not?'

Peter put on a whimsical smile. 'You mean you can cook as well.'

She threw away the contents of the refrigerator that had threatened to walk away unassisted and soon had a meal prepared, from a variety of Chinese frozen meals she had found in Peter's deep freeze. They were sitting over the several dishes as she poured the wine. Peter looked at her across the table, his facial expression asking the question that she knew she now had to answer.

'My main task at the present moment is to keep an eye on the arrangements for the forthcoming Middle East Conference, you know, advise the security part of our organisation as to who is coming and going, the connected and not so connected, looking over those people we allow to be here. Their own security people for instance. However, when dad went missing I took official leave so that I could try and find him.

Now, let's see, you've told me that you are on the engineering side of MI5, I hope you are not connected with anything dangerous.'

He forked a mouthful of the delicious meal she had prepared, and outlined his role as basically finding out what was going on in the industry of other countries, simple industrial spying, with no real risk of danger.' He eyed her cautiously before his next comment.

'I presume that it was through your work with SO16 that you found out so much about Carter and my half brother?'

'My job enabled me to look at files Peter, that's all. The FBI, along with a number of other countries, has been keeping an eye on David Luk and I expect they will now demand his extradition. It'll take months of course and then probably years to process him through the American legal system.'

'Did you know that the Israelis were also after him?' She gave him a quick glance. 'How do you know that?'

Peter then explained his conversation with Major Hessel the previous day omitting any reference to names. 'I promised confidentiality in exchange for a few answers.'

She smiled knowingly across the table at him. 'You've probably been talking to Major Hessel, a military attaché to the Israeli embassy who is over here officially as part of their security team for the Middle East Conference.

Unfortunately though my darling, my job does not enable me to divulge even to you the finer details of their arrangements.'

They finished their meal and Peter said thoughtfully, 'my paternal great grandparents were Jewish you know, came to this country in the 1880's to escape the purges of Eastern Europe and Russian pogroms.' He rose from the table, 'look, I'm going outside for a smoke, I've also got to make a confidential call to someone, do you mind.' That elfish grin came back on her face and she raised her hands in a claw like gesture towards him. 'As long as it's not another woman.'

Peter walked across the land at the back of the house and dialled a number on his mobile. 'Doug, hello it's Peter Senden here, wasn't sure if I would get an answer.'

Doug Lawson's wary voice came back. 'Released on supervisory bail, can't go anywhere, no passport, suspended from duty, not sure if we should be speaking Peter.'

'I'm on mobile, traceable of course. Look I need your help and I was hoping we could meet.'

'Meeting is out of the question Peter. What sort of help do you want?'

'Help to prove you've been set up. Do you have a PC there that's not connected to the Department network.'

'Of course I do, it connects to another line that's all, may not be secure though, the main lines are probably being tapped as I suspect this one is why, do you want to conference me?'

'That's the general idea Doug.'

They exchanged details and arranged what encryption would be used before Peter went back to the house and connected his private PC. He sat there for a moment, he knew he was taking a risk, relying on Hank Hoskins and the information that he had given to him the previous evening. Then he went to the keyboard, selected the encryption that had been arranged over the phone but with changes he knew Lawson would also make due to their open phone conversation. An arrangement they had used many times in the past. Then he checked that Katherine was busy in the kitchen before he sent the rudiments of Hank's suspicions about Major Fellows.

Questions and answers followed rapidly, both men hammering their keys in response to the other as the messages came up on their screens.

The hack into Jack Fellows's system computer at his home was arranged, Doug Lawson taking up the challenge with gleeful satisfaction.

It was getting late when Peter finished and Katherine was sitting in the kitchen reading Porter's article in yesterday's paper.

'Finished your 007 secret agent work then?'

He grinned back at her, 'how about a night cap, I presume you are staying.'

She giggled, as she switched off the kitchen lights and made for the stairs.

'I'm afraid I forgot something Watson.' She could hardly contain her giggles as they climbed the stairs and she jokingly said,

'Old Holmes here forgot to pack her strippergram police woman's uniform for you.' He joined in her mirth, not so much for her jokes, but in seeing her now in such a different light to the nervous young woman he had met at Gilbert Piltcher's cave.

Chapter 41. Car chase and a GPS handbook.

A couple of days later Peter was preparing breakfast for them both. He'd not seen or heard from Mrs.Lyonns and would ring the agency later. The whole place needed a clean up after the shooting and the people who had tramped through the house. He could imagine the insurance damage assessor's faces when they were told about the blood soaked furniture and carpet.

Katherine was still upstairs bathing and washing her hair, having phoned her father earlier.

The telephone rang. It was John Barrett. Peter had phoned him the previous evening, and told him about the retirement fund gold at the cave.

'Morning old mate, sorry to ring you at such an early hour but I'm due at the Dorchester assizes later this morning, attending some fraud case and drove down early. Roads around here are empty today, I assume due to this bomb they're still supposed to be defusing. Anyway, I have something here that I think will interest you, forgot all about it yesterday with your news. Can we meet this morning, I'll come over to the house if that's all right?'

'That's fine John, see you later.'

'Oh, by the way I have Jessica with me, just picked her up from the hospital, hope that's O.K.'

The arrangements were made and as they finished breakfast, John's car drew up on the drive. He helped Jessica out and then went round to the boot and extracted a large cardboard box as she limped to the front door with the assistance of a stick.

The women hugged and fussed over each other as they all met, an assurance to them both that the past was in the past and there would be no animosity between them over the changed relationships. The two men smiled at each other, their years of bond friendship overcoming any conscious apprehension at the changed circumstances. Peter ushered them into the drawing room, apologising for the mess and telling them to avoid sitting on the blood stained sofa and armchair that Carter and Luk had last used, now covered by a sheet.

'I believe these items may have belonged to your father.' John opened the large cardboard box and produced a brass binnacle and GPS set. 'They've been secretly marked with a UV pen so that the markings show up under ultra violet light, both items were found to have your fathers post code marked on them.'

'Where on God's earth did you get them? I thought it was strange that they were missing. I noticed that the sextant was mysteriously returned. What's been going on?'

'The sextant was probably returned because it had your fathers name engraved on it. These items were found by the Dorset police during a search of a local fisherman's home. A Mr. Pat Lyonns. Does the name ring any bells? Being Philip's executor the police called me yesterday and I went into the station and collected them this morning.'

'Are you telling me that my housekeeper deliberately stole these things?'

'I'm afraid I have to tell you that she is being held for questioning at the moment. You see the local police tracked down the motor cycle rider who caused the accident down by the marina the other week,' He looked hard at Peter before continuing. 'A local man, absolutely distraught at what had happened, it was his brother in law who was killed. I gather according to the police that the accident occurred after you were attacked with a baseball club.'

'How does that involve or connect with Mrs.Lyonns?'

'Mrs.Lyonns was their aunt. Her brother, was the diver who died in the diving accident a few years ago, an accident that the family blamed on Philip and for which they received no compensation. Not their fault, my father argued a successful case at the time and their own brief was not up to it. When your father was taken to hospital, Mrs.Lyonns and family entered his flat on the pretext of cleaning with a key she'd obtained from the regular cleaner. They were light fingered and stole those items in the belief that it was some sort of payment that they were owed. They've admitted and confessed to beating you up as some sort of recompense or revenge for their loss, but it went terribly wrong. You'll sue them of course?'

'Why should I sue them? It sounds to me as if they have paid a heavy price already for what, after all, seems to have been Philips fault.'

Katherine went out to the kitchen to prepare drinks for them and John followed, asking about progress on her father.

As they left the room, Jessica drew close to Peter and spoke to him in a low voice so as not to be overheard by the others. She smiled at the obvious relief on his face as he kissed her cheek, just as the other two entered and Katherine straight away sensed the secrecy that had been between them. She shot a quick glance at Peter so that their eyes caught for a second before she attended to the coffee cups. Peter stood and swept his hair with a hand.

'Jessica and I have an announcement to make about some wonderful news she has just given to me.' He paused, long enough to know his teasing of John was working as his eyes seemed to fill with apprehension at the news Peter was about to impart. Jessica had stood and Peter put a reassuring arm around her waist, turning to the other two, standing there, both privately fearful about what was going to be said as they waited for his announcement.

'Apparently I'm not the old bastard you've all been led think I am. Jessica has just told me that her lab has conducted preliminary DNA tests and positively proved my birthright. Philip was my father after all.'

John collapsed into one of the chairs clapping his hands and demanded Champagne, then remembered he was due to attend the court and laughingly cancelled the request. Katherine relaxed as Jessica gave Peter a playful punch in the side at his innuendo and they selected their coffee cups.

'When Peter visited me in hospital the other day, he asked if it would be possible to conduct DNA tests following on from what his half brother and Carter had told us. I managed to get the laboratory on the 'phone and they did all the tests yesterday and last night. They proved positive and I can assure you all without any doubt that Philip was Peter's genetic father.'

Katherine put down her cup.

'Have you discussed Carter's allegations with your mother?'

Peter remembered his last meeting with his mother when she had been so upset at the revelations of her past. Since David Luk's outburst he had thought a lot about the circumstances of his birth. If Carter and David knew so much about him his mother must surely have known. He had calculated from his parents wedding date and his own birthday that he must have been conceived in wedlock, in which case why had Carter seemed to be so sure that he was his son? Had his mother returned to the arms of her ex husband due to Philips homosexuality? If all the allegations Carter had made were true, why had his father blackmailed Carter to provide for his education? Perhaps there was a much deeper reason, the reason for his mothers anguish on that summer's day. From all they now knew about the man from Hong Kong, he had been an absolute despot, a murderer, a drug addict, attacking an innocent girl of fifteen and raping her. If he had been capable of carrying out such a horrendous crime once, could it be that he had committed the same crime on other occasions. Had Carter raped his mother?

'Peter! A penny for your thoughts.' Katherine brought him out of his contemplation and he looked around and smiled sheepishly at them.

'No. I haven't yet had the opportunity to speak with mother. But what the hell am I supposed to say to her when I do?'

John looked at his watch. That was a difficult one and he didn't have an answer. 'We must go in a minute.'

They said their goodbyes and John drew Peter to one side. 'We must talk later, all those letters and the blackmail we suspected, pity the old boys lived their lives with such a terrible misconception of the truth. Oh, we'd better also talk about what's happening about all that gold.' He gave Peter a slap on the back. 'Cheers mate, see you soon.'

When they had gone, Katherine laughingly admonished him for the way he had made his announcement. 'Darling, I love you so much, please don't frighten me like that again.' He looked at her, concern in his face as he kissed her and apologised.

'I love and adore you too. What happened was meant as a sort of macho joke between John and I, a gentle shot across the bows but silly of me.'

She started to clear away the coffee tray and Peter went into the study, turning the GPS over in his hand and switched it on. He watched the display as its twelve channels locked on and acquired information from the overhead satellites. It was an older model than the one he was used to and he rummaged through the bookcase for the handbook his father had enclosed with the charts and other paperwork. He hadn't looked at the handbook since putting it to one side the morning after he returned from the Downshall sanatorium and as he opened it a slip of writing paper fell out. He sat down at the desk to read it.

28 May .
My Dear Peter,
I believe I am seriously ill and not sure where you are at the moment.
I've been hired several times recently by a group of foreign business people who were interested in helping me to find a shipwreck called the Acacia Lady and its hoard of gold that I have been searching for. Look at the scrap book, it's all there.
On my last trip something happened. I didn't find the Acacia Lady, guess I never shall now but on my last dive we were on a very deep wreck that I had dived on once before and my attention was drawn to a strange light. I swam away from the other diver down there and discovered a bomb like shell, lying in the gravel with one end rotted away. It was amongst a pile of lead sheeting and my lamp could just pick out some rotting old sten guns that must have been part of the ship's cargo scattered over the seabed. When I looked inside the shell, there was a brilliant blue glow and the water around it was hot and full of bubbles.
I never believed there could be anything so awful down there but whatever it is, it must be reported to the authorities. Sadly, looking down at my hands, I'm sure it is some kind of nuclear weapon, they hurt and I can't write much more. I wanted to inform my old Royal Navy office but the telephone number had changed.
Peter, I know you deal with the right people, for God's sake tell them my story. You never knew, but I worked for the Government after I retired from the Navy, MI6 to be precise. The Dragon's Morsel was one of my projects and you will find out all about it if you can trace Simon Carter (see scrap book and letters). He once told me that the gold was guarded by a dragon so terrible it gave him nightmares. I did not believe him but I knew straight away that I'd found something that the Chinese once called the Dragon's Morsel , and guessed that it was the real purpose of the foreigners search. When I returned to the surface, I said nothing and by the time I disembarked, I was feeling very ill and told them I had flu. I drove round to the boat shed and changed and just about managed to get back here to the flat where I've sat for two days.
The Acacia Lady wreck must be nearby, when the authorities have removed the device, I hope you will continue the search that I have been making for so long. It was my retirement fund and may turn out to be yours.
Can't write any more, will give parcel to cleaner when she arrives. Look at GPS.
Look after Monica.........Tell them to get Simon Carter he is the Dragon..........

The letter ended in a scrawly signature and Peter held it in his hand and read it and re read it before pouring himself a Grouse diluted with a little water. He sat there imagining the turmoil his father must have been suffering as he wrote it.

The GPS was lying on the desk in front of him indicating its position, on the screen in latitude and longitude, but what was he to look for. He entered the navigation mode and the screen requested a position to seek. In addition to defining the present position it is also possible to enter the position of some other known point such as a harbour or navigation hazard such as a rock. Once entered, the screen will indicate a number of navigation features between the present position and the selected position, such as the speed over the ground , estimated time of arrival, course to steer, distance and course deviations. This particular GPS set could store ninety nine such positions, called waypoints.

Peter looked in the handbook and manipulated the push button controls until a list of waypoints that Philip had previously entered, appeared on the screen with their latitude and longitude definitions. He pushed the appropriate button and started to scan the list as it rolled the waypoint information up the screen.

The first twenty stored positions were designated, A.C.1., A.C.2, up to A.C.20. presumably abbreviations for Acacia Lady positions he had searched. Then the screen rolled up the next way point, DRAG MORSL, with the position marked beside it followed by various other positions that the fisherman had later stored for his lobster pots. So after all those weeks, here was the confirmation he had been seeking, the *Dragon's Morsel* was after all the *Thinman* atomic bomb. Or was it? Both Fellows and Hoskins had implied something else, some other meaning .

Peter mused over the words that had tumbled around his head since that day at Downshall Sanatorium as he took out his chart with hands that shook slightly in anticipation and marked up the positions one by one until he came to this last position. He stood silently looking at the annotations on the chart. A grid work of search boxes covering a wide area. His own position arrived at through his interpretation of the magnetic variation over those years and Philips GPS position ten miles away to the west.

Katherine came in from the kitchen where she had been stacking the dishwasher.

'Darling I've been thinking, don't you think we should go over to your mother's place and let her know what's been going on. She should be told you know, it's possible that unbeknown to you, she could be bearing the same misconception that Carter had over your birth. She's only twenty minutes away.'

Peter was torn between his mother and what he had now discovered. 'Look at this, yet another position I just don't understand it.'

Katherine looked at the chart, 'Doesn't it line up with anything?' 'Not really, look , there are now four major positions I've marked up. There's the one over to the west in Hurd Deep where your uncle stated at the enquiry that the Acacia Lady sank. Then there is the position mentioned in his letter where he said that the front end of the ship sank, that's been verified by the machine tools that have been found in that position. The third position is where the main hulk of the Acacia Lady was found two days ago and now this position which according to my father's letter is the position of the bomb. I just don't believe he could have found anything that far away.'

'What are you going to do.'

Peter looked at the chart positions again and read through Philips letter.

'My father must have been at that position otherwise he would not have died.'

Katherine pulled him round to face her. 'How exactly did your father die Peter, you've never told me.'

He sat there as though not listening. His thoughts went back at the sanatorium and his father, lying there in that sterile ward, dying from the awful dose of irradiated plutonium poisoning he had received. The events since that time as he had tried to understand what had happened and been side-tracked by the story of the gold hoard and the Acacia Lady. Now this development brought about by the Lyonns family and their revenge . Was this yet another false lead. He looked up at Katherine and kissed her, not answering her question, before standing and looking around the room. The room where Carter had died, the room where Jessica had been shot. She didn't press the question, she knew he would tell her when the time was right.

'This requires some investigation before I approach the authorities again, this time I must be sure.'

He sat looking at the chart for some minutes and then, 'I've an idea as to what may have happened, I must go up to the British Newspaper Library in West London, sounds hard of me putting this before mother but if I'm right, I think the *Dragon's Morsel* mystery may be broken.'

They sat in the Colindale reading room in West London as Peter went back to the original newspaper copies covering the official enquiry into the Acacia Lady sinking, the first connection between the men, and scanned the other pages of news. Then he went back a few months to the date of the actual sinking. The main news story was the impact of the East Coast floods following the January storms and high spring tides, with most papers filling their pages with photographs of the tragedy. It was there that he found another clue. A short report of another sinking in the same storm that had overwhelmed the Acacia Lady. Strangely the other wrecked ship, the Eastern Lady, did not receive many lines, merely to say that the ship had sunk and all hands had been saved. Nobody drowned, no insurance loss reported, but unspecified military equipment had been lost which meant a Naval Board of Enquiry. Later news items were sketchy, the Board had only released part of its findings. Not a very news worthy item he thought. He spotted an editorial in one newspaper complaining about Government censorship and that D Notices had been served at the time on the story. Then he looked through the government archive documents for 1953 that had been released in 1978 under the twenty five year rule and found the tentative connection he had been looking for. The declassified Naval Board of Enquiry report that covered the sinking of the Eastern Lady in the English Channel on the same night as the Acacia Lady. Details of its position had in fact been released twenty five years previously to the Hydrographic Department of the Navy in Taunton, so that its position could be identified as an unidentified wreck. As he read on he knew he had found the answer as he compared the reported position with the latitude and longitude from Philips GPS set. The ship had been carrying non essential military supplies in the same convoy as the Acacia Lady before she sank. There was an account by a Sub.Liet. Philip Senden of how equipment had been transferred earlier to the Eastern Lady from the Acacia Lady before she sank. The equipment list was censored and not detailed but the report went on to describe his father's bravery during the rescue that followed and resulted in the whole crew being saved. So that was it, the atomic bomb had been transferred to the Eastern Lady, probably by mistake and most likely with the full knowledge of Simon Carter.

He walked across to Katherine who had found something on the environment to read . 'Can you keep a secret ma'am?'

She looked up at him with a grin. 'So you've found what you were looking for.'

'I haven't broken the mystery of *Dragon's Morsel* if that's what you mean but I think I've discovered what happened to *Thinman* and where it is. 'I've found out that one of the other ships in the convoy sank in the same storm, in that sinking there was no loss of life and only the military equipment went down. There was a separate enquiry that, because of the military content, was held in camera. D notices were issued and there was a clamp down on information.

The press at the time let it slide by them. There was no story in it for them, no tragedy and no insurance claim as the whole lot, ship as well was covered by a British Government war indemnity. It was just another ship sunk in a storm. The Irish Ferry disaster made the headlines. Twenty five years later when the report was released for general digestion, this story didn't rock the boat, but the official admittance is there. The main point is that the co-ordinates match Philip's.'

'So what do we do now, ring Major Fellows, he's in charge isn't he?'

He sat beside her, a serious look on his face.

'Darling, I meant what I said about keeping a secret. I know about something that if I told you, could compromise your position in Special Branch.'

She pulled him around to face her. 'Peter don't be so silly. I love you, anything you say to me provided it isn't admitted murder, is between the two of us. Please, you must believe that. Anything else as far as I am concerned falls into insignificance.'

Peter held her arm and they stood. 'O.K., I'll tell you what's going on when we're in the car.'

He went to the reception desk and paid for a pile of photocopies that he tucked under one arm as they left.

In the car, he explained his doubts about Major Jack Fellows, what Hank Hoskins had told him about the CIA plot and how Doug Lawson was at that time attempting to set the trap that would expose the Major.

'What about Supt.Seiger, can't he help? What about Sir George thingy, isn't he Dick Fellows's boss?'

'No, the only one I can go to is Hank Hoskins. He's the only one in this whole God damned business that I can trust. I don't have enough authority to ring the Royal Navy, in any case whom would I ring. It would be most unlikely that the

Captain of the Seeker could just go off on a whim that's if I could even contact him.'

They sat in Katherine's Porsche, generously loaned by her father following the theft of her own car at Branscombe, the photocopies on the back seat holding the clue to the most serious potential environmental problem ever know in Britain and he did not know what to do. Did he really know if Hank was telling the whole truth or was he, Peter, being used in some way?

Then he had an idea.

'Come on, we're going to find an Internet terminal that is not linked to any of our organisations, one that's untraceable. I'm going to e-mail the US President at the White House.'

They worked at the public library computer for a few minutes, dialled into the White House Internet web site and found the address they wanted. Then Peter sent his message using as an afterthought the pseudonym *Dragon's Morsel* in the subject box.

Then they hung around for over three quarters of an hour before the reply was there on the screen.

To Dragon's Morsel from the Office of the White House.

Your code name has been verified and I can safely confirm that Cmdr. Hoskins works with the full authority of the President. If you have information pertaining to the recovery of Thinman it is imperative that you contact his office immediately.

Signed, Jonathan Erkenham, Chief adviser to the President of the USA.

This message copied to the US Embassy London. Room N13007, Wk.Stn.013750 Cmdr.H.Hoskins.USN. Z0084500/070703. Etc. Etc.

Katherine was deep into a reference book she had picked up when the message came through and Peter said. 'Wait here whilst I go outside and call Hoskins on my mobile.'

'Hi there, Hank, it's Peter Senden here, I think I've found the position of *Thinman*.' Peter stopped. He had dialled the personal mobile number for Hank Hoskins but the southern drawl at the other end of the line was not Hank. Peter spoke with caution in his voice.

'I wish to speak to Commander Hoskins. Please tell him that it's Peter Senden here and that I have some urgent information for him.'

The voice responded.

'That's O.K. Dr. Senden, I work with the Commander, you can give me the information you have on *Thinman*, where are you at the moment.' Peter hesitated.

'Sorry but this information is for the Commander only, how can I get in touch with him?' There was a pause at the other end of the line.

'Hoskins is off the project, I'm his replacement, please Dr. Senden, we need to know where you are so that we can finalise this thing.'

Peter pressed the 'call end' button on his mobile and returned to the library. He disclosed what had been said to Katherine adding,

'The guy on the other end seemed more interested to know where *I was* rather than the position for *Thinman*. Christ, I hope nothing has happened to Hank, last time we spoke he inferred that his life could be in danger from the CIA plotters.' He thought, should he tell her that there was a vague implication he could also be in danger?

Peter was anxious to get away from the place. They had been there for nearly an hour and there had probably been time enough for their location to be traced electronically. He knew that with the right mobile telephone receiving equipment their postal district location could be easily identified. With the right request it was possible for any mobile under surveillance to be pinpointed by triangulation down to about 50 yards if required. He paid the fee to the librarian and they walked out towards the library entrance and car park. As they did so, he noticed the man who had just hastily entered, well built, dressed casually, but with the hard smooth facial features of someone who was very fit, looking around but not at books, his eyes shifting constantly as he pretended to be engrossed in a small exhibition of children's art near the entrance.

Peter had seen the type many times on his travels. Presidential bodyguards, mercenaries and soldiers of fortune, they all shared that same lean healthy look.

Katherine was startled as Peter gently pushed her away and muttered. 'Walk away casually, get into the car and start it then stay there.'

She did as instructed as he turned back into the library and ducked behind one of the book racks. Peter knew he had been spotted. The man, his eyes darting furtively around the building passed through the entrance barrier and strolled casually in his direction.

Peter was pretending to read a book as the man sidled up to him.

'*Dragon's Morsel?*' He asked in a long southern drawl. Peter feigned surprise and uncertainty over the mans question.

'I'm afraid I am not aware of that title. Why don't you go over and ask the librarian or look for it through the microfiche?'

The man looked around again, his eyes taking in everything and everyone who moved and as he did so he bent towards Peter and whispered. 'Don't fuck about playing games with me pal, you know very well what I want. We can't talk here, let's be sensible and walk quietly outside.'

'I'm going nowhere until you explain what it is you want.'

'Just give me the information you have on *Thinman* and no harm will come to you.'

Peter's mind rushed over what was being said. The delayed reply from Washington had given someone the time to track down the library terminal. His mouth went suddenly dry. 'Where's Hoskins? He's the only person I'll speak to.'

'He's outside in the car, it's too risky for him to be seen at the moment. Now, are you coming or not.'

Peter felt the silencer on the gun barrel as it pressed into his side through the man's clothing. It was persuasion enough and they started to walk in the direction of the entrance. As they did so the book Peter was still carrying set off the counter alarm, distracting the man's attention for a fraction of a second, enough time for Peter to swing the heavy book upwards and across the Adams apple of the man, sending him staggering backwards.

As he ran, two muffled shots rang out and he heard the sound of the rounds as they ricocheted around the foyer. People were screaming as he ran outside to where Katherine's car was waiting, the passenger door open as he dived in and shouted, drive.'

The Porsche left rubber on the tarmac as she accelerated away and sped her way out onto the main road. 'What the hell happened in there,' she screamed above the gear changes.

Peter looked at the book he was still carrying and burst out laughing as he slung it onto the seat bench behind him.

'What's so fucking funny, what's happened, I heard gunshots back there,' she cried, keeping her eyes glued to the road as she weaved in and out of the traffic.

'Self Defence for Beginners,' he was still chuckling to himself, 'it's the title of the library book I've just used to clobber someone.'

'Well you'd better start reading it, I don't wish to alarm you lover but I think we're being followed.'

Peter adjusted the rear view mirror and watched the car for a few moments, a black Merc. 'Do you know the cork screw manoeuvre?' She nodded. 'Take a few turns at it and see if you can shake them off.'

Peter was on his mobile again as the car took a right turn at speed and headed down a quiet suburban road.

'Directories? The number for the American Embassy in London please.' He keyed in the number he was given and asked for Hoskins.' The car swung right again, pinning him to the seat.

'Peter! How you doing son?' It was Hanks voice all right but Peter had to be certain.

'Hank, I need to verify that I am speaking to you in person. Tell me, what's the *Dragon's Morsel* Hank?'

The surprised Commander responded.

'Too long a tale to explain over the phone Peter and I didn't tell you the other night, if you want to authenticate this call, only you and I would know that I gave you my new card when I visited you. I also wrote on the back of it.' Peter was satisfied.

'Someone's got your mobile Hank.'

'It vanished during the office move to the Embassy. You got trouble there?'

Peter explained what had happened, the e-mail from Washington, the man in the library, the Mercedes that was now hanging in to every move Katherine made. He half turned to Katherine. 'How fast does this thing go.' Katherine grinned, 'where to boss.'

He waved his hand and they turned sharply off Maida Vale, bumping over the speed restricting *sleeping policemen*. Speeding past small pavement cafes where the clientele jumped back from their normally quiet afternoons' ingestion of tea and Danish, tyres squealing on corners as snap decisions were made. The canal bridge at Little Venice came up too quickly and the Porsche was airborne engine screaming as Katherine struggled to hold the line before it again bit the tarmac and snaked down towards the Harrow Road heading towards the A40M elevated motorway in West London, Peter looked in the side mirror, the Mercedes had half its front missing and must have hit the metal bridge. Bits were falling off it, bouncing away along the road as it continued to pursue them. He shouted above the engine noise.

'Take a left at these traffic lights.' They had turned red as she swung the wheel into Ladbroke Grove narrowly missing a red London bus. She looked in the mirror for the now familiar Mercedes. It wasn't there.

Peter was still on the mobile. 'Hank, I think we've shaken them off.......Pull into the supermarket car park over there.......... Hank are you still there, who are these people? Can we meet somewhere?'

She rolled the Porsche into the large car park surrounding the Sainsbury supermarket.

'I'm still here Peter, from the description you gave, you're in great danger, he's one of the *Crusader* people from Lebanon. I'm restricted to the Embassy, they're after me as well. I've seen a message from Erkenham, but I'm confused, it says it's from Dragon's Morsel, now you say that you have the information. Peter, we need the information you have on *Thinman* but not on an open line.'

Katherine had hauled her handbag over from behind her seat. 'Is this any good.' She handed Peter her Nokia communicator, 'Sorry, forgot I had it.'

Peter grasped it. 'Is this thing Net wise or WAP or whatever they call it?'

She nodded, 'it's got everything, give me Hanks e-mail address, they're unlikely to have anything in that Merc that could lock into or interpret what we send.'

Peter conferred with Hank Hoskins again as the car pulled into a parking slot and stopped.

'Hank, I would like to stipulate one condition. This information must go through Royal Navy channels to HMS Seeker. I owe them that after the disappointment they had the other day.'

The Commander agreed to Peter's request and Katherine quickly logged onto her network, 'stand by your computer Hank, here comes the information you want.'

As they finished the transmission and Hoskins confirmed receipt, Peter spotted the Mercedes, doing a slow tour of the car park with three of its occupants hanging out of the windows looking wildly around as shoppers stepped back out of the way of the bits still falling off the flapping body trim.

'Got to go Hank, we've got company again.'

Katherine was still tapping away on her keyboard that she rested on her lap. Then they shot out through the chicane entrance and turned right towards the wasteland between the railway and old gasworks. Too late they realised the road was closed and she performed a hand brake turn that sent them rushing back towards the Mercedes whose driver swerved as its occupants leaned precariously out of the windows firing their handguns. Then they were out into Ladbroke Grove again, skimming around the roundabouts and over the railway bridge and turning immediately right, accelerating hard. Peter shouted, 'head south, if we can reach the A40 before the rush hour we may be able to outrun them.'

She took another right turn at speed, shouting above the noise of squealing tyres as she ducked to look at the road name. 'They're still there we're heading along Dalgarno Gardens .'

They scraped a bollard as they drove through another traffic calming junction and then passed under the railway arch and turned left into Scrubbs Lane, running straight into a jam at the traffic lights.

'Hold on to your hat Peter, south on Scrubbs Lane, I'm going for it.' She seemed to be talking to herself as she pulled over to the right, overtaking on the blind bend as traffic coming in the opposite direction pulled out of the way, horns blaring. Then she was around the traffic island on the wrong side and accelerating again. More traffic lights which Peter was pleased to see were green. Then they had to stop in traffic turning onto the A40. Westway. Katherine grabbed the rear view mirror and could only assume that the Mercedes was also stuck in traffic about twenty vehicles behind them. In her side mirror she saw two of the occupants get out and start running towards them along the outside lane of vehicles, both holding large magnum hand pieces. They seemed trapped.

Then a remarkable thing happened. The side door of a white Transit van some ten vehicles behind the Porsche and bearing the logo of a central heating company, suddenly opened. Hands came out and one of the gun toting men was grabbed and hauled inside. The other man crouched and aimed. They heard the pom pom sound of small arms gun fire as he was suddenly stumbling across the road, clutching his shoulder as he dodged the oncoming traffic and others piled out of the transit in pursuit. Then all hell was let loose as the Mercedes pulled out of the traffic, accelerating down the outside of the traffic queue, forcing the oncoming traffic to swerve onto the pavement to get out of its way. The sound of small arms fire sent pedestrians scurrying for shelter as the Mercedes became jammed in between a London taxi and an electric milk float and its occupants were surrounded by plain clothes police from the transit van, all pointing their firearms.

The lights changed and Katherine accelerated onto the main A40.

'I saw them in my side mirror,' she said, 'that was an unmarked Special Branch vehicle I requested. These days we have them cruising around in case of trouble. I've been on one of our support request channels since we left the supermarket car park and luckily that unit was on its way to the Wormwood Scrubbs Prison, just down the road.' She turned with that elfin grin. 'Thought I was talking to myself did you? Lady Superintendents *do* have some pull you know.'

They made their way back to the scene of the shooting in time to see the police patrol cars arrive and her colleagues rounding up the suspects. Then at Katherine's insistence, they drove straight to Monica Senden's cottage.

She was not expecting them and opened the door with joyful surprise, her mother eyes taking in the pair of them, the young woman and her son standing there on the door step, their happiness in each other so very obvious. As she ushered them into the living room her mind was trawling the past, the girl was familiar, but from somewhere else, another time.

The introductions were made and an old acquaintance renewed as Monica bustled around, clearing away the books and magazines she had been reading and plumping cushions on the sofa. 'Shoo Sophie.' Her Rag Doll cat looked at them reproachfully as she was swept from her usual resting place. Then Monica was talking to them about those old days, trying to remember the times in Portsmouth when Katherine had visited them as a young girl with her mother. At that time she had hoped that maybe the daughter of her friend and her own son would become closer and form a relationship. But something at that time had been wrong. She knew her son had shown interest, but the girl although seemingly normal on the surface, had shown a sort of self controlled negative sexuality, an attitude that, as his mother, she had noticed.

There was more small talk. Monica silently happy to see her son so obviously in love again and the lovely girl he had brought to see her, surely not for her approval. She continued to talk to them through the open doorway to the kitchen as she prepared a tray of tea and searched for biscuits. The talk was of Katherine's father. Monica had seen it all on the news over the last couple of days.

Peter looked at Katherine, the task he was about to undertake was a difficult one and he was not sure where to begin. She read his mind and gave him a reassuring smile before rising and joining Monica in the kitchen.

Katherine opened the new pack of biscuits and put them on a plate and Monica immediately sensed that the purpose of the visit was about to begin and that the stage curtains were being drawn back to start the show.

She hesitated with the kettle as Katherine said.

'We thought you should know that your son David has been involved in a shooting incident and is in intensive care at Odstock Hospital near Salisbury.'

Monica stopped filling the teapot, a look of concern on her face. Before she could respond, Katherine continued, 'I'm afraid we have some other bad news as well, someone else you once knew died in the shooting.' She paused as Monica's eyes caught her own. 'Mr.Simon Carter I'm afraid. I'm sorry.'

She stood there in silence as Monica took in the news, saying nothing, her mind full of pictures from the past. And it was the past. The years had made her strong so that the names that Katherine now gave her with sympathy could not be treated with the same poignancy that at one time would have prevailed.

Monica went back to filling the teapot. 'Let's go and sit down, I'd like to hear the details.'

Katherine had laid the foundations, built the first courses, put in the windows through which Monica could perceive the happenings more easily as Peter then spoke to his mother, filling in the details of the last few weeks and ending with the events in the house at Upwey. Then as softly as possible he started on the difficult thing he had come there to talk about. It had been on his mind ever since Carter had sown the uncertain seed with his assertions about Peter's illegitimacy. But how could he give her the reassurance without indicating that he had guessed her unhappy secret.

'Mother, I didn't tell you at the time, but Philip was quite disfigured by the time they fished him out of the sea after his diving accident.' Katherine listened casually, Peter had still not told her the circumstances of his father's death. Monica sat there with lips set in a thin line as the visions of both ex husbands rebounded around her tired mind. Those early happy days with each one, turning to disappointment and then grief that she still felt reflected on herself as much as those unfortunate men.

'The authorities had to check DNA samples from Philip's body with my own to ascertain our relationship as father and son for identification purposes.' He paused, hoping that the statement would have some significance for her.

If it did have any meaning, she showed no indication but asked in a hollow voice. 'And presumably from those tests they were able to establish that it was Philip they had found.''

To her own ears her voice sounded far away, different, not her own. She looked away from her son, hoping he hadn't noticed, holding down her inner anxiety at what was about to be said. What terrible questions she was going to have to find answers for.

He had noticed the tiny inflexion in her voice, the stiffening of her facial muscles and the way she was now fidgeting with her fingers. He now knew how Carter had probably used her, her misery over the years as she had tried to hide the hurt.

'Well of course they did. The DNA tests proved without any single shadow of doubt that we were father and son.'

The tension he had sensed in her was suddenly gone. Those years of wondering, of uncertainty for her, gone, blown away for ever.

Now she could at least feel free of those old ghosts. He caught a brief glance from Katherine as their eyes met. She had noticed as well.

Whatever Carter had done, or whatever their relationship had been it was now over, Monica could finally cleanse her mind, try and forget those later dormant years with Philip, remember the earlier times, the good times when they had first found their love.

The colour had returned to her cheeks as she thought over what had just been said, whether contrived or by accident she didn't know.

'I'm so sorry that Simon caused you so many problems, he was wonderful as a young man, but of course it is your father that I shall miss the most. As for David, well, I suppose I had better go and see him although I'm not sure that we will know each other.'

Early the next morning, the weather over the English Channel was not lifting. It was a grey, dismal day and the rain and sea spray ran down the bridge deck windows in constant rivulets. Captain Williams watched from the lower bridge deck wing as the small Lynx helicopter brought the American science team aboard HMS Seeker again and then went down to the mess deck to greet them. The equipment they would use had already preceded them during the night.

Within an hour, the Geiger-Muller and other radio active measurement sensors, that had been lowered to the sea bottom, were kicking their analogue needles over to full scale and the digital readouts, normally steady on background radiation noise, were now indicating large fluctuations. *Thinman* had been found at last thanks to Philips years of treasure hunting which had resulted in his death. Now perhaps his body would be released by the Coroner so that it could be decently interred at long last. To Peter, his father's death had lead to so many other things, his involvement with the *Thinman* project, Piltcher, the discovery of his half brother, a new closeness to his mother and above all his new love, Katherine Holmes.

Captain Williams turned to his comms. Yeoman. 'Signal to the USS Phoenix, *Thinman* located at 0755 UTC. State the position and handing over procedure as previously agreed. Copy to Admiral of the Fleet.' He removed his hat and ran his fingers around the inside sweat band. 'Thank God that's over with.'

Chapter 42. The Mole

Major Jack Fellows sat at his study desk in front of the large window overlooking the grounds around the house. It was late afternoon and outside it had started to drizzle as he dunked a shortbread biscuit in his cup of tea and mused over the London Daily Chronicle article. He knew there was some truth in the content of the many reports over the last couple of days but, as so often, many were blown out of all reality to sell newspapers. The stories of panic in the area as people had fled northwards, taking their relatives out of hospitals, looting, and other hidden crimes. Now the news that the nuclear bomb had been found and made safe was the new headline and journalists were already turning to other unrelated items of news. Sports and pop stars were back on the front pages of most tabloids.

People were returning to their homes and businesses, angry at what had happened. Angry that the authorities had once again muffled the truth about nuclear safety, treating them like an under class. What could they believe the next time that they were assured a nuclear accident had no significance. Nuclear management procedures across the World had to be cleaned up, removed from profit motivated cost cutting accountants. Retained in the safe hands of science, not necessarily by scientists but maybe a new brand of specialist or better still, reduced to a manageable size. Alternatively, Governments had to think the unthinkable and gradually turn away from the invisible atom with its stream of court attendants.

The Major had just returned home, earlier than usual, following a short departmental debriefing that morning, where his efforts on the *Thinman* project and liaison with the Americans had been praised by Sir George, all efforts now being concentrated on the Middle East Conference, due to be held in a couple of weeks time.

He had happily accepted the congratulations from his departmental head. Reports were now being prepared for government ministers and their departments and the scare that had occupied them for the last couple of months was over. As far as the Major was concerned, the *Crusader* Project had sunk away as he had hoped it would, no implications or clues to the role he had played and someone else implicated. He felt an elated freedom this afternoon. Everything was going to plan and money would soon start to roll in for the building plans to house his motor car collection. The insurance money he would claim when they found his wife's body, added together with the *Crusader* fund, would net him over £1,500,000. He thought about her, still lying out there in the wet grass of the Hampshire woods where he had left her early in the morning.

She had survived the fall from her mount as the harness stitching he had tampered with the evening before loosened. As he dismounted beside her she loosened off her riding helmet and looked up at him, barking out in her intolerable voice.

'Broken hip I think Jackson. Go and fetch some help. Can't move. Go on then, get on with it man.'

The horses were unsteadied and her expression turned to surprise and uncertain anxiety as he whipped the flank of her horse so that it cantered off and stood grazing at some distance from them. Then, saying nothing, he reached into his saddle bag and extracted a strange looking object, a thing that looked like a mediaeval mace or cudgel with horseshoes secured to the business end. He turned and looked at her, a cold long look as though the years of her domination were now accelerating through his head. She tried in vain to wriggle across the ground as she realised his intentions and tried to get away from him, but the pain in her hip exhausted her as she screamed out at him.

The first blow as she lay helplessly on the ground had been aimed at, and had probably broken her skull, the second and third mashed the features of her face to a pulp of blood, bone and teeth. Her arms had dropped back from protecting herself and she lay still as he delivered further frenzied blows to her body. Then he calmly remounted his horse and rode back to the stables. On the way he disposed of his weapon from a river bridge.

The stable girls were not surprised when he returned alone. He often did. They all knew that Lady Pamela Fellows usually found something to argue about when she went riding with her husband.

Now he sat there in the quiet of his study, as he calmly completed the crossword he had started earlier and turned to the business section of the newspaper, his eyes scanning his various holdings. The news out in the English Channel had not affected the Stock Exchange and the Footsie was slightly up on the news that Manchester United FC PLC had taken over one of the larger Internet merchant bankers, whether to act for them or to play was not clear.

He rose and went through to his computer room, switched on his P.C. , keyed in his network password and went into his mail box taking a cursory look over those items that had come in since the previous evening. All to do with the office except one, which appeared as a jumble of symbols, letters and numbers that made absolutely no sense at all. He tried his various encryption keys but the message whatever it was stayed there, some sort of file that meant nothing to him. He saved and used his password to enter his private financial spreadsheet to update his share holding values.

He stared at the screen in disbelief. Something had happened and all his dealings with the New York broker, Hindes and Stern had been erased. He fished the C.D. backup file out of a desk drawer and slid it into the machine. The figures were there but not on his hard disk. Two hundred thousand pounds just wiped off, the amount he had received for his part in the abortive *Crusader* project that was now clearly finished. He keyed into his Internet provider and called up the net broker web site on which he kept details of his portfolio, updating in real time. Once again, all reference to Hindes and Stern was gone. He checked back through the e-mail messages for anything from the States. There was nothing. He hesitated, what had happened, he usually had a coded overnight message from Gibson at Langley, just to confirm continuity but there was nothing.

He accessed another file, using a double guarded pair of code names, the file on his P.C. code named *Dragon's Morsel* was still there with details of transfers made to him through the Hong Kong exchange with the Chinese. He went to close it, but something happened, as though someone else was controlling the keyboard, as the file was saved to an unguarded open file. He felt the anxiety rising through his body as the keyboard responded again and he went back to the messages. Once again the strange indecipherable message came up and this time he tried to delete it. As he did so, pedophilic images started to flash on the screen, pictures from another secret library he kept. They flashed up slowly at first and then faster and faster until the screen was a blur. He tried to clear the screen but nothing on the keyboard seemed to work. The mouse and keyboard were being operated remotely from somewhere else. He switched off the processor and sat there for a few minutes, moping away the excess perspiration from his face. Then he thought, anything here could probably also appear on his office terminal. He rebooted the computer and after performing its own disc checks, all seemed normal again. But the portfolio details remained as they were, no Hindes and Stern dealings.

Doug Lawson had worked endlessly through the night at his terminal with Peter linked on in the London office. For some reason the T2 Department had not thought to disconnect Lawson from the network system. It took less than an hour to find what he was looking for. He quickly located the copy of the e-mail he was accused of sending to the Gibson group on his own terminal but with a root traced back to Fellow's home terminal. Then he had waited patiently for the Majors home terminal to be accessed.

His new piece of hacker software slid straight through, allowing him to view, manipulate and transfer information at will.

The Major looked at the screen message now occulting on his machine with deep horror.

That afternoon the Commander was looking over Peter's shoulder at the figures and let out a low whistle. 'Can you save those transactions.'

Peter grinned. 'In our department we can do anything.' His fingers worked his own keyboard and within seconds the printer was spewing out its evidence. Payments made into Fellows's account apparently from Hindes and Stern's other transaction input sources showing payments from the Chinese bank via the same banking source.

As soon as the Major realised that Lawson had hacked into his system, he knew that he had to find out how far the exposure went. Had the changes been transferred onto his office terminal ? Even as a strictly non technologist, he was aware that the department operated powerful Web loggers and system administration control software that monitored his office system. A reason why he kept his personal data stored on his home P.C.

As Peter was printing the incriminating evidence, the Major was already on the train back to London. He had to get back to his London office as quickly as possible and try to remove some of those incriminating files.

He had just arrived in the office ready to see what could be done with his terminal when his secretary put a telephone call through from his home. It was the Major's housekeeper sobbing on the other end of the line, informing him that something terrible had taken place and the police were at the house. He listened to what she had to say with growing anxiety as the beads of perspiration that had been constantly wiped away from his forehead were reconstituted.

Major Jackson Hoover Fellows looked dazed as he realised the implications of his actions with respect to what his housekeeper had just told him. The same message from Lawson was on his office terminal, indispersed with the pedophile images which he could not remove. Nothing responded, the machine wouldn't even switch off.

He sobbed loudly as he hauled the machine from its desk mounting, ripping out the connectors that were the veins and arteries feeding the brain, and crashed the apparatus to the floor. Then he donned his jacket and put on his trilby, saying good bye to the alarmed secretary in the outer registry office who was on her way into his office to investigate the noise. 'I'll bid you good afternoon Jane dear.'

The doorman doffed his hat as the Major stepped out under the great arched portico and down the shallow main entrance steps of Thames House for the last time, left the building behind him and walked along Millbank in the direction of the Palace of Westminster. Vehicles screeched to a halt as he crossed Horseferry Road as if oblivious of the traffic and then ducked across the busy Millbank and entered the Victoria Tower Gardens, beside the River Thames, just north of the Lambeth Bridge.

He walked like a sleepwalker across the lawns until his steps brought him in front of the beautiful Auguste Rodin sculpture in bronze, of Les Bourgeois de Calais, the Burghers of Calais, showing their Masonic signs of hopeless grief and horror as they surrendered their town to William III in 1347 to save it from destruction, though in this case, they appeared to look down on Fellows, full of querulous accusation and bitter malevolence as if they were judges of his dreadful deeds.

The river parapet was quite high but he managed to climb onto it and stood there looking down at the water of the Thames unaware of the Japanese tourist parties who screamed out when they realised his intentions. It was high water and the river lapped its thirsty wavelets just below him. Visions of his wife's body, as he had left it that morning, motionless and he had thought dead, filled his mind, but now he suspected she would soon be talking to the police. His secret collection of child pornography was, he acknowledged, disgusting and wrong but over the years it had beckoned him with its witch like fingers so that resistance to it was impossible.

The slightly built Japanese man had been resting his arms on the parapet as he videoed the giant London Eye Millennium wheel situated on the other bank of the river. His eyes had been glued to the tiny screen, when his peripheral vision and cries from others in his tour party caught something that shouldn't have been there. Toko Triactho, on holiday from Kokura, grabbed at the Englishman's trouser leg, but he was too light weight and late, Major Jackson Hoover Fellows jumped into the fast flowing waters of London's river and was already rapidly vanishing down stream.

As the river waters closed over his head, visions of the plans for the new car collection building came into his mind and then, the first dreadful pains made him struggle and kick towards the surface. It was too late. His thoughts as they started to dull were of the past. If only they could have had the child everything would have been different.

Back at the citadel that had been his office, an extraordinary commotion was in progress as the office was sealed off. An hour later, following a call to Sir George from the American Embassy, a relieved Doug Lawson received the news at home that he was to be unconditionally restored to his former position.

News items on the television that evening were not notable amongst all the other news. A short report on a conference at the Oussera nuclear plant in Southern Algeria that had been disrupted by a group of mercenaries who had killed a number of leading fundamentalist terrorist leaders. It had prompted outrage all over the Middle East and a combined force of Egyptian, Syrian and Israeli forces had moved in to round up the ringleaders, many of them Americans.

The MI5 man had been released and had gone into hiding. The media were clamouring for more information following an announcement on a web site in Paris that he had a story for sale, linked to Libya and the massacre in Algeria.

The Police were searching for the body of a man in the Thames. His wife lay in a serious condition, badly injured, in the North Hampshire hospital having been thrown from her horse whilst out riding that morning. Foul play was suspected as horses rarely trample their dismounted riders.

Chapter 43. Secrets and confessions.

The small Japanese lady sat with her knees demurely drawn together, her hands neatly held in her lap over the pale cream skirt of the designer suit she was wearing. Short jet black hair over dark almond eyes and chiselled pallid features were enlivened by the bright lipstick. She stood barely five feet as Peter entered the office and was introduced to her by John Barrett. A lady, beautifully coutured, probably about mid to late forties Peter guessed as she proffered a tiny hand to him.

'Peter, can I introduce Mrs.Serin Carter, Simon Carter's widow who is over here to clear up Mr.Carter's affairs in the UK.'

They all sat as she opened her handbag and placed the paper contents on the desk in front of John. A small bundle of airmail letters numbering about a dozen as she spoke in a soft even voice.

'I believe those are the letters you wished to see Mr.Barrett, they were in Simon's office, filed under a Lieut. Senden and Capt.Piltcher's names.' I hope they are the ones you telephoned me about.'

Under the serene features, Peter could detect a gentle nature but a lady used to authority. As Carter's wife she was not what he had expected. She cast a smile towards him as John gathered up the letters and started to sort them, stacking them in date order. As he worked he addressed Peter.

'Mrs. Carter has very kindly provided these letters following a call I made to her husband's office after we read through those letters in St.Mawes the other week. I hope they will provide the other side of the picture, Philip and Gilbert's letters' to Simon Carter. Hopefully we will now be able to sort out what it was that went on between them all.'

'I've spoken to Katherine's father by the way, Sir Anthony will be here shortly. I'll tell you more later.'

Peter looked up expectantly. Katherine had gone down to Cornwall a couple of days before to collect her father from the hospital and drive him home. Her bubbly phone call to Peter the previous evening had confirmed that all was well but that she would stay at Oldbury Hall for a few more days.

His thoughts of Katherine and her father were broken as Serin said, 'I'm sorry to hear about your father Dr. Senden, I can only say from my own experience that time will heal your great loss.'

Peter was at a slight loss for words as he fumbled out his own consolations to the widow.

The bright lipstick lips broke into a smile. 'Dr. Senden, there is no need to be so polite you know, we all know my husband was a rotten bastard. By healing I was referring to my own parents who died earlier this year.'

John paused his fingering of the letters and glanced quickly at Peter. 'I'm sure Dr. Senden's sentiments were meant out of consideration to yourself

Mrs.Carter in spite of the apparent animosity your husband had towards his father.'

'My husband was a conniving wicked old man, have no doubt about that. I was married to him for long enough and should know, a marriage arranged by my parents when Carter held them to ransom over an illegal business deal that he trapped them into. They were innocent and could have been ruined and then Carter offered to marry me to save their honour. A marriage of convenience you might say, I have no regrets that he is now gone. My parents have both died in the last year which is why I was recently able to leave him. That sounds hard doesn't it but he took nearly every cent they had.'

They had both listened sympathetically to her phlegmatic outburst. John shrugged his shoulders. 'Presumably your lawyer will be looking into that for you. It would seem that your husband upset many people during his lifetime.'

Peter added, 'he seemed to be under the impression that I was his son but I must tell you that DNA tests have proved conclusively that my father was Philip Senden.'

She looked away from them both as if considering her next words. 'My late husband was a killer and drug addict you know. He used to scream out in his sleep at night.'

Peter remembered his mother Monica saying a similar thing to him when he had visited her that day in early summer.

'Perhaps you would like to enlighten Dr. Senden and I, are you referring to his ship's crew whom it is alleged that he murdered.'

She looked surprised at John's remark. 'All I know is that it happened a long time ago, in Gibraltar. He confessed to me during one of his narcotic sessions, killed a man in a bar there on the waterfront in a drunken orgy.' Her fragile looking painted face was serious as she continued. 'Had you asked me before, I could have told you what those letters were all about. You will not find any direct mention however of what really went on.' She then related what had happened.

'He was on a ship with the two correspondents in those letters. It seems it was the only time in all his mischievous dealings that anyone managed to turn the tables on him. I'm afraid your father was a witness to the murder Dr.Senden but somehow they escaped unidentified. Carter knew something about the Rear Admiral, a Sub Lieutenant at the time, that was traded for keeping quiet about what had happened.' She stopped as though that was it.

Peter prompted her, 'I think I know what was traded, my father's private homosexual friendship with Gilbert Piltcher.'

She looked relieved, 'so you know about that?'

'I'm afraid so Mrs.Carter, but that is all in the past, forgotten in the light of things as they currently stand but, there were surely other things in those letters, the retirement fund for instance and the *Dragon's Morsel*.'

Her face became perplexed and she glanced over to John . 'There is more but I would find it embarrassing to discuss in front of Dr. Senden, could we talk alone.'

Peter interjected again leaning forward and talking gently to her. 'There is nothing really left that could shock me about Simon Carter, I believe you are going to tell Mr.Barrett that he raped my dear mother and led my father to believe that I was the illegitimate outcome of his vile behaviour. Eventually his befuddled mind started to believe that it was the truth.' She took a small handkerchief from her handbag and dabbed her eyes. It was answer enough.

John had listened to the conversation, sitting there, now detached for the moment as a close friend of Peter's, acting as solicitor to his client as he pushed the letter pile to one side.

'I think it is now very clear what those three old gentlemen were up to.

The letter you showed me from Captain Piltcher explained the hold that Carter had over him and your father, I presume an innocent affair that developed for a short time during the voyage from Hong Kong.' He glanced at Peter without making eye contact. 'I'm sure Peter that once your father settled down and found Monica, he probably discovered his sexuality was more in the direction of a heterosexual, the past was in the past. Piltcher on the other hand openly admits his homosexual tendencies in the letter that you gave to me. Now, let's look at the situation in Gibraltar, Carter kills someone and only your father knows about it. When they get back on board, Carter tells him that if he exposes the truth to anyone, including those on board, he will inform the Royal Navy about the homosexual affair with Piltcher. So, they are level peddling on that one.

Next, the ship runs into problems when its cargo shifts and Piltcher then discovers the gold that has apparently been smuggled on board during one of the stops.' Peter interrupted him. 'I've learned from Hank Hoskins that the gold was on board the ship from the beginning of the voyage.'

John looked up, how much did his client know that had not been divulged? He continued. 'O.K., the gold was on the ship and discovered. Our friend Piltcher threatens to expose Carter, but once again Carter uses the affair to scare the Captain into concealment. Your father has also been informed about the gold, let's say a much less serious crime than murder, so Carter agrees to a share. Your father leaves the ship which then founders and we have Piltcher's written testimony about his fear that Carter will expose him if the gold is lost. So he saves it.

The Board of Trade enquiry comes along and Carter, not knowing the gold is safe, requests the Captain to conceal the position of the wreck, offering him a further share of the gold and knowing he will receive compensation from the insurers.'

Peter had sat nodding his head in agreement with John's diagnosis. 'Christ, it's like a mushroom, pyramid selling, it goes on for ever. It must have sounded like a bonus to Piltcher, having already saved the gold, Carter then lets him off the hook with respect to his homosexual tendencies. '

'We haven't finished yet Peter. I would suggest that after a period when the whole thing had died down, Carter tried to obtain the true position of the Acacia Lady from Piltcher, suggesting that they raise the gold with Philips diving expertise. Piltcher, having saved a quantity of it for himself might have been reluctant to pass on the true position in fear of Carter exposing him again and instead gave them false positions on which your father dived. We don't know of course, but your father's marriage could have been upsetting to Piltcher and he could have been jealous or antagonistic at the time. Then another complication arose, that of your mother, which would have tormented your father to the extent that he sent threats to Carter, asking for an advance payment of what they then called the retirement fund. Exposure of the murder at that time would have had more credence than the affair which could have been treated as hearsay, your father being happily married at that stage.'

'So you think that Philip *was* blackmailing Carter?'

'No Peter, as far as I can see from the letters, his requests were considered to be an advance loan to help with your education. It probably accounts in part why he was so anxious to find the retirement fund.'

'Seems to me that they were all a conniving bunch, including my father.'

'What you have to remember Peter is that this all took place back in the mid fifties. This so called retirement fund was, according to my recent discussions with the Inland Revenue, probably worth about £2,000,000 at that time. An awful lot of money when you consider that Litlewoods top dividend on the football pools at the time was a mere £75,000. Top managers and solicitors were lucky if they were earning more than £4,500 a year. Your old farmhouse is worth a small fortune at today's prices but I bet that back then you could have picked it up for about £4,000. I don't expect that you got much change out of forty thousand when you purchased your new Jaguar. Back in the early fifties, The XK120 Sports Tourer, including the purchase tax paid at the time would have cost about thirteen hundred pounds. So you can see, what Carter dangled out to them was something that would have been hard to resist.'

'What about Sir Anthony Holmes, how did he fit in to all this.'

Serin butted in, 'I could find no correspondence with the T.Holmes that Mr.Barrett requested.'

'So he's clean and squeaky then? This still doesn't explain what Carter meant by *Dragon's Morsel*.'

John glanced up at him.

'Peter, you've been keeping certain facts to yourself over this whole thing, presumably because of your involvement with national security. However, it is not hard to diagnose from the news of the last few days that the *Dragon's Morsel* referred to the bomb that the task force found. I also believe that you became involved because it was Philip who made the first discovery of its existence out there in the Channel. I am reasonably confident now that the Coroner's inquest next week will inform us that Philip died as a result of his find, probably from nuclear irradiation as per the speculative media stories we've seen over the last few days. I'm right I believe?'

Peter nodded his head slowly, 'I'm sorry mate, couldn't tell you everything that was going on for the reasons you have just mentioned, I've had to abide by the Official Secrets Act. As for the meaning of *Dragon's Morsel*, I'm still not sure that it only refers to the bomb. I've made the same observation several times to the people I've been involved with over the last few weeks and always drawn a negative response, perhaps, maybe, yes and no. There's more to this strange metaphor than we yet know.'

Serin retrieved a small envelope from her Kurt Guiger handbag.

'I have another mystery for you. I found these compact discs of Chinese Folk Music in Simon's luggage at my stepson's flat in London. I've tried playing them but there's nothing on them. None of the tracks register and the only sound I can get is a few clicks and burring noises. I was going to dispose of them but my lawyer suggested that they may work on a computer disc drive. Do you have one here?'

John took them from her. 'I think that's Peter's department, try the machine over there, as far as I know it has something called DVD and a CD disc drive slot.'

As Peter stood, there was a knock at the door and Sally Jennings showed Sir Anthony and Katherine into the office. He looked refreshed after his few days of convalescence, greeting Peter with a warm handshake before the other introductions were made and they sat.

John fiddled with his fountain pen in front of him as he started the conversation . 'Thanks for coming over Sir Anthony, we were just trying to piece together the *Dragon's Morsel* story.' He then described what had transpired over the last ten minutes, Mrs.Carter's revelations and their summary of what had happened all those years ago.

Sir Anthony scanned the faces around him. 'I suppose that I may as well tell you my side of the story.' They all turned to him, here was someone who was actually there at the time that covered the antecedent ideas that John had promoted a few minutes before.

'I was oblivious to the dealings that had gone on between the others and stumbled by accident into their arguments. It was on the morning after the storm, a couple of days after leaving Gibraltar. The Acacia Lady was listing and a Royal Navy supply ship was standing by us waiting to take Sub.Lieut Senden and myself off the ship together with some of the Army equipment. That morning I had noticed a Geiger counter registering strange readings. The instrument had not been used since leaving the Indian Ocean. My team had finished their official measurements and packed their equipment away, ready for it to be disembarked at Gibraltar where it was to be flown back to the U.K. This instrument had been faulty and was not sent back, but I had been mystified as to why it had started to register, probably some loose connection that the storm had set up. This part of the globe, off Finisterre had not as yet been raised to any significant nuclear background radiation levels and yet it was there.

I moved cautiously through the rolling ship until the readings told me that there was something in the number two cargo hold. On entering the inspection bay I found the hold a jumbled heap of wooden crates full of machine tools and army ordnance, some of them burst open where they had shifted in the storm. Another box had a heavy lead lining that was partly opened. Then, as suddenly as the instrument had started working, it just died.

When I went back to the ward room to report my findings, I heard the raised angry voices of the other three and stood listening outside the open door, something about gold on board, a share out to be arranged in exchange for something. I entered the room, innocently enough, the arguments suddenly stopping in my awkward presence as I dutifully reported what the Geiger counter had registered. The reaction from Carter was startling. He ordered the other two out of the cabin, standing there in a fury as he faced me and took the instrument in his hands. Then he smashed it across the table.' The Knight stopped the commentary there as if uncertain how to continue as the eyes of the others waited in expectation. He turned to Katherine.

'You will have to forgive me for what I am about to tell you all.

I was never a fighter, but for some reason I hurled myself at the man, furious at what he had done. He responded with a force I did not expect, his hands around my throat, throttling me until I thought my end had come. Then, your father appeared Peter and pulled him off.

Carter then seemed to change his attitude, begging me not to disclose the readings I had taken. I was twenty three at the time, a young scientist, and I told him that it was my scientific duty to report my findings so that a team could visit the spot again and try and verify them.' Sir Anthony stopped again as though his thoughts were in the past, wringing his conscience as he then continued in a faltering quiet voice. 'I prostituted my profession. Carter knew that I had heard something about the gold and offered to cut me in for a share if I kept quiet.'

He pulled a handkerchief from his pocket and dabbed his eyes as Katherine put an arm around him. John pressed his intercom and quietly asked his secretary to arrange tea for them.

'I'm sorry, where was I? Yes, he offered me £25000 to keep quiet over something which appeared to have little importance then. I was young and it was a vast sum of money. I had no idea at the time that I would never see it of course. Later I met him and said that I was going to publish my findings.' He stopped again, obviously embarrassed. 'I can't tell you the outcome of that meeting, it bore no relevance to what we are discussing here.'

John had listened intently as had the rest of them.

'Was any agreement made in writing between the four of you about the gold. You know, percentage share or anything?'

Sir Anthony reached inside his jacket pocket, 'this is my copy of the record, the gold was for obvious reasons, defined as the retirement fund, we all gathered at his flat in West Kensington and agreed it under the most friendly circumstances. I never knew what the others personal arrangements were until your explanation just now.'

Sally brought the tea in and Peter rose and went over to the computer where he tried to boot up the first disc and frowned at what appeared on the screen.

INCORRECTLY CONFIGURED DISC.

He picked up the second disc. It had exactly the same title in English but there was some Chinese calligraphy printed on the peripheral edge. He looked across to Serin.

'Mrs.Carter, can you read Chinese?'

She sorted the discs numerically according to the Chinese characters embedded in the script and Peter inserted the first disc of the series.

He stood back and looked at the title page on the screen in silent astonishment,

TEST SEQUENCE
FILE . 8a.

There followed page after page, lines and lines of figures, strange mathematical expressions in Boolean and fuzzy logic applied to quantum wave motion formulae.

Sir Anthony was now looking at the screen over Peter's shoulder,

'That looks vaguely familiar,' he said. 'Some sort of test data on the conversion of radiation generated between the primary and secondary stages of a hydrogen bomb warhead by the look of it. That information is one of the keys to any new warhead design. Without it any other information would be useless.'

Peter inserted some of the other discs one by one and looked at the same incomprehensible lists of figures. This was probably only a fractional part of the data that both his department and Hoskins had been seeking for their respective Governments for years.

History, as usual, seemed to have repeated itself and the Chinese had again paid up and lost something through Simon Carter.

Politicians in the West could maybe now relax their guard a little as the giant Eastern Power Block sought admission to the World's trading clubs. Relaxation of the Normal Trading Relations with China might be considered by the US Congress and the final stamp of membership to the World Trade Organisation agreed with the EU and others.

In the end it would become inconceivable that any large trading block could deal on a single market stall alone whilst threatening its neighbours. Modern communications and the Internet had shrunk the World to one market. There would be no others.

Chapter 44. Conference

On most television channels that evening the main news was devoted to the historic Middle East Cease Fire Conference and the signing of the long awaited treaty that was to take place in London at Lancaster House.

Situated in St. James's and originally called York House, Lancaster House was completed in 1840 by Sir Robert Smirke and was to be the glittering venue for this important occasion.

There was no mention of nuclear secrets lost or found, that news, almost as sensitive as the miracle science it contained, would never be allowed to break. Only the very senior members of the Security Committees on both sides of the Atlantic would have access to the information.

The Prime Minister stood with the Foreign Secretary just inside the entrance as the motorcades bearing the US President and other Heads of State swept along the Mall and turned off into Stable Yard as press and TV cameras worked overtime to catch the pictures that would later be flashed around the World.

Major Hessel was the first person out of the Israeli Prime Minister's car quickly surveying the crowd before opening the door of the limousine and ushering his Prime Minister to the entrance. Listening to his ear piece for any sign from his colleague observers that would call abort and cause him to bundle the poor woman to the ground.

Once inside, the official hand shaking stills were taken and they were escorted into the conference room for the treaty signatures. Each of the principal leaders surrounded by their respective body minders and staff. Then the signatures in front of dozens of cameras as their minder's eyes darted around the audience beneath the splendour of the giant chandeliers.

Before the conference dinner, President Bill Ford retired to a private room where Peter Senden and others were lined up waiting to be presented. The introductions were made by the Foreign Secretary as the President walked along the line handshaking and thanking each person in turn. When he was introduced to Peter Senden he stopped and grinned as they shook hands.

'Dr.Senden, this historic conference and treaty signing could not have gone ahead without the fine team effort we have seen here. Your input into finding our *Thinman*, was of major importance to us all and we thank you with all sincerity. I hope that what has been done here today will have far reaching consequences for the whole world to see that creed can live in harmony with creed, nation with nation'. He had turned to proceed but stopped and turned back and in a quieter voice said.

'The *Dragon's Morsel* now lies in its proper place thanks to your assiduous attention to the matter.

As you know, due to the massive outcry over the *Thinman* accident and the potential environmental and economic catastrophe that could have occurred due to that one nuclear accident, the UN has overhauled all of its numerous committees dealing with nuclear. In future we hope that international co-operation will reduce these awful occurrences and we will all consider the safety of the world's family before our own selfish requirements.' It was a political statement that said nothing and offered no answers, except perhaps that there was still hope for the future.

Then he was gone followed by his entourage. A short peace in part of the Middle East for a while, but wondering what the next world crisis would be. They already knew in their hearts. Apart from the mid- Asia problems, China still had to sort out its differences with Taiwan and the possibility of a united Korea sent long term shivers through the Japanese government and others around the Pacific Basin. These would be difficult times for the next administration.

Peter spotted Hank Hoskins among the party as it swept on. The Commander turned and winked at him.

'Thanks for all your help son, see you sometime soon.'

Chapter 45 Dragon's Morsel.

'By the way, you've been so busy over the last few days, did you ever discover what *Dragon's Morsel* referred to?'

It was late evening after the conference and they'd just joined the Westward bound M3 motorway on their way home.
Peter drove on quietly for a few minutes before he spoke.
'It was Hank Hoskins first clue when he was thrown into the final search for what the Americans called *Thinman*.
He told me that in 1960 Mao Tse-Tung was famously recorded as saying,

'The atomic bomb is a paper tiger which the U.S. reactionaries use to scare people. It looks terrible, but in fact it isn't......All reactionaries are paper tigers.'

Recently scholars at the University of Boston have been allowed access to old Chinese documents brought over by the defector in 1989 and have prepared translations .
It appears that eight years earlier in 1952 when the young Simon Carter offered the American atom bomb secrets and documents to the Chinese, Mao was unofficially reported as saying privately, something along the lines of;
'the nuclear deterrent is a like a Chinese New Year party dragon. It twists and turns and has a giant fiery head, a cavernous ugly mouth that roars, a fat body and a long tail.
The head is the factual power of possession that can only ever be used to impress enemies. The hungry mouth devours the funds, directed away from other humanitarian causes, and feeds them to the body that contains the soul of conscience, knowledge and insight of production. The tail is the final factor, implementing the resources and directing them to the end product that is at the tiny tip of the tail. There is already proliferation and there will be more when the dragon starts to lash its tail and the world will never be the same place again. Mao went on to say something like . Our young country needs technology to enable us to produce the basic food and a quality of life for our people, not someone else's morsel. The American atomic bomb we are being offered is of no use to us, it is the smallest part of the equation and will have a terrible legacy. I would call it the *dragon's morsel*. He then went on to his famous quotation about paper tigers that was officially quoted years later.'
Katherine looked at him his face etched in serious thought.
'The metaphor used by some of the Chinese Chairman's military advisers for the American atomic bomb after that was, according to Hank, *Dragon's Morsel*. It was also the code name that they used for some of their other nuclear espionage activities.

I understand from my department that a full account of *Dragon's Morsel* will not come out until official papers are released in twenty five years time. By then the original incident will be over eighty years old and forgotten to all except the historians, who will modify the story to suit whatever political ends are required at that time'

He drove a few more miles in silence, his mind obviously taken up with what he had said.

'*Thinman* or *Dragon's Morsel* will probably be classed as the world's first nuclear accident and there have been plenty since. It's madness. We're only sixty years into the nuclear age and the World's seas are becoming polluted.'

Katherine reached over and put a finger to his lips.

'It's over darling, the outrage that the public demonstrated when the bomb was removed has ensured top priority procedures on an international scale, we're in a new century, the nuclear power of the old twentieth century has been made safe.'

He continued almost as an afterthought.

'The World will always need nucleonics you know. Its part of the physics of the universe and it's a stupid concept to postulate that we could do without it. But there's hope that the old twentieth century reliance on nuclear power and weaponry will be reduced and the legacy of accidents cleaned up.

The other day, I read about a fourth generation nuclear plant, still in development, called a pebble bed reactor. I gather it produces fuel that is easily disposed of, can't melt down and is technically unsuitable for the weapons industry. So, there are ideas being developed that could change the nuclear industries future.

There are also alternative sources of natural power and renewable power, which must be harnessed to make a world, safer and more suitable for future generations of children. Especially if they want to go on drinking fresh water.

In that way, they will still be able to occasionally pause from their squabbling and go on enjoying the beauty and happiness that this small world offers them.'

--ooOoo---

A man with a black eye patch sat at a pavement table outside the bar on the Plaza de la Cultura opposite the Teatro National of San Jose in Costa Rica's capital. The eye patch covered the terrible wound he had sustained in the head from the 7.62 mm calliper round that had shattered the side of his skull and removed one eye at Peter Senden's farmhouse.

On his damaged right hand he wore a black glove that occasionally dipped into his pocket and produced small packets of counterfeit blue triangular pills. The anxious elderly male tourists that purchased them were usually told that there was no guarantee that they would work. Half of what was supplied was coloured flour, starch and water and would probably only result in indigestion, but to those men, the pills were not freely available in their own country and were also a third of the price quoted on the Internet giving them hope of renewed virility. David Luk was free for the time being.

Seamaiden had sailed over night from the quay at Weymouth, bound again for St Mawes. The newly wed Barretts', Jessica and John, had waved Peter and Katherine off to the holiday that they were looking forward to so much.

The dawn had come up almost imperceptibly. The blackness of the night turning from dark slate and then lighter hues of grey as the sky above him gradually became lighter and the sea surface started to become defined. The mist had fallen back to give a couple of miles visibility where the horizon subtly blended the silver grey sea to white vapour and then the pale yellow in the Eastern sky as the illuminary globe started to rise. Another half hour passed and the air was feeling warmer with the light swell of the sea already reflecting the blue sky with its fading stars. The sun disc now clearly visible as its heat burnt off the surface mist and opened up the vastness of the shimmering mercury sea around him.

A summer day's dawn is a time when everything seems new and fresh in that special Eastern light, an isolated quietness that even the wind holds still to admire. An experience that early risers, if they are not rushing to their daily tasks, know well.

Peter had seen it many times at sea and always marvelled at the majestic sight. This was one of those glorious moments when the soul gratifies in the quintessence of solitude, to stand alone and drink in the magnificence of a new day.

On this day he was not alone. Katherine had emerged from the companionway, one hand balancing a plate of bacon sandwiches against the slight swell.

She smiled at him sitting there, his jersey sleeves pushed up as he steadied his hand on the tiller, his eyes watching the scene, sensing the movement of

Seamaiden as she sliced through the water with an easy motion, the small sounds of the water bubbling around her hull.

He patted the seat beside him and Katherine sat, cuddling up to him, his free arm around her.

'The World really is a beautiful place isn't it,' she said.

Peter shifted his eyes from the sails, the jib and main working in perfect harmony with the breeze and looked at her.

'Darling , you're right of course, it is beautiful. I just hope it remains that way so that our children will be able to enjoy the sea as we have. Let's hope the World does something to stop the type of near nuclear disaster that we found ourselves embroiled with.'

The *London Daily Chronicle* newspaper lay beside him screaming out its headline message.

Something had to be done to protect the innocent and indifferent population of this tiny, minuscule dot that was the Earth, floating in its golden orbit around a minor star. A blue haven in the endless enormity of space, a remarkable accident of chemistry and physics that gave life . There would be nowhere else to go once that tiny vestige of mankind was contaminated through official indifference, ignorance and neglect. A legacy of dragons. A warning that had to be heeded according to the ancient prophets.

THE END

About the Author.

Michael Kendall is an engineering physicist and businessman and worked in the international defence industries before taking early retirement. He's written numerous articles on yachting, business and technology. *Legacy of Dragons* is his first novel. and uses nuclear pollution of the oceans as the background theme to this powerful espionage story.

A winner in the national Opal/PBO 2004 sea story writers' competition and runner up in 2003, he is also a Yachtmaster, using his sailing and technical experiences for some of the background writing in *Legacy of Dragons*. He enjoys long distance walking and sails his boat mainly in the areas outlined in the novel. He lives in Hampshire

ISBN 1425107753